T0120551

TALES OF
THE
CTHULHU MYTHOS

The H. P. Lovecraft editions
from Del Rey Books

The Best of H. P. Lovecraft:
Bloodcurdling Tales of Horror and the Macabre

The Dream Cycle of H. P. Lovecraft:
Dreams of Terror and Death

The Transition of H. P. Lovecraft:
The Road to Madness

The Horror in the Museum

The Watchers Out of Time
(forthcoming)

Waking Up Screaming

Shadows of Death

Other stories in the H. P. Lovecraftian World

H. P. Lovecraft and Others:
Tales of the Cthulhu Mythos

Stories Inspired by H. P. Lovecraft:
Cthulhu 2000

Also available from The Modern Library

At the Mountains of Madness
The Definitive Edition

TALES OF THE CTHULHU MYTHOS

H.P. Lovecraft
and Others

Ballantine Books • New York

A Del Rey® Book
Published by The Random House Publishing Group

Published in the United States by Del Rey Books, an imprint of The Random House Publishing Group, a division of Random House, Inc., New York, and simultaneously in Canada by Random House of Canada Limited, Toronto.

Del Rey is a registered trademark and the Del Rey colophon
is a trademark of Random House, Inc.

www.delreybooks.com

Library of Congress Catalog Card Number: 98-96130

ISBN: 0-345-42204-X

ISBN: 978-0-345-42204-0

This edition published by arrangement with Arkham House Publishers, Inc.

Cover illustration by John Palencar

First Ballantine Books Edition: October 1998

147429898

Contents

Iä! Iä! Cthulhu Fhtagn!

"Why in the name of science-fiction did you ever print such a story as 'At the Mountains of Madness' by Lovecraft? Are you in such dire straits that you *must* print this kind of drivel? . . . If such stories as this—of two people scaring themselves half to death by looking at the carvings in some ancient ruins, and being chased by something that even the author can't describe, and full of mutterings about nameless horrors, such as the windowless solids with five dimensions, Yog-Sothoth, etc.—are what is to constitute the future yarns of *Astounding Stories*, then heaven help the cause of science-fiction."

The object of the preceding epistolary animus, taken from the letter column of the June 1936 issue of *Astounding Stories*, was of course one of two Cthulhu Mythos works by H. P. Lovecraft that were being published by the magazine during that same year. Reader response to the Lovecraft stories was not unremittingly negative, but the favorable commentary tended to be overwhelmed by wails of indignation, bemusement, dismay.

During the 1930s American magazine science fiction was largely the province of a ghettoized group of action/adventure hacks who simply transformed the Lazy X ranch into Planet X and then scribbled forth the same formula stories, substituting space pirates for cattle rustlers. For readers accustomed to hopping aboard a starship, flipping on the faster-than-light drive (never mind Einstein's special theory), and blasting the bejesus out of the eight-legged men of Betelgeuse, Lovecraft's painstakingly detailed and overtly atmospheric sojourn across the Antarctic wilderness, in which his two intrepid explorers gibber and shriek before the culminant horror, was largely incomprehensible to the SF enthusiasts of 1936.

And the difference between Lovecraft's Mythos fiction and the galaxy-bustin' ebullience of Doc Smith and his cohorts is more fundamental than a simple action-versus-atmosphere dichotomy. Many of the space-opera exponents of the era, such as E. E. Smith, Nat Schachner, and Ralph Milne Farley, had been born in the previous century when the universe was still perceived to function in terms of an immutable Newtonian order. Each star was a sun just like ours, and as nineteenth-century astronomers directed their spectroscopes to the heavens, they received back the reassuring message that the stars contained hydrogen, helium, magnesium, sodium, and other elements precisely like those found within our own solar system. Toward the end of the century, when physicists were congratulating themselves on what they thought was their complete understanding of the universe, was the ultimate human conquest of the cosmos really so improbable?

Not according to Albert Einstein, who in 1905 inaugurated the revolution in twentieth-century science that ultimately would forever shatter the tenets of classical physics. With subsequent developments in relativity, quantum mechanics, subatomic particles, and the like, the universe no longer seemed so comprehensible. Just as Copernicus and Galileo had wrenched humanity from the center of creation, so too has modern man come to realize that not only is he not at the center of the cosmos, but that he is a singularity in the cosmos. The universe with its neutron stars and quasars and black holes is strange to us, and we are a stranger in the universe.

Of all the science-fiction writers whose work appeared in the magazines during the 1930s, only H. P. Lovecraft transcends the gosh-wow insipidities of his colleagues to convey this twentieth-century sensibility of the essential mystery of the cosmos. "All my tales," wrote Lovecraft in a 1927 letter, "are based on the fundamental premise that common human laws and interests and emotions have no validity or significance in the vast cosmos-at-large," a statement that virtually encapsulates the revolution then occurring in modern science, as wide-eyed physicists were in the process of discovering a strange new world not vouchsafed by Newtonian mechanics. Thus the non-Euclidean angles of Cthulhu's sea-sunken city (see page 22) represent the same non-Euclidean geometries with which Einstein had to grapple in formulating his general theory, while the unearthly emanations from the meteorite in "The Colour Out of Space" replicate the radium experiments undertaken earlier in the century by Becquerel and the Curies. Even current developments in higher mathematics—the phenomenon of chaos—are presaged in the Mythos tales, for the supreme deity in Lovecraft's imaginary pantheon, the blind idiot god Azathoth, reigns "in the spiral black vortices of that ultimate void of Chaos." Suitably accoutred in Mandelbrot fractals and equipped with the Feigenbaum constant, Azathoth would feel eminently at home amid the permutations and perturbations of contemporary chaos theory.

To pursue further the correspondences between the Cthulhu

Mythos and twentieth-century science would be pointless, since Lovecraft's appropriation of such concepts arose not from a formal knowledge of the higher mathematics involved in, say, relativity, but rather from a sort of serendipitous temperamental insight into "the assaults of chaos and the daemons of unplumbed space." Historically Lovecraft had identified himself with a social and economic aristocracy that had been left behind by the modern twentieth century; an outsider in his own time and place, the dispossessed dreamer had become an outsider in the cosmos as well. The Argentine writer Julio Cortázar has suggested that "all completely successful short stories, especially fantastic stories, are products of neurosis, nightmares, or hallucinations neutralized through objectification and translated to a medium outside the neurotic terrain." In Lovecraft's case, his conception of the universe as a harboring place of eldritch wonders is simply his outsider complex writ large; just as Lovecraft was an outsider in his own contemporary Providence, so in the Cthulhu fiction is modern man an alien entity, lost, adrift, teetering on the brink of an awesome abyss.

Thus when Lovecraft's "At the Mountains of Madness," with its intimations of the mysterious immensities of the cosmos, was serialized in *Astounding Stories*, what readers in 1936 had considered "drivel" has been proved by the scientific revolution of this century to be true. As physician Lewis Thomas observed in a recent article, "The greatest of all the accomplishments of twentieth-century science has been the discovery of human ignorance." With the preceding statement in mind, stop for a moment, turn to page 1 of the present volume, and read the opening paragraph of "The Call of Cthulhu."

After Lovecraft's death in 1937, eldritch horrors continued to abound. Lovecraft missed by a few years the accession to *Astounding Stories* of John W. Campbell, whose editorial skills and influence would dramatically improve the entire field of American magazine science fiction. For all his prodigious talents, however, Campbell maintained an essential engineering mentality—a transcendent faith in the triumph of technology and in the absolute efficacy of human ingenuity and resourcefulness—against which Lovecraft seemed like a freakish anomaly in the science-fictional firmament.

The lonely Providence recluse and his fabled fictional legacy instead were kept alive by a coterie of friends and admirers who preserved the Cthulhu Mythos like members of some secret society guarding its sacred lore and icons. To these noble efforts at preservation, which included the founding of Arkham House in 1939 by August Derleth and Donald Wandrei, was added the more debatable proposition of imitation.

During the 1930s Lovecraft himself had concocted ersatz Mythos yarns for various revision clients, stories regarding which he significantly noted that "[I] wouldn't under any circumstances let my name be used in connexion with them." The years following Lovecraft's death, beginning with Francis T. Laney's 1942 glossary of Mythos terminology, inaugurated an era in which Cthulhu and his cosmic cohorts were scrutinized, analyzed, categorized, systematized, bent, folded, stapled—and mutilated. Thus by the 1970s, in a notably superficial book on the Mythos, an American fantasist opined the presence of "lacunae" in Lovecraft's conception, regarding which it was incumbent upon himself and others to "fill in" with new stories. Before Lovecraft's time, the market for tales of batrachian anthropophagy had always been rather limited; in the decades after his death, the pastiching of Cthulhu & Co. evolved into an industry of cyclopean proportions.

That the preponderance of such derivative work has been, in the words of the late E. Hoffmann Price, "abominable rubbish" is less significant than the very real injustice done thereby to the Mythos. Lovecraft's imaginary cosmogony was never a static system but rather a sort of aesthetic construct that remained ever adaptable to its creator's developing personality and altered interests. Thus as Gothicism gradually gave way to extraterrestrialism over the last ten years of Lovecraft's life, an early Mythos tale such as "The Dunwich Horror" (1928) is still firmly ensconced in a degenerate New England backwater, while just six years later, in "The Shadow Out of Time," Lovecraft's narrative is a dazzling Stapledonian romp through the universe past, present, and future. Similarly, as Lovecraft finally began to outgrow horror fiction in the 1930s, one again can compare "The Dunwich Horror," in which the Mythos deities are still demoniac entities to be kept at bay with grimoire-gleaned incantations, to "The Shadow Out of Time," in which the extraterrestrials have become enlightened card-carrying socialists, a direct reflection of Lovecraft's emergent interest in society and its reform. Had the man lived into the 1940s, the Mythos would have continued to evolve with its creator; there was never a rigid system that might be posthumously appropriated by the pasticheur.

Secondly, the essence of the Mythos lies not in a pantheon of imaginary deities nor in a cobwebby collection of forbidden tomes, but rather in a certain convincing cosmic attitude. *Cosmic* was Lovecraft's endlessly iterated term to describe his own central aesthetic: "I choose weird stories because they suit my inclination best—one of my strongest and most persistent wishes being to achieve, momentarily, the illusion of some strange suspension or violation of the galling limitations of time, space, and natural law which forever imprison us and frustrate our curiosity about the infinite cosmic spaces. . . ."

In a sense, Lovecraft's entire adult oeuvre is comprised of tales of cosmic wonder, but over the last ten years of his life, when he began to abandon Dunsanian exoticism and New England black magic and to seek for subject matter the mysterious abysses of outer space, he achieved a body of work to which has been posthumously applied the term Cthulhu Mythos. The Mythos, in other words, represents those cosmic wonder tales by Lovecraft in which the author had begun to direct his attention to the modern scientific universe; the Mythos deities in turn hypostatize the qualities of such a purposeless, indifferent, unutterably alien universe. And thus to all those Lovecraftian imitators who over the years have perpetrated Mythos pastiches in which eccentric New England recluses utter the right incantations in the wrong books and are promptly eaten by a giant frog named Cthulhu: the Mythos is not a concatenation of facile formulas and glossary gleanings, but rather a certain cosmic state of mind.

The preceding strictures do not apply, of course, to the present assemblage of stories, which are among the relative handful of successful works that have been influenced by the Cthulhu Mythos. A few of the earliest pieces in this volume by certain "divers hands" now seem like pop-cultural kitsch, perhaps, but everything else is quite wonderful, with the tales by Robert Bloch ("Notebook Found in a Deserted House"), Fritz Leiber, Ramsey Campbell, Colin Wilson, Joanna Russ, and Stephen King in particular exemplifying the darkly enduring power of H. P. Lovecraft over a disparate group of writers who have made their own inimitable contributions to the Mythos.

And Richard A. Lupoff, author of the final story in this collection, possibly has given us something more: "Discovery of the Ghooric Zone" is not just a distinguished Mythos tale; it is the only Mythos tale I have ever encountered by an author other than Lovecraft that conveys some sense of the iconoclastic audacity that attended the initial publication of Lovecraft's work and that so outraged the contemporary readership of *Astounding Stories*. In this brilliant narrative Lupoff has managed to include not only the requisite Mythos terminology but also the essential ambience of cosmic wonder, and then additionally has re-created some of the mind-blasting excitement of those original Mythos stories. If you would like to discover for yourself what all the shouting was about back in 1936, turn to page 438 of the present volume and begin reading about three cyborgs having sex aboard a spaceship traveling beyond Pluto to a mysterious unknown planet named Yuggoth.

JAMES TURNER

TALES OF
THE
CTHULHU MYTHOS

The Call of Cthulhu*

H. P. LOVECRAFT

(Found Among the Papers of the Late Francis Wayland Thurston, of Boston)

> Of such great powers or beings there may be conceivably a survival . . . a survival of a hugely remote period when . . . consciousness was manifested, perhaps, in shapes and forms long since withdrawn before the tide of advancing humanity . . . forms of which poetry and legend alone have caught a flying memory and called them gods, monsters, mythical beings of all sorts and kinds. . . .
>
> —ALGERNON BLACKWOOD

I. THE HORROR IN CLAY

The most merciful thing in the world, I think, is the inability of the human mind to correlate all its contents. We live on a placid island of ignorance in the midst of black seas of infinity, and it was not meant that we should voyage far. The sciences, each straining in its own direction, have hitherto harmed us little; but some day the piecing together of dissociated knowledge will open up such terrifying vistas of reality, and of our frightful position therein, that we shall either go mad from the revelation or flee from the deadly light into the peace and safety of a new dark age.

Theosophists have guessed at the awesome grandeur of the cosmic cycle wherein our world and human race form transient incidents. They have hinted at strange survivals in terms which would freeze the blood if not masked by a bland optimism. But it is not from them that there came the single glimpse of forbidden aeons which chills me when I think of it and maddens me when I dream of it. That

*Originally published in *Weird Tales*, February 1928.

glimpse, like all dread glimpses of truth, flashed out from an accidental piecing together of separated things—in this case an old newspaper item and the notes of a dead professor. I hope that no one else will accomplish this piecing out; certainly, if I live, I shall never knowingly supply a link in so hideous a chain. I think that the professor, too, intended to keep silent regarding the part he knew, and that he would have destroyed his notes had not sudden death seized him.

My knowledge of the thing began in the winter of 1926–27 with the death of my grand-uncle George Gammell Angell, Professor Emeritus of Semitic Languages in Brown University, Providence, Rhode Island. Professor Angell was widely known as an authority on ancient inscriptions, and had frequently been resorted to by the heads of prominent museums; so that his passing at the age of ninety-two may be recalled by many. Locally, interest was intensified by the obscurity of the cause of death. The professor had been stricken whilst returning from the Newport boat; falling suddenly, as witnesses said, after having been jostled by a nautical-looking negro who had come from one of the queer dark courts on the precipitous hillside which formed a short cut from the waterfront to the deceased's home in Williams Street. Physicians were unable to find any visible disorder, but concluded after perplexed debate that some obscure lesion of the heart, induced by the brisk ascent of so steep a hill by so elderly a man, was responsible for the end. At the time I saw no reason to dissent from this dictum, but latterly I am inclined to wonder—and more than wonder.

As my grand-uncle's heir and executor, for he died a childless widower, I was expected to go over his papers with some thoroughness; and for that purpose moved his entire set of files and boxes to my quarters in Boston. Much of the material which I correlated will be later published by the American Archaeological Society, but there was one box which I found exceedingly puzzling, and which I felt much averse from shewing to other eyes. It had been locked, and I did not find the key till it occurred to me to examine the personal ring which the professor carried always in his pocket. Then indeed I succeeded in opening it, but when I did so seemed only to be confronted by a greater and more closely locked barrier. For what could be the meaning of the queer clay bas-relief and the disjointed jottings, ramblings, and cuttings which I found? Had my uncle, in his latter years, become credulous of the most superficial impostures? I resolved to search out the eccentric sculptor responsible for this apparent disturbance of an old man's peace of mind.

The bas-relief was a rough rectangle less than an inch thick and about five by six inches in area; obviously of modern origin. Its designs, however, were far from modern in atmosphere and suggestion; for although the vagaries of cubism and futurism are many and wild, they do not often reproduce that cryptic regularity which lurks in prehistoric writing. And writing of some kind the bulk of these designs seemed certainly to be; though my memory, despite much familiarity with the papers and collections of my uncle, failed in any way to identify this particular species, or even to hint at its remotest affiliations.

Above these apparent hieroglyphics was a figure of evidently pictorial intent, though its impressionistic execution forbade a very clear idea of its nature. It seemed to be a sort of monster, or symbol representing a monster, of a form which only a diseased fancy could conceive. If I say that my somewhat extravagant imagination yielded simultaneous pictures of an octopus, a dragon, and a human caricature, I shall not be unfaithful to the spirit of the thing. A pulpy, tentacled head surmounted a grotesque and scaly body with rudimentary wings; but it was the *general outline* of the whole which made it most shockingly frightful. Behind the figure was a vague suggestion of a Cyclopean architectural background.

The writing accompanying this oddity was, aside from a stack of press cuttings, in Professor Angell's most recent hand; and made no pretence to literary style. What seemed to be the main document was headed "CTHULHU CULT" in characters painstakingly printed to avoid the erroneous reading of a word so unheard-of. This manuscript was divided into two sections, the first of which was headed "1925—Dream and Dream Work of H. A. Wilcox, 7 Thomas St., Providence, R.I.," and the second, "Narrative of Inspector John R. Legrasse, 121 Bienville St., New Orleans, La., at 1908 A. A. S. Mtg.—Notes on Same, & Prof. Webb's Acct." The other manuscript papers were all brief notes, some of them accounts of the queer dreams of different persons, some of them citations from theosophical books and magazines (notably W. Scott-Elliot's *Atlantis and the Lost Lemuria*), and the rest comments on long-surviving secret societies and hidden cults, with references to passages in such mythological and anthropological source-books as Frazer's *Golden Bough* and Miss Murray's *Witch-Cult in Western Europe*. The cuttings largely alluded to outré mental illnesses and outbreaks of group folly or mania in the spring of 1925.

The first half of the principal manuscript told a very peculiar tale. It appears that on March 1st, 1925, a thin, dark young man of neurotic and excited aspect had called upon Professor Angell bearing the singular clay bas-relief, which was then exceedingly damp and fresh. His card bore the name of Henry Anthony Wilcox, and my uncle had recognised him as the youngest son of an excellent family slightly known to him, who had latterly been studying sculpture at the Rhode Island School of Design and living alone at the Fleur-de-Lys Building near that institution. Wilcox was a precocious youth of known genius but great eccentricity, and had from childhood excited attention through the strange stories and odd dreams he was in the habit of relating. He called himself "physically hypersensitive," but the staid folk of the ancient commercial city dismissed him as merely "queer." Never mingling much with his kind, he had dropped gradually from social visibility, and was now known only to a small group of aesthetes from other towns. Even the Providence Art Club, anxious to preserve its conservatism, had found him quite hopeless.

On the occasion of the visit, ran the professor's manuscript, the sculptor abruptly asked for the benefit of his host's archaeological knowledge in identifying the hieroglyphics on the bas-relief. He spoke in a dreamy, stilted manner which suggested pose and alienated sympathy; and my uncle shewed some sharpness in replying, for the conspicuous freshness of the tablet implied kinship with anything but archaeology. Young Wilcox's rejoinder, which impressed my uncle enough to make him recall and record it verbatim, was of a fantastically poetic cast which must have typified his whole conversation, and which I have since found highly characteristic of him. He said, "It is new, indeed, for I made it last night in a dream of strange cities; and dreams are older than brooding Tyre, or the contemplative Sphinx, or garden-girdled Babylon."

It was then that he began that rambling tale which suddenly played upon a sleeping memory and won the fevered interest of my uncle. There had been a slight earthquake tremor the night before, the most considerable felt in New England for some years; and Wilcox's imagination had been keenly affected. Upon retiring, he had had an unprecedented dream of great Cyclopean cities of titan blocks and sky-flung monoliths, all dripping with green ooze and sinister with latent horror. Hieroglyphics had covered the walls and pillars, and from some undetermined point below had come a voice that was not a voice; a chaotic sensation which only fancy could transmute into sound, but which he attempted to render by the almost unpronounceable jumble of letters, *"Cthulhu fhtagn."*

This verbal jumble was the key to the recollection which excited and disturbed Professor Angell. He questioned the sculptor with scientific minuteness; and studied with almost frantic intensity the bas-relief on which the youth had found himself working, chilled and clad only in his night-clothes, when waking had stolen bewilderingly over him. My uncle blamed his old age, Wilcox afterward said, for his slowness in recognising both hieroglyphics and pictorial design. Many of his questions seemed highly out-of-place to his visitor, especially those which tried to connect the latter with strange cults or societies; and Wilcox could not understand the repeated promises of silence which he was offered in exchange for an admission of membership in some widespread mystical or paganly religious body. When Professor

Angell became convinced that the sculptor was indeed ignorant of any cult or system of cryptic lore, he besieged his visitor with demands for future reports of dreams. This bore regular fruit, for after the first interview the manuscript records daily calls of the young man, during which he related startling fragments of nocturnal imagery whose burden was always some terrible Cyclopean vista of dark and dripping stone, with a subterrene voice or intelligence shouting monotonously in enigmatical sense-impacts uninscribable save as gibberish. The two sounds most frequently repeated are those rendered by the letters "*Cthulhu*" and "*R'lyeh.*"

On March 23d, the manuscript continued, Wilcox failed to appear; and inquiries at his quarters revealed that he had been stricken with an obscure sort of fever and taken to the home of his family in Waterman Street. He had cried out in the night, arousing several other artists in the building, and had manifested since then only alternations of unconsciousness and delirium. My uncle at once telephoned the family, and from that time forward kept close watch of the case; calling often at the Thayer Street office of Dr. Tobey, whom he learned to be in charge. The youth's febrile mind, apparently, was dwelling on strange things; and the doctor shuddered now and then as he spoke of them. They included not only a repetition of what he had formerly dreamed, but touched wildly on a gigantic thing "miles high" which walked or lumbered about. He at no time fully described this object, but occasional frantic words, as repeated by Dr. Tobey, convinced the professor that it must be identical with the nameless monstrosity he had sought to depict in his dream-sculpture. Reference to this object, the doctor added, was invariably a prelude to the young man's subsidence into lethargy. His temperature, oddly enough, was not greatly above normal; but his whole condition was otherwise such as to suggest true fever rather than mental disorder.

On April 2nd at about 3 P.M. every trace of Wilcox's malady suddenly ceased. He sat upright in bed, astonished to find himself at home and completely ignorant of what had happened in dream or reality since the night of March 22nd. Pronounced well by his physician, he returned to his quarters in three days; but to Professor Angell he was of no further assistance. All traces of strange dreaming had vanished with his recovery, and my uncle kept no record of his night-thoughts after a week of pointless and irrelevant accounts of thoroughly usual visions.

Here the first part of the manuscript ended, but references to certain of the scattered notes gave me much material for thought—so much, in fact, that only the ingrained scepticism then forming my philosophy can account for my continued distrust of the artist. The notes in question were those descriptive of the dreams of various persons covering the same period as that in which young Wilcox had had his strange visitations. My uncle, it seems, had quickly instituted a prodigiously far-flung body of inquiries amongst nearly all the friends whom he could question without impertinence, asking for nightly reports of their dreams, and the dates of any notable visions for some time past. The reception of his request seems to have been varied; but he must, at the very least, have received more responses than any ordinary man could have handled without a secretary. This original correspondence was not preserved, but his notes formed a thorough and really significant digest. Average people in society and business—New England's traditional "salt of the earth"—gave an almost completely negative result, though scattered cases of uneasy but formless nocturnal impressions appear here and there, always between March 23d and April 2nd—the period of young Wilcox's delirium. Scientific men were little more affected, though four cases of vague description suggest fugitive glimpses of strange landscapes, and in one case there is mentioned a dread of something abnormal.

It was from the artists and poets that the pertinent answers came, and I know that panic would have broken loose had they been able to compare notes. As it was, lacking their original letters, I half suspected the compiler of having asked leading questions, or of having edited the correspondence in corroboration of what he had latently resolved to see. That is why I continued to feel that Wilcox, somehow cognisant of the old data which my uncle had possessed, had been imposing on the veteran scientist. These responses from aesthetes told a disturbing tale. From February 28th to April 2nd a large proportion of them had dreamed very bizarre things, the intensity of the dreams being immeasurably the stronger during the period of the sculptor's delirium. Over a fourth of those who reported anything, reported scenes and half-sounds not unlike those which Wilcox had described; and some of the dreamers confessed acute fear of the gigantic nameless thing visible toward the last. One case, which the note describes with emphasis, was very sad. The subject, a widely known architect with leanings toward theosophy and occultism, went violently insane on the date of young Wilcox's seizure, and expired several months later after incessant screamings to be saved from some escaped denizen of hell. Had my uncle referred to these cases by name instead of merely by number, I should have attempted some corroboration and personal investigation; but as it was, I succeeded in tracing down only a few. All of these, however, bore out the notes in full. I have often wondered if all the objects of the professor's questioning felt as puzzled as did this fraction. It is well that no explanation shall ever reach them.

The press cuttings, as I have intimated, touched on cases of panic, mania, and eccentricity during the given period. Professor Angell must have employed a cutting bureau, for the number of extracts was tremendous and the sources scattered throughout the globe. Here was a nocturnal suicide in London, where a lone sleeper had leaped from a window after a shocking cry. Here likewise a rambling letter to the editor of a paper in South America, where a fanatic deduces a dire future from visions he has seen. A despatch from California describes a theosophist colony as donning white robes en masse for some "glorious fulfilment" which never arrives, whilst items from India speak guardedly of serious native unrest toward the end of March. Voodoo orgies multiply in Hayti, and African outposts report ominous mutterings. American officers in the Philippines find certain tribes bothersome about this time, and New York policemen are mobbed by hysterical Levantines on the night of March 22–23. The west of Ireland, too, is full of wild rumour and legendry, and a fantastic painter named Ardois-Bonnot hangs a blasphemous "Dream Landscape" in the Paris spring salon of 1926. And so numerous are the recorded troubles in insane asylums, that only a miracle can have stopped the medical fraternity from noting strange parallelisms and drawing mystified conclusions. A weird bunch of cuttings, all told; and I can at this date scarcely envisage the callous rationalism with which I set them aside. But I was then convinced that young Wilcox had known of the older matters mentioned by the professor.

II. THE TALE OF INSPECTOR LEGRASSE

The older matters which had made the sculptor's dream and bas-relief so significant to my uncle formed the subject of the second half of his long manuscript. Once before, it appears, Professor Angell had seen the hellish outlines of the nameless monstrosity, puzzled over the unknown hieroglyphics, and heard the ominous syllables which can be rendered only as *"Cthulhu"*; and all this in so stirring and horrible a connexion that it is small wonder he pursued young Wilcox with queries and demands for data.

This earlier experience had come in 1908, seventeen years before, when the American Archaeological Society held its annual meeting in St. Louis. Professor Angell, as befitted one of his authority and attainments, had had a prominent part in all the deliberations; and was one of the first to be approached by the several outsiders who took advantage of the convocation to offer questions for correct answering and problems for expert solution.

The chief of these outsiders, and in a short time the focus of interest for the entire meeting, was a commonplace-looking middle-aged man who had travelled all the way from New Orleans for certain special information unobtainable from any local source. His name was John

Raymond Legrasse, and he was by profession an Inspector of Police. With him he bore the subject of his visit, a grotesque, repulsive, and apparently very ancient stone statuette whose origin he was at a loss to determine. It must not be fancied that Inspector Legrasse had the least interest in archaeology. On the contrary, his wish for enlightenment was prompted by purely professional considerations. The statuette, idol, fetish, or whatever it was, had been captured some months before in the wooded swamps south of New Orleans during a raid on a supposed voodoo meeting; and so singular and hideous were the rites connected with it, that the police could not but realise that they had stumbled on a dark cult totally unknown to them, and infinitely more diabolic than even the blackest of the African voodoo circles. Of its origin, apart from the erratic and unbelievable tales extorted from the captured members, absolutely nothing was to be discovered; hence the anxiety of the police for any antiquarian lore which might help them to place the frightful symbol, and through it track down the cult to its fountain-head.

Inspector Legrasse was scarcely prepared for the sensation which his offering created. One sight of the thing had been enough to throw the assembled men of science into a state of tense excitement, and they lost no time in crowding around him to gaze at the diminutive figure whose utter strangeness and air of genuinely abysmal antiquity hinted so potently at unopened and archaic vistas. No recognised school of sculpture had animated this terrible object, yet centuries and even thousands of years seemed recorded in its dim and greenish surface of unplaceable stone.

The figure, which was finally passed slowly from man to man for close and careful study, was between seven and eight inches in height, and of exquisitely artistic workmanship. It represented a monster of vaguely anthropoid outline, but with an octopus-like head whose face was a mass of feelers, a scaly, rubbery-looking body, prodigious claws on hind and fore feet, and long, narrow wings behind. This thing, which seemed instinct with a fearsome and unnatural malignancy, was of a somewhat bloated corpulence, and squatted evilly on a rectangular block or pedestal covered with undecipherable characters. The tips of the wings touched the back edge of the block, the seat occupied the centre, whilst the long, curved claws of the doubled-up, crouching hind legs gripped the front edge and extended a quarter of the way down toward the bottom of the pedestal. The cephalopod head was bent forward, so that the ends of the facial feelers brushed the backs of huge fore paws which clasped the croucher's elevated knees. The aspect of the whole was abnormally life-like, and the more subtly fearful because its source was so totally unknown. Its vast, awesome, and incalculable age was unmistakable; yet not one link did it shew with any known type of art belonging to civilisation's youth—or indeed to any other time. Totally separate and apart, its very material was a mystery; for the soapy, greenish-black stone with its golden or iridescent flecks and striations resembled nothing familiar to geology or mineralogy. The characters along the base were equally baffling; and no member present, despite a representation of half the world's expert learning in this field, could form the least notion of even their remotest linguistic kinship. They, like the subject and material, belonged to something horribly remote and distinct from mankind as we know it; something frightfully suggestive of old and unhallowed cycles of life in which our world and our conceptions have no part.

And yet, as the members severally shook their heads and confessed defeat at the Inspector's problem, there was one man in that gathering who suspected a touch of bizarre familiarity in the monstrous shape and writing, and who presently told with some diffidence of the odd trifle he knew. This person was the late William Channing Webb, Professor of Anthropology in Princeton University, and an explorer of no slight note. Professor Webb had been engaged, forty-eight years before, in a tour of Greenland and Iceland in search of some Runic inscriptions which he failed to unearth; and whilst high up on the West Greenland coast had encountered a singular tribe or cult of degenerate Esquimaux whose religion, a curious form of devil-worship, chilled him with its deliberate bloodthirstiness and repulsiveness. It was a faith of which other Esquimaux knew little, and which they mentioned only with shudders, saying that it had come down from horribly ancient aeons before ever the world was made. Besides nameless rites and human sacrifices there were certain queer hereditary rituals addressed to a supreme elder devil or *tornasuk*; and of this Professor Webb had taken a careful phonetic copy from an aged *angekok* or wizard-priest, expressing the sounds in Roman letters as best he knew how. But just now of prime significance was the fetish which this cult had cherished, and around which they danced when the aurora leaped high over the ice cliffs. It was, the professor stated, a very crude bas-relief of stone, comprising a hideous picture and some cryptic writing. And so far as he could tell, it was a rough parallel in all essential features of the bestial thing now lying before the meeting.

This data, received with suspense and astonishment by the assembled members, proved doubly exciting to Inspector Legrasse; and he began at once to ply his informant with questions. Having noted and copied an oral ritual among the swamp cult-worshippers his men had arrested, he besought the professor to remember as best he might the syllables taken down amongst the diabolist Esquimaux. There then followed an exhaustive comparison of details, and a moment of really awed silence when both detective and scientist agreed on the virtual identity of the phrase common to two hellish rituals so many worlds of distance apart. What, in substance, both the Esquimau wizards and the Louisiana swamp-priests had chanted to their kindred idols was something very like this—the word-divisions being guessed at from traditional breaks in the phrase as chanted aloud:

"Ph'nglui mglw'nafh Cthulhu R'lyeh wgah'nagl fhtagn."

Legrasse had one point in advance of Professor Webb, for several among his mongrel prisoners had repeated to him what older celebrants had told them the words meant. This text, as given, ran something like this:

"In his house at R'lyeh dead Cthulhu waits dreaming."

And now, in response to a general and urgent demand, Inspector Legrasse related as fully as possible his experience with the swamp worshippers; telling a story to which I could see my uncle attached profound significance. It savoured of the wildest dreams of myth-maker and theosophist, and disclosed an astonishing degree of cosmic imagination among such half-castes and pariahs as might be least expected to possess it.

On November 1st, 1907, there had come to the New Orleans police a frantic summons from the swamp and lagoon country to the south. The squatters there, mostly primitive but good-natured descendants of Lafitte's men, were in the grip of stark terror from an unknown thing which had stolen upon them in the night. It was voodoo, apparently, but voodoo of a more terrible sort than they had ever known; and some of their women and children had disappeared since the malevolent tom-tom had begun its incessant beating far within the black haunted woods where no dweller ventured. There were insane shouts and harrowing screams, soul-chilling chants and dancing devil-flames; and, the frightened messenger added, the people could stand it no more.

So a body of twenty police, filling two carriages and an automobile, had set out in the late afternoon with the shivering squatter as a guide. At the end of the passable road they alighted, and for miles splashed on in silence through the terrible cypress woods where day never came. Ugly roots and malignant hanging nooses of Spanish moss beset them, and now and then a pile of dank stones or fragment of a rotting wall intensified by its hint of morbid habitation a depression which every malformed tree and every fungous islet combined to create. At length the squatter settlement, a miserable huddle of huts, hove in sight; and hysterical dwellers ran out to cluster around the group of bobbing lanterns. The muffled beat of tom-toms was now faintly audible far, far ahead; and a curdling shriek came at infrequent intervals when the wind shifted. A reddish glare, too, seemed to filter through the pale undergrowth beyond endless avenues of forest night. Reluctant even to be left alone again, each one of the cowed squatters refused point-blank to advance another inch toward the scene of unholy worship, so Inspector Legrasse and his nineteen colleagues plunged on unguided into black arcades of horror that none of them had ever trod before.

The region now entered by the police was one of traditionally evil repute, substantially unknown and untraversed by white men. There were legends of a hidden lake unglimpsed by mortal sight, in which dwelt a huge, formless white polypous thing with luminous eyes; and squatters whispered that bat-winged devils flew up out of caverns in inner earth to worship it at midnight. They said it had been there before D'Iberville, before La Salle, before the Indians, and before even the wholesome beasts and birds of the woods. It was nightmare itself, and to see it was to die. But it made men dream, and so they knew enough to keep away. The present voodoo orgy was, indeed, on the merest fringe of this abhorred area, but that location was bad enough; hence perhaps the very place of the worship had terrified the squatters more than the shocking sounds and incidents.

Only poetry or madness could do justice to the noises heard by Legrasse's men as they ploughed on through the black morass toward the red glare and the muffled tom-toms. There are vocal qualities peculiar to men, and vocal qualities peculiar to beasts; and it is terrible to hear the one when the source should yield the other. Animal fury and orgiastic licence here whipped themselves to daemoniac heights by howls and squawking ecstasies that tore and reverberated through those nighted woods like pestilential tempests from the gulfs of hell. Now and then the less organised ululation would cease, and from what seemed a well-drilled chorus of hoarse voices would rise in singsong chant that hideous phrase or ritual:

"Ph'nglui mglw'nafh Cthulhu R'lyeh wgah'nagl fhtagn."

Then the men, having reached a spot where the trees were thinner, came suddenly in sight of the spectacle itself. Four of them reeled, one fainted, and two were shaken into a frantic cry which the mad cacophony of the orgy fortunately deadened. Legrasse dashed swamp water on the face of the fainting man, and all stood trembling and nearly hypnotised with horror.

In a natural glade of the swamp stood a grassy island of perhaps an acre's extent, clear of trees and tolerably dry. On this now leaped and twisted a more indescribable horde of human abnormality than any but a Sime or an Angarola could paint. Void of clothing, this hybrid spawn were braying, bellowing, and writhing about a monstrous ring-shaped bonfire; in the centre of which, revealed by occasional rifts in the curtain of flame, stood a great granite monolith some eight feet in height; on top of which, incongruous in its diminutiveness, rested the noxious carven statuette. From a wide circle of ten scaffolds set up at regular intervals with the flame-girt monolith as a centre hung, head downward, the oddly marred bodies of the helpless squatters who had disappeared. It was inside this circle that the ring of worshippers jumped and roared, the general direction of the mass motion being from left to right in endless Bacchanal between the ring of bodies and the ring of fire.

It may have been only imagination and it may have been only echoes which induced one of the men, an excitable Spaniard, to fancy he heard antiphonal responses to the ritual from some far and unillumined spot deeper within the wood of ancient legendry and horror. This man, Joseph D. Galvez, I later met and questioned; and he proved distractingly imaginative. He indeed went so far as to hint of the faint beating of great wings, and of a glimpse of shining eyes and a mountainous white bulk beyond the remotest trees—but I suppose he had been hearing too much native superstition.

Actually, the horrified pause of the men was of comparatively brief duration. Duty came first; and although there must have been nearly a hundred mongrel celebrants in the throng, the police relied on their firearms and plunged determinedly into the nauseous rout. For five minutes the resultant din and chaos were beyond description. Wild blows were struck, shots were fired, and escapes were made; but in the end Legrasse was able to count some forty-seven sullen prisoners, whom he forced to dress in haste and fall into line between two rows of policemen. Five of the worshippers lay dead, and two severely wounded ones were carried away on improvised stretchers by their fellow-prisoners. The image on the monolith, of course, was carefully removed and carried back by Legrasse.

Examined at headquarters after a trip of intense strain and weariness, the prisoners all proved to be men of a very low, mixed-blooded, and mentally aberrant type. Most were seamen, and a sprinkling of negroes and mulattoes, largely West Indians or Brava Portuguese from the Cape Verde Islands, gave a colouring of voodooism to the heterogeneous cult. But before many questions were asked, it became manifest that something far deeper and older than negro fetishism was involved. Degraded and ignorant as they were, the creatures held with surprising consistency to the central idea of their loathsome faith.

They worshipped, so they said, the Great Old Ones who lived ages before there were any men, and who came to the young world out of the sky. Those Old Ones were gone now, inside the earth and under the sea; but their dead bodies had told their secrets in dreams to the first men, who formed a cult which had never died. This was that cult, and the prisoners said it had always existed and always would exist, hidden in distant wastes and dark places all over the world until the time when the great priest Cthulhu, from his dark house in the mighty city of R'lyeh under the waters, should rise and bring the earth again beneath his sway. Some day he would call, when the stars were ready, and the secret cult would always be waiting to liberate him.

Meanwhile no more must be told. There was a secret which even torture could not extract. Mankind was not absolutely alone among the conscious things of earth, for shapes came out of the dark to visit the faithful few. But these were not the Great Old Ones. No man had ever seen the Old Ones. The cavern idol was great Cthulhu, but none might say whether or not the others were precisely like him. No one could read the old writing now, but things were told by word of mouth. The chanted ritual was not the secret—that was never spoken aloud, only whispered. The chant meant only this: "In his house at R'lyeh dead Cthulhu waits dreaming."

Only two of the prisoners were found sane enough to be hanged, and the rest were committed to various institutions. All denied a part in the ritual murders, and averred that the killing had been done by Black Winged Ones which had come to them from their immemorial meeting-place in the haunted wood. But of those mysterious allies no coherent account could ever be gained. What the police did extract, came mainly from an immensely aged mestizo named Castro, who claimed to have sailed to strange ports and talked with undying leaders of the cult in the mountains of China.

Old Castro remembered bits of hideous legend that paled the speculations of theosophists and made man and the world seem recent and transient indeed. There had been aeons when other Things ruled on the earth, and They had had great cities. Remains of Them, he said the deathless Chinamen had told him, were still to be found as Cyclopean stones on islands in the Pacific. They all died vast epochs of time before men came, but there were arts which could revive Them when the stars had come round again to the right positions in the cycle of eternity. They had, indeed, come themselves from the stars, and brought Their images with Them.

These Great Old Ones, Castro continued, were not composed altogether of flesh and blood. They had shape—for did not this star-fashioned image prove it?—but that shape was not made of matter. When the stars were right, They could plunge from world to world through the sky; but when the stars were wrong, They could not live. But although They no longer lived, They would never really die. They all lay in stone houses in Their great city of R'lyeh, preserved by the spells of mighty Cthulhu for a glorious resurrection when the stars and the earth might once more be ready for Them. But at that time some force from outside must serve to liberate Their bodies. The spells that preserved Them intact likewise prevented Them from making an initial move, and They could only lie awake in the dark and think whilst uncounted millions of years rolled by. They knew all that was occurring in the universe, for Their mode of speech was transmitted thought. Even now They talked in Their tombs. When, after infinities of chaos, the first men came, the Great Old Ones spoke to the sensitive among them by moulding their dreams; for only thus could Their language reach the fleshly minds of mammals.

Then, whispered Castro, those first men formed the cult around small idols which the Great Ones shewed them; idols brought in dim aeras from dark stars. That cult would never die till the stars came right again, and the secret priests would take great Cthulhu from His tomb to revive His subjects and resume His rule of earth. The time would be easy to know, for then mankind would have become as the Great Old Ones; free and wild and beyond good and evil, with laws and morals thrown aside and all men shouting and killing and revelling in joy. Then the liberated Old Ones would teach them new ways to shout and kill and revel and enjoy themselves, and all the earth would flame with a holocaust of ecstasy and freedom. Meanwhile the cult, by appropriate rites, must keep alive the memory of those ancient ways and shadow forth the prophecy of their return.

In the elder time chosen men had talked with the entombed Old ones in dreams, but then something had happened. The great stone city R'lyeh, with its monoliths and sepulchres, had sunk beneath the waves; and the deep waters, full of the one primal mystery through which not even thought can pass, had cut off the spectral intercourse. But memory never died, and high-priests said that the city would rise again when the stars were right. Then came out of the earth the black spirits of earth, mouldy and shadowy, and full of dim rumours picked up in caverns beneath forgotten sea-bottoms. But of them old Castro dared not speak much. He cut himself off hurriedly, and no amount of persuasion or subtlety could elicit more in this direction. The *size* of the Old Ones, too, he curiously declined to mention. Of the cult, he said that he thought the centre lay amidst the pathless deserts of Arabia, where Irem, the City of Pillars, dreams hidden and untouched. It was not allied to the European witch-cult, and was virtually unknown beyond its members. No book had ever really hinted of it, though the deathless Chinamen said that there were double meanings in the *Necronomicon* of the mad Arab Abdul Alhazred which the initiated might read as they chose, especially the much-discussed couplet:

> "That is not dead which can eternal lie,
> And with strange aeons even death may die."

Legrasse, deeply impressed and not a little bewildered, had inquired in vain concerning the historic affiliations of the cult. Castro, apparently, had told the truth when he said that it was wholly secret. The authorities at Tulane University could shed no light upon either cult or image, and now the detective had come to the highest authorities in the country and met with no more than the Greenland tale of Professor Webb.

The feverish interest aroused at the meeting by Legrasse's tale, corroborated as it was by the statuette, is echoed in the subsequent correspondence of those who attended; although scant mention occurs in the formal publications of the society. Caution is the first care of those accustomed to face occasional charlatanry and imposture. Legrasse for some time lent the image to Professor Webb, but at the latter's death it was returned to him and remains in his possession, where I viewed it not long ago. It is truly a terrible thing, and unmistakably akin to the dream-sculpture of young Wilcox.

That my uncle was excited by the tale of the sculptor I did not wonder, for what thoughts must arise upon hearing, after a knowledge of what Legrasse had learned of the cult, of a sensitive young man who had *dreamed* not only the figure and exact hieroglyphics of the swamp-found image and the Greenland devil tablet, but had come *in his dreams* upon at least three of the precise words of the formula uttered alike by Esquimau diabolists and mongrel Louisianans? Professor Angell's instant start on an investigation of the utmost thoroughness was eminently natural; though privately I suspected young Wilcox of having heard of the cult in some indirect way, and of having invented a series of dreams to heighten and continue the mystery at my uncle's expense. The dream-narratives and cuttings collected by the professor were, of course, strong corroboration; but the rationalism of my mind and the extravagance of the whole subject led me to adopt what I thought the most sensible conclusions. So, after thoroughly studying the manuscript again and correlating the theosophical and anthropological notes with the cult narrative of Legrasse, I made a trip to Providence to see the sculptor and give him the rebuke I thought proper for so boldly imposing upon a learned and aged man.

Wilcox still lived alone in the Fleur-de-Lys Building in Thomas Street, a hideous Victorian imitation of seventeenth-century Breton architecture which flaunts its stuccoed front amidst the lovely colonial houses on the ancient hill, and under the very shadow of the finest Georgian steeple in America. I found him at work in his rooms, and at once conceded from the specimens scattered about that his genius is indeed profound and authentic. He will, I believe, some time be heard from as one of the great decadents; for he has crystallised in clay and will one day mirror in marble those nightmares and phantasies which Arthur Machen evokes in prose, and Clark Ashton Smith makes visible in verse and in painting.

Dark, frail, and somewhat unkempt in aspect, he turned languidly at my knock and asked me my business without rising. When I told him who I was, he displayed some interest; for my uncle had excited his curiosity in probing his strange dreams, yet had never explained the reason for the study. I did not enlarge his knowledge in this regard, but sought with some subtlety to draw him out. In a short time I became convinced of his absolute sincerity, for he spoke of the dreams in a manner none could mistake. They and their subconscious residuum had influenced his art profoundly, and he shewed me a morbid statue whose contours almost made me shake with the potency of its black suggestion. He could not recall having seen the original of this thing except in his own dream bas-relief, but the outlines had formed themselves insensibly under his hands. It was, no doubt, the giant shape he had raved of in delirium. That he really knew nothing of the hidden cult, save from what my uncle's relentless catechism had let fall, he soon made clear; and again I strove to think of some way in which he could possibly have received the weird impressions.

He talked of his dreams in a strangely poetic fashion; making me see with terrible vividness the damp Cyclopean city of slimy green stone—whose *geometry*, he oddly said, was *all wrong*—and hear with frightened expectancy the ceaseless, half-mental calling from underground: *"Cthulhu fhtagn," "Cthulhu fhtagn."* These words had formed part of that dread ritual which told of dead Cthulhu's dream-vigil in his stone vault at R'lyeh, and I felt deeply moved despite my rational beliefs. Wilcox, I was sure, had heard of the cult in some casual way, and had soon forgotten it amidst the mass of his equally weird reading and imagining. Later, by virtue of its sheer impressiveness, it had found subconscious expression in dreams, in the bas-relief, and in the terrible statue I now beheld; so that his imposture upon my uncle had been a very innocent one. The youth was of a type, at once slightly affected and slightly ill-mannered, which I could never like; but I was willing enough now to admit both his genius and his honesty. I took leave of him amicably, and wish him all the success his talent promises.

The matter of the cult still remained to fascinate me, and at times I had visions of personal fame from researches into its origin and connexions. I visited New Orleans, talked with Legrasse and others of that old-time raiding-party, saw the frightful image, and even questioned such of the mongrel prisoners as still survived. Old Castro, unfortunately, had been dead for some years. What I now heard so graphically at first-hand, though it was really no more than a detailed confirmation of what my uncle had written, excited me afresh; for I felt sure that I was on the track of a very real, very secret, and very ancient religion whose discovery would make me an anthropologist of note. My attitude was still one of absolute materialism, *as I wish it still were,* and I discounted with almost inexplicable perversity the coincidence of the dream notes and odd cuttings collected by Professor Angell.

One thing I began to suspect, and which I now fear I *know,* is that my uncle's death was far from natural. He fell on a narrow hill street leading up from an ancient waterfront swarming with foreign mongrels, after a careless push from a negro sailor. I did not forget the mixed blood and marine pursuits of the cult-members in Louisiana, and would not be surprised to learn of secret methods and poison needles as ruthless and as anciently known as the cryptic rites and beliefs. Legrasse and his men, it is true, have been let alone; but in Norway a certain seaman who saw things is dead. Might not the deeper inquiries of my uncle after encountering the sculptor's data have come to sinister ears? I think Professor Angell died because he knew too much, or because he was likely to learn too much. Whether I shall go as he did remains to be seen, for I have learned much now.

III. THE MADNESS FROM THE SEA

If heaven ever wishes to grant me a boon, it will be a total effacing of the results of a mere chance which fixed my eye on a certain stray piece of shelf-paper. It was nothing on which I would naturally have stumbled in the course of my daily round, for it was an old number of an Australian journal, the *Sydney Bulletin* for April 18, 1925. It had escaped even the cutting bureau which had at the time of its issuance been avidly collecting material for my uncle's research.

I had largely given over my inquiries into what Professor Angell called the "Cthulhu Cult," and was visiting a learned friend in Paterson, New Jersey; the curator of a local museum and a mineralogist of note. Examining one day the reserve specimens roughly set on the storage shelves in a rear room of the museum, my eye was caught by an odd picture in one of the old papers spread beneath the stones. It was the *Sydney Bulletin* I have mentioned, for my friend has wide affiliations in all conceivable foreign parts; and the picture was a half-tone cut of a hideous stone image almost identical with that which Legrasse had found in the swamp.

Eagerly clearing the sheet of its precious contents, I scanned the item in detail; and was disappointed to find it of only moderate length. What it suggested, however, was of portentous significance to my flagging quest; and I carefully tore it out for immediate action. It read as follows:

MYSTERY DERELICT FOUND AT SEA

Vigilant Arrives with Helpless Armed New Zealand Yacht in Tow.
One Survivor and Dead Man Found Aboard. Tale of
Desperate Battle and Deaths at Sea.
Rescued Seaman Refuses
Particulars of Strange Experience.
Odd Idol Found in His Possession. Inquiry
to Follow.

The Morrison Co.'s freighter *Vigilant*, bound from Valparaiso, arrived this morning at its wharf in Darling Harbour, having in tow the battled and disabled but heavily armed steam yacht *Alert* of Dunedin, N. Z., which was sighted April 12th in S. Latitude 34° 21′, W. Longitude 152° 17′ with one living and one dead man aboard.

The *Vigilant* left Valparaiso March 25th, and on April 2nd was driven considerably south of her course by exceptionally heavy storms and monster waves. On April 12th the derelict was sighted; and though apparently deserted, was found upon boarding to contain one survivor in a half-delirious condition and one man who had evidently been dead for more than a week. The living man was clutching a horrible stone idol of unknown origin, about a foot in height, regarding whose nature authorities at Sydney University, the Royal Society, and the Museum in College Street all profess complete bafflement, and which the survivor says he found in the cabin of the yacht, in a small carved shrine of common pattern.

This man, after recovering his senses, told an exceedingly strange story of piracy and slaughter. He is Gustaf Johansen, a Norwegian of some intelligence, and had been second mate of the two-masted schooner *Emma* of Auckland, which sailed for Callao February 20th with a complement of eleven men. The *Emma*, he says, was delayed and thrown widely south of her course by the great storm of March 1st, and on March 22nd, in S. Latitude 49° 51′, W. Longitude 128° 34′, encountered the *Alert*, manned by a queer and evil-looking crew of Kanakas and half-castes. Being ordered peremptorily to turn back, Capt. Collins refused; whereupon the strange crew began to fire savagely and without warning upon the schooner with a peculiarly heavy battery of brass cannon forming part of the yacht's equipment. The *Emma*'s men shewed fight, says the survivor, and though the schooner began to sink from shots beneath the waterline they managed to heave alongside their enemy and board her, grappling with the savage crew on the yacht's deck, and being forced to kill them all, the number being slightly superior, because of their particularly abhorrent and desperate though rather clumsy mode of fighting.

Three of the *Emma*'s men, including Capt. Collins and First Mate Green, were killed; and the remaining eight under Second Mate Johansen proceeded to navigate the captured yacht, going ahead in

> their original direction to see if any reason for their ordering back had existed. The next day, it appears, they raised and landed on a small island, although none is known to exist in that part of the ocean; and six of the men somehow died ashore, though Johansen is queerly reticent about this part of his story, and speaks only of their falling into a rock chasm. Later, it seems, he and one companion boarded the yacht and tried to manage her, but were beaten about by the storm of April 2nd. From that time till his rescue on the 12th the man remembers little, and he does not even recall when William Briden, his companion, died. Briden's death reveals no apparent cause, and was probably due to excitement or exposure. Cable advices from Dunedin report that the *Alert* was well known there as an island trader, and bore an evil reputation along the waterfront. It was owned by a curious group of half-castes whose frequent meetings and night trips to the woods attracted no little curiosity; and it had set sail in great haste just after the storm and earth tremors of March 1st. Our Auckland correspondent gives the *Emma* and her crew an excellent reputation, and Johansen is described as a sober and worthy man. The admiralty will institute an inquiry on the whole matter beginning tomorrow, at which every effort will be made to induce Johansen to speak more freely than he has done hitherto.

This was all, together with the picture of the hellish image; but what a train of ideas it started in my mind! Here were new treasuries of data on the Cthulhu Cult, and evidence that it had strange interests at sea as well as on land. What motive prompted the hybrid crew to order back the *Emma* as they sailed about with their hideous idol? What was the unknown island on which six of the *Emma*'s crew had died, and about which the mate Johansen was so secretive? What had the vice-admiralty's investigation brought out, and what was known of the noxious cult in Dunedin? And most marvellous of all, what deep and more than natural linkage of dates was this which gave a malign and now undeniable significance to the various turns of events so carefully noted by my uncle?

March 1st—our February 28th according to the International Date Line—the earthquake and storm had come. From Dunedin the *Alert* and her noisome crew had darted eagerly forth as if imperiously summoned, and on the other side of the earth poets and artists had begun to dream of a strange, dank Cyclopean city whilst a young sculptor had moulded in his sleep the form of the dreaded Cthulhu. March 23d the crew of the *Emma* landed on an unknown island and left six men dead; and on that date the dreams of sensitive men assumed a heightened vividness and darkened with dread of a giant monster's malign pursuit, whilst an architect had gone mad and a sculptor had lapsed suddenly into delirium! And what of this storm of April 2nd—the date on which all dreams of the dank city ceased, and Wilcox emerged unharmed from the bondage of strange fever? What of all this—and of those hints of old Castro about the sunken, star-born Old Ones and their coming reign; their faithful cult *and their mastery of dreams*? Was I tottering on the brink of cosmic horrors beyond man's power to bear? If so, they must be horrors of the mind alone, for in some way the second of April had put a stop to whatever monstrous menace had begun its siege of mankind's soul.

That evening, after a day of hurried cabling and arranging, I bade my host adieu and took a train for San Francisco. In less than a month I was in Dunedin; where, however, I found that little was known of the strange cult-members who had lingered in the old sea-taverns. Waterfront scum was far too common for special mention; though there was vague talk about one inland trip these mongrels had made, during which faint drumming and red flame were noted on the distant hills. In Auckland I learned that Johansen had returned *with yellow hair turned white* after a perfunctory and inconclusive questioning at Sydney, and had thereafter sold his cottage in West Street and sailed with his wife to his old home in Oslo. Of his stirring experience he would tell his friends no more than he had told the admiralty officials, and all they could do was to give me his Oslo address.

After that I went to Sydney and talked profitlessly with seamen and members of the vice-admiralty court. I saw the *Alert*, now sold and in commercial use, at Circular Quay in Sydney Cove, but gained nothing from its non-committal bulk. The crouching image with its cuttlefish head, dragon body, scaly wings, and hieroglyphed pedestal, was preserved in the Museum at Hyde Park; and I studied it long and well, finding it a thing of balefully exquisite workmanship, and with the same utter mystery, terrible antiquity, and unearthly strangeness of material which I had noted in Legrasse's smaller specimen. Geologists, the curator told me, had found it a monstrous puzzle; for they vowed that the world held no rock like it. Then I thought with a shudder of what old Castro had told Legrasse about the primal Great Ones: "They had come from the stars, and had brought Their images with Them."

Shaken with such a mental revolution as I had never before known, I now resolved to visit Mate Johansen in Oslo. Sailing for London, I reëmbarked at once for the Norwegian capital; and one autumn day landed at the trim wharves in the shadow of the Egeberg. Johansen's address, I discovered, lay in the Old Town of King Harold Haardrada, which kept alive the name of Oslo during all the centuries that the greater city masqueraded as "Christiana." I made the brief trip by taxicab, and knocked with palpitant heart at the door of a neat and ancient building with plastered front. A sad-faced woman in black answered my summons, and I was stung with disappointment when she told me in halting English that Gustaf Johansen was no more.

He had not long survived his return, said his wife, for the doings at sea in 1925 had broken him. He had told her no more than he had told the public, but had left a long manuscript—of "technical matters" as he said—written in English, evidently in order to safeguard her from the peril of casual perusal. During a walk through a narrow lane near the Gothenburg dock, a bundle of papers falling from an attic window had knocked him down. Two Lascar sailors at once helped him to his feet, but before the ambulance could reach him he was dead. Physicians found no adequate cause for the end, and laid it to heart trouble and a weakened constitution.

I now felt gnawing at my vitals that dark terror which will never leave me till I, too, am at rest; "accidentally" or otherwise. Persuading the widow that my connexion with her husband's "technical matters" was sufficient to entitle me to his manuscript, I bore the document away and began to read it on the London boat. It was a simple, rambling thing—a naive sailor's effort at a post-facto diary—and strove to recall day by day that last awful voyage. I cannot attempt to transcribe it verbatim in all its cloudiness and redundance, but I will tell its gist enough to shew why the sound of the water against the vessel's sides became so unendurable to me that I stopped my ears with cotton.

Johansen, thank God, did not know quite all, even though he saw the city and the Thing, but I shall never sleep calmly again when I think of the horrors that lurk ceaselessly behind life in time and in space, and of those unhallowed blasphemies from elder stars which dream beneath the sea, known and favoured by a nightmare cult ready and eager to loose them on the world whenever another earthquake shall heave their monstrous stone city again to the sun and air.

Johansen's voyage had begun just as he told it to the vice-admiralty. The *Emma*, in ballast, had cleared Auckland on February 20th, and had felt the full force of that earthquake-born tempest which must have heaved up from the sea-bottom the horrors that filled men's dreams. Once more under control, the ship was making good progress when held up by the *Alert* on March 22nd, and I could feel the mate's regret as he wrote of her bombardment and sinking. Of the swarthy cult-fiends on the *Alert* he speaks with significant horror. There was some peculiarly abominable quality about them which made their destruction seem almost a duty, and Johansen shews ingenuous wonder at the charge of ruthlessness brought against his party during the proceedings of the court of inquiry. Then, driven ahead by curiosity in their captured yacht under Johansen's command, the men sight a great stone pillar sticking out of the sea, and in S. Latitude 47° 9′, W. Longitude

126° 43′ come upon a coast-line of mingled mud, ooze, and weedy Cyclopean masonry which can be nothing less than the tangible substance of earth's supreme terror—the nightmare corpse-city of R'lyeh, that was built in measureless aeons behind history by the vast, loathsome shapes that seeped down from the dark stars. There lay great Cthulhu and his hordes, hidden in green slimy vaults and sending out at last, after cycles incalculable, the thoughts that spread fear to the dreams of the sensitive and called imperiously to the faithful to come on a pilgrimage of liberation and restoration. All this Johansen did not suspect, but God knows he soon saw enough!

I suppose that only a single mountain-top, the hideous monolith-crowned citadel whereon great Cthulhu was buried, actually emerged from the waters. When I think of the *extent* of all that may be brooding down there I almost wish to kill myself forthwith. Johansen and his men were awed by the cosmic majesty of this dripping Babylon of elder daemons, and must have guessed without guidance that it was nothing of this or of any sane planet. Awe at the unbelievable size of the greenish stone blocks, at the dizzying height of the great carven monolith, and at the stupefying identity of the colossal statues and bas-reliefs with the queer image found in the shrine on the *Alert*, is poignantly visible in every line of the mate's frightened description.

Without knowing what futurism is like, Johansen achieved something very close to it when he spoke of the city; for instead of describing any definite structure or building, he dwells only on broad impressions of vast angles and stone surfaces—surfaces too great to belong to any thing right or proper for this earth, and impious with horrible images and hieroglyphs. I mention his talk about *angles* because it suggests something Wilcox had told me of his awful dreams. He had said that the *geometry* of the dream-place he saw was abnormal, non-Euclidean, and loathsomely redolent of spheres and dimensions apart from ours. Now an unlettered seaman felt the same thing whilst gazing at the terrible reality.

Johansen and his men landed at a sloping mud-bank on this monstrous Acropolis, and clambered slipperily up over titan oozy blocks which could have been no mortal staircase. The very sun of heaven seemed distorted when viewed through the polarising miasma welling out from this sea-soaked perversion, and twisted menace and suspense lurked leeringly in those crazily elusive angles of carven rock where a second glance shewed concavity after the first shewed convexity.

Something very like fright had come over all the explorers before anything more definite than rock and ooze and weed was seen. Each would have fled had he not feared the scorn of the others, and it was only half-heartedly that they searched—vainly, as it proved—for some portable souvenir to bear away.

It was Rodriguez the Portuguese who climbed up the foot of the monolith and shouted of what he had found. The rest followed him, and looked curiously at the immense carved door with the now familiar squid-dragon bas-relief. It was, Johansen said, like a great barn-door; and they all felt that it was a door because of the ornate lintel, threshold, and jambs around it, though they could not decide whether it lay flat like a trap-door or slantwise like an outside cellar-door. As Wilcox would have said, the geometry of the place was all wrong. One could not be sure that the sea and the ground were horizontal, hence the relative position of everything else seemed phantasmally variable.

Briden pushed at the stone in several places without result. Then Donovan felt over it delicately around the edge, pressing each point separately as he went. He climbed interminably along the grotesque stone moulding—that is, one would call it climbing if the thing was not after all horizontal—and the men wondered how any door in the universe could be so vast. Then, very softly and slowly, the acre-great panel began to give inward at the top; and they saw that it was balanced. Donovan slid or somehow propelled himself down or along the jamb and rejoined his fellows, and everyone watched the queer recession of the monstrously carven portal. In this phantasy of prismatic distortion it moved anomalously in a diagonal way, so that all the rules of matter and perspective seemed upset.

The aperture was black with a darkness almost material. That tenebrousness was indeed a *positive quality*; for it obscured such parts of the inner walls as ought to have been revealed, and actually burst forth like smoke from its aeon-long imprisonment, visibly darkening the sun as it slunk away into the shrunken and gibbous sky on flapping membraneous wings. The odour arising from the newly opened depths was intolerable, and at length the quick-eared Hawkins thought he heard a nasty, slopping sound down there. Everyone listened, and everyone was listening still when It lumbered slobberingly into sight and gropingly squeezed Its gelatinous green immensity through the black doorway into the tainted outside air of that poison city of madness.

Poor Johansen's handwriting almost gave out when he wrote of this. Of the six men who never reached the ship, he thinks two perished of pure fright in that accursed instant. The Thing cannot be described—there is no language for such abysms of shrieking and immemorial lunacy, such eldritch contradictions of all matter, force, and cosmic order. A mountain walked or stumbled. God! What wonder that across the earth a great architect went mad, and poor Wilcox raved with fever in that telepathic instant? The Thing of the idols, the green, sticky spawn of the stars, had awaked to claim his own. The stars were right again, and what an age-old cult had failed to do by design, a band of innocent sailors had done by accident. After vigintillions of years great Cthulhu was loose again, and ravening for delight.

Three men were swept up by the flabby claws before anybody turned. God rest them, if there be any rest in the universe. They were Donovan, Guerrera, and Ångstrom. Parker slipped as the other three were plunging frenziedly over endless vistas of green-crusted rock to the boat, and Johansen swears he was swallowed up by an angle of masonry which shouldn't have been there; an angle which was acute, but behaved as if it were obtuse. So only Briden and Johansen reached the boat, and pulled desperately for the *Alert* as the mountainous monstrosity flopped down the slimy stones and hesitated floundering at the edge of the water.

Steam had not been suffered to go down entirely, despite the departure of all hands for the shore; and it was the work of only a few moments of feverish rushing up and down between wheel and engines to get the *Alert* under way. Slowly, amidst the distorted horrors of that indescribable scene, she began to churn the lethal waters; whilst on the masonry of that charnel shore that was not of earth the titan Thing from the stars slavered and gibbered like Polypheme cursing the fleeing ship of Odysseus. Then, bolder than the storied Cyclops, great Cthulhu slid greasily into the water and began to pursue with vast wave-raising strokes of cosmic potency. Briden looked back and went mad, laughing shrilly as he kept on laughing at intervals till death found him one night in the cabin whilst Johansen was wandering deliriously.

But Johansen had not given out yet. Knowing that the Thing could surely overtake the *Alert* until steam was fully up, he resolved on a desperate chance; and, setting the engine for full speed, ran lightning-like on deck and reversed the wheel. There was a mighty eddying and foaming in the noisome brine, and as the steam mounted higher and higher the brave Norwegian drove his vessel head on against the pursuing jelly which rose above the unclean froth like the stern of a daemon galleon. The awful squid-head with writhing feelers came nearly up to the bowsprit of the sturdy yacht, but Johansen drove on relentlessly. There was a bursting as of an exploding bladder, a slushy nastiness as of a cloven sunfish, a stench as of a thousand opened graves, and a sound that the chronicler would not put on paper. For an instant the ship was befouled by an acrid and blinding green cloud, and then there was only a venomous seething astern; where—God in heaven!—the scattered plasticity of that nameless sky-spawn was nebulously *recombining* in its hateful original form, whilst its distance widened every second as the *Alert* gained impetus from its mounting steam.

That was all. After that Johansen only brooded over the idol in the cabin and attended to a few matters of food for himself and the laughing maniac by his side. He did not try to navigate after the first bold flight, for the reaction had taken something out of his soul. Then came the storm of April 2nd, and a gathering of the clouds about his consciousness. There is a sense of spectral whirling through liquid gulfs of infinity, of dizzying rides through reeling universes on a comet's tail, and of hysterical plunges from the pit to the moon and from the moon back again to the pit, all livened by a cachinnating chorus of the distorted, hilarious elder gods and the green, bat-winged mocking imps of Tartarus.

Out of that dream came rescue—the *Vigilant*, the vice-admiralty court, the streets of Dunedin, and the long voyage back home to the old house by the Egeberg. He could not tell—they would think him mad. He would write of what he knew before death came, but his wife must not guess. Death would be a boon if only it could blot out the memories.

That was the document I read, and now I have placed it in the tin box beside the bas-relief and the papers of Professor Angell. With it shall go this record of mine—this test of my own sanity, wherein is pieced together that which I hope may never be pieced together again. I have looked upon all that the universe has to hold of horror, and even the skies of spring and the flowers of summer must ever afterward be poison to me. But I do not think my life will be long. As my uncle went, as poor Johansen went, so I shall go. I know too much, and the cult still lives.

Cthulhu still lives, too, I suppose, again in that chasm of stone which has shielded him since the sun was young. His accursed city is sunken once more, for the *Vigilant* sailed over the spot after the April storm; but his ministers on earth still bellow and prance and slay around idol-capped monoliths in lonely places. He must have been trapped by the sinking whilst within his black abyss, or else the world would by now be screaming with fright and frenzy. Who knows the end? What has risen may sink, and what has sunk may rise. Loathsomeness waits and dreams in the deep, and decay spreads over the tottering cities of men. A time will come—but I must not and cannot think! Let me pray that, if I do not survive this manuscript, my executors may put caution before audacity and see that it meets no other eye.

The Return of the Sorcerer*

CLARK ASHTON SMITH

I had been out of work for several months, and my savings were perilously near the vanishing point. Therefore I was naturally elated when I received from John Carnby a favorable answer inviting me to present my qualifications in person. Carnby had advertised for a secretary, stipulating that all applicants must offer a preliminary statement of their capacities by letter, and I had written in response to the advertisement.

Carnby, no doubt, was a scholarly recluse who felt averse to contact with a long waiting-list of strangers; and he had chosen this manner of weeding out beforehand many, if not all, of those who were ineligible. He had specified his requirements fully and succinctly, and these were of such nature as to bar even the average well-educated person. A knowledge of Arabic was necessary, among other things; and luckily I had acquired a certain degree of scholarship in this unusual tongue.

I found the address, of whose location I had formed only a vague idea, at the end of a hilltop avenue in the suburbs of Oakland. It was a large, two-story house, overshaded by ancient oaks and dark with a mantling of unchecked ivy, among hedges of unpruned privet and shrubbery that had gone wild for many years. It was separated from its neighbors by a vacant, weed-grown lot on one side and a tangle of vines and trees on the other, surrounding the black ruins of a burnt mansion.

Even apart from its air of long neglect, there was something drear and dismal about the place—something that inhered in the ivy-blurred outlines of the house, in the furtive, shadowy windows, and the very forms of the misshapen oaks and oddly sprawling shrubbery. Somehow, my elation became a trifle less exuberant, as I entered the grounds and followed an unswept path to the front door.

When I found myself in the presence of John Carnby, my jubilation

---

*Originally published in *Strange Tales*, September 1931.

was still somewhat further diminished; though I could not have given a tangible reason for the premonitory chill, the dull, somber feeling of alarm that I experienced, and the leaden sinking of my spirits. Perhaps it was the dark library in which he received me as much as the man himself—a room whose musty shadows could never have been wholly dissipated by sun or lamplight. Indeed, it must have been this; for John Carnby himself was very much the sort of person I had pictured him to be.

He had all the earmarks of the lonely scholar who has devoted patient years to some line of erudite research. He was thin and bent, with a massive forehead and a mane of grizzled hair; and the pallor of the library was on his hollow, clean-shaven cheeks. But coupled with this, there was a nerve-shattered air, a fearful shrinking that was more than the normal shyness of a recluse, and an unceasing apprehensiveness that betrayed itself in every glance of his dark-ringed, feverish eyes and every movement of his bony hands. In all likelihood his health had been seriously impaired by over-application; and I could not help but wonder at the nature of the studies that had made him a tremulous wreck. But there was something about him—perhaps the width of his bowed shoulders and the bold aquilinity of his facial outlines—which gave the impression of great former strength and a vigor not yet wholly exhausted.

His voice was unexpectedly deep and sonorous.

"I think you will do, Mr. Ogden," he said, after a few formal questions, most of which related to my linguistic knowledge, and in particular my mastery of Arabic. "Your labors will not be very heavy; but I want someone who can be on hand at any time required. Therefore you must live with me. I can give you a comfortable room, and I guarantee that my cooking will not poison you. I often work at night; and I hope you will not find the irregular hours too disagreeable."

No doubt I should have been overjoyed at this assurance that the secretarial position was to be mine. Instead, I was aware of a dim, unreasoning reluctance and an obscure forewarning of evil as I thanked John Carnby and told him that I was ready to move in whenever he desired.

He appeared to be greatly pleased; and the queer apprehensiveness went out of his manner for a moment.

"Come immediately—this very afternoon, if you can," he said. "I shall be very glad to have you, and the sooner the better. I have been living entirely alone for some time; and I must confess that the solitude is beginning to pall upon me. Also, I have been retarded in my labors for lack of the proper help. My brother used to live with me and assist me, but he has gone away on a long trip."

* * *

I returned to my downtown lodgings, paid my rent with the last few dollars that remained to me, packed my belongings, and in less than an hour was back at my new employer's home. He assigned me a room on the second floor, which, though unaired and dusty, was more than luxurious in comparison with the hall-bedroom that failing funds had compelled me to inhabit for some time past. Then he took me to his own study, which was on the same floor, at the further end of the hall. Here, he explained to me, most of my future work would be done.

I could hardly restrain an exclamation of surprise as I viewed the interior of this chamber. It was very much as I should have imagined the den of some old sorcerer to be. There were tables strewn with archaic instruments of doubtful use, with astrological charts, with skulls and alembics and crystals, with censers such as are used in the Catholic Church, and volumes bound in worm-eaten leather with verdigris-mottled clasps. In one corner stood the skeleton of a large ape; in another, a human skeleton; and overhead a stuffed crocodile was suspended.

There were cases overpiled with books, and even a cursory glance at the titles showed me that they formed a singularly comprehensive collection of ancient and modern works on demonology and the black arts. There were some weird paintings and etchings on the walls, dealing with kindred themes; and the whole atmosphere of the room exhaled a medley of half-forgotten superstitions. Ordinarily I would have smiled if confronted with such things; but somehow, in this lonely, dismal house, beside the neurotic, hag-ridden Carnby, it was difficult for me to repress an actual shudder.

On one of the tables, contrasting incongruously with this mélange of mediaevalism and Satanism, there stood a typewriter, surrounded with piles of disorderly manuscript. At one end of the room there was a small, curtained alcove with a bed in which Carnby slept. At the end opposite the alcove, between the human and simian skeletons, I perceived a locked cupboard that was set in the wall.

Carnby had noted my surprise, and was watching me with a keen, analytic expression which I found impossible to fathom. He began to speak, in explanatory tones.

"I have made a life-study of demonism and sorcery," he declared. "It is a fascinating field, and one that is singularly neglected. I am now preparing a monograph, in which I am trying to correlate the magical practices and demon-worship of every known age and people. Your labors, at least for a while, will consist in typing and arranging the voluminous preliminary notes which I have made, and in helping me to track down other references and correspondences. Your knowledge of Arabic will be invaluable to me, for I am none too well-grounded in this language myself, and I am depending for certain essential data on a copy of the *Necronomicon* in the original Arabic text. I have reason to think that there are certain omissions and erroneous renderings in the Latin version of Olaus Wormius."

I had heard of this rare, well-nigh fabulous volume, but had never seen it. The book was supposed to contain the ultimate secrets of evil and forbidden knowledge; and, moreover, the original text, written by the mad Arab, Abdul Alhazred, was said to be unprocurable. I wondered how it had come into Carnby's possession.

"I'll show you the volume after dinner," Carnby went on. "You will doubtless be able to elucidate one or two passages that have long puzzled me."

The evening meal, cooked and served by my employer himself, was a welcome change from cheap restaurant fare. Carnby seemed to have lost a good deal of his nervousness. He was very talkative, and even began to exhibit a certain scholarly gaiety after we had shared a bottle of mellow Sauterne. Still, with no manifest reason, I was troubled by intimations and forebodings which I could neither analyze nor trace to their rightful source.

We returned to the study, and Carnby brought out from a locked drawer the volume of which he had spoken. It was enormously old, and was bound in ebony covers arabesqued with silver and set with darkly glowing garnets. When I opened the yellowing pages, I drew back with involuntary revulsion at the odor which arose from them—an odor that was more than suggestive of physical decay, as if the book had lain among corpses in some forgotten graveyard and had taken on the taint of dissolution.

Carnby's eyes were burning with a fevered light as he took the old manuscript from my hands and turned to a page near the middle. He indicated a certain passage with his lean forefinger.

"Tell me what you make of this," he said, in a tense, excited whisper.

I deciphered the paragraph, slowly and with some difficulty, and wrote down a rough English version with the pad and pencil which Carnby offered me. Then, at his request, I read it aloud:

> "It is verily known by few, but is nevertheless an attestable fact, that the will of a dead sorcerer hath power upon his own body and can raise it up from the tomb and perform therewith whatever action was unfulfilled in life. And such resurrections are invariably for the doing of malevolent deeds and for the detriment of others. Most readily can the corpse be animated if all its members have remained intact; and yet there are cases in which the excelling will of the wizard hath reared up from death the sundered pieces of a body hewn in many

fragments, and hath caused them to serve his end, either separately or in a temporary reunion. But in every instance, after the action hath been completed, the body lapseth into its former state."

Of course, all this was errant gibberish. Probably it was the strange, unhealthy look of utter absorption with which my employer listened, more than that damnable passage from the *Necronomicon*, which caused my nervousness and made me start violently when, toward the end of my reading, I heard an indescribable slithering noise in the hall outside. But when I finished the paragraph and looked up at Carnby, I was more than startled by the expression of stark, staring fear which his features had assumed—an expression as of one who is haunted by some hellish phantom. Somehow, I got the feeling that he was listening to that odd noise in the hallway rather than to my translation of Abdul Alhazred.

"The house is full of rats," he explained, as he caught my inquiring glance. "I have never been able to get rid of them, with all my efforts."

The noise, which still continued, was that which a rat might make in dragging some object slowly along the floor. It seemed to draw closer, to approach the door of Carnby's room, and then, after an intermission, it began to move again and receded. My employer's agitation was marked; he listened with fearful intentness and seemed to follow the progress of the sound with a terror that mounted as it drew near and decreased a little with its recession.

"I am very nervous," he said. "I have worked too hard lately, and this is the result. Even a little noise upsets me."

The sound had now died away somewhere in the house. Carnby appeared to recover himself in a measure.

"Will you please re-read your translation?" he requested. "I want to follow it very carefully, word by word."

I obeyed. He listened with the same look of unholy absorption as before, and this time we were not interrupted by any noises in the hallway. Carnby's face grew paler, as if the last remnant of blood had been drained from it, when I read the final sentences; and the fire in his hollow eyes was like phosphorescence in a deep vault.

"That is a most remarkable passage," he commented. "I was doubtful about its meaning, with my imperfect Arabic; and I have found that the passage is wholly omitted in the Latin of Olaus Wormius. Thank you for your scholarly rendering. You have certainly cleared it up for me."

His tone was dry and formal, as if he were repressing himself and holding back a world of unsurmisable thoughts and emotions. Somehow I felt that Carnby was more nervous and upset than ever, and also that my reading from the *Necronomicon* had in some mysterious manner contributed to his perturbation. He wore a ghastly brooding expression, as if his mind were busy with some unwelcome and forbidden theme.

However, seeming to collect himself, he asked me to translate another passage. This turned out to be a singular incantatory formula for the exorcism of the dead, with a ritual that involved the use of rare Arabian spices and the proper intoning of at least a hundred names of ghouls and demons. I copied it all out for Carnby, who studied it for a long time with a rapt eagerness that was more than scholarly.

"That, too," he observed, "is not in Olaus Wormius." After perusing it again, he folded the paper carefully and put it away in the same drawer from which he had taken the *Necronomicon*.

That evening was one of the strangest I have ever spent. As we sat for hour after hour discussing renditions from that unhallowed volume, I came to know more and more definitely that my employer was mortally afraid of something; that he dreaded being alone and was keeping me with him on this account rather than for any other reason. Always he seemed to be waiting and listening with a painful, tortured expectation, and I saw that he gave only a mechanical awareness to much that was said. Among the weird appurtenances of the room, in that atmosphere of unmanifested evil, of untold horror, the rational part of my mind began to succumb slowly to a recrudescence of dark ancestral fears. A scorner of such things in my normal moments, I was now ready to believe in the most baleful creations of superstitious fancy. No doubt, by some process of mental contagion, I had caught the hidden terror from which Carnby suffered.

By no word or syllable, however, did the man admit the actual feelings that were evident in his demeanor, but he spoke repeatedly of a nervous ailment. More than once, during our discussion, he sought to imply that his interest in the supernatural and the Satanic was wholly intellectual, that he, like myself, was without personal belief in such things. Yet I knew infallibly that his implications were false; that he was driven and obsessed by a real faith in all that he pretended to view with scientific detachment, and had doubtless fallen a victim to some imaginary horror entailed by his occult researches. But my intuition afforded me no clue to the actual nature of this horror.

There was no repetition of the sounds that had been so disturbing to my employer. We must have sat till after midnight with the writings of the mad Arab open before us. At last Carnby seemed to realize the lateness of the hour.

"I fear I have kept you up too long," he said apologetically. "You must go and get some sleep. I am selfish, and I forget that such hours are not habitual to others, as they are to me."

I made the formal denial of his self-impeachment which courtesy required, said good-night, and sought my own chamber with a feeling of intense relief. It seemed to me that I would leave behind me in Carnby's room all the shadowy fear and oppression to which I had been subjected.

Only one light was burning in the long passage. It was near Carnby's door; and my own door at the further end, close to the stair-head, was in deep shadow. As I groped for the knob, I heard a noise behind me, and turned to see in the gloom a small, indistinct body that sprang from the hall-landing to the top stair, disappearing from view. I was horribly startled; for even in that vague, fleeting glimpse, the thing was much too pale for a rat and its form was not at all suggestive of an animal. I could not have sworn what it was, but the outlines had seemed unmentionably monstrous. I stood trembling violently in every limb, and heard on the stairs a singular bumping sound like the fall of an object rolling downward from step to step. The sound was repeated at regular intervals, and finally ceased.

If the safety of the soul and body depended upon it, I could not have turned on the stair-light; nor could I have gone to the top steps to ascertain the agency of that unnatural bumping. Anyone else, it might seem, would have done this. Instead, after a moment of virtual petrification, I entered my room, locked the door, and went to bed in a turmoil of unresolved doubt and equivocal terror. I left the light burning; and I lay awake for hours, expecting momentarily a recurrence of that abominable sound. But the house was as silent as a morgue, and I heard nothing. At length, in spite of my anticipations to the contrary, I fell asleep and did not awaken till after many sodden, dreamless hours.

It was ten o'clock, as my watch informed me. I wondered whether my employer had left me undisturbed through thoughtfulness, or had not arisen himself. I dressed and went downstairs, to find him waiting at the breakfast table. He was paler and more tremulous than ever, as if he had slept badly.

"I hope the rats didn't annoy you too much," he remarked, after a preliminary greeting. "Something really must be done about them."

"I didn't notice them at all," I replied. Somehow, it was utterly impossible for me to mention the queer, ambiguous thing which I had seen and heard on retiring the night before. Doubtless I had been mistaken; doubtless it had been merely a rat after all, dragging something down the stairs. I tried to forget the hideously repeated noise and the momentary flash of unthinkable outlines in the gloom.

My employer eyed me with uncanny sharpness, as if he sought to penetrate my inmost mind. Breakfast was a dismal affair; and the day that followed was no less dreary. Carnby isolated himself till the middle of the afternoon, and I was left to my own devices in the well-supplied but conventional library downstairs. What Carnby was doing alone in his room I could not surmise; but I thought more than once that I heard the faint, monotonous intonations of a solemn voice. Horror-breeding hints and noisome intuitions invaded my brain. More and more the atmosphere of that house enveloped and stifled me with poisonous, miasmal mystery; and I felt everywhere the invisible brooding of malignant incubi.

It was almost a relief when my employer summoned me to his study. Entering, I noticed that the air was full of a pungent, aromatic smell and was touched by the vanishing coils of a blue vapor, as if from the burning of Oriental gums and spices in the church censers. An Ispahan rug had been moved from its position near the wall to the center of the room, but was not sufficient to cover entirely a curving violet mark that suggested the drawing of a magic circle on the floor. No doubt Carnby had been performing some sort of incantation; and I thought of the awesome formula I had translated at his request.

However, he did not offer any explanation of what he had been doing. His manner had changed remarkably and was more controlled and confident than at any former time. In a fashion almost business-like he laid before me a pile of manuscript which he wanted me to type for him. The familiar click of the keys aided me somewhat in dismissing my apprehensions of vague evil, and I could almost smile at the recherché and terrific information comprised in my employer's notes, which dealt mainly with formulae for the acquisition of unlawful power. But still, beneath my reassurance, there was a vague, lingering disquietude.

Evening came; and after our meal we returned again to the study. There was a tenseness in Carnby's manner now, as if he were eagerly awaiting the result of some hidden test. I went on with my work; but some of his emotion communicated itself to me, and ever and anon I caught myself in an attitude of strained listening.

At last, above the click of the keys, I heard the peculiar slithering in the hall. Carnby had heard it, too, and his confident look had utterly vanished, giving place to the most pitiable fear.

The sound drew nearer and was followed by a dull, dragging noise, and then by more sounds of an unidentifiable slithering and scuttling nature that varied in loudness. The hall was seemingly full of them, as if a whole army of rats were hauling some carrion booty along the floor. And yet no rodent or number of rodents could have made such sounds, or could have moved anything so heavy as the object which came behind the rest. There was something in the character of those noises, something without name or definition, which caused a slowly creeping chill to invade my spine.

"Good Lord! What is all that racket?" I cried.

"The rats! I tell you it is only rats!" Carnby's voice was a high hysterical shriek.

A moment later, there came an unmistakable knocking on the door, near the sill. At the same time I heard a heavy thudding in the locked cupboard at the further end of the room. Carnby had been standing erect, but now he sank limply into a chair. His features were ashen, and his look was almost maniacal with fright.

The nightmare doubt and tension became unbearable and I ran to the door and flung it open, in spite of a frantic remonstrance from my employer. I had no idea what I should find as I stepped across the sill into the dim-lit hall.

When I looked down and saw the thing on which I had almost trodden, my feeling was one of sick amazement and actual nausea. It was a human hand which had been severed at the wrist—a bony, bluish hand like that of a week-old corpse, with garden-mould on the fingers and under the long nails. *The damnable thing had moved!* It had drawn back to avoid me, and was crawling along the passage somewhat in the manner of a crab! And following it with my gaze, I saw that there were other things beyond it, one of which I recognized as a man's foot and another as a forearm. I dared not look at the rest. All were moving slowly, hideously away in a charnel procession, and I cannot describe the fashion in which they moved. Their individual vitality was horrifying beyond endurance. It was more than the vitality of life, yet the air was laden with a carrion taint. I averted my eyes and stepped back into Carnby's room, closing the door behind me with a shaking hand. Carnby was at my side with the key, which he turned in the lock with palsy-stricken fingers that had become as feeble as those of an old man.

"You saw them?" he asked in a dry, quavering whisper.

"In God's name, what does it all mean?" I cried.

Carnby went back to his chair, tottering a little with weakness. His lineaments were agonized by the gnawing of some inward horror, and he shook visibly like an ague patient. I sat down in a chair beside him, and he began to stammer forth his unbelievable confession, half incoherently, with inconsequential mouthings and many breaks and pauses:

"He is stronger than I am—even in death, even with his body dismembered by the surgeon's knife and saw that I used. I thought he could not return after that—after I had buried the portions in a dozen different places, in the cellar, beneath the shrubs, at the foot of the ivy-vines. But the *Necronomicon* is right . . . and Helman Carnby knew it. He warned me before I killed him, he told me he could return—*even in that condition.*

"But I did not believe him. I hated Helman, and he hated me, too.

He had attained to higher power and knowledge and was more favored by the Dark Ones than I. That was why I killed him—my own twin-brother, and my brother in the service of Satan and of Those who were before Satan. We had studied together for many years. We had celebrated the Black Mass together and we were attended by the same familiars. But Helman Carnby had gone deeper into the occult, into the forbidden, where I could not follow him. I feared him, and I could not endure his supremacy.

"It is more than a week—it is ten days since I did the deed. But Helman—or some part of him—has returned every night. . . . God! His accursed hands crawling on the floor! His feet, his arms, the segments of his legs, climbing the stairs in some unmentionable way to haunt me! . . . Christ! His awful, bloody torso lying in wait! I tell you, his hands have come even by day to tap and fumble at my door . . . and I have stumbled over his arms in the dark.

"Oh, God! I shall go mad with the awfulness of it. But he wants me to go mad, he wants to torture me till my brain gives way. That is why he haunts me in this piecemeal fashion. He could end it all at any time, with the demoniacal power that is his. He could re-knit his sundered limbs and body and slay me as I slew him.

"How carefully I buried the parts, with what infinite forethought! And how useless it was! I buried the saw and the knife, too, at the further end of the garden, as far away as possible from his evil, itching hands. But I did not bury the head with the other pieces—I kept it in that cupboard at the end of my room. Sometimes I have heard it moving there, as you heard it a while ago. . . . But he does not need the head, his will is elsewhere, and can work intelligently through all his members.

"Of course, I locked all the doors and windows at night when I found that he was coming back. . . . But it made no difference. And I have tried to exorcise him with the appropriate incantations—with all those that I knew. Today I tried that sovereign formula from the *Necronomicon* which you translated for me. I got you here to translate it. Also, I could no longer bear to be alone and I thought that it might help if there were someone else in the house. That formula was my last hope. I thought it would hold him—it is a most ancient and most dreadful incantation. But, as you have seen, it is useless. . . ."

His voice trailed off in a broken mumble, and he sat staring before him with sightless, intolerable eyes in which I saw the beginning flare of madness. I could say nothing—the confession he had made was so ineffably atrocious. The moral shock, and the ghastly supernatural horror, had almost stupefied me. My sensibilities were stunned; and it was not till I had begun to recover myself that I felt the irresistible surge of a flood of loathing for the man beside me.

I rose to my feet. The house had grown very silent, as if the macabre and charnel army of beleaguerment had now retired to its various graves. Carnby had left the key in the lock; and I went to the door and turned it quickly.

"Are you leaving? Don't go," Carnby begged in a voice that was tremulous with alarm, as I stood with my hand on the doorknob.

"Yes, I am going," I said coldly. "I am resigning my position right now; and I intend to pack my belongings and leave your house with as little delay as possible."

I opened the door and went out, refusing to listen to the arguments and pleadings and protestations he had begun to babble. For the nonce, I preferred to face whatever might lurk in the gloomy passage, no matter how loathsome and terrifying, rather than endure any longer the society of John Carnby.

The hall was empty; but I shuddered with repulsion at the memory of what I had seen, as I hastened to my room. I think I should have screamed aloud at the least sound or movement in the shadows.

I began to pack my valise with a feeling of the most frantic urgency and compulsion. It seemed to me that I could not escape soon enough from that house of abominable secrets, over which hung an atmosphere of smothering menace. I made mistakes in my haste, I stumbled over chairs, and my brain and fingers grew numb with a paralyzing dread.

I had almost finished my task, when I heard the sound of slow measured footsteps coming up the stairs. I knew that it was not Carnby, for he had locked himself immediately in his room when I had left; and I felt sure that nothing could have tempted him to emerge. Anyway, he could hardly have gone downstairs without my hearing him.

The footsteps came to the top landing and went past my door along the hall, with that same monotonous repetition, regular as the movement of a machine. Certainly it was not the soft, nervous tread of John Carnby.

Who, then, could it be? My blood stood still in my veins; I dared not finish the speculation that arose in my mind.

The steps paused; and I knew that they had reached the door of Carnby's room. There followed an interval in which I could scarcely breathe; and then I heard an awful crashing and shattering noise, and above it the soaring scream of a man in the uttermost extremity of fear.

I was powerless to move, as if an unseen iron hand had reached forth to restrain me; and I have no idea how long I waited and listened. The scream had fallen away in a swift silence; and I heard nothing now, except a low, peculiar, recurrent sound which my brain refused to identify.

It was not my own volition, but a stronger will than mine, which drew me forth at last and impelled me down the hall to Carnby's study. I felt the presence of that will as an overpowering, superhuman thing—a demoniac force, a malign mesmerism.

The door of the study had been broken in and was hanging by one hinge. It was splintered as by the impact of more than mortal strength. A light was still burning in the room, and the unmentionable sound I had been hearing ceased as I neared the threshold. It was followed by an evil, utter stillness.

Again I paused, and could go no further. But, this time, it was something other than the hellish, all-pervading magnetism that petrified my limbs and arrested me before the sill. Peering into the room, in the narrow space that was framed by the doorway and lit by an unseen lamp, I saw one end of the Oriental rug, and the gruesome outlines of a monstrous, unmoving shadow that fell beyond it on the floor. Huge, elongated, misshapen, the shadow was seemingly cast by the arms and torso of a naked man who stooped forward with a surgeon's saw in his hand. Its monstrosity lay in this: though the shoulders, chest, abdomen, and arms were all clearly distinguishable, the shadow was headless and appeared to terminate in an abruptly severed neck. It was impossible, considering the relative position, for the head to have been concealed from sight through any manner of foreshortening.

I waited, powerless to enter or withdraw. The blood had flowed back upon my heart in an ice-thick tide, and thought was frozen in my brain. An interval of termless horror, and then, from the hidden end of Carnby's room, from the direction of the locked cupboard, there came a fearsome and violent crash, and the sound of splintering wood and whining hinges, followed by the sinister, dismal thud of an unknown object striking the floor.

Again there was silence—a silence as of consummated Evil brooding above its unnameable triumph. The shadow had not stirred. There was a hideous contemplation in its attitude, and the saw was still held in its poising hand, as if above a completed task.

Another interval, and then, without warning, I witnessed the awful and unexplainable *disintegration* of the shadow, which seemed to break gently and easily into many different shadows ere it faded from view. I hesitate to describe the manner, or specify the places, in which this singular disruption, this manifold cleavage, occurred. Simultaneously, I heard the muffled clatter of a metallic implement on the Persian rug, and a sound that was not of a single body but of many bodies falling.

Once more there was silence—a silence as of some nocturnal cemetery, when grave-diggers and ghouls are done with their macabre toil, and the dead alone remain.

Drawn by the baleful mesmerism, like a somnambulist led by an unseen demon, I entered the room. I knew with a loathly prescience the sight that awaited me beyond the sill—the *double* heap of human segments, some of them fresh and bloody, and others already blue with beginning putrefaction and marked with earth-stains, that were mingled in abhorrent confusion on the rug.

A reddened knife and saw were protruding from the pile; and a little to one side, between the rug and the open cupboard with its shattered door, there reposed a human head that was fronting the other remnants in an upright posture. It was in the same condition of incipient decay as the body to which it belonged; but I swear that I saw the fading of a malignant exultation from its features as I entered. Even with the marks of corruption upon them, the lineaments bore a manifest likeness to those of John Carnby, and plainly they could belong only to a twin brother.

The frightful inferences that smothered my brain with their black and clammy cloud are not to be written here. The horror which I beheld—and the greater horror which I surmised—would have put to shame hell's foulest enormities in their frozen pits. There was but one mitigation and one mercy: I was compelled to gaze only for a few instants on that intolerable scene. Then, all at once, I felt that something had withdrawn from the room; the malign spell was broken, the overpowering volition that had held me captive was gone. It had released me now, even as it had released the dismembered corpse of Helman Carnby. I was free to go; and I fled from the ghastly chamber and ran headlong through an unlit house and into the outer darkness of the night.

Ubbo-Sathla*

CLARK ASHTON SMITH

> For Ubbo-Sathla is the source and the end. Before the coming of Zhothaqquah or Yok-Zothoth or Kthulhut from the stars, Ubbo-Sathla dwelt in the steaming fens of the new-made Earth: a mass without head or members, spawning the grey, formless efts of the prime and the grisly prototypes of terrene life. . . . And all earthly life, it is told, shall go back at last through the great circle of time to Ubbo-Sathla.
>
> —The Book of Eibon

Paul Tregardis found the milky crystal in a litter of oddments from many lands and eras. He had entered the shop of the curio-dealer through an aimless impulse, with no object in mind, other than the idle distraction of eyeing and fingering a miscellany of far-gathered things. Looking desultorily about, his attention had been drawn by a dull glimmering on one of the tables; and he had extricated the queer orb-like stone from its shadowy, crowded position between an ugly little Aztec idol, the fossil egg of a dinornis, and an obscene fetish of black wood from the Niger.

The thing was about the size of a small orange and was slightly flattened at the ends, like a planet at its poles. It puzzled Tregardis, for it was not like an ordinary crystal, being cloudy and changeable, with an intermittent glowing in its heart, as if it were alternately illumed and darkened from within. Holding it to the wintry window, he studied it for a while without being able to determine the secret of this singular and regular alternation. His puzzlement was soon complicated by a dawning sense of vague and irrecognizable familiarity, as if he had seen the thing before under circumstances that were now wholly forgotten.

---

*Originally published in *Weird Tales*, July 1933.

He appealed to the curio-dealer, a dwarfish Hebrew with an air of dusty antiquity, who gave the impression of being lost to commercial considerations in some web of cabbalistic reverie.

"Can you tell me anything about this?"

The dealer gave an indescribable, simultaneous shrug of his shoulders and his eyebrows.

"It is very old—palaeogean, one might say. I cannot tell you much, for little is known. A geologist found it in Greenland, beneath glacial ice, in the Miocene strata. Who knows? It may have belonged to some sorcerer of primeval Thule. Greenland was a warm, fertile region beneath the sun of Miocene times. No doubt it is a magic crystal; and a man might behold strange visions in its heart, if he looked long enough."

Tregardis was quite startled; for the dealer's apparently fantastic suggestion had brought to mind his own delvings in a branch of obscure lore; and, in particular, had recalled the *Book of Eibon*, that strangest and rarest of occult forgotten volumes, which is said to have come down through a series of manifold translations from a prehistoric original written in the lost language of Hyperborea. Tregardis, with much difficulty, had obtained the mediaeval French version—a copy that had been owned by many generations of sorcerers and Satanists—but had never been able to find the Greek manuscript from which the version was derived.

The remote, fabulous original was supposed to have been the work of a great Hyperborean wizard, from whom it had taken its name. It was a collection of dark and baleful myths; of liturgies, rituals, and incantations both evil and esoteric. Not without shudders, in the course of studies that the average person would have considered more than singular, Tregardis had collated the French volume with the frightful *Necronomicon* of the mad Arab, Abdul Alhazred. He had found many correspondences of the blackest and most appalling significance, together with much forbidden data that was either unknown to the Arab or omitted by him . . . or by his translators.

Was this what he had been trying to recall, Tregardis wondered—the brief, casual reference, in the *Book of Eibon*, to a cloudy crystal that had been owned by the wizard Zon Mezzamalech, in Mhu Thulan? Of course, it was all too fantastic, too hypothetic, too incredible—but Mhu Thulan, that northern portion of ancient Hyperborea, was supposed to have corresponded roughly with modern Greenland, which had formerly been joined as a peninsula to the main continent. Could the stone in his hand, by some fabulous fortuity, be the crystal of Zon Mezzamalech?

Tregardis smiled at himself with inward irony for even conceiving the absurd notion. Such things did not occur—at least, not in present-day London; and in all likelihood, the *Book of Eibon* was sheer superstitious fantasy, anyway. Nevertheless, there was something about the crystal that continued to tease and inveigle him. He ended by purchasing it, at a fairly moderate price. The sum was named by the seller and paid by the buyer without bargaining.

With the crystal in his pocket, Paul Tregardis hastened back to his lodgings instead of resuming his leisurely saunter. He installed the milky globe on his writing-table, where it stood firmly enough on one of its oblate ends. Then, still smiling at his own absurdity, he took down the yellow parchment manuscript of the *Book of Eibon* from its place in a somewhat inclusive collection of recherché literature. He opened the vermiculated leather cover with hasps of tarnished steel, and read over to himself, translating from the archaic French as he read, the paragraph that referred to Zon Mezzamalech:

> "This wizard, who was mighty among sorcerers, had found a cloudy stone, orb-like and somewhat flattened at the ends, in which he could behold many visions of the terrene past, even to the Earth's beginning, when Ubbo-Sathla, the unbegotten source, lay vast and swollen and yeasty amid the vaporing slime. . . . But of that which he beheld, Zon Mezzamalech left little record; and people say that he vanished presently, in a way that is not known; and after him the cloudy crystal was lost."

Paul Tregardis laid the manuscript aside. Again there was something that tantalized and beguiled him, like a lost dream or a memory forfeit to oblivion. Impelled by a feeling which he did not scrutinize or question, he sat down before the table and began to stare intently into the cold, nebulous orb. He felt an expectation which, somehow, was so familiar, so permeative a part of his consciousness, that he did not even name it to himself.

Minute by minute he sat, and watched the alternate glimmering and fading of the mysterious light in the heart of the crystal. By imperceptible degrees, there stole upon him a sense of dream-like duality, both in respect to his person and his surroundings. He was still Paul Tregardis—and yet he was someone else; the room was his London apartment—and a chamber in some foreign but well-known place. And in both milieus he peered steadfastly into the same crystal.

After an interim, without surprise on the part of Tregardis, the process of re-identification became complete. He knew that he was Zon Mezzamalech, a sorcerer of Mhu Thulan, and a student of all lore anterior to his own epoch. Wise with dreadful secrets that were not known to Paul Tregardis, amateur of anthropology and the occult sciences in latter-day London, he sought by means of the milky crystal to attain an even older and more fearful knowledge.

He had acquired the stone in dubitable ways, from a more than sinister source. It was unique and without fellow in any land or time. In its depths, all former years, all things that had ever been, were supposedly mirrored, and would reveal themselves to the patient visionary. And through the crystal, Zon Mezzamalech had dreamt to recover the wisdom of the gods who died before the Earth was born. They had passed to the lightless void, leaving their lore inscribed upon tablets of ultra-stellar stone; and the tablets were guarded in the primal mire by the formless, idiotic demiurge, Ubbo-Sathla. Only by means of the crystal could he hope to find and read the tablets.

For the first time, he was making trial of the globe's reputed virtues. About him an ivory-panelled chamber, filled with his magic books and paraphernalia, was fading slowly from his consciousness. Before him, on a table of some dark Hyperborean wood that had been graven with grotesque ciphers, the crystal appeared to swell and deepen, and in its filmy depth he beheld a swift and broken swirling of dim scenes, fleeting like the bubbles of a mill-race. As if he looked upon an actual world, cities, forests, mountains, seas, and meadows flowed beneath him, lightening and darkening as with the passage of days and nights in some weirdly accelerated stream of time.

Zon Mezzamalech had forgotten Paul Tregardis—had lost the remembrance of his own entity and his own surroundings in Mhu Thulan. Moment by moment, the flowing vision in the crystal became more definite and distinct, and the orb itself deepened till he grew giddy, as if he were peering from an insecure height into some never-fathomed abyss. He knew that time was racing backward in the crystal, was unrolling for him the pageant of all past days; but a strange alarm had seized him, and he feared to gaze longer. Like one who has nearly fallen from a precipice, he caught himself with a violent start and drew back from the mystic orb.

Again, to his gaze, the enormous whirling world into which he had peered was a small and cloudy crystal on his rune-wrought table in Mhu Thulan. Then, by degrees, it seemed that the great room with sculptured panels of mammoth ivory was narrowing to another and dingier place; and Zon Mezzamalech, losing his preternatural wisdom and sorcerous power, went back by a weird regression into Paul Tregardis.

And yet not wholly, it seemed, was he able to return. Tregardis, dazed and wondering, found himself before the writing-table on which he had set the oblate sphere. He felt the confusion of one who has dreamt and has not yet fully awakened from the dream. The room puzzled him vaguely, as if something were wrong with its size and furnishings; and his remembrance of purchasing the crystal from a curio-dealer was oddly and discrepantly mingled with an impression that he had acquired it in a very different manner.

He felt that something very strange had happened to him when he peered into the crystal; but just what it was he could not seem to recollect. It had left him in the sort of psychic muddlement that follows a debauch of hashish. He assured himself that he was Paul Tregardis, that he lived on a certain street in London, that the year was 1933; but such commonplace verities had somehow lost their meaning and their validity; and everything about him was shadow-like and insubstantial. The very walls seemed to waver like smoke; the people in the streets were phantoms of phantoms; and he himself was a lost shadow, a wandering echo of something long forgot.

He resolved that he would not repeat his experiment of crystal-gazing. The effects were too unpleasant and equivocal. But the very next day, by an unreasoning impulse to which he yielded almost mechanically, without reluctation, he found himself seated before the misty orb. Again he became the sorcerer Zon Mezzamalech in Mhu Thulan; again he dreamt to retrieve the wisdom of the antemundane gods; again he drew back from the deepening crystal with the terror of one who fears to fall; and once more—but doubtfully and dimly, like a failing wraith—he was Paul Tregardis.

Three times did Tregardis repeat the experience on successive days; and each time his own person and the world about him became more tenuous and confused than before. His sensations were those of a dreamer who is on the verge of waking; and London itself was unreal as the lands that slip from the dreamer's ken, receding in filmy mist and cloudy light. Beyond it all, he felt the looming and crowding of vast imageries, alien but half familiar. It was as if the phantasmagoria of time and space were dissolving about him, to reveal some veritable reality—or another dream of space and time.

There came, at last, the day when he sat down before the crystal—and did not return as Paul Tregardis. It was the day when Zon Mezzamalech, boldly disregarding certain evil and portentous warnings, resolved to overcome his curious fear of falling bodily into the visionary world that he beheld—a fear that had hitherto prevented him from following the backward stream of time for any distance. He must, he assured himself, conquer his fear if he were ever to see and read the lost tablets of the gods. He had beheld nothing more than a few fragments of the years of Mhu Thulan immediately posterior to the present—the years of his own lifetime; and there were inestimable cycles between these years and the Beginning.

Again, to his gaze, the crystal deepened immeasurably, with scenes and happenings that flowed in a retrograde stream. Again the magic ciphers of the dark table faded from his ken, and the sorcerously carven walls of his chamber melted into less than dream. Once more he grew giddy with an awful vertigo as he bent above the swirling and milling of the terrible gulfs of time in the world-like orb. Fearfully, in spite of his resolution, he would have drawn away; but he had looked and leaned too long. There was a sense of abysmal falling, a suction as of ineluctable winds, of maelstroms that bore him down through fleet unstable visions of his own past life into antenatal years and dimensions. He seemed to endure the pangs of an inverse dissolution; and then he was no longer Zon Mezzamalech, the wise and learned watcher of the crystal, but an actual part of the weirdly racing stream that ran back to re-attain the Beginning.

He seemed to live unnumbered lives, to die myriad deaths, forgetting each time the death and life that had gone before. He fought as a warrior in half-legendary battles; he was a child playing in the ruins of some olden city of Mhu Thulan; he was the king who had reigned when the city was in its prime, the prophet who had foretold its building and its doom. A woman, he wept for the bygone dead in necropoli long-crumbled; an antique wizard, he muttered the rude spells of earlier sorcery; a priest of some pre-human god, he wielded the sacrificial knife in cave-temples of pillared basalt. Life by life, era by era, he retraced the long and groping cycles through which Hyperborea had risen from savagery to a high civilization.

He became a barbarian of some troglodytic tribe, fleeing from the slow, turreted ice of a former glacial age into lands illumed by the ruddy flare of perpetual volcanoes. Then, after incomputable years, he was no longer man but a man-like beast, roving in forests of giant fern and calamite, or building an uncouth nest in the boughs of mighty cycads.

Through aeons of anterior sensation, of crude lust and hunger, of aboriginal terror and madness, there was someone—or something—that went ever backward in time. Death became birth, and birth was death. In a slow vision of reverse change, the Earth appeared to melt away, to slough off the hills and mountains of its latter strata. Always the sun grew larger and hotter above the fuming swamps that teemed with a crasser life, with a more fulsome vegetation. And the thing that had been Paul Tregardis, that had been Zon Mezzamalech, was a part of all the monstrous devolution. It flew with the claw-tipped wings of a pterodactyl, it swam in tepid seas with the vast, winding bulk of an ichthyosaurus, it bellowed uncouthly with the armored throat of some forgotten behemoth to the huge moon that burned through Liassic mists.

At length, after aeons of immemorial brutehood, it became one of the lost serpent-men who reared their cities of black gneiss and fought their venomous wars in the world's first continent. It walked undulously in antehuman streets, in strange crooked vaults; it peered at primeval stars from high, Babelian towers; it bowed with hissing litanies to great serpent-idols. Through years and ages of the ophidian era it returned, and was a thing that crawled in the ooze, that had not yet learned to think and dream and build. And the time came when there was no longer a continent, but only a vast, chaotic marsh, a sea of slime, without limit or horizon, that seethed with a blind writhing of amorphous vapors.

There, in the grey beginning of Earth, the formless mass that was Ubbo-Sathla reposed amid the slime and the vapors. Headless, without organs or members, it sloughed from its oozy sides, in a slow, ceaseless wave, the amoebic forms that were the archetypes of earthly life. Horrible it was, if there had been aught to apprehend the horror; and loathsome, if there had been any to feel loathing. About it, prone or tilted in the mire, there lay the mighty tablets of star-quarried stone that were writ with the inconceivable wisdom of the pre-mundane gods.

And there, to the goal of a forgotten search, was drawn the thing that he had been—or would sometime be—Paul Tregardis and Zon Mezzamalech. Becoming a shapeless eft of the prime, it crawled sluggishly and obliviously across the fallen tablets of the gods, and fought and ravened blindly with the other spawn of Ubbo-Sathla.

Of Zon Mezzamalech and his vanishing, there is no mention anywhere, save the brief passage in the *Book of Eibon*. Concerning Paul Tregardis, who also disappeared, there was a curt notice in several London papers. No one seems to have known anything about him: he is gone as if he had never been; and the crystal, presumably, is gone too. At least, no one has found it.

The Black Stone*

ROBERT E. HOWARD

They say foul beings of Old Times still lurk
In dark forgotten corners of the world,
And Gates still gape to loose, on certain nights,
Shapes pent in Hell.

—JUSTIN GEOFFREY

I read of it first in the strange book of Von Junzt, the German eccentric who lived so curiously and died in such grisly and mysterious fashion. It was my fortune to have access to his *Nameless Cults* in the original edition, the so-called Black Book, published in Düsseldorf in 1839, shortly before a hounding doom overtook the author. Collectors of rare literature are familiar with *Nameless Cults* mainly through the cheap and faulty translation which was pirated in London by Bridewell in 1845, and the carefully expurgated edition put out by the Golden Goblin Press of New York in 1909. But the volume I stumbled upon was one of the unexpurgated German copies, with heavy leather covers and rusty iron hasps. I doubt if there are more than half a dozen such volumes in the entire world today, for the quantity issued was not great, and when the manner of the author's demise was bruited about, many possessors of the book burned their volumes in panic.

Von Junzt spent his entire life (1795–1840) delving into forbidden subjects; he traveled in all parts of the world, gained entrance into innumerable secret societies, and read countless little known and esoteric books and manuscripts in the original; and in the chapters of the Black Book, which range from startling clarity of exposition to murky ambiguity, there are statements and hints to freeze the blood of a thinking man. Reading what Von Junzt *dared* put in print arouses uneasy speculations as to what it was that he dared *not* tell. What dark

*Originally published in *Weird Tales*, November 1931.

matters, for instance, were contained in those closely written pages that formed the unpublished manuscript on which he worked unceasingly for months before his death, and which lay torn and scattered all over the floor of the locked and bolted chamber in which Von Junzt was found dead with the marks of taloned fingers on his throat? It will never be known, for the author's closest friend, the Frenchman Alexis Ladeau, after having spent a whole night piecing the fragments together and reading what was written, burnt them to ashes and cut his own throat with a razor.

But the contents of the published matter are shuddersome enough, even if one accepts the general view that they but represent the ravings of a madman. There among many strange things I found mention of the Black Stone, that curious, sinister monolith that broods among the mountains of Hungary, and about which so many dark legends cluster. Von Junzt did not devote much space to it—the bulk of his grim work concerns cults and objects of dark worship which he maintained existed in his day, and it would seem that the Black Stone represents some order or being lost and forgotten centuries ago. But he spoke of it as one of the *keys*—a phrase used many times by him, in various relations, and constituting one of the obscurities of his work. And he hinted briefly at curious sights to be seen about the monolith on Midsummer Night. He mentioned Otto Dostmann's theory that this monolith was a remnant of the Hunnish invasion and had been erected to commemorate a victory of Attila over the Goths. Von Junzt contradicted this assertion without giving any refutatory facts, merely remarking that to attribute the origin of the Black Stone to the Huns was as logical as assuming that William the Conqueror reared Stonehenge.

This implication of enormous antiquity piqued my interest immensely, and after some difficulty I succeeded in locating a rat-eaten and moldering copy of Dostmann's *Remnants of Lost Empires* (Berlin, 1809, "Der Drachenhaus" Press). I was disappointed to find that Dostmann referred to the Black Stone even more briefly than had Von Junzt, dismissing it with a few lines as an artifact comparatively modern in contrast with the Greco-Roman ruins of Asia Minor which were his pet theme. He admitted his inability to make out the defaced characters on the monolith but pronounced them unmistakably Mongoloid. However, little as I learned from Dostmann, he did mention the name of the village adjacent to the Black Stone—Stregoicavar—an ominous name, meaning something like Witch-Town.

A close scrutiny of guide-books and travel articles gave me no further information—Stregoicavar, not on any map that I could find, lay in a wild, little-frequented region, out of the path of casual tourists. But I did find subject for thought in Dornly's *Magyar Folklore*. In his chapter on "Dream Myths" he mentions the Black Stone and tells of some curious superstitions regarding it—especially the belief that if anyone sleeps in the vicinity of the monolith, that person will be haunted by monstrous nightmares forever after; and he cited tales of the peasants regarding too-curious people who ventured to visit the Stone on Midsummer Night and who died raving mad because of *something* they saw there.

That was all I could glean from Dornly, but my interest was even more intensely roused as I sensed a distinctly sinister aura about the Stone. The suggestion of dark antiquity, the recurrent hint of unnatural events on Midsummer Night, touched some slumbering instinct in my being, as one senses, rather than hears, the flowing of some dark subterraneous river in the night.

And I suddenly saw a connection between this Stone and a certain weird and fantastic poem written by the mad poet, Justin Geoffrey: "The People of the Monolith." Inquiries led to the information that Geoffrey had indeed written that poem while traveling in Hungary, and I could not doubt that the Black Stone was the very monolith to which he referred in his strange verse. Reading his stanzas again, I felt once more the strange dim stirrings of subconscious promptings that I had noticed when first reading of the Stone.

I had been casting about for a place to spend a short vacation and I made up my mind. I went to Stregoicavar. A train of obsolete style carried me from Temesvár to within striking distance, at least, of my objective, and a three days' ride in a jouncing coach brought me to the little village which lay in a fertile valley high up in the fir-clad mountains. The journey itself was uneventful, but during the first day we passed the old battlefield of Schomvaal where the brave Polish-Hungarian knight, Count Boris Vladinoff, made his gallant and futile stand against the victorious hosts of Suleiman the Magnificent, when the Grand Turk swept over eastern Europe in 1526.

The driver of the coach pointed out to me a great heap of crumbling stones on a hill nearby, under which, he said, the bones of the brave Count lay. I remembered a passage from Larson's *Turkish Wars*: "After the skirmish" (in which the Count with his small army had beaten back the Turkish advance-guard) "the Count was standing beneath the half-ruined walls of the old castle on the hill, giving orders as to the disposition of his forces, when an aide brought to him a small lacquered case which had been taken from the body of the famous Turkish scribe and historian, Selim Bahadur, who had fallen in the fight. The Count took therefrom a roll of parchment and began to read, but he had not read far before he turned very pale and, without saying a word, replaced the parchment in the case and thrust the case into his cloak. At that very instant a hidden Turkish battery suddenly opened fire, and the balls striking the old castle, the Hungarians were horrified to see the walls crash down in ruin, completely covering the brave Count. Without a leader the gallant little army was cut to pieces, and in the war-swept years that followed, the bones of the nobleman were never recovered. Today the natives point out a huge and moldering pile of ruins near Schomvaal beneath which, they say, still rests all that the centuries have left of Count Boris Vladinoff."

I found the village of Stregoicavar a dreamy, drowsy little village that apparently belied its sinister cognomen—a forgotten back-eddy that Progress had passed by. The quaint houses and the quainter dress and manners of the people were those of an earlier century. They were friendly, mildly curious but not inquisitive, though visitors from the outside world were extremely rare.

"Ten years ago another American came here and stayed a few days in the village," said the owner of the tavern where I had put up, "a young fellow and queer-acting—mumbled to himself—a poet, I think."

I knew he must mean Justin Geoffrey.

"Yes, he was a poet," I answered, "and he wrote a poem about a bit of scenery near this very village."

"Indeed?" Mine host's interest was aroused. "Then, since all great poets are strange in their speech and actions, he must have achieved great fame, for his actions and conversations were the strangest of any man I ever knew."

"As is usual with artists," I answered, "most of his recognition has come since his death."

"He is dead, then?"

"He died screaming in a madhouse five years ago."

"Too bad, too bad," sighed mine host sympathetically. "Poor lad—he looked too long at the Black Stone."

My heart gave a leap, but I masked my keen interest and said casually: "I have heard something of this Black Stone; somewhere near this village, is it not?"

"Nearer than Christian folk wish," he responded. "Look!" He drew me to a latticed window and pointed up at the fir-clad slopes of the brooding blue mountains. "There beyond where you see the bare face of that jutting cliff stands that accursed Stone. Would that it were ground to powder and the powder flung into the Danube to be carried to the deepest ocean! Once men tried to destroy the thing, but each man who laid hammer or maul against it came to an evil end. So now the people shun it."

"What is there so evil about it?" I asked curiously.

"It is a demon-haunted thing," he answered uneasily and with the suggestion of a shudder. "In my childhood I knew a young man who came up from below and laughed at our traditions—in his foolhardiness he went to the Stone one Midsummer Night and at dawn stumbled into the village again, stricken dumb and mad. Something had shattered his brain and sealed his lips, for until the day of his death, which came soon after, he spoke only to utter terrible blasphemies or to slaver gibberish.

"My own nephew when very small was lost in the mountains and slept in the woods near the Stone, and now in his manhood he is tortured by foul dreams, so that at times he makes the night hideous with his screams and wakes with cold sweat upon him.

"But let us talk of something else, *Herr;* it is not good to dwell upon such things."

I remarked on the evident age of the tavern, and he answered with pride: "The foundations are more than four hundred years old; the original house was the only one in the village which was not burned to the ground when Suleiman's devils swept through the mountains. Here, in the house that then stood on these same foundations, it is said, the scribe Selim Bahadur had his headquarters while ravaging the country hereabouts."

I learned then that the present inhabitants of Stregoicavar are not descendants of the people who dwelt there before the Turkish raid of 1526. The victorious Moslems left no living human in the village or the vicinity hereabouts when they passed over. Men, women, and children they wiped out in one red holocaust of murder, leaving a vast stretch of country silent and utterly deserted. The present people of Stregoicavar are descended from hardy settlers from the lower valleys who came into the upper levels and rebuilt the ruined village after the Turk was thrust back.

Mine host did not speak of the extermination of the original inhabitants with any great resentment, and I learned that his ancestors in the lower levels had looked on the mountaineers with even more hatred and aversion than they regarded the Turks. He was rather vague regarding the causes of this feud, but said that the original inhabitants of Stregoicavar had been in the habit of making stealthy raids on the lowlands and stealing girls and children. Moreover, he said that they were not exactly of the same blood as his own people; the sturdy, original Magyar-Slavic stock had mixed and intermarried with a degraded aboriginal race until the breeds had blended, producing an unsavory amalgamation. Who these aborigines were, he had not the slightest idea, but maintained that they were "pagans" and had dwelt in the mountains since time immemorial, before the coming of the conquering peoples.

I attached little importance to this tale; seeing in it merely a parallel to the amalgamation of Celtic tribes with Mediterranean aborigines in the Galloway hills, with the resultant mixed race which, as Picts, has such an extensive part in Scotch legendry. Time has a curiously foreshortening effect on folklore, and just as tales of the Picts became intertwined with legends of an older Mongoloid race, so eventually to the Picts was ascribed the repulsive appearance of the squat primitives, whose individuality merged, in the telling, into Pictish tales, and was forgotten; so, I felt, the supposed inhuman attributes of the first villagers of Stregoicavar could be traced to older, outworn myths with invading Huns and Mongols.

The morning after my arrival I received directions from my host, who gave them worriedly, and set out to find the Black Stone. A few hours' tramp up the fir-covered slopes brought me to the face of the rugged, solid stone cliff which jutted boldly from the mountainside. A narrow trail wound up it, and mounting this, I looked out over the peaceful valley of Stregoicavar, which seemed to drowse, guarded on either hand by the great blue mountains. No huts or any sign of human tenancy showed between the cliffs whereon I stood and the village. I saw numbers of scattering farms in the valley but all lay on the other side of Stregoicavar, which itself seemed to shrink from the brooding slopes which masked the Black Stone.

The summit of the cliffs proved to be a sort of thickly wooded plateau. I made my way through the dense growth for a short distance and came into a wide glade; and in the center of the glade reared a gaunt figure of black stone.

It was octagonal in shape, some sixteen feet in height and about a foot and a half thick. It had once evidently been highly polished, but now the surface was thickly dinted as if savage efforts had been made to demolish it; but the hammers had done little more than to flake off small bits of stone and mutilate the characters which once had evidently marched in a spiraling line round and round the shaft to the top. Up to ten feet from the base these characters were almost completely blotted out, so that it was very difficult to trace their direction. Higher up they were plainer, and I managed to squirm part of the way up the shaft and scan them at close range. All were more or less defaced, but I was positive that they symbolized no language now remembered on the face of the earth. I am fairly familiar with all hieroglyphics known to researchers and philologists, and I can say with certainty that those characters were like nothing of which I have ever read or heard. The nearest approach to them that I ever saw were some crude scratches on a gigantic and strangely symmetrical rock in a lost valley of Yucatán. I remember that when I pointed out these marks to the archaeologist who was my companion, he maintained that they either represented natural weathering or the idle scratching of some Indian. To my theory that the rock was really the base of a long-vanished column, he merely laughed, calling my attention to the dimensions of it, which suggested, if it were built with any natural rules or architectural symmetry, a column a thousand feet high. But I was not convinced.

I will not say that the characters on the Black Stone were similar to those on the colossal rock in Yucatán; but one suggested the other. As to the substance of the monolith, again I was baffled. The stone of which it was composed was a dully gleaming black, whose surface, where it was not dinted and roughened, created a curious illusion of semi-transparency.

I spent most of the morning there and came away baffled. No connection of the Stone with any other artifact in the world suggested itself to me. It was as if the monolith had been reared by alien hands, in an age distant and apart from human ken.

I returned to the village with my interest in no way abated. Now that I had seen the curious thing, my desire was still more keenly whetted to investigate the matter further and seek to learn by what strange hands and for what strange purpose the Black Stone had been reared in the long ago.

I sought out the tavern-keeper's nephew and questioned him in regard to his dreams, but he was vague, though willing to oblige. He did not mind discussing them, but was unable to describe them with any clarity. Though he dreamed the same dreams repeatedly, and though they were hideously vivid at the time, they left no distinct impression on his waking mind. He remembered them only as chaotic nightmares through which huge whirling fires shot lurid tongues of flame and a black drum bellowed incessantly. One thing only he clearly remembered—in one dream he had seen the Black Stone, not on a mountain slope but set like a spire on a colossal black castle.

As for the rest of the villagers I found them not inclined to talk about the Stone, with the exception of the schoolmaster, a man of surprising education, who spent much more of his time out in the world than any of the rest.

He was much interested in what I told him of Von Junzt's remarks about the Stone, and warmly agreed with the German author in the alleged age of the monolith. He believed that a coven had once existed in the vicinity and that possibly all of the original villagers had been members of that fertility cult which once threatened to undermine European civilization and gave rise to the tales of witchcraft. He cited the very name of the village to prove his point; it had not been originally named Stregoicavar, he said; according to legends the builders had called it Xuthltan, which was the aboriginal name of the site on which the village had been built many centuries ago.

This fact roused again an indescribable feeling of uneasiness. The barbarous name did not suggest connection with any Scythic, Slavic, or Mongolian race to which an aboriginal people of these mountains would, under natural circumstances, have belonged.

That the Magyars and Slavs of the lower valleys believed the original inhabitants of the village to be members of the witchcraft cult was evident, the schoolmaster said, by the name they gave it, which name continued to be used even after the older settlers had been massacred by the Turks, and the village rebuilt by a cleaner and more wholesome breed.

He did not believe that the members of the cult erected the monolith, but he did believe that they used it as a center of their activities, and repeating vague legends which had been handed down since before the Turkish invasion, he advanced the theory that the degenerate villagers had used it as a sort of altar on which they offered human sacrifices, using as victims the girls and babies stolen from his own ancestors in the lower valleys.

He discounted the myths of weird events on Midsummer Night, as well as a curious legend of a strange deity which the witch-people of Xuthltan were said to have invoked with chants and wild rituals of flagellation and slaughter.

He had never visited the Stone on Midsummer Night, he said, but he would not fear to do so; whatever *had* existed or taken place there in the past, had been long engulfed in the mists of time and oblivion. The Black Stone had lost its meaning save as a link to a dead and dusty past.

It was while returning from a visit with this schoolmaster one night about a week after my arrival at Stregoicavar that a sudden recollection struck me—it was Midsummer Night! The very time that the legends linked with grisly implications to the Black Stone. I turned away from the tavern and strode swiftly through the village. Stregoicavar lay silent; the villagers retired early. I saw no one as I passed rapidly out of the village and up into the firs which masked the mountain slopes in a weird light and etched the shadows blackly. No wind blew through the firs, but a mysterious, intangible rustling and whispering was abroad. Surely on such nights in past centuries, my whimsical imagination told me, naked witches astride magic broomsticks had flown across this valley, pursued by jeering demoniac familiars.

I came to the cliffs and was somewhat disquieted to note that the illusive moonlight lent them a subtle appearance I had not noticed before—in the weird light they appeared less like natural cliffs and more like the ruins of cyclopean and Titan-reared battlements jutting from the mountain slope.

Shaking off this hallucination with difficulty, I came upon the plateau and hesitated a moment before I plunged into the brooding darkness of the woods. A sort of breathless tenseness hung over the shadows, like an unseen monster holding its breath lest it scare away its prey.

I shook off the sensation—a natural one, considering the eeriness of the place and its evil reputation—and made my way through the wood, experiencing a most unpleasant sensation that I was being followed, and halting once, sure that something clammy and unstable had brushed against my face in the darkness.

I came out into the glade and saw the tall monolith rearing its gaunt height above the sward. At the edge of the woods on the side toward the cliff was a stone which formed a sort of natural seat. I sat down, reflecting that it was probably while there that the mad poet, Justin Geoffrey, had written his fantastic "People of the Monolith." Mine host thought that it was the Stone which had caused Geoffrey's insanity, but the seeds of madness had been sown in the poet's brain long before he ever came to Stregoicavar.

A glance at my watch showed that the hour of midnight was close at hand. I leaned back, awaiting whatever ghostly demonstration might appear. A thin night wind started up among the branches of the firs, with an uncanny suggestion of faint, unseen pipes whispering an eerie and evil tune. The monotony of the sound and my steady gazing at the monolith produced a sort of self-hypnosis upon me; I grew drowsy. I fought this feeling, but sleep stole on me in spite of myself; the monolith seemed to sway and dance, strangely distorted to my gaze, and then I slept.

I opened my eyes and sought to rise, but lay still, as if an icy hand gripped me helpless. Cold terror stole over me. The glade was no longer deserted. It was thronged by a silent crowd of strange people, and my distended eyes took in strange barbaric details of costume which my reason told me were archaic and forgotten even in this backward land. Surely, I thought, these are villagers who have come here to hold some fantastic conclave—but another glance told me that these people were not of the folk of Stregoicavar. They were a shorter, more squat race, whose brows were lower, whose faces were broader and duller. Some had Slavic or Magyar features, but those features were degraded as from a mixture of some baser, alien strain I could not classify. Many wore the hides of wild beasts, and their whole appearance, both men and women, was one of sensual brutishness. They terrified and repelled me, but they gave me no heed. They formed in a vast half-circle in front of the monolith and began a sort of chant, flinging their arms in unison and weaving their bodies rhythmically from the waist upward. All eyes were fixed on the top of the Stone, which they seemed to be invoking. But the strangest of all was the dimness of their voices; not fifty yards from me hundreds of men and women were unmistakably lifting their voices in a wild chant, yet those voices came to me as a faint indistinguishable murmur as if from across vast leagues of Space—or *time*.

Before the monolith stood a sort of brazier from which a vile, nauseous yellow smoke billowed upward, curling curiously in an undulating spiral around the black shaft, like a vast unstable serpent.

On one side of this brazier lay two figures—a young girl, stark naked and bound hand and foot, and an infant, apparently only a few months old. On the other side of the brazier squatted a hideous old hag with a queer sort of black drum on her lap; this drum she beat with slow, light blows of her open palms, but I could not hear the sound.

The rhythm of the swaying bodies grew faster, and into the space between the people and the monolith sprang a naked young woman, her eyes blazing, her long black hair flying loose. Spinning dizzily on her toes, she whirled across the open space and fell prostrate before the Stone, where she lay motionless. The next instant a fantastic figure followed her—a man from whose waist hung a goatskin, and whose features were entirely hidden by a sort of mask made from a huge wolf's head, so that he looked like a monstrous, nightmare being, horribly compounded of elements both human and bestial. In his hand he held a bunch of long fir switches bound together at the larger ends, and the moonlight glinted on a chain of heavy gold looped about his neck. A smaller chain depending from it suggested a pendant of some sort, but this was missing.

The people tossed their arms violently and seemed to redouble their shouts as this grotesque creature loped across the open space with many a fantastic leap and caper. Coming to the woman who lay before the monolith, he began to lash her with the switches he bore, and she leaped up and spun into the wild mazes of the most incredible dance I have ever seen. And her tormentor danced with her, keeping the wild rhythm, matching her every whirl and bound, while incessantly raining cruel blows on her naked body. And at every blow he shouted a single word, over and over, and all the people shouted it back. I could see the working of their lips, and now the faint far-off murmur of their voices merged and blended into one distant shout, repeated over and over with slobbering ecstasy. But what that one word was, I could not make out.

In dizzy whirls spun the wild dancers, while the lookers-on, standing still in their tracks, followed the rhythm of their dance with swaying bodies and weaving arms. Madness grew in the eyes of the capering votaress and was reflected in the eyes of the watchers. Wilder and more extravagant grew the whirling frenzy of that mad dance—it became a bestial and obscene thing, while the old hag howled and battered the drum like a crazy woman, and the switches cracked out a devil's tune.

Blood trickled down the dancer's limbs, but she seemed not to feel the lashing save as a stimulus for further enormities of outrageous motion; bounding into the midst of the yellow smoke which now spread out tenuous tentacles to embrace both flying figures, she seemed to merge with that foul fog and veil herself with it. Then emerging into plain view, closely followed by the beast-thing that flogged her, she shot into an indescribable, explosive burst of dynamic mad motion, and on the very crest of that mad wave, she dropped suddenly to the sward, quivering and panting as if completely overcome by her frenzied exertions. The lashing continued with unabated violence and intensity, and she began to wriggle toward the monolith on her belly. The priest—or such I will call him—followed, lashing her unprotected body with all the power of his arm as she writhed along, leaving a heavy track of blood on the trampled earth. She reached the monolith and, gasping and panting, flung both arms about it and covered the cold stone with fierce hot kisses, as in frenzied and unholy adoration.

The fantastic priest bounded high in the air, flinging away the red-dabbled switches, and the worshippers, howling and foaming at the mouths, turned on each other with tooth and nail, rending one another's garments and flesh in a blind passion of bestiality. The priest swept up the infant with a long arm, and shouting again that Name, whirled the wailing babe high in the air and dashed its brains out against the monolith, leaving a ghastly stain on the black surface. Cold with horror, I saw him rip the tiny body open with his bare brutish fingers and fling handfuls of blood on the shaft, then toss the red and torn shape into the brazier, extinguishing flame and smoke in a crimson rain, while the maddened brutes behind him howled over and over that Name. Then suddenly they all fell prostrate, writhing like snakes, while the priest flung wide his gory hands as in triumph. I opened my mouth to scream my horror and loathing, but only a dry rattle sounded; a huge monstrous toad-like *thing* squatted on the top of the monolith!

I saw its bloated, repulsive, and unstable outline against the moonlight, and set in what would have been the face of a natural creature, its huge, blinking eyes which reflected all the lust, abysmal greed, obscene cruelty, and monstrous evil that has stalked the sons of men since their ancestors moved blind and hairless in the tree-tops. In those grisly eyes mirrored all the unholy things and vile secrets that sleep in the cities under the sea, and that skulk from the light of day in the blackness of primordial caverns. And so that ghastly thing that the unhallowed ritual of cruelty and sadism and blood had evoked from the silence of the hills, leered and blinked down on its bestial worshippers, who groveled in abhorrent abasement before it.

Now the beast-masked priest lifted the bound and weakly writhing girl in his brutish hands and held her up toward that horror on the monolith. And as that monstrosity sucked in its breath, lustfully and slobberingly, something snapped in my brain and I fell into a merciful faint.

I opened my eyes on a still white dawn. All the events of the night rushed back on me and I sprang up, then stared about me in amazement. The monolith brooded gaunt and silent above the sward which waved, green and untrampled, in the morning breeze. A few quick strides took me across the glade; here had the dancers leaped and bounded until the ground should have been trampled bare, and here had the votaress wriggled her painful way to the Stone, streaming blood on the earth. But no drop of crimson showed on the uncrushed sward. I looked, shudderingly, at the side of the monolith against which the bestial priest had brained the stolen baby—but no dark stain or grisly clot showed there.

A dream! It had been a wild nightmare—or else—I shrugged my shoulders. What vivid clarity for a dream!

I returned quietly to the village and entered the inn without being seen. And there I sat meditating over the strange events of the night. More and more was I prone to discard the dream-theory. That what I had seen was illusion and without material substance, was evident. But I believed that I had looked on the mirrored shadow of a deed perpetrated in ghastly actuality in bygone days. But how was I to know? What proof to show that my vision had been a gathering of foul specters rather than a mere nightmare originating in my own brain?

As if for answer a name flashed into my mind—Selim Bahadur! According to legend this man, who had been a soldier as well as a scribe, had commanded that part of Suleiman's army which had devastated Stregoicavar. It seemed logical enough; and if so, he had gone straight from the blotted-out countryside to the bloody field of Schomvaal, and his doom. I sprang up with a sudden shout—that manuscript which was taken from the Turk's body, and which Count Boris shuddered over—might it not contain some narration of what the conquering Turks found in Stregoicavar? What else could have shaken the iron nerves of the Polish adventurer? And since the bones of the Count had never been recovered, what more certain than that lacquered case, with its mysterious contents, still lay hidden beneath the ruins that covered Boris Vladinoff? I began packing my bag with fierce haste.

* * *

Three days later found me ensconced in a little village a few miles from the old battlefield, and when the moon rose I was working with savage intensity on the great pile of crumbling stone that crowned the hill. It was back-breaking toil—looking back now I cannot see how I accomplished it, though I labored without a pause from moonrise to dawn. Just as the sun was coming up I tore aside the last tangle of stones and looked on all that was mortal of Count Boris Vladinoff—only a few pitiful fragments of crumbling bone—and among them, crushed out of all original shape, lay a case whose lacquered surface had kept it from complete decay through the centuries.

I seized it with frenzied eagerness, and piling back some of the stones on the bones I hurried away; for I did not care to be discovered by the suspicious peasants in an act of apparent desecration.

Back in my tavern chamber I opened the case and found the parchment comparatively intact; and there was something else in the case—a small squat object wrapped in silk. I was wild to plumb the secrets of those yellowed pages, but weariness forbade me. Since leaving Stregoicavar I had hardly slept at all, and the terrific exertions of the previous night combined to overcome me. In spite of myself I was forced to stretch myself down on my bed, nor did I awake until sundown.

I snatched a hasty supper, and then in the light of a flickering candle, I set myself to read the neat Turkish characters that covered the parchment. It was difficult work, for I am not deeply versed in the language and the archaic style of the narrative baffled me. But as I toiled through it, a word or phrase here and there leaped at me and a dimly growing horror shook me in its grip. I bent my energies fiercely to the task, and as the tale grew clearer and took more tangible form my blood chilled in my veins, my hair stood up, and my tongue clove to my mouth. All external things partook of the grisly madness of that infernal manuscript until the night sounds of insects and creatures in the woods took the form of ghastly murmurings and stealthy treadings of ghoulish horrors and the sighing of the night wind changed to tittering obscene gloating of evil over the souls of men.

At last when gray dawn was stealing through the latticed window, I laid down the manuscript and took up and unwrapped the thing in the bit of silk. Staring at it with haggard eyes I knew the truth of the matter was clinched, even had it been possible to doubt the veracity of that terrible manuscript.

And I replaced both obscene things in the case, nor did I rest or sleep or eat until that case containing them had been weighted with stones and flung into the deepest current of the Danube which, God grant, carried them back into the Hell from which they came.

It was no dream I dreamed on Midsummer Midnight in the hills above Stregoicavar. Well for Justin Geoffrey that he tarried there only in the sunlight and went his way, for had he gazed upon that ghastly conclave, his mad brain would have snapped before it did. How my own reason held, I do not know.

No—it was no dream—I gazed upon a foul rite of votaries long dead, come up from Hell to worship as of old; ghosts that bowed before a ghost. For Hell has long claimed their hideous god. Long, long he dwelt among the hills, a brain-shattering vestige of an outworn age, but no longer his obscene talons clutch for the souls of living men, and his kingdom is a dead kingdom, peopled only by the ghosts of those who served him in his lifetime and theirs.

By what foul alchemy or godless sorcery the Gates of Hell are opened on that one eerie night I do not know, but mine own eyes have seen. And I know I looked on no living thing that night, for the manuscript written in the careful hand of Selim Bahadur narrated at length what he and his raiders found in the valley of Stregoicavar; and I read, set down in detail, the blasphemous obscenities that torture wrung from the lips of screaming worshippers; and I read, too, of the lost, grim black cavern high in the hills where the horrified Turks hemmed a monstrous, bloated, wallowing toad-like being and slew it with flame and ancient steel blessed in old times by Muhammad, and with incantations that were old when Arabia was young. And even staunch old Selim's hand shook as he recorded the cataclysmic, earth-shaking death-howls of the monstrosity which died not alone; for a half-score of his slayers perished with him, in ways that Selim would not or could not describe.

And that squat idol carved of gold and wrapped in silk was an image of *himself*, and Selim tore it from the golden chain that looped the neck of the slain high priest of the mask.

Well that the Turks swept that foul valley with torch and cleanly steel! Such sights as those brooding mountains have looked on belong to the darkness and abysses of lost eons. No—it is not fear of the toad-thing that makes me shudder in the night. He is made fast in Hell with his nauseous horde, freed only for an hour on the most weird night of the year, as I have seen. And of his worshippers, none remains.

But it is the realization that such things once crouched beast-like above the souls of men which brings cold sweat to my brow; and I fear to peer again into the leaves of Von Junzt's abomination. For now I understand his repeated phrase of *keys*!—age! Keys to Outer Doors—links with an abhorrent past and—who knows?—of abhorrent spheres of the *present*. And I understand why the cliffs look like battlements in the moonlight and why the tavern-keeper's nightmare-haunted nephew saw, in his dream, the Black Stone like a spire on a cyclopean black castle. If men ever excavate among those mountains, they may find incredible things below those masking slopes. For the cave wherein the Turks trapped the—*thing*—was not truly a cavern, and I shudder to contemplate the gigantic gulf of eons which must stretch between this age and the time when the earth shook herself and reared up, like a wave, those blue mountains that, rising, enveloped unthinkable things. May no man ever seek to uproot that ghastly spire men call the Black Stone!

A Key! Aye, it is a Key, symbol of a forgotten horror. That horror had faded into the limbo from which it crawled, loathsomely, in the black dawn of the earth. But what of the other fiendish possibilities hinted at by Von Junzt—what of the monstrous hand which strangled out his life? Since reading what Selim Bahadur wrote, I can no longer doubt anything in the Black Book. Man was not always master of the earth—*and is he now?*

And the thought recurs to me—if such a monstrous entity as the Master of the Monolith somehow survived its own unspeakably distant epoch so long—*what nameless shapes may even now lurk in the dark places of the world?*

The Hounds of Tindalos*

FRANK BELKNAP LONG

I

"I'm glad you came," said Chalmers. He was sitting by the window and his face was very pale. Two tall candles guttered at his elbow and cast a sickly amber light over his long nose and slightly receding chin. Chalmers would have nothing modern about his apartment. He had the soul of a mediaeval ascetic, and he preferred illuminated manuscripts to automobiles, and leering stone gargoyles to radios and adding-machines.

As I crossed the room to the settee he had cleared for me, I glanced at his desk and was surprised to discover that he had been studying the mathematical formulae of a celebrated contemporary physicist, and that he had covered many sheets of thin yellow paper with curious geometric designs.

"Einstein and John Dee are strange bedfellows," I said as my gaze wandered from his mathematical charts to the sixty or seventy quaint books that comprised his strange little library. Plotinus and Emanuel Moscopulus, St. Thomas Aquinas and Frenicle de Bessy stood elbow to elbow in the somber ebony bookcase, and chairs, table, and desk were littered with pamphlets about mediaeval sorcery and witchcraft and black magic, and all of the valiant glamorous things that the modern world has repudiated.

Chalmers smiled engagingly, and passed me a Russian cigarette on a curiously carved tray. "We are just discovering now," he said, "that the old alchemists and sorcerers were two-thirds *right*, and that your modern biologist and materialist is nine-tenths *wrong*."

"You have always scoffed at modern science," I said, a little impatiently.

---

*Originally published in *Weird Tales*, March 1929.

"Only at scientific dogmatism," he replied. "I have always been a rebel, a champion of originality and lost causes; that is why I have chosen to repudiate the conclusions of contemporary biologists."

"And Einstein?" I asked.

"A priest of transcendental mathematics!" he murmured reverently. "A profound mystic and explorer of the great *suspected*."

"Then you do not entirely despise science."

"Of course not," he affirmed. "I merely distrust the scientific positivism of the past fifty years, the positivism of Haeckel and Darwin and of Mr. Bertrand Russell. I believe that biology has failed pitifully to explain the mystery of man's origin and destiny."

"Give them time," I retorted.

Chalmers's eyes glowed. "My friend," he murmured, "your pun is sublime. Give them *time*. That is precisely what I would do. But your modern biologist scoffs at time. He has the key but he refuses to use it. What do we know of time, really? Einstein believes that it is relative, that it can be interpreted in terms of space, of *curved* space. But must we stop there? When mathematics fails us can we not advance by—insight?"

"You are treading on dangerous ground," I replied. "That is a pitfall that your true investigator avoids. That is why modern science has advanced so slowly. It accepts nothing that it cannot demonstrate. But you—"

"I would take hashish, opium, all manner of drugs. I would emulate the sages of the East. And then perhaps I would apprehend—"

"What?"

"The fourth dimension."

"Theosophical rubbish!"

"Perhaps. But I believe that drugs expand human consciousness. William James agreed with me. And I have discovered a new one."

"A new drug?"

"It was used centuries ago by Chinese alchemists, but it is virtually unknown in the West. Its occult properties are amazing. With its aid and the aid of my mathematical knowledge I believe that I can *go back through time*."

"I do not understand."

"Time is merely our imperfect perception of a new dimension of space. Time and motion are both illusions. Everything that has existed from the beginning of the world *exists now*. Events that occurred centuries ago on this planet continue to exist in another dimension of space. Events that will occur centuries from now *exist already*. We cannot perceive their existence because we cannot enter the dimension of space that contains them. Human beings as we know them are merely fractions, infinitesimally small fractions of one enormous whole. Every human being is linked with *all* the life that has preceded him on this planet. All of his ancestors are parts of him. Only time separates him from his forebears, and time is an illusion and does not exist."

"I think I understand," I murmured.

"It will be sufficient for my purpose if you can form a vague idea of what I wish to achieve. I wish to strip from my eyes the veils of illusion that time has thrown over them, and see the *beginning and the end.*"

"And you think this new drug will help you?"

"I am sure that it will. And I want you to help me. I intend to take the drug immediately. I cannot wait. I must *see.*" His eyes glittered strangely. "I am going back, back through time."

He rose and strode to the mantel. When he faced me again he was holding a small square box in the palm of his hand. "I have here five pellets of the drug Liao. It was used by the Chinese philosopher Lao Tze, and while under its influence he visioned Tao. Tao is the most mysterious force in the world; it surrounds and pervades all things; it contains the visible universe and everything that we call reality. He who apprehends the mysteries of Tao sees clearly all that was and will be."

"Rubbish!" I retorted.

"Tao resembles a great animal, recumbent, motionless, containing in its enormous body all the worlds of our universe, the past, the present, and the future. We see portions of this great monster through a slit, which we call time. With the aid of this drug I shall enlarge the slit. I shall behold the great figure of life, the great recumbent beast in its entirety."

"And what do you wish me to do?"

"Watch, my friend. Watch and take notes. And if I go back too far you must recall me to reality. You can recall me by shaking me violently. If I appear to be suffering acute physical pain you must recall me at once."

"Chalmers," I said, "I wish you wouldn't make this experiment. You are taking dreadful risks. I don't believe that there is any fourth dimension and I emphatically do not believe in Tao. And I don't approve of your experimenting with unknown drugs."

"I know the properties of this drug," he replied. "I know precisely how it affects the human animal and I know its dangers. The risk does not reside in the drug itself. My only fear is that I may become lost in time. You see, I shall assist the drug. Before I swallow this pellet I shall give my undivided attention to the geometric and algebraic symbols that I have traced on this paper." He raised the mathematical chart that rested on his knee. "I shall prepare my mind for an excursion into time. I shall approach the fourth dimension with my conscious mind before I take the drug which will enable me to exercise occult powers of perception. Before I enter the dream world of the Eastern mystic I shall acquire all of the mathematical help that modern science can offer. This mathematical knowledge, this conscious approach to an actual apprehension of the fourth dimension of time, will supplement the work of the drug. The drug will open up stupendous new vistas—the mathematical preparation will enable me to grasp them intellectually. I have often grasped the fourth dimension in dreams, emotionally, intuitively, but I have never been able to recall, in waking life, the occult splendors that were momentarily revealed to me.

"But with your aid, I believe that I can recall them. You will take down everything that I say while I am under the influence of the drug. No matter how strange or incoherent my speech may become you will omit nothing. When I awake I may be able to supply the key to whatever is mysterious or incredible. I am not sure that I shall succeed, but if I *do* succeed"—his eyes were strangely luminous—*"time will exist for me no longer!"*

He sat down abruptly. "I shall make the experiment at once. Please stand over there by the window and watch. Have you a fountain pen?"

I nodded gloomily and removed a pale green Waterman from my upper vest pocket.

"And a pad, Frank?"

I groaned and produced a memorandum book. "I emphatically disapprove of this experiment," I muttered. "You're taking a frightful risk."

"Don't be an asinine old woman!" he admonished. "Nothing that you can say will induce me to stop now. I entreat you to remain silent while I study these charts."

He raised the charts and studied them intently. I watched the clock on the mantel as it ticked out the seconds, and a curious dread clutched at my heart so that I choked.

Suddenly the clock stopped ticking, and exactly at that moment Chalmers swallowed the drug.

I rose quickly and moved toward him, but his eyes implored me not to interfere. "The clock has stopped," he murmured. "The forces that control it approve of my experiment. *Time* stopped, and I swallowed the drug. I pray God that I shall not lose my way."

He closed his eyes and leaned back on the sofa. All of the blood had left his face and he was breathing heavily. It was clear that the drug was acting with extraordinary rapidity.

"It is beginning to get dark," he murmured. "Write that. It is beginning to get dark and the familiar objects in the room are fading out. I can discern them vaguely through my eyelids, but they are fading swiftly."

I shook my pen to make the ink come and wrote rapidly in shorthand as he continued to dictate.

"I am leaving the room. The walls are vanishing and I can no longer see any of the familiar objects. Your face, though, is still visible to me. I hope that you are writing. I think that I am about to make a great leap—a leap through space. Or perhaps it is through time that I shall make the leap. I cannot tell. Everything is dark, indistinct."

He sat for a while silent, with his head sunk upon his breast. Then suddenly he stiffened and his eyelids fluttered open. "God in heaven!" he cried. "I *see!*"

He was straining forward in his chair, staring at the opposite wall. But I knew that he was looking beyond the wall and that the objects in the room no longer existed for him. "Chalmers," I cried, "Chalmers, shall I wake you?"

"Do not!" he shrieked. "I *see everything*. All of the billions of lives that preceded me on this planet are before me at this moment. I see men of all ages, all races, all colors. They are fighting, killing, building, dancing, singing. They are sitting about rude fires on lonely gray deserts, and flying through the air in monoplanes. They are riding the seas in bark canoes and enormous steamships; they are painting bison and mammoths on the walls of dismal caves and covering huge canvases with queer futuristic designs. I watch the migrations from Atlantis. I watch the migrations from Lemuria. I see the elder races—a strange horde of black dwarfs overwhelming Asia, and the Neanderthalers with lowered heads and bent knees ranging obscenely across Europe. I watch the Achaeans streaming into the Greek islands, and the crude beginnings of Hellenic culture. I am in Athens and Pericles is young. I am standing on the soil of Italy. I assist in the rape of the Sabines; I march with the Imperial Legions. I tremble with awe and wonder as the enormous standards go by and the ground shakes with the tread of the victorious *hastati*. A thousand naked slaves grovel before me as I pass in a litter of gold and ivory drawn by night-black oxen from Thebes, and the flower-girls scream *'Ave Caesar'* as I nod and smile. I am myself a slave on a Moorish galley. I watch the erection of a great cathedral. Stone by stone it rises, and through months and years I stand and watch each stone as it falls into place. I am burned on a cross head downward in the thyme-scented gardens of Nero, and I watch with amusement and scorn the torturers at work in the chambers of the Inquisition.

"I walk in the holiest sanctuaries; I enter the temples of Venus. I kneel in adoration before the Magna Mater, and I throw coins on the bare knees of the sacred courtesans who sit with veiled faces in the groves of Babylon. I creep into an Elizabethan theater and with the stinking rabble about me I applaud *The Merchant of Venice*. I walk with Dante through the narrow streets of Florence. I meet the young Beatrice, and the hem of her garment brushes my sandals as I stare enraptured. I am a priest of Isis, and my magic astounds the nations. Simon Magus kneels before me, imploring my assistance, and Pharaoh trembles when I approach. In India I talk with the Masters and run screaming from their presence, for their revelations are as salt on wounds that bleed.

"I perceive everything *simultaneously*. I perceive everything from all sides; I am a part of all the teeming billions about me. I exist in all men and all men exist in me. I perceive the whole of human history in a single instant, the past and the present.

"By simply *straining* I can see farther and farther back. Now I am going back through strange curves and angles. Angles and curves multiply about me. I perceive great segments of time through *curves*. There is *curved time*, and *angular time*. The beings that exist in angular time cannot enter curved time. It is very strange.

"I am going back and back. Man has disappeared from the earth. Gigantic reptiles crouch beneath enormous palms and swim through the loathly black waters of dismal lakes. Now the reptiles have disappeared. No animals remain upon the land, but beneath the waters, plainly visible to me, dark forms move slowly over the rotting vegetation.

"These forms are becoming simpler and simpler. Now they are single cells. All about me there are angles—strange angles that have no counterparts on the earth. I am desperately afraid.

"There is an abyss of being which man has never fathomed."

I stared. Chalmers had risen to his feet and he was gesticulating helplessly with his arms. "I am passing through unearthly angles; I am approaching—oh, the burning horror of it."

"Chalmers!" I cried. "Do you wish me to interfere?"

He brought his right hand quickly before his face, as though to shut out a vision unspeakable. "Not yet!" he cried "I will go on. I will see—what—lies—beyond—"

A cold sweat streamed from his forehead and his shoulders jerked spasmodically. "Beyond life there are"—his face grew ashen with terror—"*things* that I cannot distinguish. They move slowly through angles. They have no bodies, and they move slowly through outrageous angles."

It was then that I became aware of the odor in the room. It was a pungent, indescribable odor, so nauseous that I could scarcely endure it. I stepped quickly to the window and threw it open. When I returned to Chalmers and looked into his eyes I nearly fainted.

"I think they have scented me!" he shrieked. "They are slowly turning toward me."

He was trembling horribly. For a moment he clawed at the air with his hands. Then his legs gave way beneath him and he fell forward on his face, slobbering and moaning.

I watched him in silence as he dragged himself across the floor. He was no longer a man. His teeth were bared and saliva dripped from the corners of his mouth.

"Chalmers," I cried. "Chalmers, stop it! Stop it, do you hear?"

As if in reply to my appeal he commenced to utter hoarse convulsive sounds which resembled nothing so much as the barking of a dog, and began a sort of hideous writhing in a circle about the room. I bent and seized him by the shoulders. Violently, desperately, I shook him. He turned his head and snapped at my wrist. I was sick with horror, but I dared not release him for fear that he would destroy himself in a paroxysm of rage.

"Chalmers," I muttered, "you must stop that. There is nothing in this room that can harm you. Do you understand?"

I continued to shake and admonish him, and gradually the madness died out of his face. Shivering convulsively, he crumpled into a grotesque heap on the Chinese rug.

I carried him to the sofa and deposited him upon it. His features were twisted in pain, and I knew that he was still struggling dumbly to escape from abominable memories.

"Whiskey," he muttered. "You'll find a flask in the cabinet by the window—upper-left-hand drawer."

When I handed him the flask his fingers tightened about it until the knuckles showed blue. "They nearly got me," he gasped. He drained the stimulant in immoderate gulps, and gradually the color crept back into his face.

"That drug was the very devil!" I murmured.

"It wasn't the drug," he moaned.

His eyes no longer glared insanely, but he still wore the look of a lost soul.

"They scented me in time," he moaned. "I went too far."

"What were *they* like?" I said, to humor him.

He leaned forward and gripped my arm. He was shivering horribly. "No words in our language can describe them!" He spoke in a hoarse whisper. "They are symbolized vaguely in the myth of the Fall, and in an obscene form which is occasionally found engraved on ancient tablets. The Greeks had a name for them, which veiled their essential foulness. The tree, the snake, and the apple—these are the vague symbols of a most awful mystery."

His voice had risen to a scream. "Frank, Frank, a terrible and unspeakable *deed* was done in the beginning. Before time, the *deed*, and from the deed—"

He had risen and was hysterically pacing the room. "The deeds of the dead move through angles in dim recesses of time. They are hungry and athirst!"

"Chalmers," I pleaded to quiet him. "We are living in the third decade of the Twentieth Century."

"They are lean and athirst!" he shrieked. *"The Hounds of Tindalos!"*

"Chalmers, shall I phone for a physician?"

"A physician cannot help me now. They are horrors of the soul, and yet"—he hid his face in his hands and groaned—"they are real, Frank. I saw them for a ghastly moment. For a moment I stood on the *other side.* I stood on the pale gray shores beyond time and space. In an awful light that was not light, in a silence that shrieked, I saw *them.*

"All the evil in the universe was concentrated in their lean, hungry bodies. Or had they bodies? I saw them only for a moment; I cannot be certain. *But I heard them breathe.* Indescribably for a moment I felt their breath upon my face. They turned toward me and I fled screaming. In a single moment I fled screaming through time. I fled down quintillions of years.

"But they scented me. Men awake in them cosmic hungers. We have escaped, momentarily, from the foulness that rings them round. They thirst for that in us which is clean, which emerged from the deed without stain. There is a part of us which did not partake in the deed, and that they hate. But do not imagine that they are literally, prosaically evil. They are beyond good and evil as we know it. They are that which in the beginning fell away from cleanliness. Through the deed they became bodies of death, receptacles of all foulness. But they are not evil in *our* sense because in the spheres through which they move there is no thought, no moral, no right or wrong as we understand it. There is merely the pure and the foul. The foul expresses itself through angles; the pure through curves. Man, the pure part of him, is descended from a curve. Do not laugh. I mean that literally."

I rose and searched for my hat. "I'm dreadfully sorry for you, Chalmers," I said, as I walked toward the door. "But I don't intend to stay and listen to such gibberish. I'll send my physician to see you. He's an elderly, kindly chap, and he won't be offended if you tell him to go to the devil. But I hope you'll respect his advice. A week's rest in a good sanitarium should benefit you immeasurably."

I heard him laughing as I descended the stairs, but his laughter was so utterly mirthless that it moved me to tears.

II

When Chalmers phoned the following morning my first impulse was to hang up the receiver immediately. His request was so unusual and his voice was so wildly hysterical that I feared any further association with him would result in the impairment of my own sanity. But I could not doubt the genuineness of his misery, and when he broke down completely and I heard him sobbing over the wire, I decided to comply with his request.

"Very well," I said. "I will come over immediately and bring the plaster."

En route to Chalmers's home I stopped at a hardware store and purchased twenty pounds of plaster of Paris. When I entered my friend's room he was crouching by the window watching the opposite wall out of eyes that were feverish with fright. When he saw me he rose and seized the parcel containing the plaster with an avidity that amazed and horrified me. He had extruded all of the furniture, and the room presented a desolate appearance.

"It is just conceivable that we can thwart them!" he exclaimed. "But we must work rapidly. Frank, there is a stepladder in the hall. Bring it here immediately. And then fetch a pail of water."

"What for?" I murmured.

He turned sharply and there was a flush on his face. "To mix the plaster, you fool!" he cried. "To mix the plaster that will save our bodies and souls from a contamination unmentionable. To mix the plaster that will save the world from—Frank, *they must be kept out*!"

"Who?" I murmured.

"The Hounds of Tindalos!" he muttered. "They can only reach us through angles. We must eliminate all angles from this room. I shall plaster up all of the corners, all of the crevices. We must make this room resemble the interior of a sphere."

I knew that it would have been useless to argue with him. I fetched the stepladder, Chalmers mixed the plaster, and for three hours we labored. We filled in the four corners of the wall and the intersections of the floor and wall and the wall and ceiling, and we rounded the sharp angles of the window-seat.

"I shall remain in this room until they return in time," he affirmed when our task was completed. "When they discover that the scent leads through curves they will return. They will return ravenous and snarling and unsatisfied to the foulness that was in the beginning, before time, beyond space."

He nodded graciously and lit a cigarette. "It was good of you to help," he said.

"Will you not see a physician, Chalmers?" I pleaded.

"Perhaps—tomorrow," he murmured. "But now I must watch and wait."

"Wait for what?" I urged.

Chalmers smiled wanly. "I know that you think me insane," he said. "You have a shrewd but prosaic mind, and you cannot conceive of an entity that does not depend for its existence on force and matter. But did it ever occur to you, my friend, that force and matter are merely the barriers to perception imposed by time and space? When one knows, as I do, that time and space are identical and that they are both deceptive because they are merely imperfect manifestations of a higher reality, one no longer seeks in the visible world for an explanation of the mystery and terror of being."

I rose and walked toward the door.

"Forgive me," he cried. "I did not mean to offend you. You have a superlative intellect, but I—I have a *superhuman* one. It is only natural that I should be aware of your limitations."

"Phone if you need me," I said, and descended the stairs two steps at a time. "I'll send my physician over at once," I muttered, to myself. "He's a hopeless maniac, and heaven knows what will happen if someone doesn't take charge of him immediately."

III

The following is a condensation of two announcements which appeared in the Partridgeville Gazette *for July 3, 1928:*

Earthquake Shakes Financial District

At 2 o'clock this morning an earth tremor of unusual severity broke several plate-glass windows in Central Square and completely disorganized the electric and street railway systems. The tremor was felt in the outlying districts, and the steeple of the First Baptist Church on Angell Hill (designed by Christopher Wren in 1717) was entirely demolished. Firemen are now attempting to put out a blaze which threatens to destroy the Partridgeville Glue Works. An investigation is promised by the mayor, and an immediate attempt will be made to fix responsibility for this disastrous occurrence.

OCCULT WRITER MURDERED BY UNKNOWN GUEST

Horrible Crime in Central Square

Mystery Surrounds Death of Halpin Chalmers

At 9 A.M. today the body of Halpin Chalmers, author and journalist, was found in an empty room above the jewelry store of Smithwick and Isaacs, 24 Central Square. The coroner's investigation revealed that the room had been rented furnished to Mr. Chalmers on May 1, and that he had himself disposed of the furniture a fortnight ago. Chalmers was the author of several recondite books on occult themes, and a member of the Bibliographic Guild. He formerly resided in Brooklyn, New York.

At 7 A.M. Mr. L. E. Hancock, who occupies the apartment opposite Chalmers's room in the Smithwick and Isaacs establishment, smelt a peculiar odor when he opened his door to take in his cat and the morning edition of the *Partridgeville Gazette*. The odor he describes as extremely acrid and nauseous, and he affirms that it was so strong in the vicinity of Chalmers's room that he was obliged to hold his nose when he approached that section of the hall.

He was about to return to his own apartment when it occurred to him that Chalmers might have accidentally forgotten to turn off the gas in his kitchenette. Becoming considerably alarmed at the thought, he decided to investigate, and when repeated tappings on Chalmers's door brought no response he notified the superintendent. The latter opened the door by means of a pass key, and the two men quickly made their way into Chalmers's room. The room was utterly destitute of furniture, and Hancock asserts that when he first glanced at the floor his heart went cold within him, and that the superintendent, without saying a word, walked to the open window and stared at the building opposite for fully five minutes.

Chalmers lay stretched upon his back in the center of the room. He was starkly nude, and his chest and arms were covered with a peculiar bluish pus or ichor. His head lay grotesquely upon his chest. It had been completely severed from his body, and the features were twisted and torn and horribly mangled. Nowhere was there a trace of blood.

The room presented a most astonishing appearance. The intersections of the walls, ceiling, and floor had been thickly smeared with plaster of Paris, but at intervals fragments had cracked and fallen off, and someone had grouped these upon the floor about the murdered man so as to form a perfect triangle.

Beside the body were several sheets of charred yellow paper. These bore fantastic geometric designs and symbols and several hastily scrawled sentences. The sentences were almost illegible and so absurd in content that they furnished no possible clue to the perpetrator of the crime. "I am waiting and watching," Chalmers wrote. "I sit by the window and watch walls and ceiling. I do not believe they can reach me, but I must beware of the Doels. Perhaps *they* can help them break through. The satyrs will help, and they can advance through the scarlet circles. The Greeks knew a way of preventing that. It is a great pity that we have forgotten so much."

On another sheet of paper, the most badly charred of the seven or eight fragments found by Detective-Sergeant Douglas (of the Partridgeville Reserve), was scrawled the following:

"Good God, the plaster is falling! A terrific shock has loosened the plaster and it is falling. An earthquake perhaps! I never could have anticipated this. It is growing dark in the room. I must phone Frank. But can he get here in time? I will try. I will recite the Einstein formula. I will—God, they are breaking through! They are breaking through! Smoke is pouring from the corners of the wall. Their tongues—ahhhh—"

In the opinion of Detective-Sergeant Douglas, Chalmers was poisoned by some obscure chemical. He has sent specimens of the strange blue slime found on Chalmers's body to the Partridgeville Chemical Laboratories; and he expects the report will shed new light on one of the most mysterious crimes of recent years. That Chalmers entertained a guest on the evening preceding the earthquake is certain, for his neighbor distinctly heard a low murmur of conversation in the former's room as he passed it on his way to the stairs. Suspicion points strongly to this unknown visitor, and the police are diligently endeavoring to discover his identity.

IV

Report of James Morton, chemist and bacteriologist:

My dear Mr. Douglas:

The fluid sent to me for analysis is the most peculiar that I have ever examined. It resembles living protoplasm, but it lacks the peculiar substances known as enzymes. Enzymes catalyze the chemical reactions occurring in living cells, and when the cell dies they cause it to disintegrate by hydrolyzation. Without enzymes protoplasm should possess enduring vitality, i.e., immortality. Enzymes are the negative components, so to speak, of the unicellular organism, which is the basis of all life. That living matter can exist without enzymes biologists emphatically deny. And yet the substance that you have sent me is alive and it lacks these "indispensable" bodies. Good God, sir, do you realize what astounding new vistas this opens up?

V

Excerpt from The Secret Watcher *by the late Halpin Chalmers:*

What if, parallel to the life we know, there is another life that does not die, which lacks the elements that destroy *our* life? Perhaps in another dimension there is a *different* force from that which generates our life. Perhaps this force emits energy, or something similar to energy, which passes from the unknown dimension where *it* is and creates a new form of cell life in our dimension. No one knows that such new cell life does exist in our dimension. Ah, but I have seen *its* manifestations. I have *talked* with them. In my room at night I have talked with the Doels. And in dreams I have seen their maker. I have stood on the dim shore beyond time and matter and seen *it*. *It* moves through strange curves and outrageous angles. Someday I shall travel in time and meet *it* face to face.

The Space-Eaters*

FRANK BELKNAP LONG

> The cross is not a passive agent. It protects the pure of heart, and it has often appeared in the air above our sabbats, confusing and dispersing the powers of Darkness.
>
> —John Dee's *Necronomicon*

I

The horror came to Partridgeville in a blind fog.

All that afternoon thick vapors from the sea had swirled and eddied about the farm, and the room in which we sat swam with moisture. The fog ascended in spirals from beneath the door, and its long, moist fingers caressed my hair until it dripped. The square-paned windows were coated with a thick, dewlike moisture; the air was heavy and dank and unbelievably cold.

I stared gloomily at my friend. He had turned his back to the window and was writing furiously. He was a tall, slim man with a slight stoop and abnormally broad shoulders. In profile his face was impressive. He had an extremely broad forehead, long nose, and slightly protuberant chin—a strong, sensitive face which suggested a wildly imaginative nature held in restraint by a skeptical and truly extraordinary intellect.

My friend wrote short stories. He wrote to please himself, in defiance of contemporary taste, and his tales were unusual. They would have delighted Poe; they would have delighted Hawthorne, or Ambrose Bierce, or Villiers de l'Isle-Adam. They were studies of abnormal men, abnormal beasts, abnormal plants. He wrote of remote realms of imagination and horror, and the colors, sounds, and odors which he dared to evoke were never seen, heard, or smelt on the

*Originally published in *Weird Tales*, July 1928.

familiar side of the moon. He projected his creations against mind-chilling backgrounds. They stalked through tall and lonely forests, over ragged mountains, and slithered down the stairs of ancient houses, and between the piles of rotting black wharves.

One of his tales, "The House of the Worm," had induced a young student at a Midwestern university to seek refuge in an enormous red-brick building where everyone approved of his sitting on the floor and shouting at the top of his voice: "Lo, my beloved is fairer than all the lilies among the lilies in the lily garden." Another, "The Defilers," had brought him precisely one hundred and ten letters of indignation from local readers when it appeared in the *Partridgeville Gazette*.

As I continued to stare at him he suddenly stopped writing and shook his head. "I can't do it," he said. "I should have to invent a new language. And yet I can comprehend the thing emotionally, intuitively, if you will. If I could only convey it in a sentence somehow—the strange crawling of its fleshless spirit!"

"Is it some new horror?" I asked.

He shook his head. "It is not new to me. I have known and felt it for years—a horror utterly beyond anything your prosaic brain can conceive."

"Thank you," I said.

"All human brains are prosaic," he elaborated. "I meant no offense. It is the shadowy terrors that lurk behind and above them that are mysterious and awful. Our little brains—what can they know of vampire-like entities which may lurk in dimensions higher than our own, or beyond the universe of stars? I think sometimes they lodge in our heads, and our brains feel them, but when they stretch out tentacles to probe and explore us, we go screaming mad." He was staring at me steadily now.

"But you can't honestly believe in such nonsense!" I exclaimed.

"Of course not!" He shook his head and laughed. "You know damn well I'm too profoundly skeptical to believe in anything. I have merely outlined a poet's reactions to the universe. If a man wishes to write ghostly stories and actually convey a sensation of horror, he must believe in everything—and *anything*. By *anything* I mean the horror that transcends *everything*, that is more terrible and impossible than *everything*. He must believe that there are things from outer space that can reach down and fasten themselves on us with a malevolence that can destroy us utterly—our bodies as well as our minds."

"But this thing from outer space—how can he describe it if he doesn't know its shape—or size or color?"

"It is virtually impossible to describe it. That is what I have sought to do—and failed. Perhaps someday—but then, I doubt if it can ever be accomplished. But your artist can hint, suggest. . . ."

"Suggest what?" I asked, a little puzzled.

"Suggest a horror that is utterly unearthly; that makes itself felt in terms that have no counterparts on Earth."

I was still puzzled. He smiled wearily and elaborated his theory.

"There is something prosaic," he said, "about even the best of the classic tales of mystery and terror. Old Mrs. Radcliffe, with her hidden vaults and bleeding ghosts; Maturin, with his allegorical Faust-like hero-villains, and his fiery flames from the mouth of hell; Edgar Poe, with his blood-clotted corpses, and black cats, his telltale hearts and disintegrating Valdemars; Hawthorne, with his amusing preoccupation with the problems and horrors arising from mere human sin (as though human sins were of any significance to a coldly malign intelligence from beyond the stars). Then we have modern masters—Algernon Blackwood, who invites us to a feast of the high gods and shows us an old woman with a harelip sitting before a ouija board fingering soiled cards, or an absurd nimbus of ectoplasm emanating from some clairvoyant ninny; Bram Stoker with his vampires and werewolves, mere conventional myths, the tag-ends of mediaeval folklore; Wells with his pseudo-scientific bogies, fish-men at the bottom of the sea, ladies in the moon, and the hundred and one idiots who are constantly writing ghost stories for the magazines—what have they contributed to the literature of the unholy?

"Are we not made of flesh and blood? It is but natural that we should be revolted and horrified when we are shown that flesh and blood in a state of corruption and decay, with the worms passing over and under it. It is but natural that a story about a corpse should thrill us, fill us with fear and horror and loathing. Any fool can awake these emotions in us—Poe really accomplished very little with his Lady Ushers, and liquescent Valdemars. He appealed to simple, natural, understandable emotions, and it was inevitable that his readers should respond.

"Are we not the descendants of barbarians? Did we not once dwell in tall and sinister forests, at the mercy of beasts that rend and tear? It is but inevitable that we should shiver and cringe when we meet in literature dark shadows from our own past. Harpies and vampires and werewolves—what are they but magnifications, distortions of the great birds and bats and ferocious dogs that harassed and tortured our ancestors? It is easy enough to arouse fear by such means. It is easy enough to frighten men with the flames at the mouth of hell, because they are hot and shrivel and burn the flesh—and who does not understand and dread a fire? Blows that kill, fires that burn, shadows that horrify because their substances lurk evilly in the black corridors of our inherited memories—I am weary of the writers who would terrify us by such pathetically obvious and trite unpleasantness."

Real indignation blazed in his eyes.

"Suppose there were a greater horror? Suppose evil things from some other universe should decide to invade this one? Suppose we couldn't see them? Suppose we couldn't feel them? Suppose they were of a color unknown on Earth, or rather, of an *appearance* that was without color?

"Suppose they had a shape unknown on Earth? Suppose they were four-dimensional, five-dimensional, six-dimensional? Suppose they were a hundred-dimensional? Suppose they had no dimensions at all and yet existed? What could we do?

"They would not exist for us? They would exist for us if they gave us pain. Suppose it was not the pain of heat or cold or any of the pains we know, but a new pain? Suppose they touched something besides our nerves—reached our brains in a new and terrible way? Suppose they made themselves felt in a new and strange and unspeakable way? What could we do? Our hands would be tied. You cannot oppose what you cannot see or feel. You cannot oppose the thousand-dimensional. *Suppose they should eat their way to us through space!*"

He was speaking now with an intensity of emotion which belied his avowed skepticism of a moment before.

"That is what I have tried to write about. I wanted to make my readers feel and see that thing from another universe, from beyond space. I could easily enough hint at it or suggest it—any fool can do that—but I wanted actually to describe it. To describe a color that is not a color! a form that is formless!

"A mathematician could perhaps slightly more than suggest it. There would be strange curves and angles that an inspired mathematician in a wild frenzy of calculation might glimpse vaguely. It is absurd to say that mathematicians have not discovered the fourth dimension. They have often glimpsed it, often approached it, often apprehended it, but they are unable to demonstrate it. I know a mathematician who swears that he once saw the sixth dimension in a wild flight into the sublime skies of the differential calculus.

"Unfortunately I am not a mathematician. I am only a poor fool of a creative artist, and the thing from outer space utterly eludes me."

Someone was pounding loudly on the door. I crossed the room and drew back the latch. "What do you want?" I asked. "What is the matter?"

"Sorry to disturb you, Frank," said a familiar voice, "but I've got to talk to someone."

I recognized the lean, white face of my nearest neighbor, and stepped instantly to one side. "Come in," I said. "Come in, by all means. Howard and I have been discussing ghosts, and the things we've conjured up aren't pleasant company. Perhaps you can argue them away."

I called Howard's horrors *ghosts* because I didn't want to shock my commonplace neighbor. Henry Wells was immensely big and tall, and as he strode into the room he seemed to bring a part of the night with him.

He collapsed on a sofa and surveyed us with frightened eyes. Howard laid down the story he had been reading, removed and wiped his glasses, and frowned. He was more or less tolerant of my bucolic visitors. We waited for perhaps a minute, and then the three of us spoke almost simultaneously. "A horrible night!" "Beastly, isn't it?" "Wretched."

Henry Wells frowned. "Tonight," he said, "I—I met with a funny accident. I was driving Hortense through Mulligan Wood. . . ."

"Hortense?" Howard interrupted.

"His horse," I explained impatiently. "You were returning from Brewster, weren't you, Henry?"

"From Brewster, yes," he replied. "I was driving between the trees, keeping a sharp lookout for cars with their lights on too bright, coming right at me out of the murk, and listening to the foghorns in the bay wheezing and moaning, when something wet landed on my head. 'Rain,' I thought. 'I hope the supplies keep dry.'

"I turned round to make sure that the butter and flour were covered up, and something soft like a sponge rose up from the bottom of the wagon and hit me in the face. I snatched at it and caught it between my fingers.

"In my hands it felt like jelly. I squeezed it, and moisture ran out of it down my wrists. It wasn't so dark that I couldn't see it, either. Funny how you can see in fogs—they seem to make the night lighter. There was a sort of brightness in the air. I dunno, maybe it wasn't the fog, either. The trees seemed to stand out. You could see them sharp and clear. As I was saying, I looked at the thing, and what do you think it looked like? Like a piece of raw liver. Or like a calf's brain. Now that I come to think of it, it was more like a calf's brain. There were grooves in it, and you don't find many grooves in liver. Liver's usually as smooth as glass.

"It was an awful moment for me. 'There's someone up in one of those trees,' I thought. 'He's some tramp or crazy man or fool, and he's been eating liver. My wagon frightened him and he dropped it—a piece of it. I can't be wrong. There was no liver in my wagon when I left Brewster.'

"I looked up. You know how tall all of the trees are in Mulligan Wood. You can't see the tops of some of them from the wagon-road on a clear day. And you know how crooked and queer-looking some of the trees are.

"It's funny, but I've always thought of them as old men—tall old men, you understand, tall and crooked and very evil. I've always thought of them as wanting to work mischief. There's something unwholesome about trees that grow very close together and grow crooked.

"I looked up.

"At first I didn't see anything but the tall trees, all white and glistening with the fog, and above them a thick, white mist that hid the stars. And then something long and white ran quickly down the trunk of one of the trees.

"It ran so quickly down the tree that I couldn't see it clearly. And it was so thin anyway that there wasn't much to see. But it was like an arm. It was like a long, white, and very thin arm. But of course it wasn't an arm. Who ever heard of an arm as tall as a tree? I don't know what made me compare it to an arm, because it was really nothing but a thin line—like a wire, a string. I'm not sure that I saw it at all. Maybe I imagined it. I'm not even sure that it was as wide as a string. But it had a hand. Or didn't it? When I think of it my brain gets dizzy. You see, it moved so quickly I couldn't see it clearly at all.

"But it gave me the impression that it was looking for something that it had dropped. For a minute the hand seemed to spread out over the road, and then it left the tree and came toward the wagon. It was like a huge white hand walking on its fingers with a terribly long arm fastened to it that went up and up until it touched the fog, or perhaps until it touched the stars.

"I screamed and slashed Hortense with the reins, but the horse didn't need any urging. She was up and off before I could throw the liver, or calf's brain, or whatever it was, into the road. She raced so fast she almost upset the wagon, but I didn't draw in the reins. I'd rather lie in a ditch with a broken rib than have a long, white hand squeezing the breath out of my throat.

"We had almost cleared the wood and I was just beginning to breathe again when my brain went cold. I can't describe what happened in any other way. My brain got as cold as ice inside my head. I can tell you I was frightened.

"Don't imagine I couldn't think clearly. I was conscious of everything that was going on about me, but my brain was so cold I screamed with the pain. Have you ever held a piece of ice in the palm of your hand for as long as two or three minutes? It burnt, didn't it? Ice burns worse than fire. Well, my brain felt as though it had lain on ice for hours and hours. There was a furnace inside my head, but it was a cold furnace. It was roaring with raging cold.

"Perhaps I should have been thankful that the pain didn't last. It wore off in about ten minutes, and when I got home I didn't think I was any the worse for my experience. I'm sure I didn't think I was any the worse until I looked at myself in the glass. Then I saw the hole in my head."

Henry Wells leaned forward and brushed back the hair from his right temple.

"Here is the wound," he said. "What do you make of it?" He tapped with his fingers beneath a small round opening in the side of his head. "It's like a bullet-wound," he elaborated, "but there was no blood and you can look in pretty far. It seems to go right in to the center of my head. I shouldn't be alive."

Howard had risen and was staring at my neighbor with angry and accusing eyes.

"Why have you lied to us?" he shouted. "Why have you told us this absurd story? A long hand! You were drunk, man. Drunk—and yet you've succeeded in doing what I'd have sweated blood to accomplish. If I could have made my readers feel that horror, know it for a moment, that horror that you described in the woods, I should be with the immortals—I should be greater than Poe, greater than Hawthorne. And you—a clumsy drunken liar . . ."

I was on my feet with a furious protest.

"He's not lying," I said. "He's been shot—someone has shot him in the head. Look at this wound. My God, man, you have no call to insult him!"

Howard's wrath died and the fire went out of his eyes. "Forgive me," he said. "You can't imagine how badly I've wanted to capture that ultimate horror, to put it on paper, and he did it so easily. If he had warned me that he was going to describe something like that I would have taken notes. But of course he doesn't know he's an artist. It was an accidental *tour de force* that he accomplished; he couldn't do it again, I'm sure. I'm sorry I went up in the air—I apologize. Do you want me to go for a doctor? That *is* a bad wound."

My neighbor shook his head. "I don't want a doctor," he said. "I've seen a doctor. There's no bullet in my head—that hole was not made by a bullet. When the doctor couldn't explain it, I laughed at him. I hate doctors; and I haven't much use for fools who think I'm in the habit of lying. I haven't much use for people who won't believe me when I tell 'em I saw the long, white thing come sliding down the tree as clear as day."

But Howard was examining the wound in defiance of my neighbor's indignation. "It was made by something round and sharp," he said. "It's curious, but the flesh isn't torn. A knife or bullet would have torn the flesh, left a ragged edge."

I nodded, and was bending to study the wound when Wells shrieked, and clapped his hands to his head. "Ah-h-h!" he choked. "It's come back—the terrible, terrible cold."

Howard stared. "Don't expect me to believe such nonsense!" he exclaimed disgustedly.

But Wells was holding on to his head and dancing about the room in a delirium of agony. "I can't stand it!" he shrieked. "It's freezing up my brain. It's not like ordinary cold. It isn't. Oh, God! It's like nothing you've ever felt. It bites, it scorches, it tears. It's like acid."

I laid my hand upon his shoulder and tried to quiet him, but he pushed me aside and made for the door.

"I've got to get out of here," he screamed. "The thing wants room. My head won't hold it. It wants the night—the vast night. It wants to wallow in the night."

He threw back the door and disappeared into the fog. Howard wiped his forehead with the sleeve of his coat and collapsed into a chair.

"Mad," he muttered. "A tragic case of manic-depressive psychosis. Who would have suspected it? The story he told us wasn't conscious art at all. It was simply a nightmare-fungus conceived by the brain of a lunatic."

"Yes," I said, "but how do you account for the hole in his head?"

"Oh, that!" Howard shrugged. "He probably always had it—probably was born with it."

"Nonsense," I said. "The man never had a hole in his head before. Personally, I think he's been shot. Something ought to be done. He needs medical attention. I think I'll phone Dr. Smith."

"It is useless to interfere," said Howard. "That hole was *not* made by a bullet. I advise you to forget him until tomorrow. His insanity may be temporary, it may wear off; and then he'd blame us for interfering. If he's still emotionally disturbed tomorrow, if he comes here again and tries to make trouble, you can notify the proper authorities. Has he ever acted queerly before?"

"No," I said. "He was always quite sane. I think I'll take your advice and wait. But I wish I could explain the hole in his head."

"The story he told interests me more," said Howard. "I'm going to write it out before I forget it. Of course I shan't be able to make the horror as real as he did, but perhaps I can catch a bit of the strangeness and glamour."

He unscrewed his fountain pen and began to cover a sheet of paper with curious phrases.

I shivered and closed the door.

For several minutes there was no sound in the room save the scratching of his pen as it moved across the paper. For several minutes there was silence—and then the shrieks commenced. Or were they wails?

We heard them through the closed door, heard them above the moaning of the foghorns and the wash of the waves on Mulligan's

Beach. We heard them above the million sounds of night that had horrified and depressed us as we sat and talked in that fog-enshrouded and lonely house. We heard them so clearly that for a moment we thought they came from just outside the house. It was not until they came again and again—long, piercing wails—that we discovered in them a quality of remoteness. Slowly we became aware that the wails came from far away, as far away, perhaps, as Mulligan Wood.

"A soul in torture," muttered Howard. "A poor, damned soul in the grip of the horror I've been telling you about—the horror I've known and felt for years."

He rose unsteadily to his feet. His eyes were shining and he was breathing heavily.

I seized his shoulders and shook him. "You shouldn't project yourself into your stories that way," I exclaimed. "Some poor chap is in distress. I don't know what's happened. Perhaps a ship foundered. I'm going to put on a slicker and find out what it's all about. I have an idea we may be needed."

"We *may* be needed," repeated Howard slowly. "We may be needed indeed. It will not be satisfied with a single victim. Think of that great journey through space, the thirst and dreadful hungers it must have known! It is preposterous to imagine that it will be content with a single victim!"

Then, suddenly, a change came over him. The light went out of his eyes and his voice lost its quiver. He shivered.

"Forgive me," he said. "I'm afraid you'll think I'm as mad as the yokel who was here a few minutes ago. But I can't help identifying myself with my characters when I write. I'd described something very evil, and those yells—well, they are exactly like the yells a man would make if—if. . . ."

"I understand," I interrupted, "but we've no time to discuss that now. There's a poor chap out there"—I pointed vaguely toward the door—"with his back against the wall. He's fighting off something—I don't know what. We've got to help him."

"Of course, of course," he agreed, and followed me into the kitchen.

Without a word I took down a slicker and handed it to him. I also handed him an enormous rubber hat.

"Get into these as quickly as you can," I said. "The chap's desperately in need of us."

I had gotten my own slicker down from the rack and was forcing my arms through its sticky sleeves. In a moment we were both pushing our way through the fog.

The fog was like a living thing. Its long fingers reached up and slapped us relentlessly on the face. It curled about our bodies and ascended in great, grayish spirals from the tops of our heads. It retreated before us, and as suddenly closed in and enveloped us.

Dimly ahead of us we saw the lights of a few lonely farms. Behind us the sea drummed, and the foghorns sent out a continuous, mournful ululation. The collar of Howard's slicker was turned up over his ears, and from his long nose moisture dripped. There was grim decision in his eyes, and his jaw was set.

For many minutes we plodded on in silence, and it was not until we approached Mulligan Wood that he spoke.

"If necessary," he said, "we shall enter the wood."

I nodded. "There is no reason why we should not enter the wood," I said. "It isn't a large wood."

"One could get out quickly?"

"One could get out very quickly indeed. My God, did you hear that?"

The shrieks had grown horribly loud.

"He is suffering," said Howard. "He is suffering terribly. Do you suppose—do you suppose it's your crazy friend?"

He had voiced a question which I had been asking myself for some time.

"It's conceivable," I said. "But we'll have to interfere if he's as mad as that. I wish I'd brought some of the neighbors with me."

"Why in heaven's name didn't you?" Howard shouted. "It may take a dozen men to handle him." He was staring at the tall trees that towered before us, and I didn't think he really gave Henry Wells so much as a thought.

"That's Mulligan Wood," I said. I swallowed to keep my heart from rising to the top of my mouth. "It isn't a big wood," I added idiotically.

"Oh, my God!" Out of the fog there came the sound of a voice in the last extremity of pain. "They're eating up my brain. Oh, my God!"

I was at that moment in deadly fear that I might become as mad as the man in the woods. I clutched Howard's arm.

"Let's go back," I shouted. "Let's go back at once. We were fools to come. There is nothing here but madness and suffering and perhaps death."

"That may be," said Howard, "but we're going on."

His face was ashen beneath his dripping hat, and his eyes were thin blue slits.

"Very well," I said grimly. "We'll go on."

Slowly we moved among the trees. They towered above us, and the thick fog so distorted them and merged them together that they seemed to move forward with us. From their twisted branches the fog hung in ribbons. Ribbons, did I say? Rather were they snakes of fog—

writhing snakes with venomous tongues and leering eyes. Through swirling clouds of fog we saw the scaly, gnarled boles of the trees, and every bole resembled the twisted body of an evil old man. Only the small oblong of light cast by my electric torch protected us against their malevolence.

Through great banks of fog we moved, and every moment the screams grew louder. Soon we were catching fragments of sentences, hysterical shoutings that merged into prolonged wails. "Colder and colder and colder . . . they are eating up my brain. Colder! Ah-h-h!"

Howard gripped my arm. "We'll find him," he said. "We can't turn back now."

When we found him he was lying on his side. His hands were clasped about his head, and his body was bent double, the knees drawn up so tightly that they almost touched his chest. He was silent. We bent and shook him, but he made no sound.

"Is he dead?" I choked out. I wanted desperately to turn and run. The trees were very close to us.

"I don't know," said Howard. "I don't know. I hope that he is dead."

I saw him kneel and slide his hand under the poor devil's shirt. For a moment his face was a mask. Then he got up quickly and shook his head.

"He is alive," he said. "We must get him into some dry clothes as quickly as possible."

I helped him. Together we lifted the bent figure from the ground and carried it forward between the trees. Twice we stumbled and nearly fell, and the creepers tore at our clothes. The creepers were little malicious hands grasping and tearing under the malevolent guidance of the great trees. Without a star to guide us, without a light except the little pocket lamp which was growing dim, we fought our way out of Mulligan Wood.

The droning did not commence until we had left the wood. At first we scarcely heard it, it was so low, like the purring of gigantic engines far down in the earth. But slowly, as we stumbled forward with our burden, it grew so loud that we could not ignore it.

"What is that?" muttered Howard, and through the wraiths of fog I saw that his face had a greenish tinge.

"I don't know," I mumbled. "It's something horrible. I never heard anything like it. Can't you walk faster?"

So far we had been fighting familiar horrors, but the droning and humming that rose behind us was like nothing that I had ever heard on Earth. In excruciating fright, I shrieked aloud. "Faster, Howard, faster! For God's sake, let's get out of this!"

As I spoke, the body that we were carrying squirmed, and from its cracked lips issued a torrent of gibberish: "I was walking between the trees looking up. I couldn't see their tops. I was looking up, and then suddenly I looked down and the thing landed on my shoulders. It was all legs—all long, crawling legs. It went right into my head. I wanted to get away from the trees, but I couldn't. I was alone in the forest with the thing on my back, in my head, and when I tried to run, the trees reached out and tripped me. It made a hole so it could get in. It's my brain it wants. Today it made a hole, and now it's crawled in and it's sucking and sucking and sucking. It's as cold as ice and it makes a noise like a great big fly. But it isn't a fly. And it isn't a hand. I was wrong when I called it a hand. You can't see it. I wouldn't have seen or felt it if it hadn't made a hole and got in. You almost see it, you almost feel it, and that means that it's getting ready to go in."

"Can you walk, Wells? Can you walk?"

Howard had dropped Wells's legs, and I could hear the harsh intake of his breath as he struggled to rid himself of his slicker.

"I think so," Wells sobbed. "But it doesn't matter. It's got me now. Put me down and save yourselves."

"We've got to run!" I yelled.

"It's our one chance," cried Howard. "Wells, you follow us. Follow us, do you understand? They'll burn up your brain if they catch you. We're going to run, lad. Follow us!"

He was off through the fog. Wells shook himself free, and followed like a man in a trance. I felt a horror more terrible than death. The noise was dreadfully loud; it was right in my ears, and yet for a moment I couldn't move. The wall of fog was growing thicker.

"Frank will be lost!" It was the voice of Wells, raised in a despairing shout.

"We'll go back!" It was Howard shouting now. "It's death, or worse, but we can't leave him."

"Keep on," I called out. "They won't get me. Save yourselves!"

In my anxiety to prevent them from sacrificing themselves I plunged wildly forward. In a moment I had joined Howard and was clutching at his arm.

"What is it?" I cried. "What have we to fear?"

The droning was all about us now, but no louder.

"Come quickly or we'll be lost!" he urged frantically. "They've broken down all barriers. That buzzing is a warning. We're sensitives—we've been warned, but if it gets louder we're lost. They're strong near Mulligan Wood, and it's here they've made themselves felt. They're experimenting now—feeling their way. Later, when they've learned, they'll spread out. If we can only reach the farm. . . ."

"We'll reach the farm!" I shouted as I clawed my way through the fog.

"Heaven help us if we don't!" moaned Howard.

He had thrown off his slicker, and his seeping wet shirt clung tragically to his lean body. He moved through the blackness with long, furious strides. Far ahead we heard the shrieks of Henry Wells. Ceaselessly the foghorns moaned; ceaselessly the fog swirled and eddied about us.

And the droning continued. It seemed incredible that we should ever have found a way to the farm in the blackness. But find the farm we did, and into it we stumbled with glad cries.

"Shut the door!" shouted Howard.

I shut the door.

"We are safe here, I think," he said. "They haven't reached the farm yet."

"What has happened to Wells?" I gasped, and then I saw the wet tracks leading into the kitchen.

Howard saw them too. His eyes flashed with momentary relief.

"I'm glad he's safe," he muttered. "I feared for him."

Then his face darkened. The kitchen was unlighted and no sound came from it.

Without a word Howard walked across the room and into the darkness beyond. I sank into a chair, flicked the moisture from my eyes, and brushed back my hair, which had fallen in soggy strands across my face. For a moment I sat, breathing heavily, and when the door creaked, I shivered. But I remembered Howard's assurance: "They haven't reached the farm yet. We're safe here."

Somehow, I had confidence in Howard. He realized that we were threatened by a new and unknown horror, and in some occult way he had grasped its limitations.

I confess, though, that when I heard the screams that came from the kitchen, my faith in my friend was slightly shaken. There were low growls, such as I could not believe came from any human throat, and the voice of Howard raised in wild expostulation. "Let go, I say! Are you quite mad? Man, man, we have saved you! Don't, I say—let go of my leg. Ah-h-h!"

As Howard staggered into the room I sprang forward and caught him in my arms. He was covered with blood from head to foot, and his face was ashen.

"He's gone raving mad," he moaned. "He was running about on his hands and knees like a dog. He sprang at me, and almost killed me. I fought him off, but I'm badly bitten. I hit him in the face—knocked him unconscious. I may have killed him. He's an animal—I had to protect myself."

I laid Howard on the sofa and knelt beside him, but he scorned my aid.

"Don't bother with me!" he commanded. "Get a rope, quickly, and tie him up. If he comes to, we'll have to fight for our lives."

What followed was a nightmare. I remember vaguely that I went into the kitchen with a rope and tied poor Wells to a chair; then I bathed and dressed Howard's wounds, and lit a fire in the grate. I remember also that I telephoned for a doctor. But the incidents are confused in my memory, and I have no clear recollection of anything until the arrival of a tall, grave man with kindly and sympathetic eyes and a presence that was as soothing as an opiate.

He examined Howard, nodded, and explained that the wounds were not serious. He examined Wells, and did not nod. He explained slowly, "His pupils don't respond to light," he said. "An immediate operation will be necessary. I tell you frankly, I don't think we can save him."

"That wound in his head, Doctor," I said. "Was it made by a bullet?"

The doctor frowned. "It puzzles me," he said. "Of course it was made by a bullet, but it should have partially closed up. It goes right into the brain. You say you know nothing about it. I believe you, but I think the authorities should be notified at once. Someone will be wanted for manslaughter, unless"—he paused—"unless the wound was self-inflicted. What you tell me is curious. That he should have been able to walk about for hours seems incredible. The wound has obviously been dressed, too. There is no clotted blood at all."

He paced slowly back and forth. "We must operate here—at once. There is a slight chance. Luckily, I brought some instruments. We must clear this table and—do you think you could hold a lamp for me?"

I nodded. "I'll try," I said.

"Good!"

The doctor busied himself with preparations while I debated whether or not I should phone for the police.

"I'm convinced," I said at last, "that the wound was self-inflicted. Wells acted very strangely. If you are willing, Doctor. . . ."

"Yes?"

"We will remain silent about this matter until after the operation. If Wells lives, there would be no need of involving the poor chap in a police investigation."

The doctor nodded. "Very well," he said. "We will operate first and decide afterward."

Howard was laughing silently from his couch. "The police," he snickered. "Of what use would they be against the things in Mulligan Wood?"

There was an ironic and ominous quality about his mirth that disturbed me. The horrors that we had known in the fog seemed absurd and impossible in the cool, scientific presence of Dr. Smith, and I didn't want to be reminded of them.

The doctor turned from his instruments and whispered into my ear. "Your friend has a slight fever, and apparently it has made him delirious. If you will bring me a glass of water I will mix him a sedative."

I raced to secure a glass, and in a moment we had Howard sleeping soundly.

"Now then," said the doctor as he handed me the lamp. "You must hold this steady and move it about as I direct."

The white, unconscious form of Henry Wells lay upon the table that the doctor and I had cleared, and I trembled all over when I thought of what lay before me: I should be obliged to stand and gaze into the living brain of my poor friend as the doctor relentlessly laid it bare.

With swift, experienced fingers the doctor administered an anesthetic. I was oppressed by a dreadful feeling that we were committing a crime, that Henry Wells would have violently disapproved, that he would have preferred to die. It is a dreadful thing to mutilate a man's brain. And yet I knew that the doctor's conduct was above reproach, and that the ethics of his profession demanded that he operate.

"We are ready," said Dr. Smith. "Lower the lamp. Carefully now!"

I saw the knife moving in his competent, swift fingers. For a moment I stared, and then I turned my head away. What I had seen in that brief glance made me sick and faint. It may have been fancy, but as I stared at the wall I had the impression that the doctor was on the verge of collapse. He made no sound, but I was almost certain that he had made some horrible discovery.

"Lower the lamp," he said. His voice was hoarse and seemed to come from far down within his throat.

I lowered the lamp an inch without turning my head. I waited for him to reproach me, to swear at me perhaps, but he was as silent as the man on the table. I knew, though, that his fingers were still at work, for I could hear them as they moved about. I could hear his swift, agile fingers moving about the head of Henry Wells.

I suddenly became conscious that my hand was trembling. I wanted to lay down the lamp; I felt that I could no longer hold it.

"Are you nearly through?" I gasped in desperation.

"Hold that lamp steady!" The doctor screamed the command. "If you move that lamp again—I—I won't sew him up. I don't care if they hang me! I'm not a healer of devils!"

I knew not what to do. I could scarcely hold the lamp, and the doctor's threat horrified me.

"Do everything you can," I urged, hysterically. "Give him a chance to fight his way back. He was kind and good—once!"

For a moment there was silence, and I feared that he would not heed me. I momentarily expected him to throw down his scalpel and sponge, and dash across the room and out into the fog. It was not until I heard his fingers moving about again that I knew he had decided to give even the damned a chance.

It was after midnight when the doctor told me that I could lay down the lamp. I turned with a cry of relief and encountered a face that I shall never forget. In three-quarters of an hour the doctor had aged ten years. There were dark hollows beneath his eyes, and his mouth twitched convulsively.

"He'll not live," he said. "He'll be dead in an hour. I did not touch his brain. I could do nothing. When I saw—how things were—I—I—sewed him up immediately."

"What did you see?" I half-whispered.

A look of unutterable fear came into the doctor's eyes. "I saw—I saw. . . ." His voice broke and his whole body quivered. "I saw . . . oh, the burning shame of it . . . evil that is without shape, that is formless. . . ."

Suddenly he straightened and looked wildly about him.

"They will come here and claim him!" he cried. "They have laid their mark upon him and they will come for him. You must not stay here. This house is marked for destruction!"

I watched him helplessly as he seized his hat and bag and crossed to the door. With white, shaking fingers he drew back the latch, and in a moment his lean figure was silhouetted against a square of swirling vapor.

"Remember that I warned you!" he shouted back; and then the fog swallowed him.

Howard was sitting and rubbing his eyes.

"A malicious trick, that!" he was muttering. "To deliberately drug me! Had I known that glass of water. . . ."

"How do you feel?" I asked as I shook him violently by the shoulders. "Do you think you can walk?"

"You drug me, and then ask me to walk! Frank, you're as unreasonable as an artist. What is the matter now?"

I pointed to the silent figure on the table. "Mulligan Wood is safer," I said. "He belongs to them now!"

Howard sprang to his feet and shook me by the arm.

"What do you mean?" he cried. "How do you know?"

"The doctor saw his brain," I explained. "And he also saw something that he would not—could not describe. But he told me that they would come for him, and I believe him."

"We must leave here at once!" cried Howard. "Your doctor was right. We are in deadly danger. Even Mulligan Wood—but we need not return to the wood. There is your launch!"

"There is the launch!" I echoed, faint hope rising in my mind.

"The fog will be a most deadly menace," said Howard grimly. "But even death at sea is preferable to *this* horror."

It was not far from the house to the dock, and in less than a minute Howard was seated in the stern of the launch and I was working furiously on the engine. The foghorns still moaned, but there were no lights visible anywhere in the harbor. We could not see two feet before our faces. The white wraiths of the fog were dimly visible in the darkness, but beyond them stretched endless night, lightless and full of terror.

Howard was speaking. "Somehow I feel that there is death out there," he said.

"There is more death here," I said as I started the engine. "I think I can avoid the rocks. There is very little wind and I know the harbor."

"And of course we shall have the foghorns to guide us," muttered Howard. "I think we had better make for the open sea."

I agreed.

"The launch wouldn't survive a storm," I said, "but I've no desire to remain in the harbor. If we reach the sea, we'll probably be picked up by some ship. It would be sheer folly to remain where they can reach us."

"How do we know how far they can reach?" groaned Howard. "What are the distances of Earth to things that have traveled through space? They will overrun Earth. They will destroy us all utterly."

"We'll discuss that later," I cried as the engine roared into life. "We're going to get as far away from them as possible. Perhaps they haven't *learned* yet! While they've still limitations we may be able to escape."

We moved slowly into the channel, and the sound of the water splashing against the sides of the launch soothed us strangely. At a suggestion from me, Howard had taken the wheel and was slowly bringing her about.

"Keep her steady," I shouted. "There isn't any danger until we get into the Narrows!"

For several minutes I crouched above the engine while Howard steered in silence. Then, suddenly, he turned to me with a gesture of elation.

"I think the fog's lifting," he said.

I stared into the darkness before me. Certainly it seemed less oppressive, and the white spirals of mist that had been continually ascending through it were fading into insubstantial wisps. "Keep her head on," I shouted. "We're in luck. If the fog clears, we'll be able to see the Narrows. Keep a sharp lookout for Mulligan Light."

There is no describing the joy that filled us when we saw the light.

Yellow and bright it streamed over the water and illuminated sharply the outlines of the great rocks that rose on both sides of the Narrows.

"Let me have the wheel," I shouted as I stepped quickly forward. "This is a ticklish passage, but we'll come through now with colors flying."

In our excitement and elation we almost forgot the horror that we had left behind us. I stood at the wheel and smiled confidently as we raced over the dark water. Quickly the rocks drew nearer until their vast bulk towered above us.

"We shall certainly make it!" I cried.

But no response came from Howard. I heard him choke and gasp.

"What is the matter?" I asked suddenly, and turning, saw that he was crouching in terror above the engine. His back was turned toward me, but I knew instinctively in which direction he was gazing.

The dim shore that we had left shone like a flaming sunset. Mulligan Wood was burning. Great flames shot up from the highest of the tall trees, and a thick curtain of black smoke rolled slowly eastward, blotting out the few remaining lights in the harbor.

But it was not the flames that caused me to cry out in fear and horror. It was the shape that towered above the trees, the vast, formless shape that moved slowly to and fro across the sky.

God knows I tried to believe that I saw nothing. I tried to believe that the shape was a mere shadow cast by the flames, and I remember that I gripped Howard's arm reassuringly.

"The wood will be destroyed completely," I cried, "and those ghastly things with us will be destroyed with it."

But when Howard turned and shook his head, I knew that the dim, formless thing that towered above the trees was more than a shadow.

"If we see it clearly, we are lost!" he warned, his voice vibrant with terror. "Pray that it remains without form!"

It is older than the world, I thought, *older than all religion. Before the dawn of civilization men knelt in adoration before it. It is present in all mythologies. It is the primal symbol. Perhaps, in the dim past, thousands and thousands of years ago, it was used to—repel the invaders. I shall fight the shape with a high and terrible mystery.*

Suddenly I became curiously calm. I knew that I had hardly a minute to act, that more than our lives were threatened, but I did not tremble. I reached calmly beneath the engine and drew out a quantity of cotton waste.

"Howard," I said, "light a match. It is our only hope. You must strike a match at once."

For what seemed eternities Howard stared at me uncomprehendingly. Then the night was clamorous with his laughter.

"A match!" he shrieked. "A match to warm our little brains! Yes, we shall need a match."

"Trust me!" I entreated. "You must—it is our one hope. Strike a match quickly."

"I do not understand!" Howard was sober now, but his voice quivered.

"I have thought of something that may save us," I said. "Please light this waste for me."

Slowly he nodded. I had told him nothing, but I knew he guessed what I intended to do. Often his insight was uncanny. With fumbling fingers he drew out a match and struck it.

"Be bold," he said. "Show them that you are unafraid. Make the sign boldly."

As the waste caught fire, the form above the trees stood out with a frightful clarity.

I raised the flaming cotton and passed it quickly before my body in a straight line from my left to my right shoulder. Then I raised it to my forehead and lowered it to my knees.

In an instant Howard had snatched the brand and was repeating the sign. He made two crosses, one against his body and one against the darkness with the torch held at arm's length.

For a moment I shut my eyes, but I could still see the shape above the trees. Then slowly its form became less distinct, became vast and chaotic—and when I opened my eyes it had vanished. I saw nothing but the flaming forest and the shadows cast by the tall trees.

The horror had passed, but I did not move. I stood like an image of stone staring over the black water. Then something seemed to burst in my head. My brain spun dizzily, and I tottered against the rail.

I would have fallen, but Howard caught me about the shoulders. "We're saved!" he shouted. "We've won through."

"I'm glad," I said. But I was too utterly exhausted to really rejoice. My legs gave way beneath me and my head fell forward. All the sights and sounds of Earth were swallowed up in a merciful blackness.

II

Howard was writing when I entered the room.

"How is the story going?" I asked.

For a moment he ignored my question. Then he slowly turned and faced me. He was hollow-eyed, and his pallor was alarming.

"It's not going well," he said at last. "It doesn't satisfy me. There are problems that still elude me. I haven't been able to capture *all* of the horror of the thing in Mulligan Wood."

I sat down and lit a cigarette.

"I want you to explain that horror to me," I said. "For three weeks I have waited for you to speak. I know that you have some knowledge which you are concealing from me. What was the damp, spongy thing that landed on Wells's head in the woods? Why did we hear a droning as we fled in the fog? What was the meaning of the shape that we saw above the trees? And why, in heaven's name, didn't the horror spread as we feared it might? What stopped it? Howard, what do you think really happened to Wells's brain? Did his body burn with the farm, or did they—*claim* it? And the other body that was found in Mulligan Wood—that lean, blackened horror with riddled head—how do you explain that?" (Two days after the fire a skeleton had been found in Mulligan Wood. A few fragments of burnt flesh still adhered to the bones, and the skullcap was missing.)

It was a long time before Howard spoke again. He sat with bowed head fingering his notebook, and his body trembled all over. At last he raised his eyes. They shone with a wild light and his lips were ashen.

"Yes," he said. "We will discuss the horror together. Last week I did not want to speak of it. It seemed too awful to put into words. But I shall never rest in peace until I have woven it into a story, until I have made my readers feel and see that dreadful, unspeakable thing. And I cannot write of it until I am convinced beyond the shadow of a doubt that I understand it myself. It may help me to talk about it.

"You have asked me what the damp thing was that fell on Wells's head. I believe that it was a human brain—the essence of a human brain drawn out through a hole, or holes, in a human head. I believe the brain was drawn out by imperceptible degrees, and reconstructed again by the horror. I believe that for some purpose of its own it used human brains—perhaps to learn from them. Or perhaps it merely played with them. The blackened, riddled body in Mulligan Wood? That was the body of the first victim, some poor fool who got lost between the tall trees. I rather suspect the trees helped. I think the horror endowed them with a strange life. Anyhow, the poor chap lost his brain. The horror took it, and played with it, and then accidentally dropped it. It dropped it on Wells's head. Wells said that the long, thin, and very white arm he saw was looking for something that it had dropped. Of course Wells didn't really see the arm objectively, but the horror that is without form or color had already entered his brain and clothed itself in human thought.

"As for the droning that we heard and the shape we thought we saw above the burning forest—that was the horror seeking to make itself felt, seeking to break down barriers, seeking to enter our brains and clothe itself with our thoughts. It almost got us. If we had seen the white arm, we should have been lost."

Howard walked to the window. He drew back the curtains and gazed for a moment at the crowded harbor and the tall, white buildings that towered against the moon. He was staring at the skyline of lower Manhattan. Sheer beneath him the cliffs of Brooklyn Heights loomed darkly.

"Why didn't they conquer?" he cried. "They could have destroyed us utterly. They could have wiped us from Earth—all our wealth and power would have gone down before them."

I shivered. "Yes . . . why didn't the horror spread?" I asked.

Howard shrugged his shoulders. "I do not know. Perhaps they discovered that human brains were too trivial and absurd to bother with. Perhaps we ceased to amuse them. Perhaps they grew tired of us. But it is conceivable that the *sign* destroyed them—or sent them back through space. I think they came millions of years ago, and were frightened away by the sign. When they discovered that we had not forgotten the use of the sign they may have fled in terror. Certainly there has been no manifestation for three weeks. I think that they are gone."

"And Henry Wells?" I asked.

"Well, his body was not found. I imagine they came for him."

"And you honestly intend to put this—this obscenity into a story? Oh, my God! The whole thing is so incredible, so unheard of, that I can't believe it. Did we not dream it all? Were we ever really in Partridgeville? Did we sit in an ancient house and discuss frightful things while the fog curled about us? Did we walk through that unholy wood? Were the trees really alive, and did Henry Wells run about on his hands and knees like a wolf?"

Howard sat down quietly and rolled up his sleeve. He thrust his thin arm toward me.

"Can you argue away that scar?" he said. "There are the marks of the beast that attacked me—the man-beast that was Henry Wells. A dream? I would cut off this arm immediately at the elbow if you could convince me that it was a dream."

I walked to the window and remained for a long time staring at Manhattan. *There,* I thought, *is something substantial. It is absurd to imagine that anything could destroy it. It is absurd to imagine that the horror was really as terrible as it seemed to us in Partridgeville. I must persuade Howard not to write about it. We must both try to forget it.*

I returned to where he sat and laid my hand on his shoulder.

"You'll never give up the idea of putting it into a story?" I urged gently.

"Never!" He was on his feet, and his eyes were blazing. "Do you think I would give up now when I've almost captured it? I shall write a story that will penetrate to the inmost core of a horror that is without form and substance, but more terrible than a plague-stricken city when the cadences of a tolling bell sound an end to all hope. I shall surpass Poe. I shall surpass all the masters."

"Surpass them and be damned then," I said angrily. "That way madness lies, but it is useless to argue with you. Your egoism is too colossal."

I turned and walked swiftly out of the room. It occurred to me as I descended the stairs that I had made an idiot of myself with my fears, but even as I went down I looked fearfully back over my shoulder, as though I expected a great stone weight to descend from above and crush me to the earth. *He should forget the horror,* I thought. *He should wipe it from his mind. He will go mad if he writes about it.*

Three days passed before I saw Howard again.

"Come in," he said in a curiously hoarse voice when I knocked on his door.

I found him in dressing-gown and slippers, and I knew as soon as I saw him that he was terribly exultant.

"I have triumphed, Frank!" he cried. "I have reproduced the form that is formless, the burning shame that man has not looked upon, the crawling, fleshless obscenity that sucks at our brains!"

Before I could so much as gasp, he placed the bulky manuscript in my hands.

"Read it, Frank," he commanded. "Sit down at once and read it!"

I crossed to the window and sat down on the lounge. I sat there oblivious to everything but the typewritten sheets before me. I confess that I was consumed with curiosity. I had never questioned Howard's power. With words he wrought miracles; breaths from the unknown blew always over his pages, and things that had passed beyond Earth returned at his bidding. But could he even suggest the horror that we had known? Could he even so much as hint at the loathsome, crawling thing that had claimed the brain of Henry Wells?

I read the story through. I read it slowly, and clutched at the pillows beside me in a frenzy of loathing. As soon as I had finished it Howard snatched it from me. He evidently suspected that I desired to tear it to shreds.

"What do you think of it?" he cried exultantly.

"It is indescribably foul!" I exclaimed. "It violates privacies of the mind that should never be laid bare."

"But you will concede that I have made the horror convincing?"

I nodded and reached for my hat. "You have made it so convincing that I cannot remain and discuss it with you. I intend to walk until morning. I intend to walk until I am too weary to care, or think, or remember."

"It is a very great story!" he shouted at me, but I passed down the stairs and out of the house without replying.

III

It was past midnight when the telephone rang. I laid down the book I was reading and lowered the receiver.

"Hello. Who is there?" I asked.

"Frank, this is Howard!" The voice was strangely high-pitched. "Come as quickly as you can. *They've come back!* And Frank, the sign is powerless. I've tried the sign, but the droning is getting louder, and a dim shape. . . ." Howard's voice trailed off disastrously.

I fairly screamed into the receiver. "Courage, man! Do not let them suspect that you are afraid. Make the sign again and again. I will come at once."

Howard's voice came again, more hoarsely this time. "The shape is growing clearer and clearer. And there is nothing I can do! Frank, I have lost the power to make the sign. I have forfeited all right to the protection of the sign. I've become a priest of the Devil. That story—I should not have written that story."

"Show them that you are unafraid!" I cried.

"I'll try! I'll try! Ah, my God! The shape is. . . ."

I did not wait to hear more. Frantically seizing my hat and coat, I dashed down the stairs and out into the street. As I reached the curb a dizziness seized me. I clung to a lamp-post to keep from falling, and waved my hand madly at a fleeing taxi. Luckily the driver saw me. The car stopped, and I staggered out into the street and climbed into it.

"Quick!" I shouted. "Take me to 10 Brooklyn Heights!"

"Yes, sir. Cold night, ain't it?"

"Cold!" I shouted. "It will be cold indeed when they get in. It will be cold indeed when they start to. . . ."

The driver stared at me in amazement. "That's all right, sir," he said. "We'll get you home all right, sir. Brooklyn Heights, did you say, sir?"

"Brooklyn Heights," I groaned, and collapsed against the cushions.

As the car raced forward I tried not to think of the horror that awaited me. I clutched desperately at straws. *It is conceivable,* I thought, *that Howard has gone temporarily insane. How could the horror have found him among so many millions of people? It cannot be that* they *have deliberately sought him out. It cannot be that they would deliberately choose him from among such multitudes. He is too insignificant—all human beings are too insignificant. They would never deliberately angle for human beings. They would never deliberately trawl for human beings—but they did seek Henry Wells. And what did Howard say? "I have become a priest of the Devil." Why not* their *priest? What if Howard has become their priest on Earth? What if his story has made him their priest?*

The thought was a nightmare to me, and I put it furiously from me. *He will have courage to resist them,* I thought. *He will show them that he is not afraid.*

"Here we are, sir. Shall I help you in, sir?"

The car had stopped, and I groaned as I realized that I was about to enter what might prove to be my tomb. I descended to the sidewalk and handed the driver all the change that I possessed. He stared at me in amazement.

"You've given me too much," he said. "Here, sir . . ."

But I waved him aside and dashed up the stoop of the house before me. As I fitted a key into the door I could hear him muttering: "Craziest drunk I ever seen! He gives me four bucks to drive him ten blocks, and doesn't want no thanks or nothin'. . . ."

The lower hall was unlighted. I stood at the foot of the stairs and shouted. "I'm here, Howard! Can you come down?"

There was no answer. I waited for perhaps ten seconds, but not a sound came from the room above.

"I'm coming up!" I shouted in desperation, and started to climb the stairs. I was trembling all over. *They've got him,* I thought. *I'm too late. Perhaps I had better not—great God, what was that?*

I was unbelievably terrified. There was no mistaking the sounds. In the room above, someone was volubly pleading and crying aloud in agony. Was it Howard's voice that I heard? I caught a few words indistinctly. "Crawling—ugh! Crawling—ugh! Oh, have pity! Cold and clee-ar. Crawling—ugh! God in heaven!"

I had reached the landing, and when the pleadings rose to hoarse shrieks I fell to my knees, and made against my body, and upon the wall beside me, and in the air—the sign. I made the primal sign that had saved us in Mulligan Wood, but this time I made it crudely, not with fire, but with fingers that trembled and caught at my clothes, and I made it without courage or hope, made it darkly, with a conviction that nothing could save me.

And then I got up quickly and went on up the stairs. My prayer was that they would take me quickly, that my sufferings should be brief under the stars.

The door of Howard's room was ajar. By a tremendous effort I stretched out my hand and grasped the knob. Slowly I swung it inward.

For a moment I saw nothing but the motionless form of Howard lying upon the floor. He was lying upon his back. His knees were drawn up and he had raised his hand before his face, palms outward, as if to blot out a vision unspeakable.

Upon entering the room I had deliberately, by lowering my eyes, narrowed my range of vision. I saw only the floor and the lower section of the room. I did not want to raise my eyes. I had lowered them in self-protection because I dreaded what the room held.

I did not want to raise my eyes, but there were forces, powers at work in the room, which I could not resist. I knew that if I looked up, the horror might destroy me, but I had no choice.

Slowly, painfully, I raised my eyes and stared across the room. It would have been better, I think, if I had rushed forward immediately and surrendered to the thing that towered there. The vision of that terrible, darkly shrouded shape will come between me and the pleasures of the world as long as I remain in the world.

From the ceiling to the floor it towered, and it threw off blinding light. And pierced by the shafts, whirling around and around, were the pages of Howard's story.

In the center of the room, between the ceiling and the floor, the pages whirled about, and the light burned through the sheets, and descending in spiraling shafts entered the brain of my poor friend. Into his head, the light was pouring in a continuous stream, and above, the Master of the light moved with a slow swaying of its entire bulk. I screamed and covered my eyes with my hands, but still the Master moved—back and forth, back and forth. And still the light poured into the brain of my friend.

And then there came from the mouth of the Master a most awful sound. . . . I had forgotten the sign that I had made three times below in the darkness. I had forgotten the high and terrible mystery before which all of the invaders were powerless. But when I saw it forming itself in the room, forming itself immaculately, with a terrible integrity above the downstreaming light, I knew that I was saved.

I sobbed and fell upon my knees. The light dwindled, and the Master shriveled before my eyes.

And then from the walls, from the ceiling, from the floor, there leapt flame—a white and cleansing flame that consumed, that devoured and destroyed forever.

But my friend was dead.

The Dweller in Darkness*

AUGUST DERLETH

> Searchers after horror haunt strange, far places. For them are the catacombs of Ptolemais, and the carven mausolea of the nightmare countries. They climb to the moonlit towers of ruined Rhine castles, and falter down black cobwebbed steps beneath the scattered stones of forgotten cities in Asia. The haunted wood and the desolate mountain are their shrines, and they linger around the sinister monoliths on uninhabited islands. But the true epicure in the terrible, to whom a new thrill of unutterable ghastliness is the chief end and justification of existence, esteems most of all the ancient, lonely farmhouses of backwoods regions; for there the dark elements of strength, solitude, grotesqueness, and ignorance combine to form the perfection of the hideous.
>
> —H. P. LOVECRAFT

I

Until recently, if a traveler in north central Wisconsin took the left fork at the junction of the Brule River highway and the Chequamegon pike on the way to Pashepaho, he would find himself in country so primitive that it would seem remote from all human contact. If he drove on along the little-used road, he might in time pass a few tumble-down shacks where presumably people had once lived and which have long ago been taken back by the encroaching forest; it is not desolate country, but an area thick with growth, and over all its expanse there persists an intangible aura of the sinister, a kind of ominous oppression of the spirit quickly manifest to even the most casual traveler, for the road he has taken becomes ever more and more diffi-

---

*Originally published in *Weird Tales*, November 1944.

cult to travel, and is eventually lost just short of a deserted lodge built on the edge of a clear blue lake around which century-old trees brood eternally, a country where the only sounds are the cries of the owls, the whippoorwills, and the eerie loons at night, and the wind's voice in the trees, and—but is it always the wind's voice in the trees? And who can say whether the snapped twig is the sign of an animal passing—or of something more, some other creature beyond man's ken?

For the forest surrounding the abandoned lodge at Rick's Lake had a curious reputation long before I myself knew it, a reputation which transcended similar stories about similar primeval places. There were odd rumors about something that dwelt in the depths of the forest's darkness—by no means the conventional wild whisperings of ghosts—of something half-animal, half-man, fearsomely spoken of by such natives as inhabited the edges of that region, and referred to only by stubborn head-shakings among the Indians who occasionally came out of that country and made their way south. The forest had an evil reputation; it was nothing short of that; and already, before the turn of the century, it had a history that gave pause even to the most intrepid adventurer.

The first record of it was left in the writings of a missionary on his way through that country to come to the aid of a tribe of Indians reported to the post at Chequamegon Bay in the north to be starving. Fr. Piregard vanished, but the Indians later brought in his effects: a sandal, his rosary, and a prayerbook in which he had written certain curious words which had been carefully preserved: "I have the conviction that some creature is following me. I thought at first it was a bear, but I am now compelled to believe that it is something incredibly more monstrous than anything on this earth. Darkness is falling, and I believe I have developed a slight delirium, for I persist in hearing strange music and other curious sounds which can surely not derive from any natural source. There is also a disturbing illusion as of great footsteps which actually shake the earth, and I have several times encountered a very large footprint which varies in shape. . . ."

The second record is far more sinister. When Big Bob Hiller, one of the most rapacious lumber barons of the entire Midwest, began to encroach upon the Rick's Lake country in the middle of the last century, he could not fail to be impressed by the stand of pine in the area near the lake, and, though he did not own it, he followed the usual custom of the lumber barons and sent his men in from an adjoining piece he did own, under the intended explanation that he did not know where his line ran. Thirteen men failed to return from that first day's work on the edge of the forest area surrounding Rick's Lake; two of their bodies were never recovered; four were found—inconceivably—in the lake, several miles from where they had been cutting timber; the others were discovered at various places in the forest. Hiller thought he had a lumber war on his hands, laid his men off to mislead his unknown opponent, and then suddenly ordered them back to work in the forbidden region. After he had lost five more men, Hiller pulled out, and no hand since his time touched the forest, save for one or two individuals who took up land there and moved into the area.

One and all, these individuals moved out within a short time, saying little, but hinting much. Yet, the nature of their whispered hints was such that they were soon forced to abandon any explanation; so incredible were the tales they told, with overtones of something too horrible for description, of age-old evil which preceded anything dreamed of by even the most learned archaeologist. Only one of them vanished, and no trace of him was ever found. The others came back out of the forest and in the course of time were lost somewhere among other people in the United States—all save a half-breed known as Old Peter, who was obsessed with the idea that there were mineral deposits in the vicinity of the wood, and occasionally went to camp on its edge, being careful not to venture in.

It was inevitable that the Rick's Lake legends would ultimately reach the attention of Professor Upton Gardner of the state university; he had completed collections of Paul Bunyan, Whiskey Jack, and Hodag tales, and was engaged upon a compilation of place legends when he first encountered the curious half-forgotten tales that emanated from the region of Rick's Lake. I discovered later that his first reaction to them was one of casual interest; legends abound in out-of-the-way places, and there was nothing to indicate that these were of any more import than others. True, there was no similarity in the strictest sense of the word to the more familiar tales; for, while the usual legends concerned themselves with ghostly appearances of men and animals, lost treasure, tribal beliefs, and the like, those of Rick's Lake were curiously unusual in their insistence upon utterly outré creatures—or "a creature"—since no one had ever reported seeing more than one even vaguely in the forest's darkness, half-man, half beast, with always the hint that this description was inadequate in that it did injustice to the narrator's concept of what it was that lurked there in the vicinity of the lake. Nevertheless, Professor Gardner would in all probability have done little more than add the legends as he heard them to his collection, if it had not been for the reports—seemingly unconnected—of two curious facts, and the accidental discovery of a third.

The two facts were both newspaper accounts carried by Wisconsin papers within a week of each other. The first was a terse, half-comic report headed: SEA SERPENT IN WISCONSIN LAKE? and read: "Pilot Joseph X. Castleton, on test flight over northern Wisconsin yesterday, reported seeing a large animal of some kind bathing by night in a forest lake in the vicinity of Chequamegon. Castleton was caught in a thundershower and was flying low at the time, when, in an effort to ascertain his whereabouts, he looked down when lightning flashed, and saw what appeared to be a very large animal rising from the waters of a lake below him, and vanish into the forest. The pilot added no details to his story, but asserts that the creature he saw was not the Loch Ness monster." The second story was the utterly fantastic tale of the discovery of the body of Fr. Piregard, well-preserved, in the hollow trunk of a tree along the Brule River. At first called a lost member of the Marquette-Jolliet Expedition, Fr. Piregard was quickly identified. To this report was appended a frigid statement by the president of the State Historical Society dismissing the discovery as a hoax.

The discovery Professor Gardner made was simply that an old friend was actually the owner of the abandoned lodge and most of the shore of Rick's Lake.

The sequence of events was thus clearly inevitable. Professor Gardner instantly associated both newspaper accounts with the Rick's Lake legends; this might not have been enough to stir him to drop his researches into the general mass of legends abounding in Wisconsin for specific research of quite another kind, but the occurrence of something even more astonishing sent him posthaste to the owner of the abandoned lodge for permission to take the place over in the interests of science. What spurred him to take this action was nothing less than a request from the curator of the state museum to visit his office late one night and view a new exhibit which had arrived. He went there in the company of Laird Dorgan, and it was Laird who came to me.

But that was after Professor Gardner vanished.

For he did vanish; after sporadic reports from Rick's Lake over a period of three months, all word from the lodge ceased entirely, and nothing further was heard of Professor Upton Gardner.

Laird came to my room at the University Club late one night in October; his frank blue eyes were clouded, his lips tense, his brow furrowed, and there was everything to show that he was in a state of moderate excitation which did not derive from liquor. I assumed that he was working too hard; the first-period tests in his University of Wisconsin classes were just over; and Laird habitually took tests seriously—even as a student he had done so, and now as an instructor, he was doubly conscientious.

But it was not that. Professor Gardner had been missing almost a month now, and it was this which preyed on his mind. He said as much in so many words, adding, "Jack, I've got to go up there and see what I can do."

"Man, if the sheriff and the posse haven't discovered anything, what can you do?" I asked.

"For one thing, I know more than they do."

"If so, why didn't you tell them?"

"Because it's not the sort of thing they'd pay any attention to."

"Legends?"

"No."

He was looking at me speculatively, as if wondering whether he could trust me. I was suddenly conscious of the conviction that he *did* know something which he, at least, regarded with the gravest concern; and at the same time I had the most curious sensation of premonition and warning that I have ever experienced. In that instant the entire room seemed tense, the air electrified.

"If I go up there—do you think you could go along?"

"I guess I could manage."

"Good." He took a turn or two about the room, his eyes brooding, looking at me from time to time, still betraying uncertainty and an inability to make up his mind.

"Look, Laird—sit down and take it easy. That caged lion stuff isn't good for your nerves."

He took my advice; he sat down, covered his face with his hands, and shuddered. For a moment I was alarmed; but he snapped out of it in a few seconds, leaned back, and lit a cigarette.

"You know those legends about Rick's Lake, Jack?"

I assured him that I knew them and the history of the place from the beginning—as much as had been recorded.

"And those stories in the papers I mentioned to you . . . ?"

The stories, too. I remembered them since Laird had discussed with me their effect on his employer.

"That second one, about Fr. Piregard," he began, hesitated, stopped. But then, taking a deep breath, he began again. "You know, Gardner and I went over to the curator's office one night last spring."

"Yes, I was east at the time."

"Of course. Well, we went over there. The curator had something to show us. What do you think it was?"

"No idea. What was it?"

"That body in the tree!"

"No!"

"Gave us quite a jolt. There it was, hollow trunk and all, just the way it had been found. It had been shipped down to the museum for exhibition. But it was never exhibited, of course—for a very good reason. When Gardner saw it, he thought it was a waxwork. But it wasn't."

"You don't mean that it was the real thing?"

Laird nodded. "I know it's incredible."

"It's just not possible."

"Well, yes, I suppose it's impossible. But it was so. That's why it wasn't exhibited—just taken out and buried."

"I don't quite follow that."

He leaned forward and said very earnestly, "Because when it came in it had all the appearance of being completely preserved, as if by some natural embalming process. It wasn't. It was frozen. It began to thaw out that night. And there were certain things about it that indicated that Fr. Piregard hadn't been dead the three centuries history said he had. The body began to go to pieces in a dozen ways—but not crumbling into dust, nothing like that. Gardner estimated that he hadn't been dead over five years. Where had he been in the meantime?"

He was quite sincere. I would not at first have believed it. But there was a certain disquieting earnestness about Laird that forbade any levity on my part. If I had treated his story as a joke, as I had the impulse to do, he would have shut up like a clam, and walked out of my room to brood about this thing in secret, with Lord knows what harm to himself. For a little while I said absolutely nothing.

"You don't believe it."

"I haven't said so."

"I can feel it."

"No. It's hard to take. Let's say I believe in your sincerity."

"That's fair enough," he said grimly. "Do you believe in me sufficiently to go along up to the lodge and find out what may have happened there?"

"Yes, I do."

"But I think you'd better read these excerpts from Gardner's letters first." He put them down on my desk like a challenge. He had copied them off onto a single sheet of paper, and as I took this up he went on, talking rapidly, explaining that the letters had been those written by Gardner from the lodge. When he finished, I turned to the excerpts and read.

> I cannot deny that there is about the lodge, the lake, even the forest an aura of evil, of impending danger—it is more than that, Laird, if I could explain it, but archaeology is my forte, and not fiction. For it would take fiction, I think, to do justice to this thing I feel. . . . Yes, there are times when I have the distinct feeling that *someone* or *something* is watching me out of the forest or from the lake—there does not seem to be a distinction as I would like to understand it, and while it does not make me uneasy, nevertheless it is enough to give me pause. I managed the other day to make contact with Old Peter,

> the half-breed. He was at the moment a little the worse for firewater, but when I mentioned the lodge and the forest to him, he drew into himself like a clam. But he did put words to it: he called it the Wendigo—you are familiar with this legend, which properly belongs to the French-Canadian country.

That was the first letter, written about a week after Gardner had reached the abandoned lodge on Rick's Lake. The second was extremely terse, and had been sent by special delivery.

> Will you wire Miskatonic University at Arkham, Massachusetts, to ascertain if there is available for study a photostatic copy of a book known as the *Necronomicon*, by an Arabian writer who signs himself Abdul Alhazred? Make inquiry also for the *Pnakotic Manuscripts* and the *Book of Eibon*, and determine whether it is possible to purchase through one of the local bookstores a copy of *The Outsider and Others*, by H. P. Lovecraft, published by Arkham House last year. I believe that these books individually and collectively may be helpful in determining just what it is that haunts this place. For there *is* something; make no mistake about that; I am convinced of it, and when I tell you that I believe it has lived here not for years, but for centuries—perhaps even before the time of man—you will understand that I may be on the threshold of great discoveries.

Startling as this letter was, the third was even more so. For an interval of a fortnight went by between the second and third letters, and it was apparent that something had happened to threaten Professor Gardner's composure, for his third letter was even in this selected excerpt marked by extreme perturbation.

> Everything evil here. . . . I don't know whether it is the Black Goat with a Thousand Young or the Faceless One and/or something more that rides the wind. For God's sake . . . those accursed fragments! . . . Something in the lake, too, and at night the sounds! How still, and then suddenly those horrible flutes, those watery ululations! Not a bird, not an animal then—only those ghastly sounds. And the voices! . . . Or is it but a dream? Is it my own voice I hear in the darkness? . . .

I found myself increasingly shaken as I read those excerpts. Certain implications and hints lodged between the lines of what Professor Gardner had written were suggestive of terrible, ageless evil, and I felt that there was opening up before Laird Dorgan and myself an adventure so incredible, so bizarre, and so unbelievably dangerous that we might well not return to tell it. Yet even then there was a lurking doubt in my mind that we would say anything about what we found at Rick's Lake.

"What do you say?" asked Laird impatiently.

"I'm going."

"Good! Everything's ready. I've even got a dictaphone and batteries enough to run it. I've arranged for the sheriff of the county at Pashepaho to replace Gardner's notes, and leave everything just the way it was."

"A dictaphone," I broke in. "What for?"

"Those sounds he wrote about—we can settle that for once and all. If they're there to be heard, the dictaphone will record them; if they're just imagination, it won't." He paused, his eyes very grave. "You know, Jack, we may not come out of this thing."

"I know."

I did not say so, because I knew that Laird, too, felt the same way I did: that we were going like two dwarfed Davids to face an adversary greater than any Goliath, an adversary invisible and unknown, who bore no name and was shrouded in legend and fear, a dweller not only of the darkness of the wood but in that greater darkness which the mind of man has sought to explore since his dawn.

II

Sheriff Cowan was at the lodge when we arrived. Old Peter was with him. The sheriff was a tall, saturnine individual clearly of Yankee stock; though representing the fourth generation of his family in the area, he spoke with a twang which doubtless had persisted from generation to generation. The half-breed was a dark-skinned, ill-kempt fellow; he had a way of saying little, and from time to time grinned or snickered as at some secret joke.

"I brung up express that come some time past for the professor," said the sheriff. "From some place in Massachusetts was one of 'em, and the other from down near Madison. Didn't seem t' me 'twas worth sendin' back. So I took and brung 'em with the keys. Don't know that you fellers 'll git anyw'eres. My posse and me went through the hull woods, didn't see a thing."

"You ain't tellin' 'em everything," put in the half-breed, grinning.

"Ain't no more to tell."

"What about the carvin'?"

The sheriff shrugged irritably. "Damn it, Peter, that ain't got nothin' to do with the professor's disappearance."

"He made a drawin' of it, didn't he?"

So pressed, the sheriff confided that two members of his posse had stumbled upon a great slab or rock in the center of the wood; it was mossy and overgrown, but there was upon it an odd drawing, plainly as old as the forest—probably the work of one of the primitive Indian tribes once known to inhabit northern Wisconsin before the Dacotah Sioux and the Winnebago—

Old Peter grunted with contempt. "No Indian drawing."

The sheriff shook this off and went on. The drawing represented some kind of creature, but no one could tell what it was; it was certainly not a man, but on the other hand, it did not seem to be hairy, like a beast. Moreover, the unknown artist had forgotten to put in a face.

" 'N beside it there wuz two things," said the half-breed.

"Don't pay no attention to him," said the sheriff then.

"What two things?" demanded Laird.

"Jest things," replied the half-breed, snickering. "Heh, heh! Ain't no other way to tell it—warn't human, warn't animal, jest things."

Cowan was irritated. He became suddenly brusque; he ordered the half-breed to keep still, and went on to say that if we needed him, he would be at his office in Pashepaho. He did not explain how we were to make contact with him, since there was no telephone at the lodge, but plainly he had no high regard for the legends abounding about the area into which we had ventured with such determination. The half-breed regarded us with an almost stolid indifference, broken only by his sly grin from time to time, and his dark eyes examined our luggage with keen speculation and interest. Laird met his gaze occasionally, and each time Old Peter indolently shifted his eyes. The sheriff went on talking; the notes and drawings the missing man had made were on the desk he had used in the big room which made up almost the entire ground floor of the lodge, just where he had found them; they were the property of the State of Wisconsin and were to be returned to the sheriff's office when we had finished with them. At the threshold he turned for a parting shot to say he hoped we would not be staying too long, because "While I ain't givin' in to any of them crazy ideas—it jest ain't been so healthy for some of the people who came here."

"The half-breed knows or suspects something," said Laird at once. "We'll have to get in touch with him sometime when the sheriff's not around."

"Didn't Gardner write that he was pretty close-mouthed when it came to concrete data?"

"Yes, but he indicated the way out. Firewater."

We went to work and settled ourselves, storing our food supplies, setting up the dictaphone, getting things into readiness for a stay of at least a fortnight; our supplies were sufficient for this length of time, and if we had to remain longer, we could always go into Pashepaho for more food. Moreover, Laird had brought fully two dozen dictaphone cylinders, so that we had plenty of them for an indefinite time, particularly since we did not intend to use them except when we slept—and this would not be often, for we had agreed that one of us would watch while the other took his rest, an arrangement we were not sanguine enough to believe would hold good without fail, hence the machine. It was not until after we had settled our belongings that we turned to the things the sheriff had brought, and meanwhile, we had ample opportunity to become aware of the very definite aura of the place.

For it was not imagination that there was a strange aura about the lodge and the grounds. It was not alone the brooding, almost sinister stillness, not alone the tall pines encroaching upon the lodge, not alone the blue-black waters of the lake, but something more than that: a hushed, almost menacing air of waiting, a kind of aloof assurance that was ominous—as one might imagine a hawk might feel leisurely cruising above prey it knows will not escape its talons. Nor was this a fleeting impression, for it was obvious almost at once, and it grew with sure steadiness throughout the hour or so that we worked there; moreover, it was so plainly to be felt, that Laird commented upon it as if he had long ago accepted it, and knew that I, too, had done so! Yet there was nothing primary to which this could be attributed. There are thousands of lakes like Rick's in northern Wisconsin and Minnesota, and while many of them are not in forest areas, those which are do not differ greatly in their physical aspects from Rick's; so there was nothing in the appearance of the place which at all contributed to the brooding sense of horror which seemed to invade us from outside. Indeed, the setting was rather the opposite; under the afternoon sunlight, the old lodge, the lake, the high forest all around, had a pleasant air of seclusion—an air which made the contrast with the intangible aura of evil all the more pointed and fearsome. The fragrance of the pines, together with the freshness of the water, served also to emphasize the intangible mood of menace.

We turned at last to the material left on Professor Gardner's desk. The express packages contained, as expected, a copy of *The Outsider and Others*, by H. P. Lovecraft, shipped by the publishers, and photostatic copies of manuscript and printed pages taken from the *R'lyeh Text* and Ludvig Prinn's *De Vermis Mysteriis*—apparently sent for to supplement the earlier data dispatched to the professor by the librarian of Miskatonic University, for we found among the material brought back by the sheriff certain pages from the *Necronomicon*, in the translation by Olaus Wormius, and likewise from the *Pnakotic Manuscripts*. But it was not these pages, which for the most part were unintelligible to us, which held our attention. It was the fragmentary notes left by Professor Gardner.

It was quite evident that he had not had time to do more than put down such questions and thoughts as had occurred to him, and, while there was little assimilation manifest, yet there was about what he had written a certain terrible suggestiveness which grew to colossal proportions as everything he had not put down became obvious.

"Is the slab (a) only an ancient ruin, (b) a marker similar to a tomb, (c) or a focal point for Him? If the latter, from outside? Or from beneath? (NB: Nothing to show that the thing has been disturbed.)

"Cthulhu or Kthulhut. In Rick's Lake? Subterrene passage to Superior and the sea via the St. Lawrence? (NB: Except for the aviator's story, nothing to show that the Thing has anything to do with the water. Probably not one of the water beings.)

"Hastur. But manifestations do not seem to have been of air beings either.

"Yog-Sothoth. Of earth certainly—but he is not the 'Dweller in Darkness.' (NB: The Thing, whatever it is, must be of the earth deities, even though it travels in time and space. It could possibly be more than one, of which only the earth being is occasionally visible. Ithaqua, perhaps?)

" 'Dweller in Darkness.' Could He be the same as the Blind, Faceless One? He could be truly said to be dwelling in darkness. Nyarlathotep? Or Shub-Niggurath?

"What of fire? There must be a deity here, too. But no mention. (NB: Presumably, if the Earth and Water Beings oppose those of Air, then they must oppose those of Fire as well. Yet there is evidence here and there to show that there is more constant struggle between Air and Water Beings than between those of Earth and Air. Abdul Alhazred is damnably obscure in places. There is no clue as to the identity of Cthugha in that terrible footnote.)

"Partier says I am on the wrong track. I'm not convinced. Whoever it is that plays the music in the night is a master of hellish cadence and rhythm. And, yes, of cacophony. (CF. Bierce and Chambers.)"

That was all.

"What incredible gibberish!" I exclaimed.

And yet—and yet I knew instinctively it was not gibberish. Strange things had happened here, things which demanded an explanation which was not terrestrial; and here, in Gardner's handwriting, was evidence to show that he had not only arrived at the same conclusion, but passed it. However it might sound, Gardner had written it in all seriousness, and clearly for his own use alone, since only the vaguest and most suggestive outline seemed apparent. Moreover, the notes had a startling effect on Laird; he had gone quite pale, and now stood looking down as if he could not believe what he had seen.

"What is it?" I asked.

"Jack—he was in contact with Partier."

"It doesn't register," I answered, but even as I spoke I remembered the hush-hush that had attended the severing of old Professor Partier's connection with the University of Wisconsin. It had been given out to the press that the old man had been somewhat too liberal in his lectures in anthropology—that is, he had "Communistic leanings!"—which everyone who knew Partier realized was far from the facts. But he had said strange things in his lectures, he had talked of horrible, forbidden matters, and it had been thought best to let him out quietly. Unfortunately, Partier went out trumpeting in his contemptuous manner, and it had been difficult to hush the matter up satisfactorily.

"He's living down in Wausau now," said Laird.

"Do you suppose he could translate all this?" I asked and knew that I had echoed the thought in Laird's mind.

"He's three hours away by car. We'll copy these notes, and if nothing happens—if we can't discover anything, we'll go to see him."

If nothing happened—!

If the lodge by day had seemed brooding in an air of ominousness, by night it seemed surcharged with menace. Moreover, events began to take place with disarming and insidious suddenness, beginning in mid-evening, when Laird and I were sitting over those curious photostats sent out by Miskatonic University in lieu of the books and manuscripts themselves, which were far too valuable to permit out of their haven. The first manifestation was so simple that for some time neither of us noticed its strangeness. It was simply the sound in the trees as of rising wind, the growing song among the pines. The night was warm, and all the windows of the lodge stood open. Laird commented on the wind, and went on giving voice to his perplexity regarding the fragments before us. Not until half an hour had gone by and the sound of the wind had risen to the proportions of a gale did it occur to Laird that something was wrong, and he looked up, his eyes going from one open window to another in growing apprehension. Then I, too, became aware.

Despite the tumult of the wind, no draft of air had circulated in the room, not one of the light curtains at the window was so much as trembling!

With one simultaneous movement, both of us stepped out upon the broad verandah of the lodge.

There was no wind, no breath of air stirring to touch our hands and faces. There was only the sound in the forest. And both of us looked up to where the pines were silhouetted against the starswept heavens, expecting their tops would be bending before a high gale; but there was no movement whatever; the pines stood still, motionless; and the sound as of wind continued all around us. We stood on the verandah for half an hour, vainly attempting to determine the source of the sound—and then, as unobtrusively as it had begun, it stopped!

The hour was now approaching midnight, and Laird prepared for bed; he had slept little the previous night, and we had agreed that I was to take the first watch until four in the morning. Neither of us said much about the sound in the pines, but what was said indicated a desire to believe that there was a natural explanation for the phenomenon, if we could establish a point of contact for understanding. It was inevitable, I suppose, that even in the face of all the curious facts which had come to our attention, there should still be an earnest wish to find a natural explanation. Certainly the oldest fear and the greatest fear to which man is prey is fear of the unknown; anything capable of rationalization and explanation cannot be feared; but it was growing hourly more patent that we were facing something which defied all known rationales and credos, but hinged upon a system of belief that antedated even primitive man, and indeed, as scattered hints within the photostat pages from Miskatonic University suggested, antedated even earth itself. And there was always that brooding terror, the ominous suggestion of menace from something far beyond the grasp of such a puny intelligence as man's.

Thus it was with some trepidation that I prepared for my vigil. After Laird had gone to his room, which was at the head of the stairs, with a door opening upon a railed-in balcony looking down into the lodge room where I sat with the book by Lovecraft, reading here and there in its pages, I settled down to a kind of apprehensive waiting. It was not that I was afraid of what might take place, but rather that I was afraid that what took place might be beyond my understanding. However, as the minutes ticked past, I became engrossed in *The Outsider and Others*, with its hellish suggestions of eon-old evil, of entities coexistent with all time and conterminous with all space, and began to understand, however vaguely, a relation between the writings of this fantasist and the curious notes Professor Gardner had made. The most disturbing factor in this cognizance was the knowledge that Professor Gardner had made his notes independent of the book I now read, since it had arrived after his disappearance. Moreover, though there were certain keys to what Gardner had written in the first material he had received from Miskatonic University, there was growing now a mass of evidence to indicate that the professor had had access to some other source of information.

What was that source? Could he have learned something from Old Peter? Hardly likely. Could he have gone to Partier? It was not impossible that he had done so, though he had not imparted this information to Laird. Yet it was not to be ruled out that he had made contact with still another source of which there was no hint among his notes.

It was while I was engaged in this engrossing speculation that I became conscious of the music. It may actually have been sounding for some time before I heard it, but I do not think so. It was a curious melody that was being played, beginning as something lulling and harmonious, and then subtly becoming cacophonous and demoniac, rising in tempo, though all the time coming as from a great distance. I listened to it with growing astonishment; I was not at first aware of the sense of evil which fell upon me the moment I stepped outside and became cognizant that the music emanated from the depths of the dark forest. There, too, I was sharply conscious of its weirdness; the melody was unearthly, utterly bizarre and foreign, and the instruments which were being used seemed to be flutes, or certainly some variation of flutes.

Up to that moment there was no really alarming manifestation. That is, there was nothing but the suggestiveness of the two events which had taken place to inspire fear. There was, in short, always a good possibility that there might be a natural explanation about the sound as of wind and that of music.

But now, suddenly, there occurred something so utterly horrible, something so fraught with terror, that I was at once made prey to the most terrible fear known to man, a surging primitive horror of the unknown, of something from outside—for if I had had doubts about the things suggested by Gardner's notes and the material accompanying them, I knew instinctively that they were unfounded, for the sound that succeeded the strains of that unearthly music was of such a nature that it defied description, and defies it even now. It was simply a ghastly ululation, made by no beast known to man, and certainly by no man. It rose to an awful crescendo and fell away into a silence that was the more terrible for this soul-searing crying. It began with a two-note call, twice repeated, a frightful sound: *"Ygnaiih! Ygnaiih!"* and then became a triumphant wailing cry that ululated out of the forest and into the dark night like the hideous voice of the pit itself: *"Eh-ya-ya-ya-yahaaahaaahaaahaaa-ah-ah-ah-ngh'aaaa-ngh'aaa-ya-ya-ya . . ."*

I stood for a minute absolutely frozen to the verandah. I could not have uttered a sound if it had been necessary to save my life. The voice had ceased, but the trees still seemed to echo its frightful syllables. I heard Laird tumble from his bed, I heard him running down the stairs calling my name, but I could not answer. He came out on the verandah and caught hold of my arm.

"Good God! What was that?"

"Did you hear it?"

"I heard enough."

We stood waiting for it to sound again, but there was no repetition of it. Nor was there a repetition of the music. We returned to the sitting room and waited there, neither of us able to sleep.

But there was not another manifestation of any kind throughout the remainder of that night!

III

The occurrences of that first night more than anything else decided our direction on the following day. For, realizing that we were too ill-informed to cope with any understanding with what was taking place, Laird set the dictaphone for that second night, and we started out for Wausau and Professor Partier, planning to return on the following day. With forethought, Laird carried with him our copy of the notes Gardner had left, skeletal as they were.

Professor Partier, at first reluctant to see us, admitted us finally to his study in the heart of the Wisconsin city, and cleared books and papers from two chairs so that we could sit down. Though he had the appearance of an old man, wore a long white beard, and a fringe of white hair straggled from under his black skullcap, he was as agile as a young man; he was thin, his fingers were bony, his face gaunt, with deep black eyes, and his features were set in an expression that was one of profound cynicism, disdainful, almost contemptuous, and he made no effort to make us comfortable, beyond providing places for us to sit. He recognized Laird as Professor Gardner's secretary, said brusquely that he was a busy man preparing what would doubtless be his last book for his publishers, and he would be obliged to us if we would state the object of our visit as concisely as possible.

"What do you know of Cthulhu?" asked Laird bluntly.

The professor's reaction was astonishing. From an old man whose entire attitude had been one of superiority and aloof disdain, he became instantly wary and alert; with exaggerated care he put down the pencil he had been holding, his eyes never once left Laird's face, and he leaned forward a little over his desk.

"So," he said, "you come to me." He laughed then, a laugh which was like the cackling of some centenarian. "You come to me to ask about Cthulhu. Why?"

Laird explained curtly that we were bent upon discovering what had happened to Professor Gardner. He told as much as he thought necessary, while the old man closed his eyes, picked up his pencil once more, and tapping gently with it, listened with marked care, prompting Laird from time to time. When he had finished, Professor Partier opened his eyes slowly and looked from one to the other of us with an expression that was not unlike one of pity mixed with pain.

"So he mentioned me, did he? But I had no contact with him other than one telephone call." He pursed his lips. "He had more reference to an earlier controversy than to his discoveries at Rick's Lake. I would like now to give you a little advice."

"That's what we came for."

"Go away from that place, and forget all about it."

Laird shook his head in determination.

Partier estimated him, his dark eyes challenging his decision; but Laird did not falter. He had embarked upon this venture, and he meant to see it through.

"These are not forces with which common men have been accustomed to deal," said the old man then. "We are frankly not equipped to do so." He began then, without other preamble, to talk of matters so far removed from the mundane as to be almost beyond conception. Indeed, it was some time before I began to comprehend what he was hinting at, for his concept was so broad and breathtaking that it was difficult for anyone accustomed to so prosaic an existence as mine to grasp. Perhaps it was because Partier began obliquely by suggesting that it was not Cthulhu or his minions who haunted Rick's Lake, but clearly another; the existence of the slab and what was carved upon it clearly indicated the nature of the being who dwelled there from time to time. Professor Gardner had in final analysis got on to the right path, despite thinking that Partier did not believe it. Who was the Blind, Faceless One but Nyarlathotep? Certainly not Shub-Niggurath, the Black Goat of a Thousand Young.

Here Laird interrupted him to press for something more understandable, and then at last, realizing that we knew nothing, the professor went on, still in that vaguely irritable oblique manner, to expound mythology—a mythology of pre-human life not only on the earth, but on the stars of all the universe. "We know nothing," he repeated from time to time. "We know nothing at all. But there are certain signs, certain shunned places. Rick's Lake is one of them." He spoke of beings whose very names were awesome—of the Elder Gods who live on Betelgeuse, remote in time and space, who had cast out into space the Great Old Ones, led by Azathoth and Yog-Sothoth, and numbering among them the primal spawn of the amphibious Cthulhu, the bat-like followers of Hastur the Unspeakable, of Lloigor, Zhar, and Ithaqua, who walked the winds and interstellar space, the earth beings, Nyarlathotep and Shub-Niggurath—the evil beings who sought always to triumph once more over the Elder Gods, who had shut them out or imprisoned them—as Cthulhu long ago slept in the ocean realm of R'lyeh, as Hastur was imprisoned upon a black star near Aldebaran in the Hyades. Long before human beings walked the earth, the conflict between the Elder Gods and the Great Old Ones had taken place; and from time to time the Old Ones had made a resurgence toward power, sometimes to be stopped by direct interference by the Elder Gods, but more often by the agency of human or non-human beings serving to bring about a conflict among the beings of the elements, for, as Gardner's notes indicated, the evil Old Ones were elemental forces. And every time there had been a resurgence, the mark of it had been left deep upon man's memory—though every attempt was made to eliminate the evidence and quiet survivors.

"What happened at Innsmouth, Massachusetts, for instance?" he asked tensely. "What took place at Dunwich? In the wilds of Vermont? At the old Tuttle house on the Aylesbury pike? What of the mysterious cult of Cthulhu, and the utterly strange voyage of exploration to the Mountains of Madness? What beings dwelt on the hidden and shunned Plateau of Leng? And what of Kadath in the Cold Waste? Lovecraft knew! Gardner and many another have sought to discover those secrets, to link the incredible happenings which have taken place here and there on the face of the planet—but it is not desired by the Old Ones that mere man shall know too much. Be warned!"

He took up Gardner's notes without giving either of us a chance to say anything, and studied them, putting on a pair of gold-rimmed spectacles which made him look more ancient than ever, and going on talking, more to himself than to us, saying that it was held that the Old Ones had achieved a higher degree of development in some aspects of science than was hitherto believed possible, but that, of course, nothing was *known*. The way in which he consistently emphasized this indicated very clearly that only a fool or an idiot would disbelieve, proof or no proof. But in the next sentence, he admitted that there was certain proof—the revolting and bestial plaque bearing a representation of a hellish monstrosity walking on the winds above the earth found in the hand of Josiah Alwyn when his body was discovered on a small Pacific island months after his incredible disappearance from his home in Wisconsin; the drawings made by Professor Gardner—and, even more than anything else, that curious slab of carven stones in the forest at Rick's Lake.

"Cthugha," he murmured then, wonderingly. "I've not read the footnote to which he makes reference. And there's nothing in Lovecraft." He shook his head. "No, I don't know." He looked up. "Can you frighten something out of the half-breed?"

"We've thought of that," admitted Laird.

"Well, now, I advise a try. It seems evident that he knows something—it may be nothing but an exaggeration to which his more or less primitive mind has lent itself; but on the other hand—who can say?"

More than this Professor Partier could not or would not tell us. Moreover, Laird was reluctant to ask, for there was obviously a damnably disturbing connection between what he had revealed, however incredible it might be, and what Professor Gardner had written.

Our visit, however, despite its inconclusiveness—or perhaps because of it—had a curious effect on us. The very indefiniteness of the professor's summary and comments, coupled with such fragmentary and disjointed evidence which had come to us independently of Partier, sobered us and increased Laird's determination to get to the bottom of the mystery surrounding Gardner's disappearance, a mystery which had now become enlarged to encompass the greater mystery of Rick's Lake and the forest around it.

On the following day we returned to Pashepaho, and as luck would have it, we passed Old Peter on the road leading from town. Laird slowed down, backed up, and leaned out to meet the old fellow's speculative gaze.

"Lift?"

"Reckon so."

Old Peter got in and sat on the edge of the seat until Laird unceremoniously produced a flask and offered it to him. Then his eyes lit up; he took it eagerly and drank deeply, while Laird made small talk about life in the north woods and encouraged the half-breed to talk about the mineral deposits he thought he could find in the vicinity of Rick's Lake. In this way some distance was covered, and during this time, the half-breed retained the flask, handing it back at last when it was almost empty. He was not intoxicated in the strictest sense of the word, but he was uninhibited, and he made no protest when we took the lake road without stopping to let him out, though when he saw the lodge and knew where he was, he said thickly that he was off his route and had to be getting back before dark.

He would have started back immediately, but Laird persuaded him to come in with the promise that he would mix him a drink.

He did. He mixed him as stiff a drink as he could, and Peter downed it.

Not until he had begun to feel its effects did Laird turn to the subject of what Peter knew about the mystery of the Rick's Lake country, and instantly then the half-breed became close-mouthed, mumbling that he would say nothing, he had seen nothing, it was all a mistake, his eyes shifting from one to the other of us. But Laird persisted. He had seen the slab of carven stone, hadn't he? Yes—reluctantly. Would he take us to it? Peter shook his head violently. Not now. It was nearly dark, it might be dark before they could return.

But Laird was adamant, and finally the half-breed, convinced by

Laird's insistence that they could return to the lodge and even to Pashepaho, if Peter liked, before darkness fell, consented to lead us to the slab. Then, despite his unsteadiness, he set off swiftly into the woods along a lane that could hardly be called a trail, so faint it was, and loped along steadily for almost a mile before he drew up short and, standing behind a tree, as if he were afraid of being seen, pointed shakily to a little open spot surrounded by high trees at enough of a distance that ample sky was visible overhead.

"There—that's it."

The slab was only partly visible, for moss had grown over much of it. Laird, however, was at the moment only secondarily interested in it; it was manifest that the half-breed stood in mortal terror of the spot and wished only to escape.

"How would you like to spend the night here, Peter?" asked Laird.

The half-breed shot a frightened glance at him. "Me? Gawd, no!"

Suddenly Laird's voice steeled. "Unless you tell us what it was you saw here, that's what you're going to do."

The half-breed was not so much the worse for liquor that he could not foresee events—the possibility that Laird and I might overcome him and tie him to a tree at the edge of this open space. Plainly, he considered a bolt for it, but he knew that in his condition, he could not outrun us.

"Don't make me tell," he said. "It ain't supposed to be told. I ain't never told no one—not even the professor."

"We want to know, Peter," said Laird with no less menace.

The half-breed began to shake; he turned and looked at the slab as if he thought at any moment an inimical being might rise from it and advance upon him with lethal intent. "I can't, I can't," he muttered, and then, forcing his bloodshot eyes to meet Laird's once more, he said in a low voice, "I don't know what it was. Gawd! it was awful. It was a Thing—didn't have no face, hollered there till I thought my eardrums 'd bust, and them things that was with it—Gawd!" He shuddered and backed away from the tree, toward us. "Honest t' Gawd, I seen it there one night. It jist come, seems like, out of the air and there it was a-singin' and a-wailin' and them things playin' that damn music. I guess I was crazy for a while afore I got away." His voice broke, his vivid memory re-created what he had seen; he turned, shouting harshly, "Let's git outa here!" and ran back the way we had come, weaving among the trees.

Laird and I ran after him, catching up easily, Laird reassuring him that we would take him out of the woods in the car, and he would be well away from the forest's edge before darkness overtook him. He was as convinced as I that there was nothing imagined about the half-breed's account, that he had indeed told us all he knew; and he was silent all the way back from the highway to which we took Old Peter, pressing five dollars upon him so that he could forget what he had seen in liquor if he were so inclined.

"What do you think?" asked Laird when we reached the lodge once more.

I shook my head.

"That wailing night before last," said Laird. "The sounds Professor Gardner heard—and now this. It ties up—damnably, horribly." He turned on me with intense and fixed urgence. "Jack, are you game to visit that slab tonight?"

"Certainly."

"We'll do it."

It was not until we were inside the lodge that we thought of the dictaphone, and then Laird prepared at once to play whatever had been recorded back to us. Here at least, he reflected, was nothing dependent in any way upon anyone's imagination; here was the product of the machine, pure and simple, and everyone of intelligence knew full well that machines were far more dependable than men, having neither nerves nor imagination, knowing neither fear nor hope. I think that at most we counted upon hearing a repetition of the sounds of the previous night; not in our wildest dreams did we look forward to what we did actually hear, for the record mounted from the prosaic to the incredible, from the incredible to the horrible, and at last to a cataclysmic revelation that left us completely cut away from every credo of normal existence.

It began with the occasional singing of loons and owls, followed by a period of silence. Then there was once more that familiar rushing sound, as of wind in the trees, and this was followed by the curious cacophonous piping of flutes. Then there was recorded a series of sounds, which I put down here exactly as we heard them in that unforgettable evening hour:

> *Ygnaiih! Ygnaiih! EEE-ya-ya-ya-yahaaahaaahaaa-ah-ah-ah-ngh'aaa-ngh'aaa-ya-ya-yaaa!* (In a voice that was neither human nor bestial, but yet of both.)
>
> (An increased tempo in the music, becoming more wild and demoniac.)
>
> *Mighty Messenger—Nyarlathotep . . . from the world of Seven Suns to his earth place, the Wood of N'gai, whither may come Him Who Is Not to Be Named. . . . There shall be abundance of those from the Black Goat of the Woods, the Goat with the Thousand Young. . . .* (In a voice that was curiously human.)
>
> (A succession of odd sounds, as if audience-response: a buzzing and humming, as of telegraph wires.)

Iä! Iä! Shub-Niggurath! Ygnaiih! Ygnaiih! EEE-yaa-yaa—haa-haaa-haaaa! (In the original voice neither human nor beast, yet both.)

Ithaqua shall serve thee, Father of the million favored ones, and Zhar shall be summoned from Arcturus, by the command of 'Umr at-Tawil, Guardian of the Gate. . . . Ye shall unite in praise of Azathoth, of Great Cthulhu, of Tsathoggua. . . . (The human voice again.)

Go forth in his form or in whatever form chosen in the guise of man, and destroy that which may lead them to us. . . . (The half-bestial, half-human voice once more.)

(An interlude of furious piping, accompanied once again by a sound as of the flapping of great wings.)

Ygnaiih! Y'bthnk . . . h'ehye-n'grkdl'lh . . . Iä! Iä! Iä! (Like a chorus.)

These sounds had been spaced in such a way that it seemed as if the beings giving rise to them were moving about within or around the lodge, and the last choral chanting faded away, as if the creatures were departing. Indeed, there followed such an interval of silence that Laird had actually moved to shut off the machine when once again a voice came from it. But the voice that now emanated from the dictaphone was one which, simply because of its nature, brought to a climax all the horror so cumulative in what had gone before it; for whatever had been inferred by the half-bestial bellowings and chants, the horribly suggestive conversation in accented English, that which now came from the dictaphone was unutterably terrible:

Dorgan! Laird Dorgan! Can you hear me?

A hoarse, urgent whisper calling out to my companion, who sat white-faced now, staring at the machine above which his hand was still poised. Our eyes met. It was not the appeal, it was not everything that had gone before, it was the identity of that voice—*for it was the voice of Professor Upton Gardner!* But we had no time to ponder this, for the dictaphone went mechanically on.

"Listen to me! Leave this place. Forget. But before you go, summon Cthugha. For centuries this has been the place where evil beings from outermost cosmos have touched upon earth. I know. I am theirs. They have taken me, as they took Piregard and many others—all who came unwarily within their wood and whom they did not at once destroy. It is His wood—the Wood of N'gai, the terrestrial abode of the Blind, Faceless One, the Howler in the Night, the Dweller in Darkness, Nyarlathotep, who fears only Cthugha. I have been with him in the star spaces. I have been on the shunned Plateau of Leng—to Kadath in the Cold Waste, beyond the Gates of the Silver Key, even to Kythamil near Arcturus and Mnar, to N'kai and the Lake of Hali, to K'n-yan and fabled Carcosa, to Yaddith and Y'ha-nthlei near Innsmouth, to Yoth and Yuggoth, and from far off I have looked upon Zothique, from the eye of Algol. When Fomalhaut has topped the trees, call forth to Cthugha in these words, thrice repeated: *Ph'nglui mglw'nafh Cthugha Fomalhaut n'gha-ghaa naf'l thagn! Iä! Cthugha!* When He has come, go swiftly, lest you, too, be destroyed. For it is fitting that this accursed spot be blasted so that Nyarlathotep comes no more out of interstellar space. Do you hear me, Dorgan? Do you hear me? Dorgan! Laird Dorgan!"

There was a sudden sound of sharp protest, followed by a scuffling and tearing noise, as if Gardner had been forcibly removed, and then silence, utter and complete!

For a few moments longer Laird let the record run, but there was nothing more, and finally he started it over, saying tensely, "I think we'd better copy that as best we can. You take every other speech, and let's both copy that formula from Gardner."

"Was it . . . ?"

"I'd know his voice anywhere," he said shortly.

"He's alive then?"

He looked at me, his eyes narrowed. "We don't know that."

"But his voice!"

He shook his head, for the sounds were coming forth once more, and both of us had to bend to the task of copying, which was easier than it promised to be, for the spaces between speeches were great enough to enable us to copy without undue haste. The language of the chants and the words to Cthugha enunciated by Gardner's voice offered extreme difficulty, but by means of repeated playings, we managed to put down the approximate equivalent of the sounds. When finally we had finished, Laird shut the dictaphone off and looked at me with quizzical and troubled eyes, grave with concern and uncertainty. I said nothing; what we had just heard, added to everything that had gone before, left us no alternative. There was room for doubt about legends, beliefs, and the like—but the infallible record of the dictaphone was conclusive even if it did no more than verify half-heard credos—for it was true, there was still nothing definite; it was as if the whole were so completely beyond the comprehension of man that only in the oblique suggestion of its individual parts could something like understanding be achieved, as if the entirety were too unspeakably soul-searing for the mind of man to withstand.

"Fomalhaut rises almost at sunset—a little before, I think," mused Laird—clearly, like myself, he had accepted what we had heard without challenge other than the mystery surrounding its meaning. "It should be above the trees—presumably twenty to thirty degrees above the horizon, because it doesn't pass near enough to the zenith in this latitude to appear above these pines—at approximately an hour after darkness falls. Say nine-thirty or so."

"You aren't thinking of trying it tonight?" I asked. "After all—what does it mean? Who or what is Cthugha?"

"I don't know any more than you. And I'm not trying it tonight. You've forgotten the slab. Are you still game to go out there—after this?"

I nodded. I did not trust myself to speak, but I was not consumed by any eagerness whatever to dare the darkness that lingered like a living entity within the forest surrounding Rick's Lake.

Laird looked at his watch, and then at me, his eyes burning now with a kind of feverish determination, as if he were forcing himself to take this final step to face the unknown being whose manifestations had made the woods its own. If he expected me to hesitate, he was disappointed; however beset by fear I might be, I would not show it. I got up and went out of the lodge at his side.

IV

There are aspects of hidden life, exterior as well as of the depths of the mind, that are better kept secret and away from the awareness of common man; for there lurk in dark places of the earth horrible revenants belonging to a stratum of the subconscious which is mercifully beyond the apprehension of common man—indeed, there are aspects of creation so grotesquely shuddersome that the very sight of them would blast the sanity of the beholder. Fortunately, it is not possible even to bring back in anything but suggestion what we saw on the slab in the forest at Rick's Lake that night in October, for the thing was so unbelievable, transcending all known laws of science, that adequate words for its description have no existence in the language.

We arrived at the belt of trees around the slab while afterglow yet lingered in the western heavens, and by the illumination of a flashlight Laird carried, we examined the face of the slab itself, and the carving on it: of a vast, amorphous creature, drawn by an artist who evidently lacked sufficient imagination to etch the creature's face, for it had none, bearing only a curious, cone-like head which even in stone seemed to have a fluidity which was unnerving; moreover, the creature was depicted as having both tentacle-like appendages and hands—or growths similar to hands, not only two, but several; so that it seemed both human and non-human in its structure. Beside it had been carved two squat squid-like figures from a part of which—presumably the heads, though no outline was definitive—projected what must certainly have been instruments of some kind, for the strange, repugnant attendants appeared to be playing them.

Our examination was necessarily hurried, for we did not want to risk being seen here by whatever might come, and it may be that in the circumstances, imagination got the better of us. But I do not think so. It is difficult to maintain that consistently, sitting here at my desk, removed in space and time from what happened there; but I do maintain it. Despite the quickened awareness and irrational fear of the unknown which obsessed both of us, we kept a determined open-mindedness about every aspect of the problem we had chosen to solve. If anything, I have erred in this account on the side of science over that of imagination. In the plain light of reason, the carvings on that stone slab were not only obscene, but bestial and frightening beyond measure, particularly in the light of what Partier had hinted, and what Gardner's notes and the material from Miskatonic University had vaguely outlined, and even if time had permitted, it is doubtful if we could have looked long upon them.

We retreated to a spot comparatively near the way we must take to return to the lodge, and yet not too far from the open place where the slab lay, so that we might see clearly and still remain hidden in a place easy of access to the return path. There we took our stand and waited in that chilling hush of an October evening, while stygian darkness encompassed us, and only one or two stars twinkled high overhead, miraculously visible among the towering treetops.

According to Laird's watch, we waited exactly an hour and ten minutes before the sound as of wind began, and at once there was a manifestation which had about it all the trappings of the supernatural; for no sooner had the rushing sound begun, than the slab we had so quickly quitted began to glow—at first so indistinguishably that it seemed an illusion, and then with a phosphorescence of increasing brilliance, until it gave off such a glow that it was as if a pillar of light extended upward into the heavens. This was the second curious circumstance—the light followed the outlines of the slab, and flowed upward; it was not diffused and dispersed around the glade and into the woods, but shone heavenward with the insistence of a directed beam. Simultaneously, the very air seemed charged with evil; all around us lay thickly such an aura of fearsomeness that it rapidly became impossible to remain free of it. It was apparent that by some means unknown to us the rushing sound as of wind which now filled the air was not only associated with the broad beam of light flowing upward, *but was caused by it;* moreover, as we watched, the intensity and color of the light varied constantly, changing from a blinding white to a lambent green, from green to a kind of lavender; occasionally it was so intensely brilliant that it was necessary to avert our eyes, but for the most part it could be looked at without hurt to our eyes.

As suddenly as it had begun, the rushing sound stopped, the light became diffuse and dim; and almost immediately the weird piping as of flutes smote upon our ears. It came not from around us, but from *above,* and with one accord, both of us turned to look as far into heaven as the now fading light would permit.

Just what took place then before our eyes I cannot explain. Was it actually something that came hurtling down, streaming down, rather?—for the masses were shapeless—or was it the product of imagination that proved singularly uniform when later Laird and I found opportunity to compare notes? The illusion of great black things streaking down in the path of that light was so great that we glanced back at the slab.

What we saw there sent us screaming voicelessly from that hellish spot.

For, where but a moment before there had been nothing, there was now a gigantic protoplasmic mass, a colossal being who towered upward toward the stars, and whose actual physical being was in constant flux; and flanking it on either side were two lesser beings, equally amorphous, holding pipes or flutes in appendages and making that demoniac music which echoed and reechoed in the enclosing forest. But the thing on the slab, the Dweller in Darkness, was the ultimate in horror; for from its mass of amorphous flesh there grew at will before our eyes tentacles, claws, hands, and withdrew again; the mass itself diminished and swelled effortlessly, and where its head was and its features should have been there was only a blank facelessness all the more horrible because even as we looked there rose from its blind mass a low ululation in that half-bestial, half-human voice so familiar to us from the record made in the night!

We fled, I say, so shaken that it was only by a supreme effort of will that we were able to take flight in the right direction. And behind us the voice rose, the blasphemous voice of Nyarlathotep, the Blind, Faceless One, the Mighty Messenger, even while there rang in the channels of memory the frightened words of the half-breed, Old Peter—*It was a Thing—didn't have no face, hollered there till I thought my eardrums 'd bust, and them things that was with it—Gawd!*—echoed there while the voice of that Being from outermost space shrieked and gibbered to the hellish music of the hideous attending flute-players, rising to ululate through the forest and leave its mark forever in memory!

Ygnaiih! Ygnaiih! EEE-yayayayayaaa-haaahaaahaaahaaa-ngh'aaa-ngh'aaa-ya-ya-yaaa!

Then all was still.

And yet, incredible as it may seem, the ultimate horror awaited us.

For we had gone but halfway to the lodge when we were simultaneously aware of something following; behind us rose a hideous, horribly suggestive *sloshing* sound, as if the amorphous entity had left the slab which in some remote time must have been erected by its worshippers, and was pursuing us. Obsessed by abysmal fright, we ran as neither of us has ever run before, and we were almost upon the lodge before we were aware that the sloshing sound, the trembling and shuddering of the earth—as if some gigantic being walked upon it—had ceased, and in their stead came only the calm, unhurried tread of footsteps.

But the footsteps were not our own! And in the aura of unreality, the fearsome outsideness in which we walked and breathed, the suggestiveness of those footsteps was almost maddening!

We reached the lodge, lit a lamp, and sank into chairs to await whatever it was that was coming so steadily, unhurriedly on, mounting the verandah steps, putting its hand on the knob of the door, swinging the door open. . . .

It was Professor Gardner who stood there!

Then Laird sprang up, crying, "Professor Gardner!"

The professor smiled reservedly and put one hand up to shade his eyes. "If you don't mind, I'd like the light dimmed. I've been in the dark so long. . . ."

Laird turned to do his bidding without question, and he came forward into the room, walking with the ease and poise of a man who is as sure of himself as if he had never vanished from the face of the earth more than three months before, as if he had not made a frantic appeal to us during the night just past, as if. . . .

I glanced at Laird; his hand was still at the lamp, but his fingers were no longer turning down the wick, simply holding to it, while he gazed down unseeing. I looked over at Professor Gardner; he sat with his head turned from the lights, his eyes closed, a little smile playing about his lips; at that moment he looked precisely as I had often seen him look at the University Club in Madison, and it was as if everything that had taken place here at the lodge were but an evil dream.

But it was not a dream!

"You were gone last night?" asked the professor.

"Yes. But, of course, we had the dictaphone."

"Ah. You heard something then?"

"Would you like to hear the record, sir?"

"Yes, I would."

Laird went over and put it on the machine to play it again, and we sat in silence, listening to everything upon it, no one saying anything until it had been completed. Then the professor slowly turned his head.

"What do you make of it?"

"I don't know what to make of it, sir," answered Laird. "The speeches are too disjointed—except for yours. There seems to be some coherence there."

Suddenly, without warning, the room was surcharged with menace; it was but a momentary impression, but Laird felt it as keenly as I did, for he started noticeably. He was taking the record from the machine when the professor spoke again.

"It doesn't occur to you that you may be the victim of a hoax?"

"No."

"And if I told you that I had found it possible to make every sound that was registered on that record?"

Laird looked at him for a full minute before replying in a low voice that, of course, Professor Gardner had been investigating the phenomena of Rick's Lake woods for a far longer time than we had, and if he said so. . . .

A harsh laugh escaped the professor. "Entirely natural phenomena, my boy! There's a mineral deposit under that grotesque slab in the woods; it gives off light and also a miasma that is productive of hallucinations. It's as simple as that. As for the various disappearances—sheer folly, human failing, nothing more, but with the air of coincidence. I came here with high hopes of verifying some of the nonsense to which old Partier lent himself long ago—but—" He smiled disdainfully, shook his head, and extended his hand. "Let me have the record, Laird."

Without question, Laird gave Professor Gardner the record. The older man took it and was bringing it up before his eyes when he jogged his elbow and, with a sharp cry of pain, dropped it. It broke into dozens of pieces on the floor of the lodge.

"Oh!" cried the professor. "I'm sorry." He turned his eyes on Laird. "But then—since I can duplicate it any time for you from what I've learned about the lore of this place, by way of Partier's mouthings—" He shrugged.

"It doesn't matter," said Laird quietly

"Do you mean to say that everything on that record was just your imagination, Professor?" I broke in. "Even that chant for the summoning of Cthugha?"

The older man's eyes turned on me; his smile was sardonic. "Cthugha? What do you suppose he or that is but the figment of someone's imagination? And the inference—my dear boy, use your head. You have before you the clear inference that Cthugha has his abode on Fomalhaut, which is twenty-seven light-years away, and that, if this chant is thrice repeated when Fomalhaut has risen Cthugha will appear to somehow render this place no longer habitable by man or outside entity. How do you suppose that could be accomplished?"

"Why, by something akin to thought-transference," replied Laird doggedly. "It's not unreasonable to suppose that if we were to direct thoughts toward Fomalhaut that something there might receive them—granting that there might be life there. Thought is instant. And that they in turn may be so highly developed that dematerialization and rematerialization might be as swift as thought."

"My boy—are you serious?" The older man's voice revealed his contempt.

"You asked."

"Well, then, as the hypothetic answer to a theoretical problem, I can overlook that."

"Frankly," I said again, disregarding a curious negative shaking of Laird's head, "I don't think that what we saw in the forest tonight was just hallucination—caused by a miasma rising out of the earth or otherwise."

The effect of this statement was extraordinary. Visibly, the professor made every effort to control himself; his reactions were precisely those of a savant challenged by a cretin in one of his classes. After a few moments he controlled himself and said only, "You've been there then. I suppose it's too late to make you believe otherwise. . . ."

"I've always been open to conviction, sir, and I lean to the scientific method," said Laird.

Professor Gardner put his hand over his eyes and said, "I'm tired. I noticed last night when I was here that you're in my old room, Laird—so I'll take the room next to you, opposite Jack's."

He went up the stairs as if nothing had happened between the last time he had occupied the lodge and this.

V

The rest of the story—and the culmination of that apocalyptic night—are soon told.

I could not have been asleep for more than an hour—the time was one in the morning—when I was awakened by Laird. He stood beside my bed fully dressed and in a tense voice ordered me to get up and dress, to pack whatever essentials I had brought, and be ready for anything. Nor would he permit me to put on a light to do so, though he carried a small pocket-flash, and used it sparingly. To all my questions, he cautioned me to wait.

When I had finished, he led the way out of the room with a whispered, "Come."

He went directly to the room into which Professor Gardner had disappeared. By the light of his flash, it was evident that the bed had not been touched; moreover, in the faint film of dust that lay on the floor, it was clear that Professor Gardner had walked into the room, over to a chair beside the window, and out again.

"Never touched the bed, you see," whispered Laird.

"But why?"

Laird gripped my arm, hard. "Do you remember what Partier hinted—what we saw in the woods—the protoplasmic, amorphousness of the thing? And what the record said?"

"But Gardner told us—" I protested.

Without a further word, he turned. I followed him downstairs, where he paused at the table where we had worked and flashed the light upon it. I was surprised into making a startled exclamation which Laird hushed instantly. For the table was bare of everything but the copy of *The Outsider and Others* and three copies of *Weird Tales*, a magazine containing stories supplementing those in the book by the eccentric Providence genius, Lovecraft. All Gardner's notes, all our own notations, the photostats from Miskatonic University—everything gone!

"He took them," said Laird. "No one else could have done so."

"Where did he go?"

"Back to the place from which he came." He turned on me, his eyes gleaming in the reflected glow of the flashlight. "Do you understand what that means, Jack?"

I shook my head.

"*They* know we've been there, *they* know we've seen and learned too much. . . ."

"But how?"

"You told them."

"I? Good God, man, are you mad? How could I have told them?"

"Here, in this lodge, tonight—you yourself gave the show away, and I hate to think of what might happen now. We've got to get away."

For one moment all the events of the past few days seemed to fuse into an unintelligible mass; Laird's urgence was unmistakable, and yet the thing he suggested was so utterly unbelievable that its contemplation even for so fleeting a moment threw my thoughts into the extremest confusion.

Laird was talking now, quickly. "Don't you think it odd—how he came back? How he came out of the woods *after* the hellish thing we saw there—not before? And the questions he asked—the drift of those questions. And how he managed to break the record—our one scientific proof of something? And now, the disappearance of all the notes—of everything that might point to substantiation of what he called 'Partier's nonsense'?"

"But if we are to believe what he told us. . . ."

He broke in before I could finish. "One of them was right. Either the voice on the record calling to me—or the man who was here tonight."

"The man . . ."

But whatever I wanted to say was stilled by Laird's harsh, *"Listen!"*

From outside, from the depths of the horror-haunted dark, the earth-haven of the Dweller in Darkness, came once more, for the second time that night, the weirdly beautiful, yet cacophonous strains of flute-like music, rising and falling, accompanied by a kind of chanted ululation, and by the sound as of great wings flapping.

"Yes, I hear," I whispered.

"Listen closely!"

Even as he spoke, I understood. There was something more—the sounds from the forest were not only rising and falling—*they were approaching!*

"Now do you believe me?" demanded Laird. *"They're coming for us!"* He turned on me. "The chant!"

"What chant?" I fumbled stupidly.

"The Cthugha chant—do you remember it?"

"I took it down. I've got it here."

For an instant I was afraid that this, too, might have been taken from us, but it was not; it was in my pocket where I had left it. With shaking hands, Laird tore the paper from my grasp.

"Ph'nglui mglw'nafh Cthugha Fomalhaut n'gha-ghaa naf'l thagn! Iä! Cthugha!" he said, running to the verandah, myself at his heels.

Out of the woods came the bestial voice of the dweller in the dark. *"Ee-ya-ya-haa-haahaaa! Ygnaiih! Ygnaiih!"*

"Ph'nglui mglw'nafh Cthugha Fomalhaut n'gha-ghaa naf'l thagn! Iä! Cthugha!" repeated Laird for the second time.

Still the ghastly melee of sounds from the woods came on, in no way diminished, rising now to supreme heights of terror-fraught fury, with the bestial voice of the thing from the slab added to the wild, mad music of the pipes, and the sound as of wings.

And then, once more, Laird repeated the primal words of the chant.

On the instant that the final guttural sound had left his lips, there began a sequence of events no human eye was ever destined to witness. For suddenly the darkness was gone, giving way to a fearsome amber glow; simultaneously the flute-like music ceased, and in its place rose cries of rage and terror. Then, there appeared thousands of tiny points of light—not only on and among the trees, but on the earth itself, on the lodge and the car standing before it. For still a further moment we were rooted to the spot, and then it was borne in upon us that the myriad points of light were *living entities of flame*! For wherever they touched, fire sprang up, seeing which, Laird rushed into the lodge for such of our things as he could carry forth before the holocaust made it impossible for us to escape Rick's Lake.

He came running out—our bags had been downstairs—gasping that it was too late to take the dictaphone or anything else, and together we dashed toward the car, shielding our eyes a little from the blinding light all around. But even though we had shielded our eyes, it was impossible not to see the great amorphous shapes streaming skyward from this accursed place, nor the equally great being hovering like a cloud of living fire above the trees. So much we saw, before the frightful struggle to escape the burning woods forced us to forget mercifully the other details of that terrible, maddened flight.

Horrible as were the things that took place in the darkness of the forest at Rick's Lake, there was something more cataclysmic still, something so blasphemously conclusive that even now I shudder and tremble uncontrollably to think of it. For in that brief dash to the car, I saw something that explained Laird's doubt, I saw what had made him take heed of the voice on the record and not of the thing that came to us as Professor Gardner. The keys were there before, but I did not understand; even Laird had not fully believed. Yet it was given to us—we did not know. "It is not desired by the Old Ones that mere man shall know too much," Partier had said. And that terrible voice on the record had hinted even more clearly: *Go forth in his form or in whatever form chosen in the guise of man, and destroy that which may lead them to us. . . .* Destroy that which may lead them to us! Our record, the notes, the photostats from Miskatonic University, yes, and even Laird and myself! And the thing had gone forth, for it was Nyarlathotep, the Mighty Messenger, the Dweller in Darkness who had gone forth and who had returned into the forest to send his minions back to us. It was he who had come from interstellar space even as Cthugha, the fire being, had come from Fomalhaut upon the utterance of the command that woke him from his eon-long sleep under that amber star, the command that Gardner, the living-dead captive of the terrible Nyarlathotep, had discovered in those fantastic travelings in space and time; and it was he who returned whence he had come, with his earth-haven now forever rendered useless for him with its destruction by the minions of Cthugha!

I know, and Laird knows. We never speak of it.

If we had had any doubt, despite everything that had gone before, we could not forget that final, soul-searing discovery, the thing we saw when we shielded our eyes from the flames all around and looked away from those beings in the heavens, the line of footprints that led away from the lodge in the direction of that hellish slab deep in the black forest, *the footprints that began in the soft soil beyond the verandah in the shape of a man's footprints, and changed with each step into a hideously suggestive imprint made by a creature of incredible shape and weight, with variations of outline and size so grotesque as to have been incomprehensible to anyone who had not seen the thing on the slab—and beside them, torn and rent as if by an expanding force, the clothing that once belonged to Professor Gardner, left piece by piece along the trail back into the woods, the trail taken by the hellish monstrosity that had come out of the night, the Dweller in Darkness who had visited us in the shape and guise of Professor Gardner!*

Beyond the Threshold*

AUGUST DERLETH

I

The story is really my grandfather's.

In a manner of speaking, however, it belongs to the entire family, and beyond them, to the world; and there is no longer any reason for suppressing the singularly terrible details of what happened in that lonely house deep in the forest places of northern Wisconsin.

The roots of the story go back into the mists of early time, far beyond the beginnings of the Alwyn family line, but of this I knew nothing at the time of my visit to Wisconsin in response to my cousin's letter about our grandfather's strange decline in health. Josiah Alwyn had always seemed somehow immortal to me even as a child, and he had not appeared to change throughout the years between: a barrel-chested old man, with a heavy, full face, decorated with a closely clipped moustache and a small beard to soften the hard line of his square jaw. His eyes were dark, not overlarge, and his brows were shaggy; he wore his hair long, so that his head had a leonine appearance. Though I saw little of him when I was very young, still he left an indelible impression on me in the brief visits he paid when he stopped at the ancestral country home near Arkham, in Massachusetts—those short calls he made on his way to and from remote corners of the world: Tibet, Mongolia, the Arctic regions, and certain little-known islands in the Pacific.

I had not seen him for years when the letter came from my cousin Frolin, who lived with him in the old house grandfather owned in the heart of the forest and lake country of northern Wisconsin. "I wish you could uproot yourself from Massachusetts long enough to come out here. A great deal of water has passed under various bridges, and the

*Originally published in *Weird Tales*, September 1941.

wind has blown about many changes since last you were here. Frankly, I think it most urgent that you come. In present circumstances, I don't know to whom to turn, grandfather being not himself, and I need someone who can be trusted." There was nothing obviously urgent about the letter, and yet there was a queer constraint, there was something between lines that stood out invisibly, intangibly, to make possible only one answer to Frolin's letter—something in his phrase about the wind, something in the way he had written *grandfather being not himself*, something in the need he had expressed for *someone who can be trusted*.

I could easily take a leave of absence from my position as assistant librarian at Miskatonic University in Arkham and go west that September; so I went. I went, harassed by an almost uncanny conviction that the need for haste was great: from Boston by plane to Chicago, and from there by train to the village of Harmon, deep in the forest country of Wisconsin—a place of great natural beauty, not far from the shores of Lake Superior, so that it was possible on days of wind and weather to hear the water's sound.

Frolin met me at the station. My cousin was in his late thirties then, but he had the look of someone ten years younger, with hot, intense brown eyes, and a soft, sensitive mouth that belied his inner hardness. He was singularly sober, though he had always alternated between gravity and a kind of infectious wildness—"the Irish in him," as grandfather had once said. I met his eyes when I shook his hand, probing for some clue to his withheld distress, but I saw only that he was indeed troubled, for his eyes betrayed him, even as the roiled waters of a pond reveal disturbance below, though the surface may be as glass.

"What is it?" I asked, when I sat at his side in the coupe, riding into the country of the tall pines. "Is the old man abed?"

He shook his head. "Oh, no, nothing like that, Tony." He shot me a queer, restrained glance. "You'll see. You wait and see."

"What is it then?" I pressed him. "Your letter had the damndest sound."

"I hoped it would," he said gravely.

"And yet there was nothing I could put my finger on," I admitted. "But it was there, nevertheless."

He smiled. "Yes, I knew you'd understand. I tell you, it's been difficult—extremely difficult. I thought of you a good many times before I sat down and wrote that letter, believe me!"

"But if he's not ill . . . ? I thought you said he wasn't himself."

"Yes, yes, so I did. You wait now, Tony; don't be so impatient; you'll see for yourself. It's his mind, I think."

"His mind!" I felt a distinct wave of regret and shock at the suggestion that grandfather's mind had given way; the thought that that magnificent brain had retreated from sanity was intolerable, and I was loath to entertain it. "Surely not!" I cried. "Frolin—what the devil is it?"

He turned his troubled eyes on me once more. "I don't know. But I think it's something terrible. If it were only grandfather. But there's the music—and then there are all the other things: the sounds and smells and—" He caught my amazed stare and turned away, almost with physical effort pausing in his talk. "But I'm forgetting. Don't ask me anything more. Just wait. You'll see for yourself." He laughed shortly, a forced laugh. "Perhaps it's not the old man who's losing his mind. I've thought of that sometimes, too—with reason."

I said nothing more, but there was beginning to mushroom up inside me now a kind of tense fear, and for some time I sat by his side, thinking only of Frolin and old Josiah Alwyn living together in that old house, unaware of the towering pines all around, and the wind's sound, and the fragrant pungence of leaf-fire smoke riding the wind out of the northwest. Evening came early to this country, caught in the dark pines, and, though afterglow still lingered in the west, fanning upward in a great wave of saffron and amethyst, darkness already possessed the forest through which we rode. Out of the darkness came the cries of the great horned owls and their lesser cousins, the screech owls, making an eerie magic in the stillness broken otherwise only by the wind's voice and the noise of the car passing along the comparatively little-used road to the Alwyn house.

"We're almost there," said Frolin.

The lights of the car passed over a jagged pine, lightning-struck years ago, and standing still with two gaunt limbs arched like gnarled arms toward the road: an old landmark to which Frolin's words called my attention, since he knew I would remember it but half a mile from the house.

"If grandfather should ask," he said then, "I'd rather you said nothing about my sending for you. I don't know that he'd like it. You can tell him you were in the Midwest and came up for a visit."

I was curious anew, but forbore to press Frolin further. "He does know I'm coming, then?"

"Yes. I said I had word from you and was going down to meet your train."

I could understand that if the old man thought Frolin had sent for me about his health, he would be annoyed and perhaps angry; and yet more than this was implied in Frolin's request, more than just the simple salving of grandfather's pride. Once more that odd, intangible alarm rose up within me, that sudden, inexplicable feeling of fear.

The house looked forth suddenly in a clearing among the pines. It had been built by an uncle of grandfather's in Wisconsin's pioneering days, back in the 1850s: by one of the seafaring Alwyns of Innsmouth, that strange, dark town on the Massachusetts coast. It was an unusually unattractive structure, snug against the hillside like a crusty old woman in furbelows. It defied many architectural standards without, however, seeming ever fully free of most of the superficial facets of architecture circa 1850, making for the most grotesque and pompous appearance of structures of that day. It suffered a wide verandah, one side of which led directly into the stables where, in former days, horses, surreys, and buggies had been kept, and where now two cars were housed—the only corner of the building which gave any evidence at all of having been remodeled since it was built. The house rose two and one-half stories above a cellar floor; presumably, for darkness made it impossible to ascertain, it was still painted the same hideous brown; and judging by what light shone forth from the curtained windows, grandfather had not yet taken the trouble to install electricity, a contingency for which I had come well prepared by carrying a flashlight and an electric candle, with extra batteries for both.

Frolin drove into the garage, left the car, and carrying some of my baggage, led the way down the verandah to the front door, a massive, thick-paneled oak piece, decorated with a ridiculously large iron knocker. The hall was dark, save for a partly open door at the far end, out of which came a faint light which was yet enough to illumine spectrally the broad stairs leading to the upper floor.

"I'll take you to your room first," said Frolin, leading the way up the stairs, surefooted with habitual walking there. "There's a flashlight on the newel post at the landing," he added. "If you need it. You know the old man."

I found the light and lit it, making only enough delay so that when I caught up with Frolin, he was standing at the door of my room, which, I noticed, was almost directly over the front entrance and thus faced west, as did the house itself.

"He's forbidden us to use any of the rooms east of the hall up here," said Frolin, fixing me with his eyes, as much as to say: You see how queer he's got! He waited for me to say something, but since I did not, he went on. "So I have the room next to yours, and Hough is on the other side of me, in the southwest corner. Right now, as you might have noticed, Hough's getting something to eat."

"And grandfather?"

"Very likely in his study. You'll remember that room."

I did indeed remember that curious windowless room, built under explicit directions by Great-Uncle Leander, a room that occupied the majority of the rear of the house, the entire northwest corner and all the west width save for a small corner at the southwest, where the kitchen was, the kitchen from which a light had streamed into the lower hall at our entrance. The study had been pushed partway back into the hill slope, so the east wall could not have windows, but there was no reason save Uncle Leander's eccentricity for the windowless north wall. Squarely in the center of the east wall, indeed, built into the wall, was an enormous painting, reaching from the floor to the ceiling and occupying a width of over six feet. If this painting, apparently executed by some unknown friend of Uncle Leander's, if not by my great-uncle himself, had had about it any mark of genius or even of unusual talent, this display might have been overlooked, but it did not, it was a perfectly prosaic representation of a north country scene, showing a hillside, with a rocky cave opening out into the center of the picture, a scarcely defined path leading to the cave, an impressionistic beast which was evidently meant to resemble a bear, once common in this country, walking toward it, and overhead something that looked like an unhappy cloud lost among the pines rising darkly all around. This dubious work of art completely and absolutely dominated the study, despite the shelves of books that occupied almost every available niche in what remained of the walls in that room, despite the absurd collection of oddities strewn everywhere—bits of curiously carven stone and wood, strange mementos of great-uncle's seafaring life. The study had all the lifelessness of a museum, and yet, oddly, it responded to my grandfather like something alive, even the painting on the wall seeming to take on an added freshness whenever he entered.

"I don't think anyone who ever stepped into that room could forget it," I said with a grim smile.

"He spends most of his time there. Hardly goes out at all, and I suppose, with winter coming on, he'll come out only for his meals. He's moved his bed, too."

I shuddered. "I can't imagine sleeping in that room."

"No, nor I. But you know, he's working on something, and I sincerely believe his mind has been affected."

"Another book on his travels, perhaps?"

He shook his head. "No, a translation, I think. Something different. He found some old papers of Leander's one day, and ever since then he seems to have got progressively worse." He raised his eyebrows and shrugged. "Come on. Hough will have supper ready by this time, and you'll see for yourself."

Frolin's cryptic remarks had led me to expect an emaciated old man. After all, grandfather was in his early seventies, and even he could not be expected to live forever. But he had not changed physically at all, as far as I could see. There he sat at his supper table—still the same hardy old man, his moustache and beard not yet white, but only iron grey, and still with plenty of black in them; his face was no less heavy, his color no less ruddy. At the moment of my entrance he was eating heartily from the drumstick of a turkey. Seeing me, he raised his eyebrows a little, took the drumstick from his lips, and greeted me with no more excitement than if I had been away from him but half an hour.

"You're looking well," he said.

"And you," I said. "An old war-horse."

He grinned. "My boy, I'm on the trail of something new—some unexplored country apart from Africa, Asia, and the Arctic regions."

I flashed a glance at Frolin. Clearly, this was news to him; whatever hints grandfather might have dropped of his activities, they had not included this.

He asked then about my trip west, and the rest of the supper hour was taken up with small talk of other relatives. I observed that the old man returned insistently to long-forgotten relatives in Innsmouth: What had become of them? Had I ever seen them? What did they look like? Since I knew practically nothing of the relatives in Innsmouth, and had the firm conviction that all had died in a strange catastrophe which had washed many inhabitants of that shunned city out to sea, I was not helpful. But the tenor of these innocuous questions puzzled me no little. In my capacity as librarian at Miskatonic University, I had heard strange and disturbing hints of the business in Innsmouth, I knew something of the appearance of Federal men there, and stories of foreign agents had never had about them that essential ring of truth which made a plausible explanation for the terrible events which had taken place in that city. He wanted to know at last whether I had ever seen pictures of them, and when I said I had not, he was quite patently disappointed.

"Do you know," he said dejectedly, "there does not exist even a likeness of Uncle Leander, but the old-timers around Harmon told me years ago that he was a very homely man, that he reminded them of a *frog*." Abruptly, he seemed more animated, he began to talk a little faster. "Do you have any conception of what that means, my boy? But no, you wouldn't have. It's too much to expect. . . ."

He sat for a while in silence, drinking his coffee, drumming on the table with his fingers and staring into space with a curiously preoccupied air until suddenly he rose and left the room, inviting us to come to the study when we had finished.

"What do you make of that?" asked Frolin, when the sound of the study door closing came to us.

"Curious," I said. "But I see nothing abnormal there, Frolin. I'm afraid. . . ."

He smiled grimly. "Wait. Don't judge yet; you've been here scarcely two hours."

We went to the study after supper, leaving the dishes to Hough and his wife, who had served my grandfather for twenty years in this house. The study was unchanged, save for the addition of the old double bed, pushed up against the wall which separated the room from the kitchen. Grandfather was clearly waiting for us, or rather for me, and, if I had had occasion to think cousin Frolin cryptic, there is no word adequate to describe my grandfather's subsequent conversation.

"Have you ever heard of the Wendigo?" he asked.

I admitted that I had come upon it among other north country Indian legends: the belief in a monstrous, supernatural being, horrible to look upon, the haunter of the great forest silences.

He wanted to know whether I had ever thought of there being a possible connection between this legend of the Wendigo and the air elements, and upon my replying in the affirmative, he expressed a curiosity about how I had come to know the Indian legend in the first place, taking pains to explain that the Wendigo had nothing whatever to do with his question.

"In my capacity as a librarian, I have occasion to run across a good many out-of-the-way things," I answered.

"Ah!" he exclaimed, reaching for a book next to his chair. "Then doubtless you may be familiar with this volume."

I looked at the heavy black-bound volume whose title was stamped only on its backbone in goldleaf. *The Outsider and Others,* by H. P. Lovecraft.

I nodded. "This book is on our shelves."

"You've read it, then?"

"Oh, yes. Most interesting."

"Then you'll have read what he has to say about Innsmouth in his strange story, 'The Shadow Over Innsmouth.' What do you make of that?"

I reflected hurriedly, thinking back to the story, and presently it came to me: a fantastic tale of horrible sea-beings, spawn of Cthulhu, beast of primordial origin, living deep in the sea.

"The man had a good imagination," I said.

"Had! Is he dead, then?"

"Yes, three years ago."

"Alas! I had thought to learn from him. . . ."

"But, surely, this fiction . . ." I began.

He stopped me. "Since you have offered no explanation of what took place in Innsmouth, how can you be so sure that his narrative is fiction?"

I admitted that I could not, but it seemed that the old man had already lost interest. Now he drew forth a bulky envelope bearing many of the familiar three-cent 1869 stamps so dear to collectors, and from this took out various papers, which, he said, Uncle Leander had left with instructions for their consignment to the flames. His wish, however, had not been carried out, explained grandfather, and he had come into possession of them. He handed a few sheets to me, and requested my opinion of them, watching me shrewdly all the while.

The sheets were obviously from a long letter, written in a crabbed hand, and with some of the most awkward sentences imaginable. Moreover, many of the sentences did not seem to me to make sense, and the sheet at which I looked longest was filled with allusions strange to me. My eyes caught words like *Ithaqua, Lloigor, Hastur*; it was not until I handed the sheets back to my grandfather that it occurred to me that I had seen those words elsewhere, not too long ago. But I said nothing. I explained that I could not help feeling that Uncle Leander wrote with needless obfuscation.

Grandfather chuckled. "I should have thought that the first thing which would have occurred to you would have been similar to my own reaction, but no, you failed me! Surely it's obvious that the whole business is a code!"

"Of course! That would explain the awkwardness of his lines."

My grandfather smirked. "A fairly simple code, but adequate—entirely adequate. I have not yet finished with it." He tapped the envelope, with one index finger. "It seems to concern this house, and there is in it a repeated warning that one must be careful, and not pass beyond the threshold, for fear of dire consequences. My boy, I've crossed and recrossed every threshold in this house scores of times, and there have been no consequences. So therefore, somewhere there must exist a threshold I have not yet crossed."

I could not help smiling at his animation. "If Uncle Leander's mind was wandering, you've been off on a pretty chase," I said.

Abruptly grandfather's well-known impatience boiled to the surface. With one hand he swept my uncle's papers away; with the other he dismissed us both, and it was plain to see that Frolin and I had on the instant ceased to exist for him.

We rose, made our excuses, and left the room.

In the half-dark of the hall beyond, Frolin looked at me, saying nothing, only permitting his hot eyes to dwell upon mine for a long minute before he turned and led the way upstairs, where we parted, each to go to his own room for the night.

II

The nocturnal activity of the subconscious mind has always been of deep interest to me, since it has seemed to me that unlimited opportunities are opened up before every alert individual. I have repeatedly gone to bed with some problem vexing me, only to find it solved, insofar as I am capable of solving it, upon waking. Of those other, more devious activities of the night mind, I have less knowledge. I know that I retired that night with the question of where I had encountered my Uncle Leander's strange words before strong and foremost in mind, and I know that I went to sleep at last with that question unanswered.

Yet, when I awoke in the darkness some hours later, I knew at once that I have seen those words, those strange proper names in the book by H. P. Lovecraft which I had read at Miskatonic, and it was only secondarily that I was aware of someone tapping at my door, and called out in a hushed voice.

"It's Frolin. Are you awake? I'm coming in."

I got up, slipped on my dressing gown, and lit my electric candle. By this time Frolin was in the room, his thin body trembling a little, possibly from the cold, for the September night air flowing through my window was no longer of summer.

"What's the matter?" I asked.

He came over to me, a strange light in his eyes, and put a hand on my arm. "Can't you hear it?" he asked. "God, perhaps it *is* my mind. . . ."

"No, wait!" I exclaimed.

From somewhere outside, it seemed, came the sound of weirdly beautiful music: flutes, I thought.

"Grandfather's at the radio," I said. "Does he often listen so late?"

The expression on his face halted my words. "I own the only radio in the house. It's in my room, and it's not playing. The battery's run down, in any case. Besides, did you ever hear *such* music on the radio?"

I listened with renewed interest. The music seemed strangely muffled, and yet it came through. I observed also that it had no definite direction; while before it had seemed to come from outside, it now seemed to come from underneath the house—a curious, chant-like playing of reeds and pipes.

"A flute orchestra," I said.

"Or Pan pipes," said Frolin.

"They don't play them anymore," I said absently.

"Not on the radio," answered Frolin.

I looked up at him sharply; he returned my gaze as steadily. It occurred to me that his unnatural gravity had a reason for being, whether or not he wished to put that reason into words. I caught hold of his arms.

"Frolin—what is it? I can tell you're alarmed."

He swallowed hard. "Tony, that music doesn't come from anything in the house. It's from outside."

"But who would be outside?" I demanded.

"Nothing—no one human."

It had come at last. Almost with relief I faced this issue I had been afraid to admit to myself must be faced. *Nothing—no one human.*

"Then—what agency?" I asked.

"I think grandfather knows," he said. "Come with me, Tony. Leave the light; we can make our way in the dark."

Out in the hall, I was stopped once more by his hand tense on my arm. "Do you notice?" he whispered sibilantly. "Do you notice this, too?"

"The smell," I said. The vague, elusive smell of water, of fish and frogs and the inhabitants of watery places.

"And now!" he said.

Quite suddenly the smell of water was gone, and instead came a swift frostiness, flowing through the hall as of something alive, the indefinable fragrance of snow, the crisp moistness of snowy air.

"Do you wonder I've been concerned?" asked Frolin.

Giving me no time to reply, he led the way downstairs to the door of grandfather's study, beneath which there shone yet a fine line of yellow light. I was conscious in every step of our descent to the floor below that the music was growing louder, if no more understandable, and now, before the study door, it was apparent that the music emanated from within, and that the strange variety of odors came, too, from that study. The darkness seemed alive with menace, charged with an impending, ominous terror, which enclosed us as in a shell, so that Frolin trembled at my side.

Impulsively I raised my arm and knocked on the door.

There was no answer from within, but on the instant of my knock, the music stopped, the strange odors vanished from the air!

"You shouldn't have done that!" whispered Frolin. "If he . . ."

I tried the door. It yielded to my pressure, and I opened it.

I do not know what I expected to see there in the study, but certainly not what I did see. No single aspect of the room had changed, save that grandfather had gone to bed, and now sat there with his eyes closed and a little smile on his lips, some of his work open before him on the bed, and the lamp burning. I stood for an instant staring, not daring to believe my eyes, incredulous before the prosaic scene I looked upon. Whence then had come the music I had heard? And the odors and fragrances in the air? Confusion took possession of my thoughts, and I was about to withdraw, disturbed by the repose of my grandfather's features, when he spoke.

"Come in, then," he said, without opening his eyes. "So you heard the music, too? I had begun to wonder why no one else heard it. Mongolian, I think. Three nights ago, it was clearly Indian—north country again, Canada and Alaska. I believe there are places where Ithaqua is still worshipped. Yes, yes—and a week ago, notes I last heard played in Tibet, in forbidden Lhasa years ago, decades ago."

"Who made it?" I cried. "Where did it come from?"

He opened his eyes and regarded us standing there. "It came from here, I think," he said, placing the flat of one hand on the manuscript before him, the sheets written by my great-uncle. "And Leander's friends made it. Music of the spheres, my boy—do you credit your senses?"

"I heard it. So did Frolin."

"And what can Hough be thinking?" mused grandfather. He sighed. "I have nearly got it, I think. It only remains to determine with which of them Leander communicated."

"Which?" I repeated. "What do you mean?"

He closed his eyes and the smile came briefly back to his lips. "I thought at first it was Cthulhu; Leander was, after all, a seafaring man. But now—I wonder if it might not be one of the creatures of the air: Lloigor, perhaps—or Ithaqua, whom I believe certain of the Indians call the Wendigo. There is a legend that Ithaqua carries his victims with him in the far spaces above the earth—but I am forgetting myself again, my mind wanders." His eyes flashed open, and I found him regarding us with a peculiarly aloof stare. "It's late," he said. "I need sleep."

"What in God's name was he talking about?" asked Frolin in the hall.

"Come along," I said.

But, back in my room once more, with Frolin waiting expectantly to hear what I had to say, I did not know how to begin. How would I tell him about the weird knowledge hidden in the forbidden texts at Miskatonic University—the dread *Book of Eibon*, the obscure *Pnakotic Manuscripts*, the terrible *R'lyeh Text*, and, most shunned of all, the *Necronomicon* of the mad Arab Abdul Alhazred? How could I say to him with any conviction at all the things that crowded into my mind as a result of hearing my grandfather's strange words, the memories that boiled up from deep within—of powerful Ancient Ones, elder beings of unbelievable evil, old gods who once inhabited the earth and all the universe as we know it now, and perhaps far more—old gods of ancient good, and forces of ancient evil, of whom the latter were now in leash, and yet ever breaking forth, becoming manifest briefly, horribly, to the world of men. And their terrible names came back now, if before this hour my clue to remembrance had not been made strong enough, had been refused in the fastnesses of my inherent prejudices—Cthulhu, potent leader of the forces of the waters of earth; Yog-Sothoth and Tsathoggua, dwellers in the depths of earth; Lloigor,

Hastur, and Ithaqua, the Snow-Thing, and Wind-Walker, who were the elementals of air. It was of these beings that grandfather had spoken; and the inference he had made was too plain to be disregarded, or even to be subject to any other interpretations—that my Great-Uncle Leander, whose home, after all, had once been in the shunned and now deserted city of Innsmouth, had had traffic with at least one of these beings. And there was a further inference that he had not made, but only hinted at in something he had said earlier in the evening—that there was somewhere in the house a threshold, beyond which a man dared not walk, and what danger could lurk beyond that threshold but the path back into time, the way back to that hideous communication with the elder beings my Uncle Leander had had!

And yet somehow, the full import of grandfather's words had not dawned upon me. Though he had said so much, there was far more he had left unsaid, and I could not blame myself later for not fully realizing that grandfather's activities were clearly bent toward discovering that hidden threshold of which Uncle Leander had so cryptically written—*and crossing it!* In the confusion of thought to which I had now come in my preoccupation with the ancient mythology of Cthulhu, Ithaqua, and the elder gods, I did not follow the obvious indications to that logical conclusion, possibly because I feared instinctively to go so far.

I turned to Frolin and explained to him as clearly as I could. He listened attentively, asking a few pointed questions from time to time, and, though he paled slightly at certain details I could not refrain from mentioning, he did not seem to be as incredulous as I might have thought. This in itself was evidence of the fact that there was still more to be discovered about my grandfather's activities and the occurrences in the house, though I did not immediately realize this. However, I was shortly to discover more of the underlying reason for Frolin's ready acceptance of my necessarily sketchy outline.

In the middle of a question, he ceased talking abruptly, and there came into his eyes an expression indicating that his attention had passed from me, from the room to somewhere beyond; he sat in an attitude of listening, and, impelled by his own actions, I, too, strained to hear what he heard.

Only the wind's voice in the trees, rising now a little, I thought. A storm coming.

"Do you hear it?" he said in a shaky whisper.

"No," I said quietly. "Only the wind."

"Yes, yes—the wind. I wrote you, remember. Listen."

"Now, come, Frolin, take hold of yourself. It's only the wind."

He gave me a pitying glance and, going to the window, beckoned me after him. I followed, coming to his side. Without a word he pointed into the darkness pressing close to the house. It took me a moment to accustom myself to the night, but presently I was able to see the line of trees struck sharply against the star-swept heavens. And then, instantly, I understood.

Though the sound of the wind roared and thundered about the house, nothing whatever disturbed the trees before my eyes—not a leaf, not a treetop, not a twig, swayed by so much as a hair's breadth!

"Good God!" I exclaimed, and fell back, away from the pane, as if to shut the sight from my eyes.

"Now, you see," he said, stepping back from the window, also. "I have heard all this before."

He stood quietly, as if waiting, and I, too, waited. The sound of the wind continued unabated; it had by this time reached a frightful intensity, so that it seemed as if the old house must be torn from the hillside and hurtled into the valley below. Indeed, a faint trembling made itself manifest even as I thought this: a strange tremor, as if the house were *shuddering*, and the pictures on the walls made a slight, almost *stealthy* movement, almost imperceptible, and yet quite unmistakably visible. I glanced at Frolin, but his features were not disquieted; he continued to stand, listening and waiting, so that it was patent that the end of this singular manifestation was not yet. The wind's sound was now a terrible, demoniac howling, and it was accompanied by notes of music, which must have been audible for some time, but were so perfectly blended with the wind's voice that I was not at first aware of them. The music was similar to that which had gone before, as of pipes and occasionally stringed instruments, but was now much wilder, sounding with a terrifying abandon, with a character of unmentionable evil about it. At the same time, two further manifestations occurred. The first was the sound as of someone walking, some great being whose footsteps seemed to flow into the room from the heart of the wind itself; certainly they did not originate in the house, though there was about them the unmistakable swelling which betokened their approach to the house. The second was the sudden change in the temperature.

The night outside was warm for September in upstate Wisconsin, and the house, too, had been reasonably comfortable. Now, abruptly, coincident with the approaching footsteps, the temperature began to drop rapidly, so that in a little while the air in the room was cold, and both Frolin and I had to put on more clothing in order to keep comfortable. Still this did not seem to be the height of the manifestations for which Frolin so obviously waited; he continued to stand, saying nothing, though his eyes, meeting mine from time to time, were eloquent enough to speak his mind. How long we stood there, listening to those frightening sounds from outside, before the end came, I do not know.

But suddenly Frolin caught my arm and, in a hoarse whisper, cried, "There! There they are! Listen!"

The tempo of the weird music had changed abruptly to a diminuendo from its previous wild crescendo; there came into it now a strain of almost unbearable sweetness, with a little of melancholy to it, music as lovely as previously it had been evil, and yet the note of terror was not completely absent. At the same time, there was apparent the sound of voices, raised in a kind of swelling chant, rising from the back of the house somewhere—as if from the study.

"Great God in Heaven!" I cried, seizing Frolin. "What is it now?"

"It's grandfather's doing," he said. "Whether he knows it or not, that thing comes and sings to him." He shook his head and closed his eyes tightly for an instant before saying bitterly in a low, intense voice, "If only that accursed paper of Leander's had been burned as it ought to have been!"

"You could almost make out the words," I said, listening intently.

There *were* words—but not words I had ever heard before: a kind of horrible, primeval mouthing, as if some bestial creature with but half a tongue ululated syllables of meaningless horror. I went over and opened the door; immediately the sounds seemed clearer, so that it was evident that what I had mistaken for many voices was but one, which could nevertheless convey the illusion of many. Words—or perhaps I had better write *sounds*, bestial sounds—rose from below, a kind of awe-inspiring ululation:

"Iä! Iä! Ithaqua! Ithaqua cf'ayak vulgtmm. Iä! Uhg! Cthulhu fhtagn! Shub-Niggurath! Ithaqua naflfhtagn!"

Incredibly, the wind's voice rose to howl ever more terribly, so that I thought at any moment the house would be hurled into the void, and Frolin and myself torn from its rooms, and the breath sucked from our helpless bodies. In the confusion of fear and wonder that held me, I thought at that instant of grandfather in the study below, and beckoning Frolin, I ran from the room to the stairs, determined, despite my ghastly fright, to put myself between the old man and whatever menaced him. I ran to his door and flung myself upon it—and once more, as before, all manifestations stopped: as if by the flick of a switch, silence fell like a pall of darkness upon the house, a silence that was momentarily even more terrible.

The door gave, and once more I faced grandfather.

He was sitting still as we had left him but a short time before, though now his eyes were open, his head was cocked a little to one side, and his gaze was fixed upon the overlarge painting on the east wall.

"In God's name!" I cried. "What was that?"

"I hope to find out before long," he answered with great dignity and gravity.

His utter lack of fear quieted my own alarm to some degree, and I came a little farther into the room, Frolin following. I leaned over his bed, striving to fix his attention upon me, but he continued to gaze at the painting with singular intensity.

"What are you doing?" I demanded. "Whatever it is, there's danger in it."

"An explorer like your grandfather would hardly be content if there were not, my boy," he replied crisply, matter-of-factly.

I knew it was true.

"I would rather die with my boots on than here in this bed," he went on. "As for what we heard—I don't know how much of it *you* heard—that's something for the moment not yet explicable. But I would call to your attention the strange action of the wind."

"There was no wind," I said. "I looked."

"Yes, yes," he said a little impatiently. "True enough. And yet the wind's sound was there, and all the voices of the wind—just as I have heard it singing in Mongolia, in the great snowy spaces, over the shunned and hidden Plateau of Leng where the Tcho-Tcho people worship strange ancient gods." He turned to face me suddenly, and I thought his eyes feverish. "I did tell you, didn't I, about the worship of Ithaqua, sometimes called Wind-Walker, and by some, surely, the Wendigo, by certain Indians in upper Manitoba, and of their beliefs that the Wind-Walker takes human sacrifices and carries them over the far places of the earth before leaving them behind, dead at last? Oh, there are stories, my boy, odd legends—and something more." He leaned toward me now with a fierce intensity. "I have myself seen things—things found on a body dropped from the air—just that—things that could not possibly have been got in Manitoba, things belonging to Leng, to the Pacific Isles." He brushed me away with one arm, and an expression of disgust crossed his face. "You don't believe me. You think I'm wandering. Go on then, go back to your little sleep, and wait for your last through the eternal misery of monotonous day after day!"

"No! Say it now. I'm in no mood to go."

"I will talk to you in the morning," he said tiredly, leaning back.

With that I had to be content; he was adamant, and could not be moved. I bade him good-night once more and retreated into the hall with Frolin, who stood there shaking his head slowly, forbiddingly.

"Every time a little worse," he whispered. "Every time the wind blows a little louder, the cold comes more intensely, the voices and the music more clearly—and the sound of those terrible footsteps!"

He turned away and began to retrace the way upstairs, and, after a moment of hesitation, I followed.

In the morning my grandfather looked his usual picture of good health. At the moment of my entrance into the dining room, he was speaking to Hough, evidently in answer to a request, for the old servant stood respectfully bowed, while he heard grandfather tell him that he and Mrs. Hough might indeed take a week off, beginning today, if it was necessary for Mrs. Hough's health that she go to Wausau to consult a specialist. Frolin met my eyes with a grim smile; his color had faded a little, leaving him pale and sleepless-looking, but he ate heartily enough. His smile, and the brief indicative glance of his eyes toward Hough's retreating back, said clearly that this necessity which had come upon Hough and his wife was their way of fighting the manifestations which had so disturbed my own first night in the house.

"Well, my boy," said grandfather quite cheerfully, "you're not looking nearly as haggard as you did last night. I confess, I felt for you. I daresay also you aren't nearly so skeptical as you were."

He chuckled, as if this were a subject for joking. I could not, unfortunately, feel the same way about it. I sat down and began to eat a little, glancing at him from time to time, waiting for him to begin his explanation of the strange events of the previous night. Since it became evident shortly that he did not intend to explain, I was impelled to ask for an explanation, and did so with as much dignity as possible.

"I'm sorry if you've been disturbed," he said. "The fact of the matter is that that threshold of which Leander wrote must be in that study somewhere, and I felt quite certain I was onto it last night, before you burst into my room the second time. Furthermore, it seems undisputable that at least one member of the family has had traffic with one of those beings—Leander, obviously."

Frolin leaned forward. "Do you believe in them?"

Grandfather smiled unpleasantly. "It must be obvious that, whatever my abilities, the disturbance you heard last night could hardly have been caused by me."

"Yes, of course," agreed Frolin. "But some other agency . . ."

"No, no—it remains to be determined only which one. The water smells are the sign of the spawn of Cthulhu, but the winds might be Lloigor or Ithaqua or Hastur. But the stars aren't right for Hastur," he went on. "So we are left with the other two. There they are, then, or one of them, just across that threshold. I want to know what lies beyond that threshold, if I can find it."

It seemed incredible that my grandfather should be talking so unconcernedly about these ancient beings; his prosaic air was in itself almost as alarming as had been the night's occurrences. The temporary feeling of security I had had at the sight of him eating breakfast was washed away; I began to be conscious again of that slowly growing fear

I had known on my way to the house last evening, and I regretted having pushed my inquiry.

If my grandfather were aware of anything of this, he made no sign. He went on talking much in the manner of a lecturer pursuing a scientific inquiry for the benefit of an audience before him. It was obvious, he said, that a connection existed between the happenings at Innsmouth and Leander Alwyn's non-human contact *outside*. Did Leander leave Innsmouth originally because of the cult of Cthulhu that existed there, because he, too, was becoming afflicted with that curious facial change which overtook so many of the inhabitants of accursed Innsmouth?—those strange batrachian lineaments which horrified the Federal investigators who came to examine into the Innsmouth affair? Perhaps this was so. In any event, leaving the Cthulhu cult behind, he had made his way into the wilds of Wisconsin and somehow he had established contact with another of the elder beings, Lloigor or Ithaqua—all, to be noted, elemental forces of evil. Leander Alwyn was apparently a wicked man.

"If there is any truth to this," I cried, "then surely Leander's warning ought to be observed. Give up this mad hope of finding the threshold of which he writes!"

Grandfather gazed at me for a moment with speculative mildness; but it was plain to see that he was not actually concerning himself with my outburst. "Now I've embarked upon this exploration, I mean to keep to it. After all, Leander died a natural death."

"But, following your own theory, he had traffic with these—these things," I said. "You have none. You're daring to venture out into unknown space—it comes to that—without regard for what horrors might lie there."

"When I went into Mongolia, I encountered horrors, too. I never thought to escape Leng with my life." He paused reflectively, and then rose slowly. "No, I mean to discover Leander's threshold. And tonight, no matter what you hear, try not to interrupt me. It would be a pity, if after so long a time, I am still further delayed by your impetuosity."

"And having discovered the threshold," I cried. "What then?"

"I'm not sure I'll want to cross it."

"The choice may not be yours."

He looked at me for a moment in silence, smiled gently, and left the room.

III

Of the events of that catastrophic night, I find it difficult even at this late date to write, so vividly do they return to mind, despite the prosaic surroundings of Miskatonic University where so many of those dread secrets are hidden in ancient and little-known texts. And yet, to understand the widespread occurrences that came after, the events of that night must be known.

Frolin and I spent most of the day investigating my grandfather's books and papers, in search of verification of certain legends he had hinted at in his conversation, not only with me, but with Frolin even before my arrival. Throughout his work occurred many cryptic allusions, but only one narrative at all relative to our inquiry—a somewhat obscure story, clearly of legendary origin, concerning the disappearance of two residents of Nelson, Manitoba, and a constable of the Royal Northwest Mounted Police, and their subsequent reappearance, as if dropped from the heavens, frozen and either dead or dying, babbling of *Ithaqua*, of the *Wind-Walker*, and of many places on the face of the earth, and carrying with them strange objects, mementos of far places, which they had never been known to carry in life. The story was incredible, and yet it was related to the mythology so clearly put down in *The Outsider and Others*, and even more horribly narrated in the *Pnakotic Manuscripts*, the *R'lyeh Text*, and the terrible *Necronomicon*.

Apart from this, we found nothing tangible enough to relate to our problem, and we resigned ourselves to waiting for the night.

At luncheon and dinner, prepared by Frolin in the absence of the Houghs, my grandfather carried on as normally he was accustomed to, making no reference to his strange exploration, beyond saying that he now had definite proof that Leander had painted that unattractive landscape on the east wall of the study, and that he hoped soon, as he neared the end of the deciphering of Leander's long, rambling letter, to find the essential clue to that threshold of which he wrote, and to which he now alluded increasingly. When he rose from the dinner table, he solemnly cautioned us once more not to interrupt him in the night, under pain of his extreme displeasure, and so departed into that study out of which he never walked again.

"Do you think you can sleep?" Frolin asked me, when we were alone.

I shook my head. "Impossible. I'll stay up."

"I don't think he'd like us to stay downstairs," said Frolin, a faint frown on his forehead.

"In my room, then," I replied. "And you?"

"With you, if you don't mind. He means to see it through, and there's nothing we can do until he needs us. He may call. . . ."

I had the uncomfortable conviction that if my grandfather called for us, it would be too late, but I forbore to give voice to my fears.

The events of that evening started as before—with the strains of that weirdly beautiful music welling flute-like from the darkness around the house. Then, in a little while, came the wind, and the cold, and the ululating voice. And then, preceded by an aura of evil so great that it was almost stifling in the room—then came something more, something unspeakably terrible. We had been sitting, Frolin and I, with the light out; I had not bothered to light my electric candle, since no light we could show would illumine the source of these manifestations. I faced the window and, when the wind began to rise, looked once again to the line of trees, thinking that surely, certainly, they must bend before this great onrushing storm of wind; but again there was nothing, no movement in that stillness. And there was no cloud in the heavens; the stars shone brightly, the constellations of summer moving down to the western rim of earth to make the signature of autumn in the sky. The wind's sound had risen steadily, so that now it had the fury of a gale, and yet nothing, no movement, disturbed the line of trees dark upon the night sky.

But suddenly—so suddenly that for a moment I blinked my eyes in an effort to convince myself that a dream had shuttered my sight—in one large area of the sky the stars were gone! I came to my feet and pressed my face to the pane. It was as if a cloud had abruptly reared up into the heavens, to a height almost at the zenith; but no cloud could have come upon the sky so swiftly. On both sides and overhead stars still shone. I opened the window and leaned out, trying to follow the dark outline against the stars. *It was the outline of some great beast, a horrible caricature of man, rising to a semblance of a head high in the heavens, and there, where its eyes might have been, glowed with a deep carmine fire two stars!*—Or were they stars? At the same instant, the sound of those approaching footsteps grew so loud that the house shook and trembled with their vibrations, and the wind's demoniac fury rose to indescribable heights, and the ululation reached such a pitch that it was maddening to hear.

"Frolin!" I called hoarsely.

I heard him come to my side, and in a moment felt his tight grasp on my arm. So he, too, had seen; it was not hallucination, not dream—this giant thing outlined against the stars, and moving!

"It's moving," whispered Frolin. "Oh, God!—it's coming!"

He pulled frantically away from the window, and so did I. But in an instant, the shadow on the sky was gone, the stars shone once more. The wind, however, had not decreased in intensity one iota; indeed, if it were possible, it grew momentarily wilder and more violent; the entire house shuddered and quaked, while those thunderous footsteps echoed and re-echoed in the valley before the house. And the cold grew worse, so that breath hung a white vapor in air—a cold as of outer space.

Out of all the turmoil of mind, I thought of the legend in my grandfather's papers—the legend of *Ithaqua*, whose signature lay in the cold and snow of far northern places. Even as I remembered, everything was driven from my mind by a frightful chorus of ululation, the triumphant chanting as of a thousand bestial mouths—

"Iä! Iä! Ithaqua, Ithaqua! Ai! Ai! Ai! Ithaqua cf'ayak vulgtmm vugtlagln vulgtmm. Ithaqua fhtagn! Ugh! Iä! Iä! Ai! Ai! Ai!"

Simultaneously came a thunderous crash, and immediately after, the voice of my grandfather, raised in a terrible cry, a cry that rose into a scream of mortal terror, so that the names he would have uttered—Frolin's and mine—were lost, choked back into his throat by the full force of the horror revealed to him.

And, as abruptly as his voice ceased to sound, all other manifestations came to a stop, leaving again that ghastly, portentous silence to close around us like a cloud of doom.

Frolin reached the door of my room before I did, but I was not far behind. He fell part of the way down the stairs, but recovered in the light of my electric candle, which I had seized on my way out, and together we assaulted the door of the study, calling to the old man inside.

But no voice answered, though the line of yellow under the door was evidence that his lamp burned still.

The door had been locked from the inside, so that it was necessary to break it down before we could enter.

Of my grandfather, there was no trace. But in the east wall yawned a great cavity, where the painting, now prone upon the floor, had been—a rocky opening leading into the depths of earth—and over everything in the room lay the mark of Ithaqua—a fine carpet of snow, whose crystals gleamed as from a million tiny jewels in the yellow light of grandfather's lamp. Save for the painting, only the bed was disturbed—*as if grandfather had been literally torn out of it by stupendous force!*

I looked hurriedly to where the old man had kept Uncle Leander's manuscript—but it was gone; nothing of it remained. Frolin cried out suddenly and pointed to the painting Uncle Leander had made, and then to the opening yawning before us.

"It was here all the time—the threshold," he said.

And I saw even as he; as grandfather had seen too late—*for the painting by Uncle Leander was but the representation of the site of his home before the house had been erected to conceal that cavernous opening into the earth on the hillside, the hidden threshold against which Leander's manuscript had warned, the threshold beyond which my grandfather had vanished!*

Though there is little more to tell, yet the most damning of all the curious facts remain to be revealed. A thorough search of the cavern was subsequently made by county officials and certain intrepid adventurers from Harmon; it was found to have several openings, and it was plain that anyone or *anything* wishing to reach the house through the cavern would have had to enter through one of the innumerable hidden crevices discovered among the surrounding hills. The nature of Uncle Leander's activities was revealed after grandfather's disappearance. Frolin and I were put through a hard grilling by suspicious county officials, but were finally released when the body of my grandfather did not come to light.

But since that night, certain facts came into the open, facts which, in the light of my grandfather's hints, coupled with the horrible legends contained in the shunned books locked away here in the library of Miskatonic University, are damning and damnably inescapable.

The first of them was the series of gigantic footprints found in the earth at the place where on that fatal night the shadow had risen into the star-swept heavens—the unbelievable wide and deep depressions, as of some prehistoric monster walking there, steps a half mile apart, steps that led beyond the house and vanished at a crevice leading down into that hidden cavern in tracks identical with those found in the snow in northern Manitoba where those unfortunate travelers and the constable sent to find them had vanished from the face of the earth!

The second was the discovery of my grandfather's notebook, together with a portion of Uncle Leander's manuscript, encased in ice, found deep in the forest snows of upper Saskatchewan, and bearing every sign of having been dropped from a great height. The last entry was dated on the day of his disappearance in late September; the notebook was not found until the following April. Neither Frolin nor I dared to make the explanation of its strange appearance which came immediately to mind, and together we burned that horrible letter and the imperfect translation grandfather had made, the translation which in itself, as it was written down, with all its warnings against the terror beyond the threshold, had served to summon from *outside* a creature so horrible that its description has never been attempted by even those ancient writers whose terrible narratives are scattered over the face of the earth!

And last of all, the most conclusive, the most damning evidence—the discovery seven months later of my grandfather's body on a small Pacific island not far southeast of Singapore, and the curious report made of his condition: perfectly preserved, *as if in ice,* so cold that no one could touch him with bare hands for five days after his discovery, and the singular fact that he was found half buried in sand, *as if "he had fallen from an aeroplane!"* Neither Frolin nor I could any longer have any doubt; this was the legend of Ithaqua, who carried his victims with him into far places of the earth, in time and space, before leaving them behind. And the evidence was undeniable that my grandfather had been alive for part of that incredible journey, for if we had had any doubt, the things found in his pockets, the mementos carried from strange hidden places where he had been, and sent to us, were final and damning testimony—the gold plaque, with its miniature presentation of a struggle between ancient beings, and bearing on its surface inscriptions in cabalistic designs, the plaque which Dr. Rackham of Miskatonic University identified as having come from some place beyond the memory of man; the loathsome book in Burmese that revealed ghastly legends of that shunned and hidden Plateau of Leng, the place of the dread Tcho-Tcho people; and finally, the *revolting and bestial stone miniature of a hellish monstrosity walking on the winds above the earth*!

The Shambler from the Stars*

ROBERT BLOCH

(Dedicated to H. P. Lovecraft)

I

I am what I profess to be—a writer of weird fiction. Since earliest childhood I have been enthralled by the cryptic fascination of the unknown and the unguessable. The nameless fears, the grotesque dreams, the queer, half-intuitive fancies that haunt our minds, have always exercised for me a potent and inexplicable delight.

In literature I have walked the midnight paths with Poe or crept amidst the shadows with Machen; combed the realms of horrific stars with Baudelaire, or steeped myself with earth's inner madness amidst the tales of ancient lore. A meager talent for sketching and crayon work led me to attempt crude picturizations involving the outlandish denizens of my nighted thoughts. The same somber trend of intellect which drew me in my art interested me in obscure realms of musical composition; the symphonic strains of the *Planets Suite* and the like were my favorites. My inner life soon became a ghoulish feast of eldritch, tantalizing horrors.

My outer existence was comparatively dull. As time went on I found myself drifting more and more into the life of a penurious recluse; a tranquil, philosophical existence amidst a world of books and dreams.

A man must live. By nature constitutionally and spiritually unfitted for manual labor, I was at first puzzled about the choice of a suitable vocation. The depression complicated matters to an almost intolerable degree, and for a time I was close to utter economic disaster. It was then that I decided to write.

---

*Originally published in *Weird Tales*, September 1935.

I procured a battered typewriter, a ream of cheap paper, and a few carbons. My subject matter did not bother me. What better field than the boundless realms of a colorful imagination? I would write of horror, fear, and the riddle that is Death. At least, in the callowness of my unsophistication, this was my intention.

My first attempts soon convinced me how utterly I had failed. Sadly, miserably, I fell short of my aspired goal. My vivid dreams became on paper merely meaningless jumbles of ponderous adjectives, and I found no ordinary words to express the wondrous terror of the unknown. My first manuscripts were miserable and futile documents; the few magazines using such material being unanimous in their rejections.

I had to live. Slowly but surely I began to adjust my style to my ideas. Laboriously I experimented with words, phrases, sentence-structure. It was work, and hard work at that. I soon learned to sweat. At last, however, one of my stories met with favor; then a second, a third, a fourth. Soon I had begun to master the more obvious tricks of the trade, and the future looked brighter at last. It was with an easier mind that I returned to my dream-life and my beloved books. My stories afforded me a somewhat meager livelihood, and for a time this sufficed. But not for long. Ambition, ever an illusion, was the cause of my undoing.

I wanted to write a real story; not the stereotyped, ephemeral sort of tale I turned out for the magazines, but a real work of art. The creation of such a masterpiece became my ideal. I was not a good writer, but that was not entirely due to my errors in mechanical style. It was, I felt, the fault of my subject matter. Vampires, werewolves, ghouls, mythological monsters—these things constituted material of little merit. Commonplace imagery, ordinary adjectival treatment, and a prosaically anthropocentric point of view were the chief detriments to the production of a really good weird tale.

I must have new subject matter, truly unusual plot material. If only I could conceive of something that was teratologically incredible!

I longed to learn the songs the demons sing as they swoop between the stars, or hear the voices of the olden gods as they whisper their secrets to the echoing void. I yearned to know the terrors of the grave; the kiss of maggots on my tongue, the cold caress of a rotting shroud upon my body. I thirsted for the knowledge that lies in the pits of mummied eyes, and burned for wisdom known only to the worm. Then I could really write, and my hopes be truly realized.

I sought a way. Quietly I began a correspondence with isolated thinkers and dreamers all over the country. There was a hermit in the western hills, a savant in the northern wilds, a mystic dreamer in New

England. It was from the latter that I learned of the ancient books that hold strange lore. He quoted guardedly from the legendary *Necronomicon*, and spoke timidly of a certain *Book of Eibon* that was reputed to surpass it in the utter wildness of its blasphemy. He himself had been a student of these volumes of primal dread, but he did not want me to search too far. He had heard many strange things as a boy in witch-haunted Arkham, where the old shadows still leer and creep, and since then he had wisely shunned the blacker knowledge of the forbidden.

At length, after much pressing on my part, he reluctantly consented to furnish me with the names of certain persons he deemed able to aid me in my quest. He was a writer of notable brilliance and wide reputation among the discriminating few, and I knew he was keenly interested in the outcome of the whole affair.

As soon as his precious list came into my possession, I began a widespread postal campaign in order to obtain access to the desired volumes. My letters went out to universities, private libraries, reputed seers, and the leaders of carefully hidden and obscurely designated cults. But I was foredoomed to disappointment.

The replies I received were definitely unfriendly, almost hostile. Evidently the rumored possessors of such lore were angered that their secret should be thus unveiled by a prying stranger. I was subsequently the recipient of several anonymous threats through the mails, and I had one very alarming phone-call. This did not bother me nearly so much as the disappointing realization that my endeavors had failed. Denials, evasions, refusals, threats—these would not aid me. I must look elsewhere.

The bookstores! Perhaps on some musty and forgotten shelf I might discover what I sought.

Then I began an interminable crusade. I learned to bear my numerous disappointments with unflinching calm. Nobody in the common run of shops seemed ever to have heard of the frightful *Necronomicon*, the evil *Book of Eibon*, or the disquieting *Cultes des Goules*.

Persistence brings results. In a little old shop on South Dearborn Street, amidst dusty shelves seemingly forgotten by time, I came to the end of my search. There, securely wedged between two century-old editions of Shakespeare, stood a great black volume with iron facings. Upon it, in hand-engraved lettering, was the inscription *De Vermis Mysteriis*, or "Mysteries of the Worm."

The proprietor could not tell how it had come into his possession. Years before, perhaps, it had been included in some secondhand job-lot. He was obviously unaware of its nature, for I purchased it with a dollar bill. He wrapped the ponderous thing for me, well pleased at this unexpected sale, and bade me a very satisfied good-day.

I left hurriedly, the precious prize under my arm. What a find! I had heard of this book before. Ludvig Prinn was its author; who had perished at the inquisitorial stake in Brussels when the witchcraft trials were at their height. A strange character—alchemist, necromancer, reputed mage—he boasted of having attained a miraculous age when he at last suffered a fiery immolation at the hands of the secular arm. He was said to have proclaimed himself the sole survivor of the ill-fated Ninth Crusade, exhibiting as proof certain musty documents of attestation. It is true that a certain Ludvig Prinn was numbered among the gentlemen retainers of Montserrat in the olden chronicles, but the incredulous branded Ludvig as a crack-brained imposter, though perchance a lineal descendant of the original warrior.

Ludvig attributed his sorcerous learning to the years he had spent as a captive among the wizards and wonder-workers of Syria, and glibly he spoke of encounters with the djinns and efreets of elder Eastern myth. He is known to have spent some time in Egypt, and there are legends among the Libyan dervishes concerning the old seer's deeds in Alexandria.

At any rate, his declining days were spent in the Flemish lowland country of his birth, where he resided, appropriately enough, in the ruins of a pre-Roman tomb that stood in the forest near Brussels. Ludvig was reputed to have dwelt there amidst a swarm of familiars and fearsomely invoked conjurations. Manuscripts still extant speak of him guardedly as being attended by "invisible companions" and "Star-sent servants." Peasants shunned the forest by night, for they did not like certain noises that resounded to the moon, and they most certainly were not anxious to see what worshipped at the old pagan altars that stood crumbling in certain of the darker glens.

Be that as it may, these creatures that he commanded were never seen after Prinn's capture by the inquisitorial minions. Searching soldiers found the tomb entirely deserted, though it was thoroughly ransacked before its destruction. The supernatural entities, the unusual instruments and compounds—all had most curiously vanished. A search of the forbidding woods and a timorous examination of the strange altars did not add to the information. There were fresh blood-stains on the altars, and fresh blood-stains on the rack, too, before the questioning of Prinn was finished. A series of particularly atrocious tortures failed to elicit any further disclosures from the silent wizard, and at length the weary interrogators ceased, and cast the aged sorcerer into a dungeon.

It was in prison, while awaiting trial, that he penned the morbid, horror-hinting lines of *De Vermis Mysteriis*, known today as *Mysteries of the Worm*. How it was ever smuggled through the alert guards is a mystery in itself, but a year after his death it saw print in Cologne. It was immediately suppressed, but a few copies had already been privately distributed. These in turn were transcribed, and although there was a later censored and deleted printing, only the Latin original is accepted as genuine. Throughout the centuries a few of the elect have read and pondered on its lore. The secrets of the old archimage are known today only to the initiated, and they discourage all attempts to spread their fame, for certain very definite reasons.

This, in brief, was what I knew of the volume's history at the time it came into my possession. As a collector's item alone the book was a phenomenal find, but on its contents I could pass no judgment. It was in Latin. Since I can speak or translate only a few words of that learned tongue, I was confronted by a barrier as soon as I opened the musty pages. It was maddening to have such a treasure-trove of dark knowledge at my command and yet lack the key to its unearthing.

For a moment I despaired, since I was unwilling to approach any local classical or Latin scholar in connection with so hideous and blasphemous a text. Then came an inspiration. Why not take it east and seek the aid of my friend? He was a student of the classics, and would be less likely to be shocked by the horrors of Prinn's baleful revelations. Accordingly I addressed a hasty letter to him, and shortly thereafter received my reply. He would be glad to assist me—I must by all means come at once.

II

Providence is a lovely town. My friend's house was ancient, and quaintly Georgian. The first floor was a gem of colonial atmosphere. The second, beneath antique gables that shadowed the enormous window, served as a workroom for my host.

It was here that we pondered that grim, eventful night last April; here beside the open window that overlooked the azure sea. It was a moonless night; haggard and wan with a fog that filled the darkness with bat-like shadows. In my mind's eye I can see it still—the tiny, lamp-lit room with the big table and the high-backed chairs; the bookcases bordering the walls; the manuscripts stacked in special files.

My friend and I sat at the table, the volume of mystery before us. His lean profile threw a disturbing shadow on the wall, and his waxen face was furtive in the pale light. There was an inexplicable air of portentous revelation quite disturbing in its potency; I sensed the presence of secrets waiting to be revealed.

My companion detected it, too. Long years of occult experience had sharpened his intuition to an uncanny degree. It was not cold that made him tremble as he sat there in his chair; it was not fever that caused his eyes to flame like jewel-incarned fires. He knew, even before he opened that accursed tome, that it was evil. The musty scent that rose from those antique pages carried with it the reek of the tomb. The faded leaves were maggoty at the edges, and rats had gnawed the leather; rats which perchance had a ghastlier food for common fare.

I had told my friend the volume's history that afternoon, and had unwrapped it in his presence. Then he had seemed willing and eager to begin an immediate translation. Now he demurred.

It was not wise, he insisted. This was evil knowledge—who could say what demon-dreaded lore these pages might contain, or what ills befall the ignorant one who sought to tamper with their contents? It is not good to learn too much, and men had died for exercising the rotted wisdom that these leaves contained. He begged me to abandon the quest while the book was still unopened and to seek my inspiration in saner things.

I was a fool. Hastily I overruled his objections with vain and empty words. I was not afraid. Let us at least gaze into the contents of our prize. I began to turn the pages.

The result was disappointing. It was an ordinary-looking volume after all—yellow, crumbling leaves set with heavy black-lettered Latin texts. That was all; no illustrations, no alarming designs.

My friend could no longer resist the allurement of such a rare bibliophilic treat. In a moment he was peering intently over my shoulder, occasionally muttering snatches of Latin phrasing. Enthusiasm mastered him at last. Seizing the precious tome in both hands, he seated himself near the window and began reading paragraphs at random, occasionally translating them into English.

His eyes gleamed with a feral light; his cadaverous profile grew intent as he pored over the moldering runes. Sentences thundered in fearsome litany, then faded into tones below a whisper as his voice became as soft as a viper's hiss. I caught only a few phrases now, for in his introspection he seemed to have forgotten me. He was reading of spells and enchantments. I recall allusions to such gods of divination as Father Yig, dark Han, and serpent-bearded Byatis. I shuddered, for I knew these names of old, but I would have shuddered more had I known what was yet to come.

It came quickly. Suddenly he turned to me in great agitation, and his excited voice was shrill. He asked me if I remembered the legends of Prinn's sorcery, and the tales of the invisible servants he commanded from the stars. I assented, little understanding the cause of his sudden frenzy.

Then he told me the reason. Here, under a chapter on familiars, he had found an orison or spell, perhaps the very one Prinn had used to call upon his unseen servitors from beyond the stars! Let me listen while he read.

* * *

I sat there dully, like a stupid, uncomprehending fool. Why did I not scream, try to escape, or tear that monstrous manuscript from his hands? Instead I sat there—sat there while my friend, in a voice cracked with unnatural excitement, read in Latin a long and sonorously sinister invocation.

"Tibi, Magnum Innominandum, signa stellarum nigrarum et bufoniformis Sadoquae sigillum. . . ."

The croaking ritual proceeded, then rose on wings of nighted, hideous horror. The words seemed to writhe like flames in the air, burning into my brain. The thundering tones cast an echo into infinity, beyond the farthermost star. They seemed to pass into primal and undimensioned gates, to seek out a listener there, and summon him to earth. Was it all an illusion? I did not pause to ponder.

For that unwitting summons was answered. Scarcely had my companion's voice died away in that little room before the terror came. The room turned cold. A sudden wind shrieked in through the open window; a wind that was not of earth. It bore an evil bleating from afar, and at the sound, my friend's face became a pale white mask of newly awakened fear. Then there was a crunching at the walls, and the window-ledge buckled before my staring eyes. From out of the nothingness beyond that opening came a sudden burst of lubricious laughter—a hysterical cackling born of utter madness. It rose to the grinning quintessence of all horror, without mouth to give it birth.

The rest happened with startling swiftness. All at once my friend began to scream as he stood by the window; scream and claw wildly at empty air. In the lamplight I saw his features contort into a grimace of insane agony. A moment later, his body rose unsupported from the floor, and began to bend outward to a backbreaking degree. A second later came the sickening grind of broken bones. His form now hung in midair, the eyes glazed and the hands clutching convulsively as if at something unseen. Once again there came the sound of maniacal tittering, but this time it came from *within the room!*

The stars rocked in red anguish; the cold wind gibbered in my ears. I crouched in my chair, my eyes riveted on that astounding scene in the corner.

My friend was shrieking now; his screams blended with that gleeful, atrocious laughter from the empty air. His sagging body, dangling in space, bent backward once again as blood spurted from the torn neck, spraying like a ruby fountain.

That blood never reached the floor. It stopped in midair as the laughter ceased, and a loathsome sucking noise took its place. With a new and accelerated horror, I realized that that blood was being drained to feed the invisible entity from beyond! What creature of space had been so suddenly and unwittingly invoked? What was that vampiric monstrosity I could not see?

Even now a hideous metamorphosis was taking place. The body of my companion became shrunken, wizened, lifeless. At length it dropped to the floor and lay nauseatingly still. But in midair another and a ghastlier change occurred.

A reddish glow filled the corner by the window—a *bloody* glow. Slowly but surely the dim outlines of a Presence came into view; the blood-filled outlines of that unseen shambler from the stars. It was red and dripping; an immensity of pulsing, moving jelly; a scarlet blob with myriad tentacular trunks that waved and waved. There were suckers on the tips of the appendages, and these were opening and closing with a ghoulish lust. . . . The thing was bloated and obscene; a headless, faceless, eyeless bulk with the ravenous maw and titanic talons of a star-born monster. The human blood on which it had fed revealed the hitherto invisible outlines of the feaster. It was not a sight for sane eyes to see.

Fortunately for my reason, the creature did not linger. Spurning the dead and flabby corpse-like thing on the floor, it purposely seized the opening. There it disappeared, and I heard its far-off, derisive laughter floating on the wings of the wind as it receded into the gulfs from whence it had come.

That was all. I was left alone in the room with the limp and lifeless body at my feet. The book was gone; but there were bloody prints upon the wall, bloody swaths upon the floor, and the face of my poor friend was a bloody death's-head, leering up at the stars.

For a long time I sat alone in silence before I set to fire that room and all it contained. After that I went away, laughing, for I knew that the blaze would eradicate all trace of what remained. I had arrived only that afternoon, and there was none who knew, and none to see me go, for I departed ere the glowing flames were detected. I stumbled for hours through the twisted streets, and quaked with renewed and idiotic laughter as I looked up at the burning, ever-gloating stars that eyed me furtively through wreaths of haunted fog.

After a long while I became calm enough to board a train. I have been calm throughout the long journey home, and calm throughout the penning of this screed. I was even calm when I read of my friend's curious accidental death in the fire that destroyed his dwelling.

It is only at nights, when the stars gleam, that dreams return to drive me into a gigantic maze of frantic fears. Then I take to drugs, in a vain attempt to ban those leering memories from my sleep. But I really do not care, for I shall not be here long.

I have a curious suspicion that I shall again see that shambler from the stars. I think it will return soon without being resummoned, and I know that when it comes it will seek me out and carry me down into the darkness that holds my friend. Sometimes I almost yearn for the advent of that day, for then I shall learn once and for all, the *Mysteries of the Worm*.

The Hunter of the Dark*

H. P. LOVECRAFT

(Dedicated to Robert Bloch)

I have seen the dark universe yawning
  Where the black planets roll without aim—
Where they roll in their horror unheeded,
  Without knowledge or lustre or name.

—NEMESIS

Cautious investigators will hesitate to challenge the common belief that Robert Blake was killed by lightning, or by some profound nervous shock derived from an electrical discharge. It is true that the window he faced was unbroken, but Nature has shewn herself capable of many freakish performances. The expression on his face may easily have arisen from some obscure muscular source unrelated to anything he saw, while the entries in his diary are clearly the result of a fantastic imagination aroused by certain local superstitions and by certain old matters he had uncovered. As for the anomalous conditions at the deserted church on Federal Hill—the shrewd analyst is not slow in attributing them to some charlatanry, conscious or unconscious, with at least some of which Blake was secretly connected.

For after all, the victim was a writer and painter wholly devoted to the field of myth, dream, terror, and superstition, and avid in his quest for scenes and effects of a bizarre, spectral sort. His earlier stay in the city—a visit to a strange old man as deeply given to occult and forbidden lore as he—had ended amidst death and flame, and it must have been some morbid instinct which drew him back from his home in Milwaukee. He may have known of the old stories despite his statements

*Originally published in *Weird Tales*, December 1936.

to the contrary in the diary, and his death may have nipped in the bud some stupendous hoax destined to have a literary reflection.

Among those, however, who have examined and correlated all this evidence, there remain several who cling to less rational and commonplace theories. They are inclined to take much of Blake's diary at its face value, and point significantly to certain facts such as the undoubted genuineness of the old church record, the verified existence of the disliked and unorthodox Starry Wisdom sect prior to 1877, the recorded disappearance of an inquisitive reporter named Edwin M. Lillibridge in 1893, and—above all—the look of monstrous, transfiguring fear on the face of the young writer when he died. It was one of these believers who, moved to fanatical extremes, threw into the bay the curiously angled stone and its strangely adorned metal box found in the old church steeple—the black windowless steeple, and not the tower where Blake's diary said those things originally were. Though widely censured both officially and unofficially, this man—a reputable physician with a taste for odd folklore—averred that he had rid the earth of something too dangerous to rest upon it.

Between these two schools of opinion the reader must judge for himself. The papers have given the tangible details from a sceptical angle, leaving for others the drawing of the picture as Robert Blake saw it—or thought he saw it—or pretended to see it. Now, studying the diary closely, dispassionately, and at leisure, let us summarise the dark chain of events from the expressed point of view of their chief actor.

Young Blake returned to Providence in the winter of 1934–5, taking the upper floor of a venerable dwelling in a grassy court off College Street—on the crest of the great eastward hill near the Brown University campus and behind the marble John Hay Library. It was a cosy and fascinating place, in a little garden oasis of village-like antiquity where huge, friendly cats sunned themselves atop a convenient shed. The square Georgian house had a monitor roof, classic doorway with fan carving, small-paned windows, and all the other earmarks of early-nineteenth-century workmanship. Inside were six-panelled doors, wide floor-boards, a curving colonial staircase, white Adam-period mantels, and a rear set of rooms three steps below the general level.

Blake's study, a large southwest chamber, overlooked the front garden on one side, while its west windows—before one of which he had his desk—faced off from the brow of the hill and commanded a splendid view of the lower town's outspread roofs and of the mystical sunsets that flamed behind them. On the far horizon were the open countryside's purple slopes. Against these, some two miles away, rose the spectral hump of Federal Hill, bristling with huddled roofs and steeples whose remote outlines wavered mysteriously, taking fantastic forms as the smoke of the city swirled up and enmeshed them. Blake had a curious sense that he was looking upon some unknown, ethereal world which might or might not vanish as in a dream if ever he tried to seek it out and enter it in person.

Having sent home for most of his books, Blake bought some antique furniture suitable to his quarters and settled down to write and paint—living alone, and attending to the simple housework himself. His studio was in a north attic room, where the panes of the monitor roof furnished admirable lighting. During that first winter he produced five of his best-known short stories—"The Burrower Beneath," "The Stairs in the Crypt," "Shaggai," "In the Vale of Pnath," and "The Feaster from the Stars"—and painted seven canvases; studies of nameless, unhuman monsters, and profoundly alien, non-terrestrial landscapes.

At sunset he would often sit at his desk and gaze dreamily off at the outspread west—the dark towers of Memorial Hall just below, the Georgian court-house belfry, the lofty pinnacles of the downtown section, and that shimmering, spire-crowned mound in the distance whose unknown streets and labyrinthine gables so potently provoked his fancy. From his few local acquaintances he learned that the far-off slope was a vast Italian quarter, though most of the houses were remnants of older Yankee and Irish days. Now and then he would train his field-glasses on that spectral, unreachable world beyond the curling smoke; picking out individual roofs and chimneys and steeples, and speculating upon the bizarre and curious mysteries they might house. Even with optical aid Federal Hill seemed somehow alien, half fabulous, and linked to the unreal, intangible marvels of Blake's own tales and pictures. The feeling would persist long after the hill had faded into the violet, lamp-starred twilight, and the court-house floodlights and the red Industrial Trust beacon had blazed up to make the night grotesque.

Of all the distant objects on Federal Hill, a certain huge, dark church most fascinated Blake. It stood out with especial distinctness at certain hours of the day, and at sunset the great tower and tapering steeple loomed blackly against the flaming sky. It seemed to rest on especially high ground; for the grimy facade, and the obliquely seen north side with sloping roof and the tops of great pointed windows, rose boldly above the tangle of surrounding ridgepoles and chimney-pots. Peculiarly grim and austere, it appeared to be built of stone, stained and weathered with the smoke and storms of a century and more. The style, so far as the glass could shew, was that earliest experimental form of Gothic revival which preceded the stately Upjohn period and held over some of the outlines and proportions of the Georgian age. Perhaps it was reared around 1810 or 1815.

As months passed, Blake watched the far-off, forbidding structure with an oddly mounting interest. Since the vast windows were never lighted, he knew that it must be vacant. The longer he watched, the more his imagination worked, till at length he began to fancy curious things. He believed that a vague, singular aura of desolation hovered over the place, so that even the pigeons and swallows shunned its smoky eaves. Around other towers and belfries his glass would reveal great flocks of birds, but here they never rested. At least, that is what he thought and set down in his diary. He pointed the place out to several friends, but none of them had ever been on Federal Hill or possessed the faintest notion of what the church was or had been.

In the spring a deep restlessness gripped Blake. He had begun his long-planned novel—based on a supposed survival of the witch-cult in Maine—but was strangely unable to make progress with it. More and more he would sit at his westward window and gaze at the distant hill and the black, frowning steeple shunned by the birds. When the delicate leaves came out on the garden boughs the world was filled with a new beauty, but Blake's restlessness was merely increased. It was then that he first thought of crossing the city and climbing bodily up that fabulous slope into the smoke-wreathed world of dream.

Late in April, just before the aeon-shadowed Walpurgis time, Blake made his first trip into the unknown. Plodding through the endless downtown streets and the bleak, decayed squares beyond, he came finally upon the ascending avenue of century-worn steps, sagging Doric porches, and blear-paned cupolas which he felt must lead up to the long-known, unreachable world beyond the mists. There were dingy blue-and-white street signs which meant nothing to him, and presently he noted the strange, dark faces of the drifting crowds, and the foreign signs over curious shops in brown, decade-weathered buildings. Nowhere could he find any of the objects he had seen from afar; so that once more he half fancied that the Federal Hill of that distant view was a dream-world never to be trod by living human feet.

Now and then a battered church facade or crumbling spire came in sight, but never the blackened pile that he sought. When he asked a shopkeeper about a great stone church the man smiled and shook his head, though he spoke English freely. As Blake climbed higher, the region seemed stranger and stranger, with bewildering mazes of brooding brown alleys leading eternally off to the south. He crossed two or three broad avenues, and once thought he glimpsed a familiar tower. Again he asked a merchant about the massive church of stone, and this time he could have sworn that the plea of ignorance was feigned. The dark man's face had a look of fear which he tried to hide, and Blake saw him make a curious sign with his right hand.

Then suddenly a black spire stood out against the cloudy sky on his left, above the tiers of brown roofs lining the tangled southerly alleys.

Blake knew at once what it was, and plunged toward it through the squalid, unpaved lanes that climbed from the avenue. Twice he lost his way, but he somehow dared not ask any of the patriarchs or housewives who sat on their doorsteps, or any of the children who shouted and played in the mud of the shadowy lanes.

At last he saw the tower plain against the southwest, and a huge stone bulk rose darkly at the end of an alley. Presently he stood in a windswept open square, quaintly cobblestoned, with a high bank wall on the farther side. This was the end of his quest; for upon the wide, iron-railed, weed-grown plateau which the wall supported—a separate, lesser world raised fully six feet above the surrounding streets—there stood a grim, titan bulk whose identity, despite Blake's new perspective, was beyond dispute.

The vacant church was in a state of great decrepitude. Some of the high stone buttresses had fallen, and several delicate finials lay half lost among the brown, neglected weeds and grasses. The sooty Gothic windows were largely unbroken, though many of the stone mullions were missing. Blake wondered how the obscurely painted panes could have survived so well, in view of the known habits of small boys the world over. The massive doors were intact and tightly closed. Around the top of the bank wall, fully enclosing the grounds, was a rusty iron fence whose gate—at the head of a flight of steps from the square—was visibly padlocked. The path from the gate to the building was completely overgrown. Desolation and decay hung like a pall above the place, and in the birdless eaves and black, ivyless walls Blake felt a touch of the dimly sinister beyond his power to define.

There were very few people in the square, but Blake saw a policeman at the northerly end and approached him with questions about the church. He was a great wholesome Irishman, and it seemed odd that he would do little more than make the sign of the cross and mutter that people never spoke of that building. When Blake pressed him he said very hurriedly that the Italian priests warned everybody against it, vowing that a monstrous evil had once dwelt there and left its mark. He himself had heard dark whispers of it from his father, who recalled certain sounds and rumours from his boyhood.

There had been a bad sect there in the old days—an outlaw sect that called up awful things from some unknown gulf of night. It had taken a good priest to exorcise what had come, though there did be those who said that merely the light could do it. If Father O'Malley were alive there would be many the thing he could tell. But now there was nothing to do but let it alone. It hurt nobody now, and those that owned it were dead or far away. They had run away like rats after the threatening talk in '77, when people began to mind the way folks vanished now and then in the neighbourhood. Some day the city would step in and take the property for lack of heirs, but little good would come of anybody's touching it. Better it be left alone for the years to topple, lest things be stirred that ought to rest forever in their black abyss.

After the policeman had gone Blake stood staring at the sullen steepled pile. It excited him to find that the structure seemed as sinister to others as to him, and he wondered what grain of truth might lie behind the old tales the bluecoat had repeated. Probably they were mere legends evoked by the evil look of the place, but even so, they were like a strange coming to life of one of his own stories.

The afternoon sun came out from behind dispersing clouds, but seemed unable to light up the stained, sooty walls of the old temple that towered on its high plateau. It was odd that the green of spring had not touched the brown, withered growths in the raised, iron-fenced yard. Blake found himself edging nearer the raised area and examining the bank wall and rusted fence for possible avenues of ingress. There was a terrible lure about the blackened fane which was not to be resisted. The fence had no opening near the steps, but around on the north side were some missing bars. He could go up the steps and walk around on the narrow coping outside the fence till he came to the gap. If the people feared the place so wildly, he would encounter no interference.

He was on the embankment and almost inside the fence before anyone noticed him. Then, looking down, he saw the few people in the square edging away and making the same sign with their right hands that the shopkeeper in the avenue had made. Several windows were slammed down, and a fat woman darted into the street and pulled some small children inside a rickety, unpainted house. The gap in the fence was very easy to pass through, and before long Blake found himself wading amidst the rotting, tangled growths of the deserted yard. Here and there the worn stump of a headstone told him that there had once been burials in this field; but that, he saw, must have been very long ago. The sheer bulk of the church was oppressive now that he was close to it, but he conquered his mood and approached to try the three great doors in the facade. All were securely locked, so he began a circuit of the Cyclopean building in quest of some minor and more penetrable opening. Even then he could not be sure that he wished to enter that haunt of desertion and shadow, yet the pull of its strangeness dragged him on automatically.

A yawning and unprotected cellar window in the rear furnished the needed aperture. Peering in, Blake saw a subterrene gulf of cobwebs and dust faintly litten by the western sun's filtered rays. Debris, old barrels, and ruined boxes and furniture of numerous sorts met his eye, though over everything lay a shroud of dust which softened all sharp outlines. The rusted remains of a hot-air furnace shewed that the building had been used and kept in shape as late as mid-Victorian times.

Acting almost without conscious initiative, Blake crawled through the window and let himself down to the dust-carpeted and debris-strown concrete floor. The vaulted cellar was a vast one, without partitions; and in a corner far to the right, amid dense shadows, he saw a black archway evidently leading upstairs. He felt a peculiar sense of oppression at being actually within the great spectral building, but kept it in check as he cautiously scouted about—finding a still-intact barrel amid the dust, and rolling it over to the open window to provide for his exit. Then, bracing himself, he crossed the wide, cobweb-festooned space toward the arch. Half choked with the omnipresent dust, and covered with ghostly gossamer fibres, he reached and began to climb the worn stone steps which rose into the darkness. He had no light, but groped carefully with his hands. After a sharp turn he felt a closed door ahead, and a little fumbling revealed its ancient latch. It opened inward, and beyond it he saw a dimly illumined corridor lined with worm-eaten panelling.

Once on the ground floor, Blake began exploring in a rapid fashion. All the inner doors were unlocked, so that he freely passed from room to room. The colossal nave was an almost eldritch place with its drifts and mountains of dust over box pews, altar, hourglass pulpit, and sounding-board, and its titanic ropes of cobweb stretching among the pointed arches of the gallery and entwining the clustered Gothic columns. Over all this hushed desolation played a hideous leaden light as the declining afternoon sun sent its rays through the strange, half-blackened panes of the great apsidal windows.

The paintings on those windows were so obscured by soot that Blake could scarcely decipher what they had represented, but from the little he could make out he did not like them. The designs were largely conventional, and his knowledge of obscure symbolism told him much concerning some of the ancient patterns. The few saints depicted bore expressions distinctly open to criticism, while one of the windows seemed to shew merely a dark space with spirals of curious luminosity scattered about in it. Turning away from the windows, Blake noticed that the cobwebbed cross above the altar was not of the ordinary kind, but resembled the primordial ankh or crux ansata of shadowy Egypt.

In a rear vestry room beside the apse Blake found a rotting desk and ceiling-high shelves of mildewed, disintegrating books. Here for the first time he received a positive shock of objective horror, for the titles of those books told him much. They were the black, forbidden things which most sane people have never even heard of, or have heard of only in furtive, timorous whispers; the banned and dreaded repositories of equivocal secrets and immemorial formulae which have trickled down the stream of time from the days of man's youth, and the dim, fabulous days before man was. He had himself read many of them—a Latin version of the abhorred *Necronomicon*, the sinister *Liber Ivonis*, the infamous *Cultes des Goules* of Comte d'Erlette, the *Unaussprechlichen Kulten* of von Junzt, and old Ludvig Prinn's hellish *De Vermis Mysteriis*. But there were others he had known merely by reputation or not at all—the *Pnakotic Manuscripts*, the *Book of Dzyan*, and a crumbling volume in wholly unidentifiable characters yet with certain symbols and diagrams shudderingly recognisable to the occult student. Clearly, the lingering local rumours had not lied. This place had once been the seat of an evil older than mankind and wider than the known universe.

In the ruined desk was a small leather-bound record-book filled with entries in some odd cryptographic medium. The manuscript writing consisted of the common traditional symbols used today in astronomy and anciently in alchemy, astrology, and other dubious arts—the devices of the sun, moon, planets, aspects, and zodiacal signs—here massed in solid pages of text, with divisions and paragraphings suggesting that each symbol answered to some alphabetical letter.

In the hope of later solving the cryptogram, Blake bore off this volume in his coat pocket. Many of the great tomes on the shelves fascinated him unutterably, and he felt tempted to borrow them at some later time. He wondered how they could have remained undisturbed so long. Was he the first to conquer the clutching, pervasive fear which had for nearly sixty years protected this deserted place from visitors?

Having now thoroughly explored the ground floor, Blake ploughed again through the dust of the spectral nave to the front vestibule, where he had seen a door and staircase presumably leading up to the blackened tower and steeple—objects so long familiar to him at a distance. The ascent was a choking experience, for dust lay thick, while the spiders had done their worst in this constricted place. The staircase was a spiral with high, narrow wooden treads, and now and then Blake passed a clouded window looking dizzily out over the city. Though he had seen no ropes below, he expected to find a bell or peal of bells in the tower whose narrow, louver-boarded lancet windows his field-glass had studied so often. Here he was doomed to disappointment; for when he attained the top of the stairs he found the tower chamber vacant of chimes, and clearly devoted to vastly different purposes.

The room, about fifteen feet square, was faintly lighted by four lancet windows, one on each side, which were glazed within their screening of decaying louver-boards. These had been further fitted with tight, opaque screens, but the latter were now largely rotted away. In the centre of the dust-laden floor rose a curiously angled stone pillar some four feet in height and two in average diameter, covered on each side with bizarre, crudely incised, and wholly unrecognisable hieroglyphs. On this pillar rested a metal box of peculiarly asymmetrical form; its hinged lid thrown back, and its interior holding what looked beneath the decade-deep dust to be an egg-shaped or irregularly spherical object some four inches through. Around the pillar in a rough circle were seven high-backed Gothic chairs still largely intact, while behind them, ranging along the dark-panelled walls, were seven colossal images of crumbling, black-painted plaster, resembling more than anything else the cryptic carven megaliths of mysterious Easter Island. In one corner of the cobwebbed chamber a ladder was built into the wall, leading up to the closed trap-door of the windowless steeple above.

As Blake grew accustomed to the feeble light he noticed odd bas-reliefs on the strange open box of yellowish metal. Approaching, he tried to clear the dust away with his hands and handkerchief, and saw that the figurings were of a monstrous and utterly alien kind; depicting entities which, though seemingly alive, resembled no known life-form ever evolved on this planet. The four-inch seeming sphere turned out to be a nearly black, red-striated polyhedron with many irregular flat surfaces; either a very remarkable crystal of some sort, or an artificial object of carved and highly polished mineral matter. It did not touch the bottom of the box, but was held suspended by means of a metal band around its centre, with seven queerly designed supports extending horizontally to angles of the box's inner wall near the top. This stone, once exposed, exerted upon Blake an almost alarming fascination. He could scarcely tear his eyes from it, and as he looked at its glistening surfaces he almost fancied it was transparent, with half-formed worlds of wonder within. Into his mind floated pictures of alien orbs with great stone towers, and other orbs with titan mountains and no mark of life, and still remoter spaces where only a stirring in vague blacknesses told of the presence of consciousness and will.

When he did look away, it was to notice a somewhat singular mound of dust in the far corner near the ladder to the steeple. Just why it took his attention he could not tell, but something in its contours carried a message to his unconscious mind. Ploughing toward it, and brushing aside the hanging cobwebs as he went, he began to discern something grim about it. Hand and handkerchief soon revealed the truth, and Blake gasped with a baffling mixture of emotions. It was a human skeleton, and it must have been there for a very long time. The clothing was in shreds, but some buttons and fragments of cloth bespoke a man's grey suit. There were other bits of evidence—shoes, metal clasps, huge buttons for round cuffs, a stickpin of bygone pattern, a reporter's badge with the name of the old *Providence Telegram*, and a crumbling leather pocketbook. Blake examined the latter with care, finding within it several bills of antiquated issue, a celluloid advertising calendar for 1893, some cards with the name "Edwin M. Lillibridge," and a paper covered with pencilled memoranda.

This paper held much of a puzzling nature, and Blake read it carefully at the dim westward window. Its disjointed text included such phrases as the following:

"Prof. Enoch Bowen home from Egypt May 1844—buys old Free-Will Church in July—his archaeological work & studies in occult well known."

"Dr. Drowne of 4th Baptist warns against Starry Wisdom in sermon Dec. 29, 1844."

"Congregation 97 by end of '45."

"1846—3 disappearances—first mention of Shining Trapezohedron."

"7 disappearances 1848—stories of blood sacrifice begin."

"Investigation 1853 comes to nothing—stories of sounds."

"Fr. O'Malley tells of devil-worship with box found in great Egyptian ruins—says they call up something that can't exist in light. Flees a little light, and banished by strong light. Then has to be summoned again. Probably got this from deathbed confession of Francis X. Feeney, who had joined Starry Wisdom in '49. These people say the Shining Trapezohedron shews them heaven & other worlds, & that the Haunter of the Dark tells them secrets in some way."

"Story of Orrin B. Eddy 1857. They call it up by gazing at the crystal, & have a secret language of their own."

"200 or more in cong. 1863, exclusive of men at front."

"Irish boys mob church in 1869 after Patrick Regan's disappearance."

"Veiled article in J. March 14, '72, but people don't talk about it."

"6 disappearances 1876—secret committee calls on Mayor Doyle."

"Action promised Feb. 1877—church closes in April."

"Gang—Federal Hill Boys—threaten Dr. —— and vestrymen in May."

"181 persons leave city before end of '77—mention no names."

"Ghost stories begin around 1880—try to ascertain truth of report that no human being has entered church since 1877."

"Ask Lanigan for photograph of place taken 1851." . . .

Restoring the paper to the pocketbook and placing the latter in his coat, Blake turned to look down at the skeleton in the dust. The implications of the notes were clear, and there could be no doubt but that this man had come to the deserted edifice forty-two years before in quest of a newspaper sensation which no one else had been bold enough to attempt. Perhaps no one else had known of his plan—who could tell? But he had never returned to his paper. Had some bravely suppressed fear risen to overcome him and bring on sudden heart-failure? Blake stooped over the gleaming bones and noted their peculiar state. Some of them were badly scattered, and a few seemed oddly *dissolved* at the ends. Others were strangely yellowed, with vague suggestions of charring. This charring extended to some of the fragments of clothing. The skull was in a very peculiar state—stained yellow, and with a charred aperture in the top as if some powerful acid had eaten through the solid bone. What had happened to the skeleton during its four decades of silent entombment here Blake could not imagine.

Before he realised it, he was looking at the stone again, and letting its curious influence call up a nebulous pageantry in his mind. He saw processions of robed, hooded figures whose outlines were not human, and looked on endless leagues of desert lined with carved, sky-reaching monoliths. He saw towers and walls in nighted depths under the sea, and vortices of space where wisps of black mist floated before thin shimmerings of cold purple haze. And beyond all else he glimpsed an infinite gulf of darkness, where solid and semi-solid forms were known only by their windy stirrings, and cloudy patterns of force seemed to superimpose order on chaos and hold forth a key to all the paradoxes and arcana of the worlds we know.

Then all at once the spell was broken by an access of gnawing, indeterminate panic fear. Blake choked and turned away from the stone, conscious of some formless alien presence close to him and watching him with horrible intentness. He felt entangled with something—something which was not in the stone, but which had looked through it at him—something which would ceaselessly follow him with a cognition that was not physical sight. Plainly, the place was getting on his nerves—as well it might in view of his gruesome find. The light was waning, too, and since he had no illuminant with him he knew he would have to be leaving soon.

It was then, in the gathering twilight, that he thought he saw a faint trace of luminosity in the crazily angled stone. He had tried to look away from it, but some obscure compulsion drew his eyes back. Was there a subtle phosphorescence of radio-activity about the thing? What was it that the dead man's notes had said concerning a *Shining Trapezohedron*? What, anyway, was this abandoned lair of cosmic evil? What had been done here, and what might still be lurking in the bird-shunned shadows? It seemed now as if an elusive touch of foetor had arisen somewhere close by, though its source was not apparent. Blake seized the cover of the long-open box and snapped it down. It moved easily on its alien hinges, and closed completely over the unmistakably glowing stone.

At the sharp click of that closing a soft stirring sound seemed to come from the steeple's eternal blackness overhead, beyond the trapdoor. Rats, without question—the only living things to reveal their presence in this accursed pile since he had entered it. And yet that stirring in the steeple frightened him horribly, so that he plunged almost wildly down the spiral stairs, across the ghoulish nave, into the vaulted basement, out amidst the gathering dusk of the deserted square, and down through the teeming, fear-haunted alleys and avenues of Federal Hill toward the sane central streets and the home-like brick sidewalks of the college district.

During the days which followed, Blake told no one of his expedition. Instead, he read much in certain books, examined long years of newspaper files downtown, and worked feverishly at the cryptogram in that leather volume from the cobwebbed vestry room. The cipher, he soon saw, was no simple one; and after a long period of endeavour he felt sure that its language could not be English, Latin, Greek, French, Spanish, Italian, or German. Evidently, he would have to draw upon the deepest wells of his strange erudition.

Every evening the old impulse to gaze westward returned, and he saw the black steeple as of yore amongst the bristling roofs of a distant and half-fabulous world. But now it held a fresh note of terror for him. He knew the heritage of evil lore it masked, and with the knowledge his vision ran riot in queer new ways. The birds of spring were returning, and as he watched their sunset flights he fancied they avoided the gaunt, lone spire as never before. When a flock of them approached it, he thought, they would wheel and scatter in panic confusion—and he could guess at the wild twitterings which failed to reach him across the intervening miles.

It was in June that Blake's diary told of his victory over the cryptogram. The text was, he found, in the dark Aklo language used by certain cults of evil antiquity, and known to him in a halting way through previous researches. The diary is strangely reticent about what Blake deciphered, but he was patently awed and disconcerted by his results. There are references to a Haunter of the Dark awaked by gazing into the Shining Trapezohedron, and insane conjectures about the black gulfs of chaos from which it was called. The being is spoken of as holding all knowledge, and demanding monstrous sacrifices. Some of Blake's entries shew fear lest the thing, which he seemed to regard as summoned, stalk abroad; though he adds that the street-lights form a bulwark which cannot be crossed.

Of the Shining Trapezohedron he speaks often, calling it a window on all time and space, and tracing its history from the days it was fashioned on dark Yuggoth, before ever the Old Ones brought it to earth. It was treasured and placed in its curious box by the crinoid things of

Antarctica, salvaged from their ruins by the serpent-men of Valusia, and peered at aeons later in Lemuria by the first human beings. It crossed strange lands and stranger seas, and sank with Atlantis before a Minoan fisher meshed it in his net and sold it to swarthy merchants from nighted Khem. The Pharaoh Nephren-Ka built around it a temple with a windowless crypt, and did that which caused his name to be stricken from all monuments and records. Then it slept in the ruins of that evil fane which the priests and the new Pharaoh destroyed, till the delver's spade once more brought it forth to curse mankind.

Early in July the newspapers oddly supplement Blake's entries, though in so brief and casual a way that only the diary has called general attention to their contribution. It appears that a new fear had been growing on Federal Hill since a stranger had entered the dreaded church. The Italians whispered of unaccustomed stirrings and bumpings and scrapings in the dark windowless steeple, and called on their priests to banish an entity which haunted their dreams. Something, they said, was constantly watching at a door to see if it were dark enough to venture forth. Press items mentioned the long-standing local superstitions, but failed to shed much light on the earlier background of the horror. It was obvious that the young reporters of today are no antiquarians. In writing of these things in his diary, Blake expresses a curious kind of remorse, and talks of the duty of burying the Shining Trapezohedron and of banishing what he had evoked by letting daylight into the hideous jutting spire. At the same time, however, he displays the dangerous extent of his fascination, and admits a morbid longing—pervading even his dreams—to visit the accursed tower and gaze again into the cosmic secrets of the glowing stone.

Then something in the *Journal* on the morning of July 17 threw the diarist into a veritable fever of horror. It was only a variant of the other half-humourous items about the Federal Hill restlessness, but to Blake it was somehow very terrible indeed. In the night a thunderstorm had put the city's lighting-system out of commission for a full hour, and in that black interval the Italians had nearly gone mad with fright. Those living near the dreaded church had sworn that the thing in the steeple had taken advantage of the street-lamps' absence and gone down into the body of the church, flopping and bumping around in a viscous, altogether dreadful way. Toward the last it had bumped up to the tower, where there were sounds of the shattering of glass. It could go wherever the darkness reached, but light would always send it fleeing.

When the current blazed on again there had been a shocking commotion in the tower, for even the feeble light trickling through the grime-blackened, louver-boarded windows was too much for the thing. It had bumped and slithered up into its tenebrous steeple just in time—for a long dose of light would have sent it back into the abyss whence the crazy stranger had called it. During the dark hour praying crowds had clustered round the church in the rain with lighted candles and lamps somehow shielded with folded paper and umbrellas—a guard of light to save the city from the nightmare that stalks in darkness. Once, those nearest the church declared, the outer door had rattled hideously.

But even this was not the worst. That evening in the *Bulletin* Blake read of what the reporters had found. Aroused at last to the whimsical news value of the scare, a pair of them had defied the frantic crowds of Italians and crawled into the church through the cellar window after trying the doors in vain. They found the dust of the vestibule and of the spectral nave ploughed up in a singular way, with bits of rotted cushions and satin pew-linings scattered curiously around. There was a bad odour everywhere, and here and there were bits of yellow stain and patches of what looked like charring. Opening the door to the tower, and pausing a moment at the suspicion of a scraping sound above, they found the narrow spiral stairs wiped roughly clean.

In the tower itself a similarly half-swept condition existed. They spoke of the heptagonal stone pillar, the overturned Gothic chairs, and the bizarre plaster images; though strangely enough the metal box and the old mutilated skeleton were not mentioned. What disturbed Blake the most—except for the hints of stains and charring and bad odours—was the final detail that explained the crashing glass. Every one of the tower's lancet windows was broken, and two of them had been darkened in a crude and hurried way by the stuffing of satin pew-linings and cushion-horsehair into the spaces between the slanting exterior louver-boards. More satin fragments and bunches of horsehair lay scattered around the newly swept floor, as if someone had been interrupted in the act of restoring the tower to the absolute blackness of its tightly curtained days.

Yellowish stains and charred patches were found on the ladder to the windowless spire, but when a reporter climbed up, opened the horizontally sliding trap-door, and shot a feeble flashlight beam into the black and strangely foetid space, he saw nothing but darkness, and an heterogeneous litter of shapeless fragments near the aperture. The verdict, of course, was charlatanry. Somebody had played a joke on the superstitious hill-dwellers, or else some fanatic had striven to bolster up their fears for their own supposed good. Or perhaps some of the younger and more sophisticated dwellers had staged an elaborate hoax on the outside world. There was an amusing aftermath when the police sent an officer to verify the reports. Three men in succession found ways of evading the assignment, and the fourth went very reluctantly and returned very soon without adding to the account given by the reporters.

From this point onward Blake's diary shews a mounting tide of insidious horror and nervous apprehension. He upbraids himself for not doing something, and speculates wildly on the consequences of another electrical breakdown. It has been verified that on three occasions—during thunderstorms—he telephoned the electric light company in a frantic vein and asked that desperate precautions against a lapse of power be taken. Now and then his entries shew concern over the failure of the reporters to find the metal box and stone, and the strangely marred old skeleton, when they explored the shadowy tower room. He assumed that these things had been removed—whither, and by whom or what, he could only guess. But his worst fears concerned himself, and the kind of unholy rapport he felt to exist between his mind and that lurking horror in the distant steeple—that monstrous thing of night which his rashness had called out of the ultimate black spaces. He seemed to feel a constant tugging at his will, and callers of that period remember how he would sit abstractedly at his desk and stare out of the west window at that far-off, spire-bristling mound beyond the swirling smoke of the city. His entries dwell monotonously on certain terrible dreams, and of a strengthening of the unholy rapport in his sleep. There is mention of a night when he awaked to find himself fully dressed, outdoors, and headed automatically down College Hill toward the west. Again and again he dwells on the fact that the thing in the steeple knows where to find him.

The week following July 30 is recalled as the time of Blake's partial breakdown. He did not dress, and ordered all his food by telephone. Visitors remarked the cords he kept near his bed, and he said that sleep-walking had forced him to bind his ankles every night with knots which would probably hold or else waken him with the labour of untying.

In his diary he told of the hideous experience which had brought the collapse. After retiring on the night of the 30th he had suddenly found himself groping about in an almost black space. All he could see were short, faint, horizontal streaks of bluish light, but he could smell an overpowering foetor and hear a curious jumble of soft, furtive sounds above him. Whenever he moved he stumbled over something, and at each noise there would come a sort of answering sound from above—a vague stirring, mixed with the cautious sliding of wood on wood.

Once his groping hands encountered a pillar of stone with a vacant top, whilst later he found himself clutching the rungs of a ladder built into the wall, and fumbling his uncertain way upward toward some region of intenser stench where a hot, searing blast beat down against him. Before his eyes a kaleidoscopic range of phantasmal images played, all of them dissolving at intervals into the picture of a vast, unplumbed abyss of night wherein whirled suns and worlds of an even profounder blackness. He thought of the ancient legends of Ultimate Chaos, at whose centre sprawls the blind idiot god Azathoth, Lord of All Things, encircled by his flopping horde of mindless and amorphous dancers, and lulled by the thin monotonous piping of a daemoniac flute held in nameless paws.

Then a sharp report from the outer world broke through his stupor and roused him to the unutterable horror of his position. What it was, he never knew—perhaps it was some belated peal from the fireworks heard all summer on Federal Hill as the dwellers hail their various patron saints, or the saints of their native villages in Italy. In any event he shrieked aloud, dropped frantically from the ladder, and stumbled blindly across the obstructed floor of the almost lightless chamber that encompassed him.

He knew instantly where he was, and plunged recklessly down the narrow spiral staircase, tripping and bruising himself at every turn. There was a nightmare flight through a vast cobwebbed nave whose ghostly arches reached up to realms of leering shadow, a sightless scramble through a littered basement, a climb to regions of air and street-lights outside, and a mad racing down a spectral hill of gibbering gables, across a grim, silent city of tall black towers, and up the steep eastward precipice to his own ancient door.

On regaining consciousness in the morning he found himself lying on his study floor fully dressed. Dirt and cobwebs covered him, and every inch of his body seemed sore and bruised. When he faced the mirror he saw that his hair was badly scorched, while a trace of strange, evil odour seemed to cling to his upper outer clothing. It was then that his nerves broke down. Thereafter, lounging exhaustedly about in a dressing-gown, he did little but stare from his west window, shiver at the threat of thunder, and make wild entries in his diary.

The great storm broke just before midnight on August 8th. Lightning struck repeatedly in all parts of the city, and two remarkable fireballs were reported. The rain was torrential, while a constant fusillade of thunder brought sleeplessness to thousands. Blake was utterly frantic in his fear for the lighting system, and tried to telephone the company around 1 A.M., though by that time service had been temporarily cut off in the interest of safety. He recorded everything in his diary—the large, nervous, and often undecipherable hieroglyphics telling their own story of growing frenzy and despair, and of entries scrawled blindly in the dark.

He had to keep the house dark in order to see out the window, and it appears that most of his time was spent at his desk, peering anxiously through the rain across the glistening miles of downtown roofs at the constellation of distant lights marking Federal Hill. Now and then he would fumblingly make an entry in his diary, so that detached phrases such as "The lights must not go"; "It knows where I am"; "I must destroy it"; and "It is calling to me, but perhaps it means no injury this time"; are found scattered down two of the pages.

Then the lights went out all over the city. It happened at 2:12 A.M., according to power-house records, but Blake's diary gives no indication of the time. The entry is merely, "Lights out—God help me." On Federal Hill there were watchers as anxious as he, and rain-soaked knots of men paraded the square and alleys around the evil church with umbrella-shaded candles, electric flashlights, oil lanterns, crucifixes, and obscure charms of the many sorts common to southern Italy. They blessed each flash of lightning, and made cryptical signs of fear with their right hands when a turn in the storm caused the flashes to lessen and finally to cease altogether. A rising wind blew out most of the candles, so that the scene grew threateningly dark. Someone roused Father Merluzzo of Spirito Santo Church, and he hastened to the dismal square to pronounce whatever helpful syllables he could. Of the restless and curious sounds in the blackened tower, there could be no doubt whatever.

For what happened at 2:35 we have the testimony of the priest, a young, intelligent, and well-educated person; of Patrolman William J. Monahan of the Central Station, an officer of the highest reliability who had paused at that part of his beat to inspect the crowd; and of most of the seventy-eight men who had gathered around the church's high bank wall—especially those in the square where the eastward facade was visible. Of course there was nothing which can be proved as being outside the order of Nature. The possible causes of such an event are many. No one can speak with certainty of the obscure chemical processes arising in a vast, ancient, ill-aired, and long-deserted building of heterogeneous contents. Mephitic vapours—spontaneous combustion—pressure of gases born of long decay—any one of numberless phenomena might be responsible. And then, of course, the factor of conscious charlatanry can by no means be excluded. The thing was really quite simple in itself, and covered less than three minutes of actual time. Father Merluzzo, always a precise man, looked at his watch repeatedly.

It started with a definite swelling of the dull fumbling sounds inside the black tower. There had for some time been a vague exhalation of strange, evil odours from the church, and this had now become emphatic and offensive. Then at last there was a sound of splintering wood, and a large, heavy object crashed down in the yard beneath the frowning easterly facade. The tower was invisible now that the candles would not burn, but as the object neared the ground the people knew that it was the smoke-grimed louver-boarding of that tower's east window.

Immediately afterward an utterly unbearable foetor welled forth from the unseen heights, choking and sickening the trembling watchers, and almost prostrating those in the square. At the same time the air trembled with a vibration as of flapping wings, and a sudden east-blowing wind more violent than any previous blast snatched off the hats and wrenched the dripping umbrellas of the crowd. Nothing definite could be seen in the candleless night, though some upward-looking spectators thought they glimpsed a great spreading blur of denser blackness against the inky sky—something like a formless cloud of smoke that shot with meteor-like speed toward the east.

That was all. The watchers were half numbed with fright, awe, and discomfort, and scarcely knew what to do, or whether to do anything at all. Not knowing what had happened, they did not relax their vigil; and a moment later they sent up a prayer as a sharp flash of belated lightning, followed by an earsplitting crash of sound, rent the flooded heavens. Half an hour later the rain stopped, and in fifteen minutes more the street-lights sprang on again, sending the weary, bedraggled watchers relievedly back to their homes.

The next day's papers gave these matters minor mention in connexion with the general storm reports. It seems that the great lightning flash and deafening explosion which followed the Federal Hill occurrence were even more tremendous farther east, where a burst of the singular foetor was likewise noticed. The phenomenon was most marked over College Hill, where the crash awaked all the sleeping inhabitants and led to a bewildered round of speculations. Of those who were already awake only a few saw the anomalous blaze of light near the top of the hill, or noticed the inexplicable upward rush of air which almost stripped the leaves from the trees and blasted the plants in the gardens. It was agreed that the lone, sudden lightning-bolt must have struck somewhere in this neighbourhood, though no trace of its striking could afterward be found. A youth in the Tau Omega fraternity house thought he saw a grotesque and hideous mass of smoke in the air just as the preliminary flash burst, but his observation has not been verified. All of the few observers, however, agree as to the violent gust from the west and the flood of intolerable stench which preceded the belated stroke; whilst evidence concerning the momentary burned odour after the stroke is equally general.

These points were discussed very carefully because of their probable connexion with the death of Robert Blake. Students in the Psi Delta house, whose upper rear windows looked into Blake's study, noticed the blurred white face at the westward window on the morning of the

9th, and wondered what was wrong with the expression. When they saw the same face in the same position that evening, they felt worried, and watched for the lights to come up in his apartment. Later they rang the bell of the darkened flat, and finally had a policeman force the door.

The rigid body sat bolt upright at the desk by the window, and when the intruders saw the glassy, bulging eyes, and the marks of stark, convulsive fright on the twisted features, they turned away in sickened dismay. Shortly afterward the coroner's physician made an examination, and despite the unbroken window reported electrical shock, or nervous tension induced by electrical discharge, as the cause of death. The hideous expression he ignored altogether, deeming it a not improbable result of the profound shock as experienced by a person of such abnormal imagination and unbalanced emotions. He deduced these latter qualities from the books, paintings, and manuscripts found in the apartment, and from the blindly scrawled entries in the diary on the desk. Blake had prolonged his frenzied jottings to the last, and the broken-pointed pencil was found clutched in his spasmodically contracted right hand.

The entries after the failure of the lights were highly disjointed, and legible only in part. From them certain investigators have drawn conclusions differing greatly from the materialistic official verdict, but such speculations have little chance for belief among the conservative. The case of these imaginative theorists has not been helped by the action of superstitious Dr. Dexter, who threw the curious box and angled stone—an object certainly self-luminous as seen in the black windowless steeple where it was found—into the deepest channel of Narragansett Bay. Excessive imagination and neurotic unbalance on Blake's part, aggravated by knowledge of the evil bygone cult whose startling traces he had uncovered, form the dominant interpretation given those final frenzied jottings. These are the entries—or all that can be made of them.

"Lights still out—must be five minutes now. Everything depends on lightning. Yaddith grant it will keep up! . . . Some influence seems beating through it. . . . Rain and thunder and wind deafen. . . . The thing is taking hold of my mind. . . .

"Trouble with memory. I see things I never knew before. Other worlds and other galaxies . . . Dark . . . The lightning seems dark and the darkness seems light. . . .

"It cannot be the real hill and church that I see in the pitch-darkness. Must be retinal impression left by flashes. Heaven grant the Italians are out with their candles if the lightning stops!

"What am I afraid of? Is it not an avatar of Nyarlathotep, who in antique and shadowy Khem even took the form of man? I remember Yuggoth, and more distant Shaggai, and the ultimate void of the black planets. . . .

"The long, winging flight through the void . . . cannot cross the universe of light . . . re-created by the thoughts caught in the Shining Trapezohedron . . . send it through the horrible abysses of radiance. . . .

"My name is Blake—Robert Harrison Blake of 620 East Knapp Street, Milwaukee, Wisconsin. . . . I am on this planet. . . .

"Azathoth have mercy!—the lightning no longer flashes—horrible—I can see everything with a monstrous sense that is not sight—light is dark and dark is light . . . those people on the hill . . . guard . . . candles and charms . . . their priests. . . .

"Sense of distance gone—far is near and near is far. No light—no glass—see that steeple—that tower—window—can hear—Roderick Usher—am mad or going mad—the thing is stirring and fumbling in the tower—I am it and it is I—I want to get out . . . must get out and unify the forces. . . . It knows where I am. . . .

"I am Robert Blake, but I see the tower in the dark. There is a monstrous odour . . . senses transfigured . . . boarding at that tower window cracking and giving way. . . . Iä . . . ngai . . . ygg. . . .

"I see it—coming here—hell-wind—titan blur—black wings—Yog-Sothoth save me—the three-lobed burning eye. . . ."

The Shadow from the Steeple*

ROBERT BLOCH

William Hurley was born an Irishman and grew up to be a taxicab driver—therefore it would be redundant, in the face of both of these facts, to say that he was garrulous.

The minute he picked up his passenger in downtown Providence that warm summer evening, he began talking. The passenger, a tall thin man in his early thirties, entered the cab and sat back, clutching a briefcase. He gave an address on Benefit Street and Hurley started out, shifting both taxi and tongue into high gear.

Hurley began what was to be a one-sided conversation by commenting on the afternoon performance of the New York Giants. Unperturbed by his passenger's silence, he made a few remarks about the weather—recent, current, and expected. Since he received no reply, the driver then proceeded to discuss a local phenomenon, namely the reported escape, that morning, of two black panthers or leopards from the traveling menagerie of Langer Brothers Circus, currently appearing in the city. In response to a direct inquiry as to whether he had seen the beasts roaming at large, Hurley's customer shook his head.

The driver then made several uncomplimentary remarks about the local police force and their inability to capture the beasts. It was his considered opinion that a given platoon of law enforcement officers would be unable to catch a cold if immured in an ice-box for a year. This witticism failed to amuse his passenger, and before Hurley could continue his monologue they had arrived at the Benefit Street address. Eighty-five cents changed hands, passenger and briefcase left the cab, and Hurley drove away.

He could not know it at the time, but he thus became the last man who could or would testify to seeing his passenger alive.

The rest is conjecture, and perhaps that is for the best. Certainly it

---

*Originally published in *Weird Tales*, September 1950.

is easy enough to draw certain conclusions as to what happened that night in the old house on Benefit Street, but the weight of those conclusions is hard to bear.

One minor mystery is easy enough to clear up—the peculiar silence and aloofness of Hurley's passenger. That passenger, Edmund Fiske, of Chicago, Illinois, was meditating upon the fulfillment of fifteen years of questing; the cab-trip represented the last stage of this long journey, and he was reviewing the circumstances as he rode.

Edmund Fiske's quest had begun, on August 8, 1935, with the death of his close friend, Robert Harrison Blake, of Milwaukee.

Like Fiske himself at the time, Blake had been a precocious adolescent interested in fantasy-writing, and as such became a member of the "Lovecraft circle"—a group of writers maintaining correspondence with one another and with the late Howard Phillips Lovecraft, of Providence.

It was through correspondence that Fiske and Blake had become acquainted; they visited back and forth between Milwaukee and Chicago, and their mutual preoccupation with the weird and the fantastic in literature and art served to form the foundation for the close friendship which existed at the time of Blake's unexpected and inexplicable demise.

Most of the facts—and certain of the conjectures—in connection with Blake's death have been embodied in Lovecraft's story, "The Haunter of the Dark," which was published more than a year after the younger writer's passing.

Lovecraft had an excellent opportunity to observe matters, for it was on his suggestion that young Blake had journeyed to Providence early in 1935, and had been provided with living-quarters on College Street by Lovecraft himself. So it was both as friend and neighbor that the elder fantasy writer had acted in narrating the singular story of Robert Harrison Blake's last months.

In his story, he tells of Blake's efforts to begin a novel dealing with a survival of New England witch-cults, but modestly omits his own part in assisting his friend to secure material. Apparently Blake began work on his project and then became enmeshed in a horror greater than any envisioned by his imagination.

For Blake was drawn to investigate the crumbling black pile on Federal Hill—the deserted ruin of a church that had once housed the worshippers of an esoteric cult. Early in spring he paid a visit to the shunned structure and there made certain discoveries which (in Lovecraft's opinion) made his death inevitable.

Briefly, Blake entered the boarded-up Free-Will Church and stumbled across the skeleton of a reporter from the *Providence Telegram*, one Edwin M. Lillibridge, who had apparently attempted a similar investigation in 1893. The fact that his death was not explained seemed alarming enough, but more disturbing still was the realization that no one had been bold enough to enter the church since that date and discover the body.

Blake found the reporter's notebook in his clothing, and its contents afforded a partial revelation.

A certain Professor Bowen, of Providence, had traveled widely in Egypt, and in 1843, in the course of archaeological investigations of the crypt of Nephren-Ka, had made an unusual find.

Nephren-Ka is the "forgotten pharaoh," whose name has been cursed by the priests and obliterated from official dynastic records. The name was familiar to the young writer at the time, due largely to the work of another Milwaukee author who had dealt with the semi-legendary ruler in his tale, "Fane of the Black Pharaoh." But the discovery Bowen made in the crypt was totally unexpected.

The reporter's notebook said little of the actual nature of that discovery, but it recorded subsequent events in a precise, chronological fashion. Immediately upon unearthing his mysterious find in Egypt, Professor Bowen abandoned his research and returned to Providence, where he purchased the Free-Will Church in 1844 and made it the headquarters of what was called the "Starry Wisdom" sect.

Members of this religious cult, evidently recruited by Bowen, professed to worship an entity they called the "Haunter of the Dark." By gazing into a crystal they summoned the actual presence of this entity and did homage with blood sacrifice.

Such, at least, was the fantastic story circulated in Providence at the time—and the church became a place to be avoided. Local superstition fanned agitation, and agitation precipitated direct action. In May of 1877 the sect was forcibly broken up by the authorities, due to public pressure, and several hundred of its members abruptly left the city.

The church itself was immediately closed, and apparently individual curiosity could not overcome the widespread fear which resulted in leaving the structure undisturbed and unexplored until the reporter, Lillibridge, made his ill-fated private investigation in 1893.

Such was the gist of the story unfolded in the pages of his notebook. Blake read it, but was nevertheless undeterred in his further scrutiny of the environs. Eventually he came upon the mysterious object Bowen had found in the Egyptian crypt—the object upon which the Starry Wisdom worship had been founded—the asymmetrical metal box with its curiously hinged lid, a lid that had been closed for countless years. Blake thus gazed at the interior, gazed upon the four-inch red-black crystal polyhedron hanging suspended by seven supports. He not only gazed *at* but also *into* the polyhedron; just as the cult-worshippers had purportedly gazed, and with the same results. He was assailed by a curious psychic disturbance; he seemed to "see visions of other lands and the gulfs beyond the stars," as superstitious accounts had told.

And then Blake made his greatest mistake. He closed the box.

Closing the box—again, according to the superstitions annotated by Lillibridge—was the act that summoned the alien entity itself, the Haunter of the Dark. It was a creature of darkness and could not survive light. And in that boarded-up blackness of the ruined church, the thing emerged by night.

Blake fled the church in terror, but the damage was done. In mid-July, a thunderstorm put out the lights in Providence for an hour, and the Italian colony living near the deserted church heard bumping and thumping from inside the shadow-shrouded structure.

Crowds with candles stood outside in the rain and played candles upon the building, shielding themselves against the possible emergence of the feared entity by a barrier of light.

Apparently the story had remained alive throughout the neighborhood. Once the storm abated, local newspapers grew interested, and on the 17th of July two reporters entered the old church, together with a policeman. Nothing definite was found, although there were curious and inexplicable smears and stains on the stairs and the pews.

Less than a month later—at 2:35 A.M. on the morning of August 8th, to be exact—Robert Harrison Blake met his death during an electrical storm while seated before the window of his room on College Street.

During the gathering storm, before his death occurred, Blake scribbled frantically in his diary, gradually revealing his innermost obsessions and delusions concerning the Haunter of the Dark. It was Blake's conviction that by gazing into the curious crystal in its box he had somehow established a linkage with the non-terrestrial entity. He further believed that closing the box had summoned the creature to dwell in the darkness of the church steeple, and that in some way his own fate was now irrevocably linked to that of the monstrosity.

All this is revealed in the last messages he set down while watching the progress of the storm from his window.

Meanwhile, at the church itself, on Federal Hill, a crowd of agitated spectators gathered to play lights upon the structure. That they heard alarming sounds from inside the boarded-up building is undeniable; at least two competent witnesses have testified to the fact. One, Father Merluzzo of the Spirito Santo Church, was on hand to quiet his congregation. The other, Patrolman (now Sergeant) William J. Monahan, of Central Station, was attempting to preserve order in the face of growing panic. Monahan himself saw the blinding "blur" that seemed to issue, smoke-like, from the steeple of the ancient edifice as the final lightning-flash came.

Flash, meteor, fireball—call it what you will—erupted over the city in a blinding blaze; perhaps at the very moment that Robert Harrison Blake, across town, was writing, "Is it not an avatar of Nyarlathotep, who in antique and shadowy Khem even took the form of man?"

A few moments later he was dead. The coroner's physician rendered a verdict attributing his demise to "electrical shock," although the window he faced was unbroken. Another physician, known to Lovecraft, quarreled privately with that verdict and subsequently entered the affair the next day. Without legal authority, he entered the church and climbed to the windowless steeple where he discovered the strange asymmetrical—was it golden?—box and the curious stone within. Apparently his first gesture was to make sure of raising the lid and bringing the stone into the light. His next recorded gesture was to charter a boat, take box and curiously angled stone aboard, and drop them into the deepest channel of Narragansett Bay.

There ended the admittedly fictionalized account of Blake's death as recorded by H. P. Lovecraft. And there began Edmund Fiske's fifteen-year quest.

Fiske, of course, had known some of the events outlined in the story. When Blake had left for Providence in the spring, Fiske had tentatively promised to join him the following autumn. At first, the two friends had exchanged letters regularly, but by early summer Blake ceased correspondence altogether.

At the time, Fiske was unaware of Blake's exploration of the ruined church. He could not account for Blake's silence, and wrote Lovecraft for a possible explanation.

Lovecraft could supply little information. Young Blake, he said, had visited with him frequently during the early weeks of his stay, had consulted him about his writing, and had accompanied him on several nocturnal strolls through the city.

But during the summer, Blake's neighborliness ceased. It was not in Lovecraft's reclusive nature to impose himself upon others, and he did not seek to invade Blake's privacy for several weeks.

When he did so—and learned from the almost hysterical adolescent of his experiences in the forbidding, forbidden church on Federal Hill—Lovecraft offered words of warning and advice. But it was already too late. Within ten days of his visit came the shocking end.

Fiske learned of that end from Lovecraft on the following day. It was his task to break the news to Blake's parents. For a time he was tempted to visit Providence immediately, but lack of funds and the pressure of his own domestic affairs forestalled him. The body of his young friend duly arrived, and Fiske attended the brief ceremony of cremation.

Then Lovecraft began his own investigation—an investigation which ultimately resulted in the publication of his story. And there the matter might have rested.

But Fiske was not satisfied.

His best friend had died under circumstances which even the most skeptical must admit were mysterious. The local authorities summarily wrote off the matter with a fatuous and inadequate explanation.

Fiske determined to ascertain the truth.

Bear in mind one salient fact: all three of these men—Lovecraft, Blake, and Fiske—were professional writers and students of the supernatural or the supranormal. All three of them had extraordinary access to a bulk of written material dealing with ancient legend and superstition. Ironically enough, the use to which they put their knowledge was limited to excursions into so-called fantasy fiction, but none of them, in the light of their own experience, could wholly join their reading audience in scoffing at the myths of which they wrote.

For, as Fiske wrote to Lovecraft, "the term *myth*, as we know, is merely a polite euphemism. Blake's death was not a myth, but a hideous reality. I implore you to investigate fully. See this matter through to the end, for if Blake's diary holds even a distorted truth, there is no telling what may be loosed upon the world."

Lovecraft pledged cooperation, discovered the fate of the metal box and its contents, and endeavored to arrange a meeting with Dr. Ambrose Dexter, of Benefit Street. Dr. Dexter, it appeared, had left town immediately following his dramatic theft and disposal of the "Shining Trapezohedron," as Lovecraft called it.

Lovecraft then apparently interviewed Father Merluzzo and Patrolman Monahan, plunged into the files of the *Bulletin*, and endeavored to reconstruct the story of the Starry Wisdom sect and the entity they worshipped.

Of course he learned a good deal more than he dared to put into his magazine story. His letters to Edmund Fiske in the late fall and early spring of 1936 contain guarded hints and references to "menaces from Outside." But he seemed anxious to reassure Fiske that if there had been any menace, even in the realistic rather than the supernatural sense, the danger was now averted because Dr. Dexter had disposed of the Shining Trapezohedron, which acted as a summoning talisman. Such was the gist of his report, and the matter rested there for a time.

Fiske made tentative arrangements, early in 1937, to visit Lovecraft at his home, with the private intention of doing some further research on his own into the cause of Blake's death. But once again, circumstances intervened. For in March of that year, Lovecraft died. His unexpected passing plunged Fiske into a period of mental despondency from which he was slow to recover; accordingly, it was not until almost a year later that Edmund Fiske paid his first visit to Providence, and to the scene of the tragic episodes which brought Blake's life to a close.

For somehow, always, a black undercurrent of suspicion existed. The coroner's physician had been glib, Lovecraft had been tactful, the press and the general public had accepted matters completely—yet Blake was dead, and there had been an entity abroad in the night.

Fiske felt that if he could visit the accursed church himself, talk to Dr. Dexter and find out what had drawn him into the affair, interrogate the reporters, and pursue any relevant leads or clues, he might eventually hope to uncover the truth and at least clear his dead friend's name of the ugly shadow of mental unbalance.

Accordingly, Fiske's first step after arriving in Providence and registering at a hotel was to set out for Federal Hill and the ruined church.

The search was doomed to immediate, irremediable disappointment. For the church was no more. It had been razed the previous fall and the property taken over by the city authorities. The black and baleful spire no longer cast its spell over the Hill.

Fiske immediately took pains to see Father Merluzzo, at Spirito Santo, a few squares away. He learned from a courteous housekeeper that Father Merluzzo had died in 1936, within a year of young Blake.

Discouraged but persistent, Fiske next attempted to reach Dr. Dexter, but the old house on Benefit Street was boarded up. A call to the Physicians' Service Bureau produced only the cryptic information that Ambrose Dexter, M.D., had left the city for an indeterminate stay.

Nor did a visit with the city editor of the *Bulletin* yield any better result. Fiske was permitted to go into the newspaper's morgue and read the aggravatingly short and matter-of-fact story on Blake's death, but the two reporters who had covered the assignment and subsequently visited the Federal Hill church had left the paper for berths in other cities.

There were, of course, other leads to follow, and during the ensuing week Fiske ran them all to the ground. A copy of *Who's Who* added nothing significant to his mental picture of Dr. Ambrose Dexter. The physician was Providence-born, a lifelong resident, forty years of age, unmarried, a general practitioner, member of several medical societies—but there was no indication of any unusual "hobbies" or "other interests" which might provide a clue as to his participation in the affair.

Sergeant William J. Monahan of Central Station was sought out, and for the first time Fiske actually managed to speak to someone who admitted an actual connection with the events leading to Blake's death. Monahan was polite, but cautiously noncommittal.

Despite Fiske's complete unburdening, the police officer remained discreetly reticent.

"There's really nothing I can tell you," he said. "It's true, like Mr. Lovecraft said, that I was at the church that night, for there was a rough crowd out and there's no telling what some of them ones in the neighborhood will do when riled up. Like the story said, the old church had a bad name, and I guess Sheeley could have given you many's the story."

"Sheeley?" interjected Fiske.

"Bert Sheeley—it was his beat, you know, not mine. He was ill of pneumonia at the time, and I substituted for two weeks. Then, when he died—"

Fiske shook his head. Another possible source of information gone. Blake dead, Lovecraft dead, Father Merluzzo dead, and now Sheeley. Reporters scattered, and Dr. Dexter mysteriously missing. He sighed and persevered.

"That last night, when you saw the blur," he asked, "can you add anything by way of details? Were there any noises? Did anyone in the crowd say anything? Try to remember—whatever you can add may be of great help to me."

Monahan shook his head. "There were noises aplenty," he said. "But what with the thunder and all, I couldn't rightly make out if anything came from inside the church, like the story has it. And as for the crowd, with the women wailing and the men muttering, all mixed up with thunderclaps and wind, it was as much as I could do to hear myself yelling to keep in place, let alone make out what was being said."

"And the blur?" Fiske persisted.

"It was a blur, and that's all. Smoke, or a cloud, or just a shadow before the lightning struck again. But I'll not be saying I saw any devils, or monsters, or whatchamacallits as Mr. Lovecraft would write about in those wild tales of his."

Sergeant Monahan shrugged self-righteously and picked up the desk-phone to answer a call. The interview was obviously at an end.

And so, for the nonce, was Fiske's quest. He didn't abandon hope, however. For a day he sat by his own hotel phone and called up every "Dexter" listed in the book in an effort to locate a relative of the missing doctor; but to no avail. Another day was spent in a small boat on Narragansett Bay, as Fiske assiduously and painstakingly familiarized himself with the location of the "deepest channel" alluded to in Lovecraft's story.

But at the end of a futile week in Providence, Fiske had to confess himself beaten. He returned to Chicago, his work, and his normal pursuits. Gradually the affair dropped out of the foreground of his consciousness, but he by no means forgot it completely or gave up the notion of eventually unraveling the mystery—if mystery there was.

* * *

In 1941, during a three-day furlough from Basic Training, Pvt. First Class Edmund Fiske passed through Providence on his way to New York City and again attempted to locate Dr. Ambrose Dexter, without success.

During 1942 and 1943 Sgt. Edmund Fiske wrote, from his stations overseas, to Dr. Ambrose Dexter c/o General Delivery, Providence, R.I. His letters were never acknowledged, if indeed they were received.

In 1945, in a U.S.O. library lounge in Honolulu, Fiske read a report in—of all things—a journal on astrophysics which mentioned a recent gathering at Princeton University, at which the guest speaker, Dr. Ambrose Dexter, had delivered an address on "Practical Applications in Military Technology."

Fiske did not return to the States until the end of 1946. Domestic affairs, naturally, were the subject of his paramount consideration during the following year. It wasn't until 1948 that he accidentally came upon Dr. Dexter's name again—this time in a listing of "investigators in the field of nuclear physics" in a national weekly newsmagazine. He wrote the editors for further information, but received no reply. And another letter, dispatched to Providence, remained unanswered.

But in 1949, late in autumn, Dexter's name again came to his attention through the news columns; this time in relation to a discussion of work on the secret H-bomb.

Whatever he guessed, whatever he feared, whatever he wildly imagined, Fiske was impelled to action. It was then that he wrote to a certain Ogden Purvis, a private investigator in the city of Providence, and commissioned him to locate Dr. Ambrose Dexter. All that he required was that he be placed in communication with Dexter, and he paid a substantial retainer fee. Purvis took the case.

The private detective sent several reports to Fiske in Chicago, and they were, at first, disheartening. The Dexter residence was still untenanted. Dexter himself, according to the information elicited from governmental sources, was on a special mission. The private investigator seemed to assume from this that he was a person above reproach, engaged in confidential defense work.

Fiske's own reaction was panic.

He raised his offer of a fee and insisted that Ogden Purvis continue his efforts to find the elusive doctor.

Winter of 1950 came and, with it, another report. The private investigator had tracked down every lead Fiske suggested, and one of them led, eventually, to Tom Jonas.

Tom Jonas was the owner of the small boat which had been chartered by Dr. Dexter one evening in the late summer of 1935—the small boat which had been rowed to the "deepest channel of Narragansett Bay."

Tom Jonas had rested his oars as Dexter threw overboard the dully gleaming, asymmetrical metal box with the hinged lid open to disclose the Shining Trapezohedron.

The old fisherman had spoken freely to the private detective; his words were reported in detail to Fiske via confidential report.

"Mighty peculiar" was Jonas's own reaction to the incident. Dexter had offered him "twenty smackers to take the boat out in the middle o' midnight and heave this funny-lookin' contraption overboard. Said there was no harm in it; said it was just an old keepsake he wanted to git rid of. But all the way out he kep' starin' at the sort of jewel-thing set in some iron bands inside the box, and mumblin' in some foreign language, I guess. No, 'tweren't French or German or Italian talk, either. Polish, mebbe. I don't remember any words, either. But he acted sort of drunk. Not that I'd say anything against Dr. Dexter, understand; comes of a fine old family, even if he ain't been around these parts since, to my knowing. But I figgered he was a bit under the influence, you might say. Else why would he pay me twenty smackers to do a crazy stunt like that?"

There was more to the verbatim transcript of the old fisherman's monologue, but it did not explain anything.

"He sure seemed glad to git rid of it, as I recollect. On the way back he told me to keep mum about it, but I can't see no harm in telling at this late date; I wouldn't hold anythin' back from the law."

Evidently the private investigator had made use of a rather unethical stratagem—posing as an actual detective in order to get Jonas to talk.

This did not bother Fiske, in Chicago. It was enough to get his grasp on something tangible at last; enough to make him send Purvis another payment, with instructions to keep up the search for Ambrose Dexter. Several months passed in waiting.

Then, in late spring, came the news Fiske had waited for. Dr. Dexter was back; he had returned to his house on Benefit Street. The boards had been removed, furniture vans arrived to discharge their contents, and a manservant appeared to answer the door and to take telephone messages.

Dr. Dexter was not at home to the investigator, or to anyone. He was, it appeared, recuperating from a severe illness contracted while in government service. He took a card from Purvis and promised to deliver a message, but repeated calls brought no indication of a reply.

Nor did Purvis, who conscientiously "cased" the house and neighborhood, ever succeed in laying eyes upon the doctor himself or in finding anyone who claimed to have seen the convalescent physician on the street.

Groceries were delivered regularly; mail appeared in the box; lights glowed in the Benefit Street house nightly until all hours.

As a matter of fact, this was the only concrete statement Purvis could make regarding any possible irregularity in Dr. Dexter's mode of life—he seemed to keep electricity burning twenty-four hours a day.

Fiske promptly dispatched another letter to Dr. Dexter, and then another. Still no acknowledgment or reply was forthcoming. And after several more unenlightening reports from Purvis, Fiske made up his mind. He would go to Providence and see Dexter, somehow, come what may.

He might be completely wrong in his suspicions; he might be completely wrong in his assumption that Dr. Dexter could clear the name of his dead friend; he might be completely wrong in even surmising any connection between the two—but for fifteen years he had brooded and wondered, and it was time to put an end to his own inner conflict.

Accordingly, late that summer, Fiske wired Purvis of his intentions and instructed him to meet him at the hotel upon his arrival.

Thus it was that Edmund Fiske came to Providence for the last time; on the day that the Giants lost, on the day that the Langer Brothers lost their two black panthers, on the day that cabdriver William Hurley was in a garrulous mood.

Purvis was not at the hotel to meet him, but such was Fiske's own frenzy of impatience that he decided to act without him and drove, as we have seen, to Benefit Street in the early evening.

As the cab departed, Fiske stared up at the paneled doorway; stared at the lights blazing from the upper windows of the Georgian structure. A brass nameplate gleamed on the door itself, and the light from the windows played upon the legend AMBROSE DEXTER, M.D.

Slight as it was, this seemed a reassuring touch to Edmund Fiske. The doctor was not concealing his presence in the house from the world, however much he might conceal his actual person. Surely the blazing lights and the appearance of the nameplate augured well.

Fiske shrugged, rang the bell.

The door opened quickly. A small, dark-skinned man with a slight stoop appeared and made a question of the word, "Yes?"

"Dr. Dexter, please."

"The doctor is not in to callers. He is ill."

"Would you take a message, please?"

"Certainly." The dark-skinned servant smiled.

"Tell him that Edmund Fiske of Chicago wishes to see him at his convenience for a few moments. I have come all the way from the Middle West for this purpose, and what I have to speak to him about would take only a moment or two of his time."

"Wait, please."

The door closed. Fiske stood in the gathering darkness and transferred his briefcase from one hand to the other.

Abruptly, the door opened again. The servant peered out at him.

"Mr. Fiske—are you the gentleman who wrote the letters?"

"Letters—oh, yes, I am. I did not know the doctor ever received them."

The servant nodded. "I could not say. But Dr. Dexter said that if you were the man who had written him, you were to come right in."

Fiske permitted himself an audible sigh of relief as he stepped over the threshold. It had taken fifteen years to come this far, and now—

"Just go upstairs, if you please. You will find Dr. Dexter waiting in the study, right at the head of the hall."

Edmund Fiske climbed the stairs, turned at the top to a doorway, and entered a room in which the light was an almost palpable presence, so intense was its glare.

And there, rising from a chair beside the fireplace, was Dr. Ambrose Dexter.

Fiske found himself facing a tall, thin, immaculately dressed man who may have been fifty but who scarcely looked thirty-five; a man whose wholly natural grace and elegance of movement concealed the sole incongruity of his aspect—a very deep suntan.

"So you are Edmund Fiske."

The voice was soft, well-modulated, and unmistakably New England—and the accompanying handclasp warm and firm. Dr. Dexter's smile was natural and friendly. White teeth gleamed against the brown background of his features.

"Won't you sit down?" invited the doctor. He indicated a chair and bowed slightly. Fiske couldn't help but stare; there was certainly no indication of any present or recent illness in his host's demeanor or behavior. As Dr. Dexter resumed his own seat near the fire and Fiske moved around the chair to join him, he noted the bookshelves on either side of the room. The size and shape of several volumes immediately engaged his rapt attention—so much that he hesitated before taking a seat, and instead inspected the titles of the tomes.

For the first time in his life, Edmund Fiske found himself confronting the half-legendary *De Vermis Mysteriis*, the *Liber Ivonis*, and the almost mythical Latin version of the *Necronomicon*. Without seeking his host's permission, he lifted the bulk of the latter volume from the shelf and riffled through the yellowed pages of the Spanish translation of 1622.

Then he turned to Dr. Dexter, and all traces of his carefully contrived composure dropped away. "Then it must have been you who found these books in the church," he said. "In the rear vestry room beside the apse. Lovecraft mentioned them in his story, and I've always wondered what became of them."

Dr. Dexter nodded gravely. "Yes, I took them. I did not think it wise for such books to fall into the hands of the authorities. You know what they contain, and what might happen if such knowledge were wrongfully employed."

Fiske reluctantly replaced the great book on the shelf and took a chair facing the doctor before the fire. He held his briefcase on his lap and fumbled uneasily with the clasp.

"Don't be uneasy," said Dr. Dexter, with a kindly smile. "Let us proceed without fencing. You are here to discover what part I played in the affair of your friend's death."

"Yes, there are some questions I wanted to ask."

"Please." The doctor raised a slim brown hand. "I am not in the best of health and can give you only a few minutes. Allow me to anticipate your queries and tell you what little I know."

"As you wish." Fiske stared at the bronzed man, wondering what lay behind the perfection of his poise.

"I met your friend Robert Harrison Blake only once," said Dr. Dexter. "It was on an evening during the latter part of July, 1935. He called upon me here, as a patient."

Fiske leaned forward eagerly. "I never knew that!" he exclaimed.

"There was no reason for anyone to know it," the doctor answered. "He was merely a patient. He claimed to be suffering from insomnia. I examined him, prescribed a sedative, and acting on the merest surmise, asked if he had recently been subjected to any unusual strain or trauma. It was then that he told me the story of his visit to the church on Federal Hill and of what he had found there. I must say that I had the acumen not to dismiss his tale as the product of a hysterical imagination. As a member of one of the older families here, I was already acquainted with the legends surrounding the Starry Wisdom sect and the so-called Haunter of the Dark.

"Young Blake confessed to me certain of his fears concerning the Shining Trapezohedron—intimating that it was a focal point of primal evil. He further admitted his own dread of being somehow linked to the monstrosity in the church.

"Naturally, I was not prepared to accept this last premise as a rational one. I attempted to reassure the young man, advised him to leave Providence and forget it. And at the time I acted in all good faith. And then, in August, came news of Blake's death."

"So you went to the church," Fiske said.

"Wouldn't you have done the same thing?" parried Dr. Dexter. "If Blake had come to you with this story, told you of what he feared, wouldn't his death have moved you to action? I assure you, I did what

I thought best. Rather than provoke a scandal, rather than expose the general public to needless fears, rather than permit the possibility of danger to exist, I went to the church. I took the books. I took the Shining Trapezohedron from under the noses of the authorities. And I chartered a boat and dumped the accursed thing in Narragansett Bay, where it could no longer possibly harm mankind. The lid was up when I dropped it—for as you know, only darkness can summon the Haunter, and now the stone is eternally exposed to light.

"But that is all I can tell you. I regret that my work in recent years has prevented me from seeing or communicating with you before this. I appreciate your interest in the affair and trust my remarks will help to clarify, in a small way, your bewilderment. As to young Blake, in my capacity as examining physician, I will gladly give you a written testimony to my belief in his sanity at the time of his death. I'll have it drawn up tomorrow and send it to your hotel if you give me the address. Fair enough?"

The doctor rose, signifying that the interview was over. Fiske remained seated, shifting his briefcase.

"Now if you will excuse me," the physician murmured.

"In a moment. There are still one or two brief questions I'd appreciate your answering."

"Certainly." If Dr. Dexter was irritated, he gave no sign.

"Did you by any chance see Lovecraft before or during his last illness?"

"No. I was not his physician. In fact, I never met the man, though of course I knew of him and his work."

"What caused you to leave Providence so abruptly after the Blake affair?"

"My interests in physics superseded my interest in medicine. As you may or may not know, during the past decade or more, I have been working on problems relative to atomic energy and nuclear fission. In fact, starting tomorrow, I am leaving Providence once more to deliver a course of lectures before the faculties of eastern universities and certain governmental groups."

"That is very interesting to me, Doctor," said Fiske. "By the way, did you ever meet Einstein?"

"As a matter of fact, I did, some years ago. I worked with him on—but no matter. I must beg you to excuse me now. At another time, perhaps, we can discuss such things."

His impatience was unmistakable now. Fiske rose, lifting his briefcase in one hand and reaching out to extinguish a table lamp with the other.

Dr. Dexter crossed swiftly and lighted the lamp again.

"Why are you afraid of the dark, Doctor?" asked Fiske, softly.

"I am not af—"

For the first time the physician seemed on the verge of losing his composure. "What makes you think that?" he whispered.

"It's the Shining Trapezohedron, isn't it?" Fiske continued. "When you threw it into the bay you acted too hastily. You didn't remember at the time that even if you left the lid open, the stone would be surrounded by darkness there at the bottom of the channel. Perhaps the Haunter didn't want you to remember. You looked into the stone just as Blake did, and established the same psychic linkage. And when you threw the thing away, you gave it into perpetual darkness, where the Haunter's power would feed and grow.

"That's why you left Providence—because you were afraid the Haunter would come to you, just as it came to Blake. And because you knew that now the thing would remain abroad forever."

Dr. Dexter moved toward the door. "I must definitely ask that you leave now," he said. "If you're implying that I keep the lights on because I'm afraid of the Haunter coming after me, the way it did Blake, then you're mistaken."

Fiske smiled wryly. "That's not it at all," he answered. "I know you don't fear that. Because it's too late. The Haunter must have come to you long before this—perhaps within a day or so after you gave it power by consigning the Trapezohedron to the darkness of the Bay. It came to you, but unlike the case of Blake, it did not kill you.

"It used you. That's why you fear the dark. You fear it as the Haunter itself fears being discovered. I believe that in the darkness you look *different*. More like the old shape. Because when the Haunter came to you, it did not kill but instead, *merged*. *You* are the Haunter of the Dark!"

"Mr. Fiske, really—"

"There is no Dr. Dexter. There hasn't been any such person for many years, now. There's only the outer shell, possessed by an entity older than the world; an entity that is moving quickly and cunningly to bring destruction to all mankind. It was you who turned 'scientist' and insinuated yourself into the proper circles, hinting and prompting and assisting foolish men into their sudden 'discovery' of nuclear fission. When the first atomic bomb fell, how you must have laughed! And now you've given them the secret of the hydrogen bomb, and you'rc going on to teach them more, show them new ways to bring about their own destruction.

"It took me years of brooding to discover the clues, the keys to the so-called wild myths that Lovecraft wrote about. For he wrote in parable and allegory, but he wrote the truth. He has set it down in black and white time and again, the prophecy of your coming to earth—Blake knew it at the last when he identified the Haunter by its rightful name."

"And that is?" snapped the doctor.

"Nyarlathotep!"

The brown face creased into a grimace of laughter. "I'm afraid you're a victim of the same fantasy-projections as poor Blake and your friend Lovecraft. Everyone knows that Nyarlathotep is pure invention—part of the Lovecraft mythos."

"I thought so, until I found the clue in his poem. That's when it all fitted in; the Haunter of the Dark, your fleeing, and your sudden interest in scientific research. Lovecraft's words took on a new meaning:

> "And at the last from inner Egypt came
> The strange dark One to whom the fellahs bowed."

Fiske chanted the lines, staring at the dark face of the physician.

"Nonsense—if you must know, this dermatological disturbance of mine is the result of exposure to radiation at Los Alamos."

Fiske did not heed; he was continuing Lovecraft's poem:

> "—That wild beasts followed him and licked his hands.
> Soon from the sea a noxious birth began;
> Forgotten lands with weedy spires of gold;
> The ground was cleft, and mad auroras rolled
> Down on the quaking citadels of man.
> Then, crushing what he chanced to mould in play,
> The idiot Chaos blew Earth's dust away."

Dr. Dexter shook his head. "Ridiculous on the face of it," he asserted. "Surely, even in your—er—upset condition, you can understand that, man! The poem has no literal meaning. Do wild beasts lick my hands? Is something rising from the sea? Are there earthquakes and auroras? Nonsense! You're suffering from a bad case of what we call 'atomic jitters'—I can see it now. You're preoccupied, as so many laymen are today, with the foolish obsession that somehow our work in nuclear fission will result in the destruction of the earth. All this rationalization is a product of your imaginings."

Fiske held his briefcase tightly. "I told you it was a parable, this prophecy of Lovecraft's. God knows what he *knew* or *feared*; whatever it was, it was enough to make him cloak his meaning. And even then, perhaps, *they* got to him because he knew too much."

"*They?*"

"They from Outside—the ones you serve. You are their Messenger,

Nyarlathotep. You came, in linkage with the Shining Trapezohedron, out of inner Egypt, as the poem says. And the fellahs—the common workers of Providence who became converted to the Starry Wisdom sect—bowed before the 'strange dark one' they worshipped as the Haunter.

"The Trapezohedron was thrown into the Bay, and soon from the sea came this noxious birth—your birth, or incarnation in the body of Dr. Dexter. And you taught men new methods of destruction; destruction with atomic bombs in which the 'ground was cleft, and mad auroras rolled down on the quaking citadels of man.' Oh, Lovecraft knew what he was writing, and Blake recognized you, too. And they both died. I suppose you'll try to kill me now, so you can go on. You'll lecture, and stand at the elbows of the laboratory men urging them on and giving them new suggestions to result in greater destruction. And finally you'll blow earth's dust away."

"Please." Dr. Dexter held out both hands. "Control yourself—let me get you something! Can't you realize this whole thing is absurd?"

Fiske moved toward him, hands fumbling at the clasp of the briefcase. The flap opened, and Fiske reached inside, then withdrew his hand. He held a revolver now, and he pointed it quite steadily at Dr. Dexter's breast.

"Of course it's absurd," Fiske muttered. "No one ever believed in the Starry Wisdom sect except a few fanatics and some ignorant foreigners. No one ever took Blake's stories or Lovecraft's, or mine for that matter, as anything but a rather morbid form of amusement. By the same token, no one will ever believe there is anything wrong with you, and with so-called scientific investigation of atomic energy, or the other horrors you plan to loose on the world to bring about its doom. And that's why I'm going to kill you now!"

"Put down that gun!"

Fiske began suddenly to tremble; his whole body shook in a spectacular spasm. Dexter noted it and moved forward. The younger man's eyes were bulging, and the physician inched toward him.

"Stand back!" Fiske warned. The words were distorted by the convulsive shuddering of his jaws. "That's all I needed to know. Since you are in a human body, you can be destroyed by ordinary weapons. As so I do destroy you—Nyarlathotep!"

His finger moved.

So did Dr. Dexter's. His hand went swiftly behind him, to the master light-switch on the wall. A click, and the room was plunged into utter darkness.

Not utter darkness—for there was a glow.

The face and hands of Dr. Ambrose Dexter glowed with a phosphorescent fire in the dark. There are presumable forms of radium poisoning which can cause such an effect, and no doubt Dr. Dexter would have so explained the phenomenon to Edmund Fiske, had he the opportunity.

But there was no opportunity. Edmund Fiske heard the click, saw the fantastic flaming features, and pitched forward to thc floor.

Dr. Dexter quietly switched on the lights, went over to the younger man's side, and knelt for a long moment. He sought a pulse in vain.

Edmund Fiske was dead.

The doctor sighed, rose, and left the room. In the hall downstairs he summoned his servant.

"There has been a regrettable accident," he said. "That young visitor of mine—a hysteric—suffered a heart attack. You had better call the police, immediately. And then continue with the packing. We must leave tomorrow, for the lecture tour."

"But the police may detain you."

Dr. Dexter shook his head. "I think not. It's a clear-cut case. In any event, I can easily explain. When they arrive, notify me. I shall be in the garden."

The doctor proceeded down the hall to the rear exit and emerged upon the moonlit splendor of the garden behind the house on Benefit Street.

The radiant vista was walled off from the world, utterly deserted. The dark man stood in moonlight, and its glow mingled with his own aura.

At this moment two silken shadows leaped over the wall. They crouched in the coolness of the garden, then slithered forward toward Dr. Dexter. They made panting sounds.

In the moonlight, he recognized the shapes of two black panthers.

Immobile, he waited as they advanced, padding purposefully toward him, eyes aglow, jaws slavering and agape.

Dr. Dexter turned away. His face was turned in mockery to the moon as the beasts fawned before him and licked his hands.

Notebook Found in a Deserted House*

ROBERT BLOCH

First off, I want to write that I never did anything wrong. Not to nobody. They got no call to shut me up here, whoever they are. They got no reason to do what I'm afraid they're going to do, either.

I think they're coming pretty soon, because they've been gone outside a long time. Digging, I guess, in that old well. Looking for a gate, I heard. Not a regular gate, of course, but something else.

Got a notion what they mean, and I'm scared.

I'd look out the windows but of course they are boarded up so I can't see.

But I turned on the lamp, and I found this here notebook so I want to put it all down. Then if I get a chance maybe I can send it to somebody who can help me. Or maybe somebody will find it. Anyway, it's better to write it out as best I can instead of just sitting here and waiting. Waiting for *them* to come and get me.

I better start by telling my name, which is Willie Osborne, and that I am 12 years old last July. I don't know where I was born.

First thing I can remember is living out Roodsford way, out in what folks call the back hill country. It's real lonesome out there, with deep woods all around and lots of mountains and hills that nobody ever climbs.

Grandma use to tell me about it when I was just a little shaver. That's who I lived with, just Grandma on account of my real folks being dead. Grandma was the one who taught me how to read and write. I never been to a regular school.

Grandma knew all kinds of things about the hills and the woods and she told me some mighty queer stories. That's what I thought they was, anyway, when I was little and living all alone with her. Just stories, like the ones in books.

---

*Originally published in *Weird Tales*, May 1951.

Like stories about *them ones* hiding in the swamps, that was here before the settlers and the Indians both and how there was circles in swamps and big stones called alters where *them ones* use to make sacrefices to what they worshiped.

Grandma got some of the stories from her Grandma she said—about how *them ones* hid in the woods and swamps because they couldn't stand sunshine, and how the Indians kept out of their way. She said sometimes the Indians would leave some of their young people tied to trees in the forest as a sacrefice, so as to keep *them* contented and peacefull.

Indians knew all about *them,* and they tried to keep white folks from noticing too much or settling too close to the hills. *Them ones* didn't cause much trouble, but they might if they was crowded. So the Indians give excuses not for settling, saying there weren't enough hunting and no trails and it was too far off from the coast.

Grandma told me that was why not many places was settled even today. Nothing but a few farmhouses here and there. She told me *them ones* was still alive and sometimes on certain nights in the Spring and Fall you could see lights and hear noises far off on the tops of the hills.

Grandma said I had an Aunt Lucy and a Uncle Fred who lived out there right smack in the middle of the hills. Said my Pa used to visit them before he got married and once he heard *them* beating on a tree drum one night along about Halloween time. That was before he met Ma and they got married and she died when I come and he went away.

I heard all kinds of stories. About witches and devils and bat men that sucked your blood and haunts. About Salem and Arkham because I never been to a city and I wanted to hear tell how they were. About a place called Innsmouth with old rotten houses where people hid awful things away in the cellars and the attics. She told me bout the way graves was dug deep under Arkham. Made it sound like the whole country was full of haunts.

She use to scare me, telling about how some of these things looked and all but she never would tell me how *them ones* looked no matter how much I asked. Said she didn't want me to have any truck with such things—bad enough she and her kin knew as much as they did—allmost too much for decent God fearing people. It was lucky for me I didn't have to bother with such ideas, like my own ancestor on my father's side, Mehitabel Osborne, who got hanged for a witch back in the Salem days.

So they was just stories to me until last year when Grandma died and Judge Crubinthorp put me on the train and I went out to live with Aunt Lucy and Uncle Fred in the very same hills that Grandma use to tell about so often.

You can bet I was pretty excited, and the conductor let me ride with him all the way and told me about the towns and everything.

Uncle Fred met me at the station. He was a tall thin man with a long beard. We drove off in a buggy from the little deepo—no houses around there or nothing—right into the woods.

Funny thing about those woods. They was so still and quiet. Gave me the creeps they was so dark and lonesome. Seemed like nobody had ever shouted or laughed or even smiled in them. Couldn't imagine anyone saying anything there excep in whispers.

Trees and all was so old, too. No animals around or birds. Path kind of overgrown like nobody used it much ever. Uncle Fred drove along right fast, he didn't hardly talk to me at all but just made that old horse hump it.

Pretty soon we struck into some hills, they was awfully high ones. They was woods on them, too, and sometimes a brook come running down, but I didn't see no houses and it was always dark like at twilight, wherever you looked.

Lastly we got to the farmhouse—a little place, old frame house and barn in a clear space and trees all around kind of gloomy-like. Aunt Lucy come out to meet us, she was a nice sort of little middle-aged lady who hugged me and took my stuff in back.

But all this don't hold with what I'm supposed to write down here. It don't matter that all this last year I was living in the house here with them, eating off the stuff Uncle Fred farmed without ever going into town. No other farms around here for almost four mile and no school—so evenings Aunt Lucy would help me with my reading. I never played much.

At first I was scared of going into the woods on account of what Grandma had told me. Besides, I could tell as Aunt Lucy and Uncle Fred was scared of something from the way they locked the doors at night and never went into the woods after dark, even in summer.

But after a while, I got used to the idea of living in the woods and they didn't seem so scarey. I did chores for Uncle Fred, of course, but sometimes in afternoons when he was busy, I'd go off by myself. Particular by the time it was fall.

And that's how I heard one of the things. It was early October, I was in the glen right by the big boulder. Then the noise started. I got behind that rock fast.

You see, like I say, there isn't any animals in the woods. Nor people. Excep perhaps old Cap Pritchett the mailman who only comes through on Thursday afternoons.

So when I heard a sound that wasn't Uncle Fred or Aunt Lucy calling to me, I knew I better hide.

About that sound. It was far-away at first, kind of a dropping noise.

Sounded like the blood falling in little spurts on the bottom of the bucket when Uncle Fred hung up a butchered hog.

I looked around but I couldn't make out nothing, and I couldn't figure out the direction the noise was from either. The noise sort of stopped for a minute and they was only twilight and trees, still as death. Then the noise started again, nearer and louder.

Sounded like a lot of people running or walking all at once, moving this way. Twigs busting under feet and scrabbling in the bushes all mixed up in the noise. I scrunched down behind that boulder and kept real quiet.

I can tell that whatever makes the noise, it's real close now, right in the glen. I want to look up but dassn't because the sound is so loud and *mean*. And also there is an awful smell like something that was dead and buried being uncovered again in the sun.

All at once the noise stops again and I can tell that whatever makes it is real close by. For a minute the woods are creepy-still. Then comes the sound.

It's a voice and it's not a voice. That is, it doesn't *sound* like a voice but more like a buzzing or croaking, deep and droning. But it *has* to be a voice because it is saying words.

Not words I could understand, but words. Words that made me keep my head down, half afraid I might be seen and half afraid I might see something. I stayed there sweating and shaking. The smell was making me pretty sick, but that awful, deep droning voice was worse. Saying over and over something like

"E uh shub nigger ath ngaa ryla neb shoggoth."

I can't hope to spell it out the way it sounded, but I heard it enough times to remember. I was still listening when the smell got awful thick and I guess I must have fainted because when I woke up the voice was gone and it was getting quite dark.

I ran all the way home that night, but not before I saw where the thing had stood when it talked—and it *was* a thing.

No human being can leave tracks in the mud like goat's hoofs all green with slime that smell awful—not four or eight, but a couple *hundred*!

I didn't tell Aunt Lucy or Uncle Fred. But that night when I went to bed I had terrible dreams. I thought I was back in the glen, only this time I could see the thing. It was real tall and all inky-black, without any particular shape except a lot of black ropes with ends like hoofs on it. I mean, it had a shape but it kep changing—all bulgy and squirming into different sizes. They was a lot of mouths all over the thing like puckered up leaves on branches.

That's as close as I can come. The mouths was like leaves and the whole thing was like a tree in the wind, a black tree with lots of branches trailing the ground, and a whole lot of roots ending in hoofs. And that green slime dribbling out of the mouths and down the legs was like sap!

Next day I remembered to look in a book Aunt Lucy had downstairs. It was called a mythology. This book told about some people who lived over in England and France in the old days and was called Druids. They worshiped trees and thought they was alive. Maybe this thing was like what they worshiped—called a nature-spirit.

But these Druids lived across the ocean, so how could it be? I did a lot of thinking about it the next couple days, and you can bet I didn't go out to play in those woods again.

At last I figgered it out something like this.

Maybe those Druids got chased out of the forests over in England and France and some of them was smart enough to build boats and come across the ocean like old Leaf Erikson is supposed to have. Then they could maybe settle in the woods back here and frighten away the Indians with their magic spells.

They would know how to hide themselves away in the swamps and go right on with their heathen worshiping and call up these spirits out of the ground or wherever they come from.

Indians use to believe that white gods come from out of the sea a long time ago. What if that was just another way of telling how the Druids got here? Some real civilized Indians down in Mexico or South America—Aztecs or Inkas, I guess—said a white god come over in a boat and taught them all kinds of magic. Couldn't he of been a Druid?

That would explain Grandma's stories about *them ones*, too.

Those Druids hiding in the swamps would be the ones who did the drumming and pounding and lit the fires on the hills. And they would be calling up *them ones*, the tree spirits or whatever, out of the earth. Then they would make sacrefices. Those Druids always made sacrefices with blood, just like the old witches. And didn't Grandma tell about people who lived too near the hills disappearing and never being found again?

We lived in a spot just exactly like that.

And it was getting close to Halloween. That was the big time, Grandma always said.

I began to wonder—how soon now?

Got so scared I didn't go out of the house. Aunt Lucy made me take a tonic, said I looked peaked. Guess I did. All I know is one afternoon when I heard a buggy coming through the woods I ran and hid under the bed.

But it was only Cap Pritchett with the mail. Uncle Fred got it and come in all excited with a letter.

Cousin Osborne was coming to stay with us. He was kin to Aunt

Lucy and he had a vacation and he wanted to stay a week. He'd get here on the same train I did—the only train they was passing through these parts—on noon, October 25th.

For the next few days we was all so excited that I forgot all my crazy notions for a spell. Uncle Fred fixed up the back room for Cousin Osborne to sleep in and I helped him with the carpenter parts of the job.

Days got shorter right along, and the nights was all cold with big winds. It was pretty brisk the morning of the 25th and Uncle Fred bundled up warm to drive through the woods. He meant to fetch Cousin Osborne at noon, and it was seven mile to the station. He wouldn't take me, and I didn't beg. Them woods was too full of creaking and rustling sounds from the wind—sounds that might be something else, too.

Well, he left, and Aunt Lucy and I stayed in the house. She was putting up preserves now—plums—for over the winter season. I washed out jars from the well.

Seems like I should have told about them having two wells. A new one with a big shiny pump, close to the house. Then an old stone one out by the barn, with the pump gone. It never had been any good, Uncle Fred said, it was there when they bought the place. Water was all slimy. Something funny about it, because even without a pump, sometimes it seemed to back up. Uncle Fred couldn't figure it out, but some mornings water would be running out over the sides—green, slimy water that smelled terrible.

We kep away from it and I was by the new well, till along about noon when it started in to cloud up. Aunt Lucy fixed lunch, and it started to rain hard with thunder rolling in off the big hills in the west.

Seemed to me Uncle Fred and Cousin Osborne was going to have troubles getting home in the storm, but Aunt Lucy didn't fret about it—just made me help her put up the stock.

Come five o'clock, getting dark, and still no Uncle Fred. Then we begun to worry. Maybe the train was late, or something happened to the horse or buggy.

Six o'clock and still no Uncle Fred. The rain stopped, but you could still hear the thunder sort of growling off in the hills, and the wet branches kep dripping down in the woods, making a sound like women laughing.

Maybe the road was too bad for them to get through. Buggy might bog down in the mud. Perhaps they decided to stay in the deepo over night.

Seven o'clock and it was pitch dark outside. No rain sounds any more. Aunt Lucy was awful worried. She said for us to go out and post a lantern on the fence rail by the road.

We went down the path to the fence. It was dark and the wind had died down. Everything was still, like in the deep part of the woods. I felt kind of scared just walking down the path with Aunt Lucy—like something was out there in the quiet dark, someplace, waiting to grab me.

We lit the lantern and stood there looking down the dark road and, "What's that?" said Aunt Lucy, real sharp. I listened and heard a drumming sound far away.

"Horse and buggy," I said. Aunt Lucy perked up.

"You're right," she says, all at once. And it is, because we see it. The horse is running fast and the buggy lurches behind it, crazy-like. It don't even take a second look to see something has happened, because the buggy don't stop by the gate but keeps going up to the barn with Aunt Lucy and me running through the mud after the horse. The horse is all full of lather and foam, and when it stops it can't stand still. Aunt Lucy and I wait for Uncle Fred and Cousin Osborne to step out, but nothing happens. We look inside.

There isn't anybody in the buggy at all.

Aunt Lucy says, "Oh!" in a real loud voice and then faints. I had to carry her back to the house and get her into bed.

I waited almost all night by the window, but Uncle Fred and Cousin Osborne never showed up. Never.

The next few days was awful. They was nothing in the buggy for a clue like to what happened, and Aunt Lucy wouldn't let me go along the road into town or even to the station through the woods.

The next morning the horse was dead in the barn, and of course we would of had to walk to the deepo or all those miles to Warren's farm. Aunt Lucy was scared to go and scared to stay and she allowed as how when Cap Pritchett comes by we had best go with him over to town and make a report and then stay there until we found out what happened.

Me, I had my own ideas what happened. Halloween was only a few days away now, and maybe *them ones* had snatched Uncle Fred and Cousin Osborne for sacrefice. *Them ones* or the Druids. The mythology book said Druids could even raise storms if they wanted to with their spells.

No sense talking to Aunt Lucy, though. She was like out of her head with worry, anyway, just rocking back and forth and mumbling over and over, "They're gone" and "Fred always warned me" and "No use, no use." I had to get the meals and tend to stock myself. And nights it was hard to sleep, because I kep listening for drums. I never heard any, though, but still it was better than sleeping and having those dreams.

Dreams about the black thing like a tree, walking through the woods and sort of rooting itself to one particular spot so it could pray with all those mouths—pray down to that old god in the ground below.

I don't know where I got the idea that was how it prayed—by sort of attaching its mouths to the ground. Maybe it was on account of seeing the green slime. Or had I really seen it? I'd never gone back to look. Maybe it was all in my head—the Druid story and about *them ones* and the voice that said "shoggoth" and all the rest.

But then, where was Cousin Osborne and Uncle Fred? And what scared the horse so it up and died the next day?

Thoughts kep going round and round in my head, chasing each other, but all I knew was we'd be out of here by Halloween night.

Because Halloween was on a Thursday, and Cap Pritchett would come and we could ride to town with him.

Night before I made Aunt Lucy pack and we got all ready, and then I settled down to sleep. There was no noises, and for the first time I felt a little better.

Only the dreams come again. I dreamed a bunch of men come in the night and crawled through the parlor bedroom window where Aunt Lucy slept and got her. They tied her up and took her away, all quiet, in the dark, because they had cat-eyes and didn't need light to see.

The dream scared me so I woke up while it was just breaking into dawn. I went down the hall to Aunt Lucy right away.

She was gone.

The window was wide open like in my dream, and some of the blankets was torn.

Ground was hard outside the window and I didn't see footprints or anything. But she was gone.

I guess I cried then.

It's hard to remember what I did next. Didn't want breakfast. Went out hollering "Aunt Lucy" and not expecting any answer. I walked to the barn and the door was open and the cows were gone. Saw one or two prints going out the yard and up the road, but I didn't think it was safe to follow them.

Some time later I went over to the well and then I cried again because the water was all slimy green in the new one, just like the old.

When I saw that I knew I was right. *Them ones* must of come in the night and they wasn't even trying to hide their doings any more. Like they was sure of things.

Tonight was Halloween. I had to get out of here. If *them ones* was watching and waiting, I couldn't depend on Cap Pritchett showing up this afternoon. I'd have to chance it down the road and I'd better start walking now, in the morning, while it was still light enough to make town.

So I rummaged around and found a little money in Uncle Fred's drawer of the bureau and Cousin Osborne's letter with the address in Kingsport he wrote it from. That's where I'd have to go after I told folks in town what happened. I'd have some kin there.

I wondered if they'd believe me in town when I told them about the way Uncle Fred had disappeared and Aunt Lucy, and about *them* stealing the cattle for a sacrefice and about the green slime in the well where something had stopped to drink. I wondered if they would know about the drums and the lights on the hills tonight and if they was going to get up a party and come back this evening to try and catch *them ones* and what they meant to call up rumbling out of the earth. I wondered if they knew what a "shoggoth" was.

Well, whether they did or not, I couldn't stay and find out for myself. So I packed up my satchel and got ready to leave. Must of been around noon and everything was still.

I went to the door and stepped outside, not bothering to lock it behind me. Why should I with nobody around for miles?

Then I heard the noise down the road.

Footsteps.

Somebody walking along the road, just around the bend.

I stood still for a minute, waiting to see, waiting to run.

Then he come along.

He was tall and thin, and looked something like Uncle Fred only a lot younger and without a beard, and he was wearing a nice city kind of suit and a crush hat. He smiled when he saw me and come marching up like he knowed who I was.

"Hello, Willie," he said.

I didn't say nothing, I was so confuzed.

"Don't you know me?" he said. "I'm Cousin Osborne. Your Cousin Frank." He held out his hand to shake. "But then I guess you wouldn't remember, would you? Last time I saw you, you were only a baby."

"But I thought you were suppose to come last week," I said. "We expected you on the 25th."

"Didn't you get my telegram?" he asked. "I had business."

I shook my head. "We never get nothing here unless the mail delivers it on Thursdays. Maybe it's at the station."

Cousin Osborne grinned. "You are pretty well off the beaten track at that. Nobody at the station this noon. I was hoping Fred would come along with the buggy so I wouldn't have to walk, but no luck."

"You walked all the way?" I asked.

"That's right."

"And you come on the train?"

Cousin Osborne nodded.

"Then where's your suitcase?"

"I left it at the deepo," he told me. "Too far to fetch it along. I thought Fred would drive me back there in the buggy to pick it up." He noticed my luggage for the first time. "But wait a minute—where are you going with a suitcase, son?"

Well, there was nothing else for me to do but tell him everything that happened.

So I said for him to come into the house and set down and I'd explain.

We went back in and he fixed some coffee and I made a couple sanwiches and we ate, and then I told him about Uncle Fred going to the deepo and not coming back, and about the horse and then what happened to Aunt Lucy. I left out the part about me in the woods, of course, and I didn't even hint at *them ones*. But I told him I was scared and figgered on walking to town today before dark.

Cousin Osborne he listened to me, nodding and not saying much or interrupting.

"Now you can see why we got to go, right away," I said. "Whatever come after them will be coming after us, and I don't want to spend another night here."

Cousin Osborne stood up. "You may be right, Willie," he said. "But don't let your imagination run away with you, son. Try to separate fact from fancy. Your Aunt and Uncle have disappeared. That's fact. But this other nonsense about things in the woods coming after you—that's fancy. Reminds me of all that silly talk I heard back home, in Arkham. And for some reason there seems to be more of it around this time of year, at Halloween. Why, when I left—"

"Excuse me, Cousin Osborne," I said. "But don't you live in Kingsport?"

"Why to be sure," he told me. "But I did live in Arkham once, and I know the people around here. It's no wonder you were so frightened in the woods and got to imagining things. As it is, I admire your bravery. For a 12 year old, you've acted very sensibly."

"Then let's start walking," I said. "Here it is almost 2 and we better get moving if we want to make town before sundown."

"Not just yet, son," Cousin Osborne said. "I wouldn't feel right about leaving without looking around and seeing what we can discover about this mystery. After all, you must understand that we can't just march into town and tell the sheriff some wild nonsense about strange creatures in the woods making off with your Aunt and Uncle. Sensible folks just won't believe such things. They might think I was lying and laugh at me. Why they might even think you had something to do with your Aunt and Uncle's—well, leaving."

"Please," I said. "We got to go, right now."

He shook his head.

I didn't say any more. I might of told him a lot, about what I dreamed and heard and saw and knew—but I figgered it was no use.

Besides, there was some things I didn't want to say to him now that I had talked to him. I was feeling scared again.

First he said he was from Arkham and then when I asked him he said he was from Kingsport but it sounded like a lie to me.

Then he said something about me being scared in the woods and how could he know that? I never told him *that* part at all.

If you want to know what I really thought, I thought maybe he wasn't really Cousin Osborne at all.

And if he wasn't, then—who was he?

I stood up and walked back into the hall.

"Where you going, son?" he asked.

"Outside."

"I'll come with you."

Sure enough, he was watching me. He wasn't going to let me out of his sight. He came over and took my arm, real friendly—but I couldn't break loose. No, he hung on to me. He knew I meant to run for it.

What could I do? All alone in the house in the woods with this man, with night coming on, Halloween night, and *them ones* out there waiting.

We went outside and I noticed it was getting darker already, even in afternoon. Clouds had covered up the sun, and the wind was moving the trees so they stretched out their branches, like they was trying to hold me back. They made a rustling noise, just as if they were whispering things about me, and he sort of looked up at them and listened. Maybe he understood what they were saying. Maybe they were giving him orders.

Then I almost laughed, because he *was* listening to something and now I heard it, too.

It was a drumming sound, on the road.

"Cap Pritchett," I said. "He's the mailman. Now we can ride to town with him in the buggy."

"Let me talk to him," he says. "About your Aunt and Uncle. No sense in alarming him, and we don't want any scandal, do we? You just run along inside."

"But Cousin Osborne," I said. "We got to tell the truth."

"Of course, son. But this is a matter for adults. Now run along. I'll call you."

He was real polite about it and even smiled, but all the same he dragged me back up the porch and into the house and slammed the door. I stood there in the dark hall and I could hear Cap Pritchett slow down and call out to him, and him going up to the buggy and talking, and then all I heard was a lot of mumbling, real low. I peeked out through a crack in the door and saw them. Cap Pritchett was talking to him friendly, all right, and nothing was wrong.

Except that in a minute or so, Cap Pritchett waved and then he grabbed the reins and the buggy started off again!

Then I knew I'd have to do it, no matter what happened. I opened the door and ran out, suitcase and all, down the path and up the road after the buggy. Cousin Osborne he tried to grab me when I went by, but I ducked around him and yelled, "Wait for me, Cap—I'm coming—take me to town!"

Cap slowed down and stared back, real puzzled. "Willie!" he says. "Why I thought you was gone. He said you went away with Fred and Lucy—"

"Pay no attention," I said. "He didn't want me to go. Take me to town. I'll tell you what really happened. Please, Cap, you got to take me."

"Sure I'll take you, Willie. Hop right up here."

I hopped.

Cousin Osborne come right up to the buggy. "Here, now," he said, real sharp. "You can't leave like this. I forbid it. You're in my custody."

"Don't listen to him," I yelled. "Take me, Cap. Please!"

"Very well," said Cousin Osborne. "If you insist on being unreasonable. We'll all go. I cannot permit you to leave alone."

He smiled at Cap. "You can see the boy is unstrung," he said. "And I trust you will not be disturbed by his imaginings. Living out here like this—well, you understand—he's not quite himself. I'll explain everything on the way to town."

He sort of shrugged at Cap and made signs of tapping his head. Then he smiled again and made to climb up next to us in the buggy seat.

But Cap didn't smile back. "No, you don't," he said. "This boy Willie is a good boy. I know him. I don't know you. Looks as if you done enough explaining already, Mister, when you said Willie had gone away."

"But I merely wanted to avoid talk—you see, I've been called in to doctor the boy—he's mentally unstable—"

"Stables be damned!" Cap spit out some tobacco juice right at Cousin Osborne's feet. "We're going."

Cousin Osborne stopped smiling. "Then I insist you take me with you," he said. And he tried to climb into the buggy.

Cap reached into his jacket and when he pulled his hand out again he had a big pistol in it.

"Git down!" he yelled. "Mister, you're talking to the United States Mail and you don't tell the Government nothing, understand? Now git down before I mess your brains all over this road."

Cousin Osborne scowled, but he got away from the buggy, fast.

He looked at me and shrugged. "You're making a big mistake, Willie," he said.

I didn't even look at him. Cap said, "Gee up," and we went off down the road. The buggy wheels turned faster and faster and pretty soon the farmhouse was out of sight and Cap put his pistol away, and patted me on the shoulder.

"Stop that trembling, Willie," he said. "You're safe now. Nothing to worry about. Be in town little over an hour or so. Now you just set back and tell old Cap all about it."

So I told him. It took a long time. We kep going through the woods, and before I knew it, it was almost dark. The sun sneaked down and hid behind the hills. The dark began to creep out of the woods on each side of the road, and the trees started to rustle, whispering to the big shadows that followed us.

The horse was clipping and clopping along, and pretty soon they were other noises from far away. Might have been thunder and might have been something else. But it was getting night-time for sure, and it was the night of Halloween.

The road cut off through the hills now, and you could hardly see where the next turn would take you. Besides, it was getting dark awful fast.

"Guess we're in for a spell of rain," Cap said, looking up. "That's thunder, I reckon."

"Drums," I said.

"Drums?"

"At night in the hills you can hear them," I told him. "I heard them all this month. It's *them ones*, getting ready for the Sabbath."

"Sabbath?" Cap looked at me. "Where you hear tell about a Sabbath?"

Then I told him some more about what had happened. I told him all the rest. He didn't say anything, and before long he couldn't of answered me anyway, because the thunder was all around us, and the rain was lashing down on the buggy, on the road, everywhere. It was pitch-black outside now, and the only time we could see was when lightning flashed. I had to yell to make him hear me—yell about the things that caught Uncle Fred and come for Aunt Lucy, the things that took our cattle and then sent Cousin Osborne back to fetch me. I hollered out about what I heard in the wood, too.

In the lightning flashes I could see Cap's face. He wasn't smiling or scowling—he just looked like he believed me. And I noticed he had his pistol out again and was holding the reins with one hand even though we were racing along. The horse was so scared he didn't need the whip to keep him running.

The old buggy was lurching and bouncing, and the rain was

whistling down in the wind and it was all like an awful dream but it was real. It was real when I hollered out to Cap Pritchett about that time in the woods.

"Shoggoth," I yelled. "What's a shoggoth?"

Cap grabbed my arm, and then the lightning come and I could see his face, with his mouth open. But he wasn't looking at me. He was looking at the road and what was ahead of us.

The trees sort of come together, hanging over the next turn, and in the black it looked as if they were alive—moving and bending and twisting to block our way. Lightning flickered up again and I could see them plain, and also something else.

Something black in the road, something that wasn't a tree. Something big and black, just squatting there, waiting, with ropy arms squirming and reaching.

"Shoggoth!" Cap yelled. But I could scarcely hear him because the thunder was roaring and now the horse let out a scream and I felt the buggy jerk to one side and the horse reared up and we was almost into the black stuff. I could smell an awful smell, and Cap was pointing his pistol and it went off with a bang that was almost as loud as the thunder and almost as loud as the sound we made when we hit the black thing.

Then everything happened at once. The thunder, the horse falling, the shot, and us hitting as the buggy went over. Cap must of had the reins wrapped around his arm, because when the horse fell and the buggy turned over, he went right over the dashboard head first and down into the squirming mess that was the horse—and the black thing that grabbed it. I felt myself falling in the dark, then landing in the mud and gravel of the road.

There was thunder and screaming and another sound which I had heard only once before in the woods—a droning sound like a voice.

That's why I never looked back. That's why I didn't even think about being hurt when I landed—just got up and started to run down the road, fast as I could, run down the road in the storm and the dark with the trees squirming and twisting and shaking their heads while they pointed at me with their branches and laughed.

Over the thunder I heard the horse scream and I heard Cap scream, too, but I still didn't look back. The lightning winked on and off, and I ran through the trees now because the road was nothing but mud that dragged me down and sucked at my legs. After a while I began to scream, too, but I couldn't even hear myself for thunder. And more than thunder. I heard drums.

All at once I busted clear of the woods and got to the hills. I ran up, and the drumming got louder, and pretty soon I could see regular, not just when they was lightning. Because they was fires burning on the hill, and the booming of the drums come from there.

I got lost in the noise; the wind shrieking and the trees laughing and the drums pounding. But I stopped in time. I stopped when I saw the fires plain; red and green fires burning in all that rain.

I saw a big white stone in the center of a cleared-off space on top of the hill. The red and green fires was around and behind it, so everything stood out clear against the flames.

They was men around the alter, men with long gray beards and wrinkled-up faces, men throwing awful-smelling stuff on the fires to make them blaze red and green. And they had knives in their hands and I could hear them howling over the storm. In back, squatting on the ground, more men pounded on drums.

Pretty soon something else come up the hill—two men driving cattle. I could tell it was our cows they drove, drove them right up to the alter and then the men with the knives cut their throats for a sacrefice.

All this I could see in lightning flashes and in the fire lights, and I sort of scooched down so I couldn't get spotted by anyone.

But pretty soon I couldn't see very good any more, on account of the way they threw stuff on the fire. It set up a real thick black smoke. When this smoke come up, the men began to chant and pray louder.

I couldn't hear words, but the sounds was like what I heard back in the woods. I couldn't see too good, but I knew what was going to happen. Two men who had led the cattle went back down the other side of the hill and when they come up again they had new sacrefices. The smoke kep me from seeing plain, but these was two-legged sacrefices, not four. I might of seen better at that, only now I hid my face when they dragged them up to the white alter and used the knives, and the fire and smoke flared up and the drums boomed and they all chanted and called in a loud voice to something waiting over on the other side of the hill.

The ground began to shake. It was storming, they was thunder and lightning and fire and smoke and chanting and I was scared half out of my wits, but one thing I'll swear to—the ground began to shake. It shook and shivered and they called out to something, and in a minute something came.

It came crawling up the hillside to the alter and the sacrefice, and it was the black thing of my dreams—that black, ropy, slimy jelly tree-thing out of the woods. It crawled up and it flowed up on its hoofs and mouths and snaky arms. And the men bowed and stood back and then it got to the alter where they was something squirming on top, squirming and screaming.

The black thing sort of bent over the alter and then I heard droning sounds over the screaming as it come down. I only watched a minute, but while I watched the black thing began to swell and *grow*.

That finished me. I didn't care any more. I had to run. I got up and I run and run and run, screaming at the top of my lungs no matter who heard.

I kep running and I kep screaming forever, through the woods and the storm, away from that hill and that alter, and then all at once I knew where I was and I was back here at the farmhouse.

Yes, that's what I'd done—run in a circle and come back. But I couldn't go any further, I couldn't stand the night and the storm. So I run inside here. At first after I locked the door I just lay right down on the floor, all tuckered out from running and crying.

But in a little while I got up and hunted me some nails and a hammer and some of Uncle Fred's boards that wasn't split up into kindling.

I nailed up the door first and then boarded up all the windows. Every last one of them. Guess I worked for hours, tired as I was. When it was all done, the storm died down and it got quiet. Quiet enough for me to lie down on the couch and go to sleep.

Woke up a couple of hours ago. It was daylight. I could see it shining through the cracks. From the way the sun come in, I knew it was afternoon already. I'd slept through the whole morning, and nothing had come.

I figured now maybe I could let myself out and make town on foot, like I'd planned yesterday.

But I figgered wrong.

Before I got started taking out the nails, I heard him. It was Cousin Osborne, of course. The man who said he was Cousin Osborne, I mean.

He come into the yard, calling "Willie!" but I didn't answer. Then he tried the door and then the windows. I could hear him pounding and cussing. That was bad.

But then he began mumbling, and that was worse. Because it meant he wasn't out there alone.

I sneaked a look through the crack, but he already went around to the back of the house so I didn't see him or who was with him.

Guess that's just as well, because if I'm right, I wouldn't want to see. Hearing's bad enough.

Hearing that deep croaking, and then him talking, and then that croaking again.

Smelling that awful smell, like the green slime from the woods and around the well.

The well—they went over to the well in back. And I heard Cousin Osborne say something about, "Wait until dark. We can use the well if you find the gate. Look for the gate."

I know what that means now. The well must be a sort of entrance to the underground place—that's where those Druid men live. And the black thing.

They're out in back now, looking.

I been writing for quite a spell and already the afternoon is going. Peeking through the cracks I can see it's getting dark again.

That's when they'll come for me—when it's dark.

They'll break down the doors or the windows and come and take me. They'll take me down into the well, into the black places where the shoggoths are. There must be a whole world down under the hills, a world where they hide and wait to come out for more sacrefices, more blood. They don't want any humans around, except for sacrefices.

I saw what the black thing did on the alter. I know what's going to happen to me.

Maybe they'll miss the real Cousin Osborne back home and send somebody to find out what become of him. Maybe folks in town will miss Cap Pritchett and go on a search. Maybe they'll come here and find me. But if they don't come soon it will be too late.

That's why I wrote this. It's true, cross my heart, every word of it. And if anyone finds this notebook where I hide it, come and look down the well. The old well, out in back.

Remember what I told about *them ones*. Block up the well and clean out them swamps. No sense looking for me—if I'm not here.

I wish I wasn't so scared. I'm not even scared so much for myself, but for other folks. The ones who might come after and live around here and have the same thing happen—or worse.

You just got to believe me. Go to the woods if you don't. Go to the hill. The hill where they had the sacrefice. Maybe the stains are gone and the rain washed the footprints away. Maybe they got rid of the traces of the fire. But the alter stone must be there. And if it is, you'll know the truth. There should be some big round spots on that stone. Round spots about two feet wide.

I didn't tell about that. At the last, I did look back. I looked back at the big black thing that was a shoggoth. I looked back as it kep swelling and growing. I guess I told about how it could change shape, and how big it got. But you can't hardly imagine how big or what shape and I still dassn't tell.

All I say is look. Look and you'll see what's hiding under the earth in these hills, waiting to creep out and feast and kill some more.

Wait. They're coming now. Getting twilight and I can hear footsteps. And other sounds. Voices. And other sounds. They're banging on the door. And sure enough—they must have a tree or a plank to use for battering it down. The whole place is shaking. I can hear Cousin Osborne yelling, and that droning. The smell is awful, I'm getting sick, and in a minute—

Look at the alter. Then you'll understand what I'm trying to tell. Look at the big round marks, two feet wide, on each side. That's where the big black thing grabbed hold.

Look for the marks and you'll know what I saw, what I'm afraid of, what's waiting to grab you unless you shut it up forever under the earth.

Black marks two feet wide, but they aren't just marks.

What they really are is *fingerprints*!

The door is busting o——

The Salem Horror*

HENRY KUTTNER

When Carson first noticed the sounds in his cellar, he ascribed them to the rats. Later he began to hear the tales which were whispered by the superstitious Polish mill workers in Derby Street regarding the first occupant of the ancient house, Abigail Prinn. There was none living today who could remember the diabolical old hag, but the morbid legends which thrive in the "witch district" of Salem like rank weeds on a neglected grave gave disturbing particulars of her activities, and were unpleasantly explicit regarding the detestable sacrifices she was known to have made to a worm-eaten, crescent-horned image of dubious origin. The oldsters still muttered of Abbie Prinn and her monstrous boasts that she was high priestess of a fearfully potent god which dwelt deep in the hills. Indeed, it was the old witch's reckless boasting which had led to her abrupt and mysterious death in 1692, about the time of the famous hangings on Gallows Hill. No one liked to talk about it, but occasionally a toothless crone would mumble fearfully that the flames could not burn her, for her whole body had taken on the peculiar anesthesia of her witch-mark.

Abbie Prinn and her anomalous statue had long since vanished, but it was still difficult to find tenants for her decrepit, gabled house, with its overhanging second story and curious diamond-paned casement windows. The house's evil notoriety had spread throughout Salem. Nothing had actually happened there of recent years which might give rise to the inexplicable tales, but those who rented the house had a habit of moving out hastily, generally with vague and unsatisfactory explanations connected with the rats.

And it was a rat which led Carson to the Witch Room. The squealing and muffled pattering within the rotting walls had disturbed Carson more than once during the nights of his first week in the

---

*Originally published in *Weird Tales*, May 1937.

house, which he had rented to obtain the solitude that would enable him to complete a novel for which his publishers had been asking—another light romance to add to Carson's long string of popular successes. But it was not until sometime later that he began to entertain certain wildly fantastic surmises regarding the intelligence of the rat that scurried from under his feet in the dark hallway one evening.

The house had been wired for electricity, but the bulb in the hall was small and gave a dim light. The rat was a misshapen, black shadow as it darted a few feet away and paused, apparently watching him.

At another time Carson might have dismissed the animal with a threatening gesture and returned to his work. But the traffic on Derby Street had been unusually noisy, and he had found it difficult to concentrate upon his novel. His nerves, for no apparent reason, were taut; and somehow it seemed that the rat, watching just beyond his reach, was eyeing him with sardonic amusement.

Smiling at the conceit, he took a few steps toward the rat, and it rushed away to the cellar door, which he saw with surprise was ajar. He must have neglected to close it the last time he had been in the cellar, although he generally took care to keep the doors shut, for the ancient house was drafty. The rat waited in the doorway.

Unreasonably annoyed, Carson hurried forward, sending the rat scurrying down the stairway. He switched on the cellar light and observed the rat in a corner. It watched him keenly out of glittering little eyes.

As he descended the stairs he could not help feeling that he was acting like a fool. But his work had been tiring, and subconsciously he welcomed any interruption. He moved across the cellar to the rat, seeing with astonishment that the creature remained unmoving, staring at him. A strange feeling of uneasiness began to grow within him. The rat was acting abnormally, he felt; and the unwinking gaze of its cold shoe-button eyes was somehow disturbing.

Then he laughed to himself, for the rat had suddenly whisked aside and disappeared into a little hole in the cellar wall. Idly he scratched a cross with his toe in the dirt before the burrow, deciding that he would set a trap there in the morning.

The rat's snout and ragged whiskers protruded cautiously. It moved forward and then hesitated, drew back. Then the animal began to act in a singular and unaccountable manner—almost as though it were dancing, Carson thought. It moved tentatively forward, retreated again. It would give a little dart forward and be brought up short, then leap back hastily, as though—the simile flashed into Carson's mind—a snake were coiled before the burrow, alert to prevent the rat's escape. But there was nothing there save the little cross Carson had scratched in the dust.

No doubt it was Carson himself who blocked the rat's escape, for he was standing within a few feet of the burrow. He moved forward, and the animal hurriedly retreated out of sight.

His interest piqued, Carson found a stick and poked it exploringly into the hole. As he did so his eye, close to the wall, detected something strange about the stone slab just above the rat burrow. A quick glance around its edge confirmed his suspicion. The slab was apparently movable.

Carson examined it closely, noticed a depression on its edge which would afford a handhold. His fingers fitted easily into the groove, and he pulled tentatively. The stone moved a trifle and stopped. He pulled harder, and with a sprinkling of dry earth the slab swung away from the wall as though on hinges.

A black rectangle, shoulder-high, gaped in the wall. From its depths a musty, unpleasant stench of dead air welled out, and involuntarily Carson retreated a step. Suddenly he remembered the monstrous tales of Abbie Prinn and the hideous secrets she was supposed to have kept hidden in her house. Had he stumbled upon some hidden retreat of the long-dead witch?

Before entering the dark gap he took the precaution of obtaining a flashlight from upstairs. Then he cautiously bent his head and stepped into the narrow, evil-smelling passage, sending the flashlight's beam probing out before him.

He was in a narrow tunnel, scarcely higher than his head, and walled and paved with stone slabs. It ran straight ahead for perhaps fifteen feet, and then broadened out into a roomy chamber. As Carson stepped into the underground room—no doubt a hidden retreat of Abbie Prinn's, a hiding-place, he thought, which nevertheless could not save her on the day the fright-crazed mob had come raging along Derby Street—he caught his breath in a gasp of amazement. The room was fantastic, astonishing.

It was the floor which held Carson's gaze. The dull gray of the circular wall gave place here to a mosaic of varicolored stone, in which blues and greens and purples predominated—indeed, there were none of the warmer colors. There must have been thousands of bits of colored stone making up that pattern, for none was larger than a walnut. And the mosaic seemed to follow some definite pattern, unfamiliar to Carson; there were curves of purple and violet mingled with angled lines of green and blue, intertwining in fantastic arabesques. There were circles, triangles, a pentagram, and other, less familiar, figures. Most of the lines and figures radiated from a definite point: the center of the chamber, where there was a circular disk of dead black stone perhaps two feet in diameter.

It was very silent. The sounds of the cars that occasionally went past overhead in Derby Street could not be heard. In a shallow alcove in the wall Carson caught a glimpse of markings on the walls, and he moved slowly in that direction, the beam of his light traveling up and down the walls of the niche.

The marks, whatever they were, had been daubed upon the stone long ago, for what was left of the cryptic symbols was indecipherable. Carson saw several partly effaced hieroglyphics which reminded him of Arabic, but he could not be sure. On the floor of the alcove was a corroded metal disk about eight feet in diameter, and Carson received the distinct impression that it was movable. But there seemed no way to lift it.

He became conscious that he was standing in the exact center of the chamber, in the circle of black stone where the odd design centered. Again he noticed the utter silence. On an impulse he clicked off the ray of his flashlight. Instantly he was in dead blackness.

At that moment a curious idea entered his mind. He pictured himself at the bottom of a pit, and from above a flood was descending, pouring down the shaft to engulf him. So strong was this impression that he actually fancied he could hear a muffled thundering, the roar of the cataract. Then, oddly shaken, he clicked on the light, glanced around swiftly. The drumming, of course, was the pounding of his blood, made audible in the complete silence—a familiar phenomenon. But, if the place was so still—

The thought leaped into his mind, as though suddenly thrust into his consciousness. This would be an ideal place to work. He could have the place wired for electricity, have a table and chair brought down, use an electric fan if necessary—although the musty odor he had first noticed seemed to have disappeared completely. He moved to the tunnel mouth, and as he stepped from the room he felt an inexplicable relaxation of his muscles, although he had not realized that they had been contracted. He ascribed it to nervousness, and went upstairs to brew black coffee and write to his landlord in Boston about his discovery.

The visitor stared curiously about the hallway after Carson had opened the door, nodding to himself as though with satisfaction. He was a lean, tall figure of a man, with thick steel-gray eyebrows overhanging keen gray eyes. His face, although strongly marked and gaunt, was unwrinkled.

"About the Witch Room, I suppose?" Carson said ungraciously. His landlord had talked, and for the last week he had been unwillingly entertaining antiquaries and occultists anxious to glimpse the secret chamber in which Abbie Prinn had mumbled her spells. Carson's annoyance had grown, and he had considered moving to a quieter place; but his inherent stubbornness had made him stay on, determined to finish his novel in spite of interruptions. Now, eyeing his guest coldly, he said, "I'm sorry, but it's not on exhibition anymore."

The other looked startled, but almost immediately a gleam of comprehension came into his eyes. He extracted a card and offered it to Carson.

"Michael Leigh . . . occultist, eh?" Carson repeated. He drew a deep breath. The occultists, he had found, were the worst, with their dark hints of nameless things and their profound interest in the mosaic pattern on the floor of the Witch Room. "I'm sorry, Mr. Leigh, but—I'm really quite busy. You'll excuse me."

Ungraciously he turned back to the door.

"Just a moment," Leigh said swiftly.

Before Carson could protest he had caught the writer by the shoulders and was peering closely into his eyes. Startled, Carson drew back, but not before he had seen an extraordinary expression of mingled apprehension and satisfaction appear on Leigh's gaunt face. It was as though the occultist had seen something unpleasant—but not unexpected.

"What's the idea?" Carson asked harshly. "I'm not accustomed—"

"I'm very sorry," Leigh said. His voice was deep, pleasant. "I must apologize. I thought—well, again I apologize. I'm rather excited, I'm afraid. You see, I've come from San Francisco to see this Witch Room of yours. Would you really mind letting me see it? I should be glad to pay any sum—"

Carson made a deprecatory gesture.

"No," he said, feeling a perverse liking for this man growing within him—his well-modulated, pleasant voice, his powerful face, his magnetic personality. "No, I merely want a little peace—you have no idea how I've been bothered," he went on, vaguely surprised to find himself speaking apologetically. "It's a frightful nuisance. I almost wish I'd never found the room."

Leigh leaned forward anxiously. "May I see it? It means a great deal to me—I'm vitally interested in these things. I promise not to take up more than ten minutes of your time."

Carson hesitated, then assented. As he led his guest into the cellar he found himself telling the circumstances of his discovery of the Witch Room. Leigh listened intently, occasionally interrupting with questions.

"The rat—did you see what became of it?" he asked.

Carson looked bemused. "Why, no. I suppose it hid in its burrow. Why?"

"One never knows," Leigh said cryptically as they came into the Witch Room.

Carson switched on the light. He had had an electrical extension installed, and there were a few chairs and a table, but otherwise, the chamber was unchanged. Carson watched the occultist's face, and with surprise saw it become grim, almost angry.

Leigh strode to the center of the room, staring at the chair that stood on the black circle of stone.

"You work here?" he asked slowly.

"Yes. It's quiet—I found I couldn't work upstairs. Too noisy. But this is ideal—somehow I find it very easy to write here. My mind feels"—he hesitated—"free; that is, disassociated with other things. It's quite an unusual feeling."

Leigh nodded as though Carson's words had confirmed some idea in his own mind. He turned toward the alcove and the metal disk in the floor. Carson followed him. The occultist moved close to the wall, tracing out the faded symbols with a long forefinger. He muttered something under his breath—words that sounded like gibberish to Carson.

"Nyogtha . . . k'yarnak . . ."

He swung about, his face grim and pale. "I've seen enough," he said softly. "Shall we go?"

Surprised, Carson nodded and led the way back into the cellar.

Upstairs Leigh hesitated, as though finding it difficult to broach his subject. At length he asked, "Mr. Carson—would you mind telling me if you have had any peculiar dreams lately."

Carson stared at him, mirth dancing in his eyes. "Dreams?" he repeated. "Oh—I see. Well, Mr. Leigh, I may as well tell you that you can't frighten me. Your compatriots—the other occultists I've entertained—have already tried it."

Leigh raised his thick eyebrows. "Yes? Did they ask you whether you'd dreamed?"

"Several did—yes."

"And you told them?"

"No." Then as Leigh leaned back in his chair, a puzzled expression on his face, Carson went on slowly, "Although, really, I'm not quite sure."

"You mean?"

"I *think*—I have a vague impression—that I have dreamed lately. But I can't be sure. I can't remember anything of the dream, you see. And—oh, very probably your brother occultists put the idea into my mind!"

"Perhaps," Leigh said non-committally, getting up. He hesitated. "Mr. Carson, I'm going to ask you a rather presumptuous question. Is it necessary for you to live in this house?"

Carson sighed resignedly. "When I was first asked that question I explained that I wanted a quiet place to work on a novel, and that any quiet place would do. But it isn't easy to find 'em. Now that I have this Witch Room, and I'm turning out my work so easily, I see no reason why I should move and perhaps upset my program. I'll vacate this house when I finish my novel, and then you occultists can come in and turn it into a museum or do whatever you want with it. I don't care. But until the novel is finished I intend to stay here."

Leigh rubbed his chin. "Indeed. I can understand your point of view. But—is there no other place in the house where you can work?"

He watched Carson's face for a moment, and then went on swiftly.

"I don't expect you to believe me. You are a materialist. Most people are. But there are a few of us who know that above and beyond what men call science there is a greater science that is built on laws and principles which to the average man would be almost incomprehensible. If you have read Machen you will remember that he speaks of the gulf between the world of consciousness and the world of matter. It is possible to bridge that gulf. The Witch Room is such a bridge! Do you know what a whispering-gallery is?"

"Eh?" Carson said, staring. "But there's no—"

"An analogy—merely an analogy. A man may whisper a word in a gallery—or a cave—and if you are standing in a certain spot a hundred feet away you will hear that whisper, although someone ten feet away will not. It's a simple trick of acoustics—bringing the sound to a focal point. And this principle can be applied to other things besides sound. To any wave impulse—*even to thought!*"

Carson tried to interrupt, but Leigh kept on.

"That black stone in the center of your Witch Room is one of those focal points. The design on the floor—when you sit on the black circle there you are abnormally sensitive to certain vibrations—certain thought commands—dangerously sensitive! Why do you suppose your mind is so clear when you are working there? A deception, a false feeling of lucidity—for you are merely an instrument, a microphone, tuned to pick up certain malign vibrations the nature of which you could not comprehend!"

Carson's face was a study in amazement and incredulity. "But—you don't mean you actually *believe*—"

Leigh drew back, the intensity fading from his eyes, leaving them grim and cold. "Very well. But I have studied the history of your Abigail Prinn. She, too, understood the super-science of which I speak. She used it for evil purposes—the black art, as it is called. I have read that she cursed Salem in the old days—and a witch's curse can be a frightful thing. Will you—" He got up, gnawing at his lip. "Will you, at least, allow me to call on you tomorrow?"

Almost involuntarily Carson nodded. "But I'm afraid you'll be wasting your time. I don't believe—I mean, I have no—" He stumbled, at a loss for words.

"I merely wish to assure myself that you—oh, another thing. If you dream tonight, will you try to remember the dream? If you attempt to recapture it immediately after waking, it is often possible to recall it."

"All right. If I dream—"

That night Carson dreamed. He awoke just before dawn with his heart racing furiously and a curious feeling of uneasiness. Within the walls and from below he could hear the furtive scurryings of the rats. He got out of bed hastily, shivering in the cold grayness of early morning. A wan moon still shone faintly in a paling sky.

Then he remembered Leigh's words. He *had* dreamed—there was no question of that. But the content of his dream—that was another matter. He absolutely could not recall it to his mind, much as he tried, although there was a very vague impression of running frantically in darkness.

He dressed quickly, and because the stillness of early morning in the old house got on his nerves, went out to buy a newspaper. It was too early for shops to be open, however, and in search of a news-boy he set off westward, turning at the first corner. And as he walked a curious and inexplicable feeling began to take possession of him: a feeling of—familiarity! He had walked here before, and there was a dim and disturbing familiarity about the shapes of the houses, the outline of the roofs. But—and this was the fantastic part of it—to his knowledge he had never been on this street before. He had spent little time walking about this region of Salem, for he was indolent by nature; yet there was this extraordinary feeling of remembrance, and it grew more vivid as he went on.

He reached a corner, turned unthinkingly to the left. The odd sensation increased. He walked on slowly, pondering.

No doubt he *had* traveled by this way before and very probably he had done so in a brown study, so that he had not been conscious of his route. Undoubtedly that was the explanation. Yet as Carson turned into Charter Street he felt a nameless unease waking within him. Salem was rousing; with daylight impassive Polish workers began to hurry past him toward the mills. An occasional automobile went by.

Before him a crowd was gathered on the sidewalk. He hastened his steps, conscious of a feeling of impending calamity. With an extraordinary sense of shock he saw that he was passing the Charter Street Burying Ground, the ancient, evilly famous "Burying Point." Hastily he pushed his way into the crowd.

Comments in a muffled undertone came to Carson's ears, and a bulky blue-clad back loomed up before him. He peered over the policeman's shoulder and caught his breath in a horrified gasp.

A man leaned against the iron railing that fenced the old graveyard. He wore a cheap, gaudy suit, and he gripped the rusty bars in a clutch that made the muscles stand out in ridges on the hairy backs of his hands. He was dead, and on his face, staring up at the sky at a crazy angle, was frozen an expression of abysmal and utterly shocking horror. His eyes, all whites, were bulging hideously; his mouth was a twisted, mirthless grin.

A man at Carson's side turned a white face toward him. "Looks as if he was scared to death," he said somewhat hoarsely. "I'd hate to have seen what he saw. Ugh—look at that face!"

Mechanically Carson backed away, feeling an icy breath of nameless things chill him. He rubbed his hand across his eyes, but still that contorted, dead face swam in his vision. He began to retrace his steps, shaken and trembling a little. Involuntarily his glance moved aside, rested on the tombs and monuments that dotted the old graveyard. No one had been buried there for over a century, and the lichen-stained tombstones, with their winged skulls, fat-cheeked cherubs, and funeral urns, seemed to breathe out an indefinable miasma of antiquity. What had frightened the man to death?

Carson drew a deep breath. True, the corpse had been a frightful spectacle, but he must not allow it to upset his nerves. He could not—his novel would suffer. Besides, he argued grimly to himself, the affair was obvious enough in its explanation. The dead man was apparently a Pole, one of the group of immigrants who dwell about Salem Harbor. Passing by the graveyard at night, a spot about which eldritch legends had clung for nearly three centuries, his drink-befuddled eyes must have given reality to the hazy phantoms of a superstitious mind. These Poles were notoriously unstable emotionally, prone to mob hysteria and wild imaginings. The great Immigrant Panic of 1853, in which three witch-houses had been burned to the ground, had grown from an old woman's confused and hysterical statement that she had seen a mysterious white-clad foreigner "take off his face." What else could be expected of such people, Carson thought?

Nevertheless he remained in a nervous state, and did not return home until nearly noon. When on his arrival he found Leigh, the occultist, waiting, he was glad to see the man, and invited him in with cordiality.

Leigh was very serious. "Did you hear about your friend Abigail Prinn?" he asked without preamble, and Carson stared, pausing in the act of siphoning charged water into a glass. After a long moment he pressed the lever, sent the liquid sizzling and foaming into the whiskey. He handed Leigh the drink and took one himself—neat—before answering the question.

"I don't know what you're talking about. Has—what's she been up to?" he asked, with an air of forced levity.

"I've been checking up the records," Leigh said, "and I find Abigail Prinn was buried on December 14th, 1690, in the Charter Street Burying Ground—with a stake through her heart. What's the matter?"

"Nothing," Carson said tonelessly. "Well?"

"Well—her grave's been opened and robbed, that's all. The stake was found uprooted nearby, and there were footprints all around the grave. Shoe-prints. Did you dream last night, Carson?" Leigh snapped out the question, his gray eyes hard.

"I don't know," Carson said confusedly, rubbing his forehead. "I can't remember. I was at the Charter Street graveyard this morning."

"Oh. Then you must have heard something about the man who—"

"I saw him," Carson interrupted, shuddering. "It upset me."

He downed the whiskey at a gulp.

Leigh watched him. "Well," he said presently, "are you still determined to stay in this house?"

Carson put down the glass and stood up.

"Why not?" he snapped. "Is there any reason why I shouldn't? Eh?"

"After what happened last night—"

"After *what* happened? A grave was robbed. A superstitious Pole saw the robbers and died of fright. Well?"

"You're trying to convince yourself," Leigh said calmly. "In your heart you know—you must know—the truth. You've become a tool in the hands of tremendous terrible forces, Carson. For three centuries Abbie Prinn has lain in her grave—*undead*—waiting for someone to fall into her trap—the Witch Room. Perhaps she foresaw the future when she built it, foresaw that someday someone would blunder into that hellish chamber and be caught by the trap of the mosaic pattern. It caught you, Carson—and enabled that undead horror to bridge the gulf between consciousness and matter, to get *en rapport* with you. Hypnotism is child's play to a being with Abigail Prinn's frightful powers. She could very easily force you to go to her grave and uproot the stake that held her captive, and then erase the memory of that act from your mind so that you could not remember it even as a dream!"

Carson was on his feet, his eyes burning with a strange light. "In God's name, man, do you know what you're saying?"

Leigh laughed harshly. "God's name! The devil's name, rather—the devil that menaces Salem at this moment; for Salem is in danger, terrible danger. The men and women and children of the town Abbie Prinn cursed when they bound her to the stake—and found they couldn't burn her! I've been going through certain secret archives this morning, and I've come to ask you, for the last time, to leave this house."

"Are you through?" Carson asked coldly. "Very well. I shall stay here. You're either insane or drunk, but you can't impress me with your poppycock."

"Would you leave if I offered you a thousand dollars?" Leigh asked. "Or more, then—ten thousand? I have a considerable sum at my command."

"No, damn it!" Carson snapped in a sudden blaze of anger. "All I want is to be left alone to finish my novel. I can't work anywhere else—I don't want to, I won't—"

"I expected this," Leigh said, his voice suddenly quiet, and with a strange note of sympathy. "Man, you can't get away! You're caught in the trap, and it's too late for you to extricate yourself so long as Abbie Prinn's brain controls you through the Witch Room. And the worst part of it is that she can only manifest herself with your aid—she drains your life forces, Carson, feeds on you like a vampire."

"You're mad," Carson said dully.

"I'm afraid. That iron disk in the Witch Room—I'm afraid of that, and what's under it. Abbie Prinn served strange gods, Carson—and I read something on the wall of that alcove that gave me a hint. Have you ever heard of Nyogtha?"

Carson shook his head impatiently. Leigh fumbled in a pocket, drew out a scrap of paper. "I copied this from a book in the Kester Library," he said, "a book called the *Necronomicon*, written by a man who delved so deeply into forbidden secrets that men called him mad. Read this."

Carson's brows drew together as he read the excerpt:

> Men know him as the Dweller in Darkness, that brother of the Old Ones called Nyogtha, the Thing that should not be. He can be summoned to Earth's surface through certain secret caverns and fissures, and sorcerers have seen him in Syria and below the black tower of Leng; from the Thang Grotto of Tartary he has come ravening to bring terror and destruction among the pavilions of the great Khan. Only by the looped cross, by the Vach-Viraj incantation, and by the Tikkoun elixir may he be driven back to the nighted caverns of hidden foulness where he dwelleth.

Leigh met Carson's puzzled gaze calmly. "Do you understand now?"

"Incantations and elixirs!" Carson said, handing back the paper. "Fiddlesticks!"

"Far from it. That incantation and that elixir have been known to occultists and adepts for thousands of years. I've had occasion to use them myself in the past on certain—occasions. And if I'm right about this thing—" He turned to the door, his lips compressed in a bloodless line. "Such manifestations have been defeated before, but the difficulty lies in obtaining the elixir—it's very hard to get. But I hope . . . I'll be back. Can you stay out of the Witch Room until then?"

"I'll promise nothing," Carson said. He had a dull headache, which had been steadily growing until it obtruded upon his consciousness, and he felt vaguely nauseated. "Good-bye."

He saw Leigh to the door and waited on the steps, with an odd reluctance to return to the house. As he watched the tall occultist hurry down the street, a woman came out of the adjoining house. She caught sight of him, and her huge breasts heaved. She burst into a shrill, angry tirade.

Carson turned, staring at her with astonished eyes. His head throbbed painfully. The woman was approaching, shaking a fat fist threateningly.

"Why you scare my Sarah?" she cried, her swarthy face flushed. "Why you scare her wit' your fool tricks, eh?"

Carson moistened his lips.

"I'm sorry," he said slowly. "Very sorry. I didn't frighten your Sarah. I haven't been home all day. What frightened her?"

"T'e brown t'ing—it ran in your house, Sarah say—"

The woman paused, and her jaw dropped. Her eyes widened. She made a peculiar sign with her right hand—pointing her index and little fingers at Carson, while her thumb was crossed over the other fingers. "T'e old witch!"

She retreated hastily, muttering in Polish in a frightened voice.

Carson turned, went back into the house. He poured some whiskey into a tumbler, considered, and then set it aside untasted. He began to pace the floor, occasionally rubbing his forehead with fingers that felt dry and hot. Vague, confused thoughts raced through his mind. His head was throbbing and feverish.

At length he went down to the Witch Room. He remained there, although he did not work; for his headache was not so oppressive in the dead quiet of the underground chamber. After a time he slept.

How long he slumbered he did not know. He dreamed of Salem, and of a dimly glimpsed, gelatinous black thing that hurtled with frightful speed through the streets, a thing like an incredibly huge, jet-black amoeba that pursued and engulfed men and women who shrieked and fled vainly. He dreamed of a skull-face peering into his own, a withered and shrunken countenance in which only the eyes seemed alive, and they shone with a hellish and evil light.

He awoke at last, sat up with a start. He was very cold.

It was utterly silent. In the light of the electric bulb the green and purple mosaic seemed to writhe and contract toward him, an illusion which disappeared as his sleep-fogged vision cleared. He glanced at his wrist-watch. It was two o'clock. He had slept through the afternoon and the better part of the night.

He felt oddly weak, and a lassitude held him motionless in his chair. The strength seemed to have been drained from him. The piercing cold seemed to strike through to his brain, but his headache was gone. His mind was very clear—expectant, as though waiting for something to happen. A movement nearby caught his eye.

A slab of stone in the wall was moving. He heard a gentle grating sound, and slowly a black cavity widened from a narrow rectangle to a square. There was something crouching there in the shadow. Stark, blind horror struck through Carson as the thing moved and crept forward into the light.

It looked like a mummy. For an intolerable, age-long second the thought pounded frightfully at Carson's brain: *It looked like a mummy!* It was a skeleton-thin, parchment-brown corpse, and it looked like a skeleton with the hide of some great lizard stretched over its bones. It stirred, it crept forward, and its long nails scratched audibly against the stone. It crawled out into the Witch Room, its passionless face pitilessly revealed in the white light, and its eyes were gleaming with charnel life. He could see the serrated ridge of its brown, shrunken back. . . .

Carson sat motionless. Abysmal horror had robbed him of the power to move. He seemed to be caught in the fetters of dream-paralysis, in which the brain, an aloof spectator, is unable or unwilling to transmit the nerve-impulses to the muscles. He told himself frantically that he was dreaming, that he would presently awaken.

The withered horror arose. It stood upright, skeleton-thin, and moved to the alcove where the iron disk lay embedded in the floor. Standing with its back to Carson it paused, and a dry and sere whisper rustled out in the dead stillness. At the sound Carson would have screamed, but he could not. Still the dreadful whisper went on, in a language Carson knew was not of Earth, and as though in response an almost imperceptible quiver shook the iron disk.

It quivered and began to rise, very slowly, and as if in triumph the shriveled horror lifted its pipestem arms. The disk was nearly a foot thick, but presently as it continued to rise above the level of the floor an insidious odor began to penetrate the room. It was vaguely reptilian, musky and nauseating. The disk lifted inexorably, and a little finger of blackness crept out from beneath its edge. Abruptly Carson remembered his dream of a gelatinous black creature that hurtled through the Salem streets. He tried vainly to break the fetters of paralysis that held him motionless. The chamber was darkening, and a black vertigo was creeping up to engulf him. The room seemed to rock.

Still the iron disk lifted; still the withered horror stood with its skeleton arms raised in blasphemous benediction; still the blackness oozed out in slow amoeboid movement.

There came a sound breaking through the sere whisper of the mummy, the quick patter of racing footsteps. Out of the corner of his eye Carson saw a man come racing into the Witch Room. It was the occultist, Leigh, and his eyes were blazing in a face of deathly pallor. He flung himself past Carson to the alcove where the black horror was surging into view.

The withered thing turned with dreadful slowness. Leigh carried some implement in his left hand, Carson saw, a *crux ansata* of gold and ivory. His right hand was clenched at his side. His voice rolled out, sonorous and commanding. There were little beads of perspiration on his white face.

"Ya na kadishtu nil gh'ri . . . stell'bsna kn'aa Nyogtha . . . k'yarnak phlegethor. . . ."

The fantastic, unearthly syllables thundered out, echoing from the walls of the vault. Leigh advanced slowly, the *crux ansata* held high. And from beneath the iron disk black horror came surging!

The disk was lifted, flung aside, and a great wave of iridescent blackness, neither liquid nor solid, a frightful gelatinous mass, came pouring straight for Leigh. Without pausing in his advance he made a quick gesture with his right hand, and a little glass tube hurtled at the black thing, was engulfed.

The formless horror paused. It hesitated, with a dreadful air of indecision, and then swiftly drew back. A choking stench of burning corruption began to pervade the air, and Carson saw great pieces of the black thing flake off, shriveling as though destroyed with corroding acid. It fled back in a liquescent rush, hideous black flesh dropping as it retreated.

A pseudopod of blackness elongated itself from the central mass and like a great tentacle clutched the corpse-like being, dragged it back to the pit and over the brink. Another tentacle seized the iron disk, pulled it effortlessly across the floor, and as the horror sank from sight, the disk fell into place with a thunderous crash.

The room swung in wide circles about Carson, and a frightful nausea clutched him. He made a tremendous effort to get to his feet, and then the light faded swiftly and was gone. Darkness took him.

Carson's novel was never finished. He burned it, but continued to write, although none of his later work was ever published. His publishers shook their heads and wondered why such a brilliant writer of popular fiction had suddenly become infatuated with the weird and ghastly.

"It's powerful stuff," one man told Carson, as he handed back his novel, *Black God of Madness*. "It's remarkable in its way, but it's morbid and horrible. Nobody would read it. Carson, why don't you write the type of novel you used to do, the kind that made you famous?"

It was then that Carson broke his vow never to speak of the Witch Room, and he poured out the entire story, hoping for understanding and belief. But as he finished, his heart sank as he saw the other's face, sympathetic but skeptical.

"You dreamed it, didn't you?" the man asked, and Carson laughed bitterly.

"Yes—I dreamed it."

"It must have made a terribly vivid impression on your mind. Some dreams do. But you'll forget about it in time," he predicted, and Carson nodded.

And because he knew that he would only be arousing doubts of his sanity, he did not mention the thing that was burned indelibly on his brain, the horror he had seen in the Witch Room after wakening from his faint. Before he and Leigh had hurried, white-faced and trembling, from the chamber, Carson had cast a quick glance behind him. The shriveled and corroded patches that he had seen slough off from that being of insane blasphemy had unaccountably disappeared, although they had left black stains upon the stones. Abbie Prinn, perhaps, had returned to the hell she had served, and her inhuman god had withdrawn to hidden abysses beyond man's comprehension, routed by powerful forces of elder magic which the occultist had commanded. But the witch had left a memento behind her, a hideous thing which Carson, in that last backward glance, had seen protruding from the edge of the iron disk, as though raised in ironic salute—*a withered, claw-like hand!*

The Terror from the Depths*

FRITZ LEIBER

Remember thee!
Ay, thou poor ghost, while memory holds a seat
In this distracted globe.

—HAMLET

The following manuscript was found in a curiously embossed copper and German silver casket of highly individual modern workmanship which was purchased at an auction of unclaimed property that had been held in police custody for the prescribed number of years in Los Angeles County, California. In the casket with the manuscript were two slim volumes of verse: *Azathoth and Other Horrors* by Edward Pickman Derby, Onyx Sphinx Press, Arkham, Massachusetts, and *The Tunneler Below* by Georg Reuter Fischer, Ptolemy Press, Hollywood, California. The manuscript was penned by the second of these poets, except for the two letters and the telegram interleafed into it. The casket and its contents had passed into police custody on March 16, 1937, upon the discovery of Fischer's mutilated body by his collapsed brick dwelling in Vultures Roost under circumstances of considerable horror.

Today one will search street maps of the Hollywood Hills area in vain for the unincorporated community of Vultures Roost. Shortly after the events narrated in these pages its name (already long criticized) was changed upon the urging of prudent real-estate dealers to Paradise Crest, which was in turn absorbed by the City of Los Angeles—an event not without parallel in that general neighborhood, as when after certain scandals best forgotten, the name of Runnymede was changed to Tarzana after the chief literary creation of its most illustrious and blameless inhabitant.

The magneto-optical method of detection referred to herein, "which

*Originally published in *The Disciples of Cthulhu,* 1976.

has already discovered two new elements," is neither fraud nor fancy, but a technique highly regarded in the 1930s (though since discredited), as may be confirmed by consulting any table of elements from that period or the entries "alabamine" and "virginium" in *Webster's New International Dictionary*, second edition, unabridged. (They are not, of course, in today's tables.) While the "unknown master builder Simon Rodia" with whom Fischer's father conferred is the widely revered folk architect (now deceased) who created the matchlessly beautiful Watts Towers.

It is only with considerable effort that I can restrain myself from plunging into the very midst of a description of those unequivocably monstrous hints that have determined me to take—within the next eighteen hours and no later—a desperate and initially destructive step. There is much to write and only too little time in which to write it.

I myself need no written argument to bolster my beliefs. It is all more real to me than everyday experience. I have only to close my eyes to see Albert Wilmarth's horror-whitened long-jawed face and migraine-tormented brow. There may be something of clairvoyance in this, for I imagine his expression has not changed greatly since I last saw him. And I need not make the slightest effort to hear those hideously luring voices, like the susurrus of infernal bees and glorious wasps, which impinge upon an inner ear which I now can never and would never close. Indeed, as I listen to them, I wonder if there is anything to be gained from penning this necessarily outré document. It will be found—if it is found—in a locality where serious people do not attach any importance to strange revelations and where charlatanry is only too common. Perhaps that is well and perhaps I should make doubly sure by tearing up this sheet, for there is in my mind no doubt of the results that would follow a systematic, scientific effort to investigate those forces which have ambushed and shall soon claim (and perhaps welcome?) me.

I shall write, however, if only to satisfy a peculiar personal whim. Ever since I can remember I have been drawn to literary creation, but until this very day certain elusive circumstances and crepuscular forces have prevented my satisfactorily completing anything more than a number of poems, mostly short, and tiny prose sketches. It would interest me to discover if my new knowledge has freed me to some extent from those inhibitions. Time enough when I have completed this statement to consider the advisability of its destruction (before I perpetrate the greater and crucial destruction). Truth to tell, I am not especially moved by what may or may not happen to my fellow men; there have been *profound* influences (yes, from the depths indeed!) exerted upon my emotional growth and upon the ultimate direction of my loyalties—as will become clear to the reader in due course.

I might begin this narrative with a bald recital of the implications of the recorded findings of Professors Atwood and Pabodie's portable magneto-optic geo-scanner, or with Albert Wilmarth's horrendous revelations of the mind-shattering, planet-wide researches made during the past decade by a secret coterie of faculty members of far-off Miskatonic University in witch-haunted, shadow-beset Arkham and a few lonely colleagues in Boston and Providence, Rhode Island, or with the shivery clues that with nefarious innocence have found their way even into the poetry I have written during the past few years. If I did that, you would be immediately convinced that I was psychotic. The *reasons* that led me, step by step, to my present awesome convictions, would appear as progressive *symptoms*, and the monstrous horror behind it all would seem a shuddersome paranoid fantasy. Indeed, that will probably be your final judgement in any case, but I will nevertheless tell you what happened just as it happened to me. Then you will have the same opportunity as I had to discern, if you can, just where reality left off and imagination took up and where imagination stopped and psychosis supervened.

Perhaps within the next seventeen hours something will happen or be revealed that will in part substantiate what I shall write. I do not think so, for there is yet untold cunning in the decadent cosmic order which has entrapped me. Perhaps they will not let me finish this narrative; perhaps they will anticipate my own resolve. I am almost sure they have only held off thus far because they are sure I will do their work for them. No matter.

The sun is just now rising, red and raw, over the treacherous and crumbling hills of Griffith Park (Wilderness were a better designation). The sea fog still wraps the sprawling suburbs below, its last vestiges are sliding out of high, dry Laurel Canyon, but far off to the south I can begin to discern the black congeries of scaffold oil wells near Culver City, like stiff-legged robots massing for the attack. And if I were at the bedroom window that opens to the northwest, I would see night's shadows still lingering in the precipitous wilds of Hollywoodland above the faint, twisting, weed-encroached, serpent-haunted trails I have limped along daily for most of my natural life, tracing and retracing them ever more compulsively.

I can turn off the electric light now; my study is already pierced by shafts of low, red sunlight. I am at my table, ready to write the day through. Everything around me has the appearance of eminent normality and security. There are no signs remaining of Albert Wilmarth's frantic midnight departure with the magneto-optic apparatus he brought from the East, yet as if by clairvoyance I can see his long-jawed horror-sucked face as he clings automatically to the steering wheel of his little Austin scuttling across the desert like a frightened beetle, the geo-scanner lying on the seat beside him. This day's sun has reached him before me as he flees back toward his deeply beloved, impossibly distant New England. That sun's smoky red blaze must be in his fear-wide eyes, for I know that no power can turn him back toward the land that slips uncouth into the titan Pacific. I bear him no resentment—I have no reason to. His nerves were shattered by the terrors he bravely insisted on helping to investigate for ten long years against his steadier comrades' advice. And at the very end, I am certain, he saw horrors beyond imagining. Yet he waited to ask me to go with him and only I know how much that must have cost him. He gave me my opportunity to escape; if I had wanted to, I could have made the attempt.

But I believe my fate was decided many years ago.

My name is Georg Reuter Fischer. I was born in 1912 of Swiss parents in the city of Louisville, Kentucky, with an inwardly twisted right foot which might have been corrected by a brace, except that my father did not believe in interfering with the workings of Nature, his deity. He was a mason and stonecutter of great physical strength, vast energy, remarkable intuitive gifts (a dowser for water, oil, and metals), great natural artistry, unschooled but profoundly self-educated. A little after the Civil War, when he was a young boy, he had immigrated to this country with his father, also a mason, and upon the death of the latter, inherited a small but profitable business. Late in life he married my mother, Marie Reuter, daughter of a farmer for whom he had dowsed not only a well but a deposit of granite worth quarrying. I was the child of their age and their only child, coddled by my mother and the object of my father's more thoughtful devotion. I have few memories of our life in Louisville, but those few are eminently wholesome ones: visions of an ordered, cheerful household, of many cousins and friends, of visitings and laughter, and two great Christmas celebrations; also memories of fascinatedly watching my father at his stonecutting, bringing a profusion of flowers and leaves to life from death-pale granite.

And I will say here, because it is important to my story, that I afterward learned that our Fischer and Reuter relatives considered me exceptionally intelligent for my tender age. My father and mother always believed this, but one must allow for parental bias.

In 1917 my father profitably sold his business and brought his tiny family west, to build with his own hands a last home in this land of sunlight, crumbling sandstones, and sea-spawned hills, Southern California. This was in part because doctors had advised it as essential for the sake of my mother's failing health, slow victim of the dread tubercular scourge, but my father had always had a strong yearning for clear skies, year-round heat, and the primeval sea, a deep conviction that his destiny somehow lay west and was involved with Earth's hugest ocean: from which perhaps the moon was torn.

My father's deep-seated longing for this outwardly wholesome and bright, inwardly sinister and eaten-away landscape, where Nature herself presents the naïve face of youth masking the corruptions of age, has given me much food for thought, though it is in no way a remarkable longing. Many people migrate here, healthy as well as sick, drawn by the sun, the promise of perpetual summer, the broad if arid fields. The only unusual circumstance worthy of note is that there is a larger sprinkling than might be expected of persons of professed mystical and utopian bent. The Brothers of the Rose, the Theosophists, the Foursquare Gospelers, the Christian Scientists, Unity, the Brotherhood of the Grail, the spiritualists, the astrologers—all are here and many more besides. Believers in the need of return to primitive states and primitive wisdoms, practitioners of pseudo-disciplines dictated by pseudo-sciences—yes, even a few overly sociable hermits—one finds them everywhere; the majority awaken only my pity and distaste, so lacking in logic and avid for publicity are they. At no time—and let me emphasize this—have I been at all interested in their doings and in their ignorantly parroted principles, except possibly from the viewpoint of comparative psychology.

And they were brought here by that excessive love of sunlight which characterizes most faddists of any sort and that urge to find an unsettled, unorganized land in which utopias might take root and burgeon, untroubled by urbane ridicule and tradition-bred opposition—the same urge that led the Mormons to desert-guarded Salt Lake City, their paradise of Deseret. This seems an adequate explanation, even without bringing in the fact that Los Angeles, a city of retired farmers and small merchants, a city made hectic by the presence of the uncouth motion-picture industry, would naturally attract charlatans of all varieties. Yes, that explanation is still sufficient to me, and I am rather pleased, for even now I should hate to think that those hideously alluring voices a-mutter with secrets from beyond the rim of the cosmos *necessarily* have some dim, continent-wide *range*.

("The carven rim," they are saying now here in my study. "The proto-shoggoths, the diagramed corridor, the elder Pharos, the dreams of Cutlu . . .")

Settling my mother and myself at a comfortable Hollywood boardinghouse, where the activities of the infant film industry provided us with colorful distraction, my father tramped the hills in search of a suitable property, bringing to bear his formidable talent for locating underground water and desirable rock formations. During this period, it occurs to me now, he almost certainly pioneered those trails which it is my own invariable and ever more compulsive wont to walk. Within three months he had found and purchased the property he sought near a predominantly Alsatian and French settlement (a scatter of bungalows, no more) bearing the perhaps exaggeratedly picturesque name Vultures Roost, redolent of the Old West.

Clearing and excavation of the property revealed an upthrust stratum of fine-grained solid metamorphic rock, while a little boring provided an excellent well, to the incredulous astonishment of his initially hostile neighbors. My father kept his counsel and began, mostly with his own hands alone, to erect a brick structure of moderate size that by its layout and plans promised a dwelling of surpassing beauty. This occasioned more head-shaking and lectures on the unwisdom of building brick structures in a region where earthquakes were not unknown. They called it Fischer's Folly, I learned later. Little did they realize my father's skill and the tenacity of his masonry!

He bought a small truck and scoured the area as far south as Laguna Beach and as far north as Malibu, searching for the kilns that would provide him with bricks and tiles of requisite quality. In the end he sheathed the roof partly with copper, which has turned a beautiful green with the years. During these searches he became closely acquainted with the visionary and remarkably progressive Abbott Kinney, who was building the resort of Venice on the coast ten miles away, and with the swarthy, bright-eyed, unknown master builder Simon Rodia, self-educated like himself. All three men shared a rich vein of the poetry of stone, ceramics, and metals.

There must have been prodigious reserves of strength in the old man (for my father was that now, his hair whitely grizzled) to enable him to accomplish so much hard labor, for within two years my mother and I were able to move into our new home at Vultures Roost and take up our lives there.

I was delighted with my new surroundings and to be rejoined with my father, and only resentful of the time I must spend at school, to which my father drove me and from which he fetched me each day. I especially enjoyed rambling, occasionally with my father but chiefly by myself, through the wild, dry, rock-crowned hills, spry despite my twisted foot. My mother was fearful for me, especially because of the hairy brown and black tarantulas one sometimes encountered and the snakes, including venomous rattlers, but I was not to be restrained.

My father was happy, but also like a man in a dream as he worked unceasingly at the innumerable tasks, chiefly artistic, involved in finishing our home. It was a structure of rich beauty, though our neighbors continued to shake their heads and cluck dubiously at its hexagonal shape, partly rounded roof, thick walls of tightly mortared (though unreinforced) brick, and the area of brightly colored tile and floridly engraved stone. "Fischer's Folly," they'd whisper, and chuckle. But swarthy Simon Rodia nodded approvingly when he visited and once Abbott Kinney came to admire, driven in an expensive car by a black chauffeur with whom he seemed on terms of easy friendship.

My father's stone engravings were indeed quite fanciful and even a little disconcerting in their subject matter and location. One was in the basement's floor of natural rock, which he had smoothed. From time to time I'd watch him work on it. Desert plants and serpents seemed to be its subject matter, but as one studied it one became aware that there was much marine stuff too: serrated looping seaweeds, coiling eels, fishes that trailed tentacles, suckered octopus arms, and two giant squid eyes peering from a coral-crusted castle. And in its midst he boldly hewed in a flowery stone script, "The Gate of Dreams." My childish imagination was fired, but I was a little frightened too.

It was about this time—1921 or thereabouts—that my sleepwalking began, or at any rate showed signs of becoming disturbingly persistent. Several times my father found me at varying distances from the house along one of the paths I favored in my limping rambles and carried me tenderly back, chilled and shivering, for unlike Kentucky in summer, Southern California nights are surprisingly cold. And more than once I was found huddled and still asleep in our cellar alongside the grotesquely floor-set "Gate of Dreams" bas-relief—to which, incidentally, my mother had taken a dislike which she tried to conceal from my father.

At that time too my sleeping habits began to show other abnormalities, some of them contradictory. Although an active and apparently healthy boy of ten, I was still sleeping infancy's twelve hours or more a night. Yet despite this unusual length of slumber coupled with the restlessness my sleepwalking would seem to have indicated, I never dreamed or at any rate remembered dreams upon awakening. And with one notable exception this has been true for my entire life.

The exception occurred a little later on, when I was eleven or twelve—in 1923 or thereabouts. I remember those few dreams (there were no more than eight or nine of them) with matchless vividness. How else?—since they were my life's only ones and since . . . but I must not anticipate. At the time I was secretive about them, telling neither my father nor my mother, as if for fear my parents might worry or (children are odd!) disapprove, until one final night.

In my dream I would find myself making my way through low passages and tunnels, all crudely cut or perhaps *gnawed* from solid rock. Often I felt I was at a great distance under the earth, though why I thought this in my dream I cannot say, except that there was often a sensation of heat and an indescribable feeling of pressure from above.

This last sensation was diminished almost to nothing at times, though. And sometimes I felt there were vast amounts of water far above me, though why I suspected this I cannot say, for the strange tunnels were always very dry. Yet in my dreams I came to assume that the burrows extended limitlessly under the Pacific.

There was no obvious source of illumination in the passages. My dream explanation of how I then managed to see them was fantastic, though rather ingenious. The floor of the tunnels was colored a strange purplish-green. This I explained in my dream as being the reflection of cosmic rays (which were much in the newspapers then, firing my boyish imagination) that came down through the thick rock above from distantmost outer space. The rounded ceiling of the tunnels, on the other hand, had a weird orange-blue glow. This, I seemed to know, was caused by the reflection of certain rays unknown to science that came up through the solid rock from the Earth's incandescent, constricted core.

The eerie mixed light revealed to me the strange engravings or ridgy pictures everywhere covering the tunnels' walls. They had a strong suggestion of the marine to them and also of the monstrous, yet they were strangely *generalized*, as if they were the mathematical diagrams of oceans and their denizens and of whole universes of alien life. If *the dreams* of a monster of supernatural mentality could be given visual shape, then they would be like those endless forms I saw on the tunnels' walls. Or if *the dreams* of such a monster were half materialized and able to move through such tunnels, *they would shape the walls in such fashion.*

At first in my dreams I was not conscious of having a body. I seemed to be a viewpoint floating along the tunnels at a definitely *rhythmic* rate, now faster, now slower.

And at first I never saw anything in those tormenting tunnels, though I was continually conscious of a fear that I might—a fear mixed with a desire. This was a most disturbing and exhausting feeling, which I could hardly have concealed upon awakening save that (with one exception) I never woke until my dream had played itself out, as it were, and my feelings were temporarily exhausted.

And then in my next dream I did begin to see things—creatures—in the tunnels, floating through them in the same general rhythmic fashion as I (or my viewpoint) progressed. They were worms about as long as a man and as thick as a man's thigh, cylindrical and untapering. From end to end, as many as a centipede's legs, were pairs of tiny wings, translucent like a fly's, which vibrated unceasingly, producing an unforgettably sinister low-pitched *hum*. They had no eyes—their heads were one circular mouth lined with rows of triangular teeth like a shark's. Although blind, they seemed able to sense each other at short distances and their sudden lurching swerves then to avoid colliding with each other held a particular horror for me. (It was a little like my lurching limp.)

In my very next dream I became aware of my own dream body. In brief, I was myself one of those same winged worms. The horror I felt was extreme, yet once more the dream lasted until its intensity was damped out and I could awaken with only the memory of terror, still able (I thought) to keep my dreams a secret.

The next time I had my dream it was to see three of the winged worms writhing in a wider section of tunnel where the sensation of pressure from above was minimal. I was still observer rather than participant, floating in my worm body in a narrower side passageway. How I was able to see while in one of the blind worm bodies, my dream logic did not explain.

They were worrying a rather small human victim. Their three snouts converged upon and covered his face. Their sinister buzzing had a hungry note and there were sucking sounds.

Blond hair, white pajamas, and (projecting from the right leg of those) a foot slightly shrunken and *twisted sharply inward* told me the victim was myself.

At that instant I was shaken violently, the scene swam, and through it my mother's huge terrorized face peered down at me with my father's anxious visage close behind.

I went into convulsions of terror, flailing my limbs, and I screamed and screamed. It was hours literally before I could be quieted down, and days before my father let me tell them my nightmare.

Thereafter he made a strict rule: that no one ever try to shake me awake, no matter how bad a nightmare I seemed to be having. Later I learned he'd watch me at such times with knitted brow, suppressing the impulse to rouse me and seeing to it that no one else tried to do so.

For several nights thereafter I fought sleep, but when my nightmare was never repeated and once more I could never remember having dreamed at all when I wakened, I quieted down and my life, both sleeping and waking, became very tranquil again. In fact, even my sleepwalking became less frequent, although I continued to sleep for abnormally long hours, a practice now encouraged by my father's injunction that I never be wakened unnaturally.

But I have since come to wonder whether this apparent diminishment of my unconscious night-wandering were not because I, or some fraction of me, had become more cunningly deceitful. *Habits* have in any case a way of slipping slowly from the serious notice of those around.

At times, though, I would catch my father looking at me speculatively, as though he would have dearly liked to talk with me of various deep matters, but in the end he would always restrain this impulse (if I had divined it rightly) and content himself with encouraging me in my school studies and rambling exercise despite the latter's dangers: there *were* more rattlesnakes about my favorite paths, perhaps because opossums and raccoons were being exterminated; he made me wear high-laced shoes of stout leather.

And once or twice I got the impression that he and Simon Rodia were talking secretly about me when the latter visited.

On the whole my life was a lonely one and has remained so to this day. We had no neighbors who were friends, no friends who were neighbors. At first this was because of the relative isolation of our residence and the suspicion that Germanic names uniformly called forth in the years following the World War. But it continued even after we began to have more neighbors, tolerant newcomers. Perhaps things would have been different if my father had lived longer. (His health was good save for a touch of eyestrain—dancing colors he'd see briefly.)

But that was not to be. On that fatal Sunday in 1925 he had joined me on one of my customary walks and we had just reached one of my favorite spots when the ground gave way under his feet and he vanished from beside me, his startled exclamation dropping in pitch as he fell rapidly. For once his instinct for underground conditions had deserted him. There was a little scraping rumble as a few rocks and some gravel landslided, then silence. I approached the weed-fringed black hole on my belly and peered down fearfully.

From very far below (it sounded) I heard my father call faintly, "Georg! Get help!" His voice now had a strained, higher-pitched sound, as if his chest were being constricted.

"Father! I'm coming down," I cried, cupping my hands about my mouth, and I had thrust my twisted foot into the hole searching for support, when his frantic yet clearly enunciated words came up, his voice still higher-pitched and even more strained, as if he had to make a great effort to get sufficient breath for them: "Do *not* come down, Georg—you'll start an avalanche. Get help . . . a rope!"

After a moment's hesitation I withdrew my leg and set off for home at a hobbling gallop. My horror was heightened (or perhaps a little relieved) by a sense of the dramatic—early that year we had listened for weeks on the little crystal set I'd built to the radioed reports of the long protracted, exciting efforts (ultimately unsuccessful) to rescue Floyd Collins from where he'd got himself trapped in Sand Cave near Cave City, Kentucky. I suppose I anticipated some such drama for my father.

Most fortunately a young doctor was making a call in our neighborhood and he was foremost in the party of men I soon guided back to where my father had disappeared. No sounds at all came from the black hole, although we called and called, and I remember that a couple of men had begun to look at me dubiously, as if I'd invented the whole thing, when the courageous young doctor insisted against the advice of most on being lowered into the hole—they'd brought a strong rope *and* an electric flashlight.

He was a long time going down, descending about fifty feet in all while calls went back and forth, and almost as long being drawn up. When he emerged all smeared with sandy dirt—great orange smudges—it was to tell us (he made a point of laying his hand on my shoulder; I could see my mother hurrying up between two other women) that my father was inextricably wedged in down there with little more than his head exposed and that he was, to an absolute certainty, dead.

At that moment there was another grating rumble, and the black hole collapsed upon itself. One of the men standing on its edge was barely jerked to safety. My mother shrieked, threw herself down on the shaking brown weeds, and was drawn back too.

In the subsequent weeks it was decided that my father's body could not be recovered. Some bags of concrete and sand were dumped into what was left of the hole to seal it. My mother was forbidden to erect a monument at the spot, but in some sort of compensation—I didn't understand the logic of it—Los Angeles County presented her with a cemetery plot elsewhere. (It now holds her own body.) An unofficial funeral service conducted by a Latin-American priest was eventually held at the spot, and Simon Rodia, defying the injunction, put up a small, nonsectarian ovoid monument of his own matchlessly tough white concrete bearing my father's name and beautifully inset with a vaguely aquatic or naval design in fragmented blue and green glass. It is still there.

After my father's death I became more withdrawn and brooding than ever, and my mother, a shy consumptive woman full of hysterical fears, hardly encouraged me to become sociable. In fact, almost as long as I can remember and certainly ever since Anton Fischer's tragic and abrupt demise, nothing has ever bulked large with me save my own brooding and this brick house set in the hills with its strange, queerly set stone carvings and the hills themselves, those sandy, spongy, salt-soaked, sun-baked hills. There has been altogether too much of them in my background: I have limped too long along their crumbling rims, under their cracked and treacherous overhanging sandstones, and through the months-dry streams that thread their separating canyons. I have thought a great deal about the old days when, some Indians are said to have believed, the Strangers came down from the stars with the great meteor shower and the lizard men perished in the course of their frantic digging for water and the scaly sea men came tunneling in from their encampments beneath the vast Pacific which constituted a whole world to the west, extensive as that of the stars. I early developed too great a love for such savage fancies. Too much of my physical landscape has become the core of my mental landscape. And during the nights of my long, long sleepings, I hobbled through them both, I am somehow sure. While by day I had horrible fugitive visions of my father, underground, dead-alive, companied by the winged worms of my nightmare. Moreover, I developed the notion or fantasy that there was a network of *tunnels* underlying the paths I limped along and corresponding to them exactly, but at varying depths and coming closest to the surface at my "favorite spots."

("The legend of Yig," the voices are droning. "The violet wisps, the globular nebulas, Canis Tindalos and their foul essence, the nature of the Doels, the tinted chaos, great Cutlu's minions . . ." I have made breakfast but I cannot eat. I thirstily gulp hot coffee.)

I would hardly keep harping on my sleepwalking and on the unnaturally long hours I spent so deeply asleep that my mother would vow that my mind was elsewhere, were it not associated with a lapse in the intellectual promise I was said to have shown in earlier years. True, I got along well enough in the semi-rural grade school I trudged to and later in the suburban high school to which a bus took me; true too that I early showed interest in many subjects and flashes of excellent logic and imaginative reasoning. The trouble was that I did not seem ever able to pursue any of those flashes and make a steady and persistent effort. There would be times when my teachers would worry my mother with reports of my unpreparedness and my disregard of assignments, though when examination time came I almost invariably managed to make a creditable showing. My interests in more personal directions, too, seemed to peter out very quickly. I was certainly peculiarly deficient in the power of attention. I remember often sitting down with a favorite book or text and then finding myself, minutes or hours later, turning over pages far ahead of anything I could remember reading. Sometimes only the memory of my father's injunctions to study, to study *deeply*, would keep me prodding on.

You may not think this matter worth mentioning. There is nothing strange in a lonely sheltered child failing to show great willpower and mental energy. There is nothing strange in such a child becoming slothful, weak, and indecisive. Nothing strange—only much to pity and reproach. The powers that be know I reproached myself often enough, for as my father had encouraged me to, I felt a power and a capability somewhere in myself, but somehow inhibited. But there are only too many people with power they cannot loose. It is only *later* events that have made me see something significant in my lapsings.

My mother followed to the letter my father's directions for my higher education, which I only learned of now. Upon my graduation from high school I was sent to a venerable Eastern institution of learning not as well known as those of the Ivy League, but of equally high standing—Miskatonic University, which lies on the serpentine river of that name within the antique town of Arkham with its gambrel roofs and elm-shaded avenues quiet as the footsteps of a witch's familiar. My father had first heard of the school from an Eastern employer of his talents, a Harley Warren for whom he had done some unusual dowsing in a cemetery within a swamp of cypresses, and that man's high praise of Miskatonic had imprinted itself indelibly upon his memory. My previous school record did not permit of this (I lacked certain prerequisites) but I just barely managed—much to the surprise of all my previous teachers—to pass a stiff entrance examination which required, like that of Dartmouth, some knowledge of Greek as well as Latin. Only I knew how much furious, imagination-invoking guessing that took. I could not bear to fall utterly short of my father's hopes for me.

Unfortunately, my efforts were in vain. Before the first term ended I was back in Southern California, physically and mentally depleted by a series of attacks of nervousness, homesickness, actual ailment (anemia), an increase in the hours I devoted to sleep, and an almost incredible recurrence of my sleepwalking, which more than once carried me deep into the wild hills west of Arkham. I tried for what seemed to me a long time to stick it out, but was advised by the college doctors to give it up after some particularly bad attacks. I believe that they thought I was not cut out to be even a moderately strong individual and that they pitied me more than they sympathized with me. It is not a good thing to see a youth racked by sentiments and longings proper to a fearful child.

And they appeared to be right in this (although I know now that they were wrong), for my malady turned out *(apparently)* to be simple homesickness and nothing more. It was with a feeling of immense relief that I returned to my mother and our brick home in the hills, and with each room I reentered I gained more assurance—even, or perhaps especially, the cellar with its well-swept floor of solid rock, my father's tools and chemicals (acids, etc.), and the marinely decorated, floor-set rock inscription "The Gate of Dreams." It was as though all the time I had been at Miskatonic there had been an invisible leash dragging me back, and only now had its pressure slackened completely.

(Those voices *are* continent-wide, of course: "The essential salts, the fane of Dagon, the gray twisted brittle monstrosity, the flute-tormented pandemonium, the coral-encrusted towers of Rulay . . .")

And the hills helped me as much as my home. For a month I

roamed them daily and walked the old familiar paths between the parched and browning undergrowth, my mind full of old tales and scraps of childhood brooding. I think it was only then, only with my returning, that I first came fully to realize how much (and a little of *what*) those hills meant to me. From Mount Waterman and steep Mount Wilson with its great observatory and hundred-inch reflector down through cavernous Tujunga Canyon with its many sinuous offshoots to the flat lands and then across the squat Verdugo Hills and the closer ones with Griffith Observatory and its lesser 'scopes, to sinister, almost inaccessible Potrero and great twisting Topanga Canyons that open with the abruptness of catastrophe upon the monstrous, primeval Pacific—all of them (the hills) with few exceptions sandy, cracked, and treacherous, the earth like rock and the rock like dried earth, rotten, crumbling, and porous: all this had such a hold on me (the limper, the fearful listener) as to be obsessive. And indeed there were more and more symptoms of obsession now: I favored certain paths over others for ill-defined reasons and there were places I could not pass without stopping for a little. My fantasy or notion became stronger than ever that there were *tunnels* under the paths, traveled by beings which attracted the venomous snakes of the outer world because they were akin to them. Could some eerie reality have underlaid my childhood nightmare?—I shied away from that thought.

All this, as I say, I realized during the month after my defeated return from the East. And at the end of that month I resolved to conquer my obsession and my revolting homesickness and all the subtle weaknesses and inner hindrances that kept me from being the man my father had dreamed of. I had found that a complete break such as my father had planned for me (Miskatonic) would not work; so I determined to work out my troubles without running away: I would take courses at nearby UCLA (the University of California at Los Angeles). I would study and exercise, build up both body and mind. I remember that my determination was intense. There is something very ironic about that, for my plan, logical as it seemed, was the one sure course to further psychological entrapment.

For quite some time, however, I seemed to be getting on successfully. With systematic exercise and better-controlled diet and rest (still my twelve hours a night), I became healthier than I ever had been before. All the troubles that had beset me in the East vanished completely away. No longer did I wake shuddering from my dreamless sleepwalking; in fact, as far as I could determine at the time, that habit had gone for good. And at college, from which I returned home nightly, I made steady progress. It was then that I first began to write those imaginative and pessimistic poems tinged with metaphysical speculation that have won me some little attention from a small circle of readers. Oddly, they were sparked by the one significant item I had brought back with me from shadow-beset Arkham, a little book of verse I'd bought at a dusty secondhand store there, *Azathoth and Other Horrors* by Edward Pickman Derby, a local poet.

Now I know that my spurt of new effort during my college years was largely deceptive. Because I had decided upon a new course of life that brought me into a few new situations (though keeping me at home), I thought I was progressing vastly. I managed to keep on believing that for all my college years. That I could never study any subject profoundly, that I could never create anything that took a protracted effort, I explained by telling myself that what I was doing was "preparation" and "intellectual orientation" for some great future effort. For several years I managed to conceal from myself the fact that I could only call a tithe of my energy my own, while the residuum was being shunted down only the powers that be know what inner channels.

I thought I knew what books I was studying, but the voices now are telling me, "The runes of Nug-Soth, the clavicle of Nyarlathotep, the litanies of Lomar, the secular meditations of Pierre-Louis Montagny, the *Necronomicon*, the chants of CromYa, the overviews of Yiang-Li . . ."

(It is midday or later outside, but the house is cool. I have managed to eat a little and made more coffee. I have been down to the basement, checking my father's tools and things, his sledge, carboys of acid, et cetera, and looking at "The Gate of Dreams" and treading softly. The voices are strongest there.)

Suffice it that during my six college and "poetic" years (I couldn't carry a full load of courses) I lived not as a man, but as a fraction of a man. I had gradually given up all grand ambitions and become content to lead a life in miniature. I spent my time going to easy classes, writing fragments of prose and an occasional poem, caring for my mother (who except for her worries about me was undemanding) and for my father's house (so well built it needed hardly any care), rambling almost absentmindedly in the hills, and sleeping prodigiously. I had no friends. In fact, we had no friends. Abbott Kinney had died and Los Angeles had stolen his Venice. Simon Rodia gave up his visits, for he was now totally preoccupied with his great single-handed building project. Once on my mother's urging I went to Watts, a settlement of flower-decked humble bungalows dwarfed by his fabulous backyard towers that were rising like a blue-green Persian dream. He had trouble recalling who I was and then he watched me strangely as he worked. The money my father had left (in silver dollars) was ample for my mother and myself. In short, I had become, not unpleasantly, *resigned*.

This was all the easier for me because of my growing absorption in the doctrines of such men as Oswald Spengler who believe that culture and civilization go by cycles and that our own Faustian Western world, with all its grandiose dream of scientific progress, is headed toward a barbarism that will engulf it as surely as the Goths, Vandals, Scythians, and Huns engulfed mighty Rome and her longer-lived sister, dwindling Byzantium. As I looked from my hilltops down on bustling Los Angeles always a-building, I placidly thought of the future days when little bands of blustering, ill-kempt barbarians will walk the streets of humped and pitted asphalt and look on each of its ruined, many-purposed buildings as just another "hut"; when high-set Griffith Park Planetarium, romantically rock-built, high-walled, and firmly bastioned, will be the stronghold of some petty dictator; when industry and science will be gone and all their machines and instruments rusted and broken and their use forgotten . . . and *all* our works forgotten as completely as those of the sunken civilization of Mu in the Pacific, of the fragments of whose cities only remain Nan Matol and Rapa Nui, or Easter Island.

But *whence* did these thoughts really come? Not entirely or even principally from Spengler, I'll be bound. No, they had a *deeper* source, I greatly fear.

Yet thus I thought, thus I believed, and thus I was wooed away from the pursuits and tempting goals of our commercial world. I saw everything in terms of transciency, decadence, and decline—as if the times were as rotten and crumbling as the hills which obsessed me.

It was that I was *convinced*, not that I was morbid. No, my health was better than ever and I was neither bored nor dissatisfied. Oh, I occasionally berated myself for failure to manifest the promise my father had seen in me, but on the whole I was strangely content. I had a weird sense of power and self-satisfaction, as if I were a man in the midst of some engrossing pursuit. You know the pleasant relief and bone-deep satisfaction that comes after a day of successful hard work? Well, *that was the way I felt almost all the time, day in and day out.* And I took my happiness as a gift of the gods. It did not occur to me to ask, "*Which* gods? Are they from heaven . . . or from *the underworld*?"

Even my mother was happier, her disease arrested, her son devoted to her and leading a busy life (on a very small scale) and doing nothing to worry her beyond his occasional rambles in the snake-infested hills.

Fortune smiled on us. Our brick dwelling rode out the severe Long Beach earthquake of March 10, 1933, without sustaining the least damage. Those who still called it Fischer's Folly were nonplussed.

Last year (1936) I duly received from UCLA my bachelor's diploma in English literature, with a minor in history, my mother proudly attending the ceremony. And a month or so later she seemed as childishly delighted as I at the arrival of the first bound copies of my little book of verse, *The Tunneler Below*, printed at my own expense, and in my hubristic mood of auctorial conceit I not only sent out several copies for review but also donated two to the UCLA library and two more to that at Miskatonic. In my covering letter to the erudite Dr. Henry Armitage, librarian at the latter institution, I mentioned not only my brief attendance there, but also my inspiration by an Arkham poet. I also told him a little about the circumstances of my composition of the poems.

I joked deprecatingly to my mother about this last expansive gesture of mine, but she knew how deeply I had been hurt by my failure at Miskatonic and how strongly I desired to repair my reputation there, so when only a few weeks later a letter came addressed to me and bearing the Arkham postmark, she hurried out into the hills quite against her usual wont, to bring it to me, I having just gone out on one of my rambles.

From where I was, I barely heard, yet also recognized her mortal screams. I rushed back at my most desperate limping speed. At the very spot where my father had perished, I found her writhing on the hard, dry ground and screaming still—and near to her and whipping about, the large young rattlesnake that had bitten her on the calf, which was already swelling.

I killed the horrid thing with the stick I carry, then slashed the bite with my sharp pocketknife and sucked it out and injected antivenin from the kit I have always with me on my walks.

All to no avail. She died two days later in the hospital. Once more there was not only shock and depression, but also the dismal business of a funeral to get through (at least we already owned a grave lot), this time a more conventional ceremony, but this time I was wholly alone.

It was a week before I could bring myself to look at the letter she'd been bringing me. After all, it had been the cause of her death. I almost tore it up unread. But after I had got into it, I became more and more interested and then incredulously amazed . . . and frightened. Here it is, in its entirety:

118 Saltonstall St.,
Arkham, Mass.,
Aug. 12, 1936.

Georg Reuter Fischer, Esq.,
Vultures Roost,
Hollywood, Calif.

My dear Sir:—

Dr. Henry Armitage took the liberty of letting me peruse your *The Tunneler Below* before it was placed on general circulation in the university library. May one who serves only in the outer court of the muses' temple, and particularly outside Polyhymnia's and Erato's shrines, be permitted to express his deep appreciation of your creative achievement? And to tender respectfully the like admirations of Professor Wingate Peaslee of our psychology department and of Dr. Francis Morgan of medicine and comparative anatomy, who share my special interests, and of Dr. Armitage himself? "The Green Deeps" is in particular a remarkably well-sustained and deeply moving lyric poem.

I am an assistant professor of literature at Miskatonic and an enthusiastic amateur student of New England and other folklore. If memory serves, you were in my freshman English section six years ago. I was sorry then that the state of your health forced you to curtail your studies, and I am happy now to have before me conclusive evidence that you have completely surmounted all such difficulties. Congratulations!

And now will you allow me to pass on to another and very different matter, which is nonetheless peripherally related to your poetic work? Miskatonic is currently engaged in a broad interdepartmental research in the general area of folklore, language, and dreams, an investigation of the vocabulary of the collective unconscious, particularly as it expresses itself in poetry. The three scholars I have alluded to are among those active in this work, along with persons in Brown University, Providence, Rhode Island, who are carrying on the pioneering work of the late Professor George Gammell Angell, and from time to time I am honored to render them assistance. They have empowered me to ask you for your own help in this matter, which could be of signal importance. It is a matter of answering a few questions only, relating to the accidents of your writing and in no way impinging on its essence, and should not cut seriously into your time. Naturally any information you choose to supply will be treated as strictly confidential.

I call your attention to the following two lines in "The Green Deeps":

> Intelligence doth grow itself within
> The coral-palled, squat towers of Rulay.

Did you in composing this poem ever consider a more eccentric spelling of the last (and presumably invented?) word? "R'lyeh," say. And going back three lines, did you consider spelling "Nath" (invented?) with an initial "p"—i.e., "Pnath"?

Also in the same poem:

> The rampant dragon dreams in far Cathay
> While snake-limbed Cutlu sleeps in deep Rulay.

The name "Cutlu" (once more, invented?) is of considerable interest to us. Did you have phonetic difficulty in choosing the letters to represent the sound you had in mind? Did you perhaps simplify in the interests of poetic clarity? At any time did "Cthulhu" ever occur to you?

(As you can see, we are discovering that the language of the collective unconscious is almost unpleasantly guttural and sibilant! All hawking and spitting, like German.)

Also, there is this quatrain in your impressive lyric, "Sea Tombs":

> Their spires underlie our deepest graves;
> Lit are they by a light that man has seen.
> Only the wingless worm can go between
> Our daylight and their vault beneath the waves.

Were there some proofreading errors here?—or the equivalent. Specifically, in the second line should "that" be "no"? (And was the light you had in mind what you might call orange-blue or purple-green, or both?) And, in the next line, how does "winged" rather than "wingless" strike you?

Finally, in regard to "Sea Tombs" and also the title poem of your book, Professor Peaslee has a question which he calls a "long shot" about the subterranean and submarine tunnels which you evoke. Did you ever have fantasies of such tunnels really existing in the area where you composed the poem?—the Hollywood Hills and Santa Monica Mountains, presumably, the Pacific Ocean being nearby. Did you perhaps try actually to trace the paths overlying these fancied tunnels? And did you happen to notice (excuse the strangeness of this question) an unusual number of venomous serpents along such routes?—rattlers, I would presume (in our area it would be copperheads, and in the South water moccasins and coral snakes). If so, do take care!

If such tunnels should by some strange coincidence actually exist, it would be scientifically possible to confirm the fact without any digging or drilling (or by discovering an existent opening), it may interest you to know. Even vacuity—i.e., nothing—leaves its traces, it appears! Two Miskatonic science professors, who are part of the interdepartmental program I mentioned, have devised a highly portable apparatus for the purpose, which they call a magneto-optic geo-scanner. (That last hybrid word must sound a most clumsy and barbarous coinage to a poet, I'm sure, but you know scientists!) It is strange, is it not, to think of an investigation of dreams having geological repercussions? The clever though infelicitously named instrument is a simplified adaptation of one which has already discovered two new elements.

I shall be making a trip west early next year, to confer with a man in San Diego who happens to be the son of the scholarly recluse whose researches led to our interdepartmental program—Henry Wentworth Akeley. (The local poet—alas, deceased—to whom you pay such generous tribute, was another such pioneer, it happens oddly.) I shall be driving my own British sports car, a diminutive Austin. I am something of an automobile maniac, I must confess, even a speed demon!—however inappropriate that may be for an assistant English professor. I would be very pleased to make your further acquaintance at that time, if entirely agreeable to you. I might even bring along a geo-scanner and we could check out those hypothetical tunnels!

But I perhaps anticipate and presume too far. Pardon me. I will be very grateful for any attention you are able to give this letter and its necessarily impertinent questions.

Once more, congratulations on *The Tunneler*!

Yrs. very truly,
Albert N. Wilmarth.

It is quite impossible to describe all at once my state of mind when I finished reading this letter. I can only do so by stages. To begin with, I was flattered and gratified, even acutely embarrassed, by his apparently sincere praise of my verses—as what young poet wouldn't be? And that a psychologist and an old librarian (even an anatomist!) should admire them too—it was almost too much.

As soon as the man mentioned freshman English I realized that I had a vivid memory of him. Although I'd forgotten his name in the course of years, it came back to me like a shot when I glanced ahead at the end of the letter and saw it. He had been only an instructor then, a tall young man, cadaverously thin, always moving about with nervous rapidity, his shoulders hunched. He'd had a long jaw and a pale complexion, with dark-circled eyes which gave him a haunted look, as if he were constantly under some great strain to which he never alluded. He had the habit of jerking out a little notebook and making jottings without ceasing for a moment to discourse fluently, even brilliantly. He'd seemed incredibly well read and had had a lot to do with stimulating and deepening my interest in poetry. I even remembered his car—the other students used to joke about it with an undercurrent of envy. It had been a Model T Ford then, which he'd always driven at a brisk clip around the fringes of the Miskatonic campus, taking turns very sharply.

The program of interdepartmental research he described sounded very impressive, even exciting, but eminently plausible—I was just discovering Jung then and also semantics. And to be invited so graciously to take part in it—once again I was flattered. If I hadn't been alone while I read it, I might have blushed.

One notion I got then did stop me briefly and for a moment almost turned me angrily against the whole thing—the sudden suspicion that the purpose of the program might not be the avowed one, that (the presence in it of a psychologist and a medical doctor influenced me in this) it was some sort of investigation of the delusions of crankish, imaginative people—not so much the incidental insights as the psychopathology of poets.

But he was so very gracious and reasonable—no, I was being paranoid, I told myself. Besides, as soon as I got a ways into his detailed questions it was an altogether different reaction that filled me—one of utter amazement . . . and *fear*.

For starters, he was so incredibly accurate in his guesses (for what else could they possibly be? I asked myself uneasily) about those invented names, that he had me gasping. I *had* first thought of spelling them "R'lyeh" and "Pnath"—exactly those letters, though of course memory can be tricky about such things.

And then that *Cthulhu*—seeing it spelled that way actually made me shiver, it so precisely conveyed the deep-pitched, harsh, inhuman cry or chant I'd imagined coming up from profound black abysses, and only finally rendered as "Cutlu" rather dubiously, but fearing anything more complex would seem affectation. (And, really, you can't fit the inner rhythms of a sound like "Cthulhu" into English poetry.)

And then to find that he'd spotted those two proofreader's errors, for they'd been just that. The first I'd missed. The second ("wingless" for "winged") I'd caught, but then rather spinelessly let stand, feeling all of a sudden that I'd perpetuated something overly fantastic when I'd put a figure from my life's one nightmare (a worm with wings) into a poem.

And topping even that, how in the name of all that's wonderful could he have described unearthly colors I'd only dreamed of and never put into my poems at all? Using exactly the same color-words I'd used! I began to think that Miskatonic's interdepartmental research project must have made some epochal discoveries about dreams and dreaming and the human imagination in general, enough to turn their scholars into wizards and dumbfound Adler, Freud, and even Jung.

At that point in my reading of the letter I thought he'd hit me with everything he possibly could, but the next section managed to mine a still deeper source of horror and one most disturbingly close to everyday reality. That he should know, somehow deduce, all about my paths in the hills and my odd daydreams about them and about tunnels I'd fancied underlying them—that was truly staggering. And that he should ask *and even warn me* about venomous snakes, so that the very letter my mother was carrying unopened when she got her death sting contained a vital reference to it—really, for a moment and more then, I did wonder if I were going insane.

And finally when despite all his jaunty "fancied's" and "long shot's" and "hypothetical's" and English-professor witticisms, he began to talk as if he assumed my imaginary tunnels were real and to refer lightly to a scientific instrument that would prove it . . . well, by the time I'd finished his letter, I fully expected him to turn up the next minute—turn in sharply at our drive with a flourish of wheels and brakes in his Model T (no, Austin) and draw up in a cloud of dust at our door, the geo-scanner sitting on the front seat beside him like a fat black telescope directed downward!

And yet he'd been so damnably *breezy* about it all! I simply didn't know what to think.

(I've been down in the basement again, checking things out. This writing stirs me up and makes me frightfully restless. I went out front, and there was a rattlesnake crossing the path in the hot slanting sunlight from the west. More evidence, if any were needed, that what I fear is true. Or do I hope for it? At all events, I killed the brute. The voices vibrate with, "The half-born worlds, the alien orbs, the stirrings in blackness, the hooded forms, the nighted depths, the shimmering vortices, the purple haze . . .")

When I'd calmed down somewhat next day, I wrote Wilmarth a long letter, confirming all his hints, confessing my utter astonishment at them, and begging him to explain how he'd made them. I volunteered to assist the interdepartmental project in any way I could and invited him to be my guest when he came west. I gave him a brief history of my life and my sleep anomalies, mentioning my mother's death. I had a strange feeling of unreality as I posted the letter and waited with mixed feelings of impatience and lingering (and also regathering) incredulity for his reply.

When it came, quite a fat one, it rekindled all my first excitement, though without satisfying all my curiosity by any means. Wilmarth was still inclined to write off his and his colleagues' deductions about my word choices, dreams, and fantasies as lucky guesses, though he told me enough about the project to keep my curiosity in a fever—especially about its discoveries of obscure linkages between the life of the imagination and archaeological discoveries in far-off places. He seemed particularly interested in the fact that I generally never dreamed and that I slept for very long hours. He overflowed with thanks for my cooperation and my invitation, promising to include me on his itinerary when he drove west. And he had a lot more questions for me.

The next months were strange ones. I lived my normal life, if it can be called that, keeping up my reading and studies and library visits, even writing a little new poetry from time to time. I continued my hill-ramblings, though with a new wariness. Sometimes during them I'd stop and stare at the dry earth beneath my feet, as if expecting to trace the outlines of a trapdoor in it. And sometimes I'd be consumed by sudden, wildly passionate feelings of grief and guilt at the thought of my father locked down there and at my mother's horrible death too; I'd feel I must somehow go to them at all costs.

And yet at the same time I was living only for Wilmarth's letters and the moods of wonder, fantastic speculation, and panic—yet almost delicious terror—they evoked in me. He'd write about all sorts of things besides the project—my poetry and new readings and my ideas (he'd play the professorial mentor here from time to time), world events, the weather, astronomy, submarines, his pet cats, faculty politics at Miskatonic, town meetings at Arkham, his lectures, and the local trips he'd make. He made it all extremely interesting. Clearly he was an inveterate letter-writer and under his influence I became one too.

But most of all, of course, I was fascinated by what he'd write from time to time about the project. He told me some very interesting things about the Miskatonic Antarctic expedition of 1930–31, with its five great Dornier airplanes, and last year's somewhat abortive Australian one in which the psychologist Peaslee and his father, a one-time economist, had been involved. I remembered having read about them both in the newspapers, though the reports there had been curiously fragmentary and unsatisfying, almost as if the press were prejudiced against Miskatonic.

I got the strong impression that Wilmarth would have liked very much to have accompanied both expeditions and was very much put out at not having been able (or allowed) to, though most of the time bravely concealing his disappointment. More than once he referred to his "unfortunate nervousness," sensitivity to cold, fierce migraine attacks, and "bouts of ill health" which would put him to bed for a few days. And sometimes he'd speak with wistful admiration of the prodigious energy and stalwart constitutions of several of his colleagues, such as Professors Atwood and Pabodie, the geo-scanner's inventors, Dr. Morgan, who was a big-game hunter, and even the octogenarian Armitage.

There were occasional delays in his replies, which always filled me with anxiety and restlessness, sometimes because of these attacks of his and sometimes because he'd been away longer than he'd expected on some visit. One of the latter was to Providence to confer with colleagues and help investigate the death under mysterious circumstances involving a lightning bolt of Robert Blake, a poet like myself, short-story writer, and painter whose work had provided much material for the project.

It was just after his visit to Providence that with a curious sort of guardedness and reluctance he mentioned visiting another colleague of sorts there (who was in poor health), a Howard Phillips Lovecraft, who had fictionalized (but quite sensationally, Wilmarth warned me) some Arkham scandals and some of Miskatonic's researches and project activities. These stories had been published (when at all) in cheap pulp magazines, especially in a lurid journal called *Weird Tales* (you'll want to tear the cover off, if ever you should dare to buy a copy, he assured me). I recalled having seen the magazine on downtown newsstands in Hollywood and Westwood. I hadn't found the covers offensive. Most of their nude female figures, by some sentimental woman artist, were decorously sleek pastels and their activities only playfully perverse. Others, by one Senf, were a rather florid folk art quite reminiscent of my father's floral chiselings.

But after that, of course, I haunted secondhand bookstores, hunting down copies of *Weird Tales* (mostly) with Lovecraft stories in them, until I'd found a few and read them—one, "The Call of Cthulhu," no less. It cost me the strangest shudders, let me tell you, to see *that* name again, spelled out in cheapest print, under such very outlandish circumstances. Truly, my sense of reality was set all askew and if the tale that Lovecraft told with a strange dignity and power was anything like the truth, then Cthulhu was *real,* an other-dimensional extra-terrestrial monster dreaming in an insane, Pacific-sunken metropolis which sent out mental messages (and—who knows?—tunnels) to the world at large. In another tale, "The Whisperer in Darkness," *Albert N. Wilmarth* was a leading character, and that Akeley too he'd mentioned.

It was all fearfully unsettling and confounding. If I hadn't attended Miskatonic myself and lived in Arkham, I'd have thought surely they were a writer's projections.

As you can imagine, I continued to haunt the dusty bookstores and I *bombarded* Wilmarth with frantic questions. His replies were of a most pacifying and temporizing sort. Yes, he'd been afraid of my getting too excited, but hadn't been able to resist telling me about the stories. Lovecraft often laid on things *very* thickly indeed. I'd understand everything much better when we could really talk together and he could explain in person. Really, Lovecraft had an extremely powerful imagination and sometimes it got out of hand. No, Miskatonic had never tried to suppress the stories or take legal action, for fear of even less desirable publicity—and because the project members thought the stories might be a good preparation for the world if some of their more frightening hypotheses were verified. Really, Lovecraft was a very charming and well-intentioned person, but sometimes he went too far. And so on and so on.

Really, I don't think I could have contained myself except that, it now being 1937, Wilmarth sent me word that he was at last driving west. The Austin had been given a thorough overhaul and was "packed to the gills" with the geo-scanner, endless books and papers, and other instruments and materials, including a drug Morgan had just refined, "which induces dreaming and may, conceivably, he says, facilitate clairvoyance and clairaudience. It might make even you dream—should you consent to ingest an experimental dose."

While he was gone from 118 Saltonstall his rooms would be occupied and his cats, including his beloved Blackfellow, cared for by a close friend named Danforth, who'd spent the last five years in a mental hospital recovering from his ghastly Antarctic experience at the Mountains of Madness.

Wilmarth hated to leave at this time, he wrote, in particular he was worried about Lovecraft's failing health, but nevertheless he was on his way!

The next weeks (which dragged out to two months) were a time of particular tension, anxiety, and anticipatory excitement for me. Wilmarth had many more people and places to visit and investigations to make (including readings with the geo-scanner) than I'd ever imagined. Now he sent mostly postcards, some of them scenic, but they came thick and fast (except for a couple of worrisome hiatuses) and with his minuscule handwriting he got so much on them (even the scenic ones) that at times I almost felt I was with him on his trip, worrying about the innards of his Austin, which he called the Tin Hind after Sir Francis Drake's golden one. I on my part had only a few addresses he'd listed for me where I could write him in advance—Baltimore; Winchester, Virginia; Bowling Green, Kentucky; Memphis; Carlsbad, New Mexico; Tucson; and San Diego.

First he had to stop in Hunterdon County, New Jersey, with its quaintly backward farm communities, to investigate some possibly pre-Colonial ruins and hunt for a rumored cave, using the geo-scanner. Next, after Baltimore, there were extensive limestone caverns to check out in both Virginias. He crossed the Appalachians Winchester to Clarsksburg, a stretch with enough sharp turns to satisfy even him. Approaching Louisville, the Tin Hind was almost swallowed up in the Great Ohio Flood (which preoccupied the radio news for days; I hung over my superheterodyne set) and he was unable to visit a new correspondent of Lovecraft's there. Then there was more work for the geo-scanner near Mammoth Cave. In fact, caves seemed to dominate his journey, for after a side trip to New Orleans to confer with some occult scholar of French extraction, there were the Carlsbad Caverns and nearby but less well-known subterranean vacuities. I wondered more and more about my tunnels.

The Tin Hind held up very well, except she blew out a piston head crossing Texas ("I held her at high speed a little too long") and he lost three days getting her mended.

Meanwhile, I was finding and reading new Lovecraft stories. One, which turned up in a secondhand but quite recent science-fiction pulp, fictionalized the Australian expedition most impressively—especially the dreams old Peaslee had that led to it. In them, he'd exchanged personalities with a cone-shaped monster and was forever wandering through long stone passageways haunted by invisible whistlers. It reminded me so much of my nightmares in which I'd done the same thing with a winged worm that buzzed, that I airmailed a rather desperate letter to Tucson, telling Wilmarth all about it. I got a reply from San Diego, full of reassurances and more temporizings, and referring to old Akeley's son and some sea caverns they were looking into, and (at last!) setting a date (it would be soon!) for his arrival.

The day before that last, I made a rare find in my favorite Hollywood hunting-ground. It was a little, strikingly illustrated book by Lovecraft called *The Shadow Over Innsmouth* and issued by Visionary Press, whoever they were. I was up half the night reading it. The narrator found some sinister, scaly human beings living in a deep submarine city off New England, realized he was himself turning into one of them, and at the end had decided (for better or worse) to dive down and join them. It made me think of crazy fantasies I'd had of somehow going down into the earth beneath the Hollywood Hills and rescuing or joining my dead father.

Meanwhile mail addressed to Wilmarth care of me had begun to arrive. He'd asked my permission to include my address on the itinerary he'd sent other correspondents. There were letters and cards from (by their postmarks) Arkham and places along his route, some from abroad (mostly England and Europe, but one from Argentina), and a small package from New Orleans. The return address on most of them was his own—118 Saltonstall, so he'd eventually get them even if he missed them along his route. (He'd asked me to do the same with my own notes.) The effect was odd, as though Wilmarth were the author of everything—it almost re-aroused my first suspicions of him and the project. (One letter, though among the last to come, a thick one bearing extravagantly a six-cent airmail stamp and a ten-cent special delivery, had been addressed to George Goodenough Akeley, 176 Pleasant St., San Diego, Cal., and then forwarded care of my own address in the upper-left-hand corner.)

Late the next afternoon (Sunday, April 14—the eve of my twenty-fifth birthday, as it happened) Wilmarth arrived very much as I'd imagined it occurring when I'd finished reading his first letter, except the Tin Hind was even smaller than I'd pictured—and enameled a bright blue, though now most dusty. There *was* an odd black case on the seat beside him, though there were a lot of other things on it too—maps, mostly.

He greeted me very warmly and began to talk a blue streak almost at once, with many a jest and frequent little laughs.

The thing that really shocked me was that although I knew he was only in his thirties, his hair was white and the haunted (or hunted) look I'd remembered was monstrously intensified. And he was extremely nervous—at first he couldn't stay still a moment. It wasn't long before I became certain of something I'd never once suspected before—that his breeziness and jauntiness, his jokes and laughs, were a mask for fear, no, for sheer terror, that otherwise might have mastered him entirely.

His actual first words were, "Mr. Fischer, I presume? So glad to meet you in the flesh!—and share your most salubrious sunlight. I look as if I need it, do I not?—a horrid sight! This landscape hath a distinctly cavish, tunnelly aspect—I'm getting to be an old hand at making such geological judgements. Danforth writes that Blackfellow has quite recovered from his indisposition. But Lovecraft is in the hospital—I do not like it. Did you observe last night's brilliant conjunction?—I *like* your clear, clear skies. No, I will carry the geo-scanner (yes, it *is* that); it's somewhat crankish. But you might take the small valise. Really, so very glad!"

He did not comment on or even seem to notice my twisted right foot (something I hadn't mentioned in my letters, though he may have recalled it from six years back) or imply its or my limp's existence in any way, as by insisting on carrying the valise also. That warmed me toward him.

And before going into the house with me, he paused to praise its unusual architecture (another thing I hadn't told him about) and seemed genuinely impressed when I admitted that my father had built it by himself. (I'd feared he'd find it overly eccentric and also question whether someone could work with his hands and be a gentleman.) He also commented favorably on my father's stone carvings wherever they turned up and insisted on pausing to study them, whipping out his notebook to make some quick jottings. Nothing would do, but I must take him on a full tour of the house before he'd consent to rest or take refreshments. I left his valise in the bedroom I'd assigned him (my parents', of course), but he kept lugging the black geo-scanner around with him. It was an odd case, taller than it was wide or long, and it had three adjustable stubby legs, so that it could be set up vertically anywhere.

Emboldened by his approval of my father's carvings, I told him about Simon Rodia and the strangely beautiful towers he was building in Watts, whereupon the notebook came out again and there were more jottings. He seemed particularly impressed by the *marine* quality I found in Rodia's work.

Down in the basement (he had to go there too) he was very much struck by my father's floor-set "Gate of Dreams" stone carving and studied it longer than any of the others. (I'd been feeling embarrassed about its bold motto and odd placement.) Finally he indicated the octopus eyes staring over the castle and observed, "Cutlu, perchance?"

It was the first reference of any sort to the research project that either of us had made since our meeting and it shook me strangely, but he appeared not to notice and continued with, "You know, Mr. Fischer, I'm tempted to get a reading with Atwood and Pabodie's infernal black box right here. Would you object?"

I told him certainly not and to go right ahead, but warned him there was only solid rock under the house (I had told him about my father's dowsing and even had mentioned Harley Warren, whom it turned out Wilmarth had heard of through a Randolph Carter).

He nodded, but said, "I'll take a shot at it nonetheless. We must start somewhere, you know," and he proceeded to set up the geo-scanner carefully so it was standing vertically on its three stubby legs right in the middle of the carving. He took off his shoes first so as not to risk damaging the rather fine stonework.

Then he opened the top of the geo-scanner. I glimpsed two dials and a large eyepiece. He knelt and applied his eye to it, drawing out a black hood and draping it over his head, very much like an old-fashioned photographer focusing for a picture. "Pardon me, but the indications I must look for are difficult to see," he said muffledly. "Hello, what's this?"

There was a longish pause during which nothing happened except his shoulders shifted a bit and there were a few faint clicks. Then he emerged from under the hood, tucked it back in the black box, closed the latter, and began to put on and relace his shoes.

"The scanner's gone crankish," he explained in answer to my inquiry, "and is seeing ghost vacuities. But not to worry—it only needs new warm-up cells, I fancy, which I have with me, and will be right as rain for tomorrow's expedition! That is, if—?" He rolled his eyes up at me in smiling inquiry.

"Of course I'll be able to show you my pet trails in the hills," I assured him. "In fact, I'm bursting to."

"Capital!" he said heartily.

But as we left the basement, its rock floor rang out a bit hollowly, it sounded to me, under his high-laced leather-soled and -heeled shoes (I was wearing sneakers).

It was getting dark, so I started dinner after giving him some iced tea, which he took with lots of lemon and sugar. I cooked eggs and small beefsteaks, figuring from his haggard looks he needed the most restorative sort of food. I also built a fire in the big fireplace against the almost invariable chill of evening.

As we ate by its dancing, crackling flames, he regaled me with brief impressions of his trip west—the cold, primeval pine woods of southern New Jersey with their somberly clad inhabitants speaking an almost Elizabethan English; the very narrow dark roads of West Virginia; the freezing waters of the Ohio flooding unruffled, silent, battleship gray, and ineffably menacing under lowering skies; the profound silence of Mammoth Cave; the southern Midwest with its Depression-spawned, but already legendary, bank robbers; the nervous Creole charms of New Orleans's restored French Quarter; the lonely, incredibly long stretches of road in Texas and Arizona that made one believe one was *seeing* infinity; the great, long, blue, mystery-freighted Pacific rollers ("so different from the Atlantic's choppier, shorter-spaced waves") which he'd watched with George Goodenough Akeley, who'd turned out to be a very solid chap and knowing more about his father's frightening Vermont researches than Wilmarth had expected.

When I mentioned finding *The Shadow Over Innsmouth* he nodded and murmured, "The original of its youthful hero has disappeared *and* his cousin from the Canton asylum. Down to Y'ha-nthlei? Who knows?" But when I remembered his accumulated mail he merely nodded his thanks, wincing a little, as though reluctant to face it. He really did look shockingly tired.

When we'd finished dinner, however, and he'd taken his black coffee (also with lots of sugar) and the fire was dancing flickeringly, both yellow and blue now, he turned to me with a little, venturesomely friendly smile and a big, wonderingly wide lifting of his eyebrows, and said quietly, "And now you'll quite rightly be expecting me to tell you, my dear Fischer, all the things about the project that I've been hesitant to write, the answers I've been reluctant to give to your cogent questions, the revelations I've been putting off making until we should meet in person. Really, you have been very patient, and I thank you."

Then he shook his head thoughtfully, his eyes growing distant, as he slowly and rather sinuously and somehow unwillingly shrugged his shoulders, which paradoxically were both frail and wide, and grimaced slightly, as if tasting something strangely bitter, and said even more quietly, "if only I had more to tell you that's been *definitely proved.*

Somehow we always stop just short of that. Oh, the artifacts are real enough and certain—the Innsmouth jewelry, the Antarctic soapstones, Blake's Shining Trapezohedron, though that's lost in Narragansett Bay, the spiky baluster knob Walter Gilman brought back from his witchy dreamland (or the nontemporal fourth dimension, if you prefer), even the unknown elements, meteoric and otherwise, which defy all analysis, even the new magneto-optic probe which has given us virginium and alabamine. And it's almost equally certain that all, or almost all, those weird extraterrestrial and extra-cosmic creatures *have* existed—that's why I wanted you to read the Lovecraft stories, despite their lurid extravagances, so you'd have some picture of the entities that I'd be talking to you about. Except that they and the evidence for them *do* have a maddening way of vanishing upon extinction and from all records—Wilbur Whateley's mangled remains, his brother's vast invisible cadaver, the Plutonian old Akeley killed *and couldn't photograph*, the June 1882 meteor itself which struck Nahum Gardner's farm and which set old Armitage (young then) studying the *Necronomicon* (the start of everything at Miskatonic) and which Atwood's father saw with his own eyes and tried to analyze, or what Danforth saw down in Antarctica when he looked back at the horrible higher mountains beyond the Mountains of Madness—he's got amnesia for that now that he has regained his sanity . . . all, all gone!

"But whether any of those creatures exist *today*—there, there's the rub! The overwhelming question we can't answer, though always on the edge of doing so. The thing is," he went on with gathering urgency, "that *if they do exist*, they are so unimaginably powerful and resourceful, they might be"—and he looked around sharply—"anywhere at the moment!

"Take *Cthulhu*," he began.

I couldn't help starting as I heard that word pronounced for the first time in my life; the harsh, dark, abysmal *monosyllabic* growl it came to was so very like the sound that had originally come to me from my imagination, or my subconscious, or my otherwise unremembered dreams, or. . . .

He continued, "If Cthulhu exists, then he (or she, or it) can go anywhere he wants through space, or air, or sea, or earth itself. We know from Johansen's account (it turned his hair white) that Cthulhu can exist as a gas, be torn to atoms, and then recombine. He wouldn't need tunnels to go through solid rock, he could *seep* through it—'not in the spaces we know, but between them.' And yet in his inscrutability he might choose tunnels—there's that to be reckoned with. Or—still another possibility—perhaps he neither exists nor does not exist but is in some half state—'waits dreaming,' as Angell's old chant has it.

Perhaps his dreams, incarnated as your winged worms, Fischer, dig tunnels.

"It is those monstrous underground cavern-and-tunnel worlds, not all from Cthulhu by any means, that I have been assigned to investigate with the geo-scanner, partly because I was the first to hear of them from old Akeley and also—Merciful Creator!—from the Plutonian who masked as him—'great worlds of unknown life down there; blue-litten K'n-yan, red-litten Yoth, and black, lightless N'kai,' which was Tsathoggua's home, and even stranger inner spaces litten by colors from space and from Earth's nighted core. That's how I guessed the colors in your childhood dreams or nightmares (or personality exchanges), my dear Fischer. I've glimpsed them also in the geo-scanner, where they are, however, most fugitive and difficult to discern. . . ."

His voice trailed off tiredly, just as my own concern became most feverishly intense with his mention of "personality exchanges."

He really did look shockingly fatigued. Nevertheless I felt impelled to nerve myself to say, "Perhaps those dreams can be repeated, if I take Dr. Morgan's drug. Why not tonight?"

"Out of the question," he replied, shaking his head slowly. "In the first place, I wrote too hopefully there. At the last minute Morgan was unable to supply me with the drug. He promised to send it along by mail, but hasn't yet. In the second place, I'm inclined to think now that it would be much too dangerous an experiment."

"But at least you'll be able to check those dream colors *and* the tunnels with your geo-scanner?" I pressed on, somewhat crestfallen.

"If I can repair it . . ." he said, his head nodding and slumping to one side. The dying flames were all blue now as he whispered mumblingly, ". . . if I am *permitted* to repair it. . . ."

I had to help him to bed and then retire to my own, shaken and unsatisfied, my mind a-whirl. Wilmarth's alternating moods of breezy optimism and a seemingly *frightened* dejection were hard to adjust to. But now I realized that I was very tired myself—after all, I'd been up most of the previous night reading *Innsmouth*—and soon I slumbered.

(The voices stridently groan, "The pit of primal life, the Yellow Sign, Azathoth, the Magnum Innominandum, the shimmering violet and emerald wings, the cerulean and vermilion claws, Great Cthulhu's wasps . . ." Night has fallen. I have limpingly paced the house from the low attic with its circular portholes to the basement, where I touched my father's sledge and eyed "The Gate of Dreams." The moment draws nigh. I must write rapidly.)

I awoke to bright sunlight, feeling totally refreshed by my customary twelve hours of sleep. I found Wilmarth busily writing at the table that faced the north window of his bedroom. His smiling face looked positively youthful in the cool light, despite its neatly brushed thatch of white hair—I hardly recognized him. All his accumulated mail except for one item lay open and face downward on the far-left-hand corner of the table, while on the far-right-hand corner was an impressive pile of newly written and addressed postcards, each with its neatly affixed, fresh, one-cent stamp.

"Good morrow, Georg," he greeted me (properly pronouncing it GAY-org), "if I may so address you. And good news!—the scanner is recharged and behaving perfectly, ready for the day's downward surveying, while that letter George Goodenough forwarded is from Francis Morgan and contains a supply of the drug against tonight's inward researches! Two dosages exactly—Georg, I'll dream with you!" He waved a small paper packet.

"That's wonderful, Albert," I told him, meaning it utterly. "By the way, it's my birthday," I added.

"Congratulations!" he said joyfully. "We'll celebrate it tonight with our drafts of Morgan's drug."

And our expedition did turn out to be a glorious one, at least until almost its very end. The Hollywood Hills put on their most youthfully winning face; even the underlying crumbling, worm-eaten corruptions seemed fresh. The sun was hot, the sky bright blue, but there was a steady cool breeze from the west and occasional great high white clouds casting enormous shadows. Amazingly, Albert seemed to know the territory almost as well as I did—he'd studied his maps prodigiously and brought them along, including the penciled ones I'd sent him. And he instantly named correctly the manzanita, sumac, scrub oak, and other encroaching vegetation through which we wended our way.

Every so often and especially at my favorite pausing places, he would take readings with the geo-scanner, which he carried handily, while I had two canteens and a small backpack. While his head was under the black hood, I would stand guard, my stick ready. Once I surprised a dark and pinkly pale, fat, large serpent, which went slithering into the underbrush. Before I could tell him, he said correctly, "A king snake, foe of the crotaloids—a good omen."

And . . . on every reading, Albert's black box showed vacuities of some sort—tunnels or caves—immediately below us, at depths varying from a few to a few score meters. Somehow this did not trouble us by bright outdoor day. I think it was what we'd both been expecting. Coming out from under the hood, he'd merely nod and say, "Fifteen meters" (or the like) and note it down in his little book, and we'd tramp on. Once he let me try my luck under the hood, but all I could see through the eyepiece was what seemed like an intensification of the dancing points of colored light one sees in the dark with the eyes closed. He told me it took considerable training to learn to recognize the significant indications.

High in the Santa Monicas we lunched on beef sandwiches and the tea-flavored lemonade with which I'd filled both canteens. Sun and breeze bathed us. Hills were all around and beyond them to the west the blue Pacific. We talked of Sir Francis Drake and Magellan and of Captain Cook and his great circumpolar voyagings, and of the fabulous lands they'd all heard legends of—and of how the tunnels we were tracing were really no more strange. We spoke of Lovecraft's stories almost as if they were no more than that. Daytime viewpoints can be strangely unworrying and unconcerned.

Halfway back or so, Albert began looking very haggard once more—frighteningly so. I got him to let me carry the black box. To do that I had to abandon my flat backpack and empty canteens—he didn't seem to notice.

Almost home, we paused at my father's memorial. The sun had westered most of this way, and there were dark shadows and also shafts of ruddy light almost parallel to the ground. Albert, very weary now, was fumbling for phrases to praise Rodia's work, when there swiftly glided out of the undergrowth behind him what I first took to be a large rattlesnake. But as I lunged lurchingly toward it, lashing at it with my stick, and as it slid back into thick cover with preternatural rapidity, and as Albert whirled around, the sinuous, vanishing thing looked for an instant to me as if it were all shimmering violet-green above with beating wings and bluish-scarlet below with claws while its minatory rattle was more a skirling hum.

We raced home, not speaking of it at all, each of us concerned only that his comrade not fall behind. Somewhere mine found the strength.

His postcards had been collected from the box by the road and there were a half dozen new letters for him—and a notification of a registered package for me.

Nothing must do then but Albert must drive me down to Hollywood to pick up the package before the post office closed. His face was fearfully haggard, but he seemed suddenly flooded with a fantastic nervous energy and (when I protested that it could hardly be anything of great importance) a tremendous willpower that would brook no opposition.

He drove like a veritable demon and as though the fate of worlds depended on his speed—Hollywood must have thought it was Wallace Reid come back from the dead for another of his transcontinental racing pictures. The Tin Hind fled like a frightened one indeed, as he worked the gear lever smartly, shifting up and down. The wonders were that we weren't arrested and didn't crash. But I got to the proper window just before it closed and I signed for the package—a stoutly wrapped, tightly sealed, and heavily corded parcel from (it really startled me) Simon Rodia.

Then back again, just as fast despite my protests, the Tin Hind screeching on the corners and curves, my companion's face an implacable, watchful death's-mask, up into the crumbling and desiccated hills as the last streaks of the day faded to violet in the west and the first stars came out.

I forced Albert to rest then and drink hot black coffee freighted with sugar while I got dinner—when he'd stepped out of the car into the chilly night he'd almost fainted. I grilled steaks again—if he'd needed restorative food last night, he needed it doubly now after our exhausting hike and our Dance of Death along the dry, twisting roads, I told him roughly. ("Or Grim Reaper's Tarantella, eh, Georg?" he responded with a feeble but unvanquishable little grin.)

Soon he was prowling around again—he wouldn't stay still—and peering out the windows and then lugging the geo-scanner down into the basement, "to round out our readings," he informed me. I had just finished building and lighting a big fire in the fireplace when he came hurrying back up. Its first white flare of flame as the kindling caught showed me his ashen face and white-circled blue eyes. He was shaking all over, literally.

"I'm sorry, Georg, to be such a troublesome and seemingly ungrateful guest," he said, forcing himself with a great effort to speak coherently and calmly (though most imperatively), "but really you and I must get out of here at once. There's no place safe for us this side of Arkham—which is not safe either, but there at least we'll have the counsel and support of salted veterans of the Miskatonic project whose nerves are steadier than mine. Last night I got (and concealed from you—I was sure it had to be wrong) a reading of fifteen down there under the carving—*centimeters,* Georg, not meters. Tonight I have confirmed that reading beyond any question of a doubt, only it's shrunk to *five* under the carving. The floor there is the merest shell—it rings as hollow as a crypt in New Orleans's St. Louis One or Two—*they* have been eating at it from below and are feasting still. No, no arguments! You have time to pack one small bag—limit yourself to necessities, but bring that registered parcel from Rodia, I'm curious about it."

And with that he strode to his bedroom, whence he emerged in a short while with his packed valise and carried it and the black box out to the car.

Meanwhile I'd nerved myself to go down in the basement. The floor did ring much more hollowly than it had last night—it made me hesitate to tread upon it—but otherwise nothing appeared changed. Nevertheless it gave me a curious feeling of unreality, as if there were no real objects left in the world, only flimsy scenery, a few stage properties including a balsa sledgehammer, a registered parcel with nothing in it, and a cyclorama of nighted hills, and two actors.

I hurried back upstairs, took the steaks off the grill and set them on the table in front of the softly roaring fire (for they were done), and headed after Albert.

But he anticipated me, stepping back inside the door, looking at me sharply—his eyes were still wide and staring—and demanding, "Why aren't you packed?"

I said to him steadily, "Now look here, Albert, I thought last night the cellar floor sounded hollow, so that is not entirely a surprise. And any way you look at it, we can't drive to Arkham on nervous energy. In fact, we can't get even decently started driving east without some food inside us. You say yourself it's dangerous everywhere, even at Miskatonic, and from what we (or at least I) saw at my father's grave there may be at least one of the things loose already. So let's eat dinner—I have a hunch terror hasn't taken away your appetite entirely—and have a look inside Rodia's package, and then leave if we must."

There was a rather long pause. Then his expression relaxed into a somewhat wan smile and he said, "Very well, Georg, that does make sense. I'm frightened all right, make no mistake of that, in fact I've walked in terror for the past ten years. But in this case, to speak as honestly as I'm able, I have been even more concerned for you—it suddenly seemed such a pity, such a disservice, that I should have dragged you into this dreadful business. But as you say, one must bow to necessity, bodily and otherwise . . . and try to show a little style about it," he added with a rather doleful chuckle.

So we sat down before the dancing, golden fire and ate our steaks and fixings (I had some burgundy, he stayed with his sweet black coffee) and talked of this and that—chiefly of Hollywood, as it turned out. He'd glimpsed a bookstore on our headlong drive, and now he asked about it and that led to other things.

Our dinner done, I refilled his cup and my glass, then cleared a space and opened Rodia's parcel, using the carving knife to cut its cords and slit its seals. It contained, carefully packed in excelsior, the casket of embossed copper and German silver which sits before me now. I recognized my father's handiwork at once, which reproduced quite closely in beaten metal his stone carving in the basement, though without the "Gate of Dreams" inscription. Albert's finger indicated the Cutlu eyes, though he did not speak the name. I opened the casket. It contained several sheets of heavy bond paper. This time it was my father's handwriting I recognized. Standing side by side, Albert and I read the document, which I append here:

15 Mar 1925

My dear Son:

Today you are 13 but I write to you and wish you well when you are 25. Why I do so you will learn as you read this. The box is yours—*Leb' wohl!* I leave it with a friend to send to you if I should go in the 12 years between—Nature has given me signs that that may be: jagged flashes of rare earth colors in my eyes from time to time. Now read with care, for I am telling secrets.

When I was a boy in Louisville I had dreams by day and could not remember them. They were black times in my mind that were minutes long, the longest half an hour. Sometimes I came to in another place and doing something different, but never harmful. I thought my black daydreams were a weakness or a judgement, but Nature was wise. I was not strong and did not know enough to bear them yet. Under my father's rule I learned my craft and made my body strong and always studied when and as I could.

When I was 25 I was deep in love—this was before your mother—with a beautiful girl who died of consumption. Pining upon her grave I had a daydream, but this time by the strength of my desire I kept my mind white. I swam down through the loam and I was joined with her in full bodily union. She said this coupling must be our last, but that I now would have the power to move at will under and through the earth from time to time. We kissed farewell forever, *Lorchen* and I, and I swam down and on, her knight of dreams, exulting in my strength like some old kobold breasting the rock. It is not black down there, my son, as one would think. There are glorious colors. Water is blue, metals bright red and yellow, rocks green and brown, *undsoweiter*. After a time I swam back and up into my body, standing on the new-made grave. I was no longer pining, but profoundly grateful.

So I learned how to divine, my son, to be a fish of earth when there is need and Nature wills, to dive into the Hell of the Mountain King dancing with light. Always the finest colors and the strangest hues lay west. Rare earths they are named by scientists, who are wise, though blind. That's why I brought us here. Under the greatest of oceans, earth is a rainbow web and Nature is a spider spinning and walking it.

And now you have shown you have my power, *mein Sohn,* but in a greater form. You have black nightdreams, I know, for I have sat by you as you slept and heard you talk and seen your terror, which would soon destroy you if you could recall it, as one night showed. But Nature in her wisdom blindfolds you until you have the needed strength and learning. As you know by now, I have provided for your education at a good Eastern school praised by Harley Warren, the finest employer that I ever had, who knew a lot about the nether realms.

And now you're strong enough, *mein Sohn,* to act—and wise, I hope, as Nature's acolyte. You've studied deep and made your body strong. You have the power and the hour has come. The triton blows his horn. Rise up, *mein lieber Georg,* and follow me. Now is the time. Build upon what I've built, but build more greatly. Yours is the wider and the greater realm. Make your mind white. With or without some lovely woman's help, now burst the gate of dreams!

Your loving Father

At any other time that document would have moved and shaken me profoundly. Truth to tell, it did so move and shake me, but I had been already so moved and shaken by today's climactic events that my first thought was of how the letter applied to them.

I echoed from the letter, "Now burst the gate of dreams," and then added, suppressing another interpretation, "That means I should take Morgan's drug tonight. Let's do it, Albert, as you proposed this morning."

"Your father's last command," he said heavily, clearly much impressed by that aspect of the letter. Then, "Georg, this is a most fantastic, shattering missive! That sign he got—sounds like migraine. And his references to the rare-earth elements—that could be crucial. And colors in the earth perceived perhaps by extrasensory perception! The Miskatonic project should have started investigating dowsing years ago. We've been blind—" He broke off. "You're right, Georg, and I am strongly tempted. But the danger! How to choose? On the one hand a supreme parental injunction and our raging curiosities—for mine's a-boil. On the other hand Great Cthulhu and his minions. Oh, for an indication of how to decide!"

There was a sharp knocking at the door. We both started. After a moment's pause I moved rapidly, Albert following. With my hand on the latch I paused again. I had not heard a car stop outside. Through the stout oak came the cry, "Telegram!" I opened it.

There was revealed a skinny, somewhat jaunty-looking youth of pale complexion scattered with big freckles and with carrot red hair under his visored cap. His trousers were wrapped tightly around his legs by bicycle clips.

"Either of you Albert N. Wilmarth?" he inquired coolly.

"I am he," Albert said, stepping forward.

"Then sign for this, please."

Albert did so and tipped him, substituting a dime for a nickel at the last instant.

The youth grinned widely, said, "G'night," and sauntered off. I closed the door and turned quickly back.

Albert had torn open the flimsy envelope and drawn out and spread the missive. He was pale already, but as his eyes flashed across it, he grew paler still. It was as if he were two-thirds of a ghost already and its message had made him a full one. He held the yellow sheet out to me wordlessly:

> LOVECRAFT IS DEAD STOP THE WHIPPOORWILLS DID NOT SING STOP TAKE COURAGE STOP DANFORTH

I looked up. Albert's face was still as ghostly white, but its expression had changed from uncertainty and dread to decision and challenge.

"That tips the balance," he said. "What have I more to lose? By George, Georg, we'll have a look down into the abyss on whose edge we totter. Are you game?"

"I proposed it," I said. "Shall I fetch your valise from the car?"

"No need," he said, whipping from his inside breast pocket the small paper packet from Dr. Morgan he'd shown me that morning. "I had the hunch that we were going to use it, until that apparition at your father's tomb shattered my nerves."

I fetched small glasses. He split evenly between them the small supply of white powder, which dissolved readily in the water I added under his direction. Then he looked at me quizzically, holding his glass as if for a toast.

"No question of to whom we drink this," I said, indicating the telegram he was still holding in his other hand.

He winced slightly. "No, don't speak his name. Let's rather drink to *all* our brave comrades who have perished or suffered greatly in the Miskatonic project."

That "our" really warmed me. We touched glasses and drained them. The draft was faintly bitter.

"Morgan writes that the effects are quite rapid," he said. "First drowsiness, then sleep, and then hopefully dreams. He's tried it twice himself with Rice and doughty old Armitage, who laid the Dunwich Horror with him. The first time they visited in dream Gilman's Walpurgis hyperspace; the second, the inner city at the two magnetic poles—an area topologically unique."

Meanwhile I'd hurriedly poured a little more wine and lukewarm coffee and we'd settled ourselves comfortably in our easy chairs before the fire, the dancing flames of which became both a little blurred and a little dazzling as the drug began to take effect.

"Really, that was a most amazing missive from your father," he chatted on rapidly. "Spinning a rainbow web under the Pacific, the lines those weirdly litten tunnels—truly most vivid. Would Cthulhu be the spider? No, by Gad, I'd liefer your father's goddess Nature any day. She's kindlier at least."

"Albert," I said somewhat drowsily, thinking of personality exchanges, "could those creatures possibly be benign, or at least less malevolent than we infer?—as my father's subterranean visionings might indicate. My winged worms, even?"

"Most of our comrades did not find them so," he replied judiciously, "though of course there's our *Innsmouth* hero. What has he really found in Y'ha-nthlei? Wonder and glory? Who knows? Who can say he knows? Or old Akeley out in the stars—is his brain suffering the tortures of the damned in its shining metal cylinder? Or is it perpetually exalted by ever-changing true visions of infinity? And what did poor shoggoth-stampeded Danforth really think he saw beyond the two horrific mountain chains down there before he got amnesia? And is that last a blessing or a curse? Gad, he and I are suited to each other . . . the mind-smitten helping the nerve-shattered . . . fit nurses for felines. . . ."

"That was surely heavy news he sent you," I observed with a little yawn, indicating the telegram about Lovecraft, which he still held tightly between finger and thumb. "You know, before that wire came, I had the craziest idea—that somehow you and he were the same person. I don't mean Danforth but—"

"Don't say it!" he said sharply. Then his voice went immediately drowsy as he continued, "But the roster of the perished is longer far . . . poor Lake and poor, poor Gedney and all those others under their Southern Cross and Magellanic shroud . . . the mathematical genius Walter Gilman who lost heart most terribly . . . the nonagenarian street-slain Angell and lightning-frozen Blake in Providence . . . Edward Pickman Derby, Arkham's plump Shelley deliquescing in his witch-wife's corpse. . . . Gad, this is hardly the cheerfulest topic. . . . You know, Georg, down in San Diego young Akeley (G.G.) showed me a hidden sea-cave bluer than Capri and on its black beach of magnetite the webbed footprint of a merman . . . one of the Gnorri? . . . and then . . . oh yes, of course . . . there's Wilbur Whateley, who was almost nine feet tall . . . though he hardly counts as a Miskatonic researcher . . . but the whippoorwills didn't get him either . . . or his big brother. . . ."

I was still looking at the fire, and the dancing points of light in and around it had become the stars, thick as the Pleiades and Hyades, through which old Akeley journeyed eternally, when unconsciousness closed on me too, black as the wind-stirred, infinite gulf of darkness which Robert Blake saw in the Shining Trapezohedron, black as N'kai.

I awoke stiff and chilled. The fire at which I'd been staring was white ashes only. I felt a sharp pang of disappointment that I had not dreamed at all. Then I became aware of the low, irregular, inflected humming or buzzing that filled my ears.

I stood up with difficulty. My companion slumbered still, but his shut-eyed, death-pale face had a hideously tormented look and he writhed slowly and agonizedly from time to time as if in the grip of foulest nightmare. The yellow telegram had fallen from his fingers and lay on the floor. As I approached him I realized that the sound filling my ears was coming from between his lips, which were unceasingly a-twitch, and as I leaned my head close to them, the horridly articulate droning became recognizable words and phrases:

"The pulpy, tentacled head," I heard in horror, "*Cthulhu fhtagn,* the *wrong* geometry, the polarizing miasma, the prismatic distortion, *Cthulhu R'lyeh,* the positive blackness, the living nothingness . . ."

I could not bear to watch his dreadful agony or listen to those poisonous, *twangy* words an instant longer, so I seized him by the shoulders and shook him violently, though even as I did so there sprang into my mind my father's stern injunction never to do so.

His eyes came open wide in his white face and his mouth clamped shut as he came up with a powerful shove of his bent arms against the chair's arms which his hands had been clutching. It was as if it were happening in slow motion, though paradoxically it also seemed to be happening quite swiftly. He gave me a last mute look of utter horror and then he turned and ran, taking fantastically long strides, out through the door, which his outstretched hand threw wide ahead of him, and disappeared into the night.

I hobbled after him as swiftly as I could. I heard the motor catch at the starter's second prod. I screamed, "Wait, Albert, wait!" As I neared the Tin Hind, its lights flashed on and its motor roared and I was engulfed in acrid exhaust fumes as it screeched out the drive with a spattering of gravel and down the first curve.

I waited there then in the cold until all sight and sound of it had vanished in the night, which was already paling a little with the dawn.

And then I realized that I was still hearing those malignant, gloating, evilly resonant voices.

"*Cthulhu fhtagn,*" they were saying (and have been saying and are saying now and will forever), "the spider tunnels, the black infinities, the colors in pitch-darkness, the tiered towers of Yuggoth, the glittering centipedes, the winged worms. . . ."

Somewhere not far off I heard a low, half-articulate whirring sound.

I went back into the house and wrote this manuscript.

And now I shall place the last with its interleafed communications and also the two books of poetry that led to all this in the copper and German silver casket, and I shall carry that with me down into the basement, where I shall take up my father's sledge (wondering in which body I shall survive, if at all) and literally carry out his last letter's last injunction.

* * *

Very early on the morning of Tuesday, March 16, 1937, the householders of Paradise Crest (then Vultures Roost) were disturbed by a clashing rumble and sharp earth-shock which they attributed to an earthquake, and indeed very small tremors were registered at Griffith Observatory, UCLA, and USC, though on no other seismographs. Daylight revealed that the brick house locally known as Fischer's Folly had fallen in so completely that not one brick remained joined to another. Moreover, there appeared to be fewer bricks in view than the house would have accounted for, as if half of them had been trucked away during the night, or else fallen into some great space beneath the basement. In fact, the appearance of the ruin was of a gigantic ant lion's–pit lined by bricks instead of sand grains. The place was deemed, and actually was, dangerous, and was shortly filled in and in part cemented over, and apparently not long afterward rebuilt upon.

The body of the owner, a quietly spoken, crippled young man named Georg Reuter Fischer, was discovered flat on its face in the edge of the rubble with hands thrown out (the metal casket by one of them) as though he had been trying to flee outdoors when caught by the collapse. His death, however, was attributed to a slightly earlier accident or insane act of self-destruction involving acid, of which his eccentric father was once known to have kept a supply. It was well that easy identification was made possible by his conspicuously twisted right foot, for when the body was turned over it was discovered that something had eaten away the entire front of his face and also those portions of his skull and jaw and the entire forebrain.

Rising with Surtsey*

BRIAN LUMLEY

It appears that with the discovery of a live coelacanth—a fish thought to have been extinct for over seventy millions of years—we may have to revise our established ideas of the geological life spans of certain aquatic animals. . . .

—LINKAGE'S *WONDERS OF THE DEEP*

Surname	—Haughtree
Christian Names	—Phillip
Date of Birth	—2 Dec 1927
Age (years)	—35
Place of Birth	—Old Beldry, Yorks.
Address	—Not applicable
Occupation	—Author

WHO STATES: (Let here follow the body of the statement)

I have asked to be cautioned in the usual manner but have been told that in view of my alleged *condition* it is not necessary. . . . The implication is obvious, and because of it I find myself obliged to begin my story in the following way:

I must clearly impart to the reader—before advising any unacquainted perusal of this statement—that I was never a fanatical believer in the supernatural. Nor was I ever given to hallucinations or visions, and I have never suffered from my nerves or been persecuted by any of the mental illnesses. There is no record to support any evidence of madness in any of my ancestors—and Dr. Stewart was quite wrong to declare me insane.

It is necessary that I make these points before permitting the

*Originally published in *Dark Things*, 1971.

reading of this, for a merely casual perusal would soon bring any conventionally minded reader to the incorrect conclusion that I am either an abominable liar or completely out of my mind, and I have little wish to reinforce Dr. Stewart's opinions. . . .

Yet I admit that shortly after midnight on the 15th November 1963 the body of my brother did die by my hand; but at the same time I must clearly state that I am *not* a murderer. It is my intention in the body of this statement—which will of necessity be long, for I insist I must tell the whole story—to prove conclusively my innocence. For, indeed, I am guilty of no heinous crime, and that act of mine which terminated life in the body of my brother was nothing but the reflex action of a man who had recognized a hideous threat to the sanity of the whole world. Wherefore, and in the light of the allegation of madness leveled against me, I must now attempt to tell this tale in the most detailed fashion; I must avoid any sort of garbled sequence and form my sentences and paragraphs with meticulous care, refraining from even *thinking* on the end of it until that horror is reached. . . .

Where best to start?

If I may quote Sir Amery Wendy-Smith:

> There are fabulous legends of Star-Born creatures who inhabited this Earth many millions of years before Man appeared and who were still here, in certain black places, when he eventually evolved. They are, I am sure, to an extent here even now.

It may be remembered that those words were spoken by the eminent antiquary and archaeologist before he set out upon his last, ill-fated trip into the interior of Africa. Sir Amery was hinting, I know, at the same breed of hell-spawned horror which first began to make itself apparent to me at that ghastly time eighteen months ago; and I take this into account when I remember the way in which he returned, alone and raving, from that dark continent to civilization.

At that time my brother Julian was just the opposite of myself, insofar as he was a firm believer in dark mysteries. He read omnivorously of fearsome books uncaring whether they were factual—as Frazer's *Golden Bough* and Miss Murray's *Witch-Cult*—or fanciful—like his collection of old, nigh-priceless volumes of *Weird Tales* and similar popular magazines. Many friends, I imagine, will conclude that his original derangement was due to this unhealthy appetite for the monstrous and the abnormal. I am not of such an opinion, of course, though I admit that at one time I was.

Of Julian: he had always been a strong person physically, but had never shown much strength of character. As a boy he had had the size to easily take on any bully—but never the determination. This was also where he failed as a writer, for while his plots were good he was unable to make his characters live. Being without personality himself, it was as though he was only able to reflect his own weaknesses into his work. I worked in partnership with him, filling in plots and building life around his more or less clay figures. Up until the time of which I write, we had made a good living and had saved a reasonable sum. This was just as well, for during the period of Julian's illness, when I hardly wrote a word, I might well have found myself hard put to support both my brother and myself. Fortunately, though sadly, he was later taken completely off my hands; but that was after the onset of his trouble. . . .

It was in May 1962 that Julian suffered his actual breakdown, but the start of it all can be traced back to the 2nd of February of that year—Candlemas—a date which I know will have special meaning to anyone with even the slightest schooling in the occult. It was on that night that he dreamed his dream of titanic basalt towers—dripping with slime and ocean ooze and fringed with great sea-mats—their weirdly proportioned bases buried in grey-green muck and their non–Euclidean-angled parapets fading into the watery distances of that unquiet submarine realm.

At the time we were engaged upon a novel of eighteenth-century romance, and I remember we had retired late. Still later I was awakened by Julian's screams, and he roused me fully to listen to an hysterical tale of nightmare. He babbled of what he had seen lurking *behind* those monolithic, slimy ramparts, and I remember remarking—after he had calmed himself somewhat—what a strange fellow he was, to be a writer of romances and at the same time a reader and dreamer of horrors. But Julian was not so easily chided, and such was his fear and loathing of the dream that he refused to lie down again that night but spent the remaining hours of darkness sitting at his typewriter in the study with every light in the house ablaze.

One would think that a nightmare of such horrible intensity might have persuaded Julian to stop gorging himself with his nightly feasts of at least two hours of gruesome reading. Yet, if anything, it had the opposite effect—but now his studies were all channeled in one certain direction. He began to take a morbid interest in anything to do with oceanic horror, collecting and avidly reading such works as the German *Unter-Zee Kulten*, Gaston le Fe's *Dwellers in the Depths*, Gantley's *Hydrophinnae*, and the evil *Cthaat Aquadingen* by an unknown author. But it was his collection of fictional books which in the main claimed his interest. From these he culled most of his knowledge of the Cthulhu Mythos—which he fervently declared was not myth at all—and often expressed a desire to see an original copy of the

Necronomicon of the mad Arab Abdul Alhazred, as his own copy of Feery's *Notes* was practically useless, merely hinting at what Julian alleged Alhazred had explained in detail.

In the following three months our work went badly. We failed to make a deadline on a certain story and, but for the fact that our publisher was a personal friend, might have suffered a considerable loss financially. It was all due to the fact that Julian no longer had the urge to write. He was too taken up with his reading to work and could no longer even be approached to talk over story plots. Not only this, but that fiendish dream of his kept returning with ever increasing frequency and vividness. Every night he suffered those same silt-submerged visions of obscene terrors the like of which could only be glimpsed in such dark tomes as were his chosen reading. But did he really suffer? I found myself unable to make up my mind. For as the weeks passed, my brother seemed to become all the more uneasy and restless by day, whilst eagerly embracing the darkening skies of evening and the bed in which he sweated out the horrors of hideous dream and nightmare. . . .

We were leasing, for a reasonable monthly sum, a moderate house in Glasgow where we had separate bedrooms and a single study which we shared. Although he now looked forward to them, Julian's dreams had grown even worse and they had been particularly bad for two or three nights when, in the middle of May, it happened. He had been showing an increasing interest in certain passages in the *Cthaat Aquadingen* and had heavily underscored a section in that book which ran thus:

Rise!
O Nameless Ones:
That in Thy Season
Thine Own of Thy choosing.
Through Thy Spells and Thy Magic,
Through Dreams and Enchantry,
May know of Thy Coming;
And rush to Thy Pleasure,
For the Love of Our Master,
Knight of Cthulhu,
Deep Slumberer in Green,
Othuum . . .

This and other bits and pieces culled from various sources, particularly certain partly suppressed writings by a handful of authors, all allegedly "missing persons" or persons who had died in strange circumstances—namely: Andrew Phelan, Abel Keane, Claiborne Boyd,

Nayland Colum, and Horvath Blayne—had had a most unsettling effect upon my brother, so that he was close to exhaustion when he eventually retired late on the night that the horror really started. His condition was due to the fact that he had been studying his morbid books almost continually for a period of three days, and during that time had taken only brief snatches of sleep—and then only during the daylight hours, never at night. He would answer, if ever I attempted to remonstrate with him, that he did not *want* to sleep at night "when the time is so near" and that "there was so much that would be strange to him in Deeps." Whatever *that* was supposed to mean. . . .

After he had retired that night I worked on for an hour or so before going to bed myself. But before leaving our study I glanced at that with which Julian had last been so taken up, and I saw—as well as the above nonsense, as I then considered it—some jottings copied from the *Life of St. Brendan* by the sixth-century Abbot of Clonfert in Galway:

> All that day the brethren, even when they were no longer in view of the island, heard a loud wailing from the inhabitants thereof, and a noisome stench was perceptible at a great distance. Then St. Brendan sought to animate the courage of the brethren, saying: "Soldiers of Christ, be strong in faith unfeigned and in the armour of the spirit, for we are now on the confines of hell!"

I have since studied the *Life of St. Brendan*, and have found that which made me shudder in awful recognition—though at the reading I could not correlate the written word and my hideous disquiet; there was just something in the book which was horribly disturbing—and, moreover, I have found other references to historic oceanic eruptions; namely, those which sank Atlantis and Mu, those recorded in the *Liber Miraculorem* of the monk and chaplain Herbert of Clairvaux in France in the years 1178–80, and that which was closer to the present and which is known only through the medium of the suppressed *Johansen Narrative*. But at the time of which I write, such things only puzzled me and I could never, not even in my wildest dreams, have guessed what was to come.

I am not sure how long I slept that night before I was eventually roused by Julian and half awoke to find him crouching by my bed, whispering in the darkness. I could feel his hand gripping my shoulder, and though I was only half-awake I recall the pressure of that strong hand and something of what he said. His voice had the trance-like quality of someone under deep hypnosis, and his hand jerked each time he put emphasis on a word.

"They are *preparing*. . . . They will *rise*. . . . They have not mustered

The Greater Power, nor have they the blessing of *Cthulhu*, and the rising will not be *permanent* nor go recorded. . . . But the effort will suffice for the *Mind-Transfer*. . . . For the *Glory* of Othuum . . .

"Using those *Others* in Africa, those who took Sir Amery Wendy-Smith, *Shudde-M'ell* and his hordes, to relay their messages and dream-pictures, they have finally defeated the magic *spell* of deep water and can now *control* dreams as of old—despite the oceans which cover them! Once more they have *mastery* of dreams, but to perform the Transfer they need not even break the surface of the water—a *lessening* of the pressure will suffice.

"Ce'haie, ce'haie!!!

"*They rise even now*; and He knows me, searching me out. . . . And my mind, which they have prepared in dreams, will be here to meet Him, for I am *ready* and they need wait no longer. My ignorance is nothing—I do not *need* to know or understand! They will *show* me; as, in dreams, they have showed me the *Deep Places*. But they are unable to draw from my weak mind, or from *any* mortal brain, *knowledge of the surface*. . . . The mental images of men are not *strongly* enough transmitted. . . . And the deep water—even though, through the work of *Shudde-M'ell*, they have mostly conquered its ill effects—*still* interferes with those blurred images which they *have* managed to obtain. . . .

"*I am the chosen one*. . . . Through *His* eyes in my *body* will they again acquaint themselves *entirely* with the surface; that in time, when the stars are *right*, they may perform the *Great Rising*. . . . Ah! The Great Rising! The *damnation* of *Hastur!* The dream of *Cthulhu* for countless ages . . . When *all* the deep dwellers, the dark denizens, the *sleepers* in silted cities, will *again* confound the world with their powers. . . .

"For that is not dead which can lie *forever*, and when mysterious times have passed, *it shall be again as it once was*. . . . Soon, when the Transfer is done, He shall walk the Earth *in my guise*, and I the great deeps *in His*! So that where they ruled *before* they may one day rule *again*—aye—even the brethren of *Yibb-Tstll* and the sons of dreaming *Cthulhu* and their servants—*for the Glory of R'lyeh*. . . ."

That is as much of it as I can remember, and even then not at all clearly, and as I have said, it was nothing to me at that time but gibberish. It is only since then that I have acquainted myself with certain old legends and writings; and in particular, in connection with the latter part of my brother's fevered mouthings, the inexplicable couplet of the mad Arab Abdul Alhazred:

> "That is not dead which can eternal lie,
> And with strange aeons even death may die."

But I digress.

It took me some time, after the drone of Julian's outré monologue had died away, to realize that he was no longer in the room with me and that there was a chill morning breeze blowing through the house. In his own room his clothes still hung neatly where he had left them the night before—but Julian had gone, leaving the door to the house swinging open.

I dressed quickly and went out to search the immediate neighbourhood—with negative results. Then, as dawn was breaking, I went into a police-station to discover—to my horror—that my brother was in "protective custody." He had been found wandering aimlessly through the northern streets of the city mumbling about "giant Gods" waiting for something in the ocean deeps. He did not seem to realize that his sole attire was his dressing-gown, nor did he appear to recognize me when I was called to identify him. Indeed, he seemed to be suffering from the after-effects of some terrible shock which had left him in a trauma-like state, totally incapable of rational thought. He would only mumble unguessable things and stare blankly towards the northern wall of his cell; an awful, mad light glowing in the back of his eyes. . . .

My tasks were sufficient that morning to keep me amply occupied, and horribly so; for Julian's condition was such that on the orders of a police psychiatrist he was transferred from his police-station cell to Oakdeene Sanatorium for "observation." Nor was it easy to get him attended to at the sanatorium. Apparently the supervisors of that institute had had their own share of trouble the previous night. When I did eventually get home, around noon, my first thought was to check the daily newspapers for any reference to my brother's behaviour. I was glad, or as glad as I could be in the circumstances, to find that Julian's activities had been swamped from a more prominent place of curious interest—which they might well have otherwise claimed—by a host of far more serious events.

Strangely, those other events were similar to my brother's trouble in that they all seemed concerned with mental aberrations in previously normal people or, as at Oakdeene, increases in the activities of the more dangerous inmates of lunatic asylums all over the country. In London a businessman of some standing had hurled himself bodily from a high roof declaring that he must "fly to Yuggoth on the rim." Chandler Davies, who later died raving mad at Woodholme, painted "in a trance of sheer inspiration" an evil black and grey *G'harne Landscape* which his outraged and frightened mistress set on fire upon its completion. Stranger still, a Cotswold rector had knifed to death two members of his congregation who, he later protested to the police, "had no right to exist," and from the coast, near Harden in Durham, strange midnight swimmers had been seen to make off with a fisherman who screamed of "giant frogs" before disappearing beneath the still sea. . . . It was as if, on that queer night, some madness had descended—or, as I now believe, had risen—to blanket the more susceptible minds of certain people with utter horror.

But all these things, awful as they were, were not that which I found most disturbing. Looking back on what Julian had murmured in my bedroom while I lay in half-slumber, I felt a weird and inexplicable chill sweep over me as I read, in those same newspapers, of an amateur seismologist who believed he had traced *a submarine disturbance in the ocean between Greenland and the northern tip of Scotland. . . .*

What was it Julian had whispered about a *rising* which would not go recorded? Certainly something had been recorded happening in the depths of the sea! . . . But, of course, that was ridiculous, and I shook off the feeling of dread which had gripped me on reading the item. Whatever that deep oceanic disturbance had been, its cause could only be coincidental to my brother's behaviour.

So it was that rather than ponder the reason for so many outré happenings that ill-omened night I thanked our lucky stars that Julian had got away with so light a mention in the press; for what had occurred could have been damaging to both of us had it been given greater publicity.

Not that any of this bothered Julian! Nothing bothered him, for he stayed in that semi-conscious state in which the police had found him for well over a year. During that year his weird delusions were of such a fantastic nature that he became, as it were, the psychological pet and project of a well-known Harley Street alienist. Indeed, after the first month or so, so strong did the good doctor's interest in my brother's case become, he would accept no fee for Julian's keep or treatment; and, though I visited Julian frequently, whenever I was in London, Dr. Stewart would never listen to my protests or hear of me paying for his services. Such was his patient's weird case that the doctor declared himself extremely fortunate to be in a position where he had the opportunity to study such a fantastic mind. It amazes me now that the same man who proved so understanding in his dealings with my brother should be so totally devoid of understanding with me; yet that is the pass to which the turn of events has brought me. Still, it was plain my brother was in good hands, and in any case I could hardly afford to press the matter of payment; Dr. Stewart's fees were usually astronomical.

It was shortly after Dr. Stewart "took Julian in" that I began to study my brother's star-charts, both astronomical and astrological, and delved deep into his books on the supernatural arts and sciences. I read many peculiar volumes during that period and became reasonably familiar with the works of Fermold, Lévi, Prinn, and Gezrael, and—in certain darker reaches of the British Museum—I shuddered to the literary lunacy of Magnus, Glynnd, and Alhazred. I read the *R'lyeh Text* and the *Johansen Narrative* and studied the fables of lost Atlantis and Mu. I crouched over flaking tomes in private collections and tracked down all sources of oceanic legend and myth with which I came into contact. I read the manuscript of Andrew Phelan, the deposition of Abel Keane, the testament of Claiborne Boyd, the statement of Nayland Colum, and the narrative of Horvath Blayne. The papers of Jefferson Bates fell to my unbelieving scrutiny, and I lay awake at nights thinking of the hinted fate of Enoch Conger.

And I need never have bothered.

All the above delvings took the better part of a year to complete, by which time I was no nearer a solution to my brother's madness than when I began. No, perhaps that is not quite true. On reflection I think it quite possible that a man might go mad after exploring such dark avenues as these I have mentioned—and especially a man such as Julian, who was more than normally sensitive to begin with. But I was by no means satisfied that this was the whole answer. After all, his interest in such things had been lifelong; I could still see no reason why such an interest should suddenly accumulate so terribly. No, I was sure that the start of it all had been that Candlemas dream.

But at any rate, the year had not been totally lost. I still did not believe in such things—dark survivals of elder times; great ancient gods waiting in the ocean depths; impending doom for the human race in the form of nightmare ocean-dwellers from the beginning of time—how could I and retain my own sanity? But I had become fairly erudite regards these darker mysteries of elder Earth. And certain facets of my strange research had been of particular interest to me. I refer to what I had read of the oddly similar cases of Joe Slater, the Catskill Mountains vagabond in 1900–01, Nathaniel Wingate Peaslee of Miskatonic University in 1908–13, and Randolph Carter of Boston, whose disappearance in 1928 was so closely linked with the inexplicable case of the Swami Chandraputra in 1930. True, I had looked into other cases of alleged demonic possession—all equally well authenticated—but those I have mentioned seemed to have a special significance, as they paralleled more than roughly that case which I was researching and which involved so terribly my brother.

But time had passed quickly and it was a totally unexpected shock to me, though one of immeasurable relief and pleasure, to find in my letter-box one July morning in 1963 a letter from Dr. Stewart which told of Julian's rapid improvement. My joy and amazement can well be imagined when, on journeying down to London the very next day, to the practice of Dr. Stewart, I found my brother returned—so far as could be ascertained in such a short time—to literally complete mental recovery. Indeed, it was the doctor himself who, on my arrival, informed me that Julian's recovery was now complete, that my brother had *fully* recovered almost overnight: but I was not so sure—there appeared to be one or two anomalies.

These apart, though, the degree of recovery which had been accomplished was tremendous. When I had last seen my brother, only a month earlier, I had felt physically sickened by the unplumbed depths of his delusions. I had, on that occasion, gone to stand beside him at the barred window from which I was told he always stared blindly northwards, and in answer to my careful greeting he had said: "Cthulhu, Othuum, Dagon; the Deep Ones in Darkness; all deeply dreaming, awaiting awakening . . ." Nor had I been able to extract anything from him at all except such senseless mythological jargon.

What a transformation! Now he greeted me warmly—though I imagined his recognition of me to be a trifle slow—and after I had delightedly talked with him for a while I came to the conclusion that so far as I could discern, and apart from one new idiosyncrasy, he seemed to be the same man I had known before the onset of the trouble. This oddity I have mentioned was simply that he seemed to have developed a weird photophobia and now wore large, shielded, dark-lensed spectacles which denied one the slightest glimpse of his eyes even from the sides. But, as I later found out, there was an explanation even for these enigmatic-looking spectacles.

While Julian prepared himself for the journey back to Glasgow, Dr. Stewart took me to his study where I could sign the necessary release documents and where he could tell me of my brother's fantastic recovery. It appeared that one morning only a week earlier, on going to his exceptional patient's room, the doctor had found Julian huddled beneath his blankets. Nor would my brother come out or allow himself to be brought out until the doctor had agreed to bring him that pair of very dark-lensed spectacles. Peculiar though this muffled request had been, it had delighted the astonished alienist, constituting as it did the first conscious recognition of existence that Julian had shown since the commencement of his treatment.

And the spectacles had proved to be worth their weight in gold, for since their advent Julian had rapidly progressed to his present state of normalcy. The only point over which the doctor seemed unhappy was that to date my brother had point-blank refused to relinquish the things; he declared simply that the light *hurt his eyes!* To some degree, however, the good doctor informed me, this was only to be expected. During his long illness Julian had departed so far from the normal world, as it were, that his senses, unused, had partly atrophied—literally ceasing to function. His recovery had left him in the position of a man who, trapped in a dark cave for a long period of time, is suddenly released to face the bright outside world: which also explained in part the clumsiness which had attended Julian's every physical action during the first days of his recovery. One of the doctor's assistants had found occasion to remark upon the most odd way in which my brother had tended to wrap his arms around things which he wanted to lift or examine—even small things—as though he had forgotten what his fingers were for! Also, at first, the patient had tended to waddle rather than walk, almost in the manner of a penguin, and his recently reacquired powers of intelligent expression had lapsed at times in the queerest manner—when his speech had degenerated to nothing more than a guttural, hissing parody of the English language. But all these abnormalities had vanished in the first few days, leaving Julian's recovery as totally unexplained as had been his decline.

In the first-class compartment on the London–Glasgow train, on our way north, having exhausted the more obvious questions I had wanted to put to my restored brother—questions to which, incidentally, his answers had seemed guardedly noncommittal—I had taken out a pocketbook and started to read. After a few minutes, startled by a passing train, I had happened to glance up . . . and was immediately glad that Julian and I were alone in the compartment. For my brother had obviously found something of interest in an old newspaper, and I do not know what others might have thought of the look upon his face. . . . As he read his face bore an unpleasant and, yes, almost *evil* expression. It was made to look worse by those strange spectacles; a mixture of cruel sarcasm, black triumph, and tremendous contempt. I was taken aback, but said nothing, and later—when Julian went into the corridor for a breath of fresh air—I picked up the newspaper and turned to the section he had been reading, which perhaps had caused the weird distortion of his features. I saw at once what had affected him, and a shadow of the old fear flickered briefly across my mind as I read the article. It was not strange that what I read was new to me—I had hardly seen a newspaper since the horror began a year previously—but it was as though this was the same report I had read at that time. It was all there, almost a duplicate of the occurrences of that night of evil omen: the increased activities of lunatics all over the country, the sudden mad and monstrous actions of previously normal people, the cult activity and devil-worship in The Midlands, the sea-things sighted off Harden on the coast, and more inexplicable occurrences in the Cotswolds.

A chill as of strange ocean-floors touched my heart, and I quickly thumbed through the remaining pages of the paper—and almost dropped the thing when I came across that which I had more than half expected. For submarine disturbances had been recorded in the ocean between Greenland and the northern tip of Scotland. And more—I instinctively glanced at the date at the top-center of the page, *and saw that the newspaper was exactly one week old. . . .* It had first appeared on the stands on the very morning when Dr. Stewart had found my brother huddled beneath the blankets in the room with the barred windows.

Yet apparently my fears were groundless. On our return to the house in Glasgow the first thing my brother did, to my great delight and satisfaction, was destroy all his old books of ancient lore and sorcery; but he made no attempt to return to his writing. Rather he mooned about the house like some lost soul, in what I imagined to be a mood of frustration over those mazed months of which he said he could remember nothing. And not once, until the night of his death, did I see him without those spectacles. I believe he even wore the things to bed—but the significance of this, and something he had mumbled that night in my room, did not dawn on me until much later.

But of those spectacles: I had been assured that this photophobia would wear off, yet as the days went by it became increasingly apparent that Dr. Stewart's assurances had gone for nothing. And what was I to make of that *other* change I had noticed? Whereas before Julian had been almost shy and retiring, with a weak chin and a personality to match, he now seemed to be totally out of character, in that he asserted himself over the most trivial things whenever the opportunity arose, and his face—his lips and chin in particular—had taken on a firmness completely alien to his previous physiognomy.

It was all most puzzling, and as the weeks passed I became ever more aware that far from all being well with that altered brother of mine something was seriously wrong. Apart from his brooding, a darker horror festered within him. Why would he not admit the monstrous dreams which constantly invaded his sleep? Heaven knows he slept little enough as it was; and when he did he often roused me from my own slumbers by mumbling in the night of those same horrors which had featured so strongly in his long illness.

But then, in the middle of October, Julian underwent what I took to be a real change for the better. He became a little more cheerful and even dabbled with some old manuscripts long since left abandoned—though I do not think he did any actual work on them—and towards the end of the month he sprang a surprise. For quite some time, he told me, he had had a wonderful story in mind, but for the life of him he could not settle to it. It was a tale he would have to work on himself; and it would be necessary for him to do much research, as his material would have to be very carefully prepared. He asked that I bear with him during the period of his task and allow him as much privacy as our modest house could afford. I agreed to everything he suggested, though I could not see why he found it so necessary to have a lock put on his door; or, for that matter, why he cleared out the spacious cellar beneath the house "for future use." Not that I questioned his actions. He had asked for privacy, and as far as I could assist him he would have it. But I admit to having been more than somewhat curious.

From then on I saw my brother only when we ate—which for him was not any too often—and when he left his room to go to the library for books, a thing he did with clockwork regularity every day. With the first few of these excursions I made a point of being near the door of the house when he returned, for I was puzzled as to what form his work was going to take and I thought I might perhaps gain some insight if I could see his books of reference.

If anything, the materials Julian borrowed from the library only served to add to my puzzlement. What on Earth could he want with Lauder's *Nuclear Weapons and Engines*, Schall's *X-Rays*, Couderc's *The Wider Universe*, Ubbelohde's *Man and Energy*, Keane's *Modern Marvels of Science*, Stafford Clarke's *Psychiatry Today*, Schubert's *Einstein*, Geber's *The Electrical World*, and all the many volumes of *The New Scientist* and *The Progress of Science* with which he returned each day heavily burdened? Still, nothing he was doing gave me any cause to worry as I had in the old days, when his reading had been anything but scientific and had involved those dreadful works which he had now destroyed. But my partial peace of mind was not destined to last for very long.

One day in mid-November—elated by a special success which I had achieved in the writing of a difficult chapter in my own slowly shaping book—I went to Julian's room to inform him of my triumph. I had not seen him at all that morning, but the fact that he was out did not become apparent until, after knocking and receiving no reply, I entered his room. It had been Julian's habit of late to lock his door when he went out, and I was surprised that on this occasion he had not done so. I saw then that he had left the door open purposely so that I might see the note he had left for me on his bedside table. It was scribbled on a large sheet of white typing paper in awkward, tottering letters, and the message was blunt and to the point:

Phillip,
Gone to London for four or five days. Research. Brit. Museum . . .
Julian.

Somewhat disgruntled, I turned to leave the room and as I did so noticed my brother's diary lying open at the foot of his bed where he had thrown it. The book itself did not surprise me—before his trouble he had always kept such notes—and not being a snoop I would have left the room there and then had I not glimpsed a word—*or name*—which I recognized on the open, hand-written pages: *"Cthulhu."*

Simply that . . . yet it set my mind awhirl with renewed doubts. Was Julian's trouble reasserting itself? Did he yet require psychiatric treatment and were his original delusions returning? Remembering that Dr. Stewart had warned me of the possibility of a relapse, I considered it my duty to read all that my brother had written—which was where I met with a seemingly insurmountable problem. The difficulty was simply this: I was *unable* to read the diary, for it was written in a completely alien, cryptically cuneiform script the like of which I had ever seen only in those books which Julian had burned. There was a distinct resemblance in those weird characters to the miniscules and dot-groups of the *G'harne Fragments*—I remembered being struck by an article on them in one of Julian's books, an archaeological magazine—but only a resemblance; the diary contained nothing I could understand except that one word, *Cthulhu,* and even that had been scored through by Julian, as if on reflection, and a weird squiggle of ink had been crammed in above it as a replacement.

I was not slow to come to a decision as to what my proper course of action should be. That same day, taking the diary with me, I went down to Wharby on the noon train. That article on the *G'harne Fragments* which I had remembered reading had been the work of the curator of the Wharby Museum, Professor Gordon Walmsley of Goole; who, incidentally, had claimed the first translation of the fragments over the claim of the eccentric and long-vanished antiquarian and archaeologist Sir Amery Wendy-Smith. The professor was an authority on the Phitmar Stone—that contemporary of the famous Rosetta Stone with its key inscriptions in two forms of Egyptian hieroglyphs—and the Geph Columns Characters, and had several other translations or feats of antiquarian deciphering to his credit. Indeed, I was extremely fortunate to find him in at the museum, for he planned to fly within the week to Peru where yet another task awaited his abecedarian talents. Nonetheless, busy with arrangements as he was, he was profoundly interested in the diary; enquiring where the hieroglyphics within had been copied, and by whom and to what purpose? I lied, telling him my brother had copied the inscriptions from a black stone monolith somewhere in the mountains of Hungary; for I knew that just such a stone exists, having once seen mention of it in one of my brother's books. The professor squinted his eyes suspiciously at my lie but was so interested in the diary's strange characters that he quickly forgot whatever it was that had prompted his suspicion. From then until I was about to leave his study, located in one of the museum's rooms, we did not speak. So absorbed did he become with the diary's contents that I think he completely forgot my presence in the room. Before I left, however, I managed to extract a promise from him that the diary would be returned to my Glasgow address within three days and that a copy of his translation, if any, would accompany it. I was glad that he did not ask me why I required such a translation.

My faith in the professor's abilities was eventually borne out—but not until far too late. For Julian returned to Glasgow on the morning of the third day—earlier by twenty-four hours than I had been led to believe, and his diary still had not been returned—nor was he slow to discover its loss.

I was working half-heartedly at my book when my brother made his appearance. He must have been to his own room first. Suddenly I felt a presence in my room with me. I was so lost in my half-formed imaginings and ideas that I had not heard my door open; nonetheless I knew something was in there with me. I say *something*; and that is the way it was! I was being observed—but not, I felt, by a human being! Carefully, with the short hair of my neck prickling with an uncanny life of its own, I turned about. Standing in the open doorway with a look on his face which I can only describe as being utterly hateful was Julian. But even as I saw him, his horribly writhing features composed themselves behind those enigmatic dark glasses and he forced an unnatural smile.

"I seem to have mislaid my diary, Phillip," he said slowly. "I'm just in from London and I can't seem to find the thing anywhere. I don't suppose you've seen it, have you?" There was the suggestion of a sneer in his voice, an unspoken accusation. "I don't need the diary really, but there are one or two things in it which I wrote in code—ideas I want to use in my story. I'll let you in on a secret! It's a *fantasy* I'm writing! I mean—horror, science fiction, and fantasy—they're all the rage these days; it's about time we broke into the field. You shall see the rough work as soon as it's ready. But now, seeing as how you obviously haven't seen my diary, if you'll excuse me, I want to get some of my notes together."

He left the room quickly, before I could answer, and I would be lying if I said I was not glad to see him go. And I could not help but notice that with his departure the feeling of an alien presence also departed. My legs felt suddenly weak beneath me as a dreadful aura of foreboding settled like a dark cloud over my room. Nor did that feeling disperse—rather it tightened as night drew on.

Lying in my bed that night I found myself going again and again over Julian's strangeness, trying to make some sense of it all. A fantasy? Could it be? It was so unlike Julian; and why, if it was only a story, had his look been so terrible when he was unable to find his diary? And why write a story in a diary at all? Oh! He had liked reading weird stuff—altogether too much, as I have explained—but he had never before shown any urge to *write* it! And what of the books he had borrowed from the library? They had not seemed to be works he could possibly use in connection with the construction of a fantasy! And there was something else, something which kept making brief appearances in my mind's eye but which I could not quite bring into focus. Then I had it—the thing which had been bothering me ever since I first saw that diary: *where in the name of all that's holy had Julian learned to write in hieroglyphics?*

That cinched it!

No, I did not believe that Julian was writing a story at all. That was only an excuse he had created to put me off the track. But what track? What did he think he was doing? Oh! It was obvious; he was on the verge of another breakdown, and the sooner I got in touch with Dr. Stewart the better. All these tumultuous thoughts kept me awake until a late hour, and if my brother was noisy again that night I did not hear him. I was so mentally fatigued that when I eventually nodded off I slept the sleep of the dead.

Is it not strange how the light of day has the power to drive away the worst terrors of night? With the morning my fears were much abated and I decided to wait a few more days before contacting Dr. Stewart. Julian spent all morning and afternoon locked in the cellar, and finally—again becoming alarmed as night drew near—I determined to reason with him, if possible, over supper. During the meal I spoke to him, pointing out how strangely he seemed to be acting and lightly mentioning my fears of a relapse. I was somewhat taken aback by his answers. He argued it was my own fault he had had to resort to the cellar in which to work, stating that the cellar appeared to be the only place where he could be sure of any privacy. He laughed at my mention of a relapse, saying he had never felt better in his life! When he again mentioned "privacy" I knew he must be referring to the unfortunate incident of the missing diary and was shamed into silence. I mentally cursed Professor Walmsley and his whole museum.

Yet, in direct opposition to all my brother's glib explanations, that night was the worst; for Julian gibbered and moaned in his sleep, making it impossible for me to get any rest at all; so that when I arose, haggard and withdrawn, late on the morning of the 13th, I knew I would soon have to take some definite action.

I saw Julian only fleetingly that morning, on his way from his room to the cellar, and his face seemed pale and cadaverous. I guessed that his dreams were having as bad an effect upon him as they were on me;

yet rather than appearing tired or hag-ridden he seemed to be in the grip of some feverish excitement.

Now I became more worried than ever and even scribbled two letters to Dr. Stewart, only later to ball them up and throw them away. If Julian was genuine in whatever he was doing, I did not want to spoil his faith in me—what little of it was left—and if he was not genuine? I was becoming morbidly curious to learn the outcome of his weird activities. Nonetheless, twice that day, at noon and later in the evening, when as usual my fears got the better of me, I hammered at the cellar door demanding to know what was going on in there. My brother completely ignored these efforts of mine at communication, but I was determined to speak to him. When he finally came out of the cellar, much later that night, I was waiting for him at the door. He turned the key in the lock behind him, carefully shielding the cellar's contents from my view, and regarded me curiously from behind those horrid dark glasses before offering me the merest parody of a smile.

"Phillip, you've been very patient with me," he said, taking my elbow and leading me up the cellar steps, "and I know I must have seemed to be acting quite strangely and inexplicably. It's all very simple really, but for the moment I can't explain just what I'm about. You'll just have to keep faith with me and wait. If you're worried that I'm heading for another bout of, well, *trouble*—you can forget it. I'm perfectly all right. I just need a little more time to finish off what I'm doing—and then, the day after tomorrow, I'll take you in there"—he nodded over his shoulder—"into the cellar, and show you what I've got. All I ask is that you're patient for just one more day. Believe me, Phillip, you've got a revelation coming which will shake you to your very roots; and afterwards—you'll understand everything. Don't ask me to explain it all now—you wouldn't believe it! But seeing *is* believing, and when I take you in there you'll be able to see for yourself."

He seemed so reasonable, so sensible—if a trifle feverish—and so excited, almost like a child about to show off some new toy. Wanting to believe him, I allowed myself to be easily talked around and we went off together to eat a late meal.

Julian spent the morning of the 14th transferring all his notes—great sheaves of them which I had never suspected existed—together with odds and ends in small cardboard boxes, from his room to the cellar. After a meager lunch he was off to the library to "do some final checking" and to return a number of books lately borrowed. While he was out I went down to the cellar—only to discover that he had locked the door and taken the key with him. He returned and spent the entire afternoon locked in down there, to emerge later at night looking strangely elated. Still later, after I had retired to my room, he came and knocked on my door.

"The night is exceptionally clear, Phillip, and I thought I'd have a look at the sky . . . the stars have always fascinated me, you know? But the window in my room doesn't really show them off too well; I'd appreciate it if you'd allow me to sit in here and look out for a while?"

"By all means do, old fellow, come on in," I answered, agreeably surprised. I left my easy chair and went to stand beside him after he crossed the room to lean on the window-sill. He peered through those strange, dark lenses up and out into the night. He was, I could see, intently studying the constellations, and as I glanced from the sky to his face I mused aloud: "Looking up there, one is almost given to believe that the stars have some purpose other than merely making the night look pretty."

Abruptly my brother's manner changed. "What d'you mean by that?" He snapped, staring at me in an obviously suspicious fashion. I was taken aback. My remark had been completely innocuous.

"I mean that perhaps those old astrologers had something after all," I answered.

"Astrology is an ancient and exact science, Phillip—you shouldn't talk of it so lightly." He spoke slowly, as though restraining himself from some outburst. Something warned me to keep quiet, so I said no more. Five minutes later he left. Pondering my brother's odd manner, I sat there a while longer; and, as I looked up at the stars winking through the window across the room, I could not help but recall a few of those words he had mumbled in the darkness of my bedroom so long ago at the onset of his breakdown. He had said:

"That in time, *when the stars are right,* they may perform the Great Rising. . . ."

There was no sleep at all for me that night; the noises and mutterings, the mouthings and gibberings which came, loud and clear, from Julian's room would not permit it. In his sleep he talked of such eldritch and inexplicable things as the Deep Green Waste, the Scarlet Feaster, the Chained Shoggoth, the Lurker at the Threshold, Yibb-Tstll, Tsathoggua, the Cosmic Screams, the Lips of Bugg-Shash, and the Inhabitants of the Frozen Chasm. Towards morning, out of sheer exhaustion, I eventually nodded off into evil dreams which claimed my troubled subconscious until I awoke shortly before noon on the 15th.

Julian was already in the cellar, and as soon as I had washed and dressed, remembering his promise to "show me" what he had got, I started off down there. But at the top of the cellar steps my feet were suddenly arrested by the metallic *clack* of the letter-box flap in the front door of the house.

The diary!

Unreasonably fearing that Julian might also have heard the noise, I raced back along the passage to the door, snatched up the small stamped and addressed brown-paper parcel which lay on the inside door-mat, and fled with the thing to my room. I locked myself in and ripped open the parcel. I had tried Julian's door earlier and knew it to be unlocked. Now I planned to go in and drop the diary down behind the headboard of his bed while he was still in the cellar. In this way he might be led to believe he had merely misplaced the book. But, after laying aside the diary to pick up and read the stapled sheets which had fallen loose and fluttered to the floor, I forgot all about my planned deception in the dawning knowledge of my brother's obvious impending insanity. Walmsley had done as he had promised. I cast his brief, eagerly enquiring letter aside and quickly, in growing horror, read his translation of Julian's cryptical notes. It was all there, all the proof I needed, in neat partially annotated paragraphs; but I did not need to read it all. Certain words and phrases, lines and sentences, seemed to leap upon the paper, attracting my frantically searching eyes:

> "This shape/form? sickens me. Thanks be there is not long to wait. There is difficulty in the fact that this form/body/shape? would not obey me at first, and I fear it may have alerted—(?—?) to some degree. Also, I have to hide/protect/conceal? that of me which also came through with the transfer/journey/passage?
>
> "I know the mind of (?—?) fares badly in the Deeps . . . and of course his eyes were ruined/destroyed? completely. . . .
>
> "Curse the water that quiets/subdues? Great (?)'s power. In these few times/periods? I have looked upon/seen/observed? much and studied what I have seen and read—but I have had to gain such knowledge secretly. The mind-sendings/mental messages (telepathy?) from my kin/brothers? at (?—?) near that place which men call Devil-(?) were of little use to me, for the progress these beings/creatures? have made is fantastic in the deep times/moments/periods? since their (?) attack on those at Devil-(?).
>
> "I have seen much and I know the time is not yet ripe for the great rising/coming? They have developed weapons of (?) power. We would risk/chance? defeat—and that must never be.
>
> "But if (?????? they ???) turn their devices against themselves (??? bring ?) nation against nation (?? then??) destructive/cataclysmic? war rivaling (name—possibly *Azathoth*, as in *Pnakotic Mss*).
>
> "The mind of (?—?) has broken under the strain of the deeps. . . . It will now be necessary to contact my rightful shape in order to re-become one/re-enter? it.
>
> "*Cthulhu!* (?) triumph (???) I am eager to return to my own shape/form/body? I do not like the way this brother—(the word

brother implying falseness?) has looked at me . . . but he suspects nothing. . . ."

There was more, much more, but I skipped over the vast majority of the translation's remaining contents and finished by reading the last paragraph which, presumably, had been written in the diary shortly before Julian took himself off to London:

"(Date?) . . . six more (short periods of time?) to wait . . . Then the stars should be right/in order/positioned? and if all goes well the transfer can be performed/accomplished?"

That was all; but it was more than enough! That reference about my not "suspecting" anything, in connection with those same horrors which had been responsible for his first breakdown, was sufficient finally to convince me that my brother was seriously ill!

Taking the diary with me, I ran out of my room with one thought in my mind. Whatever Julian thought he was doing I had to stop him. Already his delvings constituted a terrible threat to his health, and who could say but that the next time a cure might not be possible? If he suffered a second attack, there was the monstrous possibility that he would remain permanently insane.

Immediately I started my frantic hammering, he opened the cellar door and I literally fell inside. I say I fell; indeed, I did—I fell from a sane world into a lunatic, alien, nightmare dimension totally outside any previous experience. As long as I live I shall never forget what I saw. The floor in the center of the cellar had been cleared, and upon it, chalked in bold red strokes, was a huge and unmistakable evil symbol. I had seen it before in those books which were now destroyed . . . and now I recoiled at what I had later read of it! Beyond the sign, in one corner, a pile of ashes was all that remained of Julian's many notes. An old iron grating had been fixed horizontally over bricks, and the makings of a fire were already upon it. A cryptographic script, which I recognized as being the blasphemous *Nyhargo Code,* was scrawled in green and blue chalk across the walls, and the smell of incense hung heavily in the air. The whole scene was ghastly, unreal, a living picture from Eliphas Lévi—nothing less than the lair of a sorcerer! Horrified, I turned to Julian—in time to see him lift a heavy iron poker and start the stunning swing downwards towards my head. Nor did I lift a finger to stop him. I could not—*for he had taken off those spectacles, and the sight of his terrible face had frozen me rigid as polar ice. . . .*

Regaining consciousness was like swimming up out of a dead, dark sea. I surfaced through shoals of night-black swimmers to an outer world where the ripples of the ocean were dimly lit by the glow from a dying orange sun. As the throbbing in my head subsided, those ripples resolved themselves into the pattern of my pin-stripe jacket—but the orange glow remained! My immediate hopes that it had all been a nightmare were shattered at once; for as I carefully raised my head from its position on my chest the whole room slowly came under my unbelieving scrutiny. Thank God Julian had his back to me and I could not see his face. Had I but *glimpsed* again, in those first moments of recovery, those hellish eyes I am certain the sight would have returned me to instant oblivion.

I could see now that the orange glow was reflected from the now blazing fire on the horizontal grill, and I saw that the poker which had been used to strike me down was buried in the heart of the flames with red-heat creeping visibly up the metal towards the wooden handle. Glancing at my watch, I saw that I had been unconscious for many hours—it was fast approaching the midnight hour. That one glance was also sufficient to tell me that I was tied to the old wicker-chair in which I had been seated, for I saw the ropes. I flexed my muscles against my bonds and noticed, not without a measure of satisfaction, that there was a certain degree of slackness in them. I had managed to keep my mind from dwelling on Julian's facial differences, but, as he turned towards me, I steeled myself to the coming shock.

His face was an impassive white mask in which shone, cold and malevolent and indescribably alien, *those eyes!* As I live and breathe, I swear they were twice the size they ought to have been—and they bulged, uniformly scarlet, outwards from their sockets in chill, yet aloof hostility.

"Ah! You've returned to us, dear brother. But why d'you stare so? Is it that you find this face so awful? Let me assure you, you don't find it half so hideous as I!"

Monstrous truth, or what I thought was the truth, began to dawn in my mazed and bewildered brain. "The dark spectacles!" I gasped. "No wonder you had to wear them, even at night. You couldn't bear the thought of people seeing those diseased eyes!"

"Diseased? No, your reasoning is only partly correct. I had to wear the glasses, yes; it was that or give myself away—which wouldn't have pleased those who sent me in the slightest, believe me. For Cthulhu, beneath the waves on the far side of the world, has already made it known to Othuum, my master, of his displeasure. They have spoken in dreams and Cthulhu is *angry*!" He shrugged. "Also, I needed the spectacles; these eyes of mine are accustomed to piercing the deepest depths of the ocean! Your surface world was an agony to me at first—but now I am used to it. In any case, I don't plan to stay here long, and when I go I will take this body with me," he plucked at himself in contempt, "for my pleasure."

I knew that what he was saying was not, could not, be possible, and I cried out to him, begging him to recognize his own madness. I babbled that modern medical science could probably correct whatever was wrong with his eyes. My words were drowned out by his cold laughter. "Julian!" I cried.

"Julian?" he answered. "Julian Haughtree?" He lowered his awful face until it was only inches from mine. "Are you blind, man? *I am Pesh-Tlen, Wizard of deep Gell-Ho to the North!*" He turned away from me, leaving my tottering mind to total up a nerve-blasting sum of horrific integers. The Cthulhu Mythos—those passages from the *Cthaat Aquadingen* and the *Life of St. Brendan*—Julian's dreams; "They can now control dreams as of old." The Mind Transfer—"They will rise"—"through his eyes in my body"—giant Gods waiting in the ocean deeps—"He shall walk the Earth in my guise"—a submarine disturbance off the coast of Greenland! *Deep Gell-Ho to the North . . .*

God in heaven! Could such things be? Was this all, in the end, not just some fantastic delusion of Julian's but an incredible fact? This thing before me! Did he—*it*—really see through the eyes of a monster from the bottom of the sea? And if so—*was it governed by that monster's mind?*

After that, it was not madness which gripped me—not then—rather was it the refusal of my whole being to accept that which was unacceptable. I do not know how long I remained in that state, but the spell was abruptly broken by the first, distant chime of the midnight hour.

At that distant clamour my mind became crystal clear and the eyes of the being called Pesh-Tlen blazed even more unnaturally as he smiled—if that word describes what he *did* with his face—in final triumph. Seeing that smile, I knew that something hideous was soon to come and I struggled against my bonds. I was gratified to feel them slacken a little more about my body. The—creature—had meanwhile turned away from me and had taken the poker from the fire. As the chimes of the hour continued to ring out faintly from afar it raised its arms, weaving strange designs in the air with the tip of the redly glowing poker, and commenced a chant or invocation of such a loathsome association of discordant tones and pipings that my soul seemed to shrink inside me at the hearing. It was fantastic that what was grunted, snarled, whistled, and hissed with such incredible fluency could ever have issued from the throat of something I had called brother, regardless what force motivated his vocal cords; but fantastic or not, I heard it. Heard it? Indeed, as that mad cacophony died away, tapering off to a high-pitched, screeching end—*I saw its result!*

Writhing tendrils of green smoke began to whirl together in one corner of the cellar. I did not see the smoke arrive, nor could I say whence it came—it was just suddenly there! The tendrils quickly became a column, rapidly thickening, spinning faster and faster, forming—*a shape!*

Outside in the night freak lightning flashed and thunder rumbled over the city in what I have since been told was the worst storm in years—but I barely heard the thunder or the heavy downpour of rain. All my senses were concentrated on the silently spinning, rapidly coalescing thing in the corner. The cellar had a high ceiling, almost eleven feet, but what was forming seemed to fill that space easily.

I screamed then, and mercifully fainted. For once again my mind had been busy totaling the facts as I knew them, and I had mentally questioned Pesh-Tlen's reason for calling up this horror from the depths—or from wherever else it came. Upstairs in my room, unless Julian had been up there and removed it, the answer lay where I had thrown it—Walmsley's translation! Had not Julian, or Pesh-Tlen, or whatever the thing was, written in that diary: *"It will now be necessary to contact my natural form in order to re-enter it"?*

My black-out could only have been momentary, for as I regained consciousness for the second time I saw that the thing in the corner had still not completely formed. It had stopped spinning and was now centrally opaque, but its outline was infirm and wavering, like a scene viewed through smoke. The creature that had been Julian was standing to one side of the cellar, arms raised towards the semi-coherent object in the corner, features strained and twitching with hideous expectancy.

"Look," it spoke coldly, half turning towards me. "See what I and the Deep Ones have done! Behold, mortal, your brother—*Julian Haughtree!*"

For the rest of my days, which I believe will not number many, I will never be able to rid my memory of that sight! While others lie drowning in sleep I will claw desperately at the barrier of consciousness, not daring to close my eyes for fear of that which lingers yet behind my eyelids. As Pesh-Tlen spoke those words—the thing in the corner finally materialized!

Imagine a black, glistening, ten-foot heap of twisting, ropey tentacles and gaping mouths. . . . Imagine the outlines of a slimy, alien face in which, sunk deep in gaping sockets, are the remains of ruptured, *human* eyes. . . . Imagine shrieking in absolute clutching, leaping fear and horror—and imagine the thing which I have here described answering your screams in a madly familiar voice; *a voice which you instantly recognize!*

"Phillip! Phillip, where are you? What's happened? I can't see. . . .

We came up out of the sea, and then I was whirled away somewhere and I heard your voice." The horror rocked back and forth. "Don't let them take me back, Phillip!"

The voice was that of my brother, all right—but not the old, *sane* Julian I had known! That was when I, too, went mad; but it was a madness with a purpose, if nothing else. When I had previously fainted, the sudden loosening of my body must have completed the work which I had started on the ropes. As I lurched to my feet they fell from me to the floor. The huge, blind monstrosity in the corner had started to lumber in my direction, vaguely twisting its tentacles before it as it came. At the same time the red-eyed demon in Julian's form was edging carefully towards it, arms eagerly outstretched.

"Julian," I screamed, "look out—only by contact can he re-enter—and then he intends to kill you, to take you back with him to the deeps."

"Back to the deeps? No! No, he can't! I won't go!" The lumbering horror with my brother's mad voice spun blindly around, its flailing tentacles knocking the hybrid sorcerer flying across the floor. I snatched the poker from the fire where it had been replaced and turned threateningly upon the sprawling half-human.

"Stand still, Julian!" I gibbered over my shoulder at the horror from the sea as the wizard before me leapt to his feet. The lumberer behind me halted. "You, Pesh-Tlen, get back." There was no plan in my bubbling mind; I only knew I had to keep the two—*things*—apart. I danced like a boxer, using the glowing poker to ward off the suddenly frantic Pesh-Tlen.

"But it's time—it's time! The contact must be now!" The red-eyed thing screeched. "Get out of my way. . . ." Its tones were barely human now. "You can't stop me. . . . I must . . . must . . . must make strong . . . strong contact! I must . . . *bhfg—ngyy fhtlhlh hegm—yeh'hhg narcchhh'yy!* You won't cheat me!"

A pool of slime, like the trail of a great snail, had quickly spread from the giant shape behind me; and, even as he screamed, Pesh-Tlen suddenly leapt forward straight onto it, his feet skidding on the evil-smelling mess. He completely lost his balance. Arms flailing he fell, face down, sickeningly, onto the rigid red-hot poker in my hand. Four inches of the glowing metal slid, like a warm knife through butter, into one of those awful eyes. There was a hissing sound, almost drowned out by the creature's single shrill scream of agony, and a small cloud of steam rose mephitically from the thing's face as it pitched to the floor.

Instantly the glistening black giant behind me let out a shriek of terror. I spun round, letting the steaming poker fall, to witness that monstrosity from the ocean floor rocking to and fro, tentacles wrapped protectively round its head. After a few seconds it became still, and the rubbery arms fell listlessly away to reveal the multimouthed face with its ruined, rotting eyes.

"You've killed him, I know it," Julian's voice said, calmer now. "He is finished and I am finished—already I can feel them recalling me." Then, voice rising hysterically: *"They won't take me alive!"*

The monstrous form trembled and its outline began to blur. My legs crumpled beneath me in sudden reaction, and I pitched to the floor. Perhaps I passed out again—I don't know for sure—but when I next looked in its direction the horror had gone. All that remained was the slime and the grotesque corpse.

I do not know where my muscles found the strength to carry my tottering and mazed body out of that house. Sanity did not drive me, I admit that, for I was quite insane. I wanted to stand beneath the stabbing lightning and scream at those awful, rain-blurred stars. I wanted to bound, to float in my madness through eldritch depths of unhallowed black blood. I wanted to cling to the writhing breasts of Yibb-Tstll. Insane—insane, I tell you, I gibbered and moaned, staggering through the thunder-crazed streets until, with a roar and a crash, sanity-invoking lightning smashed me down. . . .

You know the rest. I awoke to this world of white sheets; to you, the police psychiatrist, with your soft voice. . . . Why must you insist that I keep telling my story? Do you honestly think to make me change it? It's *true,* I tell you! I admit to killing my brother's body—but it wasn't *his mind* that I burned out! You stand there babbling of awful eye diseases. *Julian had no eye disease!* D'you really imagine that the other eye, the unburnt one which you found in that body—in my brother's face—was his? And what of the pool of slime in the cellar and the stink? Are you stupid or something? You've asked for a statement, and here it is! Watch, damn you, watch while I scribble it down . . . you damn great crimson eye . . . always watching me . . . who would have thought that the lips of Bugg-Shash could *suck* like that? Watch, you redness you . . . and look out for the Scarlet Feaster! *No, don't take the paper away. . . .*

NOTE:

Sir,

Dr. Stewart was contacted as you suggested, and after seeing Haughtree he gave his expert opinion that the man was madder than his brother had ever been. He also pointed out the possibility that the disease of Julian Haughtree's eyes had started soon after his partial mental recovery—probably brought on by constantly wearing dark spectacles. After Dr. Stewart left the police ward, Haughtree became very indignant and wrote the above statement.

Davies, our specialist, examined the body in the cellar himself and is convinced that the younger brother must, indeed, have been suffering from a particularly horrible and unknown ocular disease.

It is appreciated that there are one or two remarkable coincidences in the wild fancies of both brothers in relation to certain recent factual events—but these are, surely, only coincidences. One such event is the rise of the volcanic island of Surtsey. Haughtree must somehow have heard of Surtsey after being taken under observation. He asked to be allowed to read the following newspaper account, afterwards yelling very loudly and repeatedly: "By God! They've named it after the wrong mythos!" Thereafter he was put into a straitjacket of the arm-restricting type:

———BIRTH OF AN ISLAND———

Yesterday morning, the 16th November, the sun rose on a long, narrow island of tephra, lying in the sea to the north of Scotland at latitude 63°18′ North and longitude 20°36½′ West. Surtsey, which was born on the 15th November, was then 130 feet high and growing all the time. The fantastic "birth" of the island was witnessed by the crew of the fishing vessel *Isleifer II*, which was lying west of Geirfuglasker, southernmost of the Vestmann Islands. Considerable disturbance of the sea—which hindered clear observation—was noticed, and the phenomena, the result of submarine volcanic activity, involved such awe-inspiring sights as columns of smoke reaching to two and a half miles high, fantastic lightning storms, and the hurling of lava-bombs over a wide area of the ocean. Surtsey has been named after the giant Surter, who—in Norse Mythology—"Came from the South with Fire to fight the God Freyr at Ragnarok," which battle preceded the end of the world and the Twilight of the Gods. More details and pictures inside.

Still in the "jacket," Haughtree finally calmed himself and begged that further interesting items in the paper be read to him. Dr. Davies did the reading, and when he reached the following report Haughtree grew very excited:

———BEACHES FOULED———

Garvin Bay, on the extreme North coast, was found this morning to be horribly fouled. For a quarter of a mile deposits of some slimy, black grease were left by the tide along the sands. The stench was so great from these unrecognizable deposits that fishermen were unable to put to sea. Scientific analysis has already shown the stuff to be of an organic base, and it is thought to be some type of oil. Local shipping experts are bewildered, as no known tankers have been in the area for over three months. The tremendous variety of dead and rotting fish also washed up has caused the people of nearby Belloch to take strong sanitary precautions. It is hoped that tonight's tide will clear the affected area. . . .

At the end of the reading Haughtree said: "Julian said they wouldn't take him alive." Then, still encased in the jacket, he somehow got off the bed and flung himself through the third-story window of his room in the police ward. His rush at the window was of such tremendous ferocity and strength that he took the bars and frame with him. It all happened so quickly there was nothing anyone could do to stop him.

Submitted as an appendix to my original report.

Sgt. J. T. Muir

23 November 1963. Glasgow City Police

Cold Print*

RAMSEY CAMPBELL

> . . . for even the minions of Cthulhu dare not speak of Y'golonac; yet the time will come when Y'golonac strides forth from the loneliness of aeons to walk once more among men. . . .
>
> —REVELATIONS OF GLAAKI, VOLUME 12

Sam Strutt licked his fingers and wiped them on his handkerchief; his fingertips were grey with snow from the pole on the bus platform. Then he coaxed his book out of the polythene bag on the seat beside him, withdrew the bus-ticket from between the pages, held it against the cover to protect the latter from his fingers, and began to read. As often happened the conductor assumed that the ticket authorized Strutt's present journey; Strutt did not enlighten him. Outside, the snow whirled down the side streets and slipped beneath the wheels of cautious cars.

The slush splashed into his boots as he stepped down outside Brichester Central and, snuggling the bag beneath his coat for extra safety, pushed his way toward the bookstall, treading on the settling snowflakes. The glass panels of the stall were not quite closed; snow had filtered through and dulled the glossy paperbacks. "Look at that!" Strutt complained to a young man who stood next to him and anxiously surveyed the crowd, drawing his neck down inside his collar like a tortoise. "Isn't that disgusting? These people just don't care!" The young man, still searching the wet faces, agreed abstractedly. Strutt strode to the other counter of the stall, where the assistant was handing out newspapers. "I say!" called Strutt. The assistant, sorting change for a customer, gestured him to wait. Over the paperbacks, through the steaming glass, Strutt watched the young man rush forward and embrace a girl, then gently dry her face with a

*Originally published in *Tales of the Cthulhu Mythos*, 1969.

handkerchief. Strutt glanced at the newspaper held by the man awaiting change. BRUTAL MURDER IN RUINED CHURCH, he read; the previous night a body had been found inside the roofless walls of a church in Lower Brichester; when the snow had been cleared from this marble image, frightful mutilations had been revealed covering the corpse, oval mutilations which resembled— The man took the paper and his change away into the station. The assistant turned to Strutt with a smile: "Sorry to keep you waiting." "Yes," said Strutt. "Do you realize those books are getting snowed on? People may want to buy them, you know." "Do *you*?" the assistant replied. Strutt tightened his lips and turned back into the snow-filled gusts. Behind him he heard the ring of glass pane meeting pane.

GOOD BOOKS ON THE HIGHWAY provided shelter; he closed out the lashing sleet and stood taking stock. On the shelves the current titles showed their faces while the others turned their backs. Girls were giggling over comic Christmas cards; an unshaven man was swept in on a flake-edged blast and halted, staring around uneasily. Strutt clucked his tongue; tramps shouldn't be allowed in bookshops to soil the books. Glancing sideways to observe whether the man would bend back the covers or break the spines, Strutt moved among the shelves, but could not find what he sought. Chatting with the cashier, however, was an assistant who had praised *Last Exit to Brooklyn* to him when he had bought it last week, and had listened patiently to a list of Strutt's recent reading, though he had not seemed to recognize the titles. Strutt approached him and enquired: "Hello—any more exciting books this week?"

The man faced him, puzzled. "Any more—?"

"You know, books like this?" Strutt held up his polythene bag to show the grey Ultimate Press cover of *The Caning-Master* by Hector Q.

"Ah, no. I don't think we have." He tapped his lip. "Except—Jean Genet?"

"Who? Oh, you mean *Jennet*. No, thanks, he's dull as ditchwater."

"Well, I'm sorry, sir, I'm afraid I can't help you."

"Oh." Strutt felt rebuffed. The man seemed not to recognize him, or perhaps he was pretending. Strutt had met his kind before and had them mutely patronize his reading. He scanned the shelves again, but no cover caught his eye. At the door he furtively unbuttoned his shirt to protect his book still further, and a hand fell on his arm. Lined with grime, the hand slid down to his and touched his bag. Strutt shook it off angrily and confronted the tramp.

"Wait a minute!" the man hissed. "Are you after more books like that? I know where we can get some."

This approach offended Strutt's self-righteous sense of reading books which had no right to be suppressed. He snatched the bag out of the fingers closing on it. "So you like them too, do you?"

"Oh, yes, I've got lots."

Strutt sprang his trap. "Such as?"

"Oh, *Adam and Evan, Take Me How You Like,* all the Harrison adventures, you know, there's lots."

Strutt grudgingly admitted that the man's offer seemed genuine. The assistant at the cash-desk was eyeing them; Strutt stared back. "All right," he said. "Where's this place you're talking about?"

The other took his arm and pulled him eagerly into the slanting snow. Clutching shut their collars, pedestrians were slipping between the cars as they waited for a skidded bus ahead to be removed; flakes were crushed into the corners of the windscreens by the wipers. The man dragged Strutt amid the horns which brayed and honked, then between two store windows from which girls watched smugly as they dressed headless figures, and down an alley. Strutt recognized the area as one which he vainly combed for back-street bookshops; disappointing alcoves of men's magazines, occasional hot pungent breaths from kitchens, cars fitted with caps of snow, loud pubs warm against the weather. Strutt's guide dodged into the doorway of a public bar to shake his coat; the white glaze cracked and fell from him. Strutt joined the man and adjusted the book in its bag, snuggled beneath his shirt. He stamped the crust loose from his boots, stopping when the other followed suit; he did not wish to be connected with the man even by such a trivial action. He looked with distaste at his companion, at his swollen nose through which he was now snorting back snot, at the stubble shifting on the cheeks as they inflated and the man blew on his trembling hands. Strutt had a horror of touching anyone who was not fastidious. Beyond the doorway flakes were already obscuring their footprints, and the man said: "I get terrible thirsty walking fast like this."

"So that's the game, is it?" But the bookshop lay ahead. Strutt led the way into the bar and bought two pints from a colossal barmaid, her bosom bristling with ruffles, who billowed back and forth with glasses and worked the pumps with gusto. Old men sucked at pipes in vague alcoves, a radio blared marches, men clutching tankards aimed with jovial inaccuracy at dart-board or spittoon. Strutt flapped his overcoat and hung it next to him; the other retained his and stared into his beer. Determined not to talk, Strutt surveyed the murky mirrors which reflected gesticulating parties around littered tables not directly visible. But he was gradually surprised by the taciturnity of his table-mate; surely these people (he thought) were remarkably loquacious, in fact virtually impossible to silence? This was intolerable; sitting idly in an airless back-street bar when he could be on the move or reading—something must be done. He gulped down his beer and thumped the glass upon its mat. The other started. Then, visibly abashed, he began to sip, seeming oddly nervous. At last it was obvious that he was dawdling over the froth, and he set down his glass and stared at it. "It looks as if it's time to go," said Strutt.

The man looked up; fear widened his eyes. "Christ, I'm wet," he muttered. "I'll take you again when the snow goes off."

"That's the game, is it?" Strutt shouted. In the mirrors, eyes sought him. "You don't get that drink out of me for nothing! I haven't come this far—!"

The man swung round and back, trapped. "All right, all right, only maybe I won't find it in this weather."

Strutt found this remark too inane to comment. He rose, and buttoning his coat strode into the arcs of snow, glaring behind to ensure he was followed.

The last few shop-fronts, behind them pyramids of tins marked with misspelt placards, were cast out by lines of furtively curtained windows set in unrelieved vistas of red brick; behind the panes Christmas decorations hung like wreaths. Across the road, framed in a bedroom window, a middle-aged woman drew the curtains and hid the teenage boy at her shoulder. "Hel-*lo*, there they go," Strutt did not say; he felt he could control the figure ahead without speaking to him, and indeed had no desire to speak to the man as he halted trembling, no doubt from the cold, and hurried onward as Strutt, an inch taller than his five and a half feet and better built, loomed behind him. For an instant, as a body of snow drove toward him down the street, flakes over-exposing the landscape and cutting his cheeks like transitory razors of ice, Strutt yearned to speak, to tell of nights when he lay awake in his room, hearing the landlady's daughter being beaten by her father in the attic bedroom above, straining to catch muffled sounds through the creak of bedsprings, perhaps from the couple below. But the moment passed, swept away by the snow; the end of the street had opened, split by a traffic-island into two roads thickly draped with snow, one curling away to hide between the houses, the other short, attached to a roundabout. Now Strutt knew where he was. From a bus earlier in the week he had noticed the KEEP LEFT sign lying helpless on its back on the traffic-island, its face kicked in.

They crossed the roundabout, negotiated the crumbling lips of ruts full of deceptively glazed pools collecting behind the bulldozer treads of a redevelopment scheme, and onward through the whirling white to a patch of waste ground where a lone fireplace drank the snow. Strutt's guide scuttled into an alley and Strutt followed, intent on keeping close to the other as he knocked powdered snow from dustbin lids and flinched from back-yard doors at which dogs clawed and snarled. The man dodged left, then right, between the close labyrinthine walls, among houses whose cruel edges of jagged window-panes and thrusting askew doors even the snow, kinder to buildings than to their occupants, could not soften. A last turning, and the man slithered onto a pavement beside the remnants of a store, its front gaping emptily to frame wine-bottles abandoned beneath a HEIN 57 VARIET poster. A dollop of snow fell from the awning's skeleton to be swallowed by the drift below. The man shook, but as Strutt confronted him, pointed fearfully to the opposite pavement: "That's it, I've brought you here."

The tracks of slush splashed up Strutt's trouser legs as he ran across, checking mentally that while the man had tried to disorient him he had deduced which main road lay some five hundred yards away, then read the inscription over the shop: AMERICAN BOOKS BOUGHT AND SOLD. He touched a railing which protected an opaque window below street level, wet rust gritting beneath his nails, and surveyed the display in the window facing him: *History of the Rod*—a book he had found monotonous—thrusting out it shoulders among science-fiction novels by Aldiss, Tubb, and Harrison, which hid shamefacedly behind lurid covers; *Le Sadisme au Cinéma*; Robbe-Grillet's *Voyeur* looking lost; *The Naked Lunch*— nothing worth his journey there, Strutt thought. "All right, it's about time we went in," he urged the man inside, and with a glance up the eroded red brick at the first-floor window, the back of a dressing-table mirror shoved against it to replace one pane, entered also. The other had halted again, and for an unpleasant second Strutt's fingers brushed the man's musty overcoat. "Come on, where's the books?" he demanded, shoving past into the shop.

The yellow daylight was made murkier by the window display and the pin-up magazines hanging on the inside of the glass-panelled door; dust hung lazily in the stray beams. Strutt stopped to read the covers of paperbacks stuffed into cardboard boxes on one table, but the boxes contained only Westerns, fantasies, and American erotica, selling at half price. Grimacing at the books which stretched wide their corners like flowering petals, Strutt bypassed the hardcovers and squinted behind the counter, slightly preoccupied; as he had closed the door beneath its tongueless bell, he had imagined he had heard a cry somewhere near, quickly cut off. No doubt round here you hear that sort of thing all the time, he thought, and turned on the other: "Well, I don't see what I came for. Doesn't anybody work in this place?"

Wide-eyed, the man gazed past Strutt's shoulder; Strutt looked back and saw the frosted-glass panel of a door, one corner of the glass repaired with cardboard, black against a dim yellow light which filtered through the panel. The bookseller's office, presumably—had he heard Strutt's remark? Strutt confronted the door, ready to face impertinence.

Then the man pushed by him, searching distractedly behind the counter, fumbling open a glass-fronted bookcase full of volumes in brown paper jackets and finally extracting a parcel in grey paper from its hiding-place in one corner of a shelf. He thrust it at Strutt, muttering, "This is one, this is one," and watched, the skin beneath his eyes twitching, as Strutt tore off the paper.

The Secret Life of Wackford Squeers— "Ah, that's fine," Strutt approved, forgetting himself momentarily, and reached for his wallet; but greasy fingers clawed at his wrist. "Pay next time," the man pleaded. Strutt hesitated; could he get away with the book without paying? At that moment, a shadow rippled across the frosted glass: a headless man dragging something heavy. Decapitated by the frosted glass and by his hunched position, Strutt decided, then realized that the shopkeeper must be in contact with Ultimate Press; he must not prejudice this contact by stealing a book. He knocked away the frantic fingers and counted out two pounds; but the other backed away, stretching out his fingers in stark fear, and crouched against the office door from whose pane the silhouette had disappeared, before flinching almost into Strutt's arms. Strutt pushed him back and laid the notes in the space left on the shelf by *Wackford Squeers*, then turned on him: "Don't you intend to wrap it up? No, on second thoughts I'll do it myself."

The roller on the counter rumbled forth a streamer of brown paper; Strutt sought an undiscolored stretch. As he parcelled the book, disentangling his feet from the rejected coil, something crashed to the floor. The other had retreated toward the street door until one dangling cuff-button had hooked the corner of a carton full of paperbacks; he froze above the scattered books, mouth and hands gaping wide, one foot atop an open novel like a broken moth, and around him motes floated into beams of light mottled by the sifting snow. Somewhere a lock clicked. Strutt breathed hard, taped the package, and circling the man in distaste, opened the door. The cold attacked his legs. He began to mount the steps and the other flurried in pursuit. The man's foot was on the doorstep when a heavy tread approached across the boards. The man spun about, and below Strutt the door slammed. Strutt waited; then it occurred to him that he could hurry and shake off his guide. He reached the street and a powdered breeze pecked at his cheeks, cleaning away the stale dust of the shop. He turned away his face and, kicking the rind of snow from the headline of a sodden newspaper, made for the main road which he knew to pass close by.

Strutt woke shivering. The neon sign outside the window of his flat, a cliché but relentless as a toothache, was garishly defined against the night every five seconds, and by this and the shafts of cold Strutt knew that it was early morning. He closed his eyes again, but though his lids were hot and heavy his mind would not be lulled. Beyond the limits of his memory lurked the dream which had awoken him; he moved uneasily. For some reason he thought of a passage from the previous evening's reading: "As Adam reached the door he felt Evan's hand grip his, twisting his arm behind his back, forcing him to the floor—" His eyes opened and sought the bookcase as if for reassurance; yes, there was the book, secure within its covers, carefully aligned with its fellows. He recalled returning home one evening to find *Miss Whippe, Old-Style Governess*, thrust inside *Prefects and Fags*, straddled by *Prefects and Fags*; the landlady had explained that she must have replaced them wrongly after dusting, but Strutt knew that she had damaged them vindictively. He had bought a case that locked, and when she asked him for the key had replied: "Thanks, I think I can do them justice." You couldn't make friends nowadays. He closed his eyes again; the room and bookcase, created in five seconds by the neon and destroyed with equal regularity, filled him with their emptiness, reminding him that weeks lay ahead before the beginning of next term, when he would confront the first class of the morning and add "You know me by now" to his usual introduction "You play fair with me and I'll play fair with you," a warning which some boy would be sure to test, and Strutt would have him; he saw the expanse of white gym-short seat stretched tight down on which he would bring a gym-shoe with satisfying force—Strutt relaxed; soothed by an overwhelming echo of the pounding feet on the wooden gymnasium floor, the fevered shaking of the wall-bars as the boys swarmed ceilingward and he stared up from below, he slept.

Panting, he drove himself through his morning exercises, then tossed off the fruit juice which was always his first call on the tray brought up by the landlady's daughter. Viciously he banged the glass back on the tray; the glass splintered (he'd say it was an accident; he paid enough rent to cover, he might as well get a little satisfaction for his money). "Bet you have a fab Christmas," the girl had said, surveying the room. He'd made to grab her round the waist and curb her pert femininity—but she'd already gone, her skirt's pleats whirling, leaving his stomach hotly knotted in anticipation.

Later he trudged to the supermarket. From several front gardens came the teeth-grinding scrape of spades clearing snow; these faded and were answered by the crushed squeak of snow engulfing boots. When he emerged from the supermarket clutching an armful of cans, a snowball whipped by his face to thud against the window, a translucent beard spreading down the pane like the fluid from the noses of those boys who felt Strutt's wrath most often, for he was determined to beat this ugliness, this revoltingness, out of them. Strutt glared about him for the marksman—a seven-year-old, boarding his tricycle for a quick retreat; Strutt moved involuntarily as if to pull the boy across his knee. But the street was not deserted; even now the child's mother, in slacks and curlers peeking from beneath a headscarf, was slapping her son's hand: "I've told you, *don't* do that. —Sorry," she called to Strutt. "Yes, I'm sure," he snarled, and tramped back to his flat. His heart pumped uncontrollably. He wished fervently that he could talk to someone as he had talked to the bookseller on the edge of Goatswood who had shared his urges; when the man had died earlier that year Strutt had felt abandoned in a tacitly conspiring, hostile world. Perhaps the new shop's owner might prove similarly sympathetic? Strutt hoped that the man who had conducted him there yesterday would not be in attendance, but if he was, surely he could be got rid of—a bookseller dealing with Ultimate Press must be a man after Strutt's own heart, who would be as opposed as he to that other's presence while they were talking frankly. As well as this discussion, Strutt needed books to read over Christmas, and *Squeers* would not last him long; the shop would scarcely be closed on Christmas Eve. Thus reassured, he unloaded the cans on the kitchen table and ran downstairs.

Strutt stepped from the bus in silence; the engine's throb was quickly muffled among the laden houses. The piled snow waited for some sound. He splashed through the tracks of cars to the pavement, its dull coat depressed by countless overlapping footprints. The road twisted slyly; as soon as the main road was out of sight the side street revealed its real character. The snow laid over the house-fronts became threadbare; rusty protrusions poked through. One or two windows showed Christmas trees, their ageing needles falling out, their branches tipped with luridly sputtering lights. Strutt, however, had no eye for this but kept his gaze on the pavement, seeking to avoid stains circled by dogs' pawmarks. Once he met the gaze of an old woman staring down at a point below her window which was perhaps the extent of her outside world. Momentarily chilled, he hurried on, pursued by a woman who, on the evidence within her pram, had given birth to a litter of newspapers, and halted before the shop.

Though the orange sky could scarcely have illuminated the interior, no electric gleam was visible through the magazines, and the torn notice hanging behind the grime might read CLOSED. Slowly Strutt descended the steps. The pram squealed by, the latest flakes spreading across the newspapers. Strutt stared at its inquisitive proprietor, turned and almost fell into sudden darkness. The door had opened and a figure blocked the doorway.

"You're not shut, surely?" Strutt's tongue tangled.

"Perhaps not. Can I help you?"

"I was here yesterday. Ultimate Press book," Strutt replied to the face level with his own and uncomfortably close.

"Of course you were, yes, I recall." The other swayed incessantly like an athlete limbering up, and his voice wavered constantly from bass to falsetto, dismaying Strutt. "Well, come in before the snow gets to you," the other said and slammed the door behind them, evoking a note from the ghost of the bell's tongue.

The bookseller—this was he, Strutt presumed—loomed behind him, a head taller; down in the half-light, among the vague vindictive corners of the tables, Strutt felt an obscure compulsion to assert himself somehow, and remarked: "I hope you found the money for the book. Your man didn't seem to want me to pay. Some people would have taken him at his word."

"He's not with us today." The bookseller switched on the light inside his office. As his lined pouched face was lit up it seemed to grow; the eyes were sunk in sagging stars of wrinkles; the cheeks and forehead bulged from furrows; the head floated like a half-inflated balloon above the stuffed tweed suit. Beneath the unshaded bulb the walls pressed close, surrounding a battered desk from which overflowed fingerprinted copies of *The Bookseller* thrust aside by a black typewriter clogged with dirt, beside which lay a stub of sealing-wax and an open box of matches. Two chairs faced each other across the desk, and behind it was a closed door. Strutt seated himself before the desk, brushing dust to the floor. The bookseller paced round him and suddenly, as if struck by the question, demanded: "Tell me, why d'you read these books?"

This was a question often aimed at Strutt by the English master in the staffroom until he had ceased to read his novels in the breaks. Its sudden reappearance caught him off guard, and he could only call on his old riposte: "How d'you mean, why? Why not?"

"I wasn't being critical," the other hurried on, moving restlessly around the desk. "I'm genuinely interested. I was going to make the point that don't you want what you read about to happen, in a sense?"

"Well, maybe." Strutt was suspicious of the trend of this discussion, and wished that he could dominate; his words seemed to plunge into the snow-cloaked silence inside the dusty walls to vanish immediately, leaving no impression.

"I mean this: when you read a book don't you make it happen before you, in your mind? Particularly if you consciously attempt to visualize, but that's not essential. You might cast the book away from you, of course. I knew a bookseller who worked on this theory; you don't get much time to be yourself in this sort of area, but when he could he worked on it, though he never quite formulated— Wait a minute, I'll show you something."

He leapt away from the desk and into the shop. Strutt wondered what was beyond the door behind the desk. He half-rose but, peering back, saw the bookseller already returning through the drifting shadows with a volume extracted from among the Lovecrafts and Derleths.

"This ties in with your Ultimate Press books, really," the other said, banging the office door to as he entered. "They're publishing a book by Johannes Henricus Pott next year, so we hear, and that's concerned with forbidden lore as well, like this one; you'll no doubt be amazed to hear that they think they may have to leave some of Pott in the original Latin. This here should interest you, though; the only copy. You probably won't know the *Revelations of Glaaki*; it's a sort of Bible written under supernatural guidance. There were only eleven volumes—but this is the twelfth, written by a man at the top of Mercy Hill guided through his dreams." His voice grew unsteadier as he continued. "I don't know how it got out; I suppose the man's family may have found it in some attic after his death and thought it worth a few coppers, who knows? My bookseller—well, he knew of the *Revelations*, and he realized this was priceless; but he didn't want the seller to realize he had a find and perhaps take it to the library or the University, so he took it off his hands as part of a job lot and said he might use it for scribbling. When he read it— Well, there was one passage that for testing his theory looked like a godsend. Look."

The bookseller circled Strutt again and placed the book in his lap, his arms resting on Strutt's shoulders. Strutt compressed his lips and glanced up at the other's face; but some strength weakened, refusing to support his disapproval, and he opened the book. It was an old ledger, its hinges cracking, its yellowed pages covered by irregular lines of scrawny handwriting. Throughout the introductory monologue Strutt had been baffled; now the book was before him, it vaguely recalled those bundles of duplicated typewritten sheets which had been passed around the toilets in his adolescence. "Revelations" suggested the forbidden. Thus intrigued, he read at random. Up here in Lower Brichester the bare bulb defined each scrap of flaking paint on the door opposite, and hands moved on his shoulders, but somewhere down below he would be pursued through darkness by vast soft footsteps; when he turned to look, a swollen glowing figure was upon him— What was all this about? A hand gripped his left shoulder and the right hand turned pages; finally one finger underlined a phrase:

> Beyond a gulf in the subterranean night a passage leads to a wall of massive bricks, and beyond the wall rises Y'golonac to be served by the tattered eyeless figures of the dark. Long has he slept beyond the wall, and those which crawl over the bricks scuttle across his body

> never knowing it to be Y'golonac; but when his name is spoken or read he comes forth to be worshipped or to feed and take on the shape and soul of those he feeds upon. For those who read of evil and search for its form within their minds call forth evil, and so may Y'golonac return to walk among men and await that time when the earth is cleared off and Cthulhu rises from his tomb among the weeds, Glaaki thrusts open the crystal trapdoor, the brood of Eihort are born into daylight, Shub-Niggurath strides forth to smash the moon-lens, Byatis bursts forth from his prison, Daoloth tears away illusion to expose the reality concealed behind.

The hands on his shoulders shifted constantly, slackening and tightening. The voice fluctuated: "What did you think of that?"

Strutt thought it was rubbish, but somewhere his courage had slipped; he replied unevenly: "Well, it's—not the sort of thing you see on sale."

"You found it interesting?" The voice was deepening; now it was an overwhelming bass. The other swung round behind the desk; he seemed taller—his head struck the bulb, setting shadows peering from the corners and withdrawing, and peering again. "You're interested?" His expression was intense, as far as it could be made out; for the light moved darkness in the hollows of his face, as if the bone structure were melting visibly.

In the murk in Strutt's mind appeared a suspicion; had he not heard from his dear dead friend the Goatswood bookseller that a black magic cult existed in Brichester, a circle of young men dominated by somebody Franklin or Franklyn? Was he being interviewed for this? "I wouldn't say that," he countered.

"Listen. There was a bookseller who read this, and I told him you may be the high priest of Y'golonac. You will call down the shapes of night to worship him at the times of year; you will prostrate yourself before him and in return you will survive when the earth is cleared off for the Great Old Ones; you will go beyond the rim to what stirs out of the light. . ."

Before he could consider Strutt blurted: "Are you talking about me?" He had realized he was alone in a room with a madman.

"No, no, I meant the bookseller. But the offer now is for you."

"Well, I'm sorry, I've got other things to do." Strutt prepared to stand up.

"He refused also." The timbre of the voice grated in Strutt's ears. "I had to kill him."

Strutt froze. How did one treat the insane? Pacify them. "Now, now, hold on a minute. . . ."

"How can it benefit you to doubt? I have more proof at my disposal than you could bear. You will be my high priest, or you will never leave this room."

For the first time in his life, as the shadows between the harsh oppressive walls moved slower as if anticipating, Strutt battled to control an emotion; he subdued his mingled fear and ire with calm. "If you don't mind, I've got to meet somebody."

"Not when your fulfillment lies here between these walls." The voice was thickening. "You know I killed the bookseller—it was in your papers. He fled into the ruined church, but I caught him with my hands. . . . Then I left the book in the shop to be read, but the only one who picked it up by mistake was the man who brought you here. . . . Fool! He went mad and cowered in the corner when he saw the mouths! I kept him because I thought he might bring some of his friends who wallow in physical taboos and lose the true experiences, those places forbidden to the spirit. But he only contacted you and brought you here while I was feeding. There is food occasionally; young boys who come here for books in secret; they make sure nobody knows what they read!—and can be persuaded to look at the *Revelations*. Imbecile! He can no longer betray me with his fumbling—but I knew you would return. Now you will be mine."

Strutt's teeth ground together silently until he thought his jaws would break; he stood up, nodding, and handed the volume of the *Revelations* toward the figure; he was poised, and when the hand closed on the ledger he would dart for the office door.

"You can't get out, you know; it's locked." The bookseller rocked on his feet, but did not start toward him; the shadows now were mercilessly clear and dust hung in the silence. "You're not afraid—you look too calculating. Is it possible that you still do not believe? All right—" he laid his hands on the doorknob behind the desk: "—do you want to see what is left of my food?"

A door opened in Strutt's mind, and he recoiled from what might lie beyond. "No! No!" he shrieked. Fury followed his involuntary display of fear; he wished he had a cane to subjugate the figure taunting him. Judging by the face, he thought, the bulges filling the tweed suit must be of fat; if they should struggle, Strutt would win. "Let's get this clear," he shouted, "we've played games long enough! You'll let me out of here or I—" but he found himself glaring about for a weapon. Suddenly he thought of the book still in his hand. He snatched the matchbox from the desk, behind which the figure watched, ominously impassive. Strutt struck a match, then pinched the boards between finger and thumb and shook out the pages. "I'll burn this book!" he threatened.

The figure tensed, and Strutt went cold with fear of his next move. He touched the flame to paper, and the pages curled and were consumed so swiftly that Strutt had only the impression of bright fire and shadows growing unsteadily massive on the walls before he was shaking ashes to the floor. For a moment they faced each other, immobile. After the flames a darkness had rushed into Strutt's eyes. Through it he saw the tweed tear loudly as the figure expanded.

Strutt threw himself against the office door, which resisted. He drew back his fist, and watched with an odd timeless detachment as it shattered the frosted glass; the act seemed to isolate him, as if suspending all action outside himself. Through the knives of glass, on which gleamed drops of blood, he saw the snowflakes settle through the amber light, infinitely far; too far to call for help. A horror filled him of being overpowered from behind. From the back of the office came a sound; Strutt spun and as he did so closed his eyes, terrified to face the source of such a sound—but when he opened them he saw why the shadow on the frosted pane yesterday had been headless, and he screamed. As the desk was thrust aside by the towering naked figure, on whose surface still hung rags of the tweed suit, Strutt's last thought was an unbelieving conviction that this was happening because he had read the *Revelations*; somewhere, someone had *wanted* this to happen to him. It wasn't playing fair, he hadn't done anything to deserve this—but before he could scream out his protest his breath was cut off, as the hands descended on his face and the wet red mouths opened in their palms.

The Return of the Lloigor*

COLIN WILSON

My name is Paul Dunbar Lang, and in three weeks' time I shall be seventy-two years old. My health is excellent, but since one can never know how many more years lie ahead, I shall set down this story on paper, and perhaps even publish it, if the fit takes me. In my youth, I was a confirmed believer in the Baconian authorship of Shakespeare's plays, but I took care never to mention my views in print, out of fear of my academic colleagues. But age has one advantage; it teaches one that the opinions of other people are not really very important; death is so much more real. So if I publish this, it will not be out of desire to convince anyone of its truth; but only because I don't care whether it is believed or not.

Although I was born in England—in Bristol—I have lived in America since I was twelve years old. And for nearly forty years, I have taught English literature at the University of Virginia in Charlottesville. My *Life of Chatterton* is still the standard work on its subject, and for the past fifteen years I have been the editor of *Poe Studies*.

Two years ago in Moscow, I had the pleasure of meeting the Russian writer Irakli Andronikov, who is known mainly for his "literary research stories," a genre he may be said to have created. It was Andronikov who asked me if I had ever met W. Romaine Newbold, whose name is involved with the Voynich manuscript. Not only had I never met Professor Newbold, who died in 1926, but I had never heard of the manuscript. Andronikov outlined the story. I was fascinated. When I returned to the States, I hastened to read Newbold's *The Cipher of Roger Bacon* (Philadelphia, 1928), and Professor Manly's two articles on the subject.

The story of the Voynich manuscript is briefly this. It was found in an old chest in an Italian castle by a rare book dealer, Wilfred M.

---

*Originally published in *Tales of the Cthulhu Mythos*, 1969.

Voynich, and brought to the United States in 1912. With the manuscript, Voynich also found a letter that asserted that it had been the property of two famous scholars of the seventeenth century, and that it had been written by Roger Bacon, the Franciscan monk who died about 1294. The manuscript was 116 pages long, and was apparently written in cipher. It was clearly some kind of scientific or magical document, since it contained drawings of roots or plants. On the other hand, it also contained sketches that looked amazingly like illustrations from some modern biological textbook of minute cells and organisms—for example, of spermatozoons. There were also astronomical diagrams.

For nine years, professors, historians, and cryptographers tried to break the code. Then, in 1921, Newbold announced to the American Philosophical Society in Philadelphia that he had been able to decipher certain passages. The excitement was immense; it was regarded as a supreme feat of American scholarship. But the excitement increased when Newbold disclosed the contents of the manuscript. For it seemed that Bacon must have been many centuries ahead of his time. He had apparently invented the microscope some four hundred years before Leeuwenhoek, and had shown a scientific acumen that surpassed even that of his namesake Francis Bacon in the sixteenth century.

Newbold died before completing his work, but his "discoveries" were published by his friend Roland Kent. It was at this point that Professor Manly took up the study of the manuscript, and decided that Newbold's enthusiasm had led him to deceive himself. Examined under a microscope, it was seen that the strange nature of the characters was not entirely due to a cipher. The ink had peeled off the vellum as it dried, so that the "shorthand" was actually due to ordinary wear and tear over many centuries. With Manly's announcement of his discovery in 1931, interest in the "most mysterious manuscript in the world" (Manly's phrase) vanished, Bacon's reputation sank, and the whole thing was quickly forgotten.

Upon my return from Russia, I visited the University of Pennsylvania, and examined the manuscript. It was an odd sensation. I was not disposed to view it romantically. In my younger days, I had often felt my hair stirring as I handled a letter in Poe's handwriting, and I had spent many hours sitting in his room at the University of Virginia, trying to commune with his spirit. As I got older, I became more matter-of-fact—a recognition that geniuses are basically like other men—and I stopped imagining that inanimate objects are somehow trying to "tell a story."

Yet as soon as I handled the Voynich manuscript, I had a nasty sensation. I cannot describe it more precisely than that. It was not a sense of evil or horror or dread—just nastiness; like the sensation I used to have as a child passing the house of a woman who was reputed to have eaten her sister. It made me think of murder. This sensation stayed with me during the two hours while I examined the manuscript, like an unpleasant smell. The librarian obviously did not share my feeling. When I handed the manuscript back to her, I said jokingly: "I don't like that thing." She merely looked puzzled; I could tell she had no idea of what I meant.

Two weeks later, the two photostat copies I had ordered arrived in Charlottesville. I sent one to Andronikov, as I had promised, and had the other one bound for the university library. I spent some time poring over it with a magnifying glass, reading Newbold's book and Manly's articles. The sensation of "nastiness" did not return. But when, some months later, I took my nephew to look at the manuscript, I again experienced the same feeling. My nephew felt nothing.

While we were in the library, an acquaintance of mine introduced me to Averel Merriman, the young photographer whose work is used extensively in expensive art books of the kind published by Thames and Hudson. Merriman told me that he had recently photographed a page of the Voynich manuscript in colour. I asked if I might see it. Later that afternoon, I called on him in his hotel room and saw the photograph. What was my motive? I believe it was a sort of morbid desire to find out if the "nastiness" would come over in a colour photo. It didn't. But something more interesting did. It so happened that I was thoroughly familiar with the page Merriman had photographed. And so now, looking at it carefully, I felt sure that it was, in some subtle way, different from the original. I stared at it for a long time before I realised why. The colouring of the photograph—developed by a process invented by Merriman—was slightly "richer" than that of the original manuscript. And when I looked at certain symbols indirectly—concentrating on the line just above them—they appeared to be somehow "completed," as if the discoloration left by the flakes of ink had become visible.

I tried not to show my excitement. For some reason, I felt intensely secretive, as if Merrimen had just handed me the clue to hidden treasure. A kind of "Mr. Hyde" sensation came over me—a feeling of cunning, and a kind of lust. I asked him casually how much it would cost to photograph the whole manuscript in this way. He told me several hundred dollars. Then my idea came to me. I asked if, for a much larger sum—say a thousand dollars—he would be willing to make me large "blow-ups" of the pages—perhaps four to a page. He said he would, and I wrote him a cheque on the spot. I was tempted to ask him to send me the photographs one by one, as he did them, then felt that this might arouse his curiosity. To my nephew Julian, I explained as we left that the library of the University of Virginia had asked me to have the photographs made—a pointless lie that puzzled me. Why should I lie? Had the manuscript some dubious influence of which I had become a victim?

A month later, the registered parcel arrived. I locked the door of my study, and sat in the armchair by the window as I tore off the wrappings. I took a random photograph from the middle of the pile, and held it out to the light. I wanted to shout with pleasure at what I saw. Many of the symbols seemed to be "completed," as if their broken halves were joined by a slightly darkened area of the vellum. I looked at sheet after sheet. It was impossible to doubt. The colour photography somehow showed up markings that were invisible even to a microscope.

What followed now was routine work, although it took many months. The photographs were taped, one after the other, to a large drawing board, and then traced. The tracings were transferred, with the utmost care, to heavy drawing paper. Then, working with deliberate slowness, I sketched in the "invisible" part of the symbols, completing them. When the whole thing was finished, I bound it into a large folio, and then settled down to study it. I had completed more than half the symbols—which were, of course, four times their natural size. Now, with the aid of a kind of painstaking detective work, I was able to complete nearly all the others.

Only then, after ten months' work, did I allow myself to consider the main part of my task—the question of deciphering.

To begin with, I was totally in the dark. The symbols were complete—but what were they? I showed some of them to a colleague who had written a book on the deciphering of ancient languages. He said they bore some resemblance to later Egyptian hieroglyphics—of the period when all resemblance to "pictures" had vanished. I wasted a month pursuing this false trail. But fate was on my side. My nephew was about to return to England, and he asked me to let him have a photograph of a few pages of the Voynich manuscript. I experienced a deep reluctance, but could hardly refuse. I was still being thoroughly secretive about my work, rationalising this by telling myself that I merely wanted to insure that no one stole my ideas. Finally, I decided that perhaps the best way of preventing Julian from feeling curiosity about my labours was to make as little fuss as possible. So two days before he was due to sail, I presented him with a photograph of a page of the manuscript, and with my reconstructed version of yet another page. I did this casually, as if it were a matter that hardly interested me.

Ten days later, I received a letter from Julian that made me congratulate myself on my decision. On the boat, he had made friends with a young member of the Arab Cultural Association, who was travelling to London to take up a post. One evening, by chance, he showed him the photographs. The actual page of the Voynich manuscript meant nothing to the Arab; but when he saw my "reconstruction," he said immediately: "Ah, this is some form of Arabic." Not modern Arabic; and he was unable to read it. But he had no doubt that the manuscript had originated in the Middle East.

I rushed to the university library and found an Arabic text. A glance at it showed me the Arab had been right. The mystery of the Voynich script was solved: it seemed to be mediaeval Arabic.

It took me two weeks to learn to read Arabic—although, of course, I could not understand it. I prepared to settle down to a study of the language. If I worked at it for six hours a day, I calculated that I should be able to speak it fluently in about four months. However, this labour proved to be unnecessary. For once I had mastered the script well enough to translate a few sentences into English letters, I realised that it was not written in Arabic, but in a mixture of Latin and Greek.

My first thought was that someone had gone to a great deal of trouble to hide his thoughts from prying eyes. Then I realised that this was an unnecessary assumption. The Arabs were, of course, among the most skilled doctors in Europe in the Middle Ages. If an Arab physician were to write a manuscript, what would be more likely than that he should do so in Latin and Greek, using Arab script?

I was now so excited that I could barely eat or sleep. My housekeeper told me continually that I needed a holiday. I decided to take her advice, and take a sea voyage. I would go back to Bristol to see my family, and take the manuscript with me on the boat, where I could work undisturbed all day long.

Two days before the ship sailed, I discovered the title of the manuscript. Its title page was missing, but there was a reference on the fourteenth page that was clearly to the work itself. It was called *Necronomicon.*

The following day, I was seated in the lounge of the Algonquin Hotel in New York, sipping a martini before dinner, when I heard a familiar voice. It was my old friend Foster Damon, of Brown University, in Providence. We had met years before when he was collecting folk songs in Virginia, and my admiration for his poetry, as well as for his works on Blake, had kept us in fairly close contact ever since. I was delighted to meet him in New York. He was also staying at the Algonquin. Naturally, we had dinner together. Halfway through the meal, he asked me what I was working on.

"Have you ever heard of the *Necronomicon*?" I asked him, smiling.

"Of course."

I goggled at him. "You have? Where?"

"In Lovecraft. Isn't that what you meant?"

"Who on earth is Lovecraft?"

"Don't you know? One of our local writers in Providence. He died about thirty years ago. Haven't you come across his name?"

Now a memory stirred somewhere in my head. When I had been investigating Mrs. Whitman's house in Providence—for my book *The Shadow of Poe*—Foster had mentioned Lovecraft, with some such comment as: "You ought to read Lovecraft. He's the best American writer of horror stories since Poe." I can remember saying that I thought Bierce deserved that title, and then forgetting about it.

"Do you mean that this word *Necronomicon* actually occurs in Lovecraft?"

"I'm pretty sure of it."

"And where do you suppose Lovecraft got it?"

"I always assumed he invented it."

My interest in food vanished. This was the kind of development that no one could have foreseen. For, as far as I knew, I was the first person to read the Voynich manuscript. Or was I? How about the two scholars of the seventeenth century? Had one of them deciphered it and mentioned its name in his writings?

Obviously, the first thing to do was to check Lovecraft, and find out whether Foster's memory had served him correctly. I found myself praying that he was mistaken. After the meal, we took a taxi to a bookshop in Greenwich Village, and there I was able to locate a paperback of Lovecraft stories. Before we left the shop Foster riffed through its pages, then placed his finger on one of them:

"There it is. '*Necronomicon*, by the mad Arab, Abdul Alhazred.' "

There it was, impossible to doubt. In the taxi, on the way home, I tried not to show how shattered I felt. But soon after we got back, I excused myself and went to my room. I tried to read Lovecraft, but could not concentrate.

The next day, before sailing, I searched Brentano's for Lovecraft books, and managed to find two in hard covers, as well as several paperbacks. The hardcover books were *The Shuttered Room* and *Supernatural Horror in Literature*. In the first of these, I found a lengthy account of the *Necronomicon*, together with several quotations. But the account states, "While the book itself and most of its translators, and its author, are all imaginary, Lovecraft here employed . . . *his technique of inserting actual historical fact in the middle of large areas of purely imaginary lore.*"

Purely imaginary . . . Could it perhaps be a mere matter of coincidence of names? *Necronomicon*—the book of dead names. Not a difficult title to invent. The more I thought of it, the more likely it seemed that this was the correct explanation. And so before I went on board that afternoon, I was already feeling a great deal easier in my mind. I ate a good dinner, and read myself to sleep afterwards with Lovecraft.

I am not sure how many days went by before I began to experience a gradually increasing fascination with this new literary discovery. I know that my first impression was simply that Lovecraft was a skilful constructor of weird stories. Perhaps it was my work on the translation of the Voynich manuscript that altered my approach to him. Or possibly it was simply the realisation that Lovecraft had been uniquely obsessed by this strange world of his own creation—uniquely even when compared with such writers as Gogol and Poe. He made me think of certain writers on anthropology, however lacking in literary skill, yet made impressive by the sheer authenticity of their material.

With several hours a day in which to work, I quickly completed my translation of the Voynich manuscript. Long before the end, I had become aware that it was a fragment, and that there were mysteries involved that went beyond the cipher—a code within a code, as it were. But what struck me most powerfully—so that I sometimes had the utmost difficulty in restraining myself from rushing into the corridor and talking to the first person I met—was the incredible scientific knowledge revealed by the manuscript. Newbold had not been entirely wrong about this. The author simply knew far more than any thirteenth-century monk—or Mohammedan scholar, for that matter—could possibly know. A long and obscure passage about a "god" or demon who is somehow a vortex filled with stars is followed by a passage in which the primal constituent of matter is described as energy (using the Greek *dynamis* and *energeia*, as well as the Latin *vis*) *in limited units*. This sounds like a clear anticipation of the quantum theory. Again, the seed of man is described as being made up of units of power, each of which endows man with a lifelong characteristic. This certainly sounds remarkably like a reference to the genes. The drawing of a human spermatozoon occurs in the midst of a text that refers to the *Sefer Yezirah*, the Book of Creation in the Kabbala. Several slighting references to the *Ars Magna* of Raymond Lull support the notion that the author of the work was Roger Bacon—a contemporary of the mathematical mystic, although in one place in the text he refers to himself under the name of Martinus Hortulanus, which might be translated Martin Gardener.

What, in the last analysis, is the Voynich manuscript? It is a fragment of a work that professes to be a complete scientific account of the universe: its origin, history, geography (if I may use the term), mathematical structure, and hidden depths. The pages I possessed contained a preliminary digest of this material. In parts, it was terrifyingly knowledgeable; in other places, it seemed to be a typical mediaeval mélange of magic, theology, and pre-Copernican speculation. I got the impression that the work may have had several authors, or that the part I possessed was a digest of some other book that was imperfectly understood by Martin the Gardener. There are the usual references to Hermes Trismegistus and the Emerald Tablet, to Cleopatra's book on gold making, the *Chrysopeia*, to the gnostic serpent Ouroboros, and to a mysterious planet or star called Tormantius, which was spoken of as the home of awe-inspiring deities. There were also many references to a "Khian language" which, from their context, obviously have no connection with the Aegean island of Chios, Homer's birthplace.

It was this that set me upon the next stage of my discovery. In Lovecraft's *Supernatural Horror in Literature*, in the short section on Arthur Machen, I came across a reference to the "Chian language," connected in some way with a witchcraft cult. It also mentioned "Dôls," "voolas," and certain "Aklo letters." The latter caught my attention; there had been a reference in the Voynich manuscript to the "Aklo inscriptions." I had at first supposed Aklo to be some kind of corruption of the Kabbalastic "Agla," a word used in exorcism; now I revised my opinion. To appeal to coincidence beyond a certain point is a sign of feeble-mindedness. The hypothesis that now presented itself to my mind was this: that the Voynich manuscript was a fragment or a summary of a much longer work called the *Necronomicon*, perhaps of Kabbalistic origin. Complete copies of the book exist, or have existed, and word-of-mouth tradition may have been kept alive by secret societies such as Naundorff's infamous Church of Carmel, or the Brotherhood of Tlön described by Borges. Machen, who spent some time in Paris in the 1880s, almost certainly came into contact with Naundorff's disciple, the Abbé Boullan, who is known to have practised black magic. (He appears in Huysman's *Là-Bas*.) This could explain the traces of the *Necronomicon* to be found in his work. As to Lovecraft—he may have come across it or the verbal traditions concerning it, on his own, or perhaps even through Machen.

In that case, there might be copies of the work hidden away in some garret, or perhaps in another chest in an Italian castle. What a triumph if I could locate it, and publish it together with my translation of the Voynich manuscript! Or even if I could definitely prove that it had existed.

This was the daydream that preoccupied me during my five days on the Atlantic. And I read and reread my translation of the manuscript, hoping to discover some clue that might lead me to the complete work. But the more I read, the less clear it became. On a first reading, I had sensed an over-all pattern, some dark mythology, never stated openly, but deducible from hints. As I reread the work, I began to wonder whether all this had not been my imagination. The book seemed to dissolve into unrelated fragments.

In London, I spent a futile week in the British Museum, searching for references to the *Necronomicon* in various magical works, from Basil Valentine's *Azoth* to Aleister Crowley. The only promising reference was a footnote in E. A. Hitchcock's *Remarks upon Alchemy* (1865) to "the now unattainable secrets of the Aklo tablets." But the book contained no other reference to these tablets. Did the word "unattainable" mean that the tablets were known to be destroyed? If so, how did Hitchcock come to know about it?

The gloom of a London October, and the exhaustion that came from a persistent sore throat, had almost persuaded me to take a plane back to New York, when my luck changed. In a bookshop in Maidstone I met Fr. Anthony Carter, a Carmelite monk and editor of a small literary magazine. He had met Machen in 1944—three years before the writer's death, and had later devoted an issue of his magazine to Machen's life and work. I accompanied Fr. Carter back to the Priory near Sevenoaks, and as he drove the baby Austin at a sedate thirty miles an hour, he talked to me at length about Machen. Finally, I asked him whether, to his knowledge, Machen had ever had contact with secret societies or black magic. "Oh, I doubt it," he said, and my heart sank. Another false trail . . . "I suspect he picked up various odd traditions near his birthplace, Melincourt. It used to be the Roman Isca Silurum."

"Traditions?" I tried to keep my voice casual. "What sort of traditions?"

"Oh, you know. The sort of thing he describes in *The Hill of Dreams*. Pagan cults and that sort of thing."

"I thought that was pure imagination."

"Oh, no. He once hinted to me that he'd seen a book that revealed all kinds of horrible things about the area of Wales."

"Where? What kind of a book?"

"I've no idea. I didn't pay too much attention. I believe he saw it in Paris—or it might have been Lyons. But I remember the name of the man who showed it to him. Staislav de Guaita."

"Guaita!" I couldn't keep my voice down, and he almost steered us off the road. He looked at me with mild reproach.

"That's right. He was involved in some absurd black-magic society. Machen pretended to take it all seriously, but I'm sure he was pulling my leg. . . ."

Guaita was involved in the black-magic circle of Boullan and Naundorff. It was one more brick in the edifice.

"Where is Melincourt?"

"In Monmouthshire, I believe. Somewhere near Southport. Are you thinking of going?"

My train of thought must have been obvious. I saw no point in denying it.

The priest said nothing until the car stopped in the tree-shaded yard behind the Priory. Then he glanced at me and said mildly: "I wouldn't get too involved if I were you."

I made a noncommittal noise in my throat, and we dropped the subject. But a few hours later, back in my hotel room, I remembered his comment and was struck by it. If he believed that Machen had been pulling his leg about his "pagan cults," why warn me not to get too involved? Did he really believe in them, but prefer to keep this to himself? As a Catholic, of course, he was bound to believe in the existence of supernatural evil. . . .

I had checked in the hotel's Bradshaw before going to bed. There was a train to Newport from Paddington at 9:55, with a change for Caerleon at 2:30. At five minutes past ten, I was seated in the dining car, drinking coffee, watching the dull, soot-coloured houses of Ealing give way to the green fields of Middlesex, and feeling a depth and purity of excitement that was quite new to me. I cannot explain this. I can only say that, at this point in my search, I had a clear intuition that the important things were beginning. Until now, I had been slightly depressed, in spite of the challenges of the Voynich manuscript. Perhaps this was due to a faint distaste for the subject matter of the manuscript. I am as romantic as the next man—and I think most people are healthily romantic at bottom—but I suppose all this talk of black magic struck me ultimately as degrading nonsense—degrading to the human intellect and its capacity for evolution. But on this grey October morning, I felt something else—the stirring of the hair that Watson used to experience when Holmes shook him awake with "The game's afoot, Watson." I still had not the remotest idea what the game might consist of. But I was beginning to experience an odd intuition of its seriousness.

When I grew tired of looking at the scenery, I opened the book bag and took out a *Guide to Wales*, and two volumes of Arthur Machen; some selected stories, and the autobiographical *Far Off Things*. This latter led me to expect to find a land of enchantment in Machen's part of Wales. He writes: "I shall always esteem it as the greatest piece of fortune that has fallen to me, that I was born in the heart of Gwent." His descriptions of the "mystic tumulus," the "giant rounded billow" of the Mountain of Stone, the deep woods and the winding river, made it sound like the landscape of a dream. And in fact, Melincourt is the legendary seat of King Arthur, and Tennyson sets his *Idylls of the King* there.

The *Guide to Wales*, which I had picked up at a secondhand bookshop in the Charing Cross Road, described Southport as a little country market town "amid a pleasant, undulating, and luxuriant landscape of wood and meadow." I had half an hour to spare between trains, and decided to look at the town. Ten minutes was enough. Whatever may have been its charms in 1900 (the date of the *Guide*), it is now a typical industrial town with cranes on the skyline and the hooting of trains and boats. I drank a double whisky in the hotel next to the station, to fortify myself in the event of a similar disappointment in Caerleon. And even this did little to relieve the impact of the dreary, modernised little town in which I found myself an hour later, after a short journey through the suburbs of Southport. The town is dominated by an immense red brick monstrosity, which I guessed correctly to be a mental institution. And Chesterton's "Usk of mighty murmurings" struck me as a muddy stream whose appearance was not improved by the rain that now fell from the slate grey sky.

I checked into my hotel—an unpretentious place, without central heating—at half past three, looked at the flowered wallpaper in my bedroom—at least one survival from 1900—and decided to walk out in the rain.

A hundred yards along the main street, I passed a garage with a hand-printed notice CARS FOR HIRE. A short, bespectacled man was leaning over the engine of a car. I asked him whether there was a driver available.

"Oh yes, sir."

"This afternoon?"

"If you like, sir. Where did you want to go?"

"Just to look at the countryside."

He looked incredulous. "You are a tourist, are you, sir?"

"I suppose so, in a way."

"I'll be right with you."

His air as he wiped his hands suggested that he thought this was too good to miss. Five minutes later, he was waiting in front of the building, wearing a leather motoring jacket of a 1920ish vintage, and driving a car of the same period. The headlights actually vibrated up and down to the chatter of its engine.

"Where to?"

"Anywhere. Somewhere towards the north—towards Monmouth."

I sat huddled in the back, watching the rain, and feeling distinct signs of a cold coming on. But after ten minutes, the car warmed up, and the scenery improved. In spite of modernisation and the October drizzle, the Usk valley remained extremely beautiful. The green of the fields was striking, even compared to Virginia. The woods were, as Machen said, mysterious and shadowy, and the scenery looked almost too picturesque to be genuine, like one of those grandiose romantic landscapes by Asher Durand. And to the north and northeast lay the mountains, hardly visible through the smokey clouds; the desolate landscape of "The White People" and "The Novel of the Black Seal"—both very fresh in my mind. Mr. Evans, my driver, had the tact not to speak, but to allow me to soak up the feeling of the landscape.

I asked my driver whether he had ever seen Machen, but I had to spell the name before Mr. Evans ever recognised it. As far as I could tell, Machen seemed completely forgotten in his native town.

"You studyin' him, are you, sir?"

He used the word "studying" as if it were some remote and ritualistic activity. I acknowledged that I was; in fact, I exaggerated slightly and said that I thought of writing a book on Machen. This aroused his interest; whatever might have been his attitude to dead writers, he had nothing but respect for living ones. I told him that several of Machen's stories were set in these desolate hills that lay ahead of us, and I added casually:

"What I really want to find out is where he picked up the legends he used in his stories. I'm fairly sure he didn't invent them. Do you know of anyone around here who might know about them—the vicar, for example?"

"Oh, no. The vicar wouldn't know anythin' about legends." He made it sound as if legends were a thoroughly pagan activity.

"Can you think of anyone who might?"

"Let's see. There's the Colonel, if you could get on the right side of him. He's a funny chap, is the Colonel. If he don't like you, you'd be wastin' your breath."

I tried to find out more about this Colonel—whether he was an antiquary, perhaps; but Evans's statements remained Celtically vague. I changed the subject to the scenery, and got a steady stream of information that lasted all the way back to Melincourt. At Mr. Evans's suggestion, we drove as far north as Raglan, then turned west and drove back with the Black Mountains on our right, looking bleaker and more menacing at close quarters than from the green lowlands around Melincourt. In Pontypool, I stopped and bought a book about the Roman remains at Melincourt, and a secondhand copy of Giraldus Cambrensis, the Welsh historian and geographer, a contemporary of Roger Bacon.

Mr. Evans's taxi rates proved to be surprisingly reasonable, and I agreed to hire him for a whole day as soon as the weather improved. Then, back in the hotel, with a potation called grog, consisting of brown rum, hot water, lemon juice, and sugar, I read the London newspapers, and made cautious enquiries about the Colonel. This line of approach proving barren—the Welsh are not forthcoming with strangers—I looked him up in the phone book. Colonel Lionel Urquart,

The Leasowes, Melincourt. Then, fortified by my grog, I went into the icy phone kiosk and dialled his number. A woman's voice with an almost incomprehensible Welsh accent said the Colonel was not at home, then said he might be, and she would go and look.

After a long wait, a harsh British upper-class voice barked into the phone: "Hello, who is it?" I identified myself, but before I could finish, he snapped: "I'm sorry, I never give interviews." I explained quickly that I was a professor of literature, not a journalist.

"Ah, literature. What kind of literature?"

"At the moment, I'm interested in the local legends. Someone mentioned that you knew a great deal about them."

"Ah, they did, eh? Well, I suppose I do. What did you say your name was?"

I repeated it, and mentioned the University of Virginia, and my major publications. There were odd mumbling noises at the other end of the line, as if he were eating his moustache and finding it hard to swallow. Finally, he said:

"Look here . . . supposing you come over here a bit later this evening, around nine? We can have a drink and talk."

I thanked him, and went back to the lounge, where there was a good fire, and ordered another rum. I felt I deserved congratulations, after Mr. Evans's warnings about the Colonel. Only one thing worried me. I still had no idea of who he was, or what kind of legends interested him. I could only guess that he was the local antiquary

At half past eight, after an ample but unimaginative supper of lamb chops, boiled potatoes, and some unidentifiable green vegetable, I set out for the Colonel's house, having enquired the way from the desk clerk, who was obviously intrigued. It was still raining and windy, but my cold was held at bay by the grog.

The Colonel's house was outside the town, halfway up a steep hill. There was a rusty iron gate, and a driveway full of pools of muddy water. When I rang the doorbell, ten dogs began to bark at once, and one approached the door on the other side and snarled discouragingly. A plump Welsh woman opened the door, slapped the Doberman pinscher that growled and slavered, and led me past a pack of yelping dogs—several, I noticed, with scars and torn ears—into a dimly lit library smelling of coal smoke. I'm not sure what sort of a man I expected to meet—probably tall and British, with a sunburned face and bristly moustache—but he proved rather a surprise. Short and twisted—a riding accident had broken his right hip—his dark complexion suggested mixed blood, while the receding chin gave him a slightly reptilian look. On first acquaintance, a definitely repellant character. His eyes were bright and intelligent, but mistrustful. He struck me as a man who could generate considerable resentment. He shook my hand and asked me to sit down. I sat near the fire. A cloud of smoke immediately billowed out, making me choke and gasp.

"Needs sweeping," said my host. "Try that chair." A few moments later, something fell down the chimney along with a quantity of soot, and before the flames made it unrecognisable, I thought I recognised the skeleton of a bat. I surmised—correctly, as it turned out—that Colonel Urquart had few visitors, and therefore few occasions to use the library.

"Which of my books have you come across?" he asked me.

"I . . . er . . . to be quite honest, I only know them by hearsay."

I was relieved when he said dryly: "Like most people. Still, it's encouraging to know you're interested."

At this point, looking past his head, I noticed his name on the spine of a book. It seemed a rather luridly designed dust jacket, and the title, *The Mysteries of Mu,* was quite clearly visible in scarlet letters. So I added quickly:

"Of course, I don't know a great deal about Mu. I remember reading a book by Spence. . . ."

"Total charlatan!" Urquart snapped, and I thought his eyes took on a reddish tinge in the firelight.

"And then," I added, "Robert Graves has some curious theories about Wales and the Welsh. . . ."

"Lost tribes of Israel, indeed! I've never heard such an infantile and far-fetched idea! Anyone could tell you it's nonsense. And besides, I've proved conclusively that the Welsh are survivors from the lost continent of Mu. I have evidence to prove it. No doubt you've come across some of it."

"Not as much as I could have wished," I said, wondering what I'd let myself in for.

At this point he interrupted himself to offer me a whisky, and I had to make a quick decision—whether to plead another appointment and escape, or to stick it out. The sound of rain on the windows decided me. I would stick it out.

As he poured the whisky, he said, "I think I can guess what you are thinking. Why Mu rather than Atlantis?"

"Why, indeed," I said, in a bemused way. I wasn't even aware, at that stage, that Mu was supposed to have been situated in the Pacific.

"Quite. I asked myself exactly that question twenty years ago, when I first made my discoveries. Why Mu, when the major relics lie in South Wales and Providence?"

"Providence? Which Providence?"

"Rhode Island. I have proof that it was the centre of the religion of the survivors from Mu.

"Relics. This, for example." He handed me a chunk of green stone, almost too heavy to hold in one hand. I had never seen such stone before, although I know a little about geology. Neither had I seen anything like the drawing and inscription cut into it, except once in a temple in the jungles of Brazil. The inscription was in curved characters, not unlike Pitman's shorthand; the face in the midst of them could have been a devil mask, or a snake god, or a sea monster. As I stared at it, I felt the same distaste—the sense of *nastiness*—that I had experienced on first seeing the Voynich manuscript. I took a large swallow of my whisky. Urquart indicated the "sea monster."

"The symbol of the people of Mu. The Yambi. This stone is their colour. It's one of the ways to learn where they've been—water of that colour."

I looked at him blankly. "In what way?"

"When they destroy a place, they like to leave behind pools of water—small lakes, if possible. You can always tell them because they look slightly different from an ordinary pool of water. You get this combination of the green of stagnation, and that bluey-grey you can see here."

He turned to the bookshelf and took down an expensive art book with a title like *The Pleasures of Ruins*. He opened it and pointed at a photograph. It was in colour.

"Look at this—Sidon in Lebanon. The same green water. And look at this: Anuradhapura in Ceylon—the same green and blue. Colours of decay and death. Both places they destroyed at some point. There are six more that I know of."

I was fascinated and impressed in spite of myself; perhaps it was the stone that did it.

"But how did they do that?"

"You make the usual mistake—of thinking of them as being like ourselves. They weren't. In human terms, they were formless and invisible."

"Invisible?"

"Like wind or electricity. You have to understand they were *forces* rather than beings. They weren't even clear separate identities, as we are. That's stated in Churchward's Naacal tablets."

He proceeded to talk, and I shall not attempt to set down all he said. A lot of it struck me as sheer nonsense. But there was a crazy logic in much of it. He would snatch up books off his shelves and read me passages—most of these, as far as I could see, by all kinds of cranks. But he would then take up a textbook of anthropology or paleontology, and read some extract that seemed to confirm what he had just said.

What he told me, in brief, was this. The continent of Mu existed in the South Pacific between twenty thousand and twelve thousand years ago. It consisted of two races, one of which resembled present-day man. The other consisted of Urquart's "invisible ones from the stars."

These latter, he said, were definitely aliens on our earth, and the chief among them was called Ghatanothoa, the dark one. They sometimes took forms, such as the monster on the tablet—who was a representation of Ghatanothoa—but existed as "vortices" of power in their natural state. They were not benevolent, in our sense, for their instincts and desires were completely unlike ours. A tradition of the Naacal tablets has it that these beings created man, but this, Urquart said, must be incorrect, since archaeological evidence proved that man had evolved over millions of years. However, the men on Mu were certainly their slaves, and were apparently treated with what we would consider unbelievable barbarity. The Lloigor, or star-beings, could amputate limbs without causing death, and did this at the least sign of rebelliousness. They could also cause cancer-like tentacles to grow on their human slaves, and also used this as a form of punishment. One picture in the Naacal tablets shows a man with tentacles growing from both eye sockets.

But Urquart's theory about Mu had an extremely original touch. He told me that there was one major difference between the Lloigor and human beings. The Lloigor were deeply and wholly pessimistic. Urquart pointed out that we could hardly imagine what this meant. Human beings live on hopes of various kinds. We know we have to die. We have no idea where we came from, or where we are going to. We know that we are subject to accident and illness. We know that we seldom achieve what we want; and if we achieve it, we have ceased to appreciate it. All this we know, and yet we remain incurably optimistic, even deceiving ourselves with absurd, patently nonsensical, beliefs about life after death.

"Why am I talking to you," said Urquart, "although I know perfectly well that no professor has an open mind, and every one I've had any dealings with has betrayed me? Because I think that you might be the exception—you might grasp the truth of what I'm saying. But why should I want it known, when I have to die like everyone else? Absurd, isn't it? Yet we're *not* reasonable creatures. We live and act on an unreasonable reflex of optimism—a mere reflex, like your knee kicking when someone taps it. It's obviously completely stupid. Yet we live by it."

I found myself impressed by him, in spite of my conviction that he was slightly mad. He was certainly intelligent.

He went on to explain that the Lloigor, although infinitely more powerful than men, were also aware that optimism would be absurd in this universe. Their minds were a unity, not compartmentalised, like ours. There was no distinction in them between conscious, subconscious, and superconscious mind. So they saw things clearly all the time, without the possibility of averting the mind from the truth, or forgetting. Mentally speaking, the closest equivalent to them would be one of those suicidal romantics of the nineteenth century, steeped in gloom, convinced that life is a pit of misery, and accepting this as a basis for everyday life. Urquart denied that the Buddhists resemble the Lloigor in their ultimate pessimism—not merely because of the concept of Nirvana, which offers a kind of absolute, equivalent to the Christian God, but because no Buddhist really lives in the constant contemplation of his pessimism. He accepts it intellectually, but does not feel it with his nerves and bones. The Lloigor *lived* their pessimism.

Unfortunately—and here I found it hard to follow Urquart—the earth is not suitable for such pessimism, on a subatomic level. It is a young planet. All its energy processes are still in the uphill stage, so to speak; they are evolutionary, making for complexification, and therefore, the destruction of negative forces. A simple example of this is the way that so many of the romantics died young; the earth simply will not tolerate subversive forces.

Hence the legend that the Lloigor created men as their slaves. For why should all-powerful beings require slaves? Only because of the active hostility, so to speak, of the earth itself. To counteract this hostility, to carry out their simplest purposes, they needed creatures who worked on an optimistic basis. And so men were created, deliberately short-sighted creatures, incapable of steadily contemplating the obvious truth about the universe.

What had then happened had been absurd. The Lloigor had been increasingly weakened by their life on earth. Urquart said that the documents offer no reasons for the Lloigor's leaving their home, probably situated in the Andromeda nebula. They had gradually become less and less an active force. And their slaves had taken over, becoming the men of today. The Naacal tablets and other works that have come down from Mu are the creation of these men, not of the original "gods." The earth has favoured the evolution of its ungainly, optimistic children, and weakened the Lloigor. Nevertheless, these ancient powers remain. They have retreated under the earth and sea, in order to concentrate their power in stones and rocks, whose normal metabolism they can reverse. This has enabled them to cling to the earth for many thousands of years. Occasionally, they accumulate enough energy to erupt once again into human life, and the results are whole cities destroyed. At one time, it was the whole continent—Mu itself—and later still, Atlantis. They had always been particularly virulent when they had been able to find traces of their previous slaves. They are responsible for many archaeological mysteries—great ruined cities of South America, Cambodia, Burma, Ceylon, North Africa, even Italy. And then, according to Urquart, the two great ruined cities of North America, Grudèn Itzà, now sunk beneath the swampland around New Orleans, and Nam-Ergest, a flourishing city that once stood on the land where the Grand Canyon now yawns. The Grand Canyon, Urquart said, was not created by earth erosion, but by a tremendous underground explosion followed by a "hail of fire." He suspects that, like the great Siberian explosion, it was produced by some kind of atomic bomb. To my question of why there were not signs of an explosion around the Grand Canyon, Urquart had two replies: that it had taken place so long ago that most signs of it had been destroyed by natural forces, and second, that to any unprejudiced observer, it is plain enough that the Grand Canyon is an immense and irregular crater.

After two hours of this, and several helpings of his excellent whisky, I felt so confused that I had completely lost track of the questions I wanted to ask. I said I had to go to bed and think about it all, and the Colonel offered to run me home in his car. One of my questions came back to me as I climbed into the passenger seat of the ancient Rolls-Royce.

"What did you mean about the Welsh being survivors of Mu?"

"What I said. I am certain—I have evidence to prove—that they are descendents of the slaves of the Lloigor."

"What kind of evidence?"

"All kinds. It would take another hour to explain."

"Couldn't you give me some hint?"

"All right. Look in the paper in the morning. Tell me what strikes you."

"But what am I to look for?"

He was amused by my refusal to "wait and see." He should have known that old men are less patient than children.

"The crime figures."

"Can't you tell me more?"

"All right." We were parked outside the hotel by now, and it was still raining heavily. At this hour of the night, there was no sound but the fall of rain and the gurgling of water in the gutters. "You'll find that the crime rate in this area is three times that of the rest of England. The figures are so high that they're seldom published. Murder, cruelty, rape, every possible kind of sexual perversion—this area has the highest figures in the British Isles."

"But why?"

"I've told you. The Lloigor achieve the strength to reappear every now and then." And to make it clear that he wanted to go home, he leaned over and opened my door for me. Before I had reached the door of the hotel, he had driven off.

I asked the caretaker on duty if I could borrow a local newspaper; he produced me one from his cubbyhole, which he said I could keep. I went up to my cold room, undressed and climbed into bed—there was a hot-water bottle in it. Then I glanced through the newspaper. At first sight, I could see no evidence for Urquart's assertion. The headline was about a strike in the local dockyard, and the lead stories were about a local cattle show in which the judges had been accused of accepting bribes, and about a Southport girl swimmer who had almost broken the record for the cross-Channel swim. On the middle page, the editorial was on some question of Sunday observance. It looked innocent enough.

Then I began to notice the small paragraphs, tucked away next to the advertisements or among the sports news. The headless body that had been found floating in the Bryn Mawr reservoir has been tentatively identified as a teenage farm girl from Llandalffen. A fourteen-year-old boy sentenced to a corrective institution for inflicting injuries on a sheep with a hatchet. A farmer petitioning for divorce on the grounds that his wife seemed to be infatuated with her imbecile stepson. A vicar sentenced to a year in prison for offences against choirboys. A father who had murdered his daughter and her boyfriend out of sexual jealousy. A man in the old-folks' home who had incinerated two of his companions by pouring paraffin on their beds and setting them alight. A twelve-year-old boy who had offered his twin sisters, age seven, ice cream with rat poison sprinkled on it, and then laughed uncontrollably in the juvenile court. (The children luckily survived with bad stomach-aches.) A short paragraph saying that the police had now charged a man with the three Lovers' Lane murders.

I jotted these down in the order I read them. It was quite a chronicle for a peaceful rural area, even allowing that Southport and Cardiff, with their higher crime rates, were fairly close. Admittedly, it was not too bad a record compared to most places in America. Even Charlottesville can produce a crime record that would be regarded as a major crime wave in England. Before falling asleep, I pulled on my dressing gown, and found my way down to the lounge, where I had seen a copy of *Whitaker's Almanac*, and looked up the English crime rate. A mere 166 murders in 1967—three murders to every million people of the population; America's murder rate is about twenty times as high. Yet here, in a single issue of a small local newspaper, I had found mention of nine murders—although admittedly, some of them dated back a long way. (The Lovers' Lane murders were spread over eighteen months.)

I slept very badly that night, my mind running constantly on invisible monsters, awful cataclysms, sadistic murderers, demoniac teenagers. It was a relief to wake up to bright sunlight and a cup of morning tea. Even so, I found myself stealing a look at the maid—a pale-faced little thing with dull eyes and stringy hair—and wondering what irregular union had produced her. I had breakfast and the morning paper sent up to my room, and read it with morbid interest.

Again, the more lurid news was carefully tucked away in small paragraphs. Two eleven-year-old schoolboys were accused of being implicated in the murder of the headless girl, but claimed that a tramp "with smouldering eyes" had actually decapitated her. A Southport druggist forced to resign from the town council when accused of having "carnal knowledge" of his fourteen-year-old assistant. Evidence suggesting that a deceased midwife had been a successful baby farmer in the manner of the infamous Mrs. Dyer of Reading. An old lady of Llangwm seriously injured by a man who accused her of witchcraft—of causing babies to be born with deformities. An attempt on the life of the mayor of Chepstow by a man with some obscure grudge. . . . I omit more than half of the list, for the crimes are as dull as they are sordid.

There was no doubt that all this brooding on crime and corruption was having its effect on my outlook. I had always liked the Welsh, with their small stature and dark hair and pale skins. Now I found myself looking at them as if they were troglodytes, trying to find evidence of secret vices in their eyes. And the more I looked, the more I saw it. I observed the number of words beginning with two L's, from Lloyd's Bank to Llandudno, and thought of the Lloigor with a shudder. (Incidentally, I thought the word familiar, and found it on page 258 of the Lovecraft *Shuttered Room* volume, listed as the god "who walks the winds among the star-spaces." I also found Ghatanothoa, the Dark God, mentioned there, although not as the chief of the "star dwellers.")

It was almost intolerable, walking along that sunlit street, looking at the rural population going about their everyday business of shopping and admiring one another's babies, to feel this awful secret inside me, struggling to get out. I wanted to dismiss the whole thing as a nightmare, the invention of one half-crazed mind; then I had to acknowledge that it all followed logically from the Voynich manuscript and the Lovecraft gods. Yes, there could hardly be any doubt: Lovecraft and Machen had simply obtained some knowledge of an ancient tradition that may have existed before any known civilisation on earth.

The only other alternative was some elaborate literary hoax, organised between Machen, Lovecraft, and Voynich, who must be regarded as a forger, and that was impossible. But what an alternative! How could I believe in it and still feel sane, here in this sunlit high street, with the lilting sound of Welsh in my ears? Some evil, dark world, so alien from ours that human beings cannot even begin to understand it; strange powers whose actions seem incredibly cruel and vengeful, yet who are simply driven by abstract laws of their being that would be incomprehensible to us. Urquart, with his reptilian face and his morose intelligence. And above all, unseen forces bending the minds of these apparently innocent people around me, making them corrupt and depraved.

I had already decided what I would do that day. I would get Mr. Evans to drive me out to the "Grey Hills" mentioned by Machen, and take some photographs, and make some discreet enquiries. I even had a compass with me—one I usually kept in my car in America—in case I managed to *lose* my way.

There was a small crowd gathered outside Mr. Evans's garage and an ambulance stood by the pavement. As I approached, two attendants came out, carrying a stretcher. I saw Mr. Evans standing gloomily inside the small shop attached to the garage, watching the crowd. I asked him:

"What happened?"

"Chap upstairs committed suicide in the night. Gassed himself."

As the ambulance pulled away, I asked, "Don't you think there's rather a lot of that around here?"

"Of what?"

"Suicides, murders, and so on. Your local paper's full of it."

"I suppose so. It's the teenagers nowadays. They do what they like."

I saw there was no point in pursuing the subject. I asked him whether he was free to drive me to the Grey Hills. He shook his head.

"I promised I'd wait around to make a statement to the police. You're welcome to use the car if you want it."

And so I bought a map of the area, and drove myself. I stopped for ten minutes to admire the mediaeval bridge, mentioned by Machen, then drove slowly north. The morning was windy, but not cold, and the sunlight made the scene look totally different from the previous afternoon. Although I looked out carefully for signs of Machen's Grey Hills, I saw nothing in the pleasant, rolling landscape that seemed to answer that description. Soon I found myself passing a signpost that announced Abergavenny ten miles away. I decided to take a look at the place. By the time I arrived there, the sunlight had so far dispelled the night vapours from my head that I drove round the town—unremarkable enough architecturally—and then walked up to look at the ruined castle above it. I spoke to a couple of natives, who struck me as more English than Welsh in type. Indeed, the town is not many miles away from the Severn Valley and A. E. Housman's Shropshire.

But I was reminded of the myth of the Lloigor by a few sentences in the local guidebook about William de Braose, Lord of Brecheiniog (Brecon), "whose shadow broods darkly over the past of Abergavenny," whose "foul deeds" had apparently shocked even the lawless English of the twelfth century. I made a mental note to ask Urquart how long the Lloigor had been present in South Wales, and how far their influence extended. I drove on northwest, through the most attractive part of the valley of the Usk. At Crickhowell, I stopped in a pleasantly old-fashioned pub and drank a cool pint of mild ale, and fell into conversation with a local who proved to have read Machen. I asked him where he supposed the "Grey Hills" to be situated, and he told me confidently that it was directly to the north, in the Black Mountains, the high, wild moorland between the valleys of Usk and the Wye. So I drove on for another half hour, to the top of the pass called the Bwlch, where the scenery is among the finest in Wales, with the Brecon Beacons to the west, and woodland and hills to the south, with glimpses of the Usk reflecting the sunlight. But the Black Mountains to the east looked anything but menacing, and their description did not correspond to the page in Machen that I was using as a guide. So I turned south once again, through Abergavenny (where I ate a light lunch), and then through minor roads to Llandalffen, the road climbing steeply again.

It was here that I began to suspect that I was approaching my objective. There was a barrenness about the hills that suggested the atmosphere of "The Novel of the Black Seal." But I kept an open mind, for the afternoon had become cloudy, and I suspected it might be pure imagination. I stopped the car by the roadside, close to a stone bridge, and got out to lean on the parapet. It was a fast-flowing stream, and the glassy power of the current fascinated me until I felt almost hypnotised by it. I walked down by the side of the bridge, digging in my heels to keep my balance on the steep slope, and went down to a flat rock beside the stream. This was almost an act of bravado, for I felt a distinct discomfort, which I knew to be partly self-induced. A man of my age tends to feel tired and depressed after lunch, particularly when he has been drinking.

I had my Polaroid camera round my neck. The green of the grass and the grey of the sky made such a contrast that I decided to take a picture. I adjusted the light meter on the front of the camera, and pointed the camera upstream; then I pulled out the photograph, and slipped it under my coat to develop. A minute later, I stripped off the negative paper. The photograph was black. Obviously, it had somehow been exposed to light. I raised the camera and took a second shot, tossing the first one into the stream. As I pulled the second photograph from the camera, I had a sudden intuitive certainty that it would also be black.

I looked nervously around, and almost tripped into the stream as I saw a face looking down at me from the bridge above. It was a boy, or a youth, leaning on the parapet, watching me. My timing device stopped buzzing. Ignoring the boy, I stripped the paper off the photograph. It was black. I swore under my breath, and tossed it into the stream.

Then I looked up the slope to calculate the easiest way back, and saw the youth standing at the top. He was dressed in shabby brown clothes, completely nondescript. His face was thin and brown, reminding me of gypsies I had seen on the station in Newport. The brown eyes were expressionless. I stared back at him without smiling, at first only curious as to what he wanted.

But he made no apologetic movement, and I felt suddenly afraid that he wanted to rob me—perhaps of the camera, or the traveller's cheques in my wallet. Another look at him convinced me that he would not know what to do with either. The vacant eyes and the protruding ears indicated that I was dealing with an imbecile. And then, with sudden total certainty, I knew what he had in mind as clearly as if he had told me. He meant to rush at me down the slope, and knock me backwards into the water. But why? I glanced at the water. It was very fast, and perhaps waist-deep—perhaps a little more—but not deep enough to drown a grown man. There were rocks and stones in it, but none large enough to hurt me if I was dashed against it.

Nothing like this had ever happened to me before—at least, for the past fifty years. Weakness and fear flowed over me, so that I wanted to sit down. Only my determination not to betray fear prevented me. I made an effort, and scowled at him in an irritable manner, as I have occasionally scowled at my students. To my surprise, he smiled at me—although I think it was a smile of malice rather than of amusement—and turned away. I lost no time in scrambling up the bank to a less vulnerable position.

When I reached the road a few seconds later he was gone. The only cover within fifty yards was the other side of the bridge, or behind my car. I bent to peer under the car, to see if his feet were visible; they weren't. I overcame my panic, and went to look over the other parapet of the bridge. He wasn't there either. The only other possibility was that he had slipped under the bridge, although the water seemed to be flowing too fast. In any case, I was not going to look down there. I went back to the car, forcing myself not to hurry, and only felt safe when I was in motion.

At the top of the hill, it struck me that I had forgotten which way I was travelling. My alarm had completely erased all memory of which way I had approached the bridge, and I had parked in a gateway, at right angles to the road. I stopped on a lonely stretch of road to look at my compass. But its black pole swung gently in circles, apparently indifferent to direction. Tapping made no difference. It was not broken; the needle was still mounted on its pivot. It was simply demagnetised. I drove on until I found a signpost, discovered I was going in the right direction, and made my way to Pontypool. The problem of the compass disturbed me vaguely, but not unduly. It was only later, when I thought about it, that I realised that it should be impossible to demagnetise a compass without removing the needle and heating it, or banging it about pretty vigorously. It had been working at lunchtime, when I had glanced at it. It came to me then that the affair of the compass, like the boy, had been intended as a warning. A vague, indifferent warning, like a sleeping man brushing at a fly.

All this sounds absurd and fanciful; and I freely admit that I was half inclined to dismiss it myself. But I am inclined to trust my intuitions.

I was feeling shaken, enough to take a long swallow from my brandy flask when I arrived back at the hotel. Then I called the desk and complained about the coldness of my room, and within ten minutes, a chambermaid was making a coal fire in a grate I had not even noticed. Seated in front of it, smoking a pipe and sipping brandy, I began to feel better. After all, there was no evidence that these "powers" were actively hostile—even admitting for a moment that they existed. As a young man I was scornful about the supernatural, but as I have got older, the sharp line that divided the credible from the incredible has tended to blur; I am aware that the whole world is slightly incredible.

At six o'clock, I suddenly decided to go and see Urquart. I didn't bother to ring, for I had come to think of him as an ally, not as a stranger. So I walked in the thin drizzle to his house, and rang the front doorbell. Almost immediately, it opened, and a man came out. The Welshwoman said, "Goodbye, Doctor," and I stood and stared at her, feeling sudden fear.

"Is the Colonel all right?"

The doctor answered me. "Well enough, if he takes care. If you're a friend of his, don't stay with him too long. He needs sleep."

The Welshwoman let me in without question.

"What happened?"

"Little accident. He fell down the cellar steps, and we didn't find him for a couple of hours."

As I went upstairs, I noticed some of the dogs in the kitchen. The door was open, yet they had not barked at the sound of my voice. The upstairs corridor was damp and badly carpeted. The Doberman lay outside a door. It looked at me in a weary, subdued way, and did not stir as I went in past it.

Urquart said: "Ah, it's you, old boy. Nice of you to come. Who told you?"

"Nobody. I came to see you for a talk. What happened?"

He waited until his housekeeper closed the door.

"I got pushed down the cellar steps."

"By whom?"

"You shouldn't have to ask that."

"But what happened?"

"I went down to the cellar to get some garden twine. Halfway down the steps—a nasty, stifling feeling—I think they can produce some sort of gas. Then a definite push sideways. There's quite a drop down to the coal. Twisted my ankle, and thought I'd broken a rib. Then the door closed and latched. I shouted like a madman for two hours before the gardener heard me."

I didn't doubt his word now, or think him a crank. "But you're in obvious danger here. You ought to move to some other part of the country."

"No. They're a lot stronger than I thought. But after all, I was below ground, in the cellar. That may be the explanation. They can reach above ground, but it costs them more energy than it's worth. Anyway, there's no harm done. The ankle's only sprained and the rib isn't broken after all. It was just a gentle warning—for talking to you last night. What's been happening to you?"

"So that's it!" My own experiences now connected up. I told him what had happened to me.

He interrupted me to say, "You went down a steep bank—you see, just like me into the cellar. A thing to avoid." And when I mentioned the compass, he laughed without much humour. "That's easy for them. I told you, they can permeate matter as easily as a sponge soaks up water. Have a drink?"

I accepted, and poured him one too. As he sipped, he said, "That boy you mentioned—I think I know who it is. The grandson of Ben Chickno. I've seen him around."

"Who is Chickno?"

"Gypsy. Half his family are idiots. They all interbreed. One of his sons got five years for involvement in a murder—one of the nastiest that ever happened around here. They tortured an old couple to find out where they kept their money, then killed them. They found some of the stolen goods in the son's caravan, but he claimed they had been left there by a man on the run. He was lucky to escape a murder charge. And incidentally, the judge died a week after sentencing the son. Heart attack."

I knew my Machen better than Urquart did, and the suspicion that now came to me was natural. For Machen speaks of intercourse between certain half-imbecilic country people and his strange powers of evil. I asked Urquart, "Could this old man—Chickno—be connected with the Lloigor?"

"It depends what you mean by connected. I don't think he's important enough to know much about them. But he's the kind of person they like to encourage—a degenerate old swine. You want to ask

Inspector Davison about him; he's the head of the local force. Chickno's got a string of convictions as long as your arm—arson, rape, robbery with violence, bestiality, incest. Just a thorough degenerate."

Mrs. Dolgelly brought in his supper at this point, and intimated that it was time for me to go. At the door, I asked, "Is this man's caravan anywhere nearby?"

"About a mile away from the bridge you mentioned. You're not thinking of going there, I hope?"

Nothing was further from my thoughts, and I said so.

That evening, I wrote a long letter to George Lauerdale at Brown University. Lauerdale writes detective stories under a pseudonym, and has been responsible for two anthologies of modern poetry. I knew him to be writing a book about Lovecraft, and I needed his advice. By now, I had a feeling of being totally involved in this business. I no longer had any doubts. So was there any evidence of the Lloigor in the Providence area? I wanted to know if anyone had theories about where Lovecraft obtained his basic information. Where had he seen or heard of the *Necronomicon*? I took care to hide my real preoccupations in my letter to Lauerdale; I explained simply that I had succeeded in translating a large part of the Voynich manuscript, and that I had reason to believe that it was the *Necronomicon* referred to by Lovecraft; how could Lauerdale account for this? I went on to say that there was evidence that Machen had used real legends of Monmouthshire in his stories, and that I suspected similar legends underlying Lovecraft's work. Had he any knowledge of any such local legends? For example, were there any unpleasant stories connected with Lovecraft's "shunned house" on Benefit Street in Providence . . . ?

The day after Urquart's accident, a curious thing happened, which I shall mention only briefly, since it had no sequel. I have already mentioned the chambermaid, a pale-faced girl with stringy hair and thin legs. After breakfast, I went up to my room and found her apparently unconscious on the hearth-rug. I tried to call the desk, but got no reply. She seemed small and light, so I decided to move her onto the bed, or onto the armchair. This was not difficult; but as I lifted her, it was impossible not to become aware that she seemed to be wearing little or nothing under the brown overall-smock. This made me wonder; the weather was cold. Then, as I laid her down, she opened her eyes, and stared up at me with a cunning delight that convinced me that she had been shamming, and one of her hands caught the wrist that was trying to disengage itself from her, with the unmistakable intention of prolonging our contact.

But it was all done a little too crudely, and I started up. As I did so, I heard a step outside the door and quickly opened it. A rough-looking man with a gypsyish face was standing there, and he looked startled to see me. He started to say: "I was looking for . . . ," then he saw the girl in the room.

I said quickly, "I found her unconscious on the floor. I'll get a doctor." My only intention was to escape downstairs, but the girl overheard me and said, "No need for that," jumping up off the bed. The man turned and walked off, and she followed him a few seconds later without attempting an excuse. It took no particular subtlety to see what had been planned; he was supposed to open the door and find me in the act of making love to her. I cannot guess what was supposed to happen then; perhaps he would demand money. But I think it more likely that he would have attacked me. There was a definite family resemblance to the youth who had stared at me from the bridge. I never saw him again, and the girl seemed disposed to avoid me thereafter.

The episode made me more certain than ever that the gypsy family was more intimately involved with the Lloigor than Urquart realised. I rang his home, but was told that he was sleeping. I spent the rest of the day writing letters home, and examining the Roman remains in the town.

That evening, I saw Chickno for the first time. On the way to Urquart's, I had to pass a small public house, with a notice in the window: NO GYPSIES. Yet in the doorway of the pub stood an old man dressed in baggy clothes—a harmless-looking old man—who watched me pass with his hands in his pockets. He was smoking a cigarette which dangled loosely from his lips. He was unmistakably a gypsy.

I told Urquart about the episode of the chambermaid, but he seemed inclined to dismiss it; at worst, he thought they might have intended to blackmail me. But when I mentioned the old man, he became more interested, and made me describe him in detail. "That was Chickno, all right. I wonder what the devil he wants."

"He looked harmless," I said.

"About as harmless as a poison spider."

The encounter with Chickno disturbed me. I hope I am no more of a physical coward than the next man; but the youth by the bridge, and the chambermaid business, made me realise that we are all pretty vulnerable physically. If the chambermaid's boyfriend—or brother, or whoever it was—had chosen to hit me hard in the stomach, he could have beaten me into unconsciousness, or broken all my ribs without my making a sound. And no court would have convicted a man trying to defend a girl's "honour," especially when she alleged that she woke up from a faint to find herself being ravished. . . . The thought gave me a most unpleasant sensation in the stomach, and a real fear that I was playing with fire.

This fear explains the next event that I must describe. But I should mention that Urquart was out of bed on the third day, and that we drove out together through the Grey Hills, trying to find out whether there was any substance in Machen's mention of underground caves that were supposed to house his malicious troglodytes. We questioned the vicar in Llandalffen, and in two nearby villages, and talked to several farm-workers we met, explaining that we were interested in potholing. No one questioned our unlikely excuse, but no one had any information, although the minister in Llandalffen said he *had* heard stories of rumours of openings in hillsides, concealed by boulders.

Urquart was exhausted after his day of limping around with me, and went home at six o'clock, intending to get an early night. On my way home, I thought—or perhaps imagined—that a gypsyish-looking man followed me for several hundred yards. Someone resembling the youth was hanging around the entrance to the hotel, and walked away as I appeared. I began to feel a marked man. But after supper, feeling more comfortable, I decided to walk to the pub where I had seen old Chickno, and enquire discreetly whether he was known there.

When I was still a quarter of a mile from the place, I saw him standing in the doorway of a dairy, watching me, with no attempt to disguise the fact. I knew that if I ignored him, my feeling of insecurity would increase, and that it might cost me a sleepless night. So I did what I sometimes do to the monsters in nightmares—walked up to him and accosted him. I had the satisfaction of seeing, for a moment, that I had taken him by surprise. The watery eyes glanced away quickly—the action of a man who usually had something on his conscience.

Then, as I came up to him, I realised that the direct approach would be pointless—"Why are you following me?" He would react with the instinctive cunning of a man who is usually on the wrong side of the law, and flatly deny it. So instead, I smiled and said, "Pleasant evening." He grinned at me and said, "Oh ay." Then I stood beside him and pretended to be watching the world go past. I had another of my intuitive insights. He was slightly uncomfortable to be in the position of the hunter, so to speak; he was more used to being the quarry.

After a few moments, he said, "You're a stranger 'round here." The accent was not Welsh; it was harsher, more northern.

"Yes, I'm an American," I said. After a pause, I added, "You're a stranger too, from the sound of your accent."

"Ay. From Lancashire."

"Which part?"

"Downham."

"Ah, the village of the witches." I had given a course on the Victorian novelists, and recalled *The Lancashire Witches* by Ainsworth.

He grinned at me, and I saw that he hadn't a whole tooth in his head; the stumps were brown and broken. At close quarters, I could also see that I had been completely mistaken to think he looked harmless. Urquart's description of a poison spider was not all that far out. To begin with, he was much older than he looked at a distance—over eighty, I would have guessed. (Rumour had it later that he was over a hundred. Certainly his eldest daughter was sixty-five.) But age had not softened him or made him seem benevolent. There was a loose, degenerate look about him, and a kind of unpleasant vitality, as if he could still enjoy inflicting pain or causing fear. Even to talk with him was a slightly worrying sensation, like patting a dog you suspect has rabies. Urquart had told me some pretty disgusting rumours about him, but I could now believe them all. I recalled a story about the small daughter of a farm labourer who had accepted his hospitality one rainy night, and found it hard to keep my disgust from showing.

We stood there for several minutes more, looking at the lighted street and the few teenagers carrying portable radios who sauntered past, ignoring us.

" 'Old out your 'and," he said.

I did so. He stared at it with interest. Then he traced with his thumb the lines across the base of my right thumb.

"Long lifeline."

"I'm glad to hear that. Can you see anything else?"

He looked at me and grinned maliciously. "Nuthin' that'd interest you."

There was something unreal about this interview. I glanced at my watch. "Time for a drink." I started to walk away, then said, as if the idea had just occurred to me, "Care to join me?"

"I don't mind if I do." But the smile was so frankly insulting that anyone without ulterior motive would have taken offence. I knew what he was thinking—that I was afraid of him and wanted to try to win him over. There was some truth in the first part; none in the second. I felt that his failure to understand me gave me a slight advantage.

We walked to the pub I had intended to visit. Then I saw the notice in the window, and hesitated.

"Don't worry. That doesn't apply to me," he said.

A moment later, I saw why. The bar was half full. Several labourers were playing darts. Chickno made straight for the seat under the dartboard and sat down. A few of the men looked angry, but none said anything. They put the darts on the windowsill, and went back to the bar. Chickno grinned. I could see he enjoyed showing his power.

He said he would have a rum. I went to the bar, and the landlord served me without looking me full in the face. People moved unobtrusively to the other side of the bar, or at least as far from us as they conveniently could without being obvious. Clearly, Chickno was feared. Perhaps the death of the judge who sentenced his son had something to do with it; later, Urquart told me of other things.

One thing made me feel less worried. He could not hold his drink. I had bought him a single rum, in case he thought I was trying to get him drunk, but he looked at it and said, "Bit small, that," so I ordered a second. He had drunk the first before I brought the second over. And ten minutes later, his eyes had lost some of their cunning and sharpness.

I decided I had nothing to lose by frankness. "I've heard about you, Mr. Chickno. I'm most interested to meet you."

He said, "Ay. 'Appen you are." He sipped thoughtfully at the second rum, and sucked at a hollow tooth. Then he said: "You look a sensible fellow. Why do you stay where you're not wanted?"

I didn't pretend to misunderstand.

"I'm leaving soon—probably at the end of the week. But I came here to try and find something. Have you heard of the Voynich manuscript?" He obviously hadn't. So in spite of a feeling that I was wasting my breath—he was looking past me blankly—I told him briefly about the history of the manuscript, and how I had deciphered it. I ended by saying that Machen had also seemed to know the work, and that I suspected that its other half, or perhaps another copy, might be in this part of the world. When he answered, I saw that I had been mistaken to think him stupid or inattentive.

"So you want me to believe you're in this part lookin' for a manuscript? Is that all?" he said.

The tone had a Lancashire bluntness, but was not hostile. I said, "That's the reason I came here."

He leaned across the table, and breathed rum on me. "Look 'ere, mister, I know a lot more than you think. I know everything about you. So let's not 'ave any of this. You may be a college professor, but you don't impress me." I had a strong impression that I was looking at a rat or a weasel—a feeling that he was dangerous, and ought to be destroyed, like a dangerous snake—but I made an effort to keep this out of my eyes. I suddenly knew something else about him; he *was* impressed by the fact that I was a professor, and was enjoying his position of virtually giving me orders to go away and mind my own business.

So I drew a deep breath and said politely, "Believe me, Mr. Chickno, my main interest is in that manuscript. If I could find that, I'd be perfectly happy."

He drained his rum, and for a moment I thought he was going to walk out. But he only wanted another. I went to the bar and got him a double, and another Haig for myself.

When I sat down again, he took a good swallow of the rum. "I *know* why you're 'ere, mister. I know about your book as well. I'm not a vindictive sort of bloke. All I'm saying is that nobody's interested in you. So why don't you go back to America? You won't find the rest of your book round 'ere, I can tell you that."

Neither of us said anything for a few minutes. Then I decided to try complete frankness. "Why do they want me to go?"

For a moment, he didn't take in what I had said. Then his face became sober and serious—but only briefly. "Better not to talk of it." But after a moment, he seemed to think better of his suggestion. His eyes were malicious again. He leaned forward to me. "They're not interested in you, mister. They couldn't care less about you. It's 'im they don't like." His head jerked vaguely—I gather he meant Urquart. "He's a fool. He's had plenty of warning, and you can tell him from me, they won't bother to warn him next time."

"He doesn't think they have any power. Not enough to harm him," I said.

He seemed unable to make up his mind whether to smile or sneer. His face contorted, and for a moment, I had the illusion that his eyes had turned red, like a spider's. Then he spat out: "Then he's nothing but a bleeding——fool, and he deserves what he gets."

While I felt a twinge of fear, I also felt a touch of triumph. He had started to talk. My frankness had paid off. And unless he suddenly became cautious again, I was close to finding out some of the things I wanted to know.

He controlled himself, then said, less violently, "First of all, he's a fool because he doesn't really know anything. Not a bloody thing." He tapped my wrist with a bent forefinger.

"I suspected that," I said.

"You did, did you? Well, you were right. All this stuff about Atlantis." There was no doubt that scorn was real. But what he said next shocked me more than anything so far. He leaned forward, and said with an odd sincerity: "These things aren't out of a fairy story, you know. They're not playing games."

And I understood something that had not been clear to me so far. He knew "them," knew them with the indifferent realism of a scientist referring to the atomic bomb. I think that, up to this point, I had not really believed in "them"; I had been hoping that it was all some odd delusion; or that, like ghosts, they could not impinge on human affairs to any practical extent. His words made me understand my mistake. "These things." My hair stirred, and I felt the cold flowing down my legs to my feet.

"What *are* they doing, then?"

He emptied the glass, and said casually, "That's nuthin' to do wi' you, mate. You can't do anything about it. Nobody can." He set down the glass. "You see, this is their world anyway. We're a mistake. They want it back again." He caught the eye of the barman, and pointed to his glass.

I went over and collected another rum for him. Now I wanted to leave as soon as possible, to speak to Urquart. But it would be difficult, without running the risk of offending him.

Chickno solved my problem. After his third double rum, he abruptly ceased to be intelligible. He muttered things in a language which I took to be Romany. He mentioned a "Liz Southern" several times, pronouncing it "Sowthern," and it was only later that I recalled that this was the name of one of the Lancashire witches, executed in 1612. I never found out what he was saying, or whether he was, in fact, referring to the witch. His eyes became glassy, although he obviously thought he was still communicating something to me. Finally, I had the eerie impression that it was no longer old Chickno who was talking to me, but that he was possessed by some other creature. Half an hour later, he was dozing with his head on the table. I crossed to the barman.

"I'm sorry about this." I pointed to old Chickno.

"That's all right," he said. I think he had gathered by then that I was not a friend of the gypsy's. "I'll phone his grandson. He'll take him home."

I rang Urquart's house from the nearest phone box. His housekeeper said he was asleep. I was tempted to go over and wake him, then decided against it, and went back to the hotel wishing I had someone to talk to.

I tried to sort out my thoughts, to see some meaning in what Chickno had said. If he didn't deny the reality of the Lloigor, then why was Urquart so wrong? But I had drunk too much, and I felt exhausted. I fell asleep at midnight, but slept badly, haunted by nightmares. At two in the morning, I woke up with a horrible sense of the evil reality of the Lloigor, although it was mixed up in my mind with my nightmares about the Marquis de Sade and Jack the Ripper. My sense of danger was so strong that I switched on the light. This improved things. Then I decided that I had better write down my conversation with Chickno and give it to Urquart to read, in case he could add some of the missing parts to the jigsaw. I wrote it down in detail.

My fingers numb with the cold, I slept again, but was awakened by a faint trembling of the room, which reminded me of an earthquake tremor I experienced once in Mexico. Then I slept again until morning.

Before going in to breakfast, I enquired at the desk for mail. There was a reply to my letter from Lauerdale at Brown, and I read it as I ate my kippers.

Much of the letter was literary—a discussion of Lovecraft and his psychology. But there were pages that held far more interest for me. Lauerdale wrote: "I myself am inclined to believe, on the evidence of letters, that one of the most important experiences in Lovecraft's early life was a visit to Cohasset, a run-down fishing village between Quonochontaug and Weekapaug in Southern Rhode Island. Like Lovecraft's 'Innsmouth,' this village was later to vanish from the maps. I have been there, and its description corresponds in many ways to Lovecraft's description of Innsmouth—which Lovecraft placed in Massachusetts: 'more empty houses than people,' the air of decay, the stale fish smell. There was actually a character known as Captain Marsh living in Cohasset in 1915, when Lovecraft was there, who had spent some time in the South Seas. It may have been he who told the young Lovecraft the stories of evil Polynesian temples and undersea people. The chief of these legends—as mentioned also by Jung and Spence—is of gods from the stars (or demons) who were once lords of this earth, who lost their power through the practise of evil magic, but who will one day return and take over the earth again. In the version quoted by Jung, these gods are said to have created human beings from subhuman monsters.

"In my own opinion, Lovecraft derived the rest of the 'mythos' from Machen, perhaps from Poe, who occasionally hints at such things. 'MS. Found in a Bottle,' for example. I found no evidence that there were ever sinister rumours connected with the 'shunned house' in Benefit Street, or any other house in Providence. I shall be extremely interested to read what you have to say about Machen's sources. While I think it is just possible that Machen heard some story about some 'arcane' volume of the sort you mention, I can find no evidence that Lovecraft had firsthand acquaintance with such a book. I am sure that any connection between his *Necronomicon* and the Voynich MS. is, as you suggest, coincidence."

My hair stirred as I read the sentence about gods "who will one day return and take over the earth again," as also about the reference to Polynesian legends. For, as Churchward has written: "Easter Island, Tahiti, Samoas, . . . Hawaii, and the Marquesas are the pathetic fingers of that great land, standing today as sentinels of a silent grave." Polynesia is the remains of Mu.

All this told me little more than I knew already, or had guessed. But my encounter with Chickno raised a practical problem: how far was Urquart actually in danger? He might be right that the Lloigor had no power in themselves, or very little; but Chickno and his family were a different matter. Even taking the most sceptical view of all, that this whole thing was pure imagination and superstition, Chickno represented a very real danger. For some reason, they hated Urquart.

The desk clerk touched my sleeve: "Telephone, sir."

It was Urquart. I said, "Thank heavens you rang. I've got to talk to you."

"You've heard, then?"

"Heard what?"

"About the explosion? Chickno's dead."

"What! Are you sure?"

"Pretty sure. Although they can't find much of him."

"I'll be over right away."

That was the first I heard of the great Llandalffen explosion. I have on my desk a volume called *Stranger than Logic* by the late Frank Edwards, one of those slightly unreliable compilations of mysteries and wonders. It has a section headed "The Great Llandalffen Explosion," and what he says, substantially, is that the explosion was atomic, and was probably due to a fault in the engines of an "unidentified flying object"; he quotes the rocket scientist Willey Ley to the effect that the Siberian crater of 1908 may have been an explosion of antimatter, and draws parallels between the Llandalffen explosion and the Podkamennaya Tunguska fall. This I flatly hold to be absurd. I saw the area of the explosion, and there was not nearly enough damage for an atomic explosion, even a small one.

However, I am running ahead of my story. Urquart met me halfway to his house, and we drove out to Llandalffen. What had happened was simply that there had been a tremendous explosion at about four o'clock that morning; it may have been this that shook me awake in the early hours. The area is deserted, luckily, but a farm-labourer in a cottage three miles away was thrown out of bed by the explosion. The strangest feature of the whole affair is that it made so little actual noise; the farm-labourer thought it was an earth tremor, and went back to sleep. Two men in the village, returning home from a party, said they heard the explosion as a dull sound like distant thunder or blasting, and wondered whether a plane might have crashed with a load of bombs. The farm-labourer pedalled out to investigate at seven in the morning, but found nothing. However, he mentioned it to the farmer who employed him, and the two drove over in the farmer's car a little after nine. This time, the farmer turned off down the side road, and drove towards the gypsy caravans, which were about two miles farther on. Their first find was not, as Mr. Edwards states, a part of a human body, but part of the foreleg of a donkey, which lay in the middle of the road. Beyond this, they discovered that stone walls and trees had been flattened. Bits of the caravan and other relics were scattered for hundreds of yards around the focus of the explosion, the two-acre field in which the caravans had stood.

I saw the field myself—we were allowed to approach by the

inspector of police from Llandalffen, who knew Urquart. My first impression was that it had been an earthquake rather than an ordinary explosion. An explosion produces a crater, or clears a more-or-less flattened area, but the ground here was torn and split open as if by a convulsion from underneath. A stream flowed through the field, and it had now turned the area into a lake. On the other hand, there were certain signs that are characteristic of an explosion. Some trees were flattened, or reduced to broken stumps, but others were untouched. The wall between the field and the main road was almost intact, although it ran along the top of a raised mound or dyke, yet a wall much farther away in the next field had been scattered over a wide area.

There were also, of course, the disfigured human and animal relics that we had expected to find; shreds of skin, fragments of bone. Few of them were identifiable; the explosion seemed to have fragmented every living creature in the field. The donkey's leg found by the farmer was the largest segment recovered.

I was soon feeling severely sick, and had to go and sit in the car, but Urquart limped around for over an hour, picking up various fragments. I heard a police sergeant ask him what he was looking for, and Urquart said he didn't know. But I knew; he was hoping for some definite evidence to connect the gypsies with Mu. And somehow, I was certain that he wouldn't find it.

By now there must have been a thousand sightseers around the area, trying to approach closely enough to find out what happened. Our car was stopped a dozen or more times as we tried to drive away. Urquart told everyone who asked him that he thought a flying saucer had exploded.

In fact, we were both fairly certain what had happened. I believe that old Chickno had gone too far—that he told me too much. Urquart thinks that his chief mistake was to think of the Lloigor as somehow human, and of himself as their servant, entitled to take certain liberties. He failed to realise that he was completely dispensable, and that his naive tendency to boast and present himself as an ambassador of the Lloigor made him dangerous to them.

We reached this conclusion after I had described my talk with Chickno to Urquart. When I had finished reading him my notes, Urquart said, "No wonder they killed him."

"But he didn't say much, after all."

"He said enough. And perhaps they thought we could guess more than he said."

We had lunch in the hotel, and regretted it. Everyone seemed to know where we had been, and they stared at us and tried to overhear our conversation. The waiter spent so much time hanging about in the area of our table that the manager finally had to reprimand him. We ate as quickly as we could and went back to Urquart's house. There was a fire in the library again, and Mrs. Dolgelly brought in coffee.

I can still remember every moment of that afternoon. There was a sense of tension and foreboding, of physical danger. What had impressed Urquart most was old Chickno's scorn when I told him that Urquart thought "they" had no real power. I still remember that stream of contemptuous bad language that had made several people in the pub turn their heads. And Chickno had been proved right. "They" had plenty of power—several kinds of power. For we reached the conclusion that the devastation of the gypsy encampment was neither earthquake nor explosion, but some kind of mixture of both. An explosion violent enough to rip apart the caravans would have been heard clearly in Southport and Melincourt, and most certainly in Llandalffen, barely five miles away. The clefts and cracks in the earth suggested a convulsion of the ground. But a convulsion of the ground would not have torn apart the caravans. Urquart believed—and I finally agreed with him—that the caravans and their inhabitants *had* been literally torn apart. But in that case, what was the purpose of the convulsion of the earth? There were two possible explanations. This had happened as the "creatures" forced their way from underground. Or the "earthquake" was a deliberate false trail, a red herring. And the consequences that followed from such a supposition were so frightening that we poured ourselves whiskies, although it was only midafternoon. It meant that "they" were anxious to provide an apparently natural explanation for what had happened. And that meant they had a reason for secrecy. And, as far as we could see, there could only be one reason: they had "plans," plans for the future. I recalled Chickno's words: "This is their world anyway. . . . They want it back again."

The frustrating thing was that, in all his books on occultism and the history of Mu, Urquart had nothing that suggested an answer. It was hard to fight off a paralysed feeling of hopelessness, of not knowing where to begin. The evening paper increased the depression, for it stated confidently that the explosion had been caused by nitroglycerine! The "experts" had come up with a theory that seemed to explain the facts. Chickno's son and son-in-law had worked in stone quarries in the north, and were used to handling explosives. Nitroglycerine was occasionally used in these quarries because of its cheapness and because it is easy to manufacture. According to the newspaper report, Chickno's sons were suspected of stealing quantities of glycerine, and of nitric and sulphuric acid. Their intention, said the report, was to use them for blowing safes. They must have manufactured fairly large quantities of the nitroglycerine, and some kind of earth tremor set it off.

It was an absurd explanation; it would have taken a ton of nitroglycerine to do so much damage. In any case, a nitroglycerine explosion leaves behind characteristic signs; there were no such signs in the devastated field. A nitroglycerine explosion can be heard; no one heard it.

And yet the explanation was never seriously questioned, although there was later an official investigation into the disaster. Presumably because human beings are afraid of mysteries for which there is absolutely no explanation, the mind needs some solution, no matter how absurd, to reassure it.

There was another item in the evening paper that at first seemed irrelevant. The headline ran: "Did explosion release mystery gas?" It was only a short paragraph, which stated that many people in the area had awakened that morning with bad headaches and a feeling of lassitude, apparently signs of an impending attack of influenza. These had cleared up later in the day. Had the explosion released some gas, asked the reporter, that produced these symptoms? The newspaper's "scientific correspondent" added a note saying that sulphur dioxide could produce exactly these symptoms, and that several people had noticed such a smell in the night. Nitroglycerine, of course, contains a small quantity of sulphuric acid, which would account for the smell. . . .

Urquart said, "Soon find out about that, anyway," and rang the Southport weather bureau. They rang us back ten minutes later with the answer; the wind had been blowing from the northeast in the night. And Llandalffen lies to the north of the site of the explosion.

And still neither of us saw the significance of the item. We wasted hours searching through my translation of the Voynich manuscript for clues, then through thirty or so books on Mu and related subjects.

And then, about to reach down another volume on Lemuria and Atlantis, my eye fell on Sacheverell Sitwell's book *Poltergeists*. I stopped and stared. My mind groped for some fact I had half-forgotten. Then it came.

"My god, Urquart," I said, "I've just thought of something. Where do these creatures get their energy?" He looked at me blankly. "Is it their own natural energy? You need a physical body to generate physical energy. But how about poltergeists . . ." And then he understood, too. "Poltergeists" take energy from human beings, usually from adolescent girls. One school of thought believes that poltergeists have no independent existence; they are some kind of psychic manifestation from the unconscious mind of the adolescent, an explosion of frustration or craving for attention. The other school believes that they are "spirits" who need to borrow energy from an emotionally disturbed person; Sitwell cites cases of poltergeist disturbances in houses that have remained empty for long periods.

Could this be why so many people in the area felt tired and "fluey" when they woke up—because the energy for the explosion came *from them*?

If this was so, then the danger was not as serious as we had believed. It meant that the Lloigor had no energy of their own; they had to draw it from people—presumably sleeping people. Their powers were therefore limited.

The same thought struck us both at the same time. Except, of course, that the world is full of people. . . .

Nevertheless, we both felt suddenly more cheerful. And in this new frame of mind, we faced our fundamental task; to make the human race aware of the Lloigor. They were not indestructible, or they would not have bothered to destroy Chickno for talking about them. It might be possible to destroy them with an underground nuclear explosion. The fact that they had remained dormant for so many centuries meant that their power was limited. If we could produce definite proof of their existence, then the possibility of countering the menace was high.

The obvious starting point was the Llandalffen explosion: to make the public aware that it pointed unmistakably to the reality of these hidden forces. In a way, Chickno's death was the best thing that could have happened; they had shown their hand. We decided to visit the explosion site again in the morning, and to compile a dossier on it. We would interview the citizens of Llandalffen and find out whether any of them really *had* smelled sulphur dioxide in the night, and whether they would persist in the story when we pointed out that the wind was blowing in the opposite direction. Urquart knew a few Fleet Street journalists who had taken a vague interest in the occult and supernatural; he would contact them and hint at a big story.

When I returned to my hotel late that night, I felt happier than for many days. And I slept deeply and heavily. When I woke up, it was already long past breakfast time, and I felt exhausted. I attributed this to my long sleep, until I tried to walk to the bathroom and found that my head throbbed as if I had picked up a flu germ. I took two aspirins, had a shave, then went downstairs. To my relief, no one else showed signs of a similar exhaustion. Coffee and buttered toast in the lounge refreshed me slightly; I decided that I was suffering from ordinary strain. Then I rang Urquart.

Mrs Dolgelly said, "I'm afraid he's not up yet, sir. He's not feeling too well this morning."

"What's the matter with him?"

"Nothing much. He just seems very tired."

"I'll be right over," I said. I told the desk to ring me a taxi; I was far too tired to walk.

Twenty minutes later, I was sitting at Urquart's bedside. He looked and felt even worse than I did.

"I hate to suggest this," I said, "feeling as we both do, but I think we'd better get out of this place as soon as possible."

"Couldn't we wait until tomorrow?" he asked.

"It will be worse tomorrow. They'll exhaust us until we die of the first minor illness we pick up."

"I suppose you're right."

Although it all seemed too troublesome for words, I managed to get back to the hotel, pack my bags, and order a taxi to the station in Cardiff, where we could catch a London train at three o'clock. Urquart encountered more difficulty than I did; Mrs. Dolgelly showed unexpected strength of mind and refused to pack a case for him. He rang me, and I dragged myself back there again, wanting nothing so much as to climb back into bed. But the effort revived me; before midday, the headache had vanished, and I was feeling less exhausted, although oddly light-headed. Mrs. Dolgelly believed my explanation of an urgent telegram that made our journey a matter of life and death, although she was convinced that Urquart would collapse on the way to London.

That night, we slept in the Regent Palace Hotel. And in the morning, we both woke up feeling perfectly normal. It was Urquart who said, as we waited for our egg and bacon at breakfast, "I think we're winning, old boy."

But neither of us really believed it.

And from this point on, my story ceases to be a continuous narrative, and becomes a series of fragments, and a record of frustration. We spent weeks in the British Museum searching for clues, and later in the Bibliothèque Nationale. Books on cults in the South Seas indicate that many traditions of the Lloigor survive there, and it is well known that they will one day return and reclaim their world. One text quoted by Leduc and Poitier says that they will cause a "tearing madness" to break out among those they wish to destroy, and their footnote says that "tearing," as used in this context, means to tear with the teeth, like a man eating a chicken leg. Von Storch has records of a Haitian tribe in which the menfolk became possessed of a demon that led many of them to kill wives and children by tearing at their throats with their teeth.

Lovecraft also provided us with an important hint. In "The Call of Cthulhu" he mentions a collection of press cuttings, all of which reveal that the "entombed Old Ones" are becoming more active in the world. Later the same day, I happened to meet a girl who worked for a press-cutting agency, who told me that her job was simply to read through dozens of newspapers every day, looking out for mention of the names of clients. I asked her if she could look for items of "unusual" interest—anything hinting at the mysterious or supernatural—and she said she saw no reason why not. I gave her a copy of Charles Fort's *Lo!* to give her an idea of the kind of items I wanted.

Two weeks later, a thin buff envelope arrived, with a dozen or so press clippings in it. Most of them were unimportant—babies with two heads and similar medical curiosities, a man killed in Scotland by an enormous hailstone, reports of an abominable snowman seen on the slopes of Everest—but two or three were more relevant to our search. We immediately contacted several more press-cutting agencies in England, America, and Australia.

The result was an enormous amount of material, which finally occupied two enormous volumes. It was arranged under various headings: explosions, murders, witchcraft (and the supernatural in general), insanity, scientific observations, miscellaneous. The details of the explosion near Al-Kazimiyah in Iraq are so similar to those of the Llandalffen disaster—even to the exhaustion of the inhabitants of Al-Kazimiyah—that I have no doubt that this area is another stronghold of the Lloigor. The explosion that changed the course of the Tula Gol near Ulan Bator in Mongolia actually led the Chinese to accuse Russia of dropping an atomic bomb. The strange insanity that destroyed ninety percent of the inhabitants of the southern island of Zaforas in the Sea of Crete is still a mystery upon which the Greek military government refuses to comment. The massacre at Panagyurishte in Bulgaria on the night of March 29th, 1968, was blamed, in the first official reports, upon a "vampire cult" who "regarded the nebula in Andromeda as their true home." These are some of the major events that convinced us that the Lloigor are planning a major attack on the inhabitants of the earth.

But there were literally dozens—eventually hundreds—of less important items that fitted the pattern. The marine creature that dragged away a trout fisherman in Loch Eilt led to several newspaper articles about "prehistoric survivals"; but the Glasgow edition of the *Daily Express* (May 18, 1968) printed a story of a witch cult and their worship of a sea-devil with an overpowering smell of decay that recalled Lovecraft's Innsmouth. An item about the Melksham strangler led me to spend some days there, and I have a signed statement by Detective Sergeant Bradley agreeing that the words the killer used repeatedly before he died were "Ghatanothoa," "Nug" (another elemental described in Lovecraft), and "Rantegoz." (Rhan-Tegoth, the beast god, also mentioned in Lovecraft?) Robbins (the strangler) claimed that he was possessed by a "power from underground" when he killed the three women and amputated their feet.

It would be pointless to continue this list. We hope to have a number of selected items from it—some five hundred in all—published in a volume that will be sent to every member of Congress and every member of the British House of Commons.

There are certain items that will not be published in this volume, and which are perhaps the most disturbing of all. At 7:45 on December 7th, 1967, a small private aircraft piloted by R. D. Jones of Kingston, Jamaica, left Fort Lauderdale, Florida, for Kingston. There were three passengers aboard. The journey of about five hundred kilometres should have taken two hours. By ten o'clock, Jones's wife, waiting at the airfield, became alarmed and suggested a search. All attempts at radio contact failed. The search began during the morning. At 1:15, Jones radioed the field for permission to land, apparently unaware of the anxiety he was causing. When asked where he had been, he looked puzzled, and said, "Flying, of course." When told the time, he was amazed. *His own watch showed 10:15.* He said he had been flying in low cloud most of the way, but that he had no cause for alarm. Weather reports showed that it was an exceptionally clear day for December, and that he should have encountered no cloud. (*Gleaner,* Dec. 8th, 1967.)

The other four cases of which we possess details are similar to this first one, except that one case, the *Jeannie*, concerned a coast guard vessel off the west coast of Scotland, not an aeroplane. In this instance, the three men on board had encountered heavy "fog," discovered their radio was not working, and that, for some reason, their watches had stopped. They assumed that it was some odd magnetic disturbance. However, the vessel's other instruments worked well enough, and in due course, the boat reached Stornoway on Lewis—having been missing for twenty-two hours instead of the three or four assumed by the crew. The naval training plane *Blackjack*, off the Baja peninsula, Southern California, holds the record; it was missing for three days and five hours. The crew thought it had been away from base for seven hours or so.

We have been unable to discover what explanation was advanced by the navy for this curious episode, or by the coast guard of Great Britain for the *Jeannie* interlude. It was probably assumed that the crew got drunk at sea and fell asleep. But there is one thing we soon learned beyond all doubt: human beings do not wish to know about things that threaten their feeling of security and "normality." This was also a discovery made by the late Charles Fort; he devoted his life to analysing it. And I suppose the books of Fort present classic instances of what William James called "a certain blindness in human beings." For he invariably gives newspaper references for the incredible events he cites. Why had no one ever taken the trouble to check his references—or some of them—and then write a statement admitting his honesty or denouncing him as a fraud? Mr. Tiffany Thayer once told me that critical readers take the view that there was some "special circumstance" in each case Fort quotes which invalidates it—an unreliable witness here, an inventive reporter there, and so on. And it never strikes anyone that to use this explanation to cover a thousand pages full of carefully assembled facts amounts to pure self-delusion.

Like most people, I have always made the assumption that my fellow human beings are relatively honest, relatively open-minded, relatively curious. If anything were needed to reassure me about the curiosity about the apparently inexplicable, I would only have to glance at any airport bookstall, with its dozen or so paperbacks by Frank Edwards, et al., all bearing titles like *World of the Weird, A Hundred Events Stranger than Fiction*, and so on. It comes as a shock to discover that all this is not proof of a genuine open-mindedness about the "supernatural" but only of a desire to be titillated and shocked. These books are a kind of occult pornography, part of a game of "let's make believe the world is far less dull than it actually is."

On August 19th, 1968, Urquart and myself invited twelve "friends" to the rooms we had taken at 83 Gower Street—the house in which Darwin lived immediately after his marriage. We felt the Darwin association was appropriate, for we had no doubt that the date would long be remembered by everyone present. I shall not go into detail except to say that there were four professors—three from London, one from Cambridge—two journalists, both from respectable newspapers, and several members of the professions, including a doctor.

Urquart introduced me, and I read from a prepared statement, elaborating where I felt it to be necessary. After ten minutes, the Cambridge professor cleared his throat, said "Excuse me," and hurried out of the room. I discovered later that he thought he had been the victim of a practical joke. The others listened to the end, and for a great deal of the time, I was aware that they were also wondering whether this was all a joke. When they realised that it was not, they became definitely hostile. One of the journalists, a young man just down from the university, kept interrupting with: "Are we to understand. . . ." One of the ladies got up and left, although I heard later that this was less from disbelief than because she suddenly noticed that there were now thirteen people in the room and thought it unlucky. The young journalist was carrying two of Urquart's books on Mu, and he quoted from these with deadly effect. Urquart is certainly no master of the English language, and there was a time when I would have seen in them mainly an excuse for witty sarcasm.

But what was amazing to me was that no one present seemed to accept our "lecture" as a *warning*. They argued about it as though it were an interesting theory, or perhaps an unusual short story. Finally, after an hour of quibbling about various newspaper cuttings, a solicitor stood up and made a speech that obviously conveyed the general feeling, beginning: "I think Mr. Hough (the journalist) has expressed the misgivings we all feel. . . ." His main point, which he kept repeating, was that there was *no definite evidence*. The Llandalffen explosion could have been due to nitroglycerine or even the impact of a shower of meteors. Poor Urquart's books were treated in a manner that would have made me wince even in my most sceptical days.

There was no point in going on. We tape-recorded the whole meeting, and had it typed and duplicated, hoping that one day it will be regarded as almost unbelievable evidence of human blindness and stupidity. And then nothing more happened. The two newspapers decided not to print even a critical account of our arguments. A number of people got wind of the meeting and came to see us—bosomy ladies with ouija boards, a thin man who thought the Loch Ness monster was a Russian submarine, and a number of assorted cranks. This was the point where we decided to move to America. We still entertained some absurd hope that Americans would prove more open-minded than the English.

It did not take long to disillusion us—although it is true that we found one or two people who were at least willing to suspend judgment on our sanity. But on the whole, the results were negative. We spent an interesting day at the almost defunct fishing village of Cohasset—Lovecraft's Innsmouth; long enough to discover that it is as active a centre of Lloigor activity as Llandalffen, perhaps more so, and that we would be in extreme danger if we remained there. But we managed to locate Joseph Cullen Marsh, grandson of Lovecraft's Captain Marsh, who now lived in Popasquash. He told us that his grandfather had died insane, and believed that he had possessed certain "occult" books and manuscripts, which had been destroyed by his widow. This may have been where Lovecraft actually saw the *Necronomicon*. He also mentioned that Captain Marsh referred to the ancient Old Ones as "the Masters of Time"—an interesting comment in view of the case of the *Jeannie*, the *Blackjack*, and the rest.

Urquart is convinced that the manuscripts were not destroyed—on the curious grounds that such ancient works have a character of their own, and tend to avoid destruction. He is conducting an enormous correspondence with Captain Marsh's heirs, and his family solicitors, in an attempt to pick up the trail of the *Necronomicon*.

In the present stage . . .

Editor's Note. The above words were written by my uncle a few minutes before he received the telegram from Senator James R. Pinckney of Virginia, an old school-friend, and probably one of those my uncle mentions as being "willing to suspend judgment on his sanity." The telegram read: COME TO WASHINGTON AS SOON AS POSSIBLE, BRING CUTTINGS, CONTACT ME AT MY HOME, PINCKNEY. Senator Pinckney has confirmed to me that the Secretary for Defense had agreed to spend some time with my uncle, and that, if impressed, he might conceivably have arranged an interview with the President himself.

My uncle and Colonel Urquart were unable to get on the three-fifteen flight from Charlottesville to Washington; they went to the airport on a "stand-by" basis, hoping for cancellations. There was only one cancellation, and after some argument, Colonel Urquart agreed with my uncle that they should stick together rather than go to Washington by different routes. At this point, Captain Harvey Nichols agreed to fly them to Washington in a Cessna 311 of which he was one-quarter owner.

The plane took off from a side runway at 3:43 on February 19, 1969; the sky was perfectly clear, and weather reports were excellent. Ten minutes later, the airfield received the mystifying signal "running into low cloud." He should have been by then somewhere in the area of Gordonsville, and the weather over this area was exceptionally clear. Subsequent attempts to contact the plane by radio failed. At five o'clock, I was informed that radio contact had been lost. But during the next few hours, hope revived as widespread enquiries failed to discover any reports of a crash. By midnight, we all assumed that it would only be a matter of time before the wreck was reported.

It has never been reported. In the two months that have elapsed since then, nothing further has been heard of my uncle or of the plane. It is my own opinion—supported by many people of wide experience in flying—that the plane had an instrument failure, and somehow flew out over the Atlantic, where it crashed.

My uncle had already arranged for the publication of this book of selections from his press-cutting albums with the Black Cockerell Press of Charlottesville, and it seems appropriate that these notes of his should be used as an introduction.

In the newspaper stories that have appeared about my uncle in the past two months, it has often been assumed that he was insane, or at least, suffering from delusions. This is not my own view. I met Colonel Urquart on a great many occasions, and it is my own opinion that he was thoroughly untrustworthy. My mother described him to me as "an extremely shifty character." Even my uncle's account of him—at their first meeting—bears this out. It would be charitable to assume that Urquart believed everything he wrote in his books, but I find this hard to accept. They are cheap and sensational, and in parts obviously pure invention. (For example, he never mentions the name of the Hindu monastery—or even its location—where he made his amazing "finds" about Mu; neither does he mention the name of the priest who is supposed to have taught him to read the language of the inscriptions.)

My uncle was a simple and easy-going man, almost a caricature of the absent-minded professor. This is revealed in his naive account of the meeting at 83 Gower Street, and the reaction of his audience. He had no notion of the possibilities of human duplicity that are, in my opinion, revealed in the writings of Colonel Urquart. And typically, my uncle does not mention that it was he who paid for the Colonel's passage across the Atlantic, and for the rooms at 83 Gower Street. The Colonel's income was extremely small, while my uncle was, I suppose, comparatively well-off.

And yet there is, I think, another possibility that must be taken into account—suggested by my uncle's friend Foster Damon. My uncle was loved by his students and colleagues for his sense of dry humour, and has been many times compared to Mark Twain. And the resemblance did not end there; he also shared Twain's deep vein of pessimism about the human race.

I knew my uncle well in the last years of his life, and saw much of him even in the last months. He knew I did not believe his stories about the "Lloigor," and that I thought Urquart a charlatan. A fanatic would have tried to convince me, and perhaps refused to speak to me when I declined to be convinced. My uncle continued to treat me with the same good humour as ever, and my mother and I both noticed that his eyes often twinkled as he looked at me. Was he congratulating himself on having a nephew who was too pragmatic to be taken in by his elaborate joke?

I like to think so. For he was a good and sincere man, and is mourned by innumerable friends.

—Julian F. Lang. 1969.

My Boat*

JOANNA RUSS

Milty, have I got a story for you!

No, sit down. Enjoy the cream cheese and bagel. I guarantee this one will make a first-class TV movie; I'm working on it already. Small cast, cheap production—it's a natural. See, we start with this crazy chick, maybe about seventeen, but she's a waif, she's withdrawn from the world, see? She's had some kind of terrible shock. And she's fixed up this old apartment in a slum, really weird, like a fantasy world—long blonde hair, maybe goes around barefoot in tie-dyed dresses she makes out of old sheets, and there's this account executive who meets her in Central Park and falls in love with her on account of she's like a dryad or a nature spirit—

All right. So it stinks. I'll pay for my lunch. We'll pretend you're not my agent, okay? And you don't have to tell me it's been done; I know it's been done. The truth is—

Milty, I have to talk to someone. No, it's a lousy idea, I know, and I'm not working on it and I haven't been working on it, but what are you going to do Memorial Day weekend if you're alone and everybody's out of town?

I have to talk to someone.

Yes, I'll get off the Yiddische shtick. Hell, I don't think about it; I just fall into it sometimes when I get upset, you know how it is. You do it yourself. But I want to tell you a story and it's not a story for a script. It's something that happened to me in high school in 1952, and *I just want to tell someone.* I don't care if no station from here to Indonesia can use it; you just tell me whether I'm nuts or not, that's all.

Okay.

It was 1952, like I said. I was a senior in a high school out on the Island, a public high school but very fancy, a big drama program. They

---

*Originally published in *Fantasy and Science Fiction,* January 1976.

were just beginning to integrate, you know, the early fifties, very liberal neighborhood; everybody's patting everybody else on the back because they let five black kids into our school. Five out of eight hundred! You'd think they expected God to come down from Flatbush and give everybody a big fat golden halo.

Anyway, our drama class got integrated, too—one little black girl aged fifteen named Cissie Jackson, some kind of genius. All I remember the first day of the spring term, she was the only black I'd ever seen with a natural, only we didn't know what the hell it was, then; it made her look as weird as if she'd just come out of a hospital or something.

Which, by the way, she just had. You know Malcolm X saw his father killed by white men when he was four and that made him a militant for life? Well, Cissie's father had been shot down in front of her eyes when she was a little kid—we learned that later on—only it didn't make her militant; it just made her so scared of everybody and everything that she'd withdraw into herself and wouldn't speak to anybody for weeks on end. Sometimes she'd withdraw right out of this world and then they'd send her to the loony bin; believe me, it was all over school in two days. And she looked it; she'd sit up there in the school theater—oh, Milty, the Island high schools had *money*, you better believe it!—and try to disappear into the last seat like some little scared rabbit. She was only four-eleven anyhow, and maybe eighty-five pounds sopping wet. So maybe that's why she didn't become a militant. Hell, that had nothing to do with it. She was scared of *everybody*. It wasn't just the white-black thing, either; I once saw her in a corner with one of the other black students: real uptight, respectable boy, you know, suit and white shirt and tie and carrying a new briefcase, too, and he was talking to her about something as if his life depended on it. He was actually crying and pleading with her. And all she did was shrink back into the corner as if she'd like to disappear and shake her head No No No. She always talked in a whisper unless she was onstage and sometimes then, too. The first week she forgot her cues four times—just stood there, glazed over, ready to fall through the floor—and a couple of times she just wandered off the set as if the play was over, right in the middle of a scene.

So Al Coppolino and I went to the principal. I'd always thought Alan was pretty much a fruitcake himself—remember, Milty, this is 1952—because he used to read all that crazy stuff, *The Cult of Cthulhu, Dagon Calls, The Horror Men of Leng*— yeah, I remember that H. P. Lovecraft flick you got ten percent on for Hollywood *and* TV *and* reruns—but what did we know? Those days you went to parties, you got excited from dancing cheek to cheek, girls wore ankle socks and petticoats to stick their skirts out, and if you wore a sport shirt to school that was okay because Central High was liberal, but it better not have a pattern on it. Even so, I knew Al was a bright kid and I let him do most of the talking; I just nodded a lot. I was a big nothing in those days.

Al said, "Sir, Jim and I are all for integration and we think it's great that this is a really liberal place, but—uh—"

The principal got that look. Uh-oh.

"But?" he said, cold as ice.

"Well, sir," said Al, "it's Cissie Jackson. We think she's—um—sick. I mean wouldn't it be better if . . . I mean everybody says she's just come out of the hospital and it's a strain for all of us and it must be a lot worse strain for her and maybe it's just a little soon for her to—"

"Sir," I said, "what Coppolino means is, we don't mind integrating blacks with whites, but this isn't racial integration, sir; this is integrating normal people with a filbert. I mean—"

He said, "Gentlemen, it might interest you to know that Miss Cecilia Jackson has higher scores on her IQ tests than the two of you put together. And I am told by the drama department that she has also more talent than the two of you put together. And considering the grades both of you have managed to achieve in the fall term, I'm not at all surprised."

Al said under his breath, "Yeah, and fifty times as many problems."

Well, the principal went on and told us about how we should welcome this chance to work with her because she was so brilliant she was positively a genius, and that as soon as we stopped spreading idiotic rumors, the better chance Miss Jackson would have to adjust to Central, and if he heard anything about our bothering her again or spreading stories about her, both of us were going to get it but good, and maybe we would even be expelled.

And then his voice lost the ice, and he told us about some white cop shooting her pa for no reason at all when she was five, right in front of her, and her pa bleeding into the gutter and dying in little Cissie's lap, and how poor her mother was, and a couple of other awful things that had happened to her, and if *that* wasn't enough to drive anybody crazy—though he said, "cause problems," you know—anyhow, by the time he'd finished, I felt like a rat and Coppolino went outside the principal's office, put his face down against the tiles—they always had tiles up as high as you could reach, so they could wash off the graffiti, though we didn't use the word "graffiti" in those days—and he blubbered like a baby.

So we started a Help Cecilia Jackson campaign.

And by God, Milty, could that girl *act!* She wasn't reliable, that was the trouble; one week she'd be in there, working like a dog, voice exercises, gym, fencing, reading Stanislavsky in the cafeteria, gorgeous performances, the next week: nothing. Oh, she was there in the flesh, all right, all eighty-five pounds of her, but she would walk through everything as if her mind was someplace else: technically perfect, emotionally nowhere. I heard later those were also the times when she'd refuse to answer questions in history or geography classes, just fade out and not talk. But when she was concentrating, she could walk onto that stage and take it over as if she owned it. I never saw such a natural. At fifteen! And tiny. I mean not a particularly good voice—though I guess just getting older would've helped that—and a figure that, frankly, Milt, it was the old W. C. Fields joke, two aspirins on an ironing board. And tiny, no real good looks, but my God, you know and I know that doesn't matter if you've got the presence. And she had it to burn. She played the Queen of Sheba once, in a one-act play we put on before a live audience—all right, our parents and the other kids, who else?—and she *was* the role. And another time I saw her do things from Shakespeare. And once, of all things, a lioness in a mime class. She had it all. Real, absolute, pure concentration. And she was smart, too; by then she and Al had become pretty good friends; I once heard her explain to him (that was in the green room the afternoon of the Queen of Sheba thing when she was taking off her makeup with cold cream) just how she'd figured out each bit of business for the character. Then she stuck her whole arm out at me, pointing straight at me as if her arm was a machine gun, and said:

"For you, Mister Jim, let me tell you: the main thing is *belief*!"

It was a funny thing, Milt. She got better and better friends with Al, and when they let me tag along, I felt privileged. He loaned her some of those crazy books of his and I overheard things about her life, bits and pieces. That girl had a mother who was so uptight and so God-fearing and so respectable it was a wonder Cissie could even breathe without asking permission. Her mother wouldn't even let her straighten her hair—not ideological reasons, you understand, not then, but because—get this—*Cissie was too young.* I think her mamma must've been crazier than she was. Course I was a damn stupid kid (who wasn't?) and I really thought all blacks were real loose; they went around snapping their fingers and hanging from chandeliers, you know, all that stuff, dancing and singing. But here was this genius from a family where they wouldn't let her out at night; she wasn't allowed to go to parties or dance or play cards; she couldn't wear makeup or even jewelry. Believe me, I think if anything drove her batty it was being socked over the head so often with a Bible. I guess her imagination just had to find some way out. Her mother, by the way, would've dragged her out of Central High by the hair if she'd found out about the drama classes; we all had to swear to keep that strictly on the q.t. The theater was more sinful and wicked than dancing, I guess.

You know, I think it shocked me. It really did. Al's family was sort-of-nothing-really Catholic and mine was sort-of-nothing Jewish. I'd never met anybody with a mamma like that. I mean she would've beaten Cissie up if Cissie had ever come home with a gold circle pin on that white blouse she wore day in and day out; you remember the kind all the girls wore. And of course there were no horsehair petticoats for Miss Jackson; Miss Jackson wore pleated skirts that were much too short, even for her, and straight skirts that looked faded and all bunched up. For a while I had some vague idea that the short skirts meant she was daring, you know, sexy, but it wasn't that; they were from a much younger cousin, let down. She just couldn't afford her own clothes. I think it was the mamma and the Bible business that finally made me stop seeing Cissie as the Integration Prize Nut we had to be nice to because of the principal or the scared little rabbit who still, by the way, whispered everyplace but in drama class. I just saw Cecilia Jackson plain, I guess, not that it lasted for more than a few minutes, but I knew she was something special. So one day in the hall, going from one class to another, I met her and Al and I said, "Cissie, your name is going to be up there in lights someday. I think you're the best actress I ever met and I just want to say it's a privilege knowing you." And then I swept her a big corny bow, like Errol Flynn.

She looked at Al and Al looked at her, sort of sly. Then she let down her head over her books and giggled. She was so tiny you sometimes wondered how she could drag those books around all day; they hunched her over so.

Al said, "Aw, come on. Let's tell him."

So they told me their big secret. Cissie had a girl cousin named Gloriette, and Gloriette and Cissie together owned an honest-to-God slip for a boat in the marina out in Silverhampton. Each of them paid half the slip fee—which was about two bucks a month then, Milt—you have to remember that a marina then just meant a long wooden dock you could tie your rowboat up to.

"Gloriette's away," said Cissie, in that whisper. "She had to go visit auntie, in Carolina. And mamma's goin' to follow her next week on Sunday."

"So we're going to go out in the boat!" Al finished it for her. "You wanna come?"

"Sunday?"

"Sure, mamma will go to the bus station after church," said Cissie. "That's about one o'clock. Aunt Evelyn comes to take care of me at nine. So we have eight hours."

"And it takes two hours to get there," said Al. "First you take the subway; then you take a bus—"

"Unless we use your car, Jim!" said Cissie, laughing so hard she dropped her books.

"Well, thanks very much!" I said. She scooped them up again and smiled at me. "No, Jim," she said. "We want you to come, anyway. Al never saw the boat yet. Gloriette and me, we call it *My Boat*." Fifteen years old and she knew how to smile at you so's to twist your heart like a pretzel. Or maybe I just thought: what a wicked secret to have! A big sin, I guess, according to her family.

I said, "Sure, I'll drive you. May I ask what kind of boat it is, Miss Jackson?"

"Don't be so *damn'* silly," she said daringly. "I'm Cissie or Cecilia. Silly Jim.

"And as for *My Boat*," she added, "it's a big yacht. Enormous."

I was going to laugh at that, but then I saw she meant it. No, she was just playing. She was smiling wickedly at me again. She said we should meet at the bus stop near her house, and then she went down the tiled hall next to skinny little Al Coppolino, in her old baggy green skirt and her always-the-same white blouse. No beautiful, big white sloppy bobby socks for Miss Jackson; she just wore old loafers coming apart at the seams. She looked different, though: her head was up, her step springy, and she hadn't been whispering.

And then it occurred to me it was the first time I had ever seen her smile or laugh—offstage. Mind you, she cried easily enough, like the time in class she realized from something the teacher had said that Anton Chekhov—you know, the great Russian playwright—was dead. I heard her telling Alan later that she didn't believe it. There were lots of little crazy things like that.

Well, I picked her up Sunday in what was probably the oldest car in the world, even then—not a museum piece, Milty; it'd still be a mess—frankly I was lucky to get it started at all—and when I got to the bus station near Cissie's house in Brooklyn, there she was in her faded, hand-me-down, pleated skirt and that same blouse. I guess little elves named Cecilia Jackson came out of the woodwork every night and washed and ironed it. Funny, she and Al really did make a pair—you know, he was like the Woody Allen of Central High and I think he went in for his crazy books—sure, Milt, *very* crazy in 1952—because otherwise what could a little Italian punk do who was five foot three and so brilliant no other kid could understand half the time what he was talking about? I don't know why I was friends with him; I think it made me feel big, you know, generous and good, like being friends with Cissie. They were almost the same size, waiting there by the bus stop, and I think their heads were in the same place. I know it now. I guess he was just a couple of decades ahead of himself, like his books. And maybe if the civil rights movement had started a few years earlier—

Anyway, we drove out to Silverhampton and it was a nice drive, lots of country, though all flat—in those days there were still truck farms on the Island—and found the marina, which was nothing more than a big old quay, but sound enough; and I parked the car and Al took out a shopping bag Cissie'd been carrying. "Lunch," he said.

My Boat was there, all right, halfway down the dock. Somehow I hadn't expected it would exist, even. It was an old leaky wooden rowboat with only one oar, and there were three inches of bilge in the bottom. On the bow somebody had painted the name "My Boat" shakily in orange paint. *My Boat* was tied to the mooring by a rope about as sturdy as a piece of string. Still, it didn't look like it would sink right away; after all, it'd been sitting there for months, getting rained on, maybe even snowed on, and it was still floating. So I stepped down into it, wishing I'd had the sense to take off my shoes, and started bailing with a tin can I'd brought from the car. Alan and Cissie were taking things out of the bag in the middle of the boat. I guess they were setting out lunch. It was pretty clear that *My Boat* spent most of its time sitting at the dock while Cissie and Gloriette ate lunch and maybe pretended they were on the *Queen Mary*, because neither Alan nor Cissie seemed to notice the missing oar. It was a nice day but in-and-outish; you know, clouds one minute, sun the next, but little fluffy clouds, no sign of rain. I bailed a lot of the gunk out and then moved up into the bow, and as the sun came out I saw that I'd been wrong about the orange paint. It was yellow.

Then I looked closer: it wasn't paint but something set into the side of *My Boat* like the names on people's office doors; I guess I must've not looked too closely the first time. It was a nice, flowing script, a real professional job. Brass, I guess. Not a plate, Milt, kind of—what do they call it, parquet? Intaglio? Each letter was put in separately. Must've been Alan; he had a talent for stuff like that, used to make weird illustrations for his crazy books. I turned around to find Al and Cissie taking a big piece of cheesecloth out of the shopping bag and draping it over high poles that were built into the sides of the boat. They were making a kind of awning. I said:

"Hey, I bet you took that from the theater shop!"

She just smiled.

Al said, "Would you get us some fresh water, Jim?"

"Sure," I said. "Where, up the dock?"

"No, from the bucket. Back in the stern. Cissie says it's marked."

Oh, sure, I thought, sure. Out in the middle of the Pacific we set out our bucket and pray for rain. There was a pail there all right, and somebody had laboriously stenciled "Fresh Water" on it in green paint, sort of smudgy, but that pail was never going to hold anything ever again. It was bone-dry, empty, and so badly rusted that when you held it up to the light, you could see through the bottom in a couple of places. I said, "Cissie, it's empty."

She said, "Look again, Jim."

I said, "But look, Cissie—" and turned the bucket upside-down.

Cold water drenched me from my knees to the soles of my shoes.

"See?" she said. "Never empty." I thought: Hell, I didn't look, that's all. Maybe it rained yesterday. Still, a full pail of water is heavy and I had lifted that thing with one finger. I set it down—if it had been full before, it certainly wasn't now—and looked again.

It was full, right to the brim. I dipped my hand into the stuff and drank a little of it: cold and clear as spring water and it smelled—I don't know—of ferns warmed by the sun, of raspberries, of field flowers, of grass. I thought: my God, I'm becoming a filbert myself! And then I turned around and saw that Alan and Cissie had replaced the cheesecloth on the poles with a striped blue-and-white awning, the kind you see in movies about Cleopatra, you know? The stuff they put over her barge to keep the sun off. And Cissie had taken out of her shopping bag something patterned orange-and-green-and-blue and had wrapped it around her old clothes. She had on gold-colored earrings, big hoop things, and a black turban over that funny hair. And she must've put her loafers somewhere because she was barefoot. Then I saw that she had one shoulder bare, too, and I sat down on one of the marble benches of *My Boat* under the awning because I was probably having hallucinations. I mean she hadn't had *time*—and where were her old clothes? I thought to myself that they must've lifted a whole bagful of stuff from the theater shop, like that big old wicked-looking knife she had stuck into her amber-studded leather belt, the hilt all covered with gold and stones: red ones, green ones, and blue ones with little crosses of light winking in them that you couldn't really follow with your eyes. I didn't know what the blue ones were then, but I know now. You don't make star sapphires in a theater shop. Or a ten-inch crescent-shaped steel blade so sharp the sun dazzles you coming off its edge.

I said, "Cissie, you look like the Queen of Sheba."

She smiled. She said to me, "Jim, iss not Shee-bah as in thee Bible, but Saba. Sah-bah. You mus' remember when we meet her."

I thought to myself: Yeah, this is where little old girl genius Cissie Jackson comes to freak out every Sunday. Lost weekend. I figured this was the perfect time to get away, make some excuse, you know, and call her mamma or her auntie, or maybe just the nearest hospital. I mean just for her own sake; Cissie wouldn't hurt anybody because she wasn't mean, not ever. And anyhow she was too little to hurt anyone. I stood up.

Her eyes were level with mine. And she was standing below me.

Al said, "Be careful, Jim. Look again. Always look again." I went back to the stern. There was the bucket that said "Fresh Water," but as I looked the sun came out and I saw I'd been mistaken; it wasn't old rusty galvanized iron with splotchy, green-painted letters.

It was silver, pure silver. It was sitting in a sort of marble well built into the stern, and the letters were jade inlay. It was still full. It would always be full. I looked back at Cissie standing under the blue-and-white-striped silk awning with her star sapphires and emeralds and rubies in her dagger and her funny talk—I know it now, Milt, it was West Indian, but I didn't then—and I knew as sure as if I'd seen it that if I looked at the letters "My Boat" in the sun, they wouldn't be brass but pure gold. And the wood would be ebony. I wasn't even surprised. Although everything had changed, you understand, I'd never seen it change; it was either that I hadn't looked carefully the first time, or I'd made a mistake, or I hadn't noticed something, or I'd just forgotten. Like what I thought had been an old crate in the middle of *My Boat*, which was really the roof of a cabin with little portholes in it, and looking in I saw three bunk beds below, a closet, and a beautiful little galley with a refrigerator and a stove, and off to one side in the sink, where I couldn't really see it clearly, a bottle with a napkin around its neck, sticking up from an ice bucket full of crushed ice, just like an old Fred Astaire–Ginger Rogers movie. And the whole inside of the cabin was paneled in teakwood.

Cissie said, "No, Jim. Is not teak. Is cedar, from Lebanon. You see now why I cannot take seriously in this school this nonsense about places and where they are and what happen in them. Crude oil in Lebanon! It is cedar they have. And ivory. I have been there many, many time. I have talk' with the wise Solomon. I have been at court of Queen of Saba and have made eternal treaty with the Knossos women, the people of the double ax which is waxing and waning moon together. I have visit Akhnaton and Nofretari, and have seen great kings at Benin and at Dar. I even go to Atlantis, where the Royal Couple teach me many things. The priest and priestess, they show me how to make *My Boat* go anywhere I like, even under the sea. Oh, we have many improvin' chats upon roof of Pahlahss at dusk!"

It was real. It was all real. She was not fifteen, Milt. She sat in the bow at the controls of *My Boat*, and there were as many dials and toggles and buttons and switches and gauges on that thing as on a B-57. And she was at least ten years older. Al Coppolino, too, he looked like a picture I'd seen in a history book of Sir Francis Drake, and he had long hair and a little pointy beard. He was dressed like Drake, except for the ruff, with rubies in his ears and rings all over his fingers, and he, too, was no seventeen-year-old. He had a faint scar running from his left temple at the hairline down past his eye to his cheekbone. I could also see that under her turban Cissie's hair was braided in some very fancy way. I've seen it since. Oh, long before everybody was doing "corn rows." I saw it at the Metropolitan Museum, in silver face-mask sculptures from the city of Benin, in Africa. Old, Milt, centuries old.

Al said, "I know of other places, Princess. I can show them to you. Oh, let us go to Ooth-Nargai and Celephaïs the Fair, and Kadath in the Cold Waste—it's a fearful place, Jim, but *we* need not be afraid—and then we will go to the city of Ulthar, where is the very fortunate and lovely law that no man or woman may kill or annoy a cat."

"The Atlanteans," said Cissie in a deep, sweet voice, "they promise' that next time they show me not jus' how to go undersea. They say if you think hard, if you fix much, if you believe, then can make *My Boat* go straight up. Into the stars, Jim!"

Al Coppolino was chanting names under his breath: Cathuria, Sona-Nyl, Thalarion, Zar, Baharna, Nir, Oriab. All out of those books of his.

Cissie said, "Before you come with us, you must do one last thing, Jim. Untie the rope."

So I climbed down *My Boat*'s ladder onto the quay and undid the braided gold rope that was fastened to the slip. Gold and silk intertwined, Milt; it rippled through my hand as if it were alive; I know the hard, slippery feel of silk. I was thinking of Atlantis and Celephaïs and going up into the stars, and all of it was mixed up in my head with the senior prom and college, because I had been lucky enough to be accepted by The-College-Of-My-Choice, and what a future I'd have as a lawyer, a corporation lawyer, after being a big gridiron star, of course. Those were my plans in the old days. Dead certainties every one, right? Versus a thirty-five-foot yacht that would've made John D. Rockefeller turn green with envy and places in the world where nobody'd ever been and nobody'd ever go again. Cissie and Al stood on deck above me, the both of them looking like something out of a movie—beautiful and dangerous and very strange—and suddenly I knew I didn't want to go. Part of it was the absolute certainty that if I ever offended Cissie in any way—I don't mean just a quarrel or disagreement or something you'd get the sulks about, but a real bone-deep kind of offense—I'd suddenly find myself in a leaky rowboat with only one oar in the middle of the Pacific Ocean. Or maybe just tied up at the dock at Silverhampton; Cissie wasn't mean. At least I hoped so. I just—I guess I didn't feel *good* enough to go. And there was something about their faces, too, as if over both of them, but especially over Cissie's, like clouds, like veils, there swam other faces, other expressions, other souls, other pasts and futures, and other kinds of knowledge, all of them shifting like a heat mirage over an asphalt road on a hot day.

I didn't want that knowledge, Milt. I didn't want to go that deep. It was the kind of thing most seventeen-year-olds don't learn for years: Beauty. Despair. Mortality. Compassion. Pain.

And I was still looking up at them, watching the breeze fill out Al Coppolino's plum-colored velvet cloak and shine on his silver-and-black doublet, when a big, heavy, hard, fat hand clamped down on my shoulder and a big, fat, nasty, heavy Southern voice said:

"Hey, boy, you got no permit for this slip! What's that rowboat doin' out there? And what's yo' name?"

So I turned and found myself looking into the face of the great-granddaddy of all Southern red-neck sheriffs: face like a bulldog with jowls to match, and sunburnt red, and fat as a pig, and mountain-mean. I said, "Sir?"—every high-school kid could say that in his sleep in those days—and then we turned towards the bay, me saying, "What boat, sir?" and the cop saying just, "What the—"

Because there was nothing there. *My Boat* was gone. There was only a blue shimmering stretch of bay. They weren't out farther and they weren't around the other side of the dock—the cop and I both ran around—and by the time I had presence of mind enough to look up at the sky—

Nothing. A seagull. A cloud. A plane out of Idlewild. Besides, hadn't Cissie said she didn't yet know how to go straight up into the stars?

No, nobody ever saw *My Boat* again. Or Miss Cecilia Jackson, complete nut and girl genius, either. Her mamma came to school and I was called into the principal's office. I told them a cooked-up story, the one I'd been going to tell the cop: that they'd said they were just going to row around the dock and come back, and I'd left to see if the car was okay in the parking lot, and when I came back, they were gone. For some crazy reason I *still* thought Cissie's mamma would look like Aunt Jemima, but she was a thin little woman, very like her daughter, and as nervous and uptight as I ever saw: a tiny lady in a much-pressed, but very clean, gray business suit, like a teacher's, you know, worn-out shoes, a blouse with a white frill at the neck, a straw hat with a white band, and proper white gloves. I think Cissie knew what I expected her mamma to be and what a damned fool I was, even considering your run-of-the-mill, seventeen-year-old white liberal racist, and that's why she didn't take me along.

The cop? He followed me to my car, and by the time I got there—I was sweating and crazy scared—

He was gone, too. Vanished.

I think Cissie created him. Just for a joke.

So Cissie never came back. And I couldn't convince Mrs. Jackson that Alan Coppolino, boy rapist, hadn't carried her daughter off to some lonely place and murdered her. I tried and tried, but Mrs. Jackson would never believe me.

It turned out there was no Cousin Gloriette.

Alan? Oh, he came back. But it took him a while. A long, long while. I saw him yesterday, Milt, on the Brooklyn subway. A skinny, short guy with ears that stuck out, still wearing the sport shirt and pants he'd started out in, that Sunday more than twenty years ago, and with the real 1950s haircut nobody would wear today. Quite a few people were staring at him, in fact.

The thing is, Milt, *he was still seventeen.*

No, I know it wasn't some other kid. Because he was waving at me and smiling fit to beat the band. And when I got out with him at his old stop, he started asking after everybody in Central High just as if it had been a week later, or maybe only a day. Though when I asked him where the hell he'd been for twenty years, he wouldn't tell me. He only said he'd forgotten something. So we went up five flights to his old apartment, the way we used to after school for a couple of hours before his mom and dad came home from work. He had the old key in his pocket. And it was just the same, Milt: the gas refrigerator, the exposed pipes under the sink, the summer slipcovers nobody uses anymore, the winter drapes put away, the valance over the window muffled in a sheet, the bare parquet floors, and the old linoleum in the kitchen. Every time I'd ask him a question, he'd only smile. He knew me, though, because he called me by name a couple of times. I said, "How'd you recognize me?" and he said, "Recognize? You haven't changed." Haven't changed, my God. Then I said, "Look, Alan, what did you come back for?" and with a grin just like Cissie's, he said, "The *Necronomicon* by the mad Arab, Abdul Alhazred, what else?" but I saw the book he took with him and it was a different one. He was careful to get just the right one, looked through every shelf in the bookcase in his bedroom. There were still college banners all over the walls of his room. I know the book now, by the way; it was the one you wanted to make into a quick script last year for the guy who does the Poe movies, only I *told* you it was all special effects and animation: exotic islands, strange worlds, and the monsters' costumes alone—sure, H. P. Lovecraft. *The Dream-Quest of Unknown Kadath.* He didn't say a word after that. Just walked down the five flights with me behind him and then along the old block to the nearest subway station, but of course by the time I reached the bottom of the subway steps, he wasn't there.

His apartment? You'll never find it. When I raced back up, even the house was gone. More than that, Milt, the street is gone; the address doesn't exist anymore; it's all part of the new expressway now.

Which is why I called you. My God, I had to tell somebody! By now those two psychiatric cases are voyaging around between the stars to Ulthar and Ooth-Nargai and Dylath-Leen—

But they're not psychiatric cases. *It really happened.*

So if they're not psychiatric cases, what does that make you and me? Blind men?

I'll tell you something else, Milt: meeting Al reminded me of what Cissie once said before the whole thing with *My Boat* but after we'd become friends enough for me to ask her what had brought her out of the hospital. I didn't ask it like that and she didn't answer it like that, but what it boiled down to was that sooner or later, at every place she visited, she'd meet a bleeding man with wounds in his hands and feet who would tell her, "Cissie, go back, you're needed; Cissie, go back, you're needed." I was fool enough to ask her if he was a white man or a black man. She just glared at me and walked away. Now wounds in the hands and feet, you don't have to look far to tell what that means to a Christian Bible-raised girl. What I wonder is: will she meet Him again, out there among the stars? If things get bad enough for black power or women's liberation, or even for people who write crazy books, I don't know what, will *My Boat* materialize over Times Square or Harlem or East New York with an Ethiopian warrior-queen in it and Sir Francis Drake Coppolino, and God-only-knows-what kind of weapons from the lost science of Atlantis? I tell you, I wouldn't be surprised. I really wouldn't. I only hope He—or Cissie's idea of Him—decides that things are still okay, and they can go on visiting all those places in Al Coppolino's book. I tell you, I hope that book is a *long* book.

Still, if I could do it again. . . .

Milt, it is not a story. *It happened.* For instance, tell me one thing, how did she know the name Nofretari? That's the Egyptian Queen Nefertiti, that's how we all learned it, but how could she know the real name decades, literally decades, before anybody else? And Saba? That's real, too. And Benin? We didn't have any courses in African History in Central High, not in 1952! And what about the double-headed ax of the Cretans at Knossos? Sure, we read about Crete in high school, but nothing in our history books ever told us about the matriarchy or the labrys, that's the name of the ax. Milt, I tell you, there is even a women's lib bookstore in Manhattan *called*—

Have it your own way.

Oh, sure. She wasn't black; she was green. It'd make a great TV show. Green, blue, and rainbow-colored. I'm sorry, Milty, I know you're my agent and you've done a lot of work for me and I haven't sold much lately. I've been reading. No, nothing you'd like: existentialism, history, Marxism, some Eastern stuff—

Sorry, Milt, but we writers do read every once in a while. It's this little vice we have. I've been trying to dig deep, like Al Coppolino, though maybe in a different way.

Okay, so you want to have this Martian, who wants to invade Earth, so he turns himself into a beautiful tanned girl with long, straight blonde hair, right? And becomes a high-school student in a rich school in Westchester. And this beautiful blonde girl Martian has to get into all the local organizations like the women's consciousness-raising groups and the encounter therapy stuff and the cheerleaders and the kids who push dope, so he—she, rather—can learn about the Earth mentality. Yeah. And of course she has to seduce the principal and the coach and all the big men on campus, so we can make it into a series, even a sitcom maybe; each week this Martian falls in love with an Earthman or she tries to do something to destroy Earth or blow up something, using Central High for a base. Can I use it? Sure I can! It's beautiful. It's right in my line. I can work in everything I just told you. Cissie was right not to take me along; I've got spaghetti where my backbone should be.

Nothing. I didn't say anything. Sure. It's a great idea. Even if we only get a pilot out of it.

No, Milt, honestly, I really think it has this fantastic spark. A real touch of genius. It'll sell like crazy. Yeah, I can manage an idea sheet by Monday. Sure. "The Beautiful Menace from Mars"? Uh-huh. Absolutely. It's got sex, it's got danger, comedy, everything; we could branch out into the lives of the teachers, the principal, the other kids' parents. Bring in contemporary problems like drug abuse. Sure. Another Peyton Place. I'll even move to the West Coast again. You are a genius.

Oh, my God.

Nothing. Keep on talking. It's just—see that little skinny kid in the next booth down? The one with the stuck-out ears and the old-fashioned haircut? You don't? Well, I think you're just not looking properly, Milt. Actually I don't think I was, either; he must be one of the Met extras, you know, they come out sometimes during the intermission: all that Elizabethan stuff, the plum-colored cloak, the calf-high boots, the silver-and-black. As a matter of fact, I just remembered—the Met moved uptown a couple of years ago, so he couldn't be dressed like that, could he?

You still can't see him? I'm not surprised. The light's very bad in here. Listen, he's an old friend—I mean he's the son of an old friend—I better go over and say hello, I won't be a minute.

Milt, this young man is important! I mean he's connected with somebody very important. Who? One of the biggest and best producers in the world, that's who! He—uh—they—wanted me to—you might call it do a script for them, yeah. I didn't want to at the time, but—

No, no, you stay right here. I'll just sort of lean over and say hello. You keep on talking about the Beautiful Menace from Mars; I can listen from there; I'll just tell him they can have me if they want me.

Your ten percent? Of course you'll get your ten percent. You're my agent, aren't you? Why, if it wasn't for you, I just possibly might not have— Sure, you'll get your ten percent. Spend it on anything you like: ivory, apes, peacocks, spices, and Lebanese cedarwood!

All you have to do is collect it.

But keep on talking, Milty, won't you? Somehow I want to go over to the next booth with the sound of your voice in my ears. Those beautiful ideas. So original. So creative. So true. Just what the public wants. Of course there's a difference in the way people perceive things, and you and I, I think we perceive them differently, you know? Which is why you are a respected, successful agent and I—well, let's skip it. It wouldn't be complimentary to either of us.

Huh? Oh, nothing. I didn't say anything. I'm listening. Over my shoulder. Just keep on talking while I say hello and my deepest and most abject apologies, Sir Alan Coppolino. Heard the name before, Milt? No? I'm not surprised.

You just keep on talking. . . .

Sticks*

KARL EDWARD WAGNER

I

The lashed-together framework of sticks jutted from a small cairn alongside the stream. Colin Leverett studied it in perplexment—half a dozen odd lengths of branch, wired together at cross angles for no fathomable purpose. It reminded him unpleasantly of some bizarre crucifix, and he wondered what might lie beneath the cairn.

It was the spring of 1942—the kind of day to make the War seem distant and unreal, although the draft notice waited on his desk. In a few days Leverett would lock his rural studio, wonder if he would see it again—be able to use its pens and brushes and carving tools when he did return. It was goodby to the woods and streams of upstate New York, too. No fly rods, no tramps through the countryside in Hitler's Europe. No point in putting off fishing that trout stream he had driven past once, exploring back roads of the Otselic Valley.

Mann Brook—so it was marked on the old Geological Survey map—ran southeast of DeRuyter. The unfrequented country road crossed over a stone bridge old before the first horseless carriage, but Leverett's Ford eased across and onto the shoulder. Taking fly rod and tackle, he included pocket flask and tied an iron skillet to his belt. He'd work his way downstream a few miles. By afternoon he'd lunch on fresh trout, maybe some bullfrog legs.

It was a fine clear stream, though difficult to fish as dense bushes hung out from the bank, broken with stretches of open water hard to work without being seen. But the trout rose boldly to his fly, and Leverett was in fine spirits.

From the bridge the valley along Mann Brook began as fairly open pasture, but half a mile downstream the land had fallen into disuse and

*Originally published in *Whispers*, March 1974.

was thick with second-growth evergreens and scrub-apple trees. Another mile, and the scrub merged with dense forest, which continued unbroken. The land here, he had learned, had been taken over by the state many years back.

As Leverett followed the stream he noted the remains of an old railroad embankment. No vestige of tracks or ties—only the embankment itself, overgrown with large trees. The artist rejoiced in the beautiful dry-wall culverts spanning the stream as it wound through the valley. To his mind it seemed eerie, this forgotten railroad running straight and true through virtual wilderness.

He could imagine an old wood-burner with its conical stack, steaming along through the valley dragging two or three wooden coaches. It must be a branch of the old Oswego Midland Rail Road, he decided, abandoned rather suddenly in the 1870s. Leverett, who had a memory for detail, knew of it from a story his grandfather told of riding the line in 1871 from Otselic to DeRuyter on his honeymoon. The engine had so labored up the steep grade over Crumb Hill that he got off to walk alongside. Probably that sharp grade was the reason for the line's abandonment.

When he came across a scrap of board nailed to several sticks set into a stone wall, his darkest thought was that it might read "No Trespassing." Curiously, though the board was weathered featureless, the nails seemed quite new. Leverett scarcely gave it much thought, until a short distance beyond he came upon another such contrivance. And another.

Now he scratched at the day's stubble on his long jaw. This didn't make sense. A prank? But on whom? A child's game? No, the arrangement was far too sophisticated. As an artist, Leverett appreciated the craftsmanship of the work—the calculated angles and lengths, the designed intricacy of the maddeningly inexplicable devices. There was something distinctly uncomfortable about their effect.

Leverett reminded himself that he had come here to fish and continued downstream. But as he worked around a thicket he again stopped in puzzlement.

Here was a small open space with more of the stick lattices and an arrangement of flat stones laid out on the ground. The stones—likely taken from one of the many dry-wall culverts—made a pattern maybe twenty by fifteen feet, that at first glance resembled a ground plan for a house. Intrigued, Leverett quickly saw that this was not so. If the ground plan for anything, it would have to be for a small maze.

The bizarre lattice structures were all around. Sticks from trees and bits of board nailed together in fantastic array. They defied description; no two seemed alike. Some were only one or two sticks lashed together in parallel or at angles. Others were worked into complicated lattices of dozens of sticks and boards. One could have been a child's tree house—it was built in three planes, but was so abstract and useless that it could be nothing more than an insane conglomeration of sticks and wire. Sometimes the contrivances were stuck in a pile of stones or a wall, maybe thrust into the railroad embankment or nailed to a tree.

It should have been ridiculous. It wasn't. Instead it seemed somehow sinister—these utterly inexplicable, meticulously constructed lattices spread through a wilderness where only a tree-grown embankment or a forgotten stone wall gave evidence that man had ever passed through. Leverett forgot about trout and frog legs, instead dug into his pockets for a notebook and stub of pencil. Busily he began to sketch the more intricate structures. Perhaps someone could explain them; perhaps there was something to their insane complexity that warranted closer study for his own work.

Leverett was roughly two miles from the bridge when he came upon the ruins of a house. It was an unlovely colonial farmhouse, box-shaped and gambrel-roofed, fast falling into the ground. Windows were dark and empty; the chimneys on either end looked ready to topple. Rafters showed through open spaces in the roof, and the weathered boards of the walls had in places rotted away to reveal hewn timber beams. The foundation was stone and disproportionately massive. From the size of the unmortared stone blocks, its builder had intended the foundation to stand forever.

The house was nearly swallowed up by undergrowth and rampant lilac bushes, but Leverett could distinguish what had been a lawn with imposing shade trees. Farther back were gnarled and sickly apple trees and an overgrown garden where a few lost flowers still bloomed—wan and serpentine from years in the wild. The stick lattices were everywhere—the lawn, the trees, even the house, were covered with the uncanny structures. They reminded Leverett of a hundred misshapen spiderwebs—grouped so closely together as to almost ensnare the entire house and clearing. Wondering, he sketched page on page of them, as he cautiously approached the abandoned house.

He wasn't certain just what he expected to find inside. The aspect of the farmhouse was frankly menacing, standing as it did in gloomy desolation where the forest had devoured the works of man—where the only sign that man had been here in this century were these insanely wrought latticeworks of sticks and board. Some might have turned back at this point. Leverett, whose fascination for the macabre was evident in his art, instead was intrigued. He drew a rough sketch of the farmhouse and the grounds, overrun with the enigmatic devices, with thickets of hedges and distorted flowers. He regretted that it might be years before he could capture the eeriness of this place on scratchboard or canvas.

The door was off its hinges, and Leverett gingerly stepped within, hoping that the flooring remained sound enough to bear even his sparse frame. The afternoon sun pierced the empty windows, mottling the decaying floorboards with great blotches of light. Dust drifted in the sunlight. The house was empty—stripped of furnishings other than indistinct tangles of rubble mounded over with decay and the drifted leaves of many seasons.

Someone had been here, and recently. Someone who had literally covered the mildewed walls with diagrams of the mysterious lattice structures. The drawings were applied directly to the walls, criss-crossing the rotting wallpaper and crumbling plaster in bold black lines. Some of vertiginous complexity covered an entire wall like a mad mural. Others were small, only a few crossed lines, and reminded Leverett of cuneiform glyphics.

His pencil hurried over the pages of his notebook. Leverett noted with fascination that a number of the drawings were recognizable as schematics of lattices he had earlier sketched. Was this then the planning room for the madman or educated idiot who had built these structures? The gouges etched by the charcoal into the soft plaster appeared fresh—done days or months ago, perhaps.

A darkened doorway opened into the cellar. Were there drawings there as well? And what else? Leverett wondered if he should dare it. Except for streamers of light that crept through cracks in the flooring, the cellar was in darkness.

"Hello?" he called. "Anyone here?" It didn't seem silly just then. These stick lattices hardly seemed the work of a rational mind. Leverett wasn't enthusiastic with the prospect of encountering such a person in this dark cellar. It occurred to him that virtually anything might transpire here, and no one in the world of 1942 would ever know.

And that in itself was too great a fascination for one of Leverett's temperament. Carefully he started down the cellar stairs. They were stone and thus solid, but treacherous with moss and debris.

The cellar was enormous—even more so in the darkness. Leverett reached the foot of the steps and paused for his eyes to adjust to the damp gloom. An earlier impression recurred to him. The cellar was too big for the house. Had another dwelling stood here originally—perhaps destroyed and rebuilt by one of lesser fortune? He examined the stonework. Here were great blocks of gneiss that might support a castle. On closer look they reminded him of a fortress—for the dry-wall technique was startlingly Mycenaean.

Like the house above, the cellar appeared to be empty, although without light Leverett could not be certain what the shadows hid. There seemed to be darker areas of shadow along sections of the foundation wall, suggesting openings to chambers beyond. Leverett began to feel uneasy in spite of himself.

There was something here—a large table-like bulk in the center of the cellar. Where a few ghosts of sunlight drifted down to touch its edges, it seemed to be of stone. Cautiously he crossed the stone paving to where it loomed—waist-high, maybe eight feet long and less wide. A roughly shaped slab of gneiss, he judged, and supported by pillars of unmortared stone. In the darkness he could only get a vague conception of the object. He ran his hand along the slab. It seemed to have a groove along its edge.

His groping fingers encountered fabric, something cold and leathery and yielding. Mildewed harness, he guessed in distaste.

Something closed on his wrist, set icy nails into his flesh.

Leverett screamed and lunged away with frantic strength. He was held fast, but the object on the stone slab pulled upward.

A sickly beam of sunlight came down to touch one end of the slab. It was enough. As Leverett struggled backward and the thing that held him heaved up from the stone table, its face passed through the beam of light.

It was a lich's face—desiccated flesh tight over its skull. Filthy strands of hair were matted over its scalp, tattered lips were drawn away from broken yellowed teeth, and, sunken in their sockets, eyes that should be dead were bright with hideous life.

Leverett screamed again, desperate with fear. His free hand clawed the iron skillet tied to his belt. Ripping it loose, he smashed at the nightmarish face with all his strength.

For one frozen instant of horror the sunlight let him see the skillet crush through the mould-eaten forehead like an axe—cleaving the dry flesh and brittle bone. The grip on his wrist failed. The cadaverous face fell away, and the sight of its caved-in forehead and unblinking eyes from between which thick blood had begun to ooze would awaken Leverett from nightmare on countless nights.

But now Leverett tore free and fled. And when his aching legs faltered as he plunged headlong through the scrub-growth, he was spurred to desperate energy by the memory of the footsteps that had stumbled up the cellar stairs behind him.

II

When Colin Leverett returned from the War, his friends marked him a changed man. He had aged. There were streaks of gray in his hair; his springy step had slowed. The athletic leanness of his body had withered to an unhealthy gauntness. There were indelible lines to his face, and his eyes were haunted.

More disturbing was an alteration of temperament. A mordant cynicism had eroded his earlier air of whimsical asceticism. His fascination with the macabre had assumed a darker mood, a morbid obsession that his old acquaintances found disquieting. But it had been that kind of a war, especially for those who had fought through the Apennines.

Leverett might have told them otherwise, had he cared to discuss his nightmarish experience on Mann Brook. But Leverett kept his own counsel, and when he grimly recalled that creature he had struggled with in the abandoned cellar, he usually convinced himself it had only been a derelict—a crazy hermit whose appearance had been distorted by the poor light and his own imagination. Nor had his blow more than glanced off the man's forehead, he reasoned, since the other had recovered quickly enough to give chase. It was best not to dwell upon such matters, and this rational explanation helped restore sanity when he awoke from nightmares of that face.

Thus Colin Leverett returned to his studio, and once more plied his pens and brushes and carving knives. The pulp magazines, where fans had acclaimed his work before the War, welcomed him back with long lists of assignments. There were commissions from galleries and collectors, unfinished sculptures and wooden models. Leverett busied himself.

There were problems now. *Short Stories* returned a cover painting as "too grotesque." The publishers of a new anthology of horror stories sent back a pair of his interior drawings—"too gruesome, especially the rotted, bloated faces of those hanged men." A customer returned a silver figurine, complaining that the martyred saint was too thoroughly martyred. Even *Weird Tales*, after heralding his return to its ghoul-haunted pages, began returning illustrations they considered "too strong, even for our readers."

Leverett tried halfheartedly to tone things down, found the results vapid and uninspired. Eventually the assignments stopped trickling in. Leverett, becoming more the recluse as years went by, dismissed the pulp days from his mind. Working quietly in his isolated studio, he found a living doing occasional commissioned pieces and gallery work, from time to time selling a painting or sculpture to major museums. Critics had much praise for his bizarre abstract sculptures.

III

The War was twenty-five years history when Colin Leverett received a letter from a good friend of the pulp days—Prescott Brandon, now editor-publisher of Gothic House, a small press that specialized in books of the weird-fantasy genre. Despite a lapse in correspondence of many years, Brandon's letter began in his typically direct style:

The Eyrie/Salem, Mass./Aug. 2

To the Macabre Hermit of the Midlands:

Colin, I'm putting together a deluxe 3-volume collection of H. Kenneth Allard's horror stories. I well recall that Kent's stories were personal favorites of yours. How about shambling forth from retirement and illustrating these for me? Will need 2-color jackets and a dozen line interiors each. Would hope that you can startle fandom with some especially ghastly drawings for these—something different from the hackneyed skulls and bats and werewolves carting off half-dressed ladies.

Interested? I'll send you the materials and details, and you can have a free hand. Let us hear—Scotty.

Leverett was delighted. He felt some nostalgia for the pulp days, and he had always admired Allard's genius in transforming visions of cosmic horror into convincing prose. He wrote Brandon an enthusiastic reply.

He spent hours rereading the stories for inclusion, making notes and preliminary sketches. No squeamish sub-editors to offend here; Scotty meant what he said. Leverett bent to his task with maniacal relish.

Something different, Scotty had asked. A free hand. Leverett studied his pencil sketches critically. The figures seemed headed in the right direction, but the drawings needed something more—something that would inject the mood of sinister evil that pervaded Allard's work. Grinning skulls and leathery bats? Trite. Allard demanded more.

The idea had inexorably taken hold of him. Perhaps because Allard's tales evoked that same sense of horror; perhaps because Allard's visions of crumbling Yankee farmhouses and their depraved secrets so reminded him of that spring afternoon at Mann Brook. . . .

Although he had refused to look at it since the day he had staggered in, half-dead from terror and exhaustion, Leverett perfectly recalled where he had flung his notebook. He retrieved it from the back of a seldom-used file, thumbed through the wrinkled pages thoughtfully. These hasty sketches reawakened the sense of foreboding evil, the charnel horror of that day. Studying the bizarre lattice patterns, it seemed impossible to Leverett that others would not share his feeling of horror that the stick structures evoked in him.

He began to sketch bits of stick latticework into his pencil roughs. The sneering faces of Allard's degenerate creatures took on an added shadow of menace. Leverett nodded, pleased with the effect.

IV

Some months afterward a letter from Brandon informed Leverett he had received the last of the Allard drawings and was enormously pleased with the work. Brandon added a postscript:

For God's sake, Colin—What is it with these insane sticks you've got poking up everywhere in the illos! The damn things get really creepy after a while. How on earth did you get onto this?

Leverett supposed he owed Brandon some explanation. Dutifully he wrote a lengthy letter, setting down the circumstances of his experience at Mann Brook—omitting only the horror that had seized his wrist in the cellar. Let Brandon think him eccentric, but not madman and murderer.

Brandon's reply was immediate:

Colin—Your account of the Mann Brook episode is fascinating—and incredible! It reads like the start of one of Allard's stories! I have taken the liberty of forwarding your letter to Alexander Stefroi in Pelham. Dr. Stefroi is an earnest scholar of this region's history—as you may already know. I'm certain your account will interest him, and he may have some light to shed on the uncanny affair.

Expect 1st volume, Voices from the Shadow, *to be ready from the binder next month. The proofs looked great. Best—Scotty.*

The following week brought a letter postmarked Pelham, Massachusetts:

A mutual friend, Prescott Brandon, forwarded your fascinating account of discovering curious sticks and stone artifacts on an abandoned farm in upstate New York. I found this most intriguing, and wonder if you recall further details? Can you relocate the exact site after 30 years? If possible, I'd like to examine the foundations this spring, as they call to mind similar megalithic sites of this region. Several of us are interested in locating what we believe are remains of megalithic construction dating back to the Bronze Age, and to determine their possible use in rituals of black magic in colonial days.

Present archaeological evidence indicates that ca. 1700–2000 BC there was an influx of Bronze Age peoples into the Northeast from Europe. We know that the Bronze Age saw the rise of an extremely advanced culture, and that as seafarers they were to have no peers until the Vikings. Remains of a megalithic culture originating in the Mediterranean can be seen in the Lion Gate in Mycenae, in the

Stonehenge, and in dolmens, passage graves, and barrow mounds throughout Europe. Moreover, this seems to have represented far more than a style of architecture peculiar to the era. Rather, it appears to have been a religious cult whose adherents worshipped a sort of earth-mother, served her with fertility rituals and sacrifices, and believed that immortality of the soul could be secured through interment in megalithic tombs.

That this culture came to America cannot be doubted from the hundreds of megalithic remnants found—and now recognized—in our region. The most important site to date is Mystery Hill in N.H., comprising a great many walls and dolmens of megalithic construction—most notably the Y Cavern barrow mound and the Sacrificial Table (see postcard). Less spectacular megalithic sites include the group of cairns and carved stones at Mineral Mt., subterranean chambers with stone passageways such as at Petersham and Shutesbury, and uncounted shaped megaliths and buried "monk's cells" throughout this region.

Of further interest, these sites seem to have retained their mystic aura for the early colonials, and numerous megalithic sites show evidence of having been used for sinister purposes by colonial sorcerers and alchemists. This became particularly true after the witchcraft persecutions drove many practitioners into the western wilderness—explaining why upstate New York and western Mass. have seen the emergence of so many cultist groups in later years.

Of particular interest here is Shadrach Ireland's "Brethren of the New Light," who believed that the world was soon to be destroyed by sinister "Powers from Outside" and that they, the elect, would then attain physical immortality. The elect who died beforehand were to have their bodies preserved on tables of stone until the "Old Ones" came forth to return them to life. We have definitely linked the megalithic sites at Shutesbury to later unwholesome practices of the New Light cult. They were absorbed in 1781 by Mother Ann Lee's Shakers, and Ireland's putrescent corpse was hauled from the stone table in his cellar and buried.

Thus I think it probable that your farmhouse may have figured in similar hidden practices. At Mystery Hill a farmhouse was built in 1826 that incorporated one dolmen in its foundations. The house burned down ca. 1848–55, and there were some unsavory local stories as to what took place there. My guess is that your farmhouse had been built over or incorporated a similar megalithic site—and that your "sticks" indicate some unknown cult still survived there. I can recall certain vague references to lattice devices figuring in secret ceremonies, but can pinpoint nothing definite. Possibly they represent a development of occult symbols to be used in certain conjurations, but this is just a guess. I suggest you consult Waite's

Ceremonial Magic *or such to see if you can recognize similar magical symbols.*

Hope this is of some use to you. Please let me hear back.

Sincerely, Alexander Stefroi.

There was a postcard enclosed—a photograph of a 4½-ton granite slab, ringed by a deep groove with a spout, identified as the Sacrificial Table at Mystery Hill. On the back Stefroi had written:

You must have found something similar to this. They are not rare—we have one in Pelham removed from a site now beneath Quabbin Reservoir. They were used for sacrifice—animal and human—and the groove is to channel blood into a bowl, presumably.

Leverett dropped the card and shuddered. Stefroi's letter reawakened the old horror, and he wished now he had let the matter lie forgotten in his files. Of course, it couldn't be forgotten—even after thirty years.

He wrote Stefroi a careful letter, thanking him for his information and adding a few minor details to his account. This spring, he promised, wondering if he would keep that promise, he would try to relocate the farmhouse on Mann Brook.

V

Spring was late that year, and it was not until early June that Colin Leverett found time to return to Mann Brook. On the surface, very little had changed in three decades. The ancient stone bridge yet stood, nor had the country lane been paved. Leverett wondered whether anyone had driven past since his terror-sped flight.

He found the old railroad grade easily as he started downstream. Thirty years, he told himself—but the chill inside him only tightened. The going was far more difficult than before. The day was unbearably hot and humid. Wading through the rank underbrush raised clouds of black flies that savagely bit him.

Evidently the stream had seen severe flooding in the past years, judging from piled logs and debris that blocked his path. Stretches were scooped out to barren rocks and gravel. Elsewhere gigantic barriers of uprooted trees and debris looked like ancient and mouldering fortifications. As he worked his way down the valley, he realized that his search would yield nothing. So intense had been the force of the long-ago flood that even the course of the stream had changed. Many of the dry-wall culverts no longer spanned the brook, but sat lost and alone far back from its present banks. Others had been knocked flat and swept away, or were buried beneath tons of rotting logs.

At one point Leverett found remnants of an apple orchard groping through weeds and bushes. He thought that the house must be close by, but here the flooding had been particularly severe, and evidently even those ponderous stone foundations had been toppled over and buried beneath debris.

Leverett finally turned back to his car. His step was lighter.

A few weeks later he received a response from Stefroi to his reported failure:

> *Forgive my tardy reply to your letter of 13 June. I have recently been pursuing inquiries which may, I hope, lead to the discovery of a previously unreported megalithic site of major significance. Naturally I am disappointed that no traces remained of the Mann Brook site. While I tried not to get my hopes up, it did seem likely that the foundations would have survived. In searching through regional data, I note that there were particularly severe flash floods in the Otselic area in July 1942 and again in May 1946. Very probably your old farmhouse with its enigmatic devices was utterly destroyed not very long after your discovery of the site. This is weird and wild country, and doubtless there is much we shall never know.*
>
> *I write this with a profound sense of personal loss over the death two nights ago of Prescott Brandon. This was a severe blow to me—as I am sure it was to you and to all who knew him. I only hope the police will catch the vicious killers who did this senseless act—evidently thieves were surprised while ransacking his office. Police believe the killers were high on drugs from the mindless brutality of their crime.*
>
> *I had just received a copy of the third Allard volume,* Unhallowed Places. *A superbly designed book, and this tragedy becomes all the more insuperable with the realization that Scotty will give the world no more such treasures. In sorrow, Alexander Stefroi.*

Leverett stared at the letter in shock. He had not received news of Brandon's death—had only a few days before opened a parcel from the publisher containing a first copy of *Unhallowed Places*. A line in Brandon's last letter recurred to him—a line that seemed amusing to him at the time:

> *Your sticks have bewildered a good many fans, Colin, and I've worn out a ribbon answering inquiries. One fellow in particular—a Major George Leonard—has pressed me for details, and I'm afraid that I*

told him too much. He has written several times for your address, but knowing how you value your privacy I told him simply to permit me to forward any correspondence. He wants to see your original sketches, I gather, but these overbearing occult-types give me a pain. Frankly, I wouldn't care to meet the man myself.

VI

"Mr. Colin Leverett?"

Leverett studied the tall lean man who stood smiling at the doorway of his studio. The sports car he had driven up in was black and looked expensive. The same held for the turtleneck and leather slacks he wore, and the sleek briefcase he carried. The blackness made his thin face deathly pale. Leverett guessed his age to be late forty by the thinning of his hair. Dark glasses hid his eyes, black driving gloves his hands.

"Scotty Brandon told me where to find you," the stranger said.

"Scotty?" Leverett's voice was wary.

"Yes, we lost a mutual friend, I regret to say. I'd been talking with him just before. . . . But I see by your expression that Scotty never had time to write."

He fumbled awkwardly. "I'm Dana Allard."

"Allard?"

His visitor seemed embarrassed. "Yes—H. Kenneth Allard was my uncle."

"I hadn't realized Allard left a family," mused Leverett, shaking the extended hand. He had never met the writer personally, but there was a strong resemblance to the few photographs he had seen. And Scotty had been paying royalty checks to an estate of some sort, he recalled.

"My father was Kent's half-brother. He later took his father's name, but there was no marriage, if you follow."

"Of course." Leverett was abashed. "Please find a place to sit down. And what brings you here?"

Dana Allard tapped his briefcase. "Something I'd been discussing with Scotty. Just recently I turned up a stack of my uncle's unpublished manuscripts." He unlatched the briefcase and handed Leverett a sheaf of yellowed paper. "Father collected Kent's personal effects from the state hospital as next-of-kin. He never thought much of my uncle, or his writing. He stuffed this away in our attic and forgot about it. Scotty was quite excited when I told him of my discovery."

Leverett was glancing through the manuscript—page on page of cramped handwriting, with revisions pieced throughout like an indecipherable puzzle. He had seen photographs of Allard manuscripts. There was no mistaking this.

Or the prose. Leverett read a few passages with rapt absorption. It was authentic—and brilliant.

"Uncle's mind seems to have taken an especially morbid turn as his illness drew on," Dana hazarded. "I admire his work very greatly, but I find these last few pieces . . . well, a bit *too* horrible. Especially his translation of his mythical *Book of Elders*."

It appealed to Leverett perfectly. He barely noticed his guest as he pored over the brittle pages. Allard was describing a megalithic structure his doomed narrator had encountered in the crypts beneath an ancient churchyard. There were references to "elder glyphics" that resembled his lattice devices.

"Look here," pointed Dana. "These incantations he records here from Alorri-Zrokros's forbidden tome: 'Yogth-Yugth-Sut-Hyrath-Yogng'— Hell, I can't pronounce them. And he has pages of them."

"This is incredible!" Leverett protested. He tried to mouth the alien syllables. It could be done. He even detected a rhythm.

"Well, I'm relieved that you approve. I'd feared these last few stories and fragments might prove too much for Kent's fans."

"Then you're going to have them published?"

Dana nodded. "Scotty was going to. I just hope those thieves weren't searching for this—a collector would pay a fortune. But Scotty said he was going to keep this secret until he was ready for announcement." His thin face was sad.

"So now I'm going to publish it myself—in a deluxe edition. And I want you to illustrate it."

"I'd feel honored!" vowed Leverett, unable to believe it.

"I really liked those drawings you did for the trilogy. I'd like to see more like those—as many as you feel like doing. I mean to spare no expense in publishing this. And those stick things . . ."

"Yes?"

"Scotty told me the story on those. Fascinating! And you have a whole notebook of them? May I see it?"

Leverett hurriedly dug the notebook from his file, returned to the manuscript.

Dana paged through the book in awe. "These things are totally bizarre—and there are references to such things in the manuscript, to make it even more fantastic. Can you reproduce them all for the book?"

"All I can remember," Leverett assured him. "And I have a good memory. But won't that be overdoing it?"

"Not at all! They fit into the book. And they're utterly unique. No, put everything you've got into this book. I'm going to entitle it *Dwellers in the Earth*, after the longest piece. I've already arranged for its printing, so we begin as soon as you can have the art ready. And I know you'll give it your all."

VII

He was floating in space. Objects drifted past him. Stars, he first thought. The objects drifted closer.

Sticks. Stick lattices of all configurations. And then he was drifting among them, and he saw that they were not sticks—not of wood. The lattice designs were of dead-pale substance, like streaks of frozen starlight. They reminded him of glyphics of some unearthly alphabet—complex, enigmatic symbols arranged to spell . . . what? And there *was* an arrangement—a three-dimensional pattern. A maze of utterly baffling intricacy . . .

Then somehow he was in a tunnel. A cramped, stone-lined tunnel through which he must crawl on his belly. The dank, moss-slimed stones pressed close about his wriggling form, evoking shrill whispers of claustrophobic dread.

And after an indefinite space of crawling through this and other stone-lined burrows, and sometimes through passages whose angles hurt his eyes, he would creep forth into a subterranean chamber. Great slabs of granite a dozen feet across formed the walls and ceiling of this buried chamber, and between the slabs other burrows pierced the earth. Altar-like, a gigantic slab of gneiss waited in the center of the chamber. A spring welled darkly between the stone pillars that supported the table. Its outer edge was encircled by a groove, sickeningly stained by the substance that clotted in the stone bowl beneath its collecting spout.

Others were emerging from the darkened burrows that ringed the chamber—slouched figures only dimly glimpsed and vaguely human. And a figure in a tattered cloak came toward him from the shadow—stretched out a claw-like hand to seize his wrist and draw him toward the sacrificial table. He followed unresistingly, knowing that something was expected of him.

They reached the altar, and in the glow from the cuneiform lattices chiseled into the gneiss slab he could see the guide's face. A mouldering corpse-face, the rotted bone of its forehead smashed inward upon the foulness that oozed forth. . . .

And Leverett would awaken to the echo of his screams. . . .

He'd been working too hard, he told himself, stumbling about in the darkness, getting dressed because he was too shaken to return to sleep. The nightmares had been coming every night. No wonder he was exhausted.

But in his studio his work awaited him. Almost fifty drawings finished now, and he planned another score. No wonder the nightmares.

It was a grueling pace, but Dana Allard was ecstatic with the work he had done. And *Dwellers in the Earth* was waiting. Despite problems with typesetting, with getting the special paper Dana wanted—the book only waited on him.

Though his bones ached with fatigue, Leverett determinedly trudged through the graying night. Certain features of the nightmare would be interesting to portray.

VIII

The last of the drawings had gone off to Dana Allard in Petersham, and Leverett, fifteen pounds lighter and gut-weary, converted part of the bonus check into a case of good whiskey. Dana had the offset presses rolling as soon as the plates were shot from the drawings. Despite his precise planning, presses had broken down, one printer quit for reasons not stated, there had been a bad accident at the new printer—seemingly innumerable problems, and Dana had been furious at each delay. But the production pushed along quickly for all that. Leverett wrote that the book was cursed, but Dana responded that a week would see it ready.

Leverett amused himself in his studio constructing stick lattices and trying to catch up on his sleep. He was expecting a copy of the book when he received a letter from Stefroi:

> *Have tried to reach you by phone last few days, but no answer at your house. I'm pushed for time just now, so must be brief. I have indeed uncovered an unsuspected megalithic site of enormous importance. It's located on the estate of a long-prominent Mass. family—and as I cannot receive authorization to visit it, I will not say where. Have investigated secretly (and quite illegally) for a short time one night and was nearly caught. Came across reference to the place in collection of 17th-century letters and papers in a divinity school library. Writer denouncing the family as a brood of sorcerers and witches, references to alchemical activities and other less savory rumors—and describes underground stone chambers, megalithic artifacts etc. which are put to "foul usage and diabolic praktise." Just got a quick glimpse but his description was not exaggerated. And Colin—in creeping through the woods to get to the site, I came across dozens of your mysterious "sticks"! Brought a small one back and have it here to show you. Recently constructed and exactly like your drawings. With luck, I'll gain admittance and find out their significance—undoubtedly they have significance—though these cultists can be stubborn about sharing their secrets. Will explain my interest is scientific, no exposure to ridicule—and see what they say. Will get a closer look one way or another. And so—I'm off! Sincerely, Alexander Stefroi.*

Leverett's bushy brows rose. Allard had intimated certain dark rituals in which the stick lattices figured. But Allard had written over thirty years ago, and Leverett assumed the writer had stumbled onto something similar to the Mann Brook site. Stefroi was writing about something current.

He rather hoped Stefroi would discover nothing more than an inane hoax.

The nightmares haunted him still—familiar now, for all that its scenes and phantasms were visited by him only in dream. Familiar. The terror that they evoked was undiminished.

Now he was walking through forest—a section of hills that seemed to be close by. A huge slab of granite had been dragged aside, and a pit yawned where it had lain. He entered the pit without hesitation, and the rounded steps that led downward were known to his tread. A buried stone chamber, and leading from it stone-lined burrows. He knew which one to crawl into.

And again the underground room with its sacrificial altar and its dark spring beneath, and the gathering circle of poorly glimpsed figures. A knot of them clustered about the stone table, and as he stepped toward them he saw they pinned a frantically writhing man.

It was a stoutly built man, white hair disheveled, flesh gouged and filthy. Recognition seemed to burst over the contorted features, and he wondered if he should know the man. But now the lich with the caved-in skull was whispering in his ear, and he tried not to think of the unclean things that peered from that cloven brow, and instead took the bronze knife from the skeletal hand, and raised the knife high, and because he could not scream and awaken, did with the knife as the tattered priest had whispered. . . .

And when after an interval of unholy madness, he at last did awaken, the stickiness that covered him was not cold sweat, nor was it nightmare the half-devoured heart he clutched in one fist.

IX

Leverett somehow found sanity enough to dispose of the shredded lump of flesh. He stood under the shower all morning, scrubbing his skin raw. He wished he could vomit.

There was a news item on the radio. The crushed body of noted archaeologist, Dr. Alexander Stefroi, had been discovered beneath a fallen granite slab near Whately. Police speculated the gigantic slab had shifted with the scientist's excavations at its base. Identification was made through personal effects.

When his hands stopped shaking enough to drive, Leverett fled to Petersham—reaching Dana Allard's old stone house about dark. Allard was slow to answer his frantic knock.

"Why, good evening, Colin! What a coincidence your coming here just now! The books are ready. The bindery just delivered them."

Leverett brushed past him. "We've got to destroy them!" he blurted. He'd thought a lot since morning.

"Destroy them?"

"There's something none of us figured on. Those stick lattices—there's a cult, some damnable cult. The lattices have some significance in their rituals. Stefroi hinted once they might be glyphics of some sort, I don't know. But the cult is still alive. They killed Scotty . . . they killed Stefroi. They're onto me—I don't know what they intend. They'll kill you to stop you from releasing this book!"

Dana's frown was worried, but Leverett knew he hadn't impressed him the right way. "Colin, this sounds insane. You really have been overextending yourself, you know. Look, I'll show you the books. They're in the cellar."

Leverett let his host lead him downstairs. The cellar was quite large, flagstoned, and dry. A mountain of brown-wrapped bundles awaited them.

"Put them down here where they wouldn't knock the floor out," Dana explained. "They start going out to distributors tomorrow. Here, I'll sign your copy."

Distractedly Leverett opened a copy of *Dwellers in the Earth*. He gazed at his lovingly rendered drawings of rotting creatures and buried stone chambers and stained altars—and everywhere the enigmatic latticework structures. He shuddered.

"Here." Dana Allard handed Leverett the book he had signed. "And to answer your question, they *are* elder glyphics."

But Leverett was staring at the inscription in its unmistakable handwriting: "For Colin Leverett, Without whom this work could not have seen completion—H. Kenneth Allard."

Allard was speaking. Leverett saw places where the hastily applied flesh-toned makeup didn't quite conceal what lay beneath. "Glyphics symbolic of alien dimensions—inexplicable to the human mind, but essential fragments of an evocation so unthinkably vast that the 'pentagram' (if you will) is miles across. Once before we tried—but your iron weapon destroyed part of Althol's brain. He erred at the last instant—almost annihilating us all. Althol had been formulating the evocation since he fled the advance of iron four millennia past.

"Then you reappeared, Colin Leverett—you with your artist's knowledge and diagrams of Althol's symbols. And now a thousand new minds will read the evocation you have returned to us, unite with our minds as we stand in the Hidden Places. And the Great Old Ones will come forth from the earth, and we, the dead who have steadfastly served them, shall be masters of the living."

Leverett turned to run, but now they were creeping forth from the shadows of the cellar, as massive flagstones slid back to reveal the tunnels beyond. He began to scream as Althol came to lead him away, but he could not awaken, could only follow.

The Freshman*

PHILIP JOSÉ FARMER

The long-haired youth in front of Desmond wore sandals, ragged blue jeans, and a grimy T-shirt. A paperback, *The Collected Works of Robert Blake,* was half stuck into his rear pocket. When he turned around, he displayed in large letters on the T-shirt, M.U. His scrawny Fu Manchu mustache held some bread crumbs.

His yellow eyes—surely he suffered from jaundice—widened when he saw Desmond. He said, "This ain't the place to apply for the nursing home, Pops." He grinned, showing unusually long canines, and then turned to face the admissions desk.

Desmond felt his face turning red. Ever since he'd gotten into the line before a table marked *Toaahd Freshmen A-D,* he'd been aware of the sidelong glances, the snickers, the low-voiced comments. He stood out among these youths like a billboard in a flower garden, a corpse on a banquet table.

The line moved ahead by one person. The would-be students were talking, but their voices were subdued. For such young people, they were very restrained, excepting the smart aleck just ahead of him.

Perhaps it was the surroundings that repressed them. This gymnasium, built in the late nineteenth century, had not been repainted for years. The once-green paint was peeling. There were broken windows high on the walls; a shattered skylight had been covered with boards. The wooden floor bent and creaked, and the basketball goal rings (?) were rusty. Yet M.U. had been league champions in all fields of sports for many years. Though its enrollment was much less than that of its competitors, its teams somehow managed to win, often by large scores.

Desmond buttoned his jacket. Though it was a warm fall day, the air in the building was cold. If he hadn't known better, he would have

---

*Originally published in *Fantasy and Science Fiction,* May 1979.

thought that the wall of an iceberg was just behind him. Above him the great lights struggled to overcome the darkness that lowered like the underside of a dead whale sinking into sea depths.

He turned around. The girl just back of him smiled. She wore a flowing dashiki covered with astrological symbols. Her black hair was cut short; her features were petite and well-arranged but too pointed to be pretty.

Among all these youths there should have been a number of pretty girls and handsome men. He'd walked enough campuses to get an idea of the index of beauty of college students. But here . . . There was a girl, in the line to the right, whose face should have made her eligible to be a fashion model. Yet, there was something missing.

No, there was something added. A quality undefinable but . . . Repugnant? No, now it was gone. No, it was back again. It flitted on and off, like a bat swooping from darkness into a grayness and then up and out.

The kid in front of him had turned again. He was grinning like a fox who'd just seen a chicken.

"Some dish, heh, Pops? She likes older men. Maybe you two could get your shit together and make beautiful music."

The odor of unwashed body and clothes swirled around him like flies around a dead rat.

"I'm not interested in girls with Oedipus complexes," Desmond said coldly.

"At your age you can't be particular," the youth said, and turned away.

Desmond flushed, and he briefly fantasized knocking the kid down. It didn't help much.

The line moved ahead again. He looked at his wristwatch. In half an hour he was scheduled to phone his mother. He should have come here sooner. However, he had overslept while the alarm clock had run down, resuming its ticking as if it didn't care. Which it didn't, of course, though he felt that his possessions should, somehow, take an interest in him. This was irrational, but if he was a believer in the superiority of the rational, would he be here? Would any of these students?

The line moved jerkily ahead like a centipede halting now and then to make sure no one had stolen any of its legs. When he was ten minutes late for the phone call, he was at the head of the line. Behind the admissions table was a man far older than he. His face was a mass of wrinkles, gray dough that had been incised with fingernails and then pressed into somewhat human shape. The nose was a cuttlefish's beak stuck into the dough. But the eyes beneath the white chaotic eyebrows were as alive as blood flowing from holes in the flesh.

The hand which took Desmond's papers and punched cards was not that of an old man's. It was big and swollen, white, smooth-skinned. The fingernails were dirty.

"The Roderick Desmond, I assume."

The voice was rasping, not at all an old man's cracked quavering.

"Ah, you know me?"

"Of you, yes. I've read some of your novels of the occult. And ten years ago I rejected your request for Xeroxes of certain parts of *the* book."

The name tag on the worn tweed jacket said: R. Layamon, COTOAAHD. So this was the chairman of the Committee of the Occult Arts and History Department.

"Your paper on the non-Arabic origin of Alhazred's name was a brilliant piece of linguistic research. I knew that it wasn't Arabic or even Semitic, but I confess that I didn't know the century in which the word was dropped from the Arabic language. Your exposition of how it was retained only in connection with the Yemenite and that its original meaning was not *mad* but *one-who-sees-what-shouldn't-be-seen* was quite correct."

He paused, then said smiling, "Did your mother complain when she was forced to accompany you to Yemen?"

Desmond said, "No-n-n-o-body forced her."

He took a deep breath and said, "But how did you know she . . . ?"

"I've read some biographical accounts of you."

Layamon chuckled. It sounded like nails being shifted in a barrel. "Your paper on Alhazred and the knowledge you display in your novels are the main reasons why you're being admitted to this department despite your sixty years."

He signed the forms and handed the card back to Desmond. "Take this to the cashier's office. Oh, yes, your family is a remarkably long-lived one, isn't it? Your father died accidentally, but his father lived to be one hundred and two. Your mother is eighty, but she should live to be over a hundred. And you, you could have forty more years of life *as you've known it.*"

Desmond was enraged, but not so much that he dared let himself show it. The gray air became black, and the old man's face shone in it. It floated toward him, expanded, and suddenly Desmond was inside the gray wrinkles. It was not a pleasant place.

The tiny figures on a dimly haloed horizon danced, then faded, and he fell through a bellowing blackness. The air was gray again, and he was leaning forward, clenching the edge of the table.

"Mr. Desmond, do you have these attacks often?"

Desmond released his grip and straightened. "Too much excitement, I suppose. No, I've never had an attack, not now or ever."

The old man chuckled. "Yes, it must be emotional stress. Perhaps you'll find the means for relieving that stress here."

Desmond turned and walked away. Until he left the building, he saw only blurred figures and signs. That ancient wizard . . . how had he known his thoughts so well? Was it simply because he had read the biographical accounts, made a few inquiries, and then surmised a complete picture? Or was there more to it than that?

The sun had gone behind thick sluggish clouds. Past the campus, past many trees hiding the houses of the city, were the Tamsiqueg Hills. According to the long-extinct Indians after whom they were named, they had once been evil giants who'd waged war with the hero Mikatoonis and his magic-making friend, Chegaspat. Chegaspat had been killed, but Mikatoonis had turned the giants into stone with a magical club.

But Cotoaahd, the chief giant, was able to free himself from the spell every few centuries. Sometimes, a sorcerer could loose him. Then Cotoaahd walked abroad for a while before returning to his rocky slumber. In 1724 a house and many trees on the edge of the town had been flattened one stormy night as if colossal feet had stepped upon them. And the broken trees formed a trail which led to the curiously shaped hill known as Cotoaahd.

There was nothing about these stories that couldn't be explained by the tendency of the Indians, and the superstitious eighteenth-century whites, to legendize natural phenomena. But was it entirely coincidence that the anagram of the committee headed by Layamon duplicated the giant's name?

Suddenly, he became aware that he was heading for a telephone booth. He looked at his watch and felt panicky. The phone in his dormitory room would be ringing. It would be better to call her from the booth and save the three minutes it would take to walk to the dormitory.

He stopped. No, if he called from the booth, he would only get a busy signal.

"Forty more years of life *as you've known it,*" the chairman had said.

Desmond turned. His path was blocked by an enormous youth. He was a head taller than Desmond's six feet and so fat he looked like a smaller version of the Santa Claus balloon in Macy's Christmas-day parade. He wore a dingy sweatshirt on the front of which was the ubiquitous M.U., unpressed pants, and torn tennis shoes. In banana-sized fingers he held a salami sandwich which Gargantua would not have found too small.

Looking at him, Desmond suddenly realized that most of the students here were too thin or too fat.

"Mr. Desmond?"

"Right."

He shook hands. The fellow's skin was wet and cold, but the hand exerted a powerful pressure.

"I'm Wendell Trepan. With your knowledge, you've heard about my ancestors. The most famous, or infamous, of whom was the Cornish witch, Rachel Trepan."

"Yes. Rachel of the hamlet of Tredannick Wollas, near Poldhu Bay."

"I knew you'd know. I'm following the trade of my ancestors, though more cautiously, of course. Anyway, I'm a senior and the chair-person of the rushing committee for the Lam Kha Alif fraternity."

He paused to bite into the sandwich. Mayonnaise and salami and cheese oozing from his mouth, he said, "You're invited to the party we're holding at the house this afternoon."

The other hand reached into a pocket and brought out a card. Desmond looked at it briefly. "You want me to be a candidate for membership in your frat? I'm pretty old for that sort of thing. I'd feel out of place. . . ."

"Nonsense, Mr. Desmond. We're a pretty serious bunch. In fact, none of the frats here are like any on other campuses. You should know that. We feel you'd provide stability and, I'll admit, prestige. You're pretty well known, you know. Layamon, by the way, is a Lam Kha Alif. He tends to favor students who belong to his frat. He'd deny it, of course, and I'll deny it if you repeat this. But it's true."

"Well, I don't know. Suppose I did pledge—if I'm invited to, that is—would I have to live in the frat house?"

"Yes. We make no exceptions. Of course, that's only when you're a pledge. You can live wherever you want to when you're an active."

Trepan smiled, showing the unswallowed bite. "You're not married, so there's no problem there."

"What do you mean by that?"

"Nothing, Mr. Desmond. It's just that we don't pledge married men unless they don't live with their wives. Married men lose some of their power, you know. Of course, no way do we insist on celibacy. We have some pretty good parties, too. Once a month we hold a big bust in a grove at the foot of Cotoaahd. Most of the women guests there belong to the Ba Ghay Sin sorority. Some of them really go for the older type, if you know what I mean."

Trepan stepped forward to place his face directly above Desmond's. "We don't just have beer, pot, hashish, and sisters. There're other attractions. Brothers, if you're so inclined. Some stuff that's made from a recipe by the Marquis Manuel de Dembron himself. But most of that is kid stuff. There'll be a goat there, too!"

"A goat? A *black* goat?"

Trepan nodded, and his triple-fold jowls swung. "Yeah. Old Layamon'll be there to supervise, though he'll be masked, of course. With him as coach nothing can go wrong. Last Halloween, though . . ."

He paused, then said, "Well, it was something to see."

Desmond licked dry lips. His heart was thudding like the tomtoms that beat at the ritual of which he had only read but had envisioned many times.

Desmond put the card in his pocket. "At one o'clock?"

"You're coming? Very good! See you, Mr. Desmond. You won't regret it."

Desmond walked past the buildings of the university quadrangle, the most imposing of which was the museum. This was the oldest structure on the campus, the original college. Time had beaten and chipped away at the brick and stone of the others, but the museum seemed to have absorbed time and to be slowly radiating it back just as cement and stone and brick absorbed heat in the sunlight and then gave it back in the darkness. Also, whereas the other structures were covered with vines, perhaps too covered, the museum was naked of plant life. Vines which tried to crawl up its gray bone-colored stones withered and fell back.

Layamon's red-stone house was narrow, three stories high, and had a double-peaked roof. Its cover of vines was so thick that it seemed a wonder that the weight didn't bring it to the ground. The colors of the vines were subtly different from those on the other buildings. Seen at one angle, they looked cyanotic. From another, they were the exact green of the eyes of a Sumatran snake Desmond had seen in a colored plate in a book on herpetology.

It was this venomous reptile which was used by the sorcerers of the Yan tribes to transmit messages and sometimes to kill. The writer had not explained what he meant by "messages." Desmond had discovered the meaning in another book, which had required him to learn Malay, written in the Arabic script, before he could read it.

He hurried on past the house, which was not something a sightseer would care to look at long, and came to the dormitory. It had been built in 1888 on the site of another building and remodeled in 1938. Its gray paint was peeling. There were several broken windows, over the panes of which cardboard had been nailed. The porch floorboards bent and creaked as he passed over them. The main door was of oak, its paint long gone. The bronze head of a cat, a heavy bronze ring dangling from its mouth, served as a door knocker.

Desmond entered, passed through the main room over the worn carpet, and walked up two flights of bare-board steps. On the gray-white of a wall by the first landing someone had long ago written YOG-SOTHOTH SUCKS. Many attempts had been made to wash it off, but it was evident that only paint could hide this insulting and dangerous sentiment. Yesterday a junior had told him that no one knew who had written it, but the night after it had appeared, a freshman had been found dead, hanging from a hook in a closet.

"The kid had mutilated himself terribly before he committed suicide," the junior had said. "I wasn't here then, but I understand that he was a mess. He'd done it with a razor *and* a hot iron. There was blood all over the place, his pecker and balls were on the table, arranged to form a T-cross, you know whose symbol that is, and he'd clawed out plaster on the wall, leaving a big bloody print. It didn't even look like a human hand had done it."

"I'm surprised he lived long enough to hang himself," Desmond had said. "All that loss of blood, you know."

The junior had guffawed. "You're kidding, of course!"

It was several seconds before Desmond understood what he meant. Then he'd paled. But later he wondered if the junior wasn't playing a traditional joke on a green freshman. He didn't think he'd ask anybody else about it, however. If he had been made a fool of, he wasn't going to let it happen more than once.

He heard the phone ringing at the end of the long hall. He sighed, and strode down it, passing closed doors. From behind one came a faint tittering. He unlocked his door and closed it behind him. For a long time he stood watching the phone, which went on and on, reminding him, he didn't know why, of the poem about the Australian swagman who went for a dip in a waterhole. The bunyip, that mysterious and sinister creature of down-under folklore, the dweller in the water, silently and smoothly took care of the swagman. And the tea kettle he'd put on the fire whistled and whistled with no one to hear.

And the phone rang on and on.

The bunyip was on the other end.

Guilt spread through him as quick as a blush.

He walked across the room glimpsing something out of the corner of his eye, something small, dark, and swift that dived under the sagging mildew-odorous bed-couch. He stopped at the small table, reached out to the receiver, touched it, felt its cold throbbing. He snatched his hand back. It was foolish, but it had seemed to him that she would detect his touch and know that he was there.

Snarling, he wheeled and started across the room. He noticed that the hole in the baseboard was open again. The Coke bottle whose butt end he'd jammed into the hole had been pushed out. He stopped and reinserted it and straightened up.

When he was at the foot of the staircase, he could still hear the ringing. But he wasn't sure that it wasn't just in his head.

After he'd paid his tuition and eaten at the cafeteria—the food was better than he'd thought it would be—he walked to the ROTC building. It was in better shape than the other structures, probably because the Army was in charge of it. Still, it wasn't in the condition an inspector would require. And those cannons on caissons in the rear. Were the students really supposed to train with Spanish-American War weapons? And since when was steel subject to verdigris?

The officer in charge was surprised when Desmond asked to be issued his uniform and manuals.

"I don't know. You realize ROTC is no longer required of freshmen and sophomores?"

Desmond insisted that he wanted to enroll. The officer rubbed his unshaven jaw and blew smoke from a Tijuana Gold panatela. "Hmm. Let me see."

He consulted a book whose edges seemed to have been nibbled by rats. "Well, what do you know? There's nothing in the regulations about age. Course, there's some pages missing. Must be an oversight. Nobody near your age has ever been considered. But . . . well, if the regulations say nothing about it, then . . . what the hell! Won't hurt you, our boys don't have to go through obstacle courses or anything like that.

"But jeeze, you're sixty! Why do you want to sign up?"

Desmond did not tell him that he had been deferred from service in World War II because he was the sole support of his sick mother. Ever since then, he'd felt guilty, but at least here he could do his bit—however minute—for his country.

The officer stood up, though not in a coordinated manner. "Okay. I'll see you get your issue. It's only fair to warn you, though, that these fuckups play some mighty strange tricks. You should see what they blow out of their cannons."

Fifteen minutes later, Desmond left, a pile of uniforms and manuals under one arm. Since he didn't want to return home with them, he checked them in at the university bookstore. The girl put them on a shelf alongside other belongings, some of them unidentifiable to the noncognoscenti. One of them was a small cage covered with a black cloth.

Desmond walked to Fraternity Row. All of the houses had Arabic names, except the House of Hastur. These were afflicted with the same general decrepitude and lack of care as the university structures. Desmond turned in at a cement walk, from the cracks of which spread dying dandelions and other weeds. On his left leaned a massive wooden pole fifteen feet high. The heads and symbols carved into it had caused the townspeople to refer to it as the totem pole. It wasn't, of course, since the tribe to which it had belonged was not Northwest Coast or Alaskan Indians. It and a fellow in the university museum were the last survivors of hundreds which had once stood in this area.

Desmond, passing it, put the end of his left thumb under his nose and the tip of his index finger in the center of his forehead, and he muttered the ancient phrase of obeisance, *"Shesh-cotoaahd-ting-ononwa-senk."* According to various texts he'd read, this was required of every Tamsiqueg who walked by it during this phase of the moon. The phrase was unintelligible even to them, since it came from another tribe or perhaps from an antique stage of the language. But it indicated respect, and lack of its observance was likely to result in misfortune.

He felt a little silly doing it, but it couldn't hurt.

The unpainted wooden steps creaked as he stepped upon them. The porch was huge; the wires of the screen were rusty and useless in keeping insects out because of the many holes. The front door was open; from it came a blast of rock music, the loud chatter of many people, and the acrid odor of pot.

Desmond almost turned back. He suffered when he was in a crowd, and his consciousness of his age made him feel embarrassingly conspicuous. But the huge figure of Wendell Trepan was in the doorway, and he was seized by an enormous hand.

"Come on in!" Trepan bellowed. "I'll introduce you to the brothers!"

Desmond was pulled into a large room jammed with youths of both sexes. Trepan bulled through, halting now and then to slap somebody on the back and shout a greeting and once to pat a well-built young woman on the fanny. Then they were in a corner where Professor Layamon sat surrounded by people who looked older than most of the attendees. Desmond supposed that they were graduate students. He shook the fat swollen hand and said, "Pleased to meet you again," but he doubted that his words were heard.

Layamon pulled him down so he could be heard, and he said, "Have you made up your mind yet?"

The old man's breath was not unpleasant, but he had certainly been drinking something which Desmond had never smelled before. The red eyes seemed to hold a light, almost as if tiny candles were burning inside the eyeballs.

"About what?" Desmond shouted back.

The old man smiled and said, "You know."

He released his grip. Desmond straightened up. Suddenly, though the room was hot enough to make him sweat, he felt chilly. What was Layamon hinting at? It couldn't be that he really knew. Or could it be?

Trepan introduced him to the men and women around the chair and then took him into the crowd. Other introductions followed, most of those he met seeming to be members of Lam Kha Alif or of the sorority across the street. The only one he could identify for sure as a candidacy for pledging was a black, a Gabonese. After they left him, Trepan said, "Bukawai comes from a long line of witch doctors. He's going to be a real treasure if he accepts our invitation, though the House of Hastur and Kaf Dhal Waw are hot to get him. The department is a little weak on Central African science. It used to have a great teacher, Janice Momaya, but she disappeared ten years ago while on a sabbatical in Sierra Leone. I wouldn't be surprised if Bukawai was offered an assistant professorship even if he is nominally a freshman. Man, the other night, he taught me part of a ritual you wouldn't believe. I . . . well, I won't go into it now. Some other time. Anyway, he has the greatest respect for Layamon, and since the old fart is head of the department, Bukawai is almost a cinch to join us."

Suddenly, his lips pulled back, his teeth clenched, his skin paled beneath the dirt, and he bent over and grabbed his huge paunch. Desmond said, "What's the matter?"

Trepan shook his head, gave a deep sigh, and straightened up.

"Man, that hurt!"

"What?" Desmond said.

"I shouldn't have called him an old fart. I didn't think he could hear me, but he isn't using sound to receive. Hell, there's nobody in the world has more respect for him than me. But sometimes my mouth runs off . . . well, never again."

"You mean?" Desmond said.

"Yeah. Who'd you think? Never mind. Come with me where we can hear ourselves think."

He pulled Desmond through a smaller room, one with many shelves of books, novels, school texts, and here and there some old leather-bound volumes.

"We got a hell of a good library here, the best any house can boast of. It's one of our stellar attractions. But it's the open one."

They entered a narrow door, passed into a short hall, and stopped while Trepan took a key from his pocket and unlocked another door. Beyond it was a narrow corkscrew staircase, the steps of which were dusty. A window high above gave a weak light through dirty panes. Trepan turned on a wall light, and they went up the stairs. At the top, which was on the third floor, Trepan unlocked another door with a different key. They stepped into a small room whose walls were covered by bookshelves from floor to ceiling. Trepan turned on a light. In a corner was a small table and a folding chair. The table had a lamp and a stone bust of the Marquis de Dembron on it.

Trepan, breathing heavily after the climb, said, "Usually, only seniors and graduates are allowed here. But I'm making an exception in your case. I just wanted to show you one of the advantages of belonging to Lam Kha Alif. None of the other houses have a library like this."

Trepan was looking narrow-eyed at him. "Eyeball the books. But don't touch them. They, uh, absorb, if you know what I mean."

Desmond moved around, looking at the titles. When he was finished, he said, "I'm impressed. I thought some of these books were to be found only in the university library. In locked rooms."

"That's what the public thinks. Listen, if you pledge us, you'll have access to these books. Only don't tell the other undergrads. They'd get jealous."

Trepan, still narrow-eyed, as if he were considering something that perhaps he shouldn't, said, "Would you mind turning your back and sticking your fingers in your ears?"

Desmond said, "What?"

Trepan smiled. "Oh, if you sign up with us, you'll be given the little recipe necessary to work in here. But until then I'd just as soon you don't see it."

Desmond, smiling with embarrassment, the cause of which he couldn't account for, and also feeling excited, turned his back, facing away from Trepan, and jammed his fingertips into his ears. While he stood there in the very quiet room—was it soundproofed with insulation or with something perhaps not material?—he counted the seconds. One thousand and one, one thousand and two . . .

A little more than a minute had passed when he felt Trepan's hand on his shoulder. He turned and removed his fingers. The fat youth was holding out to him a tall but very slim volume bound in a skin with many small dark protuberances. Desmond was surprised, since he was sure he had not seen it on the shelves.

"I deactivated this," Trepan said. "Here. Take it." He looked at his wristwatch. "It'll be okay for ten minutes."

There was no title or by-line on the cover. And, now that he looked at it closely and felt it, he did not think the skin was from an animal.

Trepan said, "It's the hide of an old Atechironnon himself."

Desmond said, "Ah!" and he trembled. But he rallied.

"He must have been covered with warts."

"Yeah. Go ahead, look at it. It's a shame you can't read it, though."

The first page was slightly yellowed, which wasn't surprising for paper four hundred years old. There was no printing but large handwritten letters.

"Ye lesser Rituall of Ye Tahmmsiquegg Warlock Atechironunn," Desmond read. *"Reprodust from ye Picture-riting on ye Skin lefft unbirnt by ye Godly.*

"By his own Hand, Simon Conant. 1641.

"Let him who speaks these Words of Pictures, first lissen."

Trepan chuckled and said, "Spelling wasn't his forte, was it?"

"Simon, the half brother of Roger Conant," Desmond said. "He was the first white man to visit the Tamsiqueg and not leave with his severed thumb stuck up his ass. He was also with the settlers who raided the Tamsiqueg, but they didn't know who his sympathies were with. He fled with the badly wounded Atechironnon into the wilderness. Twenty years later, he appeared in Virginia with this book."

He slowly turned the five pages, fixing each pictograph in his photographic memory. There was one figure he didn't like to look at.

"Layamon's the only one who can read it," Trepan said.

Desmond did not tell him that he was conversant with the grammar and small dictionary of the Tamsiqueg language, written by William Cor Dunnes in 1624 and published in 1654. It contained an appendix translating the pictographs. It had cost him twenty years of search and a thousand dollars just for a Xerox copy. His mother has raised hell about the expenditure, but for once he had stood up to her. Not even the university had a copy.

Trepan looked at his watch. "One minute to go. Hey!"

He grabbed the book from Desmond's hands and said, harshly, "Turn your back and plug your ears!"

Trepan looked as if he were in a panic. He turned, and a minute later Trepan pulled one of Desmond's fingers away.

"Sorry to be so sudden, but the hold was beginning to break down. I can't figure it out. It's always been good for at least ten minutes."

Desmond had not felt anything, but that might be because Trepan, having been exposed to the influence, was more sensitive to it.

Trepan, obviously nervous, said, "Let's get out of here. It's got to cool off."

On the way down, he said, "You sure you can't read it?"

"Where would I have learned how?" Desmond said.

They plunged into a sea of noise and odors in the big room. They did not stay long, since Trepan wanted to show him the rest of the house, except the basement.

"You can see it sometime this week. Just now it's not advisable to go down there."

Desmond didn't ask why.

When they entered a very small room on the second floor, Trepan said, "Ordinarily we don't let freshmen have a room to themselves. But for you . . . well, it's yours if you want it."

That pleased Desmond. He wouldn't have to put up with someone whose habits would irk him and whose chatter would anger him.

They descended to the first floor. The big room was not so crowded now. Old Layamon, just getting up from the chair, beckoned to him. Desmond approached him slowly. For some reason, he knew he was not going to like what Layamon would say to him. Or perhaps he wasn't sure whether he would like it or not.

"Trepan showed you the frat's more precious books," the chairman said. It wasn't a question but a statement. "Especially Conant's book."

Trepan said, "How did you . . . ?" He grinned. "You felt it."

"Of course," the rusty voice said. "Well, Desmond, don't you think it's time to answer that phone?"

Trepan looked puzzled. Desmond felt sick and cold.

Layamon was now almost nose to nose with Desmond. The many wrinkles of the doughy skin looked like hieroglyphs.

"You've made up your mind, but you aren't letting yourself know it," he said. "Listen. That was Conant's advice, wasn't it? Listen. From the moment you got onto the plane to Boston, you were committed. You could have backed out in the airport, but you didn't, even though, I imagine, your mother made a scene there. But you didn't. So there's no use putting it off."

He chuckled. "That I am bothering to give you advice is a token of my esteem for you. I think you'll go far and fast. If you are able to eliminate certain defects of character. It takes strength and intelligence and great self-discipline and a vast dedication to get even a B.A. here, Desmond.

"There are too many who enroll here because they think they'll be taking snap courses. Getting great power, hobnobbing with things that are really not socially minded, to say the least, seems to them to be as easy as rolling off a log. But they soon find out that the department's standards are higher than, say, those of MIT in engineering. And a hell of a lot more dangerous.

"And then there's the moral issue. That's declared just by enrolling here. But how many have the will to push on? How many decide that they are on the wrong side? They quit, not knowing that it's too late for any but a tiny fraction of them to return to the other side. They've declared themselves, have stood up and been counted forever, as it were."

He paused to light up a brown panatela. The smoke curled around Desmond, who did not smell what he expected. The odor was not quite like that of a dead bat he had once used in an experiment.

"Every man or woman determines his or her own destiny. But I would make my decision swiftly, if I were you. I've got my eye on you, and your advancement here does depend upon my estimate of your character and potentiality.

"Good day, Desmond."

The old man walked out. Trepan said, "What was that all about?"

Desmond did not answer. He stood for a minute or so while Trepan fidgeted. Then he said good-by to the fat man and walked out slowly.

Instead of going home, he wandered around the campus. Attracted by flashing red lights, he went over to see what was going on. A car with the markings of the campus police and an ambulance from the university hospital were in front of a two-story building. Its lower floor had once been a grocery store according to the letters on the dirty plate-glass window. The paint inside and out was peeling, and plaster had fallen off the walls within, revealing the laths beneath. On the bare wooden floor were three bodies. One was the youth who had stood just in front of him in the line in the gymnasium. He lay on his back, his mouth open below the scraggly mustache.

Desmond asked one of the people pressed against the window what had happened. The gray-bearded man, probably a professor, said, "This happens every year at this time. Some kids get carried away and try something no one but an M.A. would even think of trying. It's strictly forbidden, but that doesn't stop those young fools."

The corpse with the mustache seemed to have a large round black object or perhaps a burn on its forehead. Desmond wanted to get a closer look, but the ambulance men put a blanket over the face before carrying the body out.

The gray-bearded man said, "The university police and the hospital will handle them." He laughed shortly. "The city police don't even want to come on the campus. The relatives will be notified they've OD'd from heroin."

"There's no trouble about that?"

"Sometimes. Private detectives have come here, but they don't stay long."

Desmond walked away swiftly. His mind was made up. The sight of those bodies had shaken him. He'd go home, make peace with his mother, sell all the books he'd spent so much time and money accumulating and studying, take up writing mystery novels. He'd seen the face of death, and if he did what he had thought about, only idly of course, fantasizing for psychic therapy, he would see her face. Dead. He couldn't do it.

When he entered his room in the boardinghouse, the phone was still ringing. He walked to it, reached out his hand, held it for an undeterminable time, then dropped it. As he walked toward the couch, he noticed that the Coca-Cola bottle had been shoved or pulled out of the hole in the baseboard. He knelt down and jammed it back into the hole. From behind the wall came a faint twittering.

He sat down on the sagging couch, took his notebook from his jacket pocket, and began to pencil in the pictographs he remembered so well on the sheets. It took him half an hour, since exactness of reproduction was vital. The phone did not stop ringing.

Someone knocked on the door and yelled, "I saw you go in! Answer the phone or take it off the hook! Or I'll put something on you!"

He did not reply or rise from the couch.

He had left out one of the drawings in the sequence. Now he poised the pencil an inch above the black space. Sitting at the other end of the line would be a very fat, very old woman. She was old and ugly now, but she had borne him and for many years thereafter she had been beautiful. When his father had died, she had gone to work to keep their house and to support her son in the manner to which both were accustomed. She had worked hard to pay his tuition and other expenses while he went to college. She had continued to work until he had sold two novels. Then she had gotten sickly, though not until he began bringing women home to introduce as potential wives.

She loved him, but she wouldn't let loose of him, and that wasn't genuine love. He hadn't been able to tear loose, which meant that though he was resentful he had something in him which liked being caged. Then, one day, he had decided to take the big step toward freedom. It had been done secretly and swiftly. He had despised himself for his fear of her, but that was the way he was. If he stayed here, she would be coming here. He couldn't endure that. So, he would have to go home.

He looked at the phone, started to rise, sank back.

What to do? He could commit suicide. He'd be free, and she would know how angry he'd been with her. He gave a start as the phone stopped ringing. So, she had given up for a while. But she would return to it.

He looked at the baseboard. The bottle was moving out from the hole a little at a time. Something behind the wall was working away determinedly. How many times had it started to leave the hole and found that its passage was blocked? Far too many, the thing must think, if it had a mind. But it refused to give up, and someday it might occur to it to solve its problem by killing the one who was causing the problem.

If, however, it was daunted by the far greater size of the problem maker, if it lacked courage, then it would have to keep on pushing the bottle from the hole. And . . .

He looked at the notebook, and he shook. The blank space had been filled in. There was the drawing of Cotoaahd, the thing which, now he looked at it, somehow resembled his mother.

Had he unconsciously penciled it in while he was thinking?

Or had the figure formed itself?

It didn't matter. In either case, he knew what he had to do.

While the eyes passed over each drawing, and he intoned the words of that long-dead language, he felt something move out from within his chest, crawl into his belly, his legs, his throat, his brain. The symbol of Cotoaahd seemed to burn on the sheet when he pronounced its name, his eyes on the drawing.

The room grew dark as the final words were said. He rose and turned on a table lamp and went into the tiny dirty bathroom. The face in the mirror did not look like a murderer's; it was just that of a sixty-year-old man who had been through an ordeal and was not quite sure that it was over.

On the way out of the room, he saw the Coke bottle slide free of the baseboard hole. But whatever had pushed it was not yet ready to come out.

Hours later he returned reeling from the campus tavern. The phone was ringing again. But the call, as he had expected, was not from his mother, though it was from his native city in Illinois.

"Mr. Desmond, this is Sergeant Rourke of the Busiris Police Department. I'm afraid I have some bad news for you. Uh, ah, your mother died some hours ago of a heart attack."

Desmond did not have to act stunned. He was numb throughout. Even the hand holding the receiver felt as if it had turned to granite. Vaguely, he was aware that Rourke's voice seemed strange.

"Heart attack? Heart . . . ? Are you sure?"

He groaned. His mother had died naturally. He would not have had to recite the ancient words. And now he had committed himself for nothing and was forever trapped. Once the words were used while the eyes read, there was no turning back.

But . . . if the words had been only words, dying as sound usually does, no physical reaction resulting from words transmitted through that subcontinuum, then was he bound?

Wouldn't he be free, clear of debt? Able to walk out of this place without fear of retaliation?

"It was a terrible thing, Mr. Desmond. A freak accident. Your mother died while she was talking to a visiting neighbor, Mrs. Sammins. Sammins called the police and an ambulance. Some other neighbors went into the house, and then . . . then. . . ."

Rourke's throat seemed to be clogging.

"I'd just got there and was on the front porch when it . . . it. . . ."

Rourke coughed, and he said, "My brother was in the house, too."

Three neighbors, two ambulance attendants, and two policemen had been crushed to death when the house had unaccountably collapsed.

"It was like a giant foot stepped on it. If it'd fallen in six seconds later, I'd have been caught, too."

Desmond thanked him and said he'd take the next plane out to Busiris.

He staggered to the window, and he raised it to breathe in the open air. Below, in the light of a streetlamp, hobbling along on his cane, was Layamon. The gray face lifted. Teeth flashed whitely.

Desmond wept, but the tears were only for himself.

Jerusalem's Lot*

STEPHEN KING

Oct. 2, 1850.

DEAR BONES,

How good it was to step into the cold, draughty hall here at Chapelwaite, every bone in an ache from that abominable coach, in need of instant relief from my distended bladder—and to see a letter addressed in your own inimitable scrawl propped on the obscene little cherry-wood table beside the door! Be assured that I set to deciphering it as soon as the needs of the body were attended to (in a coldly ornate downstairs bathroom where I could see my breath rising before my eyes).

I'm glad to hear that you are recovered from the *miasma* that has so long set in your lungs, although I assure you that I do sympathize with the moral dilemma the cure has affected you with. An ailing abolitionist healed by the sunny climes of slave-struck Florida! Still and all, Bones, I ask you as a friend who has also walked in the valley of the shadow, *to take all care of yourself* and venture not back to Massachusetts until your body gives you leave. Your fine mind and incisive pen cannot serve us if you are clay, and if the Southern zone is a healing one, is there not poetic justice in that?

Yes, the house is quite as finc as I had been led to believe by my cousin's executors, but rather more sinister. It sits atop a huge and jutting point of land perhaps three miles north of Falmouth and nine miles north of Portland. Behind it are some four acres of grounds, gone back to the wild in the most formidable manner imaginable—junipers, scrub vines, bushes, and various forms of creeper climb wildly over the picturesque stone walls that separate the estate from the town domain. Awful imitations of Greek statuary peer blindly through the wrack from atop various hillocks—they seem, in most cases, about to lunge

---

*Originally published by *Night Shift*, 1978.

at the passer-by. My cousin Stephen's tastes seem to have run the gamut from the unacceptable to the downright horrific. There is an odd little summer house which has been nearly buried in scarlet sumac and a grotesque sundial in the midst of what must once have been a garden. It adds the final lunatic touch.

But the view from the parlour more than excuses this; I command a dizzying view of the rocks at the foot of Chapelwaite Head and the Atlantic itself. A huge, bellied bay window looks out on this, and a huge, toadlike secretary stands beside it. It will do nicely for the start of that novel which I have talked of so long [and no doubt tiresomely].

To-day has been gray with occasional splatters of rain. As I look out all seems to be a study in slate—the rocks, old and worn as Time itself, the sky, and of course the sea, which crashes against the granite fangs below with a sound which is not precisely sound but vibration—I can feel the waves with my feet even as I write. The sensation is not a wholly unpleasant one.

I know you disapprove my solitary habits, dear Bones, but I assure you that I am fine and happy. Calvin is with me, as practical, silent, and as dependable as ever, and by midweek I am sure that between the two of us we shall have straightened our affairs and made arrangements for necessary deliveries from town—and a company of cleaning women to begin blowing the dust from this place!

I will close—there are so many things as yet to be seen, rooms to explore, and doubtless a thousand pieces of execrable furniture to be viewed by these tender eyes. Once again, my thanks for the touch of familiar brought by your letter, and for your continuing regard.

Give my love to your wife, as you both have mine.

CHARLES.

Oct. 6, 1850.

DEAR BONES,

Such a place this is!

It continues to amaze me—as do the reactions of the townfolk in the closest village to my occupancy. That is a queer little place with the picturesque name of Preacher's Corners. It was there that Calvin contracted for the weekly provisions. The other errand, that of securing a sufficient supply of cordwood for the winter, was likewise taken care of. But Cal returned with gloomy countenance, and when I asked him what the trouble was, he replied grimly enough:

"They think you mad, Mr. Boone!"

I laughed and said that perhaps they had heard of the brain fever I suffered after my Sarah died—certainly I spoke madly enough at that time, as you could attest.

But Cal protested that no-one knew anything of me except through my cousin Stephen, who contracted for the same services as I have now made provision for. "What was said, sir, was that anyone who would live in Chapelwaite must be either a lunatic or run the risk of becoming one."

This left me utterly perplexed, as you may imagine, and I asked who had given him this amazing communication. He told me that he had been referred to a sullen and rather besotted pulp-logger named Thompson, who owns four hundred acres of pine, birch, and spruce, and who logs it with the help of his five sons, for sale to the mills in Portland and to householders in the immediate area.

When Cal, all unknowing of his queer prejudice, gave him the location to which the wood was to be brought, this Thompson stared at him with his mouth ajaw and said that he would send his sons with the wood, in the good light of the day, and by the sea road.

Calvin, apparently misreading my bemusement for distress, hastened to say that the man reeked of cheap whiskey and that he had then lapsed into some kind of nonsense about a deserted village and Cousin Stephen's relations—and worms! Calvin finished his business with one of Thompson's boys, who, I take it, was rather surly and none too sober or freshly scented himself. I take it there has been some of this reaction in Preacher's Corners itself, at the general store where Cal spoke with the shop-keeper, although this was more of the gossipy, behind-the-hand type.

None of this has bothered me much; we know how rustics dearly love to enrich their lives with the smell of scandal and myth, and I suppose poor Stephen and his side of the family are fair game. As I told Cal, a man who has fallen to his death almost from his own front porch is more than likely to stir talk.

The house itself is a constant amazement. Twenty-three rooms, Bones! The wainscotting which panels the upper floors and the portrait gallery is mildewed but still stout. While I stood in my late cousin's upstairs bedroom I could hear the rats scuttering behind it, and big ones they must be, from the sound they make—almost like people walking there. I should hate to encounter one in the dark; or even in the light, for that matter. Still, I have noted neither holes nor droppings. Odd.

The upper gallery is lined with bad portraits in frames which must be worth a fortune. Some bear a resemblance to Stephen as I remember him. I believe I have correctly identified my Uncle Henry Boone and his wife Judith; the others are unfamiliar. I suppose one of them may be my own notorious grandfather, Robert. But Stephen's side of the family is all but unknown to me, for which I am heartily sorry. The same good humour that shone in Stephen's letters to Sarah and me, the same light of high intellect, shines in these portraits, bad as they are.

For what foolish reasons families fall out! A rifled *escritoire*, hard words between brothers now dead three generations, and blameless descendants are needlessly estranged. I cannot help reflecting upon how fortunate it was that you and John Petty succeeded in contacting Stephen when it seemed I might follow my Sarah through the Gates—and upon how unfortunate it was that chance should have robbed us of a face-to-face meeting. How I would have loved to hear him defend the ancestral statuary and furnishings!

But do not let me denigrate the place to an extreme. Stephen's taste was not my own, true, but beneath the veneer of his additions there are pieces [a number of them shrouded by dust-covers in the upper chambers] which are true masterworks. There are beds, tables, and heavy, dark scrollings done in teak and mahogany, and many of the bedrooms and receiving chambers, the upper study and small parlour, hold a somber charm. The floors are rich pine that glow with an inner and secret light. There is dignity here; dignity and the weight of years. I cannot yet say I like it, but I do respect it. I am eager to watch it change as we revolve through the changes of this northern clime.

Lord, I run on! Write soon, Bones. Tell me what progress you make, and what news you hear from Petty and the rest. And please do not make the mistake of trying to persuade any new Southern acquaintances as to your views *too forcibly*—I understand that not all are content to answer merely with their mouths, as is our long-winded *friend*, Mr. Calhoun.

Yr. affectionate friend,
CHARLES.

Oct. 16, 1850.

DEAR RICHARD,

Hello, and how are you? I have thought about you often since I have taken up residence here at Chapelwaite, and had half-expected to hear from you—and now I receive a letter from Bones telling me that I'd forgotten to leave my address at the club! Rest assured that I would have written eventually anyway, as it sometimes seems that my true and loyal friends are all I have left in the world that is sure and completely normal. And, Lord, how spread we've become! You in Boston, writing faithfully for *The Liberator* [to which I have also sent my address, incidentally], Hanson in England on another of his confounded *jaunts*, and poor old Bones in the very *lions' lair*, recovering his lungs.

It goes as well as can be expected here, Dick, and be assured I will render you a full account when I am not quite as pressed by certain events which are extant here—I think your legal mind may be quite intrigued by certain happenings at Chapelwaite and in the area about it.

But in the meantime I have a favour to ask, if you will entertain it. Do you remember the historian you introduced me to at Mr. Clary's fund-raising dinner for the cause? I believe his name was Bigelow. At any rate, he mentioned that he made a hobby of collecting odd bits of historical lore which pertained to the very area in which I am now living. My favour, then, is this: Would you contact him and ask him what facts, bits of folklore, or *general rumour*—if any—he may be conversant with about a small, deserted village called JERUSALEM'S LOT, near a township called Preacher's Corners, on the Royal River? The stream itself is a tributary of the Androscoggin, and flows into that river approximately eleven miles above the river's emptying place near Chapelwaite. It would gratify me intensely, and, more important, may be a matter of some moment.

In looking over this letter I feel I have been a bit short with you, Dick, for which I am heartily sorry. But be assured I will explain myself shortly, and until that time I send my warmest regards to your wife, two fine sons, and, of course, to yourself.

Yr. affectionate friend,
CHARLES.

Oct. 16. 1850

DEAR BONES,

I have a tale to tell you which seems a little strange [and even disquieting] to both Cal and me—see what you think. If nothing else, it may serve to amuse you while you battle the mosquitoes!

Two days after I mailed my last to you, a group of four young ladies arrived from the Corners under the supervision of an elderly lady of intimidatingly competent visage named Mrs. Cloris, to set the place in order and to remove some of the dust that had been causing me to sneeze seemingly at every other step. They all seemed a little nervous as they went about their chores; indeed, one flighty miss uttered a small screech when I entered the upstairs parlour as she dusted.

I asked Mrs. Cloris about this [she was dusting the downstairs hall with grim determination that would have quite amazed you, her hair done up in an old faded bandanna], and she turned to me and said with an air of determination: "They don't like the house, and I don't like the house, sir, because it has always been a *bad* house."

My jaw dropped at this unexpected bit, and she went on in a kindlier tone: "I do not mean to say that Stephen Boone was not a fine man, for he was; I cleaned for him every second Thursday all the time he was here, as I cleaned for his father, Mr. Randolph Boone, until he and his wife disappeared in eighteen and sixteen. Mr. Stephen was a good and kindly man, and so you seem, sir (if you will pardon my bluntness; I know no other way to speak), but the house is *bad* and it always *has been*, and no Boone has ever been happy here since your grandfather Robert and his brother Philip fell out over stolen [and here she paused, almost guiltily] items in seventeen and eighty-nine."

Such memories these folks have, Bones!

Mrs. Cloris continued: "The house was built in unhappiness, has been lived in with unhappiness, there has been blood spilt on its floors [as you may or may not know, Bones, my Uncle Randolph was involved in an accident on the cellar stairs which took the life of his daughter Marcella; he then took his own life in a fit of remorse. The incident is related in one of Stephen's letters to me, on the sad occasion of his dead sister's birthday], there has been disappearance and accident.

"I have worked here, Mr. Boone, and I am neither blind nor deaf. I've heard awful sounds in the walls, sir, awful sounds—thumpings and crashings and once a strange wailing that was half-laughter. It fair made my blood curdle. It's a dark place, sir." And there she halted, perhaps afraid she had spoken too much.

As for myself, I hardly knew whether to be offended or amused, curious or merely matter-of-fact. I'm afraid that amusement won the day. "And what do you suspect, Mrs. Cloris? Ghosts rattling chains?"

But she only looked at me oddly. "Ghosts there may be. But it's not ghosts in the walls. It's not ghosts that wail and blubber like the damned and crash and blunder away in the darkness. It's—"

"Come, Mrs. Cloris," I prompted her. "You've come this far. Now can you finish what you've begun?"

The strangest expression of terror, pique, and—I would swear to it—religious awe passed over her face. "Some die not," she whispered. "Some live in the twilight shadows Between to serve—Him!"

And that was the end. For some minutes I continued to tax her, but she grew only more obstinate and would say no more. At last I desisted, fearing she might gather herself up and quit the premises.

This is the end of one episode, but a second occurred the following evening. Calvin had laid a fire downstairs and I was sitting in the living-room, drowsing over a copy of *The Intelligencer* and listening to the sound of wind-driven rain on the large bay window. I felt comfortable as only one can on such a night, when all is miserable outside and all is warmth and comfort inside; but a moment later Calvin appeared at the door, looking excited and a bit nervous.

"Are you awake, sir?" he asked.

"Barely," I said. "What is it?"

"I've found something upstairs I think you should see," he responded, with the same air of suppressed excitement.

I got up and followed him. As we climbed the wide stairs, Calvin said: "I was reading a book in the upstairs study—a rather strange one—when I heard a noise in the wall."

"Rats," I said. "Is that all?"

He paused on the landing, looking at me solemnly. The lamp he held cast weird, lurking shadows on the dark draperies and on the half-seen portraits that seemed now to leer rather than smile. Outside the wind rose to a brief scream and then subsided grudgingly.

"Not rats," Cal said. "There was a kind of blundering, thudding sound from behind the book-cases, and then a horrible gurgling—horrible, sir. And scratching, as if something were struggling to get out . . . to get at me!"

You can imagine my amazement, Bones. Calvin is not the type to give way to hysterical flights of imagination. It began to seem that there was a mystery here after all—and perhaps an ugly one indeed.

"What then?" I asked him. We had resumed down the hall, and I could see the light from the study spilling forth onto the floor of the gallery. I viewed it with some trepidation; the night seemed no longer comfortable.

"The scratching noise stopped. After a moment the thudding, shuffling sounds began again, this time moving away from me. It paused once, and I swear I heard a strange, almost inaudible laugh! I went to the book-case and began to push and pull, thinking there might be a partition, or a secret door."

"You found one?"

Cal paused at the door to the study. "No—but I found this!"

We stepped in and I saw a square black hole in the left case. The books at that point were nothing but dummies, and what Cal had found was a small hiding place. I flashed my lamp within it and saw nothing but a thick fall of dust, dust which must have been decades old.

"There was only this," Cal said quietly, and handed me a yellowed foolscap. The thing was a map, drawn in spider-thin strokes of black ink—the map of a town or village. There were perhaps seven buildings, and one, clearly marked with a steeple, bore this legend beneath it: *The Worm That Doth Corrupt*.

In the upper left corner, to what would have been the northwest of this little village, an arrow pointed. Inscribed beneath it: *Chapelwaite*.

Calvin said: "In town, sir, someone rather superstitiously mentioned a deserted village called Jerusalem's Lot. It's a place they steer clear of."

"But this?" I asked, fingering the odd legend below the steeple.

"I don't know."

A memory of Mrs. Cloris, adamant yet fearful, passed through my mind. "The Worm . . ." I muttered.

"Do you know something, Mr. Boone?"

"Perhaps . . . it might be amusing to have a look for this town tomorrow, do you think, Cal?"

He nodded, eyes lighting. We spent almost an hour after this looking for some breach in the wall behind the cubby-hole Cal had found, but with no success. Nor was there a recurrence of the noises Cal had described.

We retired with no further adventure that night.

On the following morning Calvin and I set out on our ramble through the woods. The rain of the night before had ceased, but the sky was somber and lowering. I could see Cal looking at me with some doubtfulness and I hastened to reassure him that should I tire, or the journey prove too far, I would not hesitate to call a halt to the affair. We had equipped ourselves with a picnic lunch, a fine Buckwhite compass, and, of course, the odd and ancient map of Jerusalem's Lot.

It was a strange and brooding day; not a bird seemed to sing nor an animal to move as we made our way through the great and gloomy stands of pine to the south and east. The only sounds were those of our own feet and the steady pound of the Atlantic against the headlands. The smell of the sea, almost preternaturally heavy, was our constant companion.

We had gone no more than two miles when we struck an overgrown road of what I believe were once called the "corduroy" variety; this tended in our general direction and we struck off along it, making brisk time. We spoke little. The day, with its still and ominous quality, weighed heavily on our spirits.

At about eleven o'clock we heard the sound of rushing water. The remnant of road took a hard turn to the left, and on the other side of a boiling, slaty little stream, like an apparition, was Jerusalem's Lot!

The stream was perhaps eight feet across, spanned by a moss-grown footbridge. On the far side, Bones, stood the most perfect little village you might imagine, understandably weathered, but amazingly preserved. Several houses, done in that austere yet commanding form for which the Puritans were justly famous, stood clustered near the steeply sheared bank. Further beyond, along a weed-grown thoroughfare, stood three or four of what might have been primitive business establishments, and beyond that, the spire of the church marked on the map, rising up to the gray sky and looking grim beyond description with its peeled paint and tarnished, leaning cross.

"The town is well named," Cal said softly beside me.

We crossed to the town and began to poke through it—and this is where my story grows slightly amazing, Bones, so prepare yourself!

The air seemed leaden as we walked among the buildings; weighted, if you will. The edifices were in a state of decay—shutters torn off, roofs crumbled under the weight of heavy snows gone by, windows dusty and leering. Shadows from odd corners and warped angles seemed to sit in sinister pools.

We entered an old rotting tavern first—somehow it did not seem right that we should invade any of those houses to which people had retired when they wished privacy. An old weather-scrubbed sign above the splintered door announced that this had been the BOAR'S HEAD INN AND TAVERN. The door creaked hellishly on its one remaining hinge, and we stepped into the shadowed interior. The smell of rot and mould was vaporous and nearly overpowering. And beneath it seemed to lie an even deeper smell, a slimy and pestiferous smell, a smell of ages and the decay of ages. Such a stench as might issue from corrupt coffins or violated tombs. I held my handkerchief to my nose and Cal did likewise. We surveyed the place.

"My God, sir—" Cal said faintly.

"It's never been touched," I finished for him.

As indeed it had not. Tables and chairs stood about like ghostly guardians of the watch, dusty, warped by the extreme changes in temperature which the New England climate is known for, but otherwise perfect—as if they had waited through the silent, echoing decades for those long gone to enter once more, to call for a pint or a dram, to deal cards and light clay pipes. A small square mirror hung beside the rules of the tavern, *unbroken*. Do you see the significance, Bones? Small boys are noted for exploration and vandalism; there is not a "haunted" house which stands with windows intact, no matter how fearsome the eldritch inhabitants are rumoured to be; not a shadowy graveyard without at least one tombstone upended by young pranksters. Certainly there must be a score of young pranksters in Preacher's Corners, not two miles from Jerusalem's Lot. Yet the inn-keeper's glass [which must have cost him a nice sum] was intact—as were the other fragile items we found in our pokings. The only damage in Jerusalem's Lot has been done by impersonal Nature. The implication is obvious: Jerusalem's Lot is a shunned town. But why? I have a notion, but before I even dare hint at it, I must proceed to the unsettling conclusion of our visit.

We went up to the sleeping quarters and found beds made up, pewter water-pitchers neatly placed beside them. The kitchen was likewise untouched by anything save the dust of the years and that horrible, sunken stench of decay. The tavern alone would be an antiquarian's paradise; the wondrously queer kitchen stove alone would fetch a pretty price at Boston auction.

"What do you think, Cal?" I asked when we had emerged again into the uncertain daylight.

"I think it's bad business, Mr. Boone," he replied in his doleful way, "and that we must see more to know more."

We gave the other shops scant notice—there was a hostelry with mouldering leather goods still hung on rusted flatnails, a chandler's, a warehouse with oak and pine still stacked within, a smithy.

We entered two houses as we made our way toward the church at the center of the village. Both were perfectly in the Puritan mode, full of items a collector would give his arm for, both deserted and full of the same rotten scent.

Nothing seemed to live or move in all of this but ourselves. We saw no insects, no birds, not even a cobweb fashioned in a window corner. Only dust.

At last we reached the church. It reared above us, grim, uninviting, cold. Its windows were black with the shadows inside, and any Godliness or sanctity had departed from it long ago. Of that I am certain. We mounted the steps, and I placed my hand on the large iron door-pull. A set, dark look passed from myself to Calvin and back again. I opened the portal. How long since the door had been touched? I would say with confidence that mine was the first in fifty years; perhaps longer. Rust-clogged hinges screamed as I opened it. The smell of rot and decay which smote us was nearly palpable. Cal made a gagging sound in his throat and twisted his head involuntarily for clearer air.

"Sir," he asked, "are you sure that you are—?"

"I'm fine," I said calmly. But I did not feel calm, Bones, no more than I do now. I believe, with Moses, with Jereboam, with Increase Mather, and with our own Hanson [when he is in a philosophical *temperament*], that there are spiritually noxious places, buildings where the milk of the cosmos has become sour and rancid. This church is such a place; I would swear to it.

We stepped into a long vestibule equipped with a dusty coat rack and shelved hymnals. It was windowless. Oil-lamps stood in niches here and there. An unremarkable room, I thought, until I heard Calvin's sharp gasp and saw what he had already noticed.

It was an obscenity.

I daren't describe that elaborately framed picture further than this: that it was done after the fleshy style of Rubens; that it contained a grotesque travesty of a madonna and child; that strange, half-shadowed creatures sported and crawled in the background.

"Lord," I whispered.

"There's no Lord here," Calvin said, and his words seemed to hang in the air. I opened the door leading into the church itself, and the odour became a miasma, nearly overpowering.

In the glimmering half-light of afternoon the pews stretched ghost-like to the altar. Above them was a high, oaken pulpit and a shadow-struck narthex from which gold glimmered.

With a half-sob Calvin, that devout Protestant, made the Holy Sign, and I followed suit. For the gold was a large, beautifully wrought cross—but it was hung upside-down, symbol of Satan's Mass.

"We must be calm," I heard myself saying. "We must be calm, Calvin. We must be calm."

But a shadow had touched my heart, and I was afraid as I had never been. I have walked beneath death's umbrella and thought there was none darker. But there is. There is.

We walked down the aisle, our footfalls echoing above and around us. We left tracks in the dust. And at the altar there were other tenebrous *objets d'art*. I will not, cannot, let my mind dwell upon them.

I began to mount to the pulpit itself.

"Don't, Mr. Boone!" Cal cried suddenly. "I'm afraid—"

But I had gained it. A huge book lay open upon the stand, writ both in Latin and crabbed runes which looked, to my unpractised eye, either Druidic or pre-Celtic. I enclose a card with several of the symbols, redrawn from memory.

I closed the book and looked at the words stamped into the leather: *De Vermis Mysteriis*. My Latin is rusty, but serviceable enough to translate: *The Mysteries of the Worm*.

As I touched it, that accursed church and Calvin's white, upturned face seemed to swim before me. It seemed that I heard low, chanting voices, full of hideous yet eager fear—and below that sound, another, filling the bowels of the earth. An hallucination, I doubt it not—but at the same moment, the church was filled with a very real sound, which I can only describe as a huge and macabre *turning* beneath my feet. The pulpit trembled beneath my fingers; the desecrated cross trembled on the wall.

We exited together, Cal and I, leaving the place to its own darkness, and neither of us dared look back until we had crossed the rude planks spanning the stream. I will not say we defiled the nineteen hundred years man has spent climbing upward from a hunkering and superstitious savage by actually running; but I would be a liar to say that we strolled.

That is my tale. You mustn't shadow your recovery by fearing that the fever has touched me again; Cal can attest to all in these pages, up to and including the hideous *noise*.

So I close, saying only that I wish I might see you [knowing that much of my bewilderment would drop away immediately], and that I remain your friend and admirer,

CHARLES.

Oct. 17, 1850.

DEAR GENTLEMEN:

In the most recent edition of your catalogue of household items (i.e., Summer, 1850), I noticed a preparation which is titled Rat's Bane. I should like to purchase one (1) 5-pound tin of this preparation at your stated price of thirty cents ($.30). I enclose return postage. Please mail to: Calvin McCann, Chapelwaite, Preacher's Corners, Cumberland County, Maine.

Thank you for your attention in this matter.

I remain, dear Gentlemen,
CALVIN McCANN.

Oct. 19, 1850.

DEAR BONES,

Developments of a disquieting nature.

The noises in the house have intensified, and I am growing more to the conclusion that rats are not all that move within our walls. Calvin and I went on another fruitless search for hidden crannies or passages, but found nothing. How poorly we would fit into one of Mrs. Radcliffe's romances! Cal claims, however, that much of the sound emanates from the cellar, and it is there we intend to explore tomorrow. It makes me no easier to know that Cousin Stephen's sister met her unfortunate end there.

Her portrait, by the by, hangs in the upstairs gallery. Marcella Boone was a sadly pretty thing, if the artist got her right, and I do know she never married. At times I think that Mrs. Cloris was right, that it *is* a bad house. It has certainly held nothing but gloom for its past inhabitants.

But I have more to say of the redoubtable Mrs. Cloris, for I have had this day a second interview with her. As the most level-headed person from the Corners that I have met thus far, I sought her out this afternoon, after an unpleasant interview which I will relate.

The wood was to have been delivered this morning, and when noon came and passed and no wood with it, I decided to take my daily walk into the town itself. My object was to visit Thompson, the man with whom Cal did business.

It has been a lovely day, full of the crisp snap of bright autumn, and by the time I reached the Thompsons' homestead [Cal, who remained home to poke further through Uncle Stephen's library, gave me adequate directions] I felt in the best mood that these last few days have seen, and quite prepared to forgive Thompson's tardiness with the wood.

The place was a massive tangle of weeds and fallen-down buildings in need of paint; to the left of the barn a huge sow, ready for November butchering, grunted and wallowed in a muddy sty, and in the littered yard between the house and out-buildings a woman in a tattered gingham dress was feeding chickens from her apron. When I hailed her, she turned a pale and vapid face toward me.

The sudden change in expression from utter, doltish emptiness to one of frenzied terror was quite wonderful to behold. I can only think she took me for Stephen himself, for she raised her hand in the prong-fingered sign of the evil eye and screamed. The chickenfeed scattered on the ground and the fowls fluttered away, squawking.

Before I could utter a sound, a huge, hulking figure of a man clad only in long-handled underwear lumbered out of the house with a squirrel-rifle in one hand and a jug in the other. From the red light in his eye and unsteady manner of walking, I judged that this was Thompson the Woodcutter himself.

"A Boone!" he roared. "G— d—n your eyes!" He dropped the jug a-rolling and also made the Sign.

"I've come," I said with as much equanimity as I could muster under the circumstances, "because the wood has not. According to the agreement you struck with my man—"

"G— d—n your man too, say I!" And for the first time I noticed that beneath his bluff and bluster he was deadly afraid. I began seriously to wonder if he mightn't actually use his rifle against me in his excitement.

I began carefully: "As a gesture of courtesy, you might—"

"G— d—n your courtesy!"

"Very well, then," I said with as much dignity as I could muster. "I bid you good day until you are more in control of yourself." And with this I turned away and began down the road to the village.

"Don'tchee come back!" he screamed after me. "Stick wi' your evil up there! Cursed! Cursed! Cursed!" He pelted a stone at me, which struck my shoulder. I would not give him the satisfaction of dodging.

So I sought out Mrs. Cloris, determined to solve the mystery of Thompson's enmity, at least. She is a widow [and none of your confounded *matchmaking*, Bones; she is easily fifteen years my senior, and I'll not see forty again] and lives by herself in a charming little cottage at the ocean's very doorstep. I found the lady hanging out her wash, and she seemed genuinely pleased to see me. I found this a great relief; it is vexing almost beyond words to be branded pariah for no understandable reason.

"Mr. Boone," said she, offering a half-curtsey. "If you've come about washing, I take none in past September. My rheumatiz pains me so that it's trouble enough to do my own."

"I wish laundry *was* the subject of my visit. I've come for help, Mrs. Cloris. I must know all you can tell me about Chapelwaite and Jerusalem's Lot and why the townsfolk regard me with such fear and suspicion!"

"Jerusalem's Lot! You know about *that*, then."

"Yes," I replied, "and visited it with my companion a week ago."

"God!" She went pale as milk, and tottered. I put out a hand to steady her. Her eyes rolled horribly, and for a moment I was sure she would swoon.

"Mrs. Cloris, I am sorry if I have said anything to—"

"Come inside," she said. "You must know. Sweet Jesu, the evil days have come again!"

She would not speak more until she had brewed strong tea in her sunshiny kitchen. When it was before us, she looked pensively out at the ocean for a time. Inevitably, her eyes and mine were drawn to the jutting brow of Chapelwaite Head, where the house looked out over the water. The large bay window glittered in the rays of the westering sun like a diamond. The view was beautiful but strangely disturbing. She suddenly turned to me and declared vehemently:

"Mr. Boone, you must leave Chapelwaite immediately!"

I was flabbergasted.

"There has been an evil breath in the air since you took up residence. In the last week—since you set foot in the accursed place—there have been omens and portents. A caul over the face of the moon; flocks of whippoorwills which roost in the cemeteries; an unnatural birth. You *must* leave!"

When I found my tongue, I spoke as gently as I could. "Mrs. Cloris, these things are dreams. You must know that."

"Is it a dream that Barbara Brown gave birth to a child with no eyes? Or that Clifton Brockett found a flat, pressed trail five feet wide in the woods beyond Chapelwaite *where all had withered and gone white*? And can you, who have visited Jerusalem's Lot, say with truth that nothing still lives there?"

I could not answer; the scene in that hideous church sprang before my eyes.

She clamped her gnarled hands together in an effort to calm herself. "I know of these things only from my mother and her mother before her. Do you know the history of your family as it applies to Chapelwaite?"

"Vaguely," I said. "The house has been the home of Philip Boone's line since the 1780s; his brother Robert, my grandfather, located in Massachusetts after an argument over stolen papers. Of Philip's side I know little, except that an unhappy shadow fell over it, extending from father to son to grandchildren—Marcella died in a tragic accident and Stephen fell to his death. It was his wish that Chapelwaite become the home of me and mine, and that the family rift thus be mended."

"Never to be mended," she whispered. "You know nothing of the original quarrel?"

"Robert Boone was discovered rifling his brother's desk."

"Philip Boone was mad," she said. "A man who trafficked with the unholy. The thing which Robert Boone *attempted* to remove was a profane Bible writ in the old tongues—Latin, Druidic, others. A hell-book."

"De Vermis Mysteriis."

She recoiled as if struck. "You know of it?"

"I have seen it . . . touched it." It seemed again she might swoon. A hand went to her mouth as if to stifle an outcry. "Yes; in Jerusalem's Lot. On the pulpit of a corrupt and desecrated church."

"Still there; still there, then." She rocked in her chair. "I had hoped God in His wisdom had cast it into the pit of hell."

"What relation had Philip Boone to Jerusalem's Lot?"

"Blood relation," she said darkly. "The Mark of the Beast was on him, although he walked in the clothes of the Lamb. And on the night of October 31, 1789, Philip Boone disappeared . . . and the entire populace of that damned village with him."

She would say little more; in fact, seemed to know little more. She would only reiterate her plea that I leave, giving as reason something about "blood calling to blood" and muttering about "those who *watch* and those who *guard.*" As twilight drew on she seemed to grow more agitated rather than less, and to placate her I promised that her wishes would be taken under strong consideration.

I walked home through lengthening, gloomy shadows, my good mood quite dissipated and my head spinning with questions which still plague me. Cal greeted me with the news that our noises in the walls have grown worse still—as I can attest at this moment. I try to tell myself that I hear only rats, but then I see the terrified, earnest face of Mrs. Cloris.

The moon has risen over the sea, bloated, full, the colour of blood, staining the ocean with a noxious shade. My mind turns to that church again and

(here a line is struck out)

But you shall not see that, Bones. It is too mad. It is time I slept, I think. My thoughts go out to you.

Regards,
CHARLES.

(The following is from the pocket journal of Calvin McCann.)

Oct. 20, '50

Took the liberty this morning of forcing the lock which binds the book closed; did it before Mr. Boone arose. No help; it is all in cypher. A simple one, I believe. Perhaps I may break it as easily as the lock. A diary, I am certain, the hand oddly like Mr. Boone's own. Whose book, shelved in the most obscure corner of this library and locked across the pages? It seems old, but how to tell? The corrupting air has largely been kept from its pages. More later, if time; Mr. Boone set upon looking about the cellar. Am afraid these dreadful goings-on will be too much for his chancy health yet. I must try to persuade him—

But he comes.

Oct. 20, 1850.

BONES,

I can't write I cant *[sic]* write of this yet I I I

(From the pocket journal of Calvin McCann)

Oct. 20, '50

As I had feared, his health has broken—

Dear God, our Father Who art in Heaven!

Cannot bear to think of it; yet it is planted, burned on my brain like a tin-type; that horror in the cellar—!

Alone now; half-past eight o'clock; house silent but—

Found him swooned over his writing table; he still sleeps; yet for those few moments how nobly he acquitted himself while I stood paralyzed and shattered!

His skin is waxy, cool. Not the fever again, God be thanks. I daren't move him or leave him to go to the village. And if I did go, who would return with me to aid him? Who would come to this cursed house?

O, the cellar! The things in the cellar that have haunted our walls!

Oct. 22, 1850.

DEAR BONES,

I am myself again, although weak, after thirty-six hours of unconsciousness. Myself again . . . what a grim and bitter joke! I shall never be myself again, never. I have come face to face with an insanity and a horror beyond the limits of human expression. And the end is not yet.

If it were not for Cal, I believe I should end my life this minute. He is one island of sanity in all this madness.

You shall know it all.

We had equipped ourselves with candles for our cellar exploration, and they threw a strong glow that was quite adequate—hellishly adequate! Calvin tried to dissuade me, citing my recent illness, saying that the most we should probably find would be some healthy rats to mark for poisoning.

I remained determined, however; Calvin fetched a sign and answered: "Have it as you must, then, Mr. Boone."

The entrance to the cellar is by means of a trap in the kitchen floor [which Cal assures me he has since stoutly boarded over], and we raised it only with a great deal of straining and lifting.

A foetid, overpowering smell came up out of the darkness, not unlike that which pervaded the deserted town across the Royal River. The candle I held shed its glow on a steeply slanting flight of stairs leading down into darkness. They were in a terrible state of repair—in one place an entire riser was missing, leaving only a black hole—and it was easy enough to see how the unfortunate Marcella might have come to her end there.

"Be careful, Mr. Boone!" Cal said; I told him I had no intention of being anything but, and we made the descent.

The floor was earthen, the walls of stout granite, and hardly wet. The place did not look like a rat haven at all, for there were none of the things rats like to make their nests in, such as old boxes, discarded furniture, piles of paper, and the like. We lifted our candles, gaining a small circle of light, but still able to see little. The floor had a gradual slope which seemed to run beneath the main living-room and the dining-room—i.e., to the west. It was in this direction we walked. All was in utter silence. The stench in the air grew steadily stronger, and the dark about us seemed to press like wool, as if jealous of the light which had temporarily deposed it after so many years of undisputed dominion.

At the far end, the granite walls gave way to a polished wood which seemed totally black and without reflective properties. Here the cellar ended, leaving what seemed to be an alcove off the main chamber. It was positioned at an angle which made inspection impossible without stepping around the corner.

Calvin and I did so.

It was as if a rotten spectre of this dwelling's sinister past had risen before us. A single chair stood in this alcove, and above it, fastened from a hook in one of the stout overhead beams, was a decayed noose of hemp.

"Then it was here that he hung himself," Calvin muttered. "God!"

"Yes . . . with the corpse of his daughter lying at the foot of the stairs behind him."

Cal began to speak; then I saw his eyes jerked to a spot behind me; then his words became a scream.

How, Bones, can I describe the sight which fell upon our eyes? How can I tell you of the hideous tenants within our walls?

The far wall swung back, and from that darkness a face leered—a face with eyes as ebon as the Styx itself. Its mouth yawned in a toothless, agonized grin; one yellow, rotted hand stretched itself out to us. It made a hideous, mewling sound and took a shambling step forward. The light from my candle fell upon it—

And I saw the livid rope-burn about its neck!

From beyond it something else moved, something I shall dream of until the day when all dreams cease: a girl with a pallid, mouldering face and a corpse-grin; a girl whose head lolled at a lunatic angle.

They wanted us; I know it. And I know they would have drawn us into that darkness and made us their own, had I not thrown my candle directly at the thing in the partition, and followed it with the chair beneath that noose.

After that, all is confused darkness. My mind has drawn the curtain. I awoke, as I have said, in my room with Cal at my side.

If I could leave, I should fly from this house of horror with my nightdress flapping at my heels. But I cannot. I have become a pawn in a deeper, darker drama. Do not ask how I know; I only do. Mrs. Cloris was right when she spoke of blood calling to blood; and how horribly right when she spoke of those who *watch* and those who *guard*. I fear that I have wakened a Force which has slept in the tenebrous village of 'Salem's Lot for half a century, a Force which has slain my ancestors and taken them in unholy bondage as *nosferatu*—the Undead. And I have greater fears than these, Bones, but I still see only in part. If I knew . . . if I only knew all!

CHARLES.

Postscriptum—And of course I write this only for myself; we are isolated from Preacher's Corners. I daren't carry my taint there to post this, and Calvin will not leave me. Perhaps, if God is good, this will reach you in some manner. C.

(From the pocket journal of Calvin McCann)

Oct. 23, '50

He is stronger to-day; we talked briefly of the *apparitions* in the cellar; agreed they were neither hallucinations or of an *ectoplasmic* origin, but *real*. Does Mr. Boone suspect, as I do, that they have gone? Perhaps; the noises are still; yet all is ominous yet, o'ercast with a dark pall. It seems we wait in the deceptive Eye of the Storm. . . .

Have found a packet of papers in an upstairs bedroom, lying in the bottom drawer of an old roll-top desk. Some correspondence & receipted bills lead me to believe the room was Robert Boone's. Yet the most interesting document is a few jottings on the back of an advertisement for gentlemen's beaver hats. At the top is writ:

Blessed are the meek.

Below, the following apparent nonsense is writ:

b k e d s h d e r m t h e s e a k
e l m s o e r a r e s h a m d e d

I believe 'tis the key of the locked and coded book in the library. The cypher above is certainly a rustic one used in the War for Independence known as the *Fence-Rail.* When one removes the "nulls" from the second bit of scribble, the following is obtained:

b e s d r t e e k
l s e a e h m e

Read up and down rather than across, the result is the original quotation from the Beatitudes.

Before I dare show this to Mr. Boone, I must be sure of the book's contents. . . .

Oct. 24, 1850.

DEAR BONES,

An amazing occurrence—Cal, always close-mouthed until absolutely sure of himself [a rare and admirable human trait], has found the diary of my grandfather Robert. The document was in a code which Cal himself has broken. He modestly declares that the discovery was an accident, but I suspect that perseverance and hard work had rather more to do with it.

At any rate, what a somber light it sheds on our mysteries here!

The first entry is dated June 1, 1789, the last October 27, 1789—four days before the cataclysmic disappearance of which Mrs. Cloris spoke. It tells a tale of deepening obsession—nay, of madness—and makes hideously clear the relationship between Great-Uncle Philip, the town of Jerusalem's Lot, and the book which rests in that desecrated church.

The town itself, according to Robert Boone, pre-dates Chapelwaite (built in 1782) and Preacher's Corners (known in those days as Preacher's Rest and founded in 1741); it was founded by a splinter group of the Puritan faith in 1710, a sect headed by a dour religious fanatic named James Boon. What a start that name gave me! That this Boon bore relation to my family can hardly be doubted, I believe. Mrs. Cloris could not have been more right in her superstitious belief that familial blood-line is of crucial importance in this matter; and I recall with terror her answer to my question about Philip and *his* relationship to 'Salem's Lot. "Blood relation," said she, and I fear that it is so.

The town became a settled community built around the church where Boon preached—or held court. My grandfather intimates that he also held commerce with any number of ladies from the town, assuring them that this was God's way and will. As a result, the town became an anomaly which could only have existed in those isolated and queer days when belief in witches and the Virgin Birth existed hand in hand: an interbred, rather degenerate religious village controlled by a half-mad preacher whose twin gospels were the Bible and de Goudge's sinister *Demon Dwellings*; a community in which rites of exorcism were held regularly; a community of incest and the insanity and physical defects which so often accompany that sin. I suspect [and believe Robert Boone must have also] that one of Boon's bastard off-spring must have left [or have been spirited away from] Jerusalem's Lot to seek his fortune to the south—and thus founded our present lineage. I do know, by my own family reckoning, that our clan supposedly originated in that part of Massachusetts which has so lately become this Sovereign State of Maine. My great-grandfather, Kenneth Boone, became a rich man as a result of the then-flourishing fur trade. It was his money, increased by time and wise investment, which built this ancestral home long after his death in 1763. His sons, Philip and Robert, built Chapelwaite. *Blood calls to blood,* Mrs. Cloris said. Could it be that Kenneth was born of James Boon, fled the madness of his father and his father's town, only to have his sons, all-unknowing, build the Boone home *not two miles from the Boon beginnings*? If 'tis true, does it not seem that some huge and invisible Hand has guided us?

According to Robert's diary, James Boon was ancient in 1789—and he must have been. Granting him an age of twenty-five in the year of the town's founding, he would have been one hundred and four, a prodigious age. The following is quoted direct from Robert Boone's diary:

> August 4, 1789.
>
> To-day for the first time I met this Man with whom my Brother has been so unhealthily taken; I must admit this Boon controls a strange Magnetism which upset me Greatly. He is a veritable Ancient, white-bearded, and dresses in a black Cassock which struck me as somehow obscene. More disturbing yet was the Fact that he was surrounded by Women, as a Sultan would be surrounded by his Harem; and P. assures me he is active yet, although at least an Octogenarian. . . . The Village itself I had visited only once before, and will not visit again; its Streets are silent and filled with the Fear the old Man inspires from his Pulpit: I fear also that Like has mated with Like, as so many of the Faces are similar. It seemed that each way I turned I beheld the old Man's Visage . . . all are so wan; they seem Lack-Luster, as if sucked dry of all Vitality, I beheld Eyeless and Noseless Children, Women who wept and gibbered and pointed at the Sky for no Reason, and garbled talk from the Scriptures with talk of Demons; . . .
>
> P. wished me to stay for Services, but the thought of that sinister Ancient in the Pulpit before an Audience of this Town's interbred Populace repulsed me and I made an Excuse. . . .

The entries preceding and following this tell of Philip's growing fascination with James Boon. On September 1, 1789, Philip was baptized into Boon's church. His brother says: "I am aghast with Amaze and

Horror—my Brother has changed before my very Eyes—he even seems to grow to resemble the wretched Man."

First mention of the book occurs on July 23. Robert's diary records it only briefly: "P. returned from the smaller Village tonight with, I thought, a rather wild Visage. Would not speak until Bed-time, when he said that Boon had enquired after a Book titled *Mysteries of the Worm*. To please P. I promised to write Johns & Goodfellow a letter of enquiry; P. almost fawningly Grateful."

On August 12, this notation: "Rec'd two Letters in the Post today . . . one from Johns & Goodfellow in Boston. They have Note of the Tome in which P. has expressed an Interest. Only five Copies extant in this Country. The Letter is rather cool; odd indeed. Have known Henry Goodfellow for Years."

> August 13:
> P. insanely excited by Goodfellow's letter; refuses to say why. He would only say that Boon is *exceedingly anxious* to obtain a Copy. Cannot think why, since by the Title it seems only a harmless gardening Treatise. . . .
> Am worried for Philip; he grows stranger to me Daily. I wish now we had not returned to Chapelwaite. The Summer is hot, oppressive, and filled with Omens. . . .

There are only two further mentions of the infamous book in Robert's diary [he seems not to have realized the true importance of it, even at the end]. From the entry of September 4:

> I have petitioned Goodfellow to act as P.'s Agent in the matter of the Purchase, although my better Judgement cries against It. What use to demur? Has he not his own Money, should I refuse? And in return I have extracted a Promise from Philip to recant this noisome Baptism . . . yet he is so Hectic; nearly Feverish; I do not trust him. I am hopelessly *at Sea* in this Matter. . . .

Finally, September 16:

> The Book arrived to-day, with a note from Goodfellow saying he wishes no more of my Trade. . . . P. was excited to an unnatural Degree; all but snatched the Book from my Hands. It is writ in bastard Latin and a Runic Script of which I can read Nothing. The Thing seemed almost warm to the Touch, and to vibrate in my Hands, as if it contained a huge Power. . . . I reminded P. of his Promise to Recant and he only laughed in an ugly, crazed Fashion and waved that Book in my Face, crying over and over again: "We have it! We have it! The Worm! The Secret of the Worm!"

He is now fled, I suppose to his mad Benefactor, and I have not seen him more this Day. . . .

Of the book there is no more, but I have made certain deductions which seem at least probable. First, that this book was, as Mrs. Cloris has said, the subject of the falling-out between Robert and Philip; second, that it is a repository of unholy incantation, possibly of Druidic origin [many of the Druidic blood-rituals were preserved in print by the Roman conquerors of Britain in the name of scholarship, and many of these infernal cook-books are among the world's forbidden literature]; third, that Boon and Philip intended to use the book for their own ends. Perhaps, in some twisted way, they intended good, but I do not believe it. I believe they had long before bound themselves over to whatever faceless powers exist beyond the rim of the Universe; powers which may exist beyond the very fabric of Time. The last entries of Robert Boone's diary lend a dim glow of approbation to these speculations, and I allow them to speak for themselves:

October 26, 1789

A terrific Babble in Preacher's Corners to-day; Frawley, the Blacksmith, seized my Arm and demanded to know "What your Brother and that mad Antichrist are into up there." Goody Randall claims there have been *Signs* in the Sky of *great impending Disaster*. A Cow has been born with two Heads.

As for Myself, I know not what impends; perhaps 'tis my Brother's Insanity. His Hair has gone Gray almost Overnight, his Eyes are great bloodshot Circles from which the pleasing light of Sanity seems to have departed. He grins and whispers, and, for some Reason of his Own, has begun to haunt our Cellar when not in Jerusalem's Lot.

The Whippoorwills congregate about the House and upon the Grass; their combined Calling from the Mist blends with the Sea into an unearthly Shriek that precludes all thought of Sleep.

October 27, 1789

Followed P. this Evening when he departed for Jerusalem's Lot, keeping a safe Distance to avoid Discovery. The cursed Whippoorwills flock through the Woods, filling all with a deathly, psychopompotic Chant. I dared not cross the Bridge; the Town all dark except for the Church, which was litten with a ghastly red Glare that seemed to transform the high, peak'd Windows into the Eyes of the Inferno. Voices rose and fell in a Devil's Litany, sometimes laughing, sometimes sobbing. The very Ground seem'd to swell and groan beneath me, as if it bore an awful Weight, and I fled, amaz'd and full of Terror, the hellish, screaming Cries of the Whippoorwills dinning in my ears as I ran through those shadow-riven Woods.

All tends to the Climax, yet unforeseen. I dare not sleep for the Dreams that come, yet not remain awake for what lunatic Terrors may come. The night is full of awful Sounds and I fear— And yet I feel the urge to go again, to watch, *to see*. It seems that Philip himself calls me, and the old Man.
The Birds
cursed cursed cursed

Here the diary of Robert Boone ends.

Yet you must notice, Bones, near the conclusion, that he claims Philip himself seemed to call him. My final conclusion is formed by these lines, by the talk of Mrs. Cloris and the others, but most of all by those terrifying figures in the cellar, dead yet alive. Our line is yet an unfortunate one, Bones. There is a curse over us which refuses to be buried; it lives a hideous shadow-life in this house and that town. And the culmination of the cycle is drawing close again. I am the last of the Boone blood. I fear that something knows this, and that I am at the nexus of an evil endeavour beyond all sane understanding. The anniversary is All Saints' Eve, one week from today.

How shall I proceed? If only you were here to counsel me, to help me! If only you were here!

I must know all; I must return to the shunned town. May God support me!

CHARLES.

(From the pocket journal of Calvin McCann)

Oct. 25, '50

Mr. Boone has slept nearly all this day. His face is pallid and much thinner. I fear recurrence of his fever is inevitable.

While refreshing his water carafe I caught sight of two unmailed letters to Mr. Granson in Florida. He plans to return to Jerusalem's Lot; 'twill be the killing of him if I allow it. Dare I steal away to Preacher's Corners and hire a buggy? I must, and yet what if he wakes? If I should return and find him gone?

The noises have begun in our walls again. Thank God he still sleeps! My mind shudders from the import of this.

Later

I brought him his dinner on a tray. He plans on rising later, and despite his evasions, I know what he plans; yet I go to Preacher's Corners. Several of the sleeping-powders prescribed to him during his late illness remained with my things; he drank one with his tea, all-unknowing. He sleeps again.

To leave him with the Things that shamble behind our walls terrifies me; to let him continue even one more day within these walls terrifies me even more greatly. I have locked him in.

Got grant he should still be there, safe and sleeping, when I return with the buggy!

Still later

Stoned me! Stoned me like a wild and rabid dog! Monsters and fiends! These, that call themselves *men*! We are prisoners here—

The birds, the whippoorwills, have begun to gather.

October 26, 1850.

DEAR BONES,

It is nearly dusk, and I have just wakened, having slept nearly the last twenty-four hours away. Although Cal has said nothing, I suspect he put a sleeping-powder in my tea, having gleaned my intentions. He is a good and faithful friend, intending only the best, and I shall say nothing.

Yet my mind is set. Tomorrow is the day. I am calm, resolved, but also seem to feel the subtle onset of the fever again. If it is so, it *must* be tomorrow. Perhaps tonight would be better still; yet not even the fires of Hell itself could induce me to set foot in that village by shadowlight.

Should I write no more, may God bless and keep you, Bones.

CHARLES.

Postscriptum—The birds have set up their cry, and the horrible shuffling sounds have begun again. Cal does not think I hear, but I do.

C.

(From the pocket journal of Calvin McCann)

Oct. 27, '50
5 AM

He is impersuadable. Very well. I go with him.

November 4, 1850.

DEAR BONES,

Weak, yet lucid. I am not sure of the date, yet my almanac assures me by tide and sunset that it must be correct. I sit at my desk, where I sat when I first wrote you from Chapelwaite, and look out over the dark sea from which the last of the light is rapidly fading. I shall never see more. This night is my night; I leave it for whatever shadows be.

How it heaves itself at the rocks, this sea! It throws clouds of seafoam at the darkling sky in banners, making the floor beneath me tremble. In the window-glass I see my reflection, pallid as any vampire's. I have been without nourishment since the twenty-seventh of

October, and should have been without water, had not Calvin left the carafe beside my bed on that day.

O, Cal! He is no more, Bones. He is gone in my place, in the place of this wretch with his pipestem arms and skull face who I see reflected back in the darkened glass. And yet he may be the more fortunate; for no dreams haunt him as they have haunted me these last days—twisted shapes that lurk in the nightmare corridors of delirium. Even now my hands tremble; I have splotched the page with ink.

Calvin confronted me on that morning just as I was about to slip away—and I thinking I had been so crafty. I had told him that I had decided we must leave, and asked him if he would go to Tandrell, some ten miles distant, and hire a trap where we were less notorious. He agreed to make the hike and I watched him leave by the sea-road. When he was out of sight I quickly made myself ready, donning both coat and muffler [for the weather had turned frosty; the first touch of coming winter was on that morning's cutting breeze]. I wished briefly for a gun, then laughed at myself for the wish. What avails guns in such a matter?

I let myself out by the pantry-way, pausing for a last look at sea and sky; for the smell of the fresh air against the putrescence I knew I should smell soon enough; for the sight of a foraging gull wheeling below the clouds.

I turned—and there stood Calvin McCann.

"You shall not go alone," he said; and his face was as grim as ever I have seen it.

"But, Calvin—" I began.

"No, not a word! We go together and do what we must, or I return you bodily to the house. You are not well. You shall not go alone."

It is impossible to describe the conflicting emotions that swept over me: confusion, pique, gratefulness—yet the greatest of them was love.

We made our way silently past the summer house and the sundial, down the weed-covered verge and into the woods. All was dead still—not a bird sang nor a wood-cricket chirruped. The world seemed cupped in a silent pall. There was only the ever-present smell of salt, and from far away, the faint tang of woodsmoke. The woods were a blazoned riot of colour, but, to my eye, scarlet seemed to predominate all.

Soon the scent of salt passed, and another, more sinister odour took its place; that rottenness which I have mentioned. When we came to the leaning bridge which spanned the Royal, I expected Cal to ask me again to defer, but he did not. He paused, looked at that grim spire which seemed to mock the blue sky above it, and then looked at me. We went on.

We proceeded with quick yet dread footsteps to James Boon's

church. The door still hung ajar from our latter exit, and the darkness within seemed to leer at us. As we mounted the steps, brass seemed to fill my heart; my hand trembled as it touched the door-handle and pulled it. The smell within was greater, more noxious than ever.

We stepped into the shadowy anteroom and, with no pause, into the main chamber.

It was a shambles.

Something vast had been at work in there, and a mighty destruction had taken place. Pews were overturned and heaped like jackstraws. The wicked cross lay against the east wall, and a jagged hole in the plaster above it testified to the force with which it had been hurled. The oil-lamps had been ripped from their high fixtures, and the reek of whale-oil mingled with the terrible stink which pervaded the town. And down the center aisle, like a ghastly bridal path, was a trail of black ichor, mingled with sinister tendrils of blood. Our eyes followed it to the pulpit—the only untouched thing in view. Atop it, staring at us from across the blasphemous Book with glazed eyes, was the butchered body of a lamb.

"God," Calvin whispered.

We approached, keeping clear of the slime on the floor. The room echoed back our footsteps and seemed to transmute them into the sound of gigantic laughter.

We mounted the narthex together. The lamb had not been torn or eaten; it appeared, rather, to have been *squeezed* until its blood vessels had forcibly ruptured. Blood lay in thick and noisome puddles on the lectern itself, and about the base of it . . . *yet on the book it was transparent, and the crabbed runes could be read through it, as through coloured glass!*

"Must we touch it?" Cal asked, unfaltering.

"Yes. I must have it."

"What will you do?"

"What should have been done sixty years ago. I am going to destroy it."

We rolled the lamb's corpse away from the book; it struck the floor with a hideous, lolling thud. The blood-stained pages now seemed alive with a scarlet glow of their own.

My ears began to ring and hum; a low chant seemed to emanate from the walls themselves. From the twisted look on Cal's face I knew he heard the same. The floor beneath us trembled, as if the familiar which haunted this church came now unto us, to protect its own. The fabric of sane space and time seemed to twist and crack; the church seemed filled with spectres and litten with the hell-glow of eternal cold fire. It seemed that I saw James Boon, hideous and misshapen, cavorting around the supine body of a woman, and my Grand-Uncle Philip behind him, an acolyte in a black, hooded cassock, who held a knife and a bowl.

"Deum vobiscum magna vermis—"

The words shuddered and writhed on the page before me, soaked in the blood of sacrifice, prize of a creature that shambles beyond the stars—

A blind, interbred congregation swaying in mindless, daemoniac praise; deformed faces filled with hungering, nameless anticipation—

And the Latin was replaced by an older tongue, ancient when Egypt was young and the Pyramids unbuilt, ancient when this Earth still hung in an unformed, boiling firmament of empty gas:

"Gyyagin vardar Yogsoggoth! Verminis! Gyyagin! Gyyagin! Gyyagin!"

The pulpit began to rend and split, pushing upward—

Calvin screamed and lifted an arm to shield his face. The narthex trembled with a huge, tenebrous motion like a ship wracked in a gale. I snatched up the book and held it away from me; it seemed filled with the heat of the sun and I felt that I should be cindered, blinded.

"Run!" Calvin screamed. "Run!"

But I stood frozen and the alien presence filled me like an ancient vessel that had waited for years—for generations!

"Gyyagin vardar!" I screamed. "Servant of Yogsoggoth, the Nameless One! The Worm from beyond Space! Star-Eater! Blinder of Time! Verminis! Now comes the Hour of Filling, the Time of Rending! Verminis! Alyah! Alyah! Gyyagin!"

Calvin pushed me and I tottered, the church whirling before me, and fell to the floor. My head crashed against the edge of an upturned pew, and red fire filled my head—yet seemed to clear it.

I groped for the sulphur matches I had brought.

Subterranean thunder filled the place. Plaster fell. The rusted bell in the steeple pealed a choked devil's carillon in sympathetic vibration.

My match flared. I touched it to the book just as the pulpit exploded upward in a rending explosion of wood. A huge black maw was discovered beneath; Cal tottered on the edge, his hands held out, his face distended in a wordless scream that I shall hear forever.

And then there was a huge surge of gray, vibrating flesh. The smell became a nightmare tide. It was a huge outpouring of a viscid, pustulant jelly, a huge and awful form that seemed to skyrocket from the very bowels of the ground. And yet, with a sudden horrible comprehension which no man can have known, I perceived *that it was but one ring, one segment, of a monster worm that had existed eyeless for years in the chambered darkness beneath that abominated church!*

The book flared alight in my hands, and the Thing seemed to scream soundlessly above me. Calvin was struck glancingly and flung the length of the church like a doll with a broken neck.

It subsided—the thing subsided, leaving only a huge and shattered hole surrounded with black slime, and a great screaming, mewling sound that seemed to fade through colossal distances and was gone.

I looked down. The book was ashes.

I began to laugh, then to howl like a struck beast.

All sanity left me, and I sat on the floor with blood streaming from my temple, screaming and gibbering into those unhallowed shadows while Calvin sprawled in the far corner, staring at me with glazing, horror-struck eyes.

I have no idea how long I existed in that state. It is beyond all telling. But when I came again to my faculties, shadows had drawn long paths around me and I sat in twilight. Movement had caught my eye, movement from the shattered hole in the narthex floor.

A hand groped its way over the riven floorboards.

My mad laughter choked in my throat. All hysteria melted into numb bloodlessness.

With terrible, vengeful slowness, a wracked figure pulled itself up from darkness, and a half-skull peered at me. Beetles crawled over the fleshless forehead. A rotted cassock clung to the askew hollows of mouldered collarbones. Only the eyes lived—red, insane pits that glared at me with more than lunacy; they glared with the empty life of the pathless wastes beyond the edges of the Universe.

It came to take me down to darkness.

That was when I fled, screeching, leaving the body of my lifelong friend unheeded in that place of dread. I ran until the air seemed to burst like magma in my lungs and brain. I ran until I had gained this possessed and tainted house again, and my room, where I collapsed and have lain like a dead man until to-day. I ran because even in my crazed state, and even in the shattered ruin of that dead-yet-animated shape, *I had seen the family resemblance*. Yet not of Philip or of Robert, whose likenesses hang in the upstairs gallery. *That rotted visage belonged to James Boon, Keeper of the Worm!*

He still lives somewhere in the twisted, lightless wanderings beneath Jerusalem's Lot and Chapelwaite—and *It* still lives. The burning of the book thwarted *It*, but there are other copies.

Yet I am the gateway, and I am the last of the Boone blood. For the good of all humanity I must die . . . and break the chain forever.

I go to the sea now, Bones. My journey, like my story, is at an end. May God rest you and grant you all peace.

CHARLES.

* * *

The odd series of papers above was eventually received by Mr. Everett Granson, to whom they had been addressed. It is assumed that a recurrence of the unfortunate brain fever which struck him originally following the death of his wife in 1848 caused Charles Boone to lose his sanity and murder his companion and longtime friend, Mr. Calvin McCann.

The entries in Mr. McCann's pocket journal are a fascinating exercise in forgery, undoubtedly perpetrated by Charles Boone in an effort to reinforce his own paranoid delusions.

In at least two particulars, however, Charles Boone is proved wrong. First, when the town of Jerusalem's Lot was "rediscovered" (I use the term historically, of course), the floor of the narthex, although rotted, showed no sign of explosion or huge damage. Although the ancient pews *were* overturned and several windows shattered, this can be assumed to be the work of vandals from neighboring towns over the years. Among the older residents of Preacher's Corners and Tandrell there is still some idle rumor about Jerusalem's Lot (perhaps, in his day, it was this kind of harmless folk legend which started Charles Boone's mind on its fatal course), but this seems hardly relevant.

Second, Charles Boone was not the last of his line. His grandfather, Robert Boone, sired at least two bastards. One died in infancy. The second took the Boone name and located in the town of Central Falls, Rhode Island. I am the final descendant of this offshoot of the Boone line; Charles Boone's second cousin, removed by three generations. These papers have been in my committal for ten years. I offer them for publication on the occasion of my residence in the Boone ancestral home, Chapelwaite, in the hope that the reader will find sympathy in his heart for Charles Boone's poor, misguided soul. So far as I can tell, he was correct about only one thing: this place badly needs the services of an exterminator.

There are some huge rats in the walls, by the sound.

Signed,
James Robert Boone
October 2, 1971.

Discovery of the Ghooric Zone*

RICHARD A. LUPOFF

They were having sex when the warning gong sounded, Gomati and Njord and Shoten. The shimmering, fading sound indicated first long-range contact with the remote object, the long-suspected but never-before-visited tenth planet that circled far beyond the eccentric orbit of Pluto, rolling about its distant primary with irrational speed, its huge mass bathed in eternal darkness and incredible cold some sixteen billion kilometers from the remote, almost invisible, sun.

Gomati was the female member of the ship's crew. She was tall, nearly two meters from the top of her satiny smooth scalp to the tips of her glittering tin-alloy toenails. When the gong sounded she burst into a cascade of rippling laughter, high-pitched and mirthful, at the incongruity of the cosmic event's impingement upon the fleshly.

The ship had launched from Pluto, even though at this point in Pluto's orbit it was less distant from the sun than was Neptune. Fabricated in the nearly null-gravity conditions of Neptune's tiny moon Nereid, the ship had been ferried back, segment by segment, for assembly, for the cyborging of its scores of tiny biotic brains, onloading of its three-member crew, and its launch from the cratered rock surface of Pluto.

Njord, the male crew member, cursed, distracted by the radar gong, angered by Gomati's inattention, humiliated by her amusement and by her drawing away from himself and Shoten. Njord felt his organ grow flaccid at the distraction, and for the moment he regretted the decision he had made, prior to the cyborging operations of his adolescence, to retain his organic phallus and gonads. A cyborged capability might have proven more potently enduring in the circumstances, but Njord's pubescent pride had denied the possibility of his ever facing inconvenient detumescence.

---

*Originally published in *Chrysalis*, 1977.

Flung from rocky Pluto as the planet swung toward the ecliptic on its nearly eighteen-degree zoom, the ship was virtually catapulted away from the sun; it swung around Neptune, paid passing salute to the satellite of its birth with course-correcting emissions, then fled, a dart from the gravitic sling, into the black unknown.

And Shoten, most extensively cyborged of the crew members, flicked a mental command. Hooking into the ship's sensors, Shoten homed the consciousness of the navigational biotic brains onto the remote readouts that spelled the location of the distant object. The readouts confirmed suspected information about the object: its great mass, its incredible distance beyond even the aphelion of the orbit of Pluto some eight billion kilometers from the sun—the distant object circled its primary at a distance twice as great as Pluto's farthest departure from the solar epicenter.

The ship—named *Khons* in honor of an ancient celestial deity—held life-support supplies for the three crew members and fuel and power reserves for the complete outward journey, the planned landing on the distant object, the return takeoff and journey and final landing, not on Pluto—which by the time of *Khons*'s return would be far above the solar ecliptic and beyond the orbit of Neptune—but on Neptune's larger moon Triton, where a reception base had been readied before *Khons* ever had launched on its journey of exploration.

As for Njord, he grumbled under his breath, wishing almost irrelevantly that he knew the original gender of Shoten Binayakya before the latter's cyborging. Njord Freyr, born in the Laddino Imperium of earth, had retained his masculinity even as he had undergone the customary implantations, excisions, and modifications of pubescent cyborging.

Sri Gomati, of Khmeric Gondwanaland, had similarly retained her female primary characteristics in function and conformation even though she had opted for the substitution of metallic labia and clitoris, which replacement Njord Freyr found at times irritating.

But Shoten, Shoten Binayakya, fitted with multiple configurable genitalia, remained enigmatic, ambiguous as to his or her own origin: earthborn, or claiming so, yet giving allegiance neither to the Laddino Imperium governed by Yamm Kerit ben Chibcha, as did Njord Freyr, nor to Khmeric Gondwanaland, ruled by Nrisimha, the Little Lion, where lay the loyalty of Sri Gomati.

"So," Njord grated. "So, the great planet thus announces its presence." He grimaced as automatic materials-reclamation servos skittered futilely, seeking recoverable proteoids from the aborted congress.

Sri Gomati, enigmatic silvered cyberoptics glittering, turned to face the disgruntled Njord, the ambiguous Shoten. "Can you see it yet?" she asked. "Can you get a visual fix?"

Shoten Binayakya reached a cyberclaw, tapped a visual extensor control. Biotic brains keyed to obey any crew member activated the extensor, guided it toward one glittering optic. The shimmering field crept aside; input receptacles opened, ready for the insertion of fiber-optic conductors.

A click, silence.

D68/Y37/C22/FLASH

Yamm Kerit ben Chibcha's coronation was splendid. Never before had the South Polar Jerusalem seen such pomp, such display of pageantry and power. Thousands of slaves, naked and gilded and draped in jewelry and feathers, paraded up the wide boulevard before the Imperial Palace. They drew, by ropes of woven gold and weizmannium, glittering juggernauts. Fountains sprayed scented wine. Chamberlains threw fistfuls of xanthic shekels to cheering crowds.

The climax of the spectacle was the march of the anthrocyberphants, resplendent mutated elephants whose cerebellums had been surgically removed at birth and replaced with spheres of human brain material cultured from clone-cells donated (involuntarily in some cases) by the greatest scientists, scholars, and intellectuals in Yamm Kerit ben Chibcha's realm. When the anthrocyberphants were well grown and into their adolescence, their gonads were surgically removed and replaced with a variety of electronic implants, including inertial guidance computers, magnetic compass-gyroscopes, neural transceivers.

The anthrocyberphants pranced and tumbled down the grand boulevard before the Imperial Palace, trumpeting melodies from Wagner, Mendelssohn, Bach, Mozart, vain self-portraiture by Richard Strauss, erotic fantasies by Scriabin, extended lines from Britten, discordant percussives by Edgard Varèse, all in perfect orchestral harmony, all punctuated by the sounds of tympani, timbales, kettledrums, and cymbals held in writhing flexible tentacles that grew from nodes at the marchers' shoulders.

Upon the silken-draped and jewel-encrusted balcony of the Imperial Palace, the Ultimate Monarch of Laddino Imperium smiled and waved, bowed, applauded, turned to turbaned chamberlains, and grasped fistfuls of commemorative favors to toss graciously upon the marchers and the cheering crowds come to celebrate the grand ceremonial.

The Laddino Imperium included all of the grand Antarctic domain of the former Israel-in-Exile and the expanded territory of Greater Hai Brasil that had extended to claim hegemony over all of the Americas, from Hudson's Bay to Patagonia, before falling under sway of the South Polar nation. The Ultimate Monarch, Yamm Kerit ben Chibcha, bowed, waved, tossed favors to the crowd. Deep in the bowels of the earth beneath once-frozen plains and mountains, huge gyroscopes throbbed into life.

The axis of the earth began to shift through a lengthy and carefully computed cycle. None but the servants and advisors of the Ultimate Monarch had been consulted, and none but the will of Yamm Kerit ben Chibcha, the Ultimate Monarch, was considered. The ambition of Yamm Kerit ben Chibcha was to give every citizen of the planet earth, every square meter of territory, a fair and equitable access to the wealth, the beauty, the joy, the light, the warmth of the sun.

As the huge gyroscopes whirled their massive flywheels, the earth shifted its ancient tilt.

The fanatic hordes of Nrisimha, the Little Lion, poured from the city of Medina in the ancient Arabian desert, conquering all before them in the holy name of the Little Lion of God. The forces of Novum Romanum, the empire built by Fortuna Pales, and of the New Khmer Domain, created a century before by Vidya Devi, slaughtered the followers of the Little Lion Nrisimha by the hundreds of thousands, then by the millions.

How could Nrisimha continue to replace the decimated armies? How many soldiers could the single city of Medina produce? What was the secret of the fanatical hordes?

No one knew.

But they poured forth, fearless, unstoppable, unslowable, unturnable. All that the forces of resistance could do was slaughter them by the million, and they fell, they fell, but their fellows only marched across their very bodies, their strange bodies that did not putrefy like the corpses of normal soldiers but seemed instead to turn to an amorphous gel and then to sink into the earth itself, leaving behind no sign of their presence, not even uniforms or weapons or equipment, but only, in the wake of their passage, fields of strange flowers and fruits that bloomed gorgeously into towering pillars and petals and berries the size of melons, that produced sweet narcotic fumes and brought to those who harvested and ate them dreams of haunting beauty and incomparable weirdness.

Strange messengers sped across the sands of the deserts of Africa and Asia bearing the word that the Little Lion Nrisimha had come to bring peace and glory and splendor to a new Empire, to Khmeric Gondwanaland, an absolute dictatorship of unparalleled benevolence that would stretch from Siberia to Ireland and from the Arctic Circle to the Cape of Good Hope.

It took remarkably few years for the followers of the Little Lion Nrisimha to complete their conquest, and few more for the establishment of an efficient infrastructure and the appointment of regional satrapies under the absolute command of Nrisimha.

Khmeric Gondwanaland was a roaring success.

It was less than a century from the complete triumph of Yamm Kerit ben Chibcha throughout the Laddino Imperium and that of Nrisimha the Little Lion in Khmeric Gondwanaland, when the two great empires were driven into union by the eruption of attacking batrachian forces from beneath the seas of the planet. How long these strange froglike intelligences had lived in their deep and gloomy metropoli hundreds of meters beneath the surface of the earth's oceans will remain forever imponderable.

What stimulated them to rise and attack the land-dwelling nations of the earth is also unknown, although in all likelihood the steady shifting of the earth's axis brought about by the gargantuan subterranean gyroscopes of Yamm Kerit ben Chibcha was in fact the cause of the attacks.

The Deep Ones emerged and waded ashore in all regions at once. They wore only strangely crafted bangles and ornaments of uncorroded metal. They carried weapons resembling the barbed tridents of marine legendry. They dragged behind them terrible stone statues of indescribable extramundane monstrosities before which they conducted rites of blasphemous abandon and unmentionable perversion.

The Laddino Imperium and Khmeric Gondwanaland combined their respective might to deal with the menace, to drive the strange Deep Ones back into the murky realms from which they had emerged. By the year 2337 a unified earth lay once more tranquil and prosperous beneath a glowing and benevolent sun.

The menace of the Deep Ones, at least for the time, was over.

And billions of kilometers from earth, humanity renewed its heroic thrust toward the outermost regions of the solar system.

MARCH 15, 2337

"Not yet," Shoten Binayakya's voice clattered.

"Soon," Gomati countered. She hooked into *Khons*'s radar sensor, letting cyborged biots convert incoming pulses into pseudovisuals. "Look!" she exclaimed. "It's a whole system!"

Njord Freyr stirred, determined to pull his attention away from frustration, direct it toward a topic that would involve. "There, there," he heard Gomati's voice, not sure whether it was organic or synthesized, "shift your input to ultra-v!"

Njord, hooking into *Khons*'s external sensors, complied.

"Astounding!"

"Yet so."

"Not unprecedented. On the contrary," Shoten Binayakya interjected. "All the giants have complex systems of moons. Jupiter. Saturn. Uranus. Search your memory banks if you don't recall."

Surlily, Njord sped unnecessary inquiry to an implanted cyberbiot. "Mmh," he grunted. "So. Almost thirty significant satellites among them. Plus the trash. So." He nodded.

"And this new giant—?"

"Not new," Njord corrected. "It's been there all along, as long as any of the others. You know the old Laplace notion of elder planets and younger planets was abandoned about the same time as the solid atom and the flat earth."

"Good work, Freyr," Shoten shot sarcastically.

"Well then?"

Sri Gomati said, "Clearly, Njord, Shoten meant newly discovered." She paused for a fraction of a second. "And about to be newly visited."

Njord breathed a sigh of annoyance. "Well. And that old European, what's-his-name, Galapagos saw the major moons of Jupiter seven hundred years ago. All the others followed as soon as the optical telescope was developed. They didn't even need radiation sensors, no less probes to find them. Seven hundred years."

"Seven hundred twenty-seven, Njord." Sri Gomati petted him gently on his genitals.

"You and your obsession with ancient history! I don't see how you qualified for this mission, Gomati, always chasing after obscure theorizers and writers!"

"It's hardly an obsession. Galileo was one of the key figures in the history of science. And he found the four big Jovian moons in 1610. It's simple arithmetic to subtract that from 2337 and get seven-two-seven. I didn't even have to call on a cyberbiot to compute that, Njord dear."

"Argh!" The flesh remnants in Njord's face grew hot.

Shoten Binayakya interrupted the argument. "There it comes into visual range!" he exclaimed. "After these centuries, the perturbations of Uranus and Neptune solved at last. Planet X!"

Njord sneered. "You have a great predilection for the melodramatic, Shoten! Planet X, indeed!"

"Why," Shoten laughed, the sound fully synthesized, "it's a happy coincidence, Njord dear. Lowell applied the term to *his* mystery planet, meaning X the unknown. Until Tombaugh found it and named it Pluto. But now it is not only X the unknown but also X the tenth planet as well. Very neat!"

Njord began a reply but paused as the distant planet became visible through *Khons*'s sensors. It was indeed a system like those of the inner giant planets, and radar sensings pouring through *Khons*'s external devices, filtered and processed by cyberbiotic brains, overwhelmed his own consciousness.

A great dark body swam through the blackness, reflecting almost no light from the distant sun but glowing darkly, menacingly, pulsating in slow heartbeatlike waves, with a low crimson radiance that pained Njord subliminally even through the ship's mechanisms and the processing of the cyberbiots. Fascinated yet repelled, Njord stared at the glowing, pulsing globe.

About its obscene oblateness whirled a family of smaller bodies, themselves apparently dim and lifeless, yet illuminated by the raking sinister tone of their parent.

"Yuggoth," Sri Gomati's low whisper jolted Njord from his reverie. "Yuggoth," and again, "Yuggoth!"

Njord snapped, "What's that?"

"Yuggoth," repeated Sri Gomati.

The male hissed in annoyance, watched the great pulsating bulk loom larger in *Khons*'s external sensors, watched its family of moons, themselves behaving like toy planets in orbit around the glowing body's miniature sun.

"The great world must be Yuggoth," Sri Gomati crooned. "And the lesser ones Nithon, Zaman; the whirling pair—see them, see!—Thog and its twin Thok with the foul lake where puffed shoggoths splash."

"Do you know what she is raving about?" Njord demanded of Shoten Binayakya, but Shoten only shook that ambivalent satiny head, two silvery eyes shimmering, stainless steel upper and lower monodont revealed by drawn-back organic lips.

Khons's remote sensors had accumulated enough data now, the ship's cyberbiots computed and reduced the inputs, to provide a set of readouts on the new planetary grouping's characteristics. Shoten raised a telescoping cyberimplant and pointed toward a glowing screen where data crept slowly from top to bottom.

"See," the ambiguous, synthesized voice purled, "the planet's mass is gigantic. Double that of Jupiter. As great as six hundred earths! More oblate even than Jupiter also—what is its spin?" Shoten paused while more lines of information crept onto the screen. "Its rotation is even shorter than Jupiter's. Its surface speed must be—" He paused and sent a command through the ship's neurocyber network, grinned at the response that appeared on the screen.

"Think of resting on the surface of that planet and whirling about at eighty thousand kilometers an hour!"

Njord Freyr rose from his rest-couch. In fact the least extensively cyborged of the three, he retained three of his original organic limbs. He pulled himself around, using *Khons*'s interior freefall handholds to steady himself, hooked his strongly servomeched arm through two handholds, and gestured angrily from Shoten to Sri Gomati.

"We can all read the screens. I asked what this Eurasian bitch was babbling about!"

"Now, dear," Shoten Binayakya purred ambiguously.

Sri Gomati's shimmering silvery eyes seemed for once not totally masked, but fixed on some distant vision. Her hands—one fitted with an array of scientific and mechanical implements, the other implanted with a multitude of flexible cartilaginous organs equally suited for technical manipulation and erotic excesses—wove and fluttered before her face. She spoke as much to herself or to some absent, invisible entity as to Njord Freyr or Shoten Binayakya. It was as if she instructed the batches of cyberbiotic brains that populated the electronic network of the ship.

"March 15, 2337, earth standard time," she crooned. "It would please him. It would please him to know that he is remembered. That he was right in his own day. But how, I wonder, could he have known? Did he merely guess? Was he in contact with entities from beyond? Beings from this strange, gray world past the starry void, this pale, shadowy land?

"Dead four hundred years this day, Howard, does your dust lie in ancient ground still? Could some later Curwen not have raised your essential salts?"

"Madness!" Njord Freyr broke in. With his organic hand he struck Gomati's face, his palm rebounding from the hard bone and the harder metal implanted beneath her flesh.

Her glittering eyes aflash, she jerked her head away, at the same time twisting to fix him with her angry glare. A circuit of tension sprang into being between them, lips of both writhing, faces animated in mute quarrel. Beyond this, neither moved.

Only the interruption of Shoten Binayakya's commanding speech broke the tense immobility. "While you carried out your spat, dears, I had the cyberbiots plot our orbit through the new system."

"The system of Yuggoth," Gomati reiterated.

"As you wish."

The data screen went to abstract blobs for fractions of a second, then it was filled with a glowing diagram of the new system: the oblate pulsating planet, its scabrous surface features whirling in the center of the screen; the smaller rocky moons revolving rapidly about their master.

"We can land only once," Shoten purred. "We must carefully select our touchdown point. Then later expeditions may explore further. But if we choose poorly, the worlds may abandon this *Yuggoth*"—Gomati's name for the great planet was spoken sardonically—"forever." Shoten's cyborged head nodded in self-affirmation, then the synthesized words were repeated, "Yes, forever."

15032137—READOUT

The Asia-Pacific Co-prosperity Sphere continued to evolve. It was, beyond question, the center of world power, economic development, political leadership. It was also a gigantic realm sprawling across continents and oceans, including scores of great cities and billions of citizens.

Its first city was Beijing. Secondary centers of authority were established in Lhasa, Bombay, Mandalay, Quezon City, Adelaide, Christchurch, Santa Ana.

The first great leader of the Sphere, Vo Tran Quoc, had become a figure of legendary proportions within a century of his death. Schools contended as to his true identity. Despite his name, he was not Vietnamese. That much was known. One group of scholars held that he was a Maori. Another, that he was an Ainu. A third, that he was a Bengali woman, the product of rape during the war of independence of Bangladesh from Pakistan, posing as a man (or possibly having undergone a sex-change operation involving the grafting of a donated penis and testes).

At any rate, Vo Tran Quoc died.

In the wake of his death a struggle broke out. Some who contended for the power of the dead leader did so on the basis of purely personal ambition. Others, from ideological conviction. The great ideological dispute of the year 2137 dealt with the proper interpretation of an ancient political dictum.

The ancient political dictum was: Just as there is not a single thing in the world without a dual nature, so imperialism and all reactionaries have a dual nature—they are real tigers and paper tigers at the same time.

While political theorists in Beijing quarreled over the meaning of this political dictum, a new force arose with its center in the eldritch city of Angkor Wat deep in the jungles of old Cambodia. The new political force brought about a world feminist order. Its leader, following the example of Vo Tran Quoc, took the name of a mythic personage from another culture than her own.

She proclaimed a New Khmer Empire stretching from the Urals to the Rockies.

She took the name Vidya Devi. This means goddess of wisdom.

The former Slavic domain and the Maghreb suffered rivalry that led, after a century, to convergence and ultimate amalgamation. The old Roman Empire was reborn. It included all of Europe, the Near East, Africa, and North America from the Atlantic to the Pacific. (Niagara Falls now poured its waters directly into the ocean; the former west bank of the Hudson River was choice seashore property. The Rockies overlooked pounding waves that stretched to the Asian shore.)

The empire was ruled by an absolute monarch under the tutelage of the world feminist order. She was known as the Empress Fortuna Pales I.

Latin America, from Tierra del Fuego to the southern bank of the Rio Grande (but excluding Baja), was the greater Hai Brasil. The empress claimed pure Bourbon ancestry. Her name was Astrud do Muiscos.

In the Antarctic a great land-reclamation project had been undertaken. Geothermal power was used to melt the ice in a circle centered on the south pole. The cleared area measured 1.5 million square kilometers. The soil was found to be incredibly rich in minerals. It was hugely fertile. The scenic beauty of the region was incomparable. There were mountains, lakes, glaciers, to shame those of New Zealand or Switzerland or Tibet. Forests were planted and grew rapidly and luxuriantly. Imported wildlife throve. The few native species—penguins, amphibian mammals, a strange variety of bird newly discovered and named the tekeli-li*—were protected.*

The new country was called Yisroel Diaspora.

Its leader under the feminist world order was Tanit Shadrapha. This name means the healer Ishtar.

The feminist world order promoted scientific research, largely from bases in Yisroel Diaspora. Space exploration, long abandoned except for the development of orbiting weapons-systems, was resumed. Bases were established on the planet Mars and among the asteroids. A crewed ship orbited Venus, making close observations and sending robot monitors and samplers to the surface of the planet. Venus was found to be a worthless and inhospitable piece of real estate.

A landing was attempted on the surface of Mercury. The expedition was an ambitious undertaking. The lander was to touch down just on the dark side of the planetary terminator, thence to be carried into the night. During the Mercurian night it would burrow beneath the surface. By the time the terminator was reached and the ship entered the day side, it would be safely entombed and would, in effect, estivate through the searing Mercurian day.

Something went wrong. The ship landed. Excavation work began. Then, almost as if the planet were eating the ship and its crew, all disappeared beneath the surface. They were never contacted again.

* * *

On earth the dominant art form was something called cheomnaury. *This involved a blending and transformation of sensory inputs. The most favored sensory combinations were sound, odor, and flavor. The greatest* cheomnaurist *in the world was an Ecuadorian dwarf who found her way to the capital of Hai Brasil and obtained personal audience with Astrud do Muiscos herself.*

The dwarf began her performance with a presentation involving the sound of surf pounding upon the rocks of the Pacific coast where Andean granite plunges hundreds of feet into icy foam. This was blended with the warm, rich odor of chestnuts roasting over a charcoal brazier. To this the dwarf added the subtle flavor of ground coriander.

Astrud do Muiscos was pleased.

The dwarf proceeded to offer a blend of a synthesized voice such as might come from a living volcano, to which she added a scent of natron and olive unknown outside the secret embalming chamber of Egyptian temples six thousand years old, to which was added the flavor of the spithrus locusta. *The* spithrus locusta *is a marine arachnid, the flavor of whose meat is to that of ordinary broiled lobster as is that of the lobster to a common crab louse.*

Astrud do Muiscos was very pleased.

The triumph of the dwarf was a combination of white noise in the ordinary range of audibility with subtle sub- and supersonics, mixed with the odor of a quintessential coca extract and the flavor of concentrated formic acid drawn from Amazonian driver ants.

Astrud do Muiscos named the dwarf her successor to the throne of Hai Brasil.

The religion of the day, as appropriate to the climate of political realities, was a mutated form of the ancient Ishtar cult, with local variations as Ashtoroth, Astarte, and Aphrodite. There was even a sort of universal Mamacy, with its seat in ancient but restored Babylon.

MARCH 15, 2337

"I don't see why it's taken so long to get here, anyway," Njord Freyr snapped.

"You mean from Pluto?" Shoten responded. "But we are on course. We are in free-fall. Look." The cyberbiots superimposed a small box of course data beside the whirling diagram of the Yuggoth system.

"Not from Pluto!" Njord spat. "From earth! Why has it taken until 2337 to reach—Yuggoth? When space flight began almost as long ago as the era Sri Gomati babbles about. The first extraterrestrial landings took place in 1969. Mars thirty years later. Remember the stirring political slogan that we all learned as children, as children studying the history of our era? *Persons will set foot on another planet before the century ends!* That was the twentieth century, remember?"

"Every schoolchild knows," Shoten affirmed wearily.

Gomati, recovered from the shock of Njord's blow, spoke. "We could have been here two hundred years ago, Njord Freyr. But fools on earth lost heart. They began, and lost heart. They began again—and lost heart again. And again. Four times they set out, exploring the planets. Each time they lost heart, lost courage, lost interest. Were distracted by wars. Turned resources to nobler purposes.

"Humankind reached Mars as promised. And lost heart. Started once more under Shahar Shalim of the old New Maghreb. Reached Venus and Mercury. And lost heart. Reached the Asteroid Belt and the gas giants under Tanit Shadrapha of Ugarit. And lost heart.

"And now. At last. We are here." She gestured with her flowing, waving tentacles toward the diagram that glowed against the ship's dull fittings.

"What course, Shoten Binayakya?" she asked brusquely.

The whirling bodies on the screen were marked in red, the pulsing red of Yuggoth's inner flames, the beating, reflected red of the madly dashing moons. A contrasting object appeared on the screen, the flattened cone-shape of the ship *Khons*, trailing in its wake as it wove among the bodies a line to show the course of its passage. Shortly the line had woven past, circled about, curved beyond each body in the diagram, leaving the stylized representation of *Khons* in perturbated circular orbit about the entire system.

"So," purred Shoten Binayakya. And Sri Gomati and Njord Freyr in turn. "So." "So."

Shoten Binayakya flicked a pressure plate with some limb, some tool. *Khons* bucked, slithered, through a complex course correction. Shoten slapped another plate and the full exterior optics of *Khons* were activated; to the three members of the crew, hooked into the cyberbiotic system of the ship, it was as if they fell freely through the distantly star-sprayed night. Fell, fell toward red, glowing, pulsating Yuggoth and its family of gray dancing servants.

Khons, inserted into its new flight path, sped first past the outermost of Yuggoth's moons: a world of significant size. The ship's sensors and cyberbiots reported on the body: in mass and diameter not far from the dimensions of the familiar rock-and-water satellites of the outer planets. Close to five thousand kilometers through its center and marked with the nearly universal cratering of every solid world from Mercury to Pluto.

The twins, dubbed Thog and Thok by Gomati, whirled at the opposite extremes of their interwoven orbits, so *Khons* flitted past the innermost of the four moons, another apparent replica of the familiar Ganymede-Callisto-Titan-Triton model, then dropped into equatorial orbit about the dully glowing, oblate Yuggoth.

Njord, Gomati, Shoten Binayakya fell silent. The sounds of *Khons*'s automatic systems, the low hiss of recirculating air, the occasional hum or click of a servo, the slow breathing of Njord Freyr, of Sri Gomati, were the only sounds. (Shoten Binayakya's lungs had been cybermeched, whirred softly, steadily within the metal torso.)

Once more a limb flicked at a pressure plate, moved this time by feel alone. The ship, fully visible to any hypothetical viewer outside its hull, was for practical purposes totally transparent to its crew. A circuit warmed instantly to life. Radiation sensors picked up the electrical field of the planet, converted it to audio range, broadcast it within *Khons*: a howl, a moan. With each pulsation of the planet's ruddy illumination, the sound modulated through an obscene parody of some despairing sigh.

"If only Holst had known!" the synthesized voice of Shoten whispered. "If only he had known."

Yuggoth's surface sped beneath the ship, its terrible velocity of rotation making features slip away as others rushed toward the viewers, flashed beneath and dropped away, disappearing across the sprawling horizon into interstellar blackness. Great viscous plates of darkly glowing semisolid rock hundreds of kilometers across rolled and crashed majestically. Between them red-hot magma glowed balefully, great tongues of liquid rock licking upward between the pounding solid plates, the heat and brightness of the magma growing and lessening in a slow, steady rhythm that *Khons*'s cyberbiots and audio-scanners converted into a contrabass *throb-throb-throb-throb*.

"There can be no life there," Njord Freyr announced. "Nothing could live in that environment. Nothing could ever have lived there."

After a silence Sri Gomati challenged him. "The planet itself, Njord Freyr. Could it be a single organism? The sounds, the movement, the energy." She raised her organic hand to her brow, ran scores of writhing digits from the browline above her glittering silver eyes, across her satiny naked skull to the base of her neck.

"It could be a nascent sun," Shoten Binayakya whispered. "Were Jupiter larger, more energetic—you know it has been suggested that Jupiter is a failed attempt at the creation of a partner for Sol, that our own solar system is an unsuccessful venture at the formation of a double star."

"And Yuggoth?" Gomati dropped her tentacular hand to her lap.

Njord Freyr's voice contained only a tincture of sarcasm. "Sent by some remote godling to undo Jupiter's failure, hey? How do we know that it's always been here? Before now we knew it existed at all only through courtesy of Neptune's and Pluto's perturbations. How do we know this Yuggoth isn't a new arrival in the system? Nobody knew that Neptune or Pluto existed until a few centuries ago!"

"Or perhaps," purred Shoten, "perhaps our system is a failed triple star. Ah, think of the show if we had three suns to light our worlds instead of one!"

Again Shoten Binayakya flicked at a pressure plate. Once more *Khons* shifted, jounced. There was a steady acceleration and the ship slid from its orbit around the ruddy pulsating planet, fell away from Yuggoth and toward the spinning worldlets that occupied the central orbit around the planet.

"They must be," Gomati crooned softly, "they must be. Thog and Thok, Thog and Thok. How could he know, centuries past? Let some Curwen find the salts and let him tell!"

"You're babbling again!" Njord almost shouted. "I thought we were selected for stability for this mission. How did you ever get past the screening?"

Distracted, Sri Gomati slowly dragged her fascinated gaze from the spinning moons, turned silver eyes toward Njord Freyr. "Somehow he knew," she mumbled. Her lips drew back in a slow smile showing her bright steel monodonts. "And somehow we will find the Ghooric zone where the fungi blossom!"

As if in a trance she turned slowly away, leaned forward, eyes glittering metallically, leaned and reached her hands, the cyborged and the genetically custom-formed, as if to touch the two red-gray worldlets.

"He wrote horror stories," Gomati said, her voice dead-level as if trance-ridden. "He wrote of an unknown outer planet that he called Yuggoth, and of others—Nithon, Zaman, Thog, and Thok—and of horrid, puffy beasts called shoggoths that splashed obscenely in the pools of the Ghooric zone.

"He died four hundred years ago today, Howard did. But first he wrote of one Curwen who could restore the dead if only he could obtain their essential salts. What he called their essential salts." She paused and giggled. "Maybe he had a prevision of cloning!"

MAR 15, 2037—A VIDEOTAPE

Open with a logo recognizable as representing world politics.

The old century ended with a definite shift of world power. The westward movement of two millennia continued. Mesopotamia, Hellas, Italia, Franco-Germania, England, America. Now the power in America shifted from an Atlantic to a Pacific orientation.

The new powers to contend with were Japan, China, Soviet Asia.

Western Europe and the eastern United States lapsed into terminal decadence as loci of civilization. Europe from the Danube to the Urals passed from Habsburg and Romanoff glitter to a brief democratic flicker to a drab gray dusk as Soviet Europe and then into Slavic night. Like its predecessor of fifteen centuries, the Soviet Empire split in half; like the Western half of the predecessor, the Western Soviet Empire was overrun by barbarians. But it did not fall to the barbarians. Not really. It fell to its own internal rot. And like the eastern half of the predecessor, the Eastern Soviet Empire throve.

By the hundredth anniversary of that death in the Jane Brown Memorial Hospital, the landmass of the earth eastward from the Urals to the Rockies came under unified government. It included dozens of half-forgotten countries. Tibet. Afghanistan. India. Laos. Australia. Tonga. The Philippines. Manchuria. Mongolia. California. Baja.

It was called the Asia-Pacific Co-prosperity Sphere.

Europe from the Urals to the English Channel became a peninsula of forests and farms. What small vigor remained was concentrated in the region from the Danube to the Urals. Slavic influence, walled off in the East by the great and burgeoning Asian renaissance, spread northward and westward. After a pause at the limits of a region running from the Scandinavian Peninsula to the Iberian, the Slavic Empire launched its rude invasion fleet. It crossed the English Channel. There was little resistance. The few defenders of British sovereignty, under the leadership of a fellow called Harald, were defeated at a place called Runnymede.

The next westward hop was to America. It took the Slavs a while to prepare themselves for that. But when they made their move they were greeted with flowers and flags. They did not have to conquer. They only had to occupy and administer.

The third power of the world in this time took form to the south of the Slavic domain. Arab leaders, glutted with petrobux, bought arms and hired mercenaries. Governments could not achieve unity, but a shadowy group known by the cryptic name of opec *did. The governments as such withered. The shadowy* opec *exercised more and more power. It did so more and more openly.*

Slowly the influence of opec *spread westward and southward until all of the old Near East and Africa were under its sway.*

Then was proclaimed the New Maghreb.

Cut to logo representing heroic leadership.

The most powerful person in the world was the Chairperson of the Asia-Pacific Co-prosperity Sphere, Vo Tran Quoc.

The leader of the second power, the Slavic Empire, was called Svarozits Perun. This name means thunderbolt of God.

The head of opec *and de facto ruler of the New Maghreb was called Shahar Shalim. This name means* dawn of peace.

Cut to logo representing sex.

The major sexual attitude of the time was androgyny, rivaled but not equaled by the cult of pansexuality. Androgyny implies a recognition of the full sexual potential of each individual. Former distinctions were abandoned. It was no longer regarded as improper to pursue a relationship of male to male or female to female; nor was it required to have two partners in a relationship. Practices ranging from onanism to mass interplay were accepted.

The pansexualists held that androgyny was needlessly limiting in scope. If one could relate to any man or woman—why not to a giraffe? A condor? A cabbage? A bowl of sand? A machine?

The ocean?

The sky?

To the cosmos?

To God?

Cut to logo representing music.

The most popular musical composition as of Mar 15, 2037, was ironically a hundred-year-old tune, complete with lyrics. Searches of nearly forgotten records revealed the names of the composer and lyricist. An old 78-rpm shellac-disk rendition of the tune was discovered in a watertight vault beneath a flooded city. The sound was transcribed and released once again to the world.

The original lyrics had been written by one Jacob Jacobs. A second version, in English, was used on the shellac disk. These words were by Sammy Cahn and Saul Chaplin. The music was by Sholom Secunda. The singers were Patti, Maxene, and LaVerne Andrews. The song was "Bei Mir Bist du Schön."

Cut to logo representing geodynamics.

The latter years of the twentieth century and the early decades of the twenty-first were marked by changes in weather patterns and geodynamics. Accustomed to the reliable round of winter and summer, rainy season and dry season, the flow of rivers and the currents and tides of the oceans, man had come to look upon the earth as a stable and dependable home.

He was mistaken.

A trivial shift in air patterns, a minor trembling of the planetary mantle, a minute increase or diminution of the sun's warmth received by the planet, and the mighty works of man crumbled like sand castles in the surf.

An example. Earthquakes were more or less expected in certain regions: the Pacific coast of North America, Japan, and eastern China, a Eurasian belt running from Yugoslavia through Greece and Turkey to Iran. Tragedies were masked with heroism, fear hidden behind the false face of humor. "When California falls into the ocean this piece of Arizona desert will be choice waterfront property."

Nobody expected New England and maritime Canada to crumble, but when the big quake hit, they did. From the St. Lawrence to the Hudson. It started with a tremor and rumble, grew to a scream and smash, ended with a gurgle and then the soft, even lapping of the Atlantic waters.

Among the bits of real estate that wound up on the ocean floor—a very minor bit—was a chunk of old Providence-Plantations known as Swan Point Cemetery. Now the Deep Ones indeed swam over the single stone marker of the Lovecraft family plot. Winfield, Sarah, Howard, *the marker was inscribed. Currents could flow all the way from Devil's Reef and Innsmouth Harbor to far Ponape in the Pacific, and the Deep Ones visited Swan Point.*

In the field of religion, there was a revival of the ancient cults of the sea-gods, especially that of Dagon.

MARCH 15, 2337

Khons slithered through another correction, took up a complex orbit that circled one moon, crossed to the other, circled, returned, describing over and over the conventional sign for the infinite.

Shoten tapped a plate, and the large viewing screen inside *Khons* glowed once more, seeming to stand unsupported against the background of the two moons and the distant star-sprayed blackness. Every now and again the progress of the two whirling moons and *Khons*'s orbit around and between them would bring Yuggoth itself swinging across the view of the three crew members so that one or both of the worldlets and the ship's data screen swept opaquely across the dark, pulsating oblateness.

Shoten commanded, and cyberbiots magnified the surface features of the moons on the data screen. The omnipresent craters sprang up, but then, as the magnification increased, it became obvious that they were not the sharp-edged features of the typical airless satellite but the shortened, rounded curves typical of weathering. Shoten gestured, and the focus slid across the surface of the nearer body. Above the horizon distant stars faded and twinkled.

"Air!" Shoten declared. And Njord and Gomati, agreeing, "Air." "Air."

Shoten Binayakya dropped *Khons* into a lower orbit, circling only one of the twin moons, that which Gomati had arbitrarily named as Thog. Again the magnification of the screen increased. In the center of a crater outlines appeared, forms of structures reared ages before by purposeful intelligence.

Amazed, Njord Freyr asked, "Could there be life?"

Shoten turned a metallic face toward him, shook slowly that ambiguous head. "Not now. No movement, no radiation, no energy output. But once . . ." There was a silence. Breathing, whirring, the soft clicks and hums of *Khons*. "But once . . ." Shoten Binayakya said again in that cold, synthesized voice.

Sri Gomati gestured. "This is where we must land. After all the explorations of the planets and their moons, even the futile picking among the rubbish of the Asteroid Belt by the great Astrud do Muiscos—to find signs of life at last! This is where we must land!"

Shoten Binayakya nodded agreement without waiting even for the assent of Njord Freyr. A limb flicked out, tapped. *Khons* bucked and started circling downward toward the reticulated patterns on the surface of Thog.

With a jolt and a shudder *Khons* settled onto the surface of the moon, well within the weathered walls of the crater and within a kilometer or less of the structured protuberances. Shoten quiesced the cyberbiots to mere maintenance level of *Khons*, leaving only the receptors and telemeters warm, then asked the others to prepare to exit.

Njord Freyr and Sri Gomati slipped breathers over their heads and shoulders. Shoten ordered a variety of internal filtration modifications within the recirculation system that provided life support. They took readings from *Khons*'s external sensors, slid back hatches, made their way from *Khons*, stood facing what, it was now obvious, were relics of incredible antiquity.

Abreast, the three moved toward the ruins: Njord on motorized, gyrostabilized cyborged wheel assemblies; Shoten Binayakya rumbling on tread-laying gear, stable, efficient; Sri Gomati striding left foot, right foot, organic legs encased in puff-jointed pressure suit like some anachronistic caricature of a Bipolar Technocompetitive Era spaceman.

They halted a few meters from the first row of structures. Like the crater rims, the walls, columns, arches, were weather-rounded, tumbled, softened. A metallic telescoping tentacle whiplashed out from the hub of one of Njord's cyborg-wheels. A crumbled cube of some now-soft stonelike material fell away to ashes, to dust.

Njord turned bleak silver eyes to the others. "Once, perhaps . . ."

"Come along," Gomati urged, "let's get to exploring these ruins!" Excitement colored her voice. "There's no telling what evidence they may contain of their builders. We may learn whether these worlds and their inhabitants originated in our own system or whether they came from—elsewhere."

At Gomati's final word she turned her face skyward, and the others followed suit. It was the worldlet Thog's high noon or the equivalent of noon. The sun was so remote—sixteen billion kilometers, twice as far as it was from Pluto at the latter's aphelion and 120 times as distant as it was from earth—that to the three standing on the surface of Thog, it was utterly lost in the star-dotted blackness.

But Yuggoth itself hung directly overhead, obscenely bloated and oblate, its surface filling the heavens, looking as if it were about to crash shockingly upon *Khons* and the three explorers, and all the time pulsing, pulsing, pulsing like an atrocious heart, throbbing, throbbing. And now Thog's twin worldlet, dubbed Thok by the female crew member, swept in Stygian silhouette across the tumultuous face of Yuggoth, Thok's black roundness varied by the serrations of crater-rims casting their deep shadows on the pale, pink-pulsating gray rocks of Thog.

The blackness enveloped first *Khons*, then sped across the face of Thog, swept over the three explorers, blotting out the pulsing ruddiness of Yuggoth and plunging them into utter blackness.

Gomati's fascination was broken by the purring synthetic voice of Shoten Binayakya. "An interesting occultation," Shoten said, "but come, we have our mission to perform. *Khons* is taking automatic measurements and telemetering information back to Neptune. And here," the silvery eyes seemed to flicker in distant starlight as a cybernetic extensor adjusted devices on the mechanical carapace, "my own recording and telemetering devices will send data back to the ship."

MARCH 15, 1937—A SNAPSHOT

Dr. Dustin stood by the bed. The patient was semiconscious. His lips moved, but no one could hear what he said. Two old women sat by the bed. One was his aunt Annie. The other was Annie's dear friend Edna, present as much to comfort the grieving aunt as to visit the dying nephew.

Dr. Dustin leaned over the bed. He checked the patient's condition. He stood for a while trying to understand the patient's words, but he could not. From time to time the patient moved his hand feebly. It looked as if he was trying to slap something.

The old woman named Annie had tears on her face. She reached into a worn black purse for her handkerchief and wiped the tears away as best she could. She grasped Dr. Dustin's hand and held it between her own. She asked him, "Is there any hope? Any?"

The doctor shook his head. "I'm sorry, Mrs. Gamwell." And to the other woman, almost bowing, "Miss Lewis.

"I'm sorry," the doctor said again.

The old woman named Annie released the doctor's hand. The other old woman, Edna, reached toward Annie. They sat facing each other. They embraced clumsily, as people must when sitting face to face. Each old woman tried to comfort the other.

The doctor sighed and walked to the window. He looked outside. It was early morning. The sun had risen, but it was visible only as a pale watery glow in the east. The sky was gray with clouds. The ground was covered with patches of snow, ice, slush. More snow was falling.

The doctor wondered why it seemed that he lost patients only in winter, or during rainstorms, or at night. Never on a bright spring or summer day. He knew that that was not really true. Patients died when they died. When their fatal condition, whatever it was, happened to complete the running of its course. Still, it seemed *always to happen in the dark of the night or in the dark of the year.*

He heard someone whistling.

He turned and saw two young residents passing the doorway. One of them was whistling. He was whistling a popular tune that the doctor had heard on the radio. He couldn't remember what program he had heard it on. Possibly the program was "The Kate Smith Show" or "Your Hit Parade." The tune was very catchy, even though the words were in some language that eluded Dr. Dustin's ear. The song was called "Bei Mir Bist du Schön."

Three thousand miles away, the Spanish were engaged in a confusing civil war. The old king had abdicated years before, and a republic had been proclaimed. But after the direction of the new government became clear, a colonel serving in the Spanish colonial forces in Africa returned with his troops—largely Berbers and Rifs—to change things.

He would overthrow the republic. He would end the nonsense of democracy, atheism, lewdness, that the republic tolerated. He would restore discipline, piety, modesty. He would reinstitute the monarchy.

At the moment it appeared that the republican forces were winning. They had just recaptured the cities of Trijuque and Guadalajara. They had taken rebel prisoners. These included Spanish monarchists. They included African troops as well. Strangely, some of the prisoners spoke only Italian. They said they were volunteers. They said they had been ordered to volunteer. And they always obeyed their orders.

In China, forces of the Imperial Japanese Army were having easy going. Their opposition was weak. The Chinese were divided. They had been engaged in a civil war. It was not much like the one in Spain. It had been going on much longer. It had begun with the death of President Sun Yat-sen in 1924. The Japanese were not the only foreign power to intervene in China.

Germany had owned trading concessions in China until the Treaty of Versailles ended them. Germany was burgeoning now and had ambitions to regain her lost privileges.

Other countries had felt their interests threatened by the Chinese civil war. England had sent troops. France had used her influence. France was worried that she might lose her valuable colonies in Indochina. Russia had tried to influence China's internal politics. There had been grave danger of war between Russia and China. Especially when the Chinese sacked the Russian Embassy in Beijing and beheaded six of its staff.

The United States had intervened. American gunboats plied Chinese waterways. The gunboat Panay *was sunk by aerial gunfire and bombing. The* Panay *was on the Yangtze river when this happened. The Yangtze is a Chinese river. But the* Panay *was sunk by Japanese forces. This pleased China. Japan apologized and paid compensation.*

Joe Louis and Joe DiMaggio, two young athletes, were in training. Both of them had very good years in 1937.

A wealthy daredevil pilot named Howard Hughes flew across the United States in seven hours and twenty-eight minutes. This set off a new wave of excitement and "air-mindedness." In Santa Monica, California, the Douglas Aircraft Company was completing its new airliner. This would carry forty passengers. It had four engines. It would be capable of speeds up to 237 miles per hour.

More conservative people felt that the zeppelin would never yield to the airplane. The great airship Hindenburg *was on the Atlantic run. It was huge. It was beautiful. There was a piano in its cocktail lounge. The European terminus of its flights was Tempelhof Airdrome in Germany. The American terminus of its flights was Lakehurst, New Jersey.*

On the morning of March 15, Rabbi Louis I. Newman found eleven large orange swastikas painted on the walls of Temple Rodeph Sholom, 7 West 83rd Street, New York. This was the third such incident at Temple Rodeph Sholom. Rabbi Newman suspected that the swastikas were painted in retaliation for Secretary of State Hull's protests against abusive statements in the German press.

At Turn Hall, Lexington Avenue and 85th Street, the head of the Silver Shirts of New York replied. His name was George L. Rafort. He said the swastikas were painted by Jewish troublemakers. He knew this because the arms of the eleven swastikas pointed backward. He said, "This is a mistake no Nazi would make."

In Providence, Rhode Island, the snow continued to fall. The city's hills were slippery. There were accident cases in the hospitals.

In the Jane Brown Memorial Hospital on College Hill, Howard Lovecraft opened his eyes. No one knew what he saw. Certainly Dr. Cecil Calvert Dustin did not. Howard slapped the coverlet of his bed. He moved his lips. A sound emerged. He might have said, "Feather." Perhaps he had been slapping at an errant feather. Or perhaps the word was "Father." He might have said, "Father, you look just like a young man."

MARCH 15, 2337

They rolled, clanked, strode forward a few meters more, halted once again at the very edge of the ancient ruins. Shoten Binayakya sent two core samplers downward from mechanized instrumentation compartments, one to sample soil, the other to clip some material from the ruins themselves. Carbon dating would proceed automatically within Shoten's cyborged componentry.

Sri Gomati gazed at the ruins. They had the appearance, in the faint distant starlight, of stairs and terraces walled with marble balustrades. Gomati ran her optical sensors to maximum image amplification to obtain meaningful sight in the darkness of the occultation of Yuggoth.

And then—it is highly doubtful that the discovery would have been made by the single brief expedition, working in the ruddy, pulsating light of Yuggoth; it was surely that planet's occultation by Thok that must receive credit for the find—Gomati turned at the gasp of Njord Freyr. Her eyes followed the path of his pointing, armor-gauntleted hand.

From some opening deep under the rubble before them a dim but baleful light emerged, pulsating obscenely. But unlike the crimson pulsations of Yuggoth above the explorers, this light beneath their feet was of some shocking, awful green.

Without speaking the three surged forward, picking their way through the ruined and crumbled remnants of whatever ancient city had once flung vaulted towers and fluted columns into the black sky above the tiny world. They reached the source of the radiance barely in time, for as the disk sped across the face of Yuggoth, the black shadow that blanketed the landing site of the ship *Khons* and the ruins where the crew poked and studied, fled across the pale gray face of Thog leaving them standing once more in the red pulsating glare of the giant planet.

In the obscene half-daylight, the hideous metallic glare of bronze-green was overwhelmed and disappeared into the general throbbing ruddiness. But by now Shoten Binayakya had shot a telescoping core-probe into the opening from which the light emerged, and with mechanical levers pried back the marblelike slab whose cracked and chipped corner had permitted the emergence of the glow.

Servos revved, the stone slab crashed aside. Steps led away, into the bowels of the worldlet Thog. In the dark, shadowy recess the red pulsating light of giant Yuggoth and the baleful metallic green fought and shifted distressingly.

"The Ghooric zone," Sri Gomati whispered to herself, "the Ghooric zone."

They advanced down the stairs, leaving behind the baleful pulsations of Yuggoth, lowering themselves meter by meter into the bronze-green lighted depths of Thog. The track-laying cybermech of Shoten Binayakya took the strangely proportioned stairway with a sort of clumsy grace. Njord Freyr, his wheeled undercarriage superbly mobile on the level surface of Thog, now clutched desperately to the fluted carapace of Shoten.

Sri Gomati walked with ease, gazing out over the subsurface world of Thog. Seemingly kilometers below their entry a maze of dome on dome and tower on tower lay beside—she shook her head, adjusted metallic optics. There seemed to be a subterranean sea here within the depths of tiny Thog, a sea whose dark and oily waters lapped and gurgled obscenely at a black and gritty beach.

At the edge of that sea, that body which must be little more than a lake by earthly standards, on that black and grainy beach, great terrible creatures rolled and gamboled shockingly.

"Shoggoths!" Sri Gomati ran ahead of the others, almost tumbling from the unbalustraded stairway. "Shoggoths! Exactly as he said, splashing beside a foul lake! Shoggoths!" Exalted, she reached the end of the stairway, ran through towering columns past walls of sprawling bas-relief that showed hideous deities destroying intruders upon their shrines while awful acolytes crept away toward enigmatic vehicles in search of morsels to appease their obscene gods.

Gomati heard the grinding, clanking sounds of Shoten Binayakya following her, the steady whir of Njord Freyr's undercarriage. She turned and faced them. "This is the year 2337," she shouted, "the four hundredth anniversary of his death! How could he know? How could he ever have known?"

And she ran down hallways beneath vaulted gambrel roofs, ran past more carvings and paintings showing strange, rugose cone-shaped beings and terrible, tentacle-faced obscenities that loomed frighteningly above cowering prey. Then Gomati came to another hallway, one lit with black tapers that flared and guttered terribly.

The air in the room was utterly still, the shadows of fluted columns solemn against walls carved and lettered in a script whose awesome significance had been forgotten before earth's own races were young. And in the center of the room, meter-tall tapers of Stygian gloom marking its four extremities, stood a catafalque, and on the catafalque, skin as white as a grave-worm, eyes shut, angular features in somber repose, lay the black-draped figure of a man.

Sri Gomati raced to the foot of the catafalque, stood gazing into the flickering darkness of the hall, then advanced to stand beside the head of the body. Her silvery eyes shimmered and she began to laugh, to giggle and titter obscenely, and yet to weep at the same time, for some cybersurgeon long before had seen fit to leave those glands and ducts intact.

And Sri Gomati stood tittering and snuffling until Njord Freyr rolled beside her on his cyborged power-wheels and the ambiguous Shoten Binayakya ground and clanked beside her on tread-laying undercarriage, and they took her to return to the spaceship *Khons*.

But strangest of all is this. The stairway by which they attempted to return to the surface of the worldlet Thog and the safety of their spaceship *Khons* had crumbled away under the weight of untold eons and that of the cybermechanisms of the exploration party, and when they tried to climb those crumbling stairs they found themselves trapped in the Ghooric zone kilometers beneath the surface of the worldlet Thog.

And there, beside the oily, lapping sea, the foul lake where puffed shoggoths splash, they remained, the three, forever.

Cthulhu noster qui es in maribus, sanctificetur nomen tuum; adveniat regnum tuum; fiat voluntas tua sicut in R'lyeh et in Y'ha-nthlei.

—Olaus Wormius

"Lovecraft's fiction is one of the cornerstones of modern horror. These dream stories are a perfect introduction to his work: a unique and visionary world of wonder, terror, and delirium."

—Clive Barker

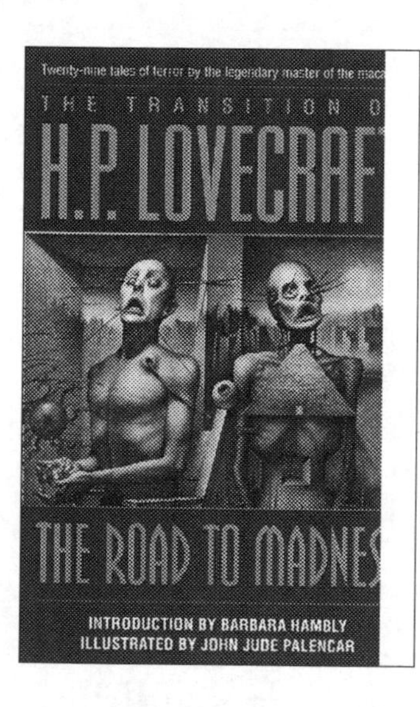

Twenty-nine tales of terror by the legendary master of the macabre, including:

IMPRISONED WITH THE PHARAOHS—Houdini seeks to reveal the demons that inhabit the Egyptian night.

AT THE MOUNTAINS OF MADNESS—An unsuspecting expedition uncovers a city of untold terror, buried beneath an Antarctic wasteland.

Plus, for the first time in any Del Rey edition:

HERBERT WEST: REANIMATOR—Mad experiments yield hideous results in this, the inspiration for the cult film *Re-Animator.*

COOL AIR—An icy apartment hides secrets no man dares unlock.

THE TERRIBLE OLD MAN—The intruders seek a fortune but find only death!

Published by Del Rey Books.
Available wherever books are sold.

"A master craftsman, Lovecraft brings compelling visions of nightmarish fear, invisible worlds, and the demons of the unconscious. If one author truly represents the very best in American literary horror, it is H. P. Lovecraft."

—John Carpenter

This volume collects, for the first time, the entire Dream Cycle and related tales as penned by H. P. Lovecraft, the master of twentieth-century horror, including some of his most fantastic visions:

THE DOOM THAT CAME TO SARNATH—Hate, genocide, and a deadly curse.

THE NAMELESS CITY—Death lies beneath the shifting sands, in a story linking the Dream Cycle with the legendary Cthulhu Mythos.

THE CATS OF ULTHAR—In Ulthar, no man may kill a cat . . . and woe unto any who tries.

THE DREAM QUEST OF UNKNOWN KADATH—The epic nightmare adventure with tendrils stretching throughout the entire Dream Cycle.

Printed in the United States
by Baker & Taylor Publisher Services